Edward Poste

Gaii Institutionum Iuris Civilis Commentaii Quatuor

Edward Poste

Gaii Institutionum Iuris Civilis Commentaii Quatuor

Reprint of the original, first published in 1871.

1st Edition 2022 | ISBN: 978-3-36812-472-4

Verlag (Publisher): Outlook Verlag GmbH, Zeilweg 44, 60439 Frankfurt, Deutschland
Vertretungsberechtigt (Authorized to represent): E. Roepke, Zeilweg 44, 60439 Frankfurt, Deutschland
Druck (Print): Books on Demand GmbH, In de Tarpen 42, 22848 Norderstedt, Deutschland

GAII

INSTITUTIONUM IURIS CIVILIS COMMENTARII QUATUOR

OR

MENTS OF ROMAN LAW

BY GAIUS

VITH A TRANSLATION AND COMMENTARY

BY

EDWARD POSTE, M.A.

BARRISTER AT LAW

AND FELLOW OF ORIEL COLLEGE, OXFORD

Oxford

AT THE CLARENDON PRESS

M.DCCC.LXXI

PREFACE.

In the year 1816, Niebuhr noticed in the library of the Cathedral Chapter at Verona a manuscript in which certain compositions of Saint Jerome had been written over some prior writings, which in certain places had themselves been superposed on some still earlier inscription. On communication with Von Savigny, Niebuhr came to the conclusion that the lowest or earliest inscription was an elementary treatise on Roman law by Gaius, a treatise hitherto only known, or principally known, to Roman lawyers by a barbarous epitome of its contents inserted in the code of Alaric, king of the Visigoths. The palimpsest or rewritten manuscript originally contained 129 folios, three of which are now lost. One folio belonging to the Fourth Book (§ 136–§ 144) having been detached by some accident from its fellows, had been published by Maffei in his Historia Teologica, A.D. 1740, and republished by Haubold in the very year in which Niebuhr discovered the rest of the codex.

Each page of the MS. generally contains twenty-four lines, each line thirty-nine letters; but sometimes as many as forty-five. On sixty pages, or about a fourth of the whole, the codex is doubly palimpsest, i. e. there are three inscriptions on the parchment. About a tenth of the whole is lost or completely illegible, but part of this may be restored from Justinian's Institutes, or from other sources; accordingly, of the whole Institutions about one thirteenth is wanting, one half of which belongs to the Fourth Book.

From the style of the handwriting the MS. is judged to be older than Justinian or the sixth century after Christ; but probably did not precede that monarch by a long interval. The word Dimissum, often used in the code of Alaric in the unclassical sense of legatum, occurs in 2 § 195, and looks like an annotation transferred by a transcriber from the margin to the text. As this use of the word is very barbarous and comparatively recent, Huschke is inclined to believe that the century preceding Justinian is the earliest date that can be assigned to the MS.

In a year after Niebuhr's discovery the whole text of Gaius had been copied out by Goeschen and Hollweg, who had been sent to Verona for that purpose by the Prussian Royal Academy of Sciences, and in 1820 the first edition was published. Since that time the text has been gradually purified by the labours—the wonderful learning, ingenuity, and patience—of many distinguished German jurists and scholars.

Little is known about Gaius, not even his family name (cognomen), or gentile name (nomen), for Gaius is merely an individual name (praenomen). The word 'Gaius' is a trisyllable in the classical period, for instance, in the versification of Catullus, Martial, and Statius; e.g. Martial, 11, 36:

> 'Quincunces et sex cyathos bessesque bibamus,
> Gaius ut fiat Julius et Proculus'

(i.e. the sextarius of 12 cyathi being the potatory unit, 'Drink 5 of wine to 7 of water, 6 of wine to 6 of water, and 8 of wine to 4 of water, to spell the name of Gaius Julius Proculus'); but at a later period, e.g. in the versification of Ausonius, it is contracted into a dissyllable.

Respecting his date, we know that he flourished under the emperors Hadrian (A.D. 117–138), Antoninus Pius (A.D. 138–161), Marcus Aurelius Antoninus (A.D. 161–180), and Commodus (A.D. 180–192). Gaius himself mentions that he was a contemporary of Hadrian, Dig. 34, 5, 7, pr. He apparently wrote the First Book of his Institutions under Antoninus Pius, whom he mentions, § 53, § 74, § 102, without the epithet Divus (Departed), but in the Second Book, § 195, with this epithet. The Antoninus mentioned, § 126, is probably Marcus Aurelius Philosophus. Respecting the rules of Cretio, 2 § 177, Gaius appears not to be cognizant of a constitution of Marcus Aurelius mentioned by Ulpian, 22, 34. That he survived to the time of Commodus appears from his having written a treatise on the Sc. Orphitianum, an enactment passed under that emperor.

As the opinions of Gaius are not quoted by the subsequent jurists whose fragments are preserved in the Digest, it has been inferred that Gaius was a public teacher of jurisprudence (jus publice docens), who never in his lifetime obtained the highest distinction of the legal profession, the title of juris auctor (jus publice respondens), see p. 22. Valentinian, however, after his death raised Gaius to the position of juris auctor, that is, gave to his writings pre-eminent auctoritas, or exclusive legislative authority, equal to that of four other jurists, Papinian, Ulpian, Paulus, and Modestinus.

Besides his Institutions, Gaius was the author of many other treatises, of which fragments are preserved in the Digest, and some of which are alluded to by Gaius in the Institutions. For instance, he wrote a treatise on Edictum Urbicum, 1 § 188, which, as opposed to Edictum Provinciale, probably embraced the edicts of the Praetor urbanus, the Praetor peregrinus, and the Aedilis curulis; a commentary on the Twelve Tables, another on the lex Papia Poppaea, another on the works of Quintus Mucius, besides a treatise on Res quotidianae, and the above-named treatise on Sc. Orphitianum and another on Sc. Tertullianum.

The name of the recently discovered work, perhaps in mastery of the subject and its union of the opposite virtues of brevity and clearness the best elementary treatise of jurisprudence the world has ever seen, does not appear in the MS.; but from the proem to Justinian's Institutes appears to have been INSTITUTIONES, or, to distinguish it from the systems of Rhetoric which also bore this name, INSTITUTIONES IURIS CIVILIS. From the way in which it is mentioned by Justinian, we may infer that for 350 years the *élite* of the youth of Rome were initiated in the mysteries of jurisprudence by the manual of Gaius, much as English law students have for many years commenced their labours under the inferior auspices of Blackstone. It is probably in allusion to the familiarity of the Roman youth with the writings of Gaius that Justinian repeatedly calls him (e.g. Inst. proem, 6; Inst. 4, 18, 5; and in the Constitution prefixed to the Digest, and addressed ad Antecessores, § 1,) 'our friend Gaius' (Gaius noster). The shortness of the time that sufficed Tribonian and his colleagues for the composition of Justinian's Institutes (apparently a few months towards the close of the three years devoted to the compilation of the Digest, Inst. proem) is less surprising when we see how closely Tribonian has followed the arrangement of Gaius, and how largely, when no change of legislation prohibited, he has appropriated his very words.

Certain internal evidences, as already noticed, fix the date at which portions of the Institutions were composed. The emperor Hadrian is spoken of as Departed or Deceased (Divus) except in 1 § 47 and 2 § 57. Antoninus Pius is sometimes (1 § 53, 1 § 102) named without this epithet, but in 2 § 195 has the style of Divus. Marcus Aurelius was probably named, 2 § 126, and the Institutions were probably published before his death, for 2 § 177, as above mentioned, contains no notice of a constitution of his, recorded by Ulpian, that bears on the matter in question. Paragraphs 3 § 24 § 25 would hardly have been penned after the Sc. Orphitianum, A.D. 178, or the Sc. Tertullianum, A.D. 158.

On the continent the discovery of the Institutions of Gaius inaugurated quite a new era in the study of Roman law, throwing a flood of light on much that had been hitherto obscure. If English scholars have hitherto fallen behind their continental brothers, it has been principally in their inattention to Roman jurisprudence. Most of them would probably be surprised to hear, what however would not be very far from the truth, that the knowledge of the laws under which Horace and Cicero lived is almost as accessible to any one interested in the inquiry, as is the knowledge of the laws of England of the present day to the English layman. There are signs, however, which promise that this neglect of one of the most valuable branches of classic literature will not be much longer chargeable on English universities and English scholars.

For the Latin text of Gaius I should have been glad to have been able to avail myself of the edition understood to be preparing for publication under the auspices of the Berlin Academy of Sciences, as the result of a new examination of the Veronese MS. by Studemund and Mommsen. An improved version of the text emanating from the labours of such eminent critics cannot fail to be of the highest interest. Some foretaste of the fruits of their labours has been given to the public by Krueger, from whose pamphlet some extracts are given in the Addenda. In the meantime I have thought it best to reprint the very judicious edition of Gaius given by Gneist in his Syntagma Iuris Romani, with, however, a few variations, which are indicated in an Appendix.

In the text of Gaius, the words or portions of words which are purely conjectural are denoted by italics. The orthography of the Veronese MS. is extremely inconstant. Some of these inconstancies it will be seen are retained: e.g. the spelling oscillates between the forms praegnas and praegnans, nanctus and nactus, erciscere and herciscere, prendere and prehendere, diminuere and deminuere, parentum and parentium, vulgo and volgo, apud and aput, sed and set, proxumus and proximus, affectus and adfectus, inponere and imponere, &c. Some irregularities likely to embarrass the reader, e.g. the substitution of v for b in debitor and probare, the substitution of b for v in servus and vitium, have been tacitly corrected. The numeration of the paragraphs was introduced by Goeschen in his first edition of Gaius, and for convenience of reference has been retained by all subsequent editors. The rubrics or titles marking the larger divisions of the subject, with the exception of a few at the beginning, are not found in the Veronese MS. Those that are found are not very apposite, and are supposed not to be the work of Gaius, but of a transcriber. To distinguish them from the others they are accompanied with a translation. The remainder are of my own invention, or are taken from the corresponding sections of Justinian's Institutes.

The present edition is partly addressed to law students who desire to prepare themselves for the intelligent appreciation of the laws of their own country by an acquaintance with the only other system of legal conceptions known to the world, and partly to those not destined to the legal profession who consider some initiation in the principles of jurisprudence as an essential part of a liberal education.

The text is accompanied with a translation which, though principally intended for those who profess little knowledge of Latin, it is hoped may be found useful even to advanced scholars unfamiliar with the conceptions and language of Roman jurisprudence.

The commentary, notwithstanding an anxiety not to alarm the student by its dimensions, occasionally refers to corresponding institutions, like or unlike, of English jurisprudence. The scruples against swelling the bulk of the work by this course were overcome by the conviction that besides being a ready mode of interpreting what might be enigmatic, the citation of likenesses or contrasts from an independent legislation would, if psychologists say truly, be rather an assistance to the memory than a burden.

An elementary treatise can scarcely make any profession of originality. I have availed myself of lights wherever I could obtain them. And, not to crowd the following pages with references to the writers to whom I am indebted, I must here once for all acknowledge my obligation, not to mention many authors from whom I have borrowed isolated views or quotations, to Austin's Lectures on Jurisprudence, to Ortolan's elegant and lucid commentary on the Institutes of Justinian, to Puchta's learned Cursus der Institutionen, and above all to the various writings of Von Savigny, a rival of the brightest names of the golden period of Roman jurisprudence.

As the Institutions of Gaius were intended to be an introductory initiation in Roman law, I have not thought it necessary to write an introduction to an introduction; but to the student who is making his first acquaintance with the subject I would give the following advice. He may find his labours lightened and his path made easier if he studies the various divisions of the Institutions of Gaius in the following order. He will do well (on the teleological principle that the Beginning is explained by the End) to begin with Procedure (Actiones, Book IV), the final manifestation and application of the rules of Substantive law: to proceed to Obligations (3 § 88–§ 225), the rules of which appeal to the common sense of mankind, and are the most cosmopolitan part of the code: and from thence to the modes of acquiring Ownership, 2 § 1–§ 96. The arbitrary and local, but proportionately curious and picturesque, law of Persons (Book I) may next be studied. The law of Wills (2 § 97–§ 289), somewhat formidable from its dimensions but tolerably clear in its details, may follow. The law of Intestate succession, obscure in parts and not very interesting nor necessary to the understanding of other portions, may be left to the last.

CHRONOLOGICAL TABLE.

B.C.

753. Foundation of Rome.

578—535. Servius Tullius. Division into thirty Tribes. Institution of Comitia Tributa, Census, Comitia Centuriata.

494. First secession of the Plebs. Appointment of Tribunes of the Plebs.

451. Laws of the Ten Tables promulgated.

450—449. Two additional Tables of Laws. The Patricians incorporated in the local Tribes. Lex Valeria Horatia gives legislative power to Comitia Tributa.

366. First appointment of a Praetor.

339. Q. Publilius Philo, Dictator, abolishes the veto of the Comitia Centuriata on the legislative measures of the Comitia Tributa.

326. Partial abolition of Nexum.

312. Cnaeus Flavius publishes a calendar of Dies Fasti and Nefasti.

287. Last secession of the Plebs. Q. Hortensius, Dictator, abolishes the veto of the Senate on the legislative measures of the Comitia Tributa.

269. First issue of silver coins at Rome.

264. First gladiatorial exhibition at Rome.

244. Lex Silia about this time.

B.C.

234. Lex Calpurnia about this time.

204. Lex Cincia.

170. Lex Aebutia.

122. C. Gracchus gives judicial functions to the Equites.

90. Lex Julia confers the franchise on all the Latins.

89. The franchise granted to all the confederate towns of Italy, and the Latin franchise to the Transpadani.

27. Octavianus receives the titles of Augustus and Imperator.

A.D.

4. Lex Aelia Sentia.

9. Lex Papia Poppaea.

19. Lex Junia Norbana.

62. Sc. Trebellianum.

69—79. Vespasian.

98—117. Trajan.

117—138. Hadrian.

131. Edictum Perpetuum promulgated.

138—161. Antoninus Pius.

161—180. Marcus Aurelius Antoninus Philosophus.

180—192. Commodus.

294. Judicia Ordinaria abolished by Diocletian.

527—565. Justinian.

CONTENTS.

BOOK I.

STATUS OR UNEQUAL RIGHTS [DE PERSONIS].

BOOK II.

EQUAL RIGHTS [DE REBUS].

BOOK III.

BOOK IV.

PROCEDURE [DE ACTIONIBUS].

EXPLANATION OF ABBREVIATIONS.

Inst. Institutes of Justinian.

Dig. Digest or Pandects of Justinian.

Cod. Codex of Justinian.

The meaning of the numbers that follow these abbreviations will be obvious to any one who opens a volume of the Corpus Juris.

Pr. stands for principio, meaning, in the first paragraph of a title of the Institutes, or of a fragment of a title of the Digest.

The Commentaries of Gaius are referred to by numbers indicating the book and the paragraph: e.g. 2 § 5, indicates the 5th paragraph of Book 2.

When Ulpian or Paulus is quoted, the works referred to are the Regulae of Ulpian and the Sententiae Receptae of Paulus.

ELEMENTS OF ROMAN LAW.

BOOK I.

DE PERSONIS.

The following treatise is a portion of a particular jurisprudence; it is an exposition of the Civil law of Rome, that is to say, of her Private law (jus privatum) as opposed to her Public law (jus publicum) in both acceptations, in other words, as opposed both to her Criminal law and to her Constitutional law.

Law is the common subject both of Jurisprudence and of Political or Legislative science: but these sciences differ herein, that Jurisprudence treats of laws as they are, Political or Legislative science treats of laws as they ought to be. To the statesman or legislator laws are only means to an end; to the jurist they are what figure is to the geometer, i.e. a subject-matter independent and final, into whose investigation the relation of means to end never enters except occasionally and incidentally, e.g. so far as the end proposed by the lawgiver may be indicated by jurisprudence as a clue to guide the judicature in the interpretation of a law. Statesmanship or legislation may be regarded as a master science to which jurisprudence is ancillary, as furnishing the statesman or legislator with an exact knowledge of the instruments and materials at his disposition, and of the methods which he may employ.

The expounder of Roman law, and indeed of any law, must constantly make use of certain terms, expressing generalizations of jurisprudence, and more or less technical; and the due understanding of these terms, accordingly, is necessary to the due understanding of any systematic exposition of law. As Gaius has omitted to supply any preliminary definitions of his leading terms, instead of occupying ourselves with the orts and scraps of philosophy or forensic rhetoric that oddly garnish the entrance to Justinian's Institutes, or the more copious but equally ill-selected aphorisms huddled together at the beginning of his Digest, and attempting to wring from them more significance than they really contain; it may be expedient to unfold, independently of our Roman authorities, the import of some of the pivot terms of the subject; and we shall find the definitions we require already elaborated for us in the writings of Austin, to whose valuable but unfortunately unfinished Lectures on Jurisprudence I am mainly indebted for the leading definitions and divisions that will be employed in this commentary.

A few definitions will suffice. The words which denote the instruments and materials of legislation and the subject-matter of jurisprudence are Law, Sanction, Title, Right, Obligation. The definitions of these five terms may, indeed, be regarded as a single definition, for the things denoted by these five words are merely the same thing looked at from different sides: at least they are correlative ideas, indissolubly connected parts of the same indivisible whole. The definitions of these terms which we proceed to give are their definitions, it is to be observed, as used in jurisprudence, that is, in the exposition not of natural or moral laws but of positive or political laws, and are accordingly unconnected with the hypotheses of any particular school of Ethical speculation.

A Law is a command; that is to say, it is the signification by a lawgiver to a person obnoxious to evil of the lawgiver's wish that such person should do or forbear to do some act, with the intimation of an evil that will be inflicted in case the wish be disregarded.

Points to be noted here are the author and the subject of law. Every law is set by a sovereign person or a sovereign body of persons to a member or members of the independent political society wherein that person or body is sovereign or supreme: it is set by a monarch or sovereign number to a person or persons in a state of subjection to its author. A Sovereign is a determinate human superior, who receives habitual obedience or submission from the bulk of a given society, and is not in the habit of obedience to a like superior.

A Sanction is the evil annexed to the command of the lawgiver.

Obligation or duty is obnoxiousness to the evil annexed to the command of the lawgiver.

Right is the capacity of exacting by the power of the sovereign certain acts or forbearances; or, it is the capacity of the person benefited by a doing or forbearance commanded by the lawgiver to enforce that performance or forbearance from the person to whom it is onerous, that is, to whom it is commanded, by an appeal to the sovereign power to whom such person is subject.

Dealing at present with the Civil code, we shall confine ourselves, in treating of Rights, to rights of subject against subject, that is, to rights which imply a common superior. Whether a sovereign can have rights against his own subject, whether, that is, the conception of rights permits the same person to be party and sovereign, is a question that may be left to the theory of the Political code. The question whether a sovereign, in his civil courts of judicature, shall accord rights to a foreign potentate, that is, to one who owes him no allegiance, may be left to the theory of the salutary but sanctionless code called the Comity of nations.

Title is the fact, event, or circumstance defining or designating the person on whom the lawgiver confers a right or on whom he imposes an obligation. The word Title is employed in a limited application by English lawyers, to denote the mode of acquiring a Real right; but we use it without any limitation to any branch of law, to denote universally the fact originating any right, real or personal, and not only to denote the fact originating any right, but also the fact originating any obligation, civil or criminal; nay, further, not only to denote the mode in which any right or obligation is originated, or begins, but also to denote the mode in which any right or obligation is terminated or comes to an end. To use the nomenclature of Bentham, a Title is a fact Dispositive of Rights and Obligations. The generic term Dispositive splits into Investitive and Divestitive. Title, then, is a fact Investitive or Divestitive of Rights and Obligations. Investitive again splits into Collative and Impositive, and Divestitive into Privative and Exonerative. Title, then, definitively, is any fact Collative or Privative of a Right and Impositive or Exonerative of an Obligation.

Every Right implies a Law by which it is created, a Title to which it is annexed, a Sovereign by whom it is enforced, a Sanction by means of which it is enforced, a person in whom it resides, and a person on whom a correlative obligation is incumbent. The same, mutatis mutandis, may be said of every relative Obligation. We say of every relative obligation, for not all obligations are relative. Obligations are either relative or absolute; relative are those which imply a private person invested with a corresponding right, absolute those which do not involve a private person invested with a correlative right. For instance, the duties violated by smuggling, by polygamy, by breach of prison, by cruelty to brute animals, are not obligations to a private person but to the Sovereign, and the rights of the Sovereign, if he has any, have no limits but the limits of his might, and bear no resemblance to the rights contemplated by the Civil code, which are acts or forbearances, enforcible by appeal to a common human superior; for the Sovereign, ex vi termini, has no human superior. All rights, then, imply correlative obligations, but not all obligations imply correlative rights.

Every legislation or system of laws is composed of a vast number of particular laws, having the same or analogous features, just as every tissue is composed of an infinity of threads, and every vegetable or animal organism of an infinity of cells: and having before our eyes the cardinal points of any individual law, by considering the division or differentiation of these cardinal points we may anticipate the leading divisions of the general mass of legislation.

Having given the definitions of these cardinal points, we will now notice some of their fundamental divisions.

The primary division of Rights, the one most necessary for forming clear conceptions on the subject, a division which, as far as my acquaintance with juristic literature extends, Austin was the first to make clear and luminous, is the division into Sanctioned rights and Sanctioning rights. This division of Rights depends on a corresponding division of the Titles to which they are annexed.

Sanctioned, or primary, or final rights, are such rights as exist antecedently to any Wrong, rights whose Title or origin from which they spring, and which defines the person on whom they are conferred, is some circumstance other than a Wrong. Sanctioning, secondary, or instrumental rights, are rights engendered by a Wrong committed by some other person, rights conferred upon a person whose title to them is the fact that he has suffered a Wrong.

Wrong is the violation of right or duty, and may be defined as disobedience, intentional or negligent, to the command of the sovereign, entitling the wrongdoer to the Sanction, that is, to the evil threatened by the lawgiver. Examples of Sanctioned rights are the right of a proprietor to enjoy the fruits of ownership, the right of a contractor to the performance of the promise made by the person with whom he contracted, the right of every respectable member of society to have his honour unstained, his character unimpeached. The corresponding Sanctioning rights, or rights of the injured party to redress, are the right of the dispossessed proprietor to be reinstated in possession, the right of the deceived contractor to have damages for non-performance or to have specific performance enforced by the court, the right of the slandered person to recover damages for slander.

The divergence of Rights into two classes, rights antecedent to wrong, and rights consequent on wrong, which we have referred to a divergence of Titles, flows immediately from the essence of Law, and may be deduced from its definition.

The essence of every Law is the injunction or prohibition of some given act and the menace of an evil in the case of non-compliance. Every law, that is to say, is at once Imperative and Punitory; it is only Imperative by being Punitory. So far as law is Imperative, it confers primary or sanctioned rights, and imposes primary or sanctioned duties: so far as it is Punitory, it confers secondary or sanctioning rights, and imposes secondary or sanctioning duties. A primary obligation may be defined as the burden imposed by the law in its first or imperative clause; a secondary obligation as the burden imposed by the law in its alternative or punitory clause.

Sanctioning rights only exist for the sake of Sanctioned rights. Accordingly, the latter may be called principal or final, the former instrumental or ancillary. So far as the existence of Sanctioned rights is dependent on the existence of Sanctioning rights, we might invert the epithets primary and secondary, which we have applied to them. I have no Sanctioned rights independently of the injunction or prohibition which declares that some act or omission is a violation of my right, and vindicates it by a Sanction civil or criminal. That is, my Sanctioned right or duty owes its existence to the injunction or prohibition of certain acts and to the remedy or punishment to be applied in case of disobedience.

Accordingly, though looking at them as means and ends, we have called Sanctioning rights Secondary and Sanctioned rights Primary; yet if we looked at the order of existence, we might call Sanctioning rights Primary and Sanctioned rights Secondary.

Again, Sanctioning rights and duties are directly enforced by the courts, Sanctioned rights and duties only indirectly. Sanctioning rights and duties are not only immediately enforced, but also universally and invariably, except when there is a miscarriage of justice. Sanctioned rights and duties cannot be secured from violation, even when the administration of justice is perfect: the sovereign can only induce, persuade, incline, to the observance of primary rights and duties, by holding out the inexorable alternative of secondary rights and duties; he cannot compel. As only secondary rights are directly enforced by the judicature, it might be alleged that these are the only genuine rights; that primary rights are merely imaginary, a fiction of philosophic jurisprudence: and it must be admitted that some secondary rights are the more prominent and constant object of the jurist than the corresponding primary rights. Thus the portion of primary rights that hereafter, as opposed to Acquired rights, we shall call Primordial rights (right to life, health, liberty, reputation, etc.) are never so much as mentioned by Gaius, nor, so far as I am aware, by any Roman jurist, but are only deducible from the corresponding Sanctioning rights, the rights that arise from violence, assault and battery, defamation, and the like. This obscuration of the Primary right in comparison with the corresponding Secondary right is, however, not invariable. The Primary rights of Status, Property, Obligation, are commonly recognized both in popular and juristic language as clearly as the corresponding Secondary rights, and we are quite justified in extending the division of Sanctioned and Sanctioning rights from these types where it is more strongly marked through the universal sphere of rights, that is, to those regions where the Primary rights have engaged a less amount of attention.

A second fundamental division of rights, common to all legislations, and ever present to the mind of Roman jurists, is the division into Real and Personal, or jus in rem and jus in personam. This division of rights depends on a division of the corresponding obligations. Every right residing in one person implies the existence of another person or persons on whom a corresponding duty is incumbent. The corresponding duty is sometimes incumbent on a determinate person or persons, sometimes on persons indeterminate, in other words, on the world at large. In the former case it is usually positive, that is to say, a duty of actual performance; in the latter case it is usually negative, that is to say, a duty of abstention or forbearance. Jus in personam is a right to acts on the part of a certain person, Jus in rem is a right to forbearance on the part of all persons. Examples of Real right are Status, Franchise, Ownership: examples of Personal right are Obligations (in a narrower acceptation than we have hitherto assumed) arising from contract or delict. Jus in rem may be defined as a right correlating with obligations at once universal and negative: Jus in personam a right correlating with obligations at once particular and positive. Jus in personam implies the relation of debtor and creditor; Jus in rem is well expressed by the Aeschylean Furies in describing the exclusive character of their office:—

γεινομέναισι λάχη τάδ' ἐφ' ἁμὶν ἐκράνθη·
ἀθανάτων δ' ἀπέχειν χέρας, οὐδέ τις ἐστὶ
ξυνδαίτωρ μετάκοινος.

'At our birth this domain to us the Fates allotted.
The immortals off must hold their hands,
Nor is there banqueter our feast to share.'

It is to be observed that the expressions Jus in rem and Jus in personam are not classical. The classical expressions on which they are modelled are actio in rem, actio in personam, action to inforce a Real right, action to inforce a Personal right. Jurisprudence, however, requires terms to express this leading classification of Rights, and, as such terms are not supplied by the Roman jurists, the above mentioned, as, though barbarous, they seem on the whole to be most eligible, have been adopted, and will be employed in the course of this commentary.

A third important division of Rights is expressed in the terms Jura rerum and Jura personarum, rights given by the law of Things, and rights given by the law of Persons. But we may adjourn the consideration of this division until we examine the rights of Status, as we shall immediately proceed to do, Status forming the subject of the first book of the commentaries of Gaius.

The evil which constitutes a Sanction may consist in the loss of any of the rights protected by the sovereign. It may be the privation of political rights, the privation or diminution of property, or the privation of primordial rights—incarceration, compulsory labour, banishment, death.

The motives which sway the legislator in determining the nature and amount of the sanction are various. Sometimes the motive is simply the reparation of a harm inflicted. Sometimes the apportionment of the remedy is intended as an inducement to the aggrieved party to recur to the public judicature instead of redressing his own grievance, and, to use a common expression, taking the law into his own hands—an urgently pressing motive in the infant beginnings of society. Sometimes the end of the lawgiver is the prevention of the prohibited act by terrorism, by the menace of the sanction and the execution of the menace. Sometimes the sanction is retributive or vindictive, the expression of the conscience or moral sentiments of the society. In humane legislations a collateral end of the sanction is often the reformation of the offender: this motive is confined to sanctions of the criminal code.

To a division of Sanctions corresponds an important division of jurisprudence. Some Sanctions may be enforced or remitted at the discretion of a private party, others are enforced at the discretion of the Sovereign or state, and by the Sovereign or state alone can the liability of the wrongdoer be remitted. This founds the division of the code or statute-book into the Civil code and the Criminal code.

But even the Civil code presents, more strongly marked in Roman law than in modern systems, a similar division of Sanctions. The principal end or object of some Sanctions, as above stated, is the redress of injury in the past, compensation or indemnity to the injured person for his violated primary right: the end of others is the prevention of injury in the future, terrorism, or the deterrence of future wrongdoers by exemplary punishment of a past offender. On this division of civil sanctions is based the division of civil suits into Rei persecutio and Poenae persecutio, a suit to recover property, and a suit to recover a penalty. A judgment may be bilaterally penal, that is, may both impoverish the defendant and enrich the plaintiff; or it may be unilaterally penal, that is, may impoverish the defendant without enriching the plaintiff, e. g. in a suit for indemnification, when the defendant has not gained in proportion to the loss he has inflicted on the plaintiff. A suit which is Rei persecutio may be unilaterally penal. Bilaterally penal suits, though common in Roman law, are unfrequent in modern legislations.

The sanction of a right or obligation, whether primary or secondary, is a motive addressed to the will of the person who owes the obligation, and is the prevision or anticipation of an intending wrongdoer, that his unlawful gain will be extorted from him, and, commonly, an additional evil, loss, or pain will be inflicted on him by the irresistible power of the sovereign. The sanction of the primary obligation is the secondary obligation, and it is imaginable that the sanction of the secondary obligation should be a tertiary obligation, and so on; but this series of sanctioned and sanctioning obligations cannot proceed without a limit: if it did, every sanction might be defied and every obligation broken, and there would be no ultimate basis of obligation. But, in fact, the series comes to a speedy end. When once the secondary obligation is ascertained by a Judgment or Condemnation, unless this judgment is satisfied by a voluntary submission of the party condemned, the ultimate sanction soon quits the form of obligation, and presents itself in the shape of Execution, that is, of physical compulsion, to which the assent of the party obliged is immaterial. Indeed, in the criminal code we can scarcely speak of primary and secondary obligation, as the sanction usually in the first instance assumes the form of physical compulsion.

For a further consideration of the classification of Rights, see 2 § 1, commentary; and for a further elucidation of the import of Title, see 2 § 79, commentary.

De *iure gentium et civili.*

§ 1. *Omnes populi qui legibus et moribus reguntur partim suo proprio, partim communi omnium hominum iure utuntur: nam quod quis*que populus ipse sibi ius constituit, id ipsius proprium est vocaturque ius civile, quasi ius proprium ip*sius civitatis; quod vero naturalis* ratio inter omnes homines constituit, id apud omnes populos peraeque custoditur vocaturque ius gentium, quasi quo iure omnes gentes utuntur. Populus itaque Romanus partim suo proprio, partim communi omnium hominum iure utitur. quae singula qualia sint, suis locis proponemus.

§ 2. Constant autem iura ex legibus, plebiscitis, senatusconsultis, constitutionibus Principum, edictis eorum qui ius edicendi habent, responsis prudentium.

§ 3. Lex est quod populus iubet atque constituit. plebiscitum est quod plebs iubet atque constituit. plebs autem a populo eo distat, quod populi appellatione universi cives significantur, connumeratis e*tiam* patriciis; plebis autem appellatione sine patriciis ceteri cives significantur. Unde olim patricii dicebant plebiscitis se non teneri, quia sine auctoritate eorum facta essent. sed postea lex Hortensia lata est, qua cautum est ut plebiscita universum populum tenerent. itaque eo modo legibus exaequata sunt.

§ 4. Senatusconsultum est quod senatus iubet atque constituit, idque legis vicem optinet, quamvis fu*er*it quaesitum.

§ 5. Constitutio Principis est quod Imperator decreto vel edicto

On gentile law and civil law.

§ 1. The laws of every people governed by statutes and customs are partly peculiar to itself, partly common to all mankind. The rules enacted by a given state for its own members are peculiar to itself, and are called civil law; the rules prescribed by natural reason are observed by all nations alike, and are called gentile law. So the laws of the people of Rome are partly peculiar to itself, partly common to all nations; and this distinction shall be traced, as occasion offers, through all the branches of the code.

§ 2. Roman law consists of statutes, plebiscites, senatusconsults, constitutions of the emperors, edicts of magistrates authorized to issue them, and opinions of jurists.

§ 3. A statute is a command and ordinance of the people: a plebiscite is a command and ordinance of the commonalty. The commonalty and the people are thus distinguished: the people are all the citizens, including the patricians; the commonalty are all the citizens, except the patricians. Whence in former times the patricians maintained that they were not subject to the plebiscites, as passed without their authority; but afterwards a statute called the lex Hortensia was enacted, which provided that the plebiscites should bind the people, and thus plebiscites were made coordinate with statutes.

§ 4. A senatusconsult is a command and ordinance of the senate, and is assimilated in force to a statute, a point which was formerly controverted.

§ 5. A constitution is an ordinance of the emperor by decree,

vel epistula constituit. nec umquam dubitatum est, quin id legis vicem optineat, cum ipse Imperator per legem imperium accipiat.

edict, or letter; and was always recognized as having the force of a statute, as the statute which invests the emperor with his office confers upon him the whole power of the people.

§ 6. Ius autem edicendi habent magistratus populi Romani. sed amplissimum ius est in edictis duorum Praetorum, urbani et peregrini: quorum in provinciis iurisdictionem Praesides earum habent; item in edictis Aedilium curulium, quorum iurisdictionem in provinciis populi Romani Quaestores habent; nam in provincias Caesaris omnino Quaestores non mittuntur, et ob id hoc edictum in his provinciis non proponitur.

§ 6. Power to issue edicts is vested in magistrates of the people of Rome, the amplest authority belonging to the edicts of the two praetors, the home praetor and the foreign praetor, whose provincial jurisdiction is vested in the presidents of the provinces, and to the edicts of the curule ediles, whose jurisdiction in the provinces of the people of Rome is vested in quaestors: in the provinces of the emperor no quaestors are appointed, and in these provinces, accordingly, the edict of the ediles is not published.

§ 7. Responsa prudentium sunt sententiae et opiniones eorum quibus permissum est iura condere. quorum omnium si in unum sententiae concurrant, id quod ita sentiunt legis vicem optinet; si vero dissentiunt, iudici licet quam velit sententiam sequi: idque rescripto divi Hadriani significa*tur*.

§ 7. The answers of jurists are the decisions and opinions of persons authorized to interpret the law. If they are unanimous, their decision has the force of law; if they disagree, the judge may follow whichever opinion he chooses, as is ruled by a rescript of the late emperor Hadrian.

I. § 1. Jurisprudence treats exclusively of positive law: the exclusive origin of positive law is positive legislation; the term positive legislation including both the express or direct enactments of the political sovereign, and the implied, indirect, circuitous enactments imported by the sovereign's acquiescence in the ruling of subordinate authorities.

The rules and principles denoted by the terms praetor-made law, jurist-made law, judge-made law, are only law because they are impliedly adopted, confirmed, and ratified by the silent acquiescence of the sovereign legislature.

When Roman jurists spoke of Gentile law or Natural law they intended to denote a certain portion of Roman positive law, that is, of law administered by Roman tribunals and enforced by the Roman executive. Accordingly, when Gaius speaks of Gentile law as enacted by Nature (id quod naturalis ratio inter omnes homines constituit), and Civil law as enacted by the Roman legislature, he uses language which, though probably traditional in the writings of Roman jurists, is inappropriate and misleading; for the enactments of Nature differ from the enactments, express or tacit, of political sovereigns in many important particulars.

Austin illustrates the character of Positive or Political law by contrasting it in certain points with the law of Honour and the law of Fashion.

Unlike the purely Ethical law, or a law set by a man to himself, which has nothing in the nature of a sanction to compel him to observe it, the law of Honour and the law of Fashion have certain earthly sanctions annexed to them, whereby the party on whom the obligation is imposed is inclined to act agreeably to their injunctions and prohibitions. The transgressor of these laws is harmed in consequence of the displeasure which his breach of law provokes; and all parties obnoxious to the displeasure of the society whose sentiments and opinions constitute the law are inclined by the evil which will probably follow disobedience to act or forbear agreeably to the dictates of the law. But along with this resemblance between the law of Honour and Positive law there is the following difference. The law of Honour or of Fashion is set by an indeterminate lawgiver; a political law is set by a determinate lawgiver, a given earthly potentate. The sanction annexed to the law of Honour or of Fashion is applied against the party whose conduct deviates from the law by another indeterminate party of his own spontaneous movement; not by an assignable functionary authorized by the indeterminate lawgiver to enforce the law; not, like the sanction of political law, by a minister of justice appointed by a determinate political sovereign to execute the commands which he issues. In these respects the Natural or Gentile law of Roman jurists differs from Moral law and from the law of Opinion, and shows itself to be a genuine portion of Positive or Political law.

The organ by which the Jus gentium of the Romans was promulgated, which made it by quasi enactment a portion of Roman Positive law, was principally the Edict of the Praetor peregrinus. The relations of Roman citizens with aliens (peregrini), that is, with the members of foreign states formerly subjugated by Rome and now living under the protection of Roman law, were subject to the jurisdiction of a special minister of justice called Praetor peregrinus, who, like the Praetor urbanus, published an annual edict announcing the principles on which justice would be administered. These principles composed Jus gentium as opposed to Jus civium. Jus gentium, that is to say, was not really, as Roman jurists imagined or represented, a collection of the principles common to the legislation of all nations, but a body of rules which the Roman praetor thought worthy to govern the intercourse of Roman citizens with the members of all, originally independent but now subject, foreign nations. Accordingly, if for the definition given by Gaius we substitute the definition 'Quod edicto suo praetor peregrinus omnibus gentibus constituit,' we shall be much nearer the truth.

Gradually the rules regulating the intercourse of citizens with aliens were extended to the intercourse of citizens with citizens, in cases where the rigorous conditions of jus civile were not exactly satisfied, and the precepts of jus gentium were transferred from the edict of praetor peregrinus to the edict of praetor urbanus.

Another organ of quasi publication, whereby the rules of jus gentium were transformed from ideal law to positive law—from laws of Utopia to laws of Rome—were the writings of the jurists, who, at first with the tacit, afterwards with the express permission of the legislature, engaged, nominally in interpreting, really in extending the law, about the time of Cicero (De Legibus, 1, 5), transferred to the edict of the praetor the activity which they had formerly displayed in developing the statutes of the Comitia and the law of the Twelve Tables.

The portion of the edict most fertile in germs of natural law would be the clauses in which the praetor announced, as he did in some cases, that he would instruct the judex, whom he appointed to hear and determine a controversy, to govern himself by a consideration of what was aequum et bonum, i. e. by his views of equity and expediency: and if any of the oral formularies of the earliest system of procedure (legis actiones) contained these or equivalent terms, such formularies may be regarded as a third source of Gentile or Natural law.

Jus civile, i. e. jus civium, was the law of the Twelve Tables, augmented by subsequent legislation, by juristic interpretation, and by consuetudinary law. The institutions of jus civile may be exemplified by such titles to property as Mancipatio and In Jure Cessio, contracts by the form of Nexum and Sponsio, title to intestate succession by Agnatio or civil relationship; while corresponding institutions of jus gentium were the acquisition of property by Tradition, contract by Stipulation without the solemn term Spondeo, title to intestate succession by Cognatio or natural relationship. Other departments of life were not subject to parallel institutes of Civil law and Natural law, but the mutual relations of citizens with citizens as well as of citizens with aliens were exclusively controlled by Gentile law: e.g. the contracts called Consensual, such as buying and selling, letting and hiring, partnership; and contracts called Real, such as the contract of loan for use or loan for consumption.

Gentile titles to Property (jus in rem), titles which ultimately superseded civil titles, are explained at large in Book II.

In respect of Obligation (jus in personam), Gentile law may be divided into two classes, according to the degree in which it was recognized by Civil law:—

A. A portion of Gentile law was recognized as a ground of Action. To this class belong (1) the simple or Formless contracts to which we have alluded, (2) obligations to indemnify grounded on delict, (3) right quasi ex contractu to recover property when it has been lost by one side and gained by the other without any title, Dig. 12, 6, 14, and Dig. 25, 2, 25. Actions founded on this obligation to restore (condictiones), although it was a naturalis obligatio, Dig. 12, 6, 15, were as rigorous (stricti juris) as any in the Civil code. In these cases the obligatio, though naturalis as founded in Jus gentium, yet, as actionable, was said to be civilis obligatio, Dig. 19, 5, 5, 1.

The two eminently Civil spheres of the law of obligation were (1) specialty or Formal contracts, and (2) bilaterally penal suits. Yet even into these provinces Gentile law forced a partial entrance. We shall see that aliens could be parties to a Stipulatio or Verbal contract, though not by the Civil formulary, Spondeo 3 § 93; and to Transcriptio 3 § 133, and Syngrapha 3 § 134, certain forms of Literal contract; and could be made plaintiffs or defendants in bilaterally penal suits by means of the employment of certain Fictions, 4 § 37. This, however, was rather the extension of Civil law to aliens than the intrusion of Gentile law into a Civil province.

B. Other rights and obligations of Gentile law were not admitted as direct grounds for maintaining an action, yet were otherwise noticed by the institutes of Civil jurisprudence and indirectly enforced. Thus a merely naturalis obligatio, though not actionable, might (1) furnish a ground of an equitable defence (exceptio): for instance, on payment of a merely natural debt the receiver has a right of retention, and can bar the suit to recover it back as a payment made in error (condictio indebiti soluti) by pleading the naturalis obligatio, Dig. 12, 6, 64; or the defendant can meet a claim by Compensatio, 4 § 61, cross demand or set-off, of a debt that merely rests on naturalis obligatio, Dig. 40, 7, 20, 2: or a naturalis obligatio might (2) form the basis of an accessory obligation, such as Suretyship (fidejussio) Dig. 46, 1, 6, 2, or Guaranty (constitutum) Dig. 13, 5, 1, 7, or Mortgage (pignus) Dig. 20, 1, 5, pr. or Novation, 3 § 176, Dig. 46, 2, 1, 1, all Civil institutions and direct grounds of action. Though these rights and obligations of Gentile law are imperfect (obligatio tantum naturalis) as not furnishing immediate grounds of action, yet, as being partially and indirectly enforced by Roman tribunals, they clearly compose a portion of Positive law.

Some Roman jurists distinguished Jus naturale and Jus gentium. Thus Ulpian denotes by Jus naturale the law governing the relation of the sexes, i.e. the relation of husband and wife, parent and children, relations anterior to political society, and without which the race could not have been perpetuated: while by Jus gentium he denotes relations that imply the existence of political society.

Modern writers would denote by Jus gentium the generally recognized principles of justice, principles which may be discovered by an induction of positive laws, that is, by a comparison of actually existing legislations, to be universally admitted, or, if not universally, by a majority or by a number of nations; while by Natural law they would denote a philosophic ideal, what might be otherwise denominated the moral law or the divine law, the law that ought to be everywhere established, though perhaps never yet adopted in actual legislation. Gaius, however, in the following commentary uses the terms Jus naturale and Jus gentium as perfectly synonymous and interchangeable.

§ 3. To explain the various sources of Roman law is to write the history of the successive changes in the centre of gravity of sovereign power at Rome. These changes are principally at first the changing relations of Populus and Plebs, at which we may take a hasty glance, as the account given by Gaius is inadequate and misleading.

There was a time when the three tribes of the Populus, the Ramnes, a Latin or Pelasgic race seated on the Palatine hill, the Tities or Quirites, a Sabine race seated on the Capitoline and Quirinal hills, and the Luceres, an Etrurian race seated on the Caelian hill, composed the whole of the Roman state. These three tribes of the Populus were divided into thirty Curiae, and the Curiae into three hundred Gentes. The heads of the Gentes or clans composed the Senate; the heads of the Families composing the Gentes constituted the popular body, or Comitia Curiata.

The Plebs or Plebes, a conquered Latin population, whose first beginnings were located in the suburbs (esquiliae) adjoining these hills, and named outsiders (exquilini) as opposed to the burgesses or insiders (inquilini), and whose large after-growth was settled by bonus Ancus on the Aventine (in memory of which Catullus calls the joint Populus and Plebs, Romulique Ancique gentem), shared the same jus privatum but not the same jus publicum, that is, were not admitted to any share of political power, and formed outside of the city a separate free but dependent corporation. At this time it was true, as Gaius says, that the Plebeians and Patricians were separate bodies.

But this was not so after the legislation of Servius Tullius, to whom is ascribed the division of the people into local Tribes, and into classified Centuries.

The local tribes, probably thirty in number, were a territorial division, including the whole population, patrician as well as plebeian, and forming the basis of the organization of the legislative assembly called Comitia Tributa.

The centuries were a division both civil and military, and the civil division was a classification of the whole population according to their fortune or census.

Those of the highest census were distributed into eighteen centuries of Knights, six patrician and twelve plebeian, which supplied eighteen corresponding centuries of cavalry.

The remainder of the population were divided into five classes, according to their diminishing census, the first class being distributed into eighty centuries, the three next into twenty each, and the fifth into thirty; and each of these classes contributed a corresponding number of centuries (companies) to the infantry, whose equipment, differing in costliness, at once indicated the branch of the service for which they were destined and the class from which they sprang.

Each civil century had a single vote in the Comitia Centuriata, and from the number of centuries into which the classes were respectively distributed, it is obvious that in this assembly the wealthy classes had a great predominance; that is, the Comitia Centuriata was a timocratic assembly, or one in which the ascendency belonged to wealth, as the Comitia Tributa was a democratic assembly, or one in which the ascendency belonged to numbers. The Comitia Tributa were called Plebs, the Comitia Centuriata were called Populus; the enactments of the latter body were called leges, the enactments of the former were called plebiscites.

The subsequent stages in the growth of the commonalty and the changes in the centre of sovereign power are indicated by three legislative measures which demand our consideration.

B.C. 449, a lex Valeria Horatia, passed after a second secession of the plebs, enacted, Ut quod tributim plebes jussisset populum teneret, Livy, 3, 55, 'that the enactments of the Comitia Tributa should bind the populus.'

B.C. 339, a lex Publilia, carried by the dictator Publilius Philo, enacted, Ut plebiscita omnes Quirites tenerent, Livy, 8, 12, 'that plebiscites should bind all Quirites.'

A second, Ut legum quae comitiis centuriatis ferrentur, ante initum suffragium patres auctores fierent, 'that the bills proposed at the Comitia Centuriata should be sanctioned by the fathers before they were submitted to the vote.'

B.C. 287, a lex Hortensia, passed after a secession of the plebs to the Janiculum, enacted, Ut eo jure quod plebs statuisset omnes Quirites tenerentur, Gellius, 15, 27, 'that plebiscites should bind all Quirites.'

The interpretation of these apparently identical and, as it seems, imperfectly recited laws, appears to be as follows:—

By the lex Valeria Horatia the Comitia Tributa received a legislative initiative, but, to have force of law, the enactments required to be confirmed by the vote of Comitia Centuriata (Comitia Curiata, according to Niebuhr) and sanctioned by the auctoritas of the Senate.

By one lex Publilia the necessity of the confirmation of plebiscites by the Comitia Centuriata (Comitia Curiata according to

Niebuhr) was abolished, though the sanction of the Senate was still required to give them legal force.

By the second lex Publilia, Niebuhr supposes that the Comitia Curiata were deprived of their veto on the laws passed at the Comitia Centuriata, their confirmation being reduced to a formality; but it was probably merely a ratification of the existing state of the law, giving the Senate the exclusive initiative in the legislation of the Comitia Centuriata.

By the lex Hortensia, plebiscites were declared to have the force of law without requiring to be sanctioned by the auctoritas of the Senate.

After this period the Comitia Tributa and Comitia Centuriata coexisted as concurrent legislative bodies, the Comitia Tributa chiefly dealing with matters of private law, the Comitia Centuriata with public matters, such as elections and questions of peace and war or alliance.

As Rome grew in opulence, the sums fixed for the census of the higher classes of the Comitia Centuriata ceased to denote a considerable fortune, and this fact alone would divest this assembly of much of its timocratic character. Some further change supervened, introducing the Tribal division into the organization of the Comitia Centuriata; but the nature of this change is one of the obscurest questions in Roman history, and one which we have no space to investigate.

Plebiscites as well as the enactments of Comitia Centuriata were called Leges, and were named after the tribunes by whom they were carried, as the leges proper (rarely called populiscita) were named after the consul or dictator by whom they were carried. Thus Lex Canuleia, Lex Aquilia, 3 § 210, Lex Atinia, Inst. 2, 6, 2, Lex Furia testamentaria, 2 § 225, were plebiscites named after tribunes, the Lex Valeria Horatia was named after two consuls, the Lex Publilia and Lex Hortensia were named after dictators.

§ 4. The legislative power of the senate was in the time of the republic a matter of controversy. It is certain that it had a power of issuing certain administrative decrees or instructions to magistrates that was hardly distinguishable from legislation. Under the emperors matters were changed. Legislation by the Comitia, though spoken of by Gaius in the present tense, had ceased to be a reality after the time of Tiberius, and the last recorded lex was passed in the reign of Nerva. As early as the time of Augustus the auctoritas of the senate began to be regarded as the essential process in making a law, and the subsequent rogatio of the Comitia as a mere formality, which was finally omitted. Senatusconsults, like laws, were sometimes named after the consuls who proposed them, and are sometimes even called leges: thus the measure which Gaius calls Sc. Claudianum, 1 § 84, is subsequently referred to by him under the name of lex, 1 § 86. Ulpian says, Non ambigitur senatum jus facere posse, Dig. 1, 3, 9, 'it is unquestioned that what the senate decrees becomes part of the civil law.' Of course, these senatusconsults were merely a disguised form of imperial constitution. The sovereignty had passed from both patricians and plebeians to the hands of an autocrat. A measure was recommended by the emperor in an oratio or epistola to the senate, and then proposed by the consul who convoked the senate, and voted by the senate without opposition. Even this form was finally disused. No senatusconsult relating to matters of civil law occurs after the time of Septimus Severus.

§ 5. The nature of the different forms of imperial constitution has been much controverted, and certainly varied at different periods. They may be characterized as legislative, judicial, and interpretative.

Edicts were legislative ordinances issued by the emperor in virtue of the jurisdiction appertaining to him as highest magistrate, and were analogous to the edicts of the praetors and ediles.

Decreta were judicial decisions made by the emperor as the highest appellate tribunal: or in virtue of his magisterial jurisdiction, and analogous to the extraordinaria cognitio of the praetor.

Epistolae or rescripta were answers to inquiries addressed to the emperor by private parties or by judges. They may be regarded as interpretations of law by the emperor as the most authoritative juris peritus.

The words of Gaius explaining why constitutions had the force of law seem to be imperfect, and may be supplemented from Justinian: Sed et quod principi placuit legis habet vigorem: cum lege regia, quae de imperio ejus lata est, populus ei et in eum omne suum imperium et potestatem concessit, Inst. 1, 2, 6. 'Imperial constitutions have the effect of law, because by the lex regia, whereby the emperor is invested with his office, the people confers on him all its sovereignty and power.' The lex imperii,

Cod. 6, 23, 3, was called by later jurists lex regia, in memory of the lex curiata, whereby the kings were invested with regal power. The king was proposed by the senate and elected by the Comitia Curiata, and the election was ratified in a second assembly presided over by the king; e. g. Numam Pompilium regem, patribus auctoribus, sibi ipse populus adscivit, qui ut huc venit, quanquam populus curiatis eum comitiis regem esse jusserat, tamen ipse de suo imperio curiatam legem tulit, Cic. De Republ. 2, 13. A fragment of a bronze tablet, on which was inscribed the lex investing Vespasian with sovereign powers, was discovered at Rome in the fourteenth century, and is still preserved in the capitol.

§ 6. All the higher magistrates of Rome were accustomed to issue edicts or proclamations. Thus the consuls convoked the comitia, the army, the senate, by edict: the censors proclaimed the approaching census by edict: the ediles issued regulations for the market by edict: and magistrates with jurisdiction published edicts announcing the rules they would observe in the administration of justice, the Edicts of the Praetor urbanus, Praetor peregrinus, Aedilis curulis being called Edicta urbana, while the Edicts of the governors of provinces were called Edicta provincialia. These edicts, besides being orally proclaimed, were written on white tablets (in albo) and suspended in the forum: apud forum palam ubi de plano legi possit, Probus, 'in the forum in an open space where persons standing on the ground may read.' Such an edict was always published on entering on office (est enim tibi jam, cum magistratum inieris et in concionem adscenderis, edicendum quae sis observaturus in jure dicendo, Cic. De Fin. 2, 22), and was then called Edictum perpetuum, as opposed to occasional proclamations, Edictum repentinum. A clause (pars, caput, clausula, edictum) retained from a former edict was called Edictum tralatitium, Gellius, 3, 18; and though doubtless the edicts gradually changed according to changing emergencies, each succeeding praetor with very slight modifications substantially reproduced the edict of his predecessor. In the reign of Hadrian the jurist Salvius Julianus, called by Justinian Praetoriani edicti ordinator, reduced the edict to its definitive form, and if the yearly publication was not discontinued (cf. Gaius, jus edicendi habent), at all events Julian's coordination of Praetorian law was embodied in all subsequent publications. Such was the origin of Jus honorarium (praetorium, aedilicium), as opposed to Jus civile: and from what has preceded, it needs hardly be stated that the antithesis, Jus civile, Jus honorarium, is nearly coincident with the antithesis, Jus civile, Jus gentium.

It may be observed that Gaius does not attribute to edicts the force of a statute: and this theoretical inferiority of Jus honorarium, for after all it was only theoretical, had a vast influence in modelling the forms and proceedings of Roman jurisprudence. The remedy or redress administered to a plaintiff who based his claim on Jus civile differed from that administered on an appeal to Jus honorarium, as we shall see when we come to treat of Bonitary ownership, Bonorum possessio, Actio in factum, Exceptio. This difference of remedy preserved Jus civile pure and uncontaminated, or at least always distinguishable from Jus honorarium; but this perpetuation of the memory of the various origins of the law, like the analogous distinction of Equity and Common law in English jurisprudence, was purchased by sacrificing for an insufficient object simplicity of rule and uniformity of process.

In the first period of the empire, that is, in the first three centuries of our era, it was the policy of the emperors to maintain a certain show of republican institutions, and the administration of the empire was nominally divided between the princeps or emperor and the people as represented by the senate. Thus, at Rome there were two sets of magistrates, the old republican magistrates with little real power, consuls, praetors, censors, tribunes, quaestors, in outward form elected by the people; and the imperial nominees with much greater real authority, under the name of praefecti, the praefectus urbi, praefectus praetorio, praefectus vigilum, praefectus annonae, praefectus aerario; for though nominally the people and princeps had their separate treasuries under the name of aerarium and fiscus, yet the treasury of the people was not managed by quaestors as in the time of the republic, but by an official appointed by the emperor. Similarly the provinces were divided between the people and the prince, the people administering those which were peaceful and unwarlike, the prince those which required the presence of an army. The governor of a province, whether of the people or the emperor, was called Praeses Provinciae, though the title properly belonged to the governor of an imperial province. The Praeses of a popular province was a Proconsul, and the chief subordinate functionaries were Legati, to whom was delegated the civil jurisdiction, and quaestors, who exercised a jurisdiction corresponding to that of the ediles in Rome. The emperor himself was in theory the Proconsul of an imperial province; but the actual governor, coordinate with the Proconsul of a senatorial province, was the Legatus Caesaris, while the financial administration and fiscal jurisdiction were committed to a functionary called Procurator Caesaris, instead of the republican Quaestor. Sometimes the same person united the office of Procurator and Legatus, as, for instance, Pontius Pilate.

§ 7. The opinions of a jurist had originally only the weight that was due to his knowledge and genius; but on the transfer of sovereign power from the hands of the people to those of a monarch, the latter recognized the expediency of being able to direct and inspire the oracles of jurisprudence; and accordingly Augustus converted the profession of jurist into a sort of political function, giving the decisions of certain authorized jurists the force of law, intending, doubtless, that the blue ribbon of the profession should never be conferred on any lawyer who had antiquarian notions of constitutional law, or whose instincts did not make him a zealous propagandist of the doctrines of despotism. Ante tempora Augusti publice respondendi jus non a principibus dabatur, sed qui fiduciam studiorum suorum habebant, consulentibus respondebant. Neque responsa utique signata dabant, sed plerumque judicibus ipsi scribebant aut testabantur qui illos consulebant. Primus divus Augustus, ut major juris auctoritas haberetur, constituit ut ex auctoritate ejus responderent, et ex illo tempore peti hoc pro beneficio coepit, Dig. 1, 2, 47. 'Until Augustus, the public decision of legal questions was not a right conferred by imperial grant, but any one who relied on his knowledge advised the clients who chose to consult him. Nor were juristic opinions always given in a letter closed and sealed, but were generally laid before the judge in the writing or by the attestation of one of the suitors. Augustus, in order to increase their weight, enacted that they should be clothed with his authority, and henceforth this office was sought for as an imperial favour.' Those jurists who had the Jus respondendi were called Juris auctores. Their auctoritas resided, in the first instance, in their responsa, or the written opinions they gave when consulted on a single case; but in the second instance, doubtless, in their writings, which in fact were mainly a compilation of their responsa, a fact which has left its traces in the disjointed and incoherent style which disagreeably characterizes Roman juristic literature. In the course of centuries the accumulation of juristic writings of coordinate authority was a serious embarrassment to the tribunals. To remedy this evil, A.D. 426, Theodosius and Valentinian enacted what is called the law of citations, Cod. Theodosianus, 3, limiting legal authority to the opinions of five jurists, Gaius, Papinian, Ulpian, Paulus, Modestinus, and of any other jurists whom these writers quoted, provided that such quotations should be verified by reference to the original writings of those juris auctores. In case of a divergence of opinion, the authorities were to be counted, and the majority was to prevail. In case of an equal division of authorities, the voice of Papinian was to prevail. A.D. 533, Justinian published his Digest or Pandects, a compilation of extracts from the writings of the jurists, to which he gives legislative authority. Every sentence, accordingly, of these passages is called a lex, and the remainder of their writings is pronounced to be absolutely void of authority. To prevent the recurrence of the evil which his codification was intended to remove, and confident in the lucidity and adequacy of his Digest and Code, Justinian prohibits for the future the composition of any juristic treatise or commentary on the laws. If any one should disregard the prohibition, the books are to be destroyed and the author punished as guilty of forgery (falsitas), Cod. 1, 17, 2, 21.

Besides the sources of law enumerated by Gaius, the Institutes of Justinian mention Custom or Usage, the source of consuetudinary or customary law (jus non scriptum, consensu receptum, moribus introductum). To this branch of law are referred, with other rules, the invalidity of donations between husband and wife, Dig. 24, 1, 1, the power of making a will for an infant successor who dies before the age of puberty (pupillaris substitutio), Dig. 28, 6, 2, and universal succession in Coemption and Adrogation, 3 § 82. We may suppose that Customary law, like Roman law in general, would fall into two divisions, Civil law and Gentile law, the former embracing what Roman writers sometimes speak of as mores majorum. Before the time of Gaius, however, most, if not all, of Customary law must have been taken up into the edict of the praetor or the writings of the jurists, Cic. De Invent. 2, 22; i. e. unwritten law must have changed its character and have been transformed into written law.

DE IURIS DIVISIONE.

§ 8. Omne autem ius quo utimur vel ad personas pertinet, vel ad res, vel ad actiones. sed prius videamus de personis.

ON THE BRANCHES OF THE LAW.

§ 8. The whole of the law by which we are governed relates either to persons, or to things, or to procedure; and let us first examine the law of persons.

§ 8. What are the leading divisions of law—what are the main masses into which legislation naturally breaks itself—what are the joints and articulations which separate the whole code into various subordinate codes, like the different limbs and members of an organic whole—what is the import of the Gaian division into jus personarum, jus rerum, jus actionum, or rather, to adhere to the classical phrases, jus ad personas pertinens, jus ad res pertinens, jus ad actiones pertinens?

By jus ad actiones pertinens, to begin with the easier part of the problem, there is no doubt that the inventor of the division intended to designate the law of PROCEDURE as opposed to the law of rights; the adjective code, to use Bentham's phraseology, as opposed to the substantive code. There is as little doubt that in the Commentaries of Gaius this design is not executed with precision, and that, instead of the law of procedure, the last portion of his treatise rather contains the law of sanctioning rights, as opposed to the law of primary rights.

It is more difficult to determine the principle of the other division, the relation of the law of Persons to the law of Things. They both deal with the rights and duties of persons in the ordinary modern acceptation of the word: why, then, we may inquire, are certain rights and duties of persons separated from the rest and dealt with under the distinguishing category of jura personarum? It is not enough to say with Austin that the law of Things is the universal or general portion of the law, the law of Persons a particular and exceptional branch; that it is treated separately on account of no essential or characteristic difference, but merely because it is commodious to treat separately what is special and exceptional from what is general and universal. This answer furnishes no positive character of the law of Persons, but only the negative character of anomaly, i.e. of unlikeness to the larger portion of the law; but it would be difficult to show that the law of Persons is more exceptional, anomalous, eccentric, than the Civil dispositions as opposed to the Natural or Gentile dispositions of the law of Things.

We must look to the details of the law of Persons, and observe whether its dispositions have any common character as contrasted with the dispositions of the law of Things. The law of Persons, in other words, the law of Status, classifies men as slaves and free, as citizens (privileged) and aliens (unprivileged), as paterfamilias (superior) and filiusfamilias (dependent). The law of Things looks at men as playing the parts of contractors or of neighbouring proprietors; in other words, the law of Persons considers men as UNEQUALS, the law of Things considers them as EQUALS: the one may be defined as the law of relations of inequality, the other as the law of relations of equality.

It may induce us to believe that the law of unequal relations and the law of equal relations is a fundamental division of the general code, if we consider how essential are the ideas of equality and inequality to the fundamental conception of law. If we ventured on a Platonic myth, we might say that Zeus, wishing to confer the greatest possible gift on the human race, took the most opposite and uncombinable things in the universe, Equality and Inequality, and, welding them together indissolubly, called the product by the name of political society or positive law.

The assumption will hardly be controverted, that in the relations of subject to subject, Positive law, like Ethical law, recognizes, as an ideal at least, the identity of the just (lawful) with the equal. Inequality, however, is no less essentially involved in positive law. We have seen that there is no right and no duty by positive law without a legislator and sovereign to whom the person owing the duty is in subjection. On the one side weakness, on the other irresistible power. Positive rights and duties, then, imply both the relation of subject to subject, and the relation of subject to sovereign or wielder of the sanction, in other words, both the relation of equal to equal, and the relation of unequal to unequal. It is the more surprising that Austin should apparently have failed to seize with precision this conception of the law of Persons, as he makes the remark, in which the whole truth seems implicitly contained, that the bulk of the law of Persons composes the Public, Political, or Constitutional code (jus publicum). Political society or government essentially implies subordination. It implies on the one hand, sovereign power reposing in various legislative bodies, distributed, delegated, and vested in various corporations, magistrates, judges, and other functionaries; on the other hand, private persons or subjects subordinate to the sovereign power and to its delegates and ministers. The different forms of government are so many forms of subordination, so many relations of superior and inferior, that is, so many relations of unequals. Public law, then, is a law of Status, and the law of Persons or law of Status in the private code is the intrusion of a portion of the public code into the private code; or, in barbarous and semi-civilized legislations, the disfigurement of private law by the introduction of relations that properly belong to public law. For instance, the most salient institution of the ancient Roman law of Persons, the power of life and death over wife and child that vested in the father of the household, was the concession to a subject of an attribute that properly belongs to the sovereign or a public functionary. Another institution, slavery, placed one subject over another in the position of despotic sovereign. The relation of civis to peregrinus, so far as any rights at all were accorded to peregrinus, may be conjectured to have originally been that of patronus to cliens, that is to say, of political superior to political inferior.

Government or positive law has usually commenced in the invasion by the stronger of the (moral) rights of the weaker; but so necessary is inequality to equality, or subordination to coordination, that the (moral) crimes of ancient conquerors are regarded with less aversion by philosophic historians, as being the indispensable antecedents of subsequent civilization. The beginnings, then, of positive law have been universally the less legitimate form of inequality, inequality between subject and subject, leaving its traces in dispositions of the civil code: but the advance of civilization is the gradual elimination of inequality from the law, until little remains but that between magistrate and private person, or sovereign and subject. Modern society has advanced so far on the path of equalization, in the recognition of all men as equal before the law, that the distinctions of status, as they existed in the Roman law of persons, are almost obliterated from the private code. Slavery has vanished; parental and marital power are of the mildest form; civilized countries accord the same rights to cives and peregrini; guardians (tutores) in modern jurisprudence, as in the later period of Roman law, are considered as discharging a public function, and accordingly the relation of guardian and ward may be regarded as a portion of the public code.

Having been led to mention Public or Constitutional law, it may aid to clear our conceptions if we observe that some of its dispositions are necessarily, and by the nature of the case, deficient in the characters of Positive law. It is rigorously true to say that the powers of subordinate political functionaries are a status. They imply rights and duties on the part of superior and inferior, enforced by appeal to the common sovereign. But, when tracing the hierarchy of government, we come to the top of the scale; when we speak of the limitations of the sovereign power, we have passed from the sphere of Positive law. The sovereign is free from the fetters of positive law; he has no legal obligations, for they would imply a superior. Like a private individual who sets an ethical law to himself, the sovereign is not constrained to observe constitutional law by aught that resembles a positive sanction. The existence of a law to bind the sovereign being assumed, the sovereign, the author of the law, can abrogate it at pleasure. Like the Aeschylean Jove, *παρ' ἑαυτῷ τὸ δίκαιον ἔχων*, 'with his own fingers warping law,' *ἰδίοις νόμοις Ζεὺς ἀθέτως κρατύνει*, 'with self-set law' the sovereign 'sways uncontrolled;' or in the words of another poet, *ἡ πόλις ἐβούλεθ', ᾗ νόμων οὐδὲν μέλει*, 'such the state's pleasure, whom no law restrains.' Nor has the sovereign any rights like those of a subject by positive law; and this absence of protection by positive sanctions may be expressed by the aphorism—the sovereign's might is his right. The sovereign body, of course, cannot emancipate itself from the law of prudence, nor from the ethical law, nor from the divine law, but these are the only laws from which it is not emancipated. Constitutional law cannot be enforced against the sovereign body by any but moral sanctions. Whereas, then, the law of Persons that belongs to private law is just as much positive law as the law of Things, and political functionaries who exercise a delegated power fall under a positive law of Persons, the absolute sovereign is not invested with legal status. When it approaches the limitations of the sovereign Constitutional law changes its character, it ceases to be positive law, and becomes a law of opinion; or, in other words, public law, so far as it relates to the sovereign, is not properly law, but only a collection of ethical maxims.

In speaking of Constitutional law as a law of status, we must be understood as using the language of theoretical jurisprudence, not of Roman law: the classical jurists use the term status to denote exclusively relations of private persons, denoting by the status of civitas the rights, political or civil, of the private citizen, not the political attributes of the magistrate.

Before we terminate our general remarks on the nature of status, it is necessary to distinguish from the law of Persons a department of law with which, in consequence of a verbal ambiguity, it is sometimes confounded. Blackstone deserves credit for having recognized Public law as a part of the law of Persons; but he also included under the law of Persons that department of primary rights to which belong the right of free locomotion, the right of using the bodily organs, the right to health, the right to reputation, and other rights which perhaps more commonly emerge in the redress meted out for their violation, that is, in the corresponding sanctioning rights, the right of redress for bodily violence, for false imprisonment, for bodily injury, for defamation, and the like. These, however, are not the special and exceptional rights of certain eminently privileged classes, but the ordinary rights of all the community, at least of all who live under the protection of the law; they belong to filiusfamilias as well as to paterfamilias, to peregrinus and latinus as well as to civis. The rights in question, that is to say, do not belong to the law of unequal rights, or the law of Persons, but to the law of equal rights, or the law of Things.

The anomalous institution of slavery, however, furnishes a ground for controverting this arrangement; for, as by this legalized iniquity of ancient law, the slave, living, as he did, not so much under the protection as under the oppression of the law, was denuded of all the rights of humanity, including those of which we speak, we cannot say that these rights belong to servus as well as to liber. The same, however, may be said of contract rights and rights of ownership, for the slave had neither part nor lot in these any more than in the right of a man to the use of his own limbs. In defining, therefore, jura rerum to be the equal rights of all, we must be understood to mean, of all who have any rights. Perhaps, indeed, instead of saying that jura rerum are the rights of men regarded as equal, it would be more exact to say, that while jus personarum regards exclusively the unequal capacities, that is, the unequal rights of persons, jus rerum treats of rights irrespectively both of the equality and the inequality of the persons in whom they are vested, leaving their equal or unequal distribution to be determined by jus personarum.

In order to mark the natural position of these rights in the civil code, I have avoided designating them, with Blackstone, by the name of Personal rights, a term which I am precluded from using by yet another reason. I have employed the terms Personal right and Real right to mark the antithesis of rights against a single debtor and rights against the universe. Now the rights in question are rights that imply a negative obligation incumbent on all the world, that is to say, in our sense of the words they are not Personal, but Real.

From inability to find a better name, I have called them PRIMORDIAL rights, a name which is open to objection, as it may seem to imply a superior dignity of these rights, or an independence, in contrast with other rights, of positive legislation, characters which the name is not intended to connote. The strangeness of the name has one advantage, that it prevents any misconception as to the department of rights it is employed to designate.

DE CONDICIONE HOMINUM.	ON DIVERSITIES OF CONDITION.
§ 9. Et quidem summa divisio de iure personarum haec est, quod omnes homines aut liberi sunt aut servi.	§ 9. The first division of men by the law of persons is into freemen and slaves.
§ 10. Rursus liberorum hominum alii ingenui sunt, alii libertini.	§ 10. Freemen are divided into freeborn and freedmen.
§ 11. Ingenui sunt, qui liberi nati sunt; libertini, qui ex iusta servitute manumissi sunt.	§ 11. The freeborn are free by birth; freedmen by manumission from legal slavery.
§ 12. Rursus libertinorum *tria sunt genera: nam aut cives Romani, aut Latini, aut dediticiorum* numero sunt. de quibus singulis dispiciamus; ac prius *de* dediticiis.	§ 12. Freedmen, again, are divided into three classes, citizens of Rome, Latins, and persons on the footing of enemies surrendered at discretion. Let us examine each class in order, and commence with freedmen assimilated to enemies surrendered at discretion.

§ 12. As Gaius has not marked very strongly the divisions of the present book, it may be worth while to consider what are the leading branches of the doctrine of Status. Status falls under three heads,—liberty (libertas), citizenship (civitas), and domestic position (familia).

Under the first head, men are divided into free (liberi) and slaves (servi): the free, again, are either free by birth (ingenui) or by manumission (libertini). We have here, then, three classes to consider: ingenui, libertini, servi.

Under the second head men were originally divided into citizens (cives) and aliens (peregrini). The rights of citizens fall into two branches, political and civil, the former being electoral and legislative power (jus suffragii) and capacity for office (jus honorum), the latter relating to property (commercium) or to marriage (connubium). Aliens were of course devoid of the political portion of these rights (suffragium and honores); they were also devoid of proprietary and family rights as limited and protected by the civil law (commercium and connubium), though they enjoyed corresponding rights under the jus gentium. At a subsequent period a third class were intercalated between cives and peregrini, namely, latini, devoid of the political portion of the franchise, and enjoying only a portion of the private franchise, commercium without connubium. Here also, then, we have three classes, cives, latini, peregrini.

The powers of the head of a family were nominally three, potestas, manus, mancipium: potestas, however, was either potestas dominica, power over his slaves, or potestas patria, power over his children, which, at the period when Roman law is known to us, were different in kind; so that the rights of paterfamilias were really fourfold. Manus or marital power placed the wife on the footing of filiafamilias, which was the same as that of filiusfamilias. Paterfamilias had a legal power of selling (mancipare) his children into bondage; and mancipium, as denoting a person, designated a filiusfamilias who had been sold by his parent as a bondsman to another paterfamilias. In respect of his purchaser, such a bondsman was assimilated to a slave: in respect of the rest of the world, he was free and a citizen, though probably his political capacities were suspended as long as his bondage (mancipii causa) lasted. As slaves are treated of under the head of libertas, and the status of the wife (manus) was exactly the same as that of the son, we may say, that in respect of domestic dependence or independence (familia), as well as in respect of libertas and civitas, men are divided into three classes,—paterfamilias, filiusfamilias, and mancipium; paterfamilias alone being independent (sui juris), the other two being dependent (alieni juris) in unequal degrees.

These nine classes are not examined by Gaius with equal minuteness. Under the first head he principally examines the libertini: the classes under the second head, cives, latini, peregrini, are only noticed indirectly, i.e. so far as they present a type for the classification of libertini; and the bulk of the first book of the Commentary is devoted to domestic relations.

DE DEDITICIIS VEL LEGE AELIA SENTIA.

§ 13. Lege itaque Aelia Sentia cavetur, ut qui servi a dominis poenae nomine vincti *sint*, quibusve stigmata inscripta sint, deve quibus ob noxam quaestio tormentis habita *sit* et in ea noxa fuisse convicti sint, quique *ut* ferro aut cum bestiis depugnarent traditi sint, inve ludum custodiamve coniecti fuerint, et postea vel ab *eodem* domino vel ab alio manumissi, eiusdem condicionis liberi fiant, cuius condicionis sunt peregrini dediticii.

§ 14. Vocantur autem *peregrini dediticii* hi qui quondam adversus populum Romanum armis susceptis pugnaverunt, deinde, *ut* victi sunt, se dediderunt.

§ 15. Huius ergo turpitudinis servos quocumque modo et cuiuscumque aetatis manumissos, etsi pleno iure dominorum fuerint, numquam aut cives Romanos aut Latinos fieri dicemus, sed omni modo dediticiorum numero constitui intellegemus.

§ 16 Si vero in nulla tali turpitudine sit servus, manumissum modo civem Romanum, modo Latinum fieri dicemus.

§ 17. Nam in cuius persona tria haec concurrunt, ut maior sit annorum triginta, et ex iure Quiritium domini, et iusta ac legitima manumissione liberetur, id est vindicta aut censu aut *testamento* is civis Romanus fit: sin vero aliquid eorum deerit, Latinus erit.

FREEDMEN ASSIMILATED TO SURRENDERED FOES AND DISPOSITIONS OF THE LEX AELIA SENTIA.

§ 13. The law Aelia Sentia enacts that slaves who have been punished by their proprietors with chains, or have been branded, or have been examined with torture on a criminal charge, and have been convicted, or have been delivered to fight with men or beasts, or have been committed to a gladiatorial school or a public prison, if subsequently manumitted by the same or by another proprietor, shall acquire by manumission the status of enemies surrendered at discretion.

§ 14. Surrendered enemies are people who having taken up arms and fought against the people of Rome and having been defeated have surrendered.

§ 15. Slaves tainted with this degree of criminality, by whatever mode they are manumitted and at whatever age, and notwithstanding the plenary dominion of their proprietor, never become citizens of Rome or Latins, but can only acquire the status of enemies who have surrendered.

§ 16. If unstained by offences of so deep a dye, manumission sometimes makes the slave a citizen of Rome, sometimes a Latin.

§ 17. A slave in whose person these three conditions are united, thirty years of age, quiritary ownership of the manumitter, liberation by a civil and statutory mode of manumission, i.e. by default in a fictitious vindication, by entry on the censor's register, by testamentary disposition, becomes a citizen of Rome: a slave who fails to satisfy one of these conditions becomes only a Latin.

DE MANUMISSIONE VEL CAUSAE PROBATIONE.

§ 18. Quod autem de aetate servi requiritur, lege Aelia Sentia introductum est. nam ea lex minores xxx annorum servos non aliter voluit manumissos cives Romanos fieri, quam si vindicta, aput consilium iusta causa manumissionis adprobata, liberati fuerint.

§ 19. Iusta autem causa manumissionis est veluti si quis filium filiamve, aut fratrem sororemve naturalem, aut alumnum, aut *paedagogum*, aut servum procuratoris habendi gratia, aut ancillam matrimonii causa, aput consilium manumittat.

§ 20. Consilium autem adhibetur in urbe Roma quidem quinque senatorum et quinque equitum Romanorum puberum; in provinciis autem viginti recuperatorum civium Romanorum. idque fit ultimo die conventus: sed Romae certis diebus aput consilium manumittuntur. Maiores vero triginta annorum servi semper manumitti solent, adeo ut vel in transitu manumittantur, veluti cum Praetor aut Proconsule in balneum vel in *th*eatrum eat.

§ 21. Praeterea minor triginta annorum servus manumissione potest civis Romanus fieri, si ab eo domino qui solvendo non erat, *testamento* eum liberum et heredem relictum— [*desunt lin.* 24.]

ON MANUMISSION AND PROOF OF ADEQUATE GROUNDS OF MANUMISSION.

18. The requisition of a certain age of the slave was introduced by the lex Aelia Sentia, by the terms of which law, unless he is thirty years old, a slave cannot on manumission become a citizen of Rome, unless the mode of manumission is fictitious vindication, preceded by proof of adequate motive before a body of judicial assessors of the praetor.

§ 19. It is an adequate motive of manumission if, for instance, the slave whose manumission is justified before the council is a natural child or natural brother or sister or foster child of the manumitter's, or a governor of the manumitter's child, or is destined to be employed as an agent in business, or is a female destined to become the manumitter's wife.

§ 20. The council of assessors is composed at Rome of five senators and five Roman knights above the age of puberty: in the provinces of twenty recuperators, who must be Roman citizens, and who hold their session on the last day of the assize. At Rome the council holds its session on certain days appointed for the purpose. A slave above the age of thirty can be manumitted at any time, and even in the streets, when the praetor or proconsul is on his way to the bath or theatre.

§ 21. Under the age of thirty a slave becomes by manumission a citizen of Rome, when his owner being insolvent leaves a will, in which he gives him his freedom and institutes him his heir (2 § 154), provided that no other devisee accepts the succession.

§ 22. — *manumissi sunt*, Latini *Iuniani dicuntur*: Latini ideo, *quia* adsimulati *sunt Latinis coloniariis*; Iuniani ideo, quia per legem Iuniam libertatem *acceperunt*, *cum* olim servi viderentur esse.

§ 22. Slaves manumitted in writing, or in the presence of witnesses, or at a banquet, are called Latini Juniani: Latini because they are assimilated in status to Latin colonists (§ 131), Juniani because they owe their freedom to the lex Junia, before whose enactment they were slaves in the eye of the law.

§ 23. Non *tamen* illis permittit lex Iunia nec ipsis testamentum facere, nec ex testamento alieno capere, nec tutores testamento dari.

§ 23. These freedmen, however, are not permitted by the lex Junia either to dispose of their property by will or to take by devise or bequest, or to be appointed testamentary guardians.

§ 24. Quod autem diximus ex testamento eos *capere non* posse, *ita* intelleg*endum est, ut nihil* directo heredi*tatis* legatorumve nomine *eos* posse capere dicamus; *a*lioquin per fideicommissum capere possunt.

§ 24. Their incapacity to take under a will must only be understood as an incapacity to take directly as successors or legatees, not to take indirectly as beneficiaries of a trust.

§ 25. Hi vero qui dediticiorum numero sunt nullo m*odo ex testamento* capere possunt, non magis quam qui liber peregrinusque *est*. nec ipsi *testamentum* facere possunt secundum *quod plerisque* placuit.

§ 25. Freedmen classed with surrendered enemies are incapable of taking under a will in any form, as are other free aliens, and are incompetent to make a will according to the prevalent opinion.

§ 26. Pessima itaque libertas eorum est qui dediticiorum numero sunt: nec ulla lege aut senatusconsulto aut constitutione principali aditus illis ad civitatem Romanam datur.

§ 26. It is only the lowest grade of freedom, then, that is enjoyed by freedmen assimilated to surrendered aliens, nor does any statute, senatusconsult, or constitution open to them a way of obtaining Rom a citizenship.

§ 27. Quin et in urbe Roma vel intr*a* centesimum urbis Romae miliarium mo*r*ari prohibentur; et *si contra fecerint*, ipsi bonaque eorum publice venire iubentur ea condicione, ut ne in urbe Roma vel intra centesimum urbis Romae miliarium serviant, n*eve* u*mquam manumittantur*; *et* si *manumissi* fuerint, servi populi Romani esse iubentur. et haec ita lege Aelia Sentia comprehensa sunt.

§ 27. Further, they are forbidden to reside in Rome or within the hundredth milestone from Rome; and if they disobey the prohibition, their persons and goods are directed to be sold on the condition that they shall be held in servitude beyond the hundredth milestone from Rome, and shall be incapable of subsequent manumission, and, if manumitted, shall be slaves of the people of Rome: and these provisions are dispositions of the lex Aelia Sentia.

§ 17. Manumission was either a public or a private act. When manumission, besides freeing a slave from the dominion of his proprietor, converted him into a citizen of Rome, it was not a matter of merely private interest to be accomplished by the sole volition of the proprietor. Accordingly, the three modes of manumission which conferred the Roman franchise on the manumitted slave, testamento, censu, vindictâ, involved in different forms the intervention of the State.

Wills were originally executed at the Comitia calata, 2 § 101, where the dispositions of the testator, including his donations of freedom, received legislative sanction, being converted into a private law by the ratification of the sovereign assembly. When a new form of will was introduced, 2 § 102, testators retained their power of manumission, although the people here at the utmost were only symbolically represented by the witnesses of a mancipation. Bequests of liberty were either direct or indirect. A direct bequest of liberty (directo data libertas) made the manumitted slave a freedman of the testator (libertus orcinus, Inst. 2, 24, 2): an indirect bequest, that is, a request to the successor to manumit the slave (fideicommissaria libertas) made the slave on manumission a freedman of the successor, 2 § 266.

In manumission by the Census the interests of the State were represented by the censor. Censu manumittebantur olim qui lustrali censu Romae jussu dominorum inter cives Romanos censum profitebantur, Ulpian 1, 8. 'Registry by the censor was an ancient mode of manumission by the quinquennial census at Rome when a slave was ordered by his owner to make his return of property on the register of Roman citizens.' Ex jure civili potest esse contentio, quum quaeritur, is qui domini voluntate census sit, continuone an ubi lustrum conditum liber sit, Cic. De Orat. 1, 40. 'It is a question of civil law, when a slave is registered with his owner's sanction, whether his freedom dates from the actual inscription on the register or from the close of the censorial period.' Ulpian speaks of the census as a thing of the past. Since the Christian era only three had been held, the last under Vespasian, A.D. 74. The only census which ever took place after this was in the reign of the Emperor Decius, A.D. 249.

Soon after manumission by census fell into desuetude, a new form, marking the progress of Christianity, was gradually established, and may be regarded as a substitute for the older form, manumission in ecclesiis. A constitution of Constantine, A.D. 316, recognizing its validity, mentions that it had been long in practice, Cod. 1, 13. It was a proceeding before the bishop in the presence of the congregation, accompanied with a written record, and was practised down to the days of feudalism. Cujacius mentions that the following inscription was to be seen over the door of the ancient cathedral of Orleans: Ex beneficio Sanctae Crucis, per Joannem episcopum et per Albertum Sanctae Crucis casatum, factus est liber Lemtbertus, teste hac sancta ecclesia—'By the grace of the Holy Cross, and by the ministry of Bishop Joannes, Albertus, vassal of the Holy Cross, manumitted Lemtbertus in the presence of this holy Church.'

In manumission by Vindicta the State was represented by the Praetor. The vindicta or festuca was a rod or staff, representing a lance, the symbol of dominion, with which the parties in a real action (vindicatio) touched the subject of litigation as they solemnly pronounced their claim. Accordingly it was used in a suit respecting freedom (liberalis causa), for this, as status is a real right (jus in rem), was a form of real action, and was sometimes prosecuted by way of genuine litigation, sometimes was merely a solemn grant of liberty, that is, a species of alienation by surrender in the presence of the magistrate (in jure cessio). In a liberalis causa the slave to be manumitted, being the subject of the fictitious litigation, could not himself be a party, but was advocated by a vindex or adsertor libertatis, who in later times was usually represented by the praetor's lictor. The adsertor grasping the slave with one of his hands, and touching him with the vindicta, asserted his freedom, 4 § 16. The proprietor quitting his grasp of the slave (manu mittens) and confessing by silence or express declaration the justice of the claim, the magistrate pronounced the slave to be free. This procedure belonging to the praetor's voluntary, not his contentious, jurisdiction, did not require the praetor to be seated on his elevated platform in the comitium (pro tribunali), but might be transacted by him on the level ground (de plano); and as the mere presence of the praetor constituted a court (jus), he was usually seized upon for the purpose of manumissions as he was preparing to take a drive (gestatio), or to bathe, or to go to the theatre.

§ 18. The lex Aelia Sentia passed in the reign of Augustus, in the same year with the lex Julia de maritandis ordinibus, A.D. 4, and named after the consuls Sextus Aelius Catus and Caius Sentius Saturninus, was intended to throw obstacles in the way of acquiring the Roman franchise. One of its enactments provided that a slave under the age of thirty could not be made a citizen unless manumitted by V ndicta, after proof of adequate motive before a certain judicial board. We may inquire what would be the effect of manumission if the causae probatio were omitted. Inscription on the censor's register was probably entirely null and void, as this ceremony was either a mode of making a Roman citizen or it was nothing. Testamentary manumission, as we learn from Ulpian, left the man legally a slave, but gave him actual liberty (possessio libertatis, in libertate esse, as opposed to libertas), a condition recognized and protected by the praetor. Manumission by Vindicta probably gave the slave freedom without the franchise, i. e. made him a peregrinus; at least it is not obvious why he should have been worse off than testamento manumissus, and the following passage of Ulpian implies that their condition was not exactly the same: 'Eadem lege cautum est ut minor triginta annorum servus vindicta manumissus civis Romanus non fiat, nisi apud consilium causa probata fuerit, id est sine consilio manumissum caescris' (sic. For this word some conjecture: Lex Aelia Sentia. Perhaps we should read something to the following effect: peregrinum facit, nam nec civitatem adipisci nec) 'servum manere putat; testamento vero manumissum perinde haberi jubet, atque si domini voluntate in libertate esset, ideoque latinus fit,' 1, 12. The subsequent lex Junia Norbana apparently provided that, in the absence of causae probatio, the minor triginta annis manumissus, whether testamento or vindicta, should belong to the new class which it introduced, namely, the Latini. Hence, by an intelligible anachronism, Gaius, § 29, § 31, speaks of Latini made by the lex Aelia Sentia.

§ 19. Alumnus denotes a slave child reared by the manumitter, as appears from the following passage: Alumnos magis mulieribus conveniens est manumittere, sed et in viris receptum est, satisque est permitti eum manumitti in quo nutriendo propensiorem animum fecerint, Dig. 40, 2, 14. 'Foster children are more naturally manumitted by women than by men, though not exclusively; and it suffices to allow the manumission of a child who has won his proprietor's affection in the course of his education.'

§ 20. The Equites Romani, who at Rome composed a moiety of the judicial assessors, are opposed to Equites equo publico. Eques Romanus was such merely by his census: Eques equo publico, in the latter days of Rome, was a youth nominated by the emperor to the turmae equitum; not, however, intended for actual service with the legions, but merely marked out as an expectant of future employment in higher public functions, military or civil. The title of Princeps juventutis, often conferred by the emperors on their successors designate, denoted the leader of the Equites equo publico. In the time of Augustus the list of judices (album judicum) consisted of three panels (decuriae), Senatores, Equites Romani, and Equites equo publico. Augustus added a fourth, the Ducenarii, those whose census amounted to 200,000 sesterces, who judged minor cases; and subsequently Caligula added a fifth.

Recuperators are judges not taken from the panel (album judicum).

§ 21. Ulpian adds, 1, 14, that a slave who otherwise would only have become dediticius, or a freedman of the lowest class, if he is instituted the heres necessarius of an insolvent, becomes civis Romanus.

§ 22. When manumission was a purely private act, it could not confer the Roman franchise; it could only make a dediticius or a latinus.

The codex Alaricianus or Breviarium Alaricianum, a code promulgated A.D. 506 by Alaric king of the Visigoths of Spain and Gaul, contained, besides extracts from the codex Theodosianus (promulgated A.D. 436), a selection from the Sententiae of Paulus and an epitome of these institutes of Gaius. From this epitome it appears that in the paragraphs now obliterated Gaius proceeded to explain the modes of private manumission by which a slave became Latinus Junianus, and instanced writing (per epistolam), attestation of witnesses (inter amicos), invitation of the slave to sit with other guests at the table of his master (convivii adhibitione).

The lex Junia Norbana, probably passed in the reign of Tiberius, A.D. 19, fifteen years after the lex Aelia Sentia, in the consulate of Marcus Junius Silanus and Lucius Norbanus Balbus, defined and modified the status conferred by such acts of private manumission, converting Praetoris tuitione liber into ipso jure liber, or possessio libertatis into genuine libertas; with, however, sundry grievous stints and deductions. Under this statute the freedman was nominally assimilated to Latinus coloniarius, the citizen of a Roman colony in Latium; that is, had a moiety of the private rights composing civitas Romana or jus Quiritium, possessing commercium without connubium. As incapable of connubium or civil marriage, the

Latinus was incapable of patria potestas over his children and of agnatio or civil relationship. Though incapable of civil marriage he was of course capable of gentile marriage (matrimonium, uxorem liberorum quaerendorum causa ducere) and of natural relationship (cognatio), just as an alien (peregrinus), though, by want of commercium, incapable of dominion ex jure Quiritium, was capable of bonitary ownership (in bonis habere) under the jus gentium.

In virtue of commercium, the Latinus Junianus was capable of Quiritary ownership, of civil acquisition and alienation (usucapio, mancipatio, in jure cessio), contract (obligatio), and action (condictio, vindicatio), like a Roman citizen; but in respect of testamentary succession his rights were very limited. He was said to have testamentary capacity (testamentifactio), Ulpian, 20, 9; but this only meant that he could perform the part of witness, or familiae emptor, or libripens (2 § 104), i. e. could assist another person to make a valid will; not that he could take under a will either as heir or as legatee, or could dispose of his own property by will, Ulpian, 20, 14. At his death all his property belonged to his patron, as if it were the peculium of a slave, 3 § 56. In fact, as Justinian says: Licet ut liberi vitam suam peragebant, attamen ipso ultimo spiritu simul animam atque libertatem amittebant, Inst. 3, 7, 4. 'Though free in their lifetime, the same moment that deprived them of life reduced them to the condition of slaves.'

Although in the person of libertus himself, Latinitas was almost a mockery, yet it was not so for his posterity; these disabilities only attached to the original freedman, not to his issue. The son of the dediticius or Latinus Junianus, though reduced to absolute penury by the confiscation of the parental property to the patron, began, and continued, the world with the ordinary capacities, respectively, of peregrinus and Latinus coloniarius, and was under no legal obligations to the patron of his father.

Long before the time of Gaius, Latinitas or Latium had only a juristic, not an ethnographic signification. Soon after the social war all Italy received the civitas Romana. Originally Gallia Cispadana (Southern Lombardy) had civitas Romana, while Gallia Transpadana (Northern Lombardy) had only Latinitas, but Gallia Transpadana afterwards obtained civitas. Latinitas was a definite juristic conception, and Latin status was conferred as a boon on many provincial towns and districts that had no connection with

Latium or its races. Vitellius is carped at by Tacitus for his lavish grants of Latinity (Latium vulgo dilargiri, Hist. 3, 55). Hadrian made many similar grants (Latium multis civitatibus dedit, Spartian, Had. 21), and Vespasian conferred Latin rights on the whole of Spain, Pliny, Hist. Nat. 3, 4.

QUIBUS MODIS LATINI AD CIVITATEM ROMANAM PERVENI*ANT*.

§ 28. Latini multis modis ad civitatem Romanam perveniunt.

§ 29. S*tatim* enim ea*dem* lege Aelia Sentia cautum est, ut minores triginta annorum manumissi *et* Latini facti, si uxores duxerint vel cives Romanas, vel Latinas coloniarias, *vel eius*dem condicionis cuius et ipsi essent, idque testati fuerint adhibitis non minus quam septem testibus civibus Romanis puberibus, et filium procreaverint, *et* is filius anniculus *fuerit*, per*mitt*atur *eis, si velint*, per *e*am legem adire Praetorem vel in provinciis Praesidem provinciae, et adprobare se *ex* lege A*elia Sentia* uxorem duxisse et ex ea filium anniculum habere; et si is aput quem causa probata est id ita esse pronuntiaverit, tunc et ipse Latinus et uxor eius, si et ipsa eiusdem *condicionis sit, et ipsorum filius, si et ipse eiusdem* condicionis sit, cives Romani esse iubentur.

§ 30. Ideo autem in ips*orum filio* adiecimus 'si et ipse e*ius*dem condicionis sit,' q*uia* si uxor Latini civis Romana *est*, qui ex ea nascitur ex novo senatusconsulto quod auctore divo Hadriano factum est, civis Romanus nascitur.

MODES BY WHICH LATIN FREEDMEN BECOME ROMAN CITIZENS.

§ 28. Latins have many avenues to the Roman franchise.

§ 29. For instance, the same lex Aelia Sentia enacts that when a slave below the age of thirty becomes by manumission a Latin, if he take to himself as wife a citizen of Rome, or a Latin colonist, or a freedwoman of his own condition, and thereof procure attestation by not less than seven witnesses, citizens of Rome above the age of puberty, on begetting a son who attains the age of a year, he shall be permitted if he choose to avail himself of his privilege under that statute to apply to the praetor, or, if he reside in a province, to the president of the province, and to prove that he has conformed to the requirement of the lex Aelia Sentia by marrying a wife, and begetting by her a son who has completed the first year of his age: and thereupon if the magistrate to whom the proof is submitted pronounce the truth of the declaration, that Latin and his wife, if she is of the same condition, and their son, if he is of the same condition, are declared by the statute to be Roman citizens.

§ 30. The reason why I added, when I mentioned the son, if of the same condition, was this, that if the wife of the Latin is a citizen of Rome, the son, in virtue of the recent senatusconsult made on the motion of the late Emperor Hadrian, is a citizen of Rome from the date of his birth.

§ 31. Hoc tamen ius adipiscendae civitatis Romanae etiamsi *soli* minores *tri*ginta annorum manumissi et Latini facti ex lege Aelia Sentia habuerunt, tamen postea senatusconsulto quod Pegaso et Pusione Consulibus factum est, et*iam* maioribus triginta annorum manumissis Latinis factis concessum est.

§ 31. This capacity of acquiring Roman citizenship, though by the lex Aelia Sentia exclusively granted to freedmen who only became Latins in consequence of being under thirty years of age at the time of their manumission, by a subsequent senatusconsult, made in the consulship of Pegasus and Pusio, was extended to all freedmen who acquire the status of Latins, even though thirty years old when manumitted.

§ 32. Ceterum etiamsi an*te de*cesserit Latinus, *quam* annic*uli f*i*li*i causam probarit, potest mat*er* eius causam probare, et sic et ipsa fi*et* civis Rom*ana* [*desunt* 39. *lin.*]

§ 32. If the Latin die before proving the title of his son, on his son's attaining the age of a year the mother may prove the title, and thereupon both she and her son become citizens of Rome.

§§ 33, 34, 35. *si quis alicuius et* in bonis et ex iure Quiritium sit, manumissus, ab eodem scilicet, et Latinus fieri p*otest et* ius Quiritium consequi.

§§ 33, 34, 35. A slave in whom his owner has both bonitary and quiritary property, if twice manumitted by his owner, may acquire by the first manumission the Latin status, and by the second the Roman franchise.

§ 29. The decision (sententia) of the judex in a judicium ordinarium was either condemnatio or absolutio of the defendant. In real actions this was apparently preceded by pronuntiatio, a declaration of the rights of the parties. This appears from the following, among other passages: Sed et si fundum vindicem meum esse, tuque confessus sis, perinde teneberis atque si dominii mei fundum esse pronunciatum esset, Dig. 42, 2, 6, 2. Si quum de hereditate inter me et te controversia esset, juravero hereditatem meam esse, id consequi debeo quod haberem si secundum me de hereditate pronuntiatum esset, Dig. 12, 2, 10, 3. When the pronuntiatio was for the plaintiff, if the defendant obeyed the arbitrium or provisional order of the judex by making restitution, there was no subsequent condemnatio. In the form of real action, called a praejudicium, that is, a simple issue of fact, the pronunciatio formed the whole result of the trial, and was not followed by sententia. Similarly, when a Latinus laid his claim of Roman franchise before the praetor under this enactment of the lex Aelia Sentia, the result of the extraordinaria cognitio of the praetor, as appears by this paragraph, was merely a pronuntiatio without any subsequent decretum.

§ 35. Besides the method provided by the lex Aelia Sentia, Latinus or Latina might attain the Roman franchise under the following conditions:—

1. By erroris causae probatio, i. e. if, intending to comply with the statute, Latinus marry Peregrina, believing her to be Latina, § 70; or Latina marry Peregrinus, believing him to be Latinus, § 69; or if Civis, believing himself to be Latinus, marry Latina, § 71; or if Civis marry Latina, believing her to be Civis Romana, § 67; on proof of this mistake, the Latinus or Latina and their offspring acquire the franchise.

2. By magistracy in a Latin colony Latinus becomes Civis Romanus, § 95.

3. By remanumission (iteratio), i. e. after acquiring Latinity by one of the private modes of manumission, a subsequent manumission by one of the public modes, vindicta, censu, or testamento, converted Latinus into Civis, § 35, and Ulpian, 3, 4.

4. By six years' service in the Roman guards (si inter vigiles Romae sex annos militaverit, Ulp. 3, 5). A decree of the senate made three years' service a sufficient title.

5. By building a house in Rome (aedificio, Ulp. 3, 1).

6. By building a ship of 10,000 modii and importing corn to Rome for six years, Ulp. 3, 6.

7. By building a mill and bakehouse for the supply of Rome (pistrino, Ulp. 3, 1).

8. By bearing three children, Ulp. 3, 1.

9. By imperial grant (beneficio principali, Ulp. 3, 2).

Civitas Romana and Jus Quiritium are synonymous, but the former term was always used when the franchise was conferred on a Peregrinus, the latter generally when it was conferred on Latinus Junianus: e. g. Quare rogo, des ei civitatem, est enim peregrinae conditionis, manumissus a peregrina. . . . Idem rogo, des jus Quiritium libertis Antoniae Maximillae . . . quod a te, petente patrona, peto, Pliny to Trajan, 10, 4. Ago gratias, domine, quod et jus Quiritium libertis necessariae mihi feminae et civitatem Romanam Harpocrati, iatraliptae meo, sine mora indulsisti, ibid. 10, 5. Civitas Romana, however, was sometimes used in speaking of the enfranchisement of Latinus, as we see from Gaius 1, § 28.

QUI, QUIBUS EX CAUSIS, MANUMITTERE NON POSSINT.

§ 36. *Non tamen cuicumque volenti manumittere licet.*

§ 36. Not every owner who is so disposed is capable of manumission.

§ 37. *nam is qui* in fraudem creditorum vel in fraudem patroni manumitt*it*, nihil agit, quia lex Aelia Sentia impedit libertatem.

§ 37. An owner who would defraud his creditors or his own patron by an intended manumission, attempts in vain to manumit, because the lex Aelia Sentia defeats the manumission.

§ 38. Item eadem lege minori xx annorum domino non aliter manumittere permittitur, quam si vindicta aput consilium iusta causa manumissionis adprobata fuerit.

§ 38. Again, by a disposition of the same statute, before attaining twenty years of age, the only process by which an owner can manumit, is fictitious vindication preceded by proof of adequate motive before the council of assessors.

§ 39. Iustae autem causae manumissionis sunt: veluti si quis patrem aut matrem aut paedagogum aut conlactaneum manumittat. sed et illae causae, quas superius in serv*o* minore xxx annorum exposuimus, ad hunc quoque casum de quo loquimur adferri possunt. item ex diverso hae ca*u*sae, quas in minore xx annorum domino rettulimus, porrigi possunt et ad servum minorem xxx annorum.

§ 39. It is an adequate motive of manumission if the father, for instance, or mother, or governor, or foster-brother of the manumitter, is the slave to be manumitted. In addition to these, the motives recently specified respecting the slave under thirty years of age, may be alleged when the manumitting owner is under twenty; and, reciprocally, the motives valid when the manumitting owner is under twenty, are admissible when the manumitted slave is under thirty.

§ 40. Cum ergo certus modus manumittendi minoribus xx annorum dominis per legem Aeliam Sentiam constitutus sit, evenit, ut qui XIIII annos aetatis expleverit, licet testamentum facere possit, et in eo heredem sibi instituere legataque relinquere possit, tamen, si adhuc minor sit annorum xx, libertatem servo dare non potest.

§ 40. As, then, the lex Aelia Sentia prescribes a certain mode of manumission for owners under the age of twenty, it follows that, though after completing his fourteenth year, a person is competent to make a will, and therein to institute an heir and leave bequests; yet, until he has attained the age of twenty, he cannot therein enfranchise a slave.

§ 41. Et quamvis Latinum facere velit minor xx annorum dominus, tamen nihilominus debet aput consilium causam probare, et ita postea inter amicos manumittere.

§ 41. And even to confer the Latin status, if he is under the age of twenty, the owner must satisfy the council of the adequacy of his motive before he manumits the slave in the presence of witnesses.

§ 41. Justinian permitted minors to enfranchise by will as soon as they could make a valid will, i.e. at the age of 14, Novella, 119, 2. He mentions that the lowest class of freedmen (dediticia libertas) had long been obsolete, and formally abolished the second class (latina libertas), converting most of the modes of making Latinus into modes of making Civis Romanus, and declaring the rest inoperative, Cod. 7, 6.

DE LEGE FURIA CANINIA.

§ 42. Praeterea lege Furia Caninia certus modus constitutus est in servis testamento manumittendis.

§ 42. Moreover, by the lex Furia Caninia a certain limit is fixed to the number of slaves who can receive testamentary manumission.

§ 43. Nam ei qui plures quam duos neque plures quam decem servos habebit, usque ad partem dimidiam eius numeri manumittere permittitur. *ei* vero qui plures quam x *n*eque plures quam xxx servos habebit, usque ad tertiam partem eius numeri manumittere permittitur. at ei qui plures quam xxx, neque plures quam centum habebit, usque ad partem quartam *manumittere permittitur, nec latior licentia* datur. novissime ei qui plures quam C habebit, nec plures quam D, *amplius non* permittitur, quam ut quintam partem, neque plures *manumittat.* sed praescribit lex, ne cui plures manumittere liceat quam C. *igitur* si quis unum servum omnino aut duos habet, *de eo hac lege nihil cautum est;* et ideo liberam habet potestatem manumittendi.

§ 43. An owner who has more than two slaves and not more than ten is allowed to manumit as many as half that number; he who has more than ten and not more than thirty is allowed to manumit a third of that number; he who has more than thirty and not more than a hundred is allowed to manumit a fourth; lastly, he who has more than a hundred and not more than five hundred is allowed to manumit a fifth: and, however many a man possesses, he is never allowed to manumit more than this number, for the law prescribes that no one shall manumit more than a hundred. On the other hand, if a man has only one or only two, the law is silent, and the owner has unrestricted power of manumission.

§ 44. Ac nec ad eos *quidem* omnino haec lex pertinet, qui sine tes*tamento* manumittunt. itaque licet iis, qui vindicta aut censu aut inter amicos manumittunt, totam familiam suam liberare, scilicet si alia causa non inpediat libertatem.

§ 44. Nor does the statute apply to any but testamentary manumission, so that by means of fictitious vindication or inscription on the censor's register, or by attestation of friends, a proprietor of slaves may manumit his whole household, provided that there is no other let or hindrance to impede their manumission.

§ 45. Sed quod *de* numero servorum testamento manumittendorum diximus, ita intell*egemus, ut ex eo* numero, ex quo dimidia aut tertia aut quarta aut quinta pars liberari *potest, utique tot manumittere* liceat, quot ex antecedenti numero licuit. et hoc ipsa *lege pro*visum est. erat

§ 45. But the limitation of the number of slaves that a testator is allowed to manumit is subject to the following proviso: that out of each of the numbers from which a half, a third, a fourth, a fifth, may respectively be enfranchised, as many may always be enfranchised

enim sane absurdum, ut x servorum domino quinque liberare liceret, quia usque ad dimidiam partem *ex eo* numero manumittere ei conceditur, *ulterius autem* XII servos habenti non plures liceret manumittere quam IIII. at eis qui plures quam x neque [*desunt lin.* 24].

as out of the preceding number, a proviso expressed in the statute; indeed, it would have been irrational if the owner of ten slaves had been entitled to enfranchise five, and the owner of twelve could only manumit four . . . .

§ 46. Nam et si testamento scriptis in orbem servis libertas data sit, quia nullus ordo manumissionis invenitur, nulli liberi erunt; quia lex Fu*ri*a Caninia quae in fraudem eius facta sint rescindit. sunt etiam specialia senatusconsulta, quibus rescissa sunt ea quae in fraudem eius legis excogitata sunt.

§ 46. If a testator manumits in excess of the permitted number, and arranges their names in a circle, as no order of manumission can be discovered, none of them can obtain their freedom, as both the lex Furia Caninia itself and certain subsequent decrees of the senate declare null and void all dispositions contrived for the purpose of eluding the statute.

§ 47. In summa sciendum est, *cum* lege Aelia Sentia cautum sit, ut *qui* creditorum fraudandorum causa manumissi sint liberi non fiant, etiam hoc ad peregrinos pertinere (senatus ita censuit ex auctoritate Hadriani); cetera vero iura eius legis ad peregrinos non pertinere.

§ 47. Finally, it is to be noted that the provision in the lex Aelia Sentia making manumissions in fraud of creditors inoperative, was extended to aliens by a decree of the senate passed on the proposition of the Emperor Hadrian; whereas the remaining dispositions of that statute are inapplicable to aliens.

§ 47. The lex Furia Caninia, passed A.D. 8, four years after the lex Aelia Sentia, in the consulate of Furius Camillus and Caius Caninius Gallus, was abrogated by Justinian.

DE HIS QUI SUI VEL ALIENI IURIS SINT.

§ 48. Sequitur de iure personarum alia divisio. nam quaedam personae sui iuris sunt, quaedam alieno iuri sunt subiectae.

§ 48. Another division in the law of Persons classifies men as either dependent or independent.

§ 49. Sed rursus earum personarum, quae alieno iuri subiectae sunt, aliae in potestate, aliae in manu, aliae in mancipio sunt.

§ 49. Those who are dependent or subject to a superior, are either in his power, in his hand, or in his mancipation.

§ 50. Videamus nunc de iis quae alieno iuri subiect*ae* sint: si cognoverimus quae istae personae sint, simul intellegemus quae sui iuris sint.

§ 50. Let us first explain what persons are dependent on a superior, and then we shall know what persons are independent.

§ 51. Ac prius dispiciamus de iis qui in aliena potestate sunt.

§ 51. Of persons subject to a superior, let us first examine who are in his power.

§ 52. In potestate itaque sunt servi dominorum. quae quidem potestas iuris gentium est: nam aput omnes peraeque gentes animadvertere possumus dominis in servos vitae necisque potestatem esse. et quod*cu*mque per servum adquiritur, id domino adquiritur.

§ 53. Sed hoc tempore neque civibus Romanis, nec ullis aliis hominibus qui sub imperio populi Romani sunt, licet supra modum et sine causa in servos suos saevire. Nam ex constitutione *sacratissimi Imperatoris* Antonini qui sine causa servum suum occiderit, non minus teneri iubetur, quam qui alienum servum occiderit. Sed et maior quoque asperitas dominorum per eiusdem Principis constitutionem coercetur. Nam consultus a quibusdam Praesidibus provinciarum de his servis, qui ad fana deorum vel ad statuas Principum confugiunt, praecepit, ut si intolerabilis videatur dominorum saevitia, cogantur servos suos vendere. Et utrumque recte fit; male enim nostro iure uti non debemus: qua ratione et prodi*g*is interdi*c*itur bonorum suorum administratio.

§ 54. Ceterum cum aput cives Romanos duplex sit dominium, (nam vel in bonis vel ex iure Quiritium vel ex utroque iure cuiusque servus esse intellegitur), ita demum servum in potestate domini esse dicemus, si in bonis eius sit, etiamsi simul ex iure Quiritium eiusdem non sit. nam qui nudum ius Quiritium in servo habet, is potestatem habere non intellegitur.

§ 52. Slaves are in the power of their proprietors, a power recognized by Gentile law, for all nations present the spectacle of masters invested with power of life and death over slaves; and by the Roman law the owner is entitled to everything acquired by servile labour.

§ 53. But in the present day neither citizens of Rome, nor any other persons under the empire of the people of Rome, are permitted to indulge in excessive or causeless harshness towards their slaves. By a constitution of the Emperor Pius Antoninus, a man who kills a slave of whom he is owner, is as liable to punishment as a man who kills a slave of whom he is not owner: and inordinate cruelty on the part of owners is checked by another constitution whereby the same emperor, in answer to enquiries from presidents of provinces concerning slaves who take refuge at temples of the gods, or statues of the emperor, commanded that on proof of intolerable cruelty a proprietor should be compelled to sell his slaves: and both ordinances are just, for it is proper that the abuse of a lawful right should be restrained, a principle recognized in the interdiction of prodigals from the administration of their fortune.

§ 54. Citizens of Rome having two kinds of dominion, bonitary and quiritary, or a union of bonitary and quiritary dominion, a slave is in the power of an owner who has bonitary dominion over him, even unaccompanied with quiritary dominion; if an owner has only naked quiritary dominion he is not deemed to have the slave in his power.

The condition of the slave was at its worst in the golden period of Roman history. As soon as Rome found her power irresistible she proceeded to conquer the world, and each stage of conquest was the reduction of a vast portion of mankind to slavery. 30,000

Tarentines were sent as slaves to Rome by Fabius Cunctator, the captor of Tarentum ; 150,000 Epirots by Paulus Aemilius, the subjugator of Epirus. Julius Caesar retrieved his shattered fortunes by enormous operations in the slave market during his campaigns in Gaul. Thus, unfortunately for the slave, the slave market was continually glutted and slave life was cheap. The condition of the slave gradually but slowly improved under the emperors. A lex Petronia of uncertain date required a slave-owner to obtain the permission of a magistrate before exposing a slave to be torn to pieces by wild beasts, and only allowed such permission to be granted for some offence committed by the slave, Dig. 48, 8, 11, 2. Claudius prohibited killing slaves who fell sick, and enacted that the exposure of a slave to perish in his sickness should operate as a manumission, conferring Latinitas, Sueton. Claud. 25, Cod. 7. 6. 3. Hadrian deprived proprietors of the power of putting slaves to death without a judicial sentence, Spartian, Had. 18. Antoninus Pius declared a proprietor who killed a slave to be guilty of murder, and subject to the penalty of the lex Cornelia de sicariis. We read in Justinian's Digest: Qui hominem occiderit punitur non habita differentia cujus conditionis hominem interemit, Dig. 48, 8, 12. 'Homicide is punished without regard to the status of the person killed.' The punishment was generally capital. Legis Corneliae de sicariis et veneficis poena insulae deportatio est et omnium bonorum ademptio. Sed solent hodie capite puniri nisi honestiore loco positi fuerint quam ut poenam legis sustineant: humiliores enim solent vel bestiis subici, altiores vero deportantur in insulam, Dig. 48, 8, 3, 5. 'The law of Cornelius Sylla touching assassins and poisoners, punishes with transportation to an island and forfeiture of all property. But at present the punishment is usually capital, unless the criminal is of exalted station; humbler criminals are thrown to wild beasts, only criminals of higher rank are transported.' Hadrian prohibited the castration of a slave, consenting or not consenting, under penalty of death, Dig. 48, 8, 4, 2. Antoninus Pius also protected slaves against cruelty and personal violation, Dig. 1, 6, 2. The Digest, 1, 6, 1, quoting Gaius, 1 § 53, after sine causa, interpolates, legibus cognita, thus placing slaves under the protection of the law, and almost recognizing in slaves some of the primordial rights of humanity, except that, as already observed, obligation does not necessarily imply a correlative right. Roman law to the end, unlike other legislations which have recognized forms of slavery, refused to admit any rights in the slave. Florentinus, however, not long after the time of Gaius, admitted that slavery was a violation of the law of nature. Servitus est constitutio juris gentium qua quis dominio alieno contra naturam subicitur, Dig. 1, 5, 4. 'Slavery is an institution of Gentile law, making one man the property of another, in contravention of Natural law.' Ulpian says the same: Quod attinet ad jus civile, servi pro nullis habentur, non tamen et jure naturali; quia quod ad jus naturale attinet, omnes homines aequales sunt, Dig. 50, 17, 32. 'Before the Civil law a slave is nothing, but not before the Natural law; for in the eye of Natural law all men are equal.' The belief in a Natural law, more venerable than any Civil law, was very prevalent in the ancient world, and one of the principal contributions of Philosophy to civilization.

The absolute privation of all rights was sometimes expressed by saying that a slave has no persona, caput, or status: e.g. Servos quasi nec personam habentes, Nov. Theod. 17. 'Slaves being regarded as impersonal men.' Servus manumissus capite non minuitur quia nullum caput habet, Inst. 1, 16, 4. 'A slave by manumission loses no rights, having none to lose.' Cum servus manumittitur, quia servile caput nullum jus habet, ideo nec minui potest, eo die enim incipit statum habere, Dig. 4, 5, 4. 'A slave who is manumitted, having no rights, cannot lose any, for all his rights date from the day of his manumission.' The word 'persona,' however, is sometimes applied to slaves: e.g. in personam servilem nulla cadit obligatio, Dig. 50, 17, 22. 'A slave can owe no obligation;' see also Gaius, 1 § 17. So is caput in one of the above quoted passages.

DE PATRIA POTESTATE.

§ 55. Item in potestate nostra sunt liberi nostri quos iustis nuptiis procreavimus. quod ius proprium civium Romanorum est. fere enim nulli alii sunt homines, qui talem in filios suos habent potestatem, qualem nos habemus. idque div*us* Hadrian*us* edicto quod proposuit de his, qui sibi liberisque suis ab eo civitatem Romanam petebant, significavit. nec m*e* prae*terit* Galatarum gentem credere, in potestatem parentum liberos esse.

§ 55. Again, a man has power over his own children begotten in civil wedlock, a right peculiar to citizens of Rome, for there is scarcely any other nation where fathers are invested with such power over their children as at Rome; and this the late Emperor Hadrian declared in the edict he published respecting certain petitioners for a grant of the Roman franchise to themselves and their children; though I am aware that among the Galatians parents are invested with power over their children.

§ 55. The most peculiar portion of the Roman law of status is that which refers to patria potestas, or the relation of paterfamilias to filiusfamilias. Patria potestas was founded on consuetudinary law (quum jus potestatis moribus sit receptum, Dig. 1, 6, 8), and may be considered under two heads, (1) as regarding the person of the son, (2) as regarding proprietary rights acquirable by the son.

1. Over the person of the child the father had originally a power of life and death. Patribus jus vitae in liberos necisque potestas olim erat permissa, Cod. 8, 47, 10. So the lex Pompeia de parricidiis, enumerating the persons who could be guilty of parricide, or the murder of a blood relation, omits the father, Dig. 48, 9. Compare also the formula of Adrogatio, § 98, commentary. But in later times this power was withdrawn. Hadrian condemned to deportation a father who in the hunting-field killed his son who had committed adultery with his stepmother, Dig. 48, 9, 5. Constantine, A.D. 319, included killing by a father under the crime of parricide, Cod. 9, 17. Fathers retained the power of moderate chastisement, but severe punishment could only be inflicted by the magistrate, Cod. 8, 47, 3. Si atrocitas facti jus domesticae emendationis excedat, placet enormis delicti reos dedi judicum notioni, Cod. 9, 15. Trajan compelled a father to emancipate a son whom he treated with inhumanity, Dig. 37, 12, 5. It was originally at the option of the parent whether he would rear an infant or expose it to perish, but in later times exposition was unlawful. Unusquisque sobolem suam nutriat: quod si exponendam putaverit, animadversioni quae constituta est subjacebit, Valentinian, Valens, and Gratian, A.D. 374, Cod. 8, 52, 2. 'Every parent must rear his offspring, and exposition will be punished according to law.'

Originally also parents had the power of selling (mancipandi) their children into bondage, thus producing a capitis minutio, or degradation of status. In fact, the patriarchs of the Roman race were slave-dealers who, like some savage tribes in Africa and elsewhere, trafficked in the bodies of their own children. We must note, however, that the bondage into which a Roman father sold his children was, at least at the time at which this institution is known to us, a limited degree of subjection: the mancipation could only be made to another Roman citizen, and the bondsman continued to be liber and civis. But this power also was withdrawn in more civilized times. A law of Diocletian and Maximian declares the sale, donation, pledging of children to be unlawful, Cod. 4, 43, 1.

A rescript of one of the Antonines commences in the following terms: Rem illicitam et inhonestam admisisse te confiteris, quia proponis filios ingenuos a te venundatos, Cod. 7, 16, 1: 'You are guilty, by your own admission, of an unlawful and disgraceful act, as you state that you sold your freeborn children.' Justinian increased the penalties of the law against creditors who took possession of the freeborn child of a debtor as a security for a debt. He enacted that the creditor should forfeit the debt, should pay an equal sum to the child or parent, and in addition should undergo corporal punishment, Novella, 134, 7. In the time of Gaius, the only genuine sale of a child into bondage was in the case of noxal surrender, i.e. when a father sued for the trespass of a child, in lieu of damages, surrendered his delinquent son or daughter as a bondsman (mancipium) to the plaintiff, § 140. The sale of the child in adoption and emancipation was merely fictitious; even noxal surrender was practically obsolete in the time of Justinian, by whom it was formally abolished, Inst. 4, 8, 7. Constantine, however, in cases of extreme poverty permitted parents to sell their children immediately after birth (sanguinolentos), and this constitution was retained in the code of Justinian, Cod. 4, 43, 2.

2. In respect of property, filiusfamilias was capable of obligation but not of right; he could be debtor but not creditor; in any transaction where an independent person (sui juris) would have been creditor, filiusfamilias was merely a conduit-pipe through which a right vested in his father as creditor or proprietor. Even in domestic relations filiusfamilias could only figure as inferior, not as superior; he owed obedience, but could not exercise command (jus, in the special sense which it has in the phrases, sui juris, alieni juris); he could only be an instrument by which his father acquired a right of command. Thus, filiusfamilias had commercium, and could take by mancipatio, but the property he thus took vested in his father; he could make a valid contract, but the contractual right vested in his father; he had testamentifactio, that is, he could be witness, libripens, familiae emptor, but he could not make a will, for he had no property to leave; and if he took under a will as legatee or heir, the legacy or succession vested in his father. He had the other element of civitas, connubium; that is, he could contract a civil marriage and beget civil children; but the patria potestas over these children vested not in the father but in the grandfather, and if the marriage was accompanied with power of

hand (manus), marital power over the wife, this vested not in the husband but in the husband's father. Any property which the son was allowed by his father to manage was called his peculium, i.e. was held on the same terms as property which a slave administered by permission of his proprietor. In respect of debts which he incurred, the son did not act as conduit-pipe, but (except for a loan of money, which the Sc. Macedonianum made irrecoverable,) was liable in his own person. Filiusfamilias ex omnibus causis tanquam paterfamilias obligatur, et ob id agi cum eo tanquam cum patrefamilias potest, Dig. 44, 7, 39. 'A son under power incurs obligation by the same titles, and may be sued on the same grounds of action as an independent person.' The same rule applied to the son as to the slave: Melior conditio nostra per servos fieri potest, deterior fieri non potest, Dig. 50, 17, 133. 'The melioration of his proprietor's condition is in the power of a slave, but not the deterioration.'

In his political functions (munus publicum), filiusfamilias was entirely beyond the sphere of patria potestas. Quod ad jus publicum attinet non sequitur jus potestatis, Dig. 36, 1, 14, 1. 'The magisterial power of a filiusfamilias is unaffected by patria potestas.' Thus, a son could act as praetor, ibid, or as judex, Dig. 5, 1, 17, in a suit to which his father was a party. He could even preside as magistrate over his own adoption or emancipation: Si consul vel praeses filiusfamilias sit, posse eum apud semetipsum vel emancipari vel in adoptionem dari constat, Dig. 1, 7, 3, (which makes it doubtful how far political functions were suspended even by the state of mancipium or bondage). He could also be appointed guardian (tutor), for guardianship (tutela) was regarded as a public office. Filiusfamilias in publicis causis loco patrisfamilias habetur, veluti si vel magistratum gerat vel tutor detur, Dig. 1, 6, 9. 'A filiusfamilias in his public relations is deemed independent, for instance, as magistrate or as guardian.'

The above-stated incapacities of filiusfamilias were subject, however, to certain exceptions and modifications, which may now be briefly considered.

a. In certain cases filiusfamilias had an anomalous right of suing in his own name (suo nomine), i.e. not merely as procurator or attorney of his father, and even in opposition to his father's wishes. Filiusfamilias suo nomine nullam actionem habet nisi injuriarum, et quod vi aut clam, et depositi, et commodati, ut Julianus putat, Dig. 44, 7, 9. 'A filiusfamilias can only sue in his own name for outrage, by interdict for violent or clandestine disturbance, for deposit, for loan, according to Julian.' These suits, which, in spite of the statement in the text, were not the only, though perhaps the oldest, actions maintainable by a person under power, deserve a brief explanation. Without the right to Honour, one of the primordial rights of humanity, a man is scarcely a freeman, and, accordingly, this right vests definitively in filiusfamilias, and does not again pass out of him to vest in his father. Any dishonouring outrage, therefore, gave filiusfamilias a right of bringing a civil action, called actio injuriarum, in his own name and, if the offence was atrocious, or his father's character dubious, without his father's consent, Dig. 47, 10, 17, 13, although any pecuniary damages that he thereby recovered, being in the nature of property, were recovered for his father. The son under power was recognized, then, as invested with a vindictive right, though not with a proprietary right. The actio injuriarum was an action in bonum et aequum concepta (compare Dig. 44, 10, 11, 1, and Dig. 44, 7, 34, pr.), that is, the terms of the formula (conceptio) directed the judex to assess the damages not on any principle of civil law, but by his own sense of natural equity (aequum et bonum), and this form may have helped to make the action maintainable by one who on the principles of civil law was incompetent to sue. The interdict quod vi aut clam was maintainable by filiusfamilias on the same principle as the actio injuriarum, being a means of vindicating a dishonouring outrage inflicted on filiusfamilias by some violent disturbance of real property in defiance of his prohibitio or summons to stay operations and let the matter abide the result of a judicial trial. On the same principle a filiusfamilias disinherited or passed over in the will of his mother or maternal grandfather, as such disinheritance or pretermission was an implied imputation of turpitude or unworthiness and therefore dishonouring, might without the consent of his father (Dig. 5, 2, 22, pr.) vindicate his honour by impeaching the will of inofficiositas (immorality, or want of natural affection) although such querela inofficiosi testamenti, being in another point of view an hereditatis petitio or real action, was not properly maintainable by a filiusfamilias. If the plaintiff filiusfamilias could show that the disinheritance or omission was not due to his own demerits, he invalidated the will by a fictitious presumption of the testator's lunacy and made the testator intestate; and thus filiusfamilias vindicated his own character, but whatever share he recovered in the intestate succession vested in his father.

The right of filiusfamilias to sue by actio commodati or depositi was founded on a different principle. Suppose that filiusfamilias had borrowed or hired a thing that he afterwards lent or deposited; his father, not being responsible for his son's debts, would not be interested in the recovery of the thing, and therefore was not entitled to sue the depositary or borrower: the son, however, would be answerable to the original lender or letter, and accordingly was allowed to sue in his own name. To avoid, however, contravening the civil law by affirming a proprietary right vested in a filiusfamilias, he did not sue by a formula in jus concepta, i. e. of the form, si paret oportere, 'if the plaintiff establish a right,' but by a formula in factum, of the form, si paret factum esse, 'if the plaintiff establish a fact.' It is remarkable that Gaius instances precisely the actio commodati and the actio depositi as having two forms, one in jus and another in factum (4 § 47); and we may conjecture that the latter was invented to be used under these very circumstances by filiusfamilias.

b. The latter periods of Roman law present a gradual emancipation of filiusfamilias by successive inventions of new kinds of peculium. As early as the time of Augustus the earnings of a filiusfamilias in military service were called castrense peculium and belonged to him in absolute proprietorship. Filiifamilias in castrensi peculio vice patrumfamiliarum funguntur, Dig. 4, 6, 2. 'A filiusfamilias in respect of his military acquisitions has the right of a paterfamilias.' Subsequently the earnings of filiifamilias in the civil service of the State, in holy orders, in the liberal professions, were assimilated to their earnings in the army, under the name of peculium quasi castrense. Further, whatever came to the son from his mother or from the maternal line, or from any source but the paternal estate, was called peculium adventicium, and in this the father had only a usufruct or life estate, while the son had the reversion in fee (proprietas). Only such peculium as was derived from the paternal estate (ex re patris) continued, under the name of peculium profecticium, subject to the old rules and belonged in absolute property to the father.

The Gallic race, of which the Galatians were a branch, are mentioned by Caesar as having the institution of patria potestas: Viri in uxores, sicuti in liberos, vitae necisque habent potestatem, De Bello Gall. 6, 19. 'Husbands and fathers have power of life and death over wives and children.' St. Paul in his Epistle to the Galatians alludes to the peculiarity of their law: 'The heir, as long as he is a child, differeth nothing from a servant, though he be lord of all;' 4, 1.

DE NUPTIIS.

§ 56. *Habent autem in potestate liberos cives Romani*, si cives Romanas uxores duxerint, vel etiam Latinas peregrinasve cum quibus conubium habeant. cum enim conubium id efficiat, ut liberi patris condicionem sequantur, evenit ut non *solum* cives Romani fiant, set *et* in potestate patris sint.

§ 56. A Roman citizen contracts civil wedlock and begets children subject to his power when he takes to wife a citizen of Rome or a Latin or alien with whom a Roman has capacity of civil wedlock; for as civil wedlock has the effect of giving to the children the paternal condition, they become by birth not only citizens of Rome, but also subject to the power of the father.

§ 57. Unde et veteranis quibusdam concedi solet principalibus constitutionibus conubium cum his Latinis peregrinisve quas primas post missionem uxores duxerint. et qui ex eo matrimonio nascuntur, et cives Romani et in potestatem parentum fiunt.

§ 57. And for this purpose veterans often obtain by imperial constitution a power of civil wedlock with the first Latin or alien woman they take to wife after their discharge from service, and the children of such marriages are born citizens of Rome and subject to paternal power.

§ 58. *Sciendum autem est non omnes nobis uxores ducere licere:* nam a quarundam nuptiis abstinere debemus.

§ 58. We must observe that it is not any woman that can be taken to wife, for some marriages are prohibited.

§ 59. Inter eas enim personas quae parentum liberorumve locum inter se optinent nuptiae contrahi non possunt, nec inter eas conubium est, velut inter patrem et filiam, *vel* matrem et filium, *vel* avum et neptem: et si tales personae inter se coierint, nefarias *atque incestas nuptias contraxisse dicuntur. et haec a*deo ita sunt, ut quamvis per adoptionem parentum liberorumve loco sibi esse coeperint, non possint inter se matrimonio coniungi, in tantum, ut et dissoluta adoptione idem iuris maneat: itaque eam quae nobis adoptione filiae aut neptis loco esse coeperit non poterimus uxorem ducere, quamvis eam emancipaverimus.

§ 59. Persons related as ascendent and descendent are incapable of lawful marriage or civil wedlock, father and daughter, for instance, mother and son, grandfather and granddaughter: and if such relations unite, their unions are called incestuous and nefarious; and so absolute is the rule that merely adoptive ascendents and descendents are so utterly prohibited from intermarriage that dissolution of the adoption does not dissolve the prohibition: so that an adoptive daughter or granddaughter cannot be taken to wife even after emancipation.

§ 60. Inter eas quoque personas

§ 60. Collateral relatives also are

quae ex transverso gradu cognatione iunguntur est quaedam similis observatio, sed non tanta.

§ 61. Sane inter fratrem et sororem prohibitae sunt nuptiae, sive eodem patre eademque matre nati fuerint, sive alterutro eorum. sed si qua per adoptionem soror mihi esse coeperit, quamdiu quidem constat adoptio, sane inter me et eam nuptiae non possunt consistere; cum vero per emancipationem adoptio dissoluta sit, potero eam uxorem ducere; set *et* si ego emancipatus fuero, nihil inpedimento erit nuptiis.

§ 62. Fratris filiam uxorem ducere licet: idque primum in usum venit, cum divus Claudius Agrippinam, fratris sui filiam, uxorem duxisset. sororis vero filiam uxorem ducere non licet. et haec ita principalibus constitutionibus significantur. Item amitam et materteram uxorem ducere non licet.

§ 63. Item eam quae *nobis quondam socrus* aut nurus aut privigna aut noverca fuit. ide*o autem* diximus quondam, quia si adhuc constant eae nuptiae per quas talis adfinitas quaesita est, alia ratione *inter nos* nupti*ae* esse non possunt, quia neque eadem duobus nupta esse potest, neque idem duas uxores habere.

§ 64. Ergo si quis nefarias atque incestas nuptias contraxerit, neque uxorem habere videtur, neque libe*ros. hi enim* qui ex eo coitu nascuntur, matrem quidem habere videntur, patrem vero non utique: nec ob id in potestate eius sunt, *sed* quales sunt ii quos mater vulgo concepit. *nam nec hi* patrem habere *omnino* intelleguntur, cum *his etiam* incertus sit; unde solent spurii *f*ilii appellari, vel a Graeca voce quasi σποράδην concepti, vel quasi sine patre filii.

subject to similar prohibitions, but not so stringent.

§ 61. Brother and sister, indeed, are prohibited from intermarriage whether they are born of the same father and mother or have only one parent in common: but though an adoptive sister cannot, during the subsistence of the adoption, become a man's wife, yet if the adoption is dissolved by her emancipation, or if the man is emancipated, there is no impediment to their intermarriage.

§ 62. A man may marry his brother's daughter, a practice first introduced when Claudius married his brother's daughter Agrippina, but may not marry his sister's daughter, a distinction laid down in imperial constitutions, nor may he marry his father's sister or his mother's sister.

§ 63. He may not marry one who has been his wife's mother or his son's wife or his wife's daughter or his father's wife. I say, one who has been so allied, because during the continuance of the marriage that produced the alliance there would be another impediment to the union, for a man cannot have two wives nor a woman two husbands.

§ 64. A man who contracts a nefarious and incestuous marriage is not deemed to have either a wife or children; for the offspring of such a union are deemed to have a mother but no father, and therefore are not subject to paternal power; resembling children born in promiscuous intercourse, who are deemed to have no father, because their true father is uncertain, and who are called bastards either from the Greek word denoting illicit intercourse or because they are fatherless.

In any treatise on the law of marriage that we open we shall meet the expression, the marriage contract; and this suggests the inquiry, is marriage a contract, and, if so, to which class of Roman contracts, Verbal, Literal, Real, Consensual, 3 § 89, is Roman marriage to be referred? Most writers assume that it was a Consensual contract, on the strength of texts like the following: Nuptias non concubitus sed consensus facit, Dig. 35, 1, 15. 'Marriage does not depend on cohabitation, but on consent.' Ortolan, however, remarks that consensual contracts could be formed by absent contractors, Inst. 3, 2, whereas a marriage could not be contracted in the absence of the wife, Paul, 2, 19, 18; and shows that, besides the consent of the parties, delivery of possession of the wife to the husband was required, from which he infers that Roman marriage was not a Consensual but a Real contract. It is true that marriage might be contracted in the absence of the husband: Vir absens uxorem ducere potest, femina absens nubere non potest, Paul, 2, 19, 8; but this was only under certain conditions. Mulierem absenti per literas ejus vel per nuntium posse nubere placet, si in domum ejus deduceretur; eam vero quae abesset ex literis vel nuntio deduci a marito non posse: deductione enim opus esse in mariti non in uxoris domum quasi in domicilium matrimonii, Dig. 23, 21, 5. 'A man in his absence may marry by letter or message, provided the woman is led to his house: a woman in her absence cannot marry by letter or message, for the leading must be to the husband's house, as the domicile of the married pair.' And precisely the same conditions were sufficient in other cases to constitute delivery of possession. Si venditorem quod emerim deponere in mea domo jusserim, possidere me certum est, quanquam id nemo dum attigerit, Dig. 41, 2, 18, 2. 'If a vendor deposit any article in my house by my order, I have possession of it though I have never touched it.' Consensus, then, in the above-quoted passage, is not opposed to delivery of possession, but to cohabitation, or to the use of certain words or certain documents, or to the solemn and graceful ceremonial with which custom surrounded the matrimonial union.

Real contracts, however, are executory on one side and executed on the other, whereas in the conjugal relation both parties are on the same footing in respect of execution; and we may ask whether marriage is a contract at all; whether it does not rather fall under the opposite category of alienation or conveyance.

Instead of finding its analogon in locatio-conductio or societas (consensual contracts) or pignus or commodatum (real contracts), may we not rather, with Savigny, find it in transfer of dominion or other creations of real right, such as adoption, the concession of patria potestas, or emancipation, investiture with independent status? Did not tradition, or delivery of possession, operate to engender, not a personal right, as in real contract, but a real right, as in alienation of ownership, 2 § 65? This seems the truer view, and if we use the expression, marriage contract, we must use the term contract not in a specific sense, as opposed to conveyance, but in a generic sense, as embracing both contract proper and conveyance. Contract proper and conveyance, though generally contrasted in jurisprudence, have much in common. If contract in its narrower sense is defined to be the concurrence of two manifestations of will creating a jus in personam, and conveyance the concurrence of two manifestations of will creating a jus in rem, the concurrence of two manifestations of will creating a jus is an element common to both terms of the comparison, and this common element may be denominated in a generic sense a contract. Contract in the narrower sense may then be distinguished as an obligative contract and conveyance as a translative contract, and the latter head will include the contract of marriage, if we continue to employ this expression.

As in respect of property or dominion we find in Roman law the distinction of Quiritary and Bonitary, that is, of civil and gentile, ownership, so in respect of the conjugal relation we find the distinction of civil marriage (connubium, justae nuptiae, justum matrimonium) and gentile marriage (nuptiae, matrimonium), of which the former alone was valid at civil law (connubium est uxoris jure ducendae facultas, Ulpian, 5, 3; 'connubium is the capacity of marriage valid by civil law') and capable of producing patria potestas and agnatio, though the latter produced legitimate children (justi as opposed to naturales liberi) and cognatio or natural relationship.

Capacity of civil marriage (connubium) is (*a*) absolute and (*b*) relative. (*a*) Only citizens have the absolute capacity of civil marriage, and such Latins and aliens as are specially privileged, § 56: slaves are incapable both of civil and gentile marriage. (*b*) Capacity of civil marriage is, however, always relative to another person as forming the other party to the union. A citizen only has connubium with a citizen or with such Latins and aliens as are specially privileged; and, before the lex Papia Poppoea was passed, a freeborn citizen (ingenuus) had no connubium with a citizen by manumission (libertinus). Lege Papia cavetur omnibus ingenuis praeter senatores eorumque liberos libertinam uxorem habere licere, Dig. 23, 2, 23. 'The lex Papia permits all freeborn citizens, except senators and their children, to marry freedwomen.'

§ 58. The prohibition of marriage between collateral relations, originally perhaps extended as far as there were legal names for the relationship, i. e. as far as the sixth degree, for Tacitus mentions that second cousins were once incapable of intermarriage, sobrinarum diu ignorata matrimonia, Ann. 12, 6; the prohibition was subsequently reduced to the fourth degree, i. e. to the intermarriage of first cousins (consobrini), Ulpian, 5, 6; and finally to the third degree; with this restriction, however, that if one of the collaterals was only removed by one degree from the common ancestor (stipes communis), he was regarded as a quasi ascendent (loco parentis) and incapable of intermarriage at any degree: thus, a man could not marry his brother's or sister's granddaughter, though only related in the fourth degree, Cod. 5, 4, 13. Degrees in the direct line were reckoned by counting the generations or births to which a person owed his descent from an ancestor: thus, a man is one degree from his father, two from his grandfather: in the transverse or collateral line, by adding the degrees which separate each collateral from the common stock; thus, a man is two degrees from his sister, three from his niece.

§ 62. Constantine restored the ancient law and prohibited marriage with a brother's daughter as incestuous, Cod. Theod. 1, 2.

§ 63. Alliance (affinitas) is the relationship of a person to the kin (cognates) of a spouse. The husband is allied to the kin of the wife, the wife to the kin of the husband; but there is no alliance between the kin of the husband and the kin of the wife. The following are some of the names given to these relationships. In the ascending line the father and mother of the wife or husband are socer and socrus (father-in-law, mother-in-law), and in relation to them the husband of the daughter and wife of the son are gener and nurus (son-in-law, daughter-in-law). In the descending line the children of the spouse are privignus and privigna (step-son, step-daughter), and in relation to them the husband of the mother and the wife of the father are vitricus and noverca (step-father and step-mother). In the collateral line the husband's brother is levir (brother-in-law), the husband's sister is glos (sister-in-law). Intermarriage with allies in the direct line, or their ascendents or descendents, was absolutely prohibited; collateral alliance was no impediment in the time of Gaius, but at a later period marriage with a deceased brother's wife or a deceased wife's sister was forbidden, Cod. 5, 5, 5.

DE ERRORIS CAUSAE PROBATIONE.

§ 65. *Aliquando autem evenit, ut liberi qui statim ut na*ti sunt parentum in potestate non fiant, ii postea tamen redigantur in potestatem.

§ 65. It sometimes happens that children when first born are not in their father's power, but are subsequently brought into subjection to him.

§ 66. Itaque *si Latinus* ex lege Aelia Sentia uxore ducta filium procreaverit, aut Latinum ex Latina, aut civem Romanum ex cive Romana, non habebit eum in potestate: *at causa probata civitatem Romanam consequitur cum filio*: simul ergo eum in potestate sua habere incipit.

§ 66. Thus, under the lex Aelia Sentia a Latin who marries and begets a son of Latin status by a Latin mother, or a citizen of Rome by a Roman mother, is not invested with power over him; but on proof of his above-mentioned statutory title, he becomes a citizen of Rome along with his son, who is henceforth subject to his power.

§ 67. Item si civis Romanus Latinam aut peregrinam uxorem duxerit per ignorantiam, cum eam civem Romanam esse crederet, et filium procreaverit, hic non est in potestate, quia ne quidem civis Romanus est, sed aut Latinus aut peregrinus, id est eius condicionis cuius et mater fuerit, quia non aliter quisquam ad patris condicionem accedit, quam si inter patrem et matrem eius conubium sit: sed ex senatusconsulto permittitur causam erroris probare, et ita uxor quoque et filius a*d* civitatem Romanam perveniunt, et ex eo tempore incipit filius in potestate patris esse. Idem iuris est, si eam per ignorantiam uxorem duxerit quae dedi*ti*ciorum numero est, nisi quod uxor non fit civis Romana.

§ 67. Again, if a Roman citizen marry a Latin or an alien woman in a mistaken belief that she is a citizen of Rome, the son whom he begets is not in his power, not being born a citizen of Rome, but a Latin or an alien, that is to say, of the same status as his mother, for a child is not born into the condition of his father unless his parents had capacity of civil marriage: but a senatusconsult allows the father to prove a cause of justifiable error, and then the wife and son become citizens of Rome, and the son is thenceforth in the power of the father. The same relief is given when a Roman citizen under a like misconception marries a freedwoman having the status of a surrendered foe, except that the wife does not become a citizen of Rome.

§ 68. Item si civis Romana per errorem nupta sit peregrino tamquam civi Romano, permittitur ei causam erroris probare, et ita filius quoque et maritus ad civitatem Ro-

§ 68. Again, a female citizen of Rome who marries an alien in the false belief that he is a Roman citizen is permitted to prove a cause of justifiable error, and thereupon her

manam perveniunt, et aeque simul incipit filius in potestate patris esse. Idem iuris est si peregrino tamquam Latino ex lege Aelia Sentia nupta sit: nam et de hoc specialiter senatusconsulto cavetur. Idem iuris est aliquatenus, si ei qui dediticiorum numero est, tamquam civi Romano aut Latino e lege Aelia Sentia nupta sit: nisi quod scilicet qui dediticiorum numero est, in sua condicione permanet, et ideo filius, quamvis fiat civis Romanus, in potestatem patris non redigitur.

son and husband become citizens of Rome, and simultaneously the son becomes subject to the power of his father. Similar relief is given if she marry an alien as a Latin intending to comply with the conditions of the lex Aelia Sentia, for this case is specially provided for in the senatusconsult. Similar relief is given to a certain extent if she marry a freedman having the status of a surrendered foe instead of a Roman citizen, or instead of a Latin, whom she intended to marry according to the provision of the lex Aelia Sentia, except that the freedman husband continues of the same status, and therefore the son, though he becomes a citizen of Rome, does not fall under parental power.

§ 69. Item si Latina peregrino, quem Latinum esse crederet, nupserit, potest ex *senatusconsulto* filio *nato* causam *erroris* probare, *et ita omnes* fiunt cives Romani, *et* filius in potestate patris esse incipit.

§ 69. Also a Latin freedwoman married to an alien whom she believed to be a Latin is permitted by the senatusconsult, on the birth of a son, to prove a cause of justifiable error, and thereupon they all become Roman citizens, and the son becomes subject to paternal power.

§ 70. *Idem iuris omnino est*, si Latinus per errorem peregrinam quasi Latin*am* aut civem Romanam e lege Aelia Sentia uxorem duxerit.

§ 70. Exactly the same relief is given if a Latin freedman mistakenly marry an alien woman instead of a Latin freedwoman, or a citizen of Rome, when he intended to comply with the lex Aelia Sentia.

§ 71. Praeterea si civis Romanus, qui se credidisse*t* Latinum, *duxisset* Latinam, permittitur e*i* filio nato erroris causam *pro*bare, *tamquam si ex* lege Aelia Sentia uxorem duxisset. Item h*is qui licet* cives Romani essent, peregrinos se esse credidisse*nt* et peregrinas uxores duxissent, permittitur ex senatusconsulto filio nato causam erroris probare: quo facto peregrina uxor civis Romana *fit* et filius *quoque ita* non solum *ad civitatem Romanam pervenit*, sed *etiam* i*n* potestatem patris *redigitur*.

§ 71. Further, a Roman citizen who marries a Latin freedwoman, believing himself to be a Latin, is permitted on the birth of a son to prove the cause of his mistake as if he had married according to the provisions of the lex Aelia Sentia. So, too, a Roman citizen who marries an alien, believing himself to be an alien, is permitted by the senatusconsult on the birth of a son to prove the cause of the mistake, and then the alien wife becomes a Roman citizen, and the son becomes a Roman citizen and subject to the power of the father.

§ 72. Quaecumque de filio esse diximus, eadem et de filia dicta intellegemus.

§ 72. Whatever has been said of a son applies to a daughter.

§ 73. Et quantum ad erroris causam probandam attinet, nihil interest cuius aetatis filius sive filia *sit* .... Latinus .... qui .... nisi minor anniculo *sit* filius filiave, causa probari non potest. nec me praeterit in aliquo rescripto divi Hadriani ita esse constitutum, tamquam quod ad erroris quoque *causam* probandam [*desunt* 2. *lin.*] Imperator .... tuendam dedit.

§ 73. And as to the proof of the cause of error, the age of the son or daughter is immaterial, except that, if the marriage was contracted with an intention to satisfy the requirements of the lex Aelia Sentia, the child must be a year old before the cause can be proved. I am aware that a rescript of the late Emperor Hadrian speaks as if proof of the cause of error ....

§ 74. *Item* peregrino [3½ *lin.*] uxorem duxisset et filio nato alias civitatem Romanam consecutus esset, deinde cum q*uaereretur* an *causam* probare *posset*, *re*scripsit Imperator Antoninus perinde posse eum *causam pro*bare, atque si peregrinus mansisset. ex quo colligimus etiam peregrinum *causam* probare posse.

§ 74. When an alien, believed to be a Roman citizen, married a Roman wife, and subsequently to the birth of a son acquired the Roman franchise, the question arising whether he could prove the cause of error, a rescript of Antoninus Pius decided that he was just as competent to prove as if he had continued an alien: from which may be gathered that an alien is competent to prove the cause of error.

§ 75. *Ex iis* qu*ae* diximus ap*paret* .... error*e* .... *pere*grinus [1½ *lin.*] quid*em* .... errorem .... matrimonium .... ea quae superius .... nul*lus er*ror intervenerit .... null*o* cas*u* ....

§ 75. It appears that an alien cannot acquire the Roman franchise under the lex Aelia Sentia, but may by proof of having contracted a marriage under a justifiable error.

Mistake or error sometimes conferred a right which a party could not have acquired if he had not acted under a mistake. Thus, the lender of money to a filiusfamilias without the father's consent had no legal claim to recover, unless he lent believing the borrower to be independent (sui juris), and possession could not mature by usucapion into ownership, unless it had a bona fide inception, i. e. unless it commenced in an honest misunderstanding. The relief of error had similarly important results in questions of status.

The subjection of a child to patria potestas by erroris causae probatio operated to invalidate a previously executed will, like the subsequent birth (agnatio) of a child in civil wedlock (suus postumus), 2 § 142.

DE STATU LIBERORUM.

§ 76. [2 *lin.*] uxorem duxerit, *sicut supra quoque* dixi*mus*, ius*tum* matrimonium contrahi et tunc ex iis *qui* nasci*tur*, civis Romanus est et in potestate patris erit.

§ 76. When a Roman takes to wife an alien privileged as I described (§ 56), he contracts a civil marriage, and his son is born a Roman citizen and subject to his power.

§ 77. Itaque si civis Romana peregrino *nupserit, is qui nascitur, licet omni modo peregrinus sit, tamen interveniente conubio iustus* filius *est*, *tamquam* si ex peregrina eum procreasset. hoc *tamen tempore e* senatusconsulto quod auctore divo Hadriano factum est, *et*si non fuerit conubium inter civem Romanam et peregrinum, qui nascitur iustus patris filius est.

§ 77. So if a female Roman marry an alien with whom she has capacity of civil marriage, her son is an alien and a lawful son of his father, just as if his mother had been an alien. At the present day, by a senatusconsult passed on the proposition of the late Emperor Hadrian, even without civil marriage the offspring of a Roman woman and alien is a lawful son of his father.

§ 78. Quod autem diximus inter civem Romanam peregrinum*que matrimonio contracto eum qui* nascitur, peregrin*um* [*desunt* 11 *lin.*]

§ 78. The rule that when a female Roman citizen marries an alien with whom she has no capacity of civil marriage the offspring is an alien is a statutory enactment: the rule that when a female alien marries a Roman citizen with whom she has no right of civil marriage the offspring is an alien is a disposition of Gentile law.

§ 79. A*deo autem* hoc ita es*t*, u*t* [*desunt* 3 *lin.*] sed etiam, qui Latini nominantur: sed ad alios Latinos pertinet, qui proprios populos propriasque civitate*s* habebant et erant peregrinorum numero.

§ 79. And so the offspring of a Latin freedwoman by a Roman citizen with whom she has no capacity of civil marriage is a Latin, although this is not provided in the statute; for the Latins mentioned in the statute are Latins in another sense, Latins by race and members of a foreign state, that is to say, aliens.

§ 80. *Eadem ratione* ex contrario ex Latino et cive R*omana qui nascitur*, civis Romanus nascitur. fuerunt tamen qui putaverunt ex lege Aelia Sentia contracto matrimonio Latinum nasci, *q*uia videtur eo casu per legem Aeliam Sentiam et Iuniam conubi*um* inter eos dari, et semper conubium efficit, ut qui nascitur patris condicioni accedat: aliter vero contracto matrimonio

§ 80. By the same principle, conversely, the son of a Latin and a Roman woman is by birth a Roman citizen. Some, however, thought that if the marriage was contracted in accordance with the lex Aelia Sentia, the offspring is a Latin by birth, because in this hypothesis the lex Aelia Sentia and Junia Norbana confer a capacity of civil marriage, and a civil marriage

eum qui nascitur iure gentium matris condicionem sequi. at *vero hodie civis Romanus* est; *scilicet* hoc iure utimur ex senatusconsulto, quo auctore divo Hadriano significatur, ut *omni modo* ex Latino et cive Romana natus civis Romanus nascatur.

always transmits to the offspring the status of the father: if the marriage was otherwise contracted, they held the offspring acquires by Gentile law the status of his mother. However, it is now certain that the offspring is a Roman citizen in either case; for the senatusconsult passed on the proposition of the late Emperor Hadrian enacts that the son of a Latin and a Roman woman is under every hypothesis a Roman citizen.

§ 81. *His convenienter etiam ill*ud senatusconsulto divo Hadriano auctore significatur, ut ex Latino *et* per*e*grina, item contra ex peregrino *et Latina qui nascitur*, matris condicionem sequatur.

§ 81. Consistently herewith Hadrian's senatusconsult provides that the offspring of the marriage of a Latin freedman with an alien woman or of an alien with a Latin freedwoman follows the mother's condition.

§ 82. Illud quoque his conveniens est, quod ex ancilla et libero iure gentium servus nascitur, et ex libera et servo liber nascitur.

§ 82. Consistently herewith the offspring of a female slave and a freedman is by Gentile law a slave, the offspring of a freedwoman and a slave is free.

§ 83. Animadvertere tamen debemus, ne iuris gentium regulam vel lex aliqua vel quod legis vicem optinet, aliquo casu commutaverit.

§ 83. We must observe, however, whether the law of nations in any given instance is overruled by a statute or ordinance having the authority of a statute.

§ 84. Ecce enim ex senatusconsulto Claudiano poterat civis Romana quae alieno servo volente domino eius coi*i*t, ipsa ex pactione libera permanere, sed servum procreare: nam quod inter eam et dominum istius servi convenerit, ex senatusconsulto ratum esse iubetur. sed postea divus Hadrianus iniquitate r*ei* et inelegantia iuris motus restituit iuris gentium regulam, ut cum ipsa mulier libera permaneat, liberum pariat.

§ 84. For instance, the Sc. Claudianum permitted to a female citizen of Rome having intercourse with a slave with his owner's consent, to continue herself in virtue of the convention free, while she gave birth to a slave, her agreement to that effect with the owner being made valid by the senatusconsult. Subsequently, however, the late Emperor Hadrian was induced by the injustice and anomaly of the ordinance to re-establish the rule of Gentile law, that as the mother continues free the offspring follows her status.

§ 85. Ex lege .... *ex* ancilla et libero poterant liberi nasci: nam ea lege cavetur, ut si quis cum aliena ancilla quam credebat libe-

§ 85. By the (same) law the offspring of a female slave by a freeman might be free, for that law provided that the offspring of a

ram esse coierit; si quidem masculi nascantur, liberi sint, si vero feminae, ad eum pertineant cuius mater ancilla fuerit. sed et in hac specie divus Vespasianus inelegantia iuris motus restituit iuris gentium regulam, ut omni modo, etiam si masculi nascantur, servi sint eius cuius et mater fuerit.

freeman by another person's female slave whom he believed to be free shall be free if they are male, but shall belong to their mother's proprietor if they are female: but here too the late Emperor Vespasian was moved by the anomalous character of the rule to re-establish the canon of Gentile law, and declared that the offspring in every case, whether male or female, should be slaves and the property of their mother's owner.

§ 86. Sed illa pars eiusdem legis salva est, ut ex libera et servo alieno, quem sciebat servum esse, servi nascantur. itaque apud quos talis lex non est, qui nascitur iure gentium matris condicionem sequitur et ob id liber est.

§ 86. But another clause of that law continues in force, providing that the offspring of a freewoman by another person's slave whom she knows to be a slave are born slaves, though where this law is not established the offspring by Gentile law follow the mother's condition and are free.

§ 87. Quibus autem casibus matris et non patris condicionem sequitur qui nascitur, iisdem casibus in potestate eum patris, etiamsi is civis Romanus sit, non esse plus quam manifestum est. et ideo superius rettulimus, quibusdam casibus per errorem non iusto contracto matrimonio senatum intervenire et emendare vitium matrimonii, eoque modo plerumque efficere, ut in potestatem patris filius redigatur.

§ 87. When the child follows the mother's condition instead of the father's, it is obvious that he is not subject to the power of the father, even though the father is a Roman citizen: but in some cases, as I mentioned above (§ 67), when a mistake was the occasion of a non-civil marriage being contracted, the senate interferes and purges the defect of the marriage, and this generally has the effect of subjecting the son to the power of the father.

The rules relating to the status of the offspring of parents of unequal status are at first sight chaotic and bewildering, but they are reducible to a few canons. The most general canon is the rule of Gentile law, that children follow the condition of the mother. This is subject to two exceptions.

1. Children born in civil wedlock follow the condition of the father.

2. Children born in gentile (lawful) wedlock of a Roman mother and alien father follow the condition of the father: this was a special enactment of the lex Mensia. These rules are stated in the following passages: Lex naturae haec est ut qui nascitur sine legi-

timo matrimonio matrem sequatur nisi lex specialis aliud inducat, Dig. 1, 5. 'By the law of nature children not born in civil wedlock follow the status of the mother, in the absence of a special statute to the contrary.' Connubio interveniente liberi semper patrem sequuntur: non interveniente connubio, matris conditioni accedunt, excepto eo qui ex peregrino et cive Romana peregrinus nascitur, quoniam lex Mensia ex alterutro peregrino natum deterioris parentis conditionem sequi jubet, Ulpian, 5, 8. 'In civil wedlock the children have the status of the father, in the absence of civil wedlock of the mother; except that the children of an alien father and Roman mother are aliens, as the lex Mensia makes the children aliens when either parent is an alien.'

The Sc. Claudianum introduced some special enactments respecting the intercourse of freewomen with slaves, which, however, were subsequently abolished.

a. If a freewoman had intercourse with a slave with the consent of his proprietor she retained her freedom, though degraded to the class of a freedwoman, but her issue was the slave of the proprietor. The slavery of the issue was abolished by Hadrian, § 84.

b. If a freewoman persisted in intercourse with the slave of another person against the will and in spite of the prohibition of the proprietor, after three denunciations on his part she was awarded to him by the magistrate as a slave, and her issue, whether born before or after the adjudication, became slaves of the same person, who also acquired her estate by a species of universal succession. This merciless law, which, from the minuteness with which the details are developed (Paulus, 2, 21), appears to have been often applied, was not abrogated till the time of Justinian, Inst. 3, 12, 1.

c. If a freeman had intercourse with a slave whom he supposed to be free, her male children were born into freedom. This relief of error was abolished by Vespasian as anomalous (inelegans), § 85.

§ 77. The paragraph is imperfect and, perhaps for that reason, its drift is obscure. In what sense could a Roman woman be said to have connubium with an alien? We may conjecture that at one time such marriages, by some special statute or positive enactment, were invalid, and not even admitted as valid by Gentile law; that is, that the children were deemed to be bastards. Individuals who obtained a special release from this incapacity would have connubium, and the children of the marriage would by the general rule follow the status of the father. Hadrian seems to have repealed the general disability and made the marriage valid in all cases, i. e. a good gentile marriage even without the grant of connubium; but the lex Mensia, of uncertain date, declared that in this case Gentile law should not operate to give the children the status of the mother.

§ 80. There was not much plausibility in the view that a marriage under the lex Aelia Sentia, merely because it was statutory (regulated by statute), was therefore a civil marriage; and we may regard the senatusconsult of Hadrian, which denied its civil character, as purely declaratory.

§ 88. Sed si ancilla ex cive Romano conceperit, deinde manumissa civis Romana facta sit, et tunc pariat, licet civis Romanus sit qui nascitur, sicut pater eius, non tamen in potestatem patris est, quia neque ex iusto coitu conceptus est, neque ex ullo senatusconsulto talis coitus quasi iustus constituitur.

§ 88. If a female slave conceive by a Roman citizen and become by manumission a citizen of Rome before giving birth to a son, her son, though a citizen of Rome like his father, is not in his father's power, because he was not begotten in civil wedlock, and there is no senatusconsult which cures the defect of the intercourse in which he was begotten.

§ 89. Quod autem placuit, si ancilla ex cive Romano conceperit, deinde manumissa pepererit, qui nascitur liberum nasci, *na*turali ratione fit. nam hi qui illegitime concipiuntur, statum sumunt ex eo tempore quo nascuntur: itaque si ex libera nascuntur, liberi fiunt, nec interest ex quo mater eos conceperit, cum ancilla fuerit. at hi qui legitime concipiuntur, ex conceptionis tempore statum sumunt.

§ 89. The decision that when a female slave conceives by a Roman citizen and is manumitted before childbirth, her offspring is born free, is a rule of natural law; for in illegitimate or non-civil conception the status of the offspring depends on the moment of birth, and the mother's freedom at the moment of birth makes the offspring free, and the status of the father is immaterial: but in legitimate or civil conception the status of the child is determined by the time of conception.

§ 90. Itaque si cu*i* mulieri *civi Romanae praegnanti* aqua et igni *inter*dictum fuerit, eoque modo peregrina *fiat, et* tunc pariat, conplures distinguunt et puta*nt*, si quidem ex iustis nuptiis conceperit, civem Romanum ex ea nasci, si vero volgo conceperit, peregrinum ex ea nasci.

§ 90. Accordingly, if a female citizen of Rome being pregnant is interdicted from fire and water, and becoming thus an alien gives birth to a child, many jurists distinguish and hold that her offspring is a Roman citizen if begotten in civil wedlock, but if in promiscuous intercourse, an alien.

§ 91. Item si qua mulier civis Romana praegnas ex senatusconsulto Claudiano ancilla facta sit ob id, quod alieno servo *coierit* denuntiante domino eius, conpl*ures distingu*unt et existimant, si quidem ex iustis nuptiis conceperit, civem Romanum ex ea nasci, si vero volgo conceper*it*, *servum* nasci eius cuius mater facta est ancill*a*.

§ 91. So if a female citizen of Rome being pregnant is reduced to slavery under the Sc. Claudianum for having intercourse with a slave against the prohibition of his owner, many jurists make a distinction and hold that her offspring, if conceived in civil wedlock is a citizen of Rome, if conceived in illicit intercourse is a slave of the person who becomes proprietor of the mother.

§ 92. *Item peregr*ina quoque si vulgo conceperit, deinde civis Romana *facta sit, et par*i*at*, civem Romanum parit; si vero ex peregrino, *cui* secundum leges moresque peregrinorum coniuncta *est*, videtur ex senatusconsulto quod auctore divo Hadriano factum *est* peregrinus *nasci*, n*isi* patri *e*ius civitas Romana q*uaesita* sit.

§ 92. Also if an alien woman conceive in illicit intercourse and afterwards becomes a Roman citizen and gives birth to a child, the child is a Roman citizen; but if she conceived by an alien, to whom she was married in accordance with alien laws and customs, it seems that under Hadrian's senatusconsult her offspring is born an alien, unless the father also has acquired the Roman franchise.

Supposing the status of a parent changes during the period of gestation (if, for instance, the mother is a slave at the time of conception and free at the time of birth), what effect has this on the status of the issue? The following rule was adopted: in cases where the child follows the status of the father, that is, when it is begotten in civil marriage, the status of the father at the time of conception determines the status of the child; where the child follows the status of the mother, that is, when it is begotten in gentile marriage or in promiscuous intercourse, the status of the child is determined by the status of the mother at the moment of birth. In his qui jure contracto matrimonio nascuntur, conceptionis tempus spectatur; in his autem qui non legitime concipiuntur, editionis, Ulpian, 5, 10. 'Children born in civil wedlock have their status fixed at the time of conception; children born out of civil wedlock have their status fixed at the time of delivery.' That is to say, the legal position of the issue is made to follow the analogy of its physical condition. The physical influence of the father terminates with conception: his subsequent health, life, or death, does not affect the physical state of the child; but the child is affected by every change in the physical condition of the mother, her health, life, or death, up to the moment of birth. In imitation of this analogy, the status of the child, when it depended on the status of the father, was not affected by any change in that status subsequent to the period of conception; but when it depended on the status of the mother it varied with every change in that status up to the moment of birth. By the time of Gaius, though the change is not mentioned in the text, this rule was modified in favour of liberty, and it was established that if the mother was free either at the date of conception or at the date of birth or at any intermediate period, the issue was born free. Si libera conceperit et ancilla facta peperit, liberum parit, id enim favor libertatis exposcit. Si ancilla conceperit et medio tempore manumissa sit, rursus facta ancilla peperit, liberum parit, media enim tempora libertati prodesse, non nocere etiam possunt, Paulus, 2, 24, 2.

§ 88. The issue of a mother who was a slave at the date of conception but is a citizen at the date of birth, though it is born a Roman citizen, is not subject to patria potestas, because it does not satisfy the definition in § 55, liberi quos justis nuptiis procreavimus, 'a child begotten in civil wedlock.'

§ 90. Aquae et ignis interdictio was originally a permission to avoid punishment under the penal code by voluntary exile. Subsequently it was employed as a punishment, and under the emperors assumed the form of deportatio in insulam. It was attended with confiscation of goods, and involved loss of civitas but not of libertas, § 161.

§ 92. The offspring of a wedded mother who was an alien at the date of conception and is a citizen at the date of birth, according to the general rule of gentile law, should be born a Roman citizen; but this would contravene the above-mentioned lex Mensia, which enacted that the issue of a marriage is an alien whenever either parent is an alien. We may from this passage conjecture that what Ulpian calls the lex Mensia (a law not elsewhere quoted) was identical with what Gaius calls the senatusconsult of Hadrian, and was a comprehensive ordinance, regulating the conditions and effect of gentile marriages.

§ 93. Si peregrinus *cum liberis civitate Romana donatus fuerit, non aliter filii* in potestate *eius fiunt, quam si Imperator eos in potestatem redegerit*. quod ita demum is facit, si causa cognita aestimaverit hoc

§ 93. If an alien and his children receive a grant of Roman citizenship, the children do not fall under the power of the father except by express ordinance of the emperor, which he only makes if, on hearing

filiis expedire: diligentius atque exactius *enim* causam cognoscit de impuberibus absentibusque. et haec ita edicto divi Hadriani significantur.

the facts of the case, he deems it expedient for the interest of the children, and only after a careful and minute inquiry if they are infants and absent, as an edict of the Emperor Hadrian intimates.

§ 94. Item si *quis* cum uxore praegnante civitate Romana donatus sit, quamvis is qui nascitur, ut supra diximus, *civis* Romanus sit, tamen in potestate patris non fit: idque subscriptione divi Hadriani significatur. qua de causa qui intellegit uxorem suam esse praegnatem, dum civitatem sibi et uxori ab Imperatore petit, simul ab eodem petere debet, ut eum qui natus erit in potestate sua habeat.

§ 94. Also if an alien and his pregnant wife receive a grant of Roman citizenship, the child, though a Roman citizen, as above mentioned, is not born in the power of his father according to a rescript of the late Emperor Hadrian; wherefore, if he knows his wife to be pregnant, an alien who petitions the emperor for the Roman franchise for himself and his wife ought at the same time to petition that his son may be subjected to his power.

§ 95. Alia causa est eorum qui Latini sunt *et* cum liberis suis ad civitatem Romanam perveniunt: nam horum i*n potestate fiunt* liberi. quod ius quibusdam pe*regrinis* . . . . [*desunt lin.* 4.]

§ 95. The rule is different for Latins who with their children are made citizens of Rome, for their children fall under their power, and a similar right is conceded to certain aliens under the denomination of greater Latinity.

§ 96. Magistratum gerunt, civitatem Romanam consequuntur; minus latum [*Latium?*] est, cum hi tantum qui vel magistratum vel honorem gerunt ad civitatem Romanam perveniunt. idque conpluri*bus* epistulis Principum significatur. [1 *lin.*]

§ 96. Greater Latinity is the right whereby the magistrates of certain towns acquire the Roman franchise along with their wives and children: lesser Latinity is the right whereby the magistrates themselves acquire the Roman franchise, but not their wives and children, a distinction intimated by several imperial rescripts.

The grant of civitas was either made to communities or to individuals. It was a lucrative source of revenue to the emperors. The fees to be paid were not small, Acts of the Apostles, 22, 28, and the new-made civis was regarded as a manumitted slave of the emperor, and was expected to remember the emperor in his will. The philosophic emperor, Marcus Aurelius, under whom Gaius flourished, granted the Roman franchise to all who were ready to pay the fees, data cunctis promiscue civitas Romana, Aurelius Victor, 16. Antoninus Caracalla, A.D. 211–217, after raising from one-twentieth to one-tenth the tax on manumissions and the testamentary succession and legacy duty, which was only levied on Roman citizens, exhausted for a time this source of revenue by conferring at a stroke the Roman franchise on every free subject of the empire: In orbe Romano qui sunt, ex constitutione imperatoris Antonini cives Romani effecti sunt, Dig. 1, 5, 17. This was not a general manumission of slaves nor an abolition of the status of Latin or alien, but a grant of the franchise to all existing Latins and aliens, imposing in effect a capitation tax on the individuals, and leaving those orders to be again replenished by subsequent manumissions of Latini and dediticii. The value of the privileges of civis Romanus was gradually declining. The political portions of civitas had been extinguished by the establishment of the empire, and Rome was destined at last to undergo the fate she had inflicted on so many other cities. She was sacked by Alaric, king of the Goths, A.D. 410. She was entered by Genseric, king of the Vandals, and, after a sack of fourteen days, left a heap of ruins, A.D. 455. The splendour of the title of civis Romanus was sadly dimmed before Justinian made it acquirable by every form of manumission.

§ 94. Subscriptio was an imperial rescript written under the petition to which it was an answer: a rescript written on a separate document was called epistola. The latter was addressed to public functionaries, the former to private individuals, and by its connection with the petition enabled a tribunal to which it was submitted to investigate the truth of the allegations on which it was founded.

The grant of patria potestas by the sovereign power to the new-made citizen may be assimilated to the legislative grant of patria potestas in adrogatio.

§ 96. The terms greater Latinity, lesser Latinity (Latium majus, Latium minus), are not legible in the manuscript of Gaius, but both Niebuhr and Mommsen suppose that they formed the subject of the present paragraph.

DE ADOPTIONIBUS.

§ 97. *Non solum tamen naturales liberi, secundum ea quae* diximus, in potestate nostra sunt, verum et hi quos adoptamus.

§ 98. Adoptio autem duobus modis fit, aut populi auctoritate, aut inperio magistratus, vel*ut* Praetoris.

§ 97. Not only natural children are subject, as mentioned, to paternal power, but also adoptive children.

§ 98. Adoption is of two forms, adoption by permission of the sovereign and adoption by the judicial authority of a magistrate, for instance, by the judicial authority of the praetor.

§ 99. Populi auctoritate adoptamus eos qui sui iuris sunt: quae species adoptionis dicitur adrogatio, quia et is qui adoptat rogatur, id est interrogatur an velit eum quem adoptaturus sit iustum sibi filium esse; et is qui adoptatur rogatur an id fieri patiatur; et populus rogatur an id fieri iubeat. Imperio magistratus adoptamus eos qui in potestate parentium sunt, sive primum gradum liberorum optineant, qualis est filius et filia, sive inferiorem, qualis est nepos, neptis, pronepos, proneptis.

§ 99. Permission of the sovereign is required for the adoption of an independent person, and this form is called adrogation, because the adopter is interrogated whether he wishes to have the person adopted for his lawful son, the person adopted is interrogated whether he thereto consents, and the legislature is interrogated whether such is its command. The judicial authority of a magistrate gives validity to the adoption of a person subject to the power of an ascendent, whether a descendent in the first degree, as a son or daughter, or in a remoter degree, as a grandson or granddaughter, great-grandson or great-granddaughter.

§ 100. Et quidem illa adoptio quae per populum fit nusquam nisi Romae fit: at haec etiam in provinciis aput Praesides earum fieri solet.

§ 100. Adoption by the sanction of the legislature can only be solemnized at Rome, the other process can be performed in the provinces in the court of the president.

§ 101. Item per populum feminae non adoptantur; nam id magis placuit. Aput Praetorem vero vel in provinciis aput Proconsulem Legatumve etiam feminae solent adoptari.

§ 101. Adoption by legislative sanction is inapplicable to females, as has finally been ruled; but females may be adopted by the other mode of adoption, at Rome in the court of the praetor, in provinces of the people in the court of the proconsul, in provinces of the emperor in the court of the legate.

§ 102. Item inpuberem aput populum adoptari aliquando prohibitum est, aliquando permissum est. nunc ex epistula optimi Imperatoris Antonini quam scripsit Pontificibus, si iusta causa adoptionis esse videbitur, cum quibusdam condicionibus permissum est. aput Praetorem vero, et in provinciis aput Proconsulem Legatumve, cuiuscumque aetatis adoptare possumus.

§ 102. The legislative adoption of a child below the age of puberty was at one time prohibited, at another permitted; at the present day, by the epistle of the Emperor Antoninus addressed to the pontifices, on evidence of a just cause of adoption, it is permitted, subject to certain conditions. In the court of the praetor at Rome, in the court of the proconsul in a province of the people, and in the court of the legate in a province of the emperor, a person of any age may be adopted.

§ 103. Illud vero utriusque adoptionis commune est, quia et hi qui

§ 103. Both forms of adoption agree in this point, that persons

generare non possunt, quales sunt spadones, adoptare possunt.

incapable of procreation by natural impotence are permitted to adopt.

§ 104. Feminae vero nullo modo adoptare possunt, quia ne quidem naturales liberos in potestate habent.

§ 104. Women cannot adopt by either form of adoption, for even their natural children are not subject to their power.

§ 105. Item si quis per populum sive apud Praetorem vel aput Praesidem provinciae adoptaverit, potest eundem alii in adoptionem dare.

§ 105. He who has adopted a person either by the sanction of the legislature or by the judicial authority of the praetor or of the president of a province, can transfer his adoptive son to another adoptive father.

§ 106. Set illa quaestio est, an minor natu maiorem natu adoptare possit: *idque* utriusque adoptionis commune est.

§ 106. Whether a younger person can adopt an older is a disputed point in both forms of adoption.

§ 107. Illud proprium est eius adoptionis quae per populum fit, quod is qui liberos in potestate habet, si se adrogandum dederit, non solum ipse potestati adrogatoris subicitur, set etiam liberi eius in eiusdem fiunt potestate *t*anquam nepotes.

§ 107. It is peculiar to adoption by the sanction of the legislature, that children in the power of the person adrogated, as well as their father, fall under the power of the adrogator, assuming the position of grandchildren.

Adrogation, or the adoption of an independent person (paterfamilias), reducing him to a dependent status (filiusfamilias), was a legislative act of the Comitia Curiata; but though, as representing the people, this assembly was legally omnipotent, it was unconstitutional to deprive a person either of the franchise or of domestic independence without his own consent. We learn from Cicero the formula by which this assent was ascertained: Sed quum hoc juris a majoribus proditum sit ut nemo civis Romanus aut libertatem (Mommsen conjectures: sui potestatem, but this in popular language may have been included under libertatem) aut civitatem possit amittere, nisi ipse auctor factus sit, quod tu ipse potuisti in tua causa discere: credo enim, quanquam in ista adoptione legitime factum est nihil, tamen te esse interrogatum, auctorne esses, ut in te P. Fonteius vitae necisque potestatem haberet ut in filio—quaero si aut negasses aut tacuisses, si tamen id triginta curiae jussissent, nam id jussum esset ratum? De Domo, 29. 'As it is an immemorial rule of law that no citizen of Rome shall be deprived of independence or the franchise against his will, as you have had occasion of learning by your own experience, for I suppose that, illegal as your adrogation was in all points, you at least were asked whether you consented to become subject to the adrogator's power of life and death as if you were his son;—if you had opposed or been silent, and the thirty Curiae had nevertheless passed the law, tell me, would their enactment have had any binding force?' The form in which the law was proposed to the legislative assembly is given by Gellius: Adrogantur hi qui, cum sui juris sunt, in alienam sese potestatem tradunt ejusque rei ipsi auctores fiunt. Sed adrogationes non temere nec inexplorate committuntur: nam comitia, arbitris pontificibus, praebentur, quae curiata appellantur, aetasque ejus qui adrogare vult, an liberis potius gignundis idonea sit, bonaque ejus qui adrogatur ne insidiose adpetita sint, consideratur, jusque jurandum a Q. Mucio, pontifice maximo, conceptum dicitur, quod in adrogando juraretur. . . . . Adrogatio autem dicta quia genus hoc in alienam familiam transitus per populi rogationem fit. Ejus rogationis verba haec sunt. Velitis, jubeatis, uti L. Valerius L. Titio tam jure legeque filius siet, quam si ex eo patre matreque familias ejus natus esset, utique ei vitae necisque in eum potestas siet, uti patri endo filio est. Haec ita uti dixi, ita vos, Quirites, rogo. 5, 19. 'Adrogation is the subjection of an independent person with his own consent to the power of a superior, and is not transacted in the dark or without investigation. The Comitia Curiata, at which the College of Pontiffs is present, are convened, and examine whether the age of the adrogator does not rather qualify him for the natural procreation of children, and whether the estate of the adrogatus is not the object of fraudulent cupidity, and an oath, said to be framed by Q. Mucius, the high pontiff, has to be taken by the adrogator. . . . Adrogation, the name given to this transit into a strange family, is derived from the interrogation of the legislative body, which is in the following form: 'Is it your will and command that L. Valerius shall be as completely by law and statute the son of L. Titius, as if he were born of L. Titius and his wife, and that L. Titius shall have power of life and death over L. Valerius as a father has over his son? As I have said, so you, Quirites, I ask?' Those who voted in affirmation of the measure proposed said (at least in other similar assemblies): Uti rogas; those who voted against it said: Antiquo. Women were originally incapable of being adrogated, because they were incapable of appearing in the Comitia Curiata, Quoniam cum feminis nulla comitiorum communio est, Gellius, ibid; but this incapacity vanished as soon as the lex Curiata, as form of adrogation, was superseded by imperial rescript (principale rescriptum), Dig. 1, 7, 21. Women, being incapable of exercising parental power, could not, properly speaking, adrogate; but they were permitted by quasi adrogation to establish the same legal relation as existed between a mother and her natural children, Cod. 8, 48, 5. An adrogator was usually required to be sixty years old, Dig. 1, 7, 15, and to be eighteen years (plena pubertate) older than adrogatus, Inst. 1, 11, 4. Originally a youth must have attained the age of puberty before he could be adrogated, § 102: Sed adrogari non potest nisi jam vesticeps . . . . quoniam tutoribus in pupillos tantam esse auctoritatem potestatemque fas non est, ut caput liberum fidei suae commissum alienae ditioni subiciant, Gellius, ibid. 'A youth cannot be adrogated before he has assumed the toga virilis, because a guardian has no authority or power to subject an independent person, with whose charge he is entrusted, to the domination of a stranger.' The purple-edged praetexta was generally laid aside by boys along with the bulla aurea which they wore round their neck, on the first Liberalia, the 17th March, Ovid, Fasti, 3, 771, after the completion of their fourteenth year. Females did not lay aside the praetexta till their marriage. Antoninus Pius permitted the adrogation of youths below the age of puberty (impubes, investis) under certain conditions; e.g. the adrogator entered into a stipulation, originally with a public slave, in later times with a public notary (tabularius), in the event of the death of adrogatus before the age of puberty, to restore his estate to his natural heirs, and, in the event of emancipation, to adrogatus himself: and adrogatus became entitled to a fourth part of the estate of adrogator (called quarta Antonini) of which he could not be deprived by disinherison or by unmerited emancipation. In the time of Justinian the adrogator only acquired in any case an usufruct or life estate in the property of adrogatus, which reverted to adrogatus after the death of adrogator; that is to say, the property of adrogatus was transformed by adrogation into peculium adventicium.

The form of adoption is explained below, § 134, under the head of dissolution of patria potestas, for as patria potestas is vested by adoption in the adoptive father, so it is divested from the natural father. The contrasted forms of adrogation and adoption are mentioned in juxtaposition by Suetonius: Gaium et Lucium adoptavit, domi per assem et libram emptos a patre Agrippa . . . Tertium nepotem Agrippam simulque privignum Tiberium adoptavit in foro lege curiata, Augustus, 64. 'Augustus adopted his daughter's sons, Gaius and Lucius, by (fictitious vindication after) a private conveyance by bronze and balance from their father Agrippa. His third grandson Agrippa and his stepson Tiberius he adrogated in the forum by a law of the Comitia Curiata.' These comitia had long been merely fictitious forms, the thirty curiae being symbolized by thirty lictors.

The effect of adoption was much reduced by a constitution of Justinian. If the adoption was by an ascendent, maternal or paternal, it retained its old character: but if it was by a stranger it neither created nor extinguished patria potestas; it did not transfer the adopted son from his old family into a new family, and therefore it neither destroyed nor created any tie of agnation: its only effect was to give to the adoptive son, in the event of intestacy, a claim against the estate of the intestate adoptive father; Cod. 8, 48, 10.

Besides the two modes of originating patria potestas which we have hitherto examined, birth in civil wedlock and adoption, subsequently to the time of Gaius a third mode was introduced, called by modern jurists Legitimation. This was the promotion of naturales liberi, children born in concubinatus, or cohabitation without matrimony, to the position of justi liberi, children born in lawful wedlock, which, after the extension of the franchise by Caracalla, would mean the same as children born in civil wedlock. Concubinatus was a relation partially recognized by the law, and children born in concubinage, though they had no right, by title of cognation, to the succession of their father, were recognized as cognates of their mother, and differed from children born in promiscuous intercourse (stuprum), inasmuch as their father was not considered incertus.' There were three modes of the legitimation of natural children, subsequent marriage, destination to the municipal senate (curiae oblatio), and imperial rescript. Legitimation by subsequent marriage was introduced by Constantine, A.D. 335. Legitimation by destination to the senate was introduced by Theodosius and Valentinian, A.D. 443, with the design of replenishing the order of municipal senators (curiales, decuriones), much reduced in the time of the later emperors in consequence of the general disinclination to belong to a class, subject, along with various apparent privileges, to many onerous and intolerable obligations. To fill the gaps in this order, a father was permitted to legitimate his natural child by making him a senator of his municipality (civitas), and was relieved from the restrictions limiting the amount devisable by testators to natural children, Cod. 5, 27, 3. Legitimation by imperial rescript was introduced by Justinian.

The laws recognizing concubinatus were abrogated by Leo Philosophus, A.D. 887. It was in answer to a proposition of the bishops to introduce legitimation by subsequent wedlock that the English Lords at the Parliament of Merton used the celebrated expression: Nolumus leges Angliae mutari, 20 Hen. 3, c. 9, A.D. 1236.

DE MANU.

§ 108. *Nunc de his personis videamus quae in manu nostra sunt.* *quod* et ipsum ius proprium civium Romanorum est.

§ 108. Let us next proceed to consider what persons are subject to the Hand, another right only vested in citizens of Rome.

§ 109. Sed in potestate quidem et masculi et feminae esse solent: in manum autem feminae tantum conveniunt.

§ 109. Power is a right over males as well as females: Hand relates exclusively to females.

§ 110. Olim itaque tribus modis in manum conveniebant, usu, farreo, coemptione.

§ 110. In former days there were three modes of becoming subject to Hand, possession, confarreation, coemption.

§ 111. Usu in manum conveniebat quae anno continuo nupta perseverab*at*; q*uae enim* velut annua possessione usucapiebatur, in familiam viri transibat filiaeque locum optinebat. itaque lege duodecim tabularum cautum *erat*, si qua nollet eo modo in manum mariti conv*enire, ut quotan*nis trinoctio abesset a*t*que *ita usum* cuiusque anni interrumperet. set hoc totum ius partim legibus sublatum est, partim ipsa desuetudine oblitteratum est.

§ 111. Possession invested the husband with right of Hand after a whole year of unbroken cohabitation. Such annual possession operated a kind of usucapion, and brought the wife into the family of the husband, where it gave her the status of a daughter. Accordingly, the law of the Twelve Tables provided that a wife who wished to avoid subjection to the Hand of the husband should annually absent herself three nights from his roof to bar the annual usucapion: but this proceeding is partly abolished by statute, partly obliterated by mere disuse.

§ 112. Farreo in manu*m* conveniunt *per* quoddam genus sacrificii .... in quo farreus panis adhibetur: unde etiam confarreatio dicitur. *sed con*plura praeterea huius iuris ordinandi gratia cum certis et

§ 112. Confarreation, another mode in which subjection to Hand originates, is a sacrifice in which they use a cake of spelt, whence the ceremony derives its name, and various other acts and things are

sollemnibus verbis, praesentibus decem testibus aguntur et fiunt. quo*d* ius etiam nostris temporibus in usu est: nam flamines maiore*s*, id est Diales, Martiales, Quirinales, sic*ut* *reges* sacrorum, nisi *sint* co*n*farreati*s* nup*tiis* *nati*, *inaugurari* *non* videm*us* . . . . co*n*farreatio . . . .

required to be done and made with a traditional form of words, in the presence of ten witnesses: and this ceremony is still in use, for the functions of the greater flamens, that is, the flamens of Jove, of Mars, of Quirinus, and the duties of the ritual king, can only be performed by persons born in marriage solemnized by confarreation.

§ 113. *Coemptione* *in* *man*u*m* conv*e*niun*t* per mancipatione*m*, *id est* per quandam imaginariam venditionem, *adhi*bitis non m*i*nu*s* quam v. testibus, civibus Romanis puberibus, item libripend*e*, *asse* *is* *sibi* *emit* mulierem, cuius in manum convenit.

§ 113. In coemption the right of Hand over a woman is vested in a person to whom she is conveyed by a mancipation or imaginary sale in the presence of at least five witnesses, citizens of Rome above the age of puberty, besides a balance holder, for an As or ingot of bronze.

§ 114. Potest autem coemptionem facere mulier non solum cum marito suo, sed etiam cum extraneo: *unde* aut matrimonii causa facta coemptio dicitur, aut fiduciae causa. *quae* enim cum marito suo facit coemptionem, *ut* aput eum filiae loco sit, dicitur matrimonii causa fecisse coemptionem: quae vero alterius rei causa facit coemptionem *cum* viro *suo* *aut* cum extraneo, velut tutelae evitandae causa, dicitur fiduciae causa fecisse coemptionem.

§ 114. By coemption a woman may convey herself either to a husband or to a stranger, and accordingly there are two forms of coemption, matrimonial and fiduciary. A coemption with a husband in order to acquire the status of daughter in his house is a matrimonial coemption: a coemption for another purpose, whether with a husband or with a stranger, for liberation, for instance, from guardianship, is a fiduciary coemption.

§ 115. Quod est tale: si qua velit quos habe*t* tutores reponere, ut alium nanciscatur, ii*s* *auctori*bus coemptionem facit; deinde a coemptionatore remancipata ei cui ipsa velit, et ab eo vindicta manumissa, incipit eum habere tu*t*orem, *a* quo manumissa est: qui tutor fiduciarius dicitur, sicut inferius appare*b*it.

§ 115. This is accomplished by the following process: the woman who desires to set aside her present guardians and substitute another makes a coemption of herself to some one with their sanction: thereupon the party to this coemption remancipates her to the person intended to be substituted as guardian, and this person manumits her by fictitious vindication, and in virtue of this manumission becomes her guardian, being called a fiduciary guardian, as will hereafter be explained.

§ 115 *a*. Olim etiam testamenti faciendi gratia *f*iduciari*a* fiebat coemptio. tunc enim non aliter

§ 115 *a*. In former times testamentary capacity was acquired by fiduciary coemption, for no woman

feminae testamenti faciendi ius habebant, exceptis quib*us*dam personis, quam si coemptionem fecisse*nt* remancipataeque *et* manumissae fuissent. set hanc nece*ssitatem* coemptionis *faciendae* ex auctoritate divi Hadriani senatus remisit . . . . femina . . . .

§ 115 *b*. *Licet autem mulier* fiduciae causa *cum viro suo fecerit co*emp*tionem*, nihilominus filiae loco incipit esse: nam si omnino qualibet ex causa u*x*or in manu viri *sit*, plac*uit* eam *iura* filiae nancisci.

was competent to dispose of her property by will, with the exception of certain persons, unless she had made a coemption, been remancipated, and then manumitted: but this necessity of coemption was abolished by a senatusconsult made on the motion of Hadrian.

§ 115 *b*. Even if a woman makes only a fiduciary coemption with her husband, she acquires the status of his daughter, for it is held that from whatever cause a woman is in the hand of her husband, she acquires the position of his daughter.

Marital power (manus) was entirely assimilated to patria potestas. By manus the husband had power of life and death over the wife, Livy, 39, 18; Tac. Ann. 13, 32; and all the property of the wife, even more absolutely than by the common law of English jurisprudence, vested in the husband, 2 § 98.

Manus was perhaps originally an essential accompaniment of civil wedlock, and the patriarchs of the Roman nation could probably not conceive of the conjugal union as disjoined from manus. Yet at a very early period of Roman history these elements of marriage were recognized as separable, and in later times they were almost universally dissociated, and wedlock was unaccompanied by manus. In a marriage celebrated without confarreation and without coemption, before the expiration of the first year of cohabitation, there was civil wedlock without manus, and the Twelve Tables provided a method (trinoctio abesse) by which this state could be indefinitely prolonged: a filiusfamilias was capable of civil wedlock, but had no manus, for marital power, like every other civil right, passed out of the dependent husband to vest in the father; and as soon as gentile marriages were recognized by the legislator the Romans were still more familiarized with the spectacle of lawful matrimony without manus. As the ages advanced the wife acquired more and more independence; manus was almost obsolete in the time of Gaius, and it has quite vanished from the legislation of Justinian.

Confarreation was a form of marriage which made the issue eligible for certain high sacerdotal functions, and may therefore be regarded as characteristic of the patrician caste. Originally it probably produced marital power in its full extent; but when Augustus,

B.C. 10, after a vacancy of seventy-five years, renewed the priesthood of Jove (flaminium diale) he limited by statute the legal effect of confarreation in that particular instance, § 136; and Tiberius, A.D. 23, extended the limitation to all future cases of confarreation. Henceforth it only operated a change of family in respect of sacred rites (sacra): the woman ceased to have the domestic gods and domestic worship of her father, and took in exchange the domestic gods and domestic worship of her husband. But in secular matters her family was unchanged: she remained, if filiafamilias, subject to patria potestas, and did not become quasi filiafamilias in the household of her husband: her old ties of agnation in her father's family were not snapped, and no new ties of agnation in her husband's family were acquired. Divorce (diffarreatio) was almost impossible, and this indissolubility of the connection contributed to the unpopularity of confarreatio. Moreover, it was a religious ceremonial, requiring the presence of the pontifex maximus and flamen dialis, and as such it vanished with vanishing paganism.

The exact nature of Coemption, in consequence of the defective state of the Veronese manuscript, must remain a mystery. Coemption was a form of mancipation, § 113, but in virtue of the provision of the Twelve Tables, Cum nexum faxit mancipiumque, uti lingua nuncupassit, ita jus esto, the nature of every mancipation depended on the mancipii lex, the accompanying nuncupation or verbal declaration of its conditions, intentions, purposes; as in English conveyancing the nature of a grant is limited and determined by the habendum and tenendum of the deed. We are informed that in coemption the formula was not the same as in other mancipations, § 123, but we are not informed what it was. Even in Cicero's time many advocates were ignorant of the legal effect of a coemption because they were ignorant of the precise terms of the formula in which it was concluded, De Orat. 1, 56. The word itself may suggest a conjecture that it was a conveyance of the husband to the wife as well as of the wife to the husband; and this is supported by Servius on Georgics, 1, 34, and Isidorus, 5, 24, no great authorities, but who quoted apparently from Ulpian: Antiquus nuptiarum erat ritus, quo se maritus et uxor invicem emebant, ne videretur ancilla uxor, 'An ancient nuptial form wherein husband and wife made a mutual purchase, to bar the inference that the wife became a slave.' Plutarch informs us that the wife asserted her equality by the terms, Ubi tu Caius, ego Caia, Quaest. Rom. 28: 'Where thou art master, I am mistress.' Boethius on Cicero Topica, 3, 14, quoting from Ulpian, says: Sese in coemendo invicem interrogabant, vir ita: an sibi mulier materfamilias esse vellet? illa respondebat velle. Item mulier interrogabat, an vir sibi paterfamilias esse vellet? ille respondebat velle. Itaque mulier viri conveniebat in manum, et erat mulier materfamilias viro, loco filiae. 'The man and woman interrogated one another. He asked her if she wished to be mother of his household; she answered, Yes. She asked him if he wished to be father of her household; he answered, Yes. And thus the woman passed into the Hand of the man, and was called the mother of his household, with the status of filiafamilias.' According to Cicero, the wife was only called materfamilias when subject to Hand: Genus est uxor, ejus duae formae, una matrumfamilias, quae in manum convenerant, altera earum quae tantummodo uxores habentur, Top. 4. Gellius says the same: Idonei vocum antiquarum enarratores tradiderunt .... matremfamilias appellatam esse eam solam quae in mariti manu mancipioque, aut in ejus in cujus maritus manu mancipioque esset, quoniam non in matrimonium tantum sed in familiam quoque mariti et in sui heredis locum venisset, Gellius, 18, 6. 'Competent interpreters of the ancient language say that materfamilias was a title only given to a wife in the hand and mancipation of her husband, or of the person who held her husband in hand and mancipation, as she was not only a wife, but a member of the family of the husband, having acquired therein the status of self-successor.' Boethius further limits the title to a wife who has become subject to manus by coemption: Quae autem in manum per coemptionem convenerant, hae matresfamilias vocabantur, quae vero usu et farreatione minime, ibid. However this may have been, in one sense the name was a misnomer, for a wife subject to hand was not sui juris (materfamilias), but alieni juris (filiafamilias).

If the wife was subject to the power of her father she required his consent (auctoritas) before she could make a coemption with her husband: Secundo capite legis Juliae de adulteriis permittitur patri si in filia sua quam in potestate habet, aut in ea quae eo auctore, cum in potestate esset, viro in manum convenerit, adulterum domi suae generive sui deprehenderit, isque in eam rem socerum adhibuerit, ut is pater eum adulterum sine fraude sua occidat, ita ut filiam in continenti occidat, Collatio, 4, 22. 'The second section of the lex Julia on adultery permits a father who finds his daughter, who is in his power or with his consent in the hand of her husband, committing adultery in his house or in the house of her husband, if called in for the purpose by his son-in-law, to kill the adulterer with impunity, provided that at the same time he also puts his daughter to death.' If the wife was independent of parental control, she required the sanction of her guardians, that is, her agnates, before she could make a coemption with her husband: In manum convenerat usu an coemptione? Usu non potuit, nihil enim potest de tutela legitima nisi omnium tutorum auctoritate deminui. Coemptione? omnibus ergo auctoribus, Cic. Pro Flacco, 34. 'Had the wife become subject to marital power by cohabitation or by coemption? Certainly not by either, for the rights of agnatic guardians cannot be defeated without the concurrence of all the guardians.'

Coemption was sometimes employed for other purposes than matrimony, and was then called fiduciary coemption. Sometimes the intention was to extinguish the obligation of onerous sacred rites attached to the estate of an heiress: Jure consultorum ingenio senes ad coemptiones faciendas interimendorum sacrorum causa reperti sunt, Cic. Pro Murena, 12. 'Juristic ingenuity invented coemptions with aged men for extinguishing sacred rites.' Savigny gives the following conjectural explanation of the process. The obligation to the sacra attached to the Quiritary ownership of the universitas of the woman's estate. This, by the effect of coemption, vested in the coemptionator, an old man approaching dissolution (senex coemptionalis), with whom a fictitious marriage was contracted, and who took the estate as universal successor. He forthwith expelled the woman from his manus by remancipation and manumission, and then, according to covenant, restored to her the estate in portions, that is, released from the ritual obligations, which only attached to the universitas. On his death, as Quiritary owner of the empty universitas, the obligation to the rites was extinguished, for the succession (hereditas) to the coemptionator did not pass to the woman, as she by remancipation had ceased to be [such was the hypothesis of Savigny before the discovery of Gaius: instructed by Gaius we must rather say, as mere fiduciary coemption had not the effect of making her] his filiafamilias and sua heres. Universal succession was an institution which Roman law only admitted in certain cases: as operated by contract it was only admitted in case of Manus and Adoptio. If universal succession was required for the purpose of extinguishing the obligation to sacred rites attaching to the estate of an heiress, we might have supposed that adrogatio would have been a less offensive mockery than a fictitious marriage (fiduciary coemption); adrogatio, however, was inapplicable, because, as we have seen, up to a late period of Roman law women were incapable of being adrogated. At other times coemption was employed to enable a woman to select a guardian, § 195, or by breaking the ties of agnation to acquire testamentary capacity, § 115 *a*. The coemptionator (party to the coemption) in virtue of his manus could sell the woman into bondage as if she were filiafamilias: accordingly, he mancipated her to a third person, who, by manumitting her, became her patron, and, as patron, in accordance with the Twelve Tables, § 165, her statutory guardian, and was called her fiduciary guardian, § 115. It may occur to us that as coemptio required the sanction of a father or guardian, this process could not be of much use in getting rid of a guardian or defeating the claims of agnatic guardians to a woman's intestate succession; but it must be remembered that the nearest agnate, who alone was heir and guardian, was a variable person, and that a given nearest agnate might be not indisposed to allow a woman to acquire the free disposition of her property and to defeat the claims of those who, after his death, would be nearest agnates and presumptive heirs.

Agnatic guardianship of female wards was abolished by a lex Claudia, § 171, and the rupture of the ties of agnation by means of coemption ceased to be necessary to the validity of a woman's will by a senatusconsult of Hadrian, § 115 *a*.

The origination of manus by length of continuous possession (usus), i. e. by usucapion, shows plainly enough that early Roman law regarded the wife as a mere chattel of the husband. The law of the Twelve Tables allowed the wife to bar the usucapion by an absence for three nights in each year, which gives rise to a question of computation. The Roman year consisted of 365 days; the day of 24 hours was measured from midnight to midnight. Where the expiration of a certain term was an element of Title, the following distinction was observed: if a right was to be acquired by the expiration of a certain period, it was acquired as soon as the last day of the period began; for instance, if the period was a year, the right was acquired immediately after midnight of the 364th day. This applied to acquisition of ownership by usucapion, Dig. 44, 3, 15, and Dig. 41, 3, 6; acquisition of testamentary capacity by attaining to years of puberty, Dig. 28, 1, 5; acquisition of manumissive capacity, Dig. 40, 1, 1; acquisition by a Latin of the franchise by bringing up a yearling (anniculus) issue of a lawful marriage, Dig. 50, 16, 132. Anniculus trecentesimo sexagesimo quinto die dicitur, incipiente plane, non exacto die, quia annum civiliter non ad momenta temporum sed ad dies numeramus, Dig. 50, 16, 134. 'A child is said to be a yearling on its 365th day, at the beginning, not at the close of the day; for civil computation of the year does not recognize the minor subdivision into minutes or hours, but only reckons by whole days.'

When, on the contrary, a right was forfeited or extinguished by lapse of a certain period, as in the loss of a right of action under a statute of limitations, Dig. 44, 7, 6, the period was not completed until the last day was ended. The following passage from Gellius shows that the vesting of manus by cohabitation was regarded as a loss of independence by the wife, not as an acquisition of power by the husband, for the latter computation was employed. Q. quoque Mucium jure consultum dicere solitum legi, lege non isse usurpatum mulierem, quae, quum kalendis Januariis apud virum matrimonii causa esse coepisset, ante diem quartum kalendas Januarias sequentes usurpatum isset: non enim posse impleri trinoctium, quod abesse a viro usurpandi causa ex duodecim tabulis deberet, quoniam tertiae noctis posteriores sex horae alterius anni essent qui inciperet ex kalendis, 3, 2. 'I have read that, according to Quintus Mucius, the statutory requirements for the interruption of usucapion are not satisfied if a woman married on the 1st of January and did not leave her husband's house until the 29th of December, as she could not then be absent for three days before the end of the year, the interval required by the Twelve Tables, because the last six hours of the third night belong to the first day of the following year.' This implies that the year of cohabitation was not completed before midnight of the 31st of December, and that the wife could satisfy the law by leaving on the 28th. If the vesting of manus had been regarded as an acquisition of a right by the husband, the year would have been complete immediately after midnight of December 30, and the wife could not have accomplished a sufficient interruption of possession (usurpatio) unless she left her husband's house before midnight on the 27th.

§ 114. Fiducia was a declaration of the conditions, purposes, and trusts of a mancipation. Besides its use in coemption, it was employed, as we shall see presently, in emancipation and adoption, and was the earliest form of constituting the contracts of deposit and mortgage, 2, § 59.

DE MANCIPIO.

§ 116. Superest ut exponamus quae personae in mancipio sint.

§ 116. It remains to examine what it is to be held in mancipation.

§ 117. Omnes igitur liberorum personae, *sive* masculi*ni* siv*e* femi*nini sexus, quae* in potestate parentis sunt, mancipari ab hoc eodem modo possunt, quo etiam servi mancipari possunt.

§ 117. All children, male or female, in the power of their father are liable to be mancipated by their father just as his slaves may be mancipated.

§ 118. Idem iuris est in earum personis quae in manu sunt. nam feminae a coemptionatoribus eodem modo possunt *mancipari quo liberi a parente mancipantur; adeo* quidem, *ut quam*vis *ea sola* aput coemptionatorem f*i*liae loco sit *quae ei* nupta sit, *tamen* nihilo minus etiam quae ei nup*ta* non *sit*, nec ob id filiae loco sit, ab eo mancipari possit.

§ 118. A woman in the hand is subject to the same mode of alienation, and may be mancipated by the person who has acquired her by coemption just as a child may be mancipated by its father: and although the acquirer by coemption has not the power of a father over her unless he is her husband, nevertheless, even when he is not her husband, and therefore has not the status of a father, he can dispose of her by mancipation.

§ 118 *a*. Plerumque solum et a parentibus et a coemptionatoribus mancipantur, cum velint parentes coemptionatoresque *e* suo iure eas personas dimittere, sicut inferius evidentius apparebit.

§ 118 *a*. Almost the sole occasion of mancipation by a parent or acquirer by coemption is when the parent or acquirer by coemption designs to liberate the person mancipated from his lawful control, as will presently be more fully explained.

§ 119. Est autem mancipatio, ut supra quoque diximus, imaginaria quaedam venditio: quod et ipsum ius proprium civium Romanorum est. eaque res ita agitur. adhibitis non minus qu*am* quinque testibus civibus Romanis puberibus, et praeterea alio eiusdem condicionis qui libram aeneam teneat, qui appellatur libripens, is qu*i* mancipio accipit rem, *aes* tenens ita dicit: HUNC EGO HOMINEM EX IURE QUIRITIUM MEUM ESSE AIO, ISQUE MIHI EMPTUS EST HOC AERE AENEAQUE LIBRA: deinde aere percutit libram, idque aes dat ei a quo mancipio accipit, quasi pretii loco.

§ 119. Mancipation, as before stated, is an imaginary sale which is only within the competence of Roman citizens, and consists in the following process: in the presence of not fewer than five witnesses, citizens of Rome above the age of puberty, and another person of the same condition, who holds a bronze balance in his hands and is called the balance holder, the alienee holding a bronze ingot in his hand, pronounces the following words: THIS MAN I CLAIM AS BELONGING TO ME BY RIGHT QUIRITARY AND BE HE PURCHASED TO ME BY THIS INGOT AND THIS SCALE OF BRONZE. He then strikes the scale with the ingot, which he delivers to the mancipator as by way of purchase money.

§ 120. Eo modo et serviles et liberae personae mancipantur. animalia quoque quae mancipi sunt, quo in numero habentur boves, equi, muli, asini; item praedia tam urbana quam rustica quae et ipsa mancipi sunt, qualia sunt Italica, eodem modo solent mancipari.

§ 120. By this formality both slaves and free persons may be mancipated, and also such animals as are mancipable, namely, oxen, horses, mules, and asses: immovables also, urban and rustic, if subject to quiritary dominion, such as Italic lands and houses, are aliened by the same outward form.

§ 121. In eo solo praediorum mancipatio a ceterorum mancipatione differt, quod personae serviles et liberae, item animalia quae mancipi sunt, nisi in praesentia sint, mancipari non possunt: adeo quidem, ut eum *qui* mancipio accipit adprehendere id ipsu*m* quod e*i* mancipio datur necesse sit: unde etiam mancipatio dicitur, quia manu res capitur. praedia vero absentia solent mancipari.

§ 121. The only point wherein the mancipation of immovables differs from the mancipation of movables is this, that persons, whether slaves or free, and animals that are mancipable, must be present to be mancipated: indeed the alienee must grasp the movable to be conveyed with his hand, and from this manual prehension the name of mancipation is derived; whereas immovables need not be present to be mancipated.

§ 122. Ideo autem aes et libra adhibetur, quia olim aereis tantum nummis utebantur; et erant asses, dupondii, semis*ses et quadrantes*, nec ullus aureus vel argenteus *nummus in* usu erat, sicut ex lege XII tabularum intellegere possumus; eorumque nummorum vis et potes*tas* non in numero erat, sed in pondere n*ummorum*. *vel*uti asses librales erant, et dipondii *tum* erant *bilibres; unde etiam* dipondius dictus *est quasi duo* pondo: *quod* nomen adhuc in usu retinetur. semisse*s quoque* et quadrante*s* pro rata scilicet portione *li*bra*e aeris habe*ba*nt certum pondus*. *item* qui daba*nt olim pecuniam non ad*numeraba*n*t eam, sed a*pp*endeba*n*t. unde servi quibus perm*ittitur* ad*mini*s*t*ratio *pecu*niae d*ispensatores* appellati sunt et ad*huc appellan*tur.

§ 122. The reason of using a bronze ingot and a weighing scale is the fact that the ancient currency consisted entirely of bronze ingots, the as, the double as, the half as, the quarter as, and there was no gold or silver in circulation, as appears by the law of the Twelve Tables: and the value of the currency was not measured by number of coins but by weight of metal. Thus the as was a pound of bronze, the double as two pounds, whence its name (dupondius), which still survives; the half as and quarter as those respective fractions of a pound. Accordingly, money payments were not made by counting, but by weighing, whence slaves entrusted with pecuniary transactions are still called dispensators.

§ 123. Si tamen quaerat ali*quis*, *qu*are a coemptio*ne differat mancipatio*, ea quidem quae coemptionem

§ 123. If it is asked in what respect coemptive conveyance differs from mancipation, the answer is

facit, *non deducitur in* servilem condicionem, a *parentibus vero et a coemptionatoribus* mancipati mancipataeve servorum loco constituuntur, adeo quidem, ut ab eo cuius in mancipio sunt neque hereditatem neque legata aliter capere possint, quam *si* simul eodem testamento liberi esse iubeantur sicuti iuris est in persona servorum. sed differentiae ratio manifesta *est*, cum a parentibus et a coemptionatoribus iisdem verbis mancipio accipiuntur quibus servi; quod non similiter *fit* in *coemptione*.

this, that coemption does not reduce to a servile condition, whereas mancipation reduces to so completely a servile condition that a person held in mancipation cannot take as heir or legatee under the will of the person to whom he is mancipated, unless thereby at the same time enfranchised, thus labouring under the same incapacity as a slave: the reason too of the difference is plain, as the form of words employed in mancipation by a parent or previous acquirer by coemption is identical with that used in the mancipation of slaves, but it is not so in coemptive conveyance.

In what respects did domestic bondage (mancipium or mancipii causa) differ from slavery (servitus)? Bondage was an institute of Civil law, slavery an institute of the law of nations, § 52. Bondage was the result of mancipation by a parent or coemptionator, and only a Roman citizen was capable of becoming a bondsman. The bondsman was civis Romanus, though what became of his political capacities during his bondage is uncertain; and he was liber, though alieni juris: he was free in respect of the rest of the world, he was only a bondsman in respect of his domestic superior (paterfamilias). Hence the status of mancipium was relative; a man could only be mancipium in relation to a given domestic lord: whereas the status of slavery was absolute; a man might be a slave without a proprietor (servus sine domino): for instance, a person condemned for a capital crime, who was called the slave of punishment (servus poenae, Inst. 1, 12, 3), or a slave abandoned (derelictus) by his proprietor. Accordingly, falling into servitus was maxima capitis diminutio, while falling into mancipii causa was minima capitis diminutio, § 162. The bondsman had no proprietary rights against his superior, 2, § 86, but he had some of the Primordial rights; for instance, he could sue his superior for outrage, § 141; and he was capable of civil wedlock and could beget Roman citizens, though during his bondage his patria potestas was in abeyance, § 135 *a*. Release from bondage, as from slavery, was by manumission, and the manumitter became the patron of the released person, § 195, but the manumitted bondsman became ingenuus, whereas

the manumitted slave became libertinus. Bondage did not exist in the time of Justinian.

§ 120. Under the first emperors the body of the Roman world consisted of three members, the imperial city, Rome, Italy, and the provinces, the two former being highly privileged in comparison with the third. After the Social War all Italy had acquired the Roman franchise, but Italic soil was not a purely local appellation, as jus Italicum was conceded to many provincial cities. Jus Italicum, or Italian privileges, implied (1) a free municipal constitution with elective magistrates (generally called duumviri juri dicundo) possessed of independent jurisdiction; and, what was still more important, (2) immunity from direct taxation, whether in the form of capitation tax (tributum capitis), imposed on all who were not holders of land (tributarii), or in the form of land tax (tributum agri), imposed on holders of land (possessores), and paid in provinces of the people to the aerarium under the name of stipendium, in provinces of the emperor to the fiscus under the name of tributum, 2, § 21. Italic soil was (3) subject to Quiritary ownership (dominium ex jure Quiritium) and acquirable and transferable by usucapion and mancipation. Under the later emperors, as early as the time of Diocletian, the Roman world was equalized, not by the elevation of the depressed members, but by depression of those formerly favoured: Italy was shorn of her privileges, and all the empire became provincial.

§ 122. Chemical analysis shows that the aes of which Roman coins consisted was bronze, a mixture of copper (cuprum), tin, and lead. Brass, a mixture of copper and calamine (cadmeia) or zinc, was called orichalcum. Silver currency was first introduced B.C. 269.

§ 123. As coemptio was a form of mancipatio, how does it happen that manus, the result of coemptio, differs from mancipium, the result of mancipatio? Because, Gaius answers, the formula of words used in the mancipatio that entered into coemptio was specifically different from the formula employed on other occasions of mancipation.

QUIBUS MODIS IUS POTESTATIS SOLVATUR.

§ 124. Videamus nunc, quib*us* *modis ii qui a*lieno iur*i* *sub*iecti sunt eo iure liberentur.

§ 124. Let us now examine the modes whereby persons dependent on a superior are freed from their dependence.

§ 125. *Ac* prius de his dispiciamus qui in potestate sunt.

§ 125. And, first, let us consider persons subject to power.

§ 126. Et quidem *servi quemadmodum potestate liberentur, ex his intellegere* possumus quae de servis manumittendis superius exposuimus.

§ 126. The mode of liberating slaves from their proprietor's power was expounded above, when we treated of servile manumission.

§ 127. Hi vero qui *in potestate parentis sunt mortuo eo sui iuris fiunt. Sed hoc* distinctionem recipit. nam *mortuo patre sane* omnimodo filii filiaeve sui iuris efficiuntur. mortuo vero avo *non omnimodo nepotes neptesque* sui *iuris fiunt, sed ita, si post mortem avi* in patris sui potestatem recasuri non *sunt. itaque si moriente avo pater eorum et vivat et in potestate* patris fuerit, tunc post *obitum avi* in potestate pat*ris sui fiunt : si vero is*, quo tempore av*us* moritur, *aut iam mortuus est, aut exiit de potestate patris, tunc hi, quia* in potestatem eius cadere non possunt, sui iuris fiunt.

§ 127. Children under paternal power become independent at the parent's death, subject, however, to this reservation : the death of a father always releases his sons and daughters from dependence : the death of a grandfather only releases his grandchildren from dependence, provided that it does not subject them to the power of their father : for if at the death of the grandfather the father is alive and in his power, the grandchildren, after the grandfather's death, are in the power of the father ; but if at the time of the grandfather's death the father is dead or not subject to the grandfather, the grandchildren will not fall under his power, but become independent.

§ 128. Cum autem is cui ob aliquod maleficium ex lege poenali aqua et igni interdicitur civitatem Romanam amittat, sequitur, ut qui eo modo ex numero civium Romanorum tollitur, proinde ac mortuo eo desinant liberi in potestate eius esse : nec enim ratio patitur, ut peregrinae condicionis homo civem Romanum in potestate habeat. Pari ratione et si ei qui in potestate parentis sit aqua et igni interdictum fuerit, desinit in potestate parentis esse, quia aeque ratio non patitur, ut peregrinae condicionis homo in potestate sit civis Romani parentis.

§ 128. As interdiction from fire and water for an offence against the criminal code involves loss of citizenship, such removal of a man from the list of Roman citizens operates, like his death, to liberate his children from his power, for it is inconsistent with civil law that an alien should exercise parental power over a citizen of Rome : conversely, the interdiction from fire and water of a person subject to parental power terminates the power of the parent, because it is a similar inconsistency that a person of alien status should be subject to the parental power of a Roman citizen.

§ 129. Quod si ab hostibus captus fuerit parens, quamvis serv*us inte*rim hostium fiat, pendet ius liberorum propter ius postliminii, *quia* hi qui ab hostibus capti sunt, si reversi fuerint, omn*ia* pristina iura recipiunt.

§ 129. Though the hostile capture of the parent makes him a slave of the enemy, the status of his children is suspended by his right of retrospective rehabilitation, for on escape from captivity a man recovers all

itaque reversus habebit liberos in potestate. si vero illic mortuus sit, erunt quidem liberi sui iuris; sed utrum ex hoc tempore quo mortuus est aput hostes parens, an ex illo quo ab hostibus captus est, dubitari potest. Ipse quoque filius neposve si ab hostibus captus fuerit, similiter dicemus propter ius postliminii potestatem quoque parentis in suspenso esse.

former rights: accordingly, if the father returns he will have his children in his power; if he dies in captivity his children will be independent, but whether their independence dates from the death of the parent or from his capture by the enemy may be disputed. Conversely, if a son or grandson is captured by the enemy, his right of subsequent recovery of status causes the power of his ascendent to be provisionally suspended.

§ 130. Praeterea exeunt liberi virilis sexus de patris potestate si flamines Diales inaugurentur, et feminini sexus si virgines Vestales capiantur.

§ 130. Further, a son is liberated from parental power by his inauguration as flamen of Jove, a daughter by her selection for the office of Vestal virgin.

§ 131. Olim quoque, quo tempore populus Romanus in Latinas regiones colonias deducebat, *qui iussu* parentis *profectus erat in Latinam coloniam*, e *patria potestate exire videbatur, cum qui ita civitate Romana cesserant acci*perentur alterius civitatis cives.

§ 131. Formerly, too, when Rome used to send colonies into the Latin territory, an order of the parent to depart for a Latin colony was held to liberate a son from parental power, because such departure was held to make the son a citizen of a foreign state.

§ 128. Relegation was a milder form of punishment than deportation, and involved no loss of civitas nor of domestic rights, Inst. 1, 12, 2.

§ 129. Postliminium is the recovery of rights by a person returned from captivity, or the recovery of rights over a person or thing recovered from hostile possession. The word postliminium seems to be derived from pot, the root of potestas or possessio, and limen or stlimen = ligamen, and therefore would denote the bridging over of the interval of captivity by a fiction of continued capacity or possession, as a doorway is bridged over by a lintel (limen).

§ 130. In imitation of the ancient law Justinian enacted that certain dignities should release from patria potestas; for instance, patriciatus and the episcopate, the latter because it made a man spiritual father of all mankind, Novella, 81.

§ 131. The Latini or members of coloniae Latinae were an intermediate class between cives and peregrini. They differed from peregrini in that they had commercium, i. e. capacity of Quiritary ownership with its incidents, and they differed from cives in not having connubium, and consequently being incapable of patria potestas, Cic. Pro Caecina, 35. A Roman citizen could only become a Latin with his own consent. Qui cives Romani in colonias Latinas proficiscebantur, fieri non poterant Latini ni erant auctores facti nomenque dederant, Cic. De Domo, 30. 'Roman citizens who went to Latin colonies did not lose their citizenship without voluntary enrolment among the colonists.' See also Cic. Pro Balbo, 11.

§ 132. Emancipatione *quoque desinunt liberi in potestatem parentium esse. sed* filius quidem *tertia demum mancipatione, ceteri* vero liberi, sive masculini sexus sive feminini, una mancipatione exeunt de parentium potestate: lex enim xii. tantum in persona filii de tribus mancipationibus loquitur, *his* verbis: SI PATER FILIUM *TER VENUMDABIT, FILIUS A PATRE* LIBER ESTO. *eaque* res ita agitur. mancipat pater filium alicui: is *eum* vindicta manu*mittit:* eo fact*o* revertitur in potestatem patris. is eum iterum mancipat vel eidem vel alii; *set in usu est eidem* mancipari: isque *eum* postea simi*liter vindicta manumittit: quo facto rursus* in potestatem patris *sui* reverti*tur. tunc* tertio pater eum mancipat vel eidem vel alii; set hoc in usu est, ut eidem manci*petur: eaque* mancipati*one desinit* in *potestate patris esse, et*iamsi nondum manumissus sit, set adhuc in causa mancip*ii* [*lin.* 24].

§ 132. Emancipation also liberates children from the power of the parent, a son being liberated by three mancipations, other issue, male or female, by a single mancipation; for the law of the Twelve Tables only mentions three mancipations in the case of the son, which it does in the following terms: IF A FATHER SELL A SON THREE TIMES, THE SON SHALL BE FREE FROM THE FATHER. The ceremony is as follows: the father mancipates his son to some one; the alienee manumits him by fictitious vindication, whereupon he reverts into the power of his father; the father again mancipates him to the same or a different alienee, usually to the same, who again manumits him by fictitious vindication, whereupon he reverts a second time into the power of his father; the father then mancipates him a third time to the same or a different alienee, usually to the same, and by this third mancipation the son ceases to be in the power of the father even before manumission and while in the status of a person held in mancipation. [The alienee or fiduciary father should then remancipate him to the natural father, in order that thereupon the natural father by manumitting him may acquire the rights of patron instead of the fiduciary father.]

§ 133. *Liberum autem arbitrium est ei qui filium et ex eo nepotem in potestate habebit, filium quidem potestate dimittere, nepotem vero in*

§ 133. A grandfather who has both a son, and by his son a grandson, in his power, may either release his son from his power and retain

potestate retinere; vel ex diverso filium quidem in potestate retinere, nepotem vero manumittere; vel omnes sui iuris efficere. eadem et de pronepote dicta esse intellegemus.

§ 134. *Praeterea parentes liberis in adoptionem datis in potestate eos habere desinunt; et in filio quidem,* si *in adoptionem datur, tres mancipationes et duae* intercedentes manumissiones proinde fiunt, ac fieri solent cum ita eum pater de potestate dimittit, ut sui iuris efficiatur. deinde aut patri remancipatur, et ab eo is qui adoptat vindicat aput praetorem filium suum esse, et illo contra non vin*d*icante *a* praetore vindicanti filius addicitur, aut *non* remancipatur patri, *sed ei qui adoptat in iure ceditur ab eo apud quem in tertia* mancipatione est: set sane commodius est patri remancipari. in ceteris vero liberorum personis, seu masculini seu femini sexus, una scilicet mancipatio sufficit, et aut remancipantur parenti aut *non* remancipantur. Eadem et in provinciis aput praesidem provinciae solent fieri.

§ 135*a*. Qui ex filio semel iterumve mancipato conceptus est, licet post tertiam mancipationem patris sui nascatur, tamen in avi potestate est, et ideo ab eo et *e*mancipari et in adoptionem dari potest. At is qui ex eo filio conceptus est qui in tertia mancipatione est, non nascitur in avi potestate. set eum Labeo quidem existimat in eiusdem mancipio esse cuius et pater sit. utimur autem hoc iure, ut quam diu pater eius in mancipio sit, pendeat ius eius: et si quidem pater eius ex mancipatione manumissus erit, cadit in eius potestatem; si vero is, dum in mancipio sit, decesserit, sui iuris fit.

the grandson, or retain the son and manumit the grandson, or emancipate both son and grandson; and a great grandfather has a similar latitude of choice.

§ 134. A father is also divested of power over his children by giving them in adoption. To give a son in adoption, the first stage is three mancipations and two manumissions, as in emancipation; after this the son is either remancipated to the father, and by the adopter claimed as son from him by vindication before the praetor, and in default of counterclaim by the natural father is awarded by the praetor to the adoptive father as his son; or without remancipation to the natural father is directly claimed by the adoptive father by vindication from the alienee of the third mancipation (fiduciary father); but it is more convenient to interpose a remancipation to the natural father. In the case of other issue, male or female, a single mancipation suffices, with or without remancipation to the natural father. In the provinces a similar ceremony can be performed before the president of the province.

§ 135*a*. A grandson begotten after the first or second mancipation of the son, though born after the third mancipation, is subject to the power of the grandfather, and may by him be given in adoption or emancipated: a grandson begotten after the third mancipation is not born in the power of the grandfather, but, according to Labeo, is born in mancipation to the person to whom his father is mancipated. The rule, however, which has obtained acceptance is, that so long as the father is in mancipation the status of the child is in suspension, and if the father is manumitted the child falls under his power; if the father dies in mancipation the child becomes independent.

§ 135*b*. Et de .... licet .... [1 *lin.*] ut supra diximus, quod in filio faciunt tres mancipationes, hoc facit una mancipatio in nepote.

§ 135*b*. .... as before mentioned, the result of three mancipations of the son is obtained by a single mancipation of the grandson.

§ 136. *Mulieres, quamvis in manu sint, nisi coemtionem* fecerin*t, potestate parentis non liberantur.* hoc *in Flaminica Diali senatusconsulto confirmatur*, quo *ex auctoritate consulum* Maximi et Tuberonis *cavetur*, *ut* haec quod *ad* sacra tan*tu*m videatur in manu esse, quod vero ad cetera perinde habeatur, atque si in manum no*n convenisset. Sed mulieres quae in manum conveniunt per coemptionem a* potestate parentis liberantur: nec interest, an in viri sui manu *sint, an* extranei*; quamvis* ha*e* solae loco filiarum habeantur quae in viri manu *sunt*.

§ 136. A wife subjected to the hand of a husband by confarreation is not thereby freed from the power of her father; and this is declared by the senatusconsult of the consuls Maximus and Tubero respecting the priestess of Jove, which limits the marital hand to the sphere of sacred rites, and declares the status of the wife unaffected in other respects by subjection to the hand of the husband. Subjection to hand by coemption liberates from the power of the parent, and it is immaterial whether it is a coemption subjecting the woman to the hand of a husband or to the hand of a stranger, although the status of quasi daughter only belongs to a woman in the hand of a husband.

§ 132. The epitomator of Gaius in the code of Alaric mentions as present at an emancipation, besides the five witnesses and libripens, a seventh person whom he calls antestatus, who is not elsewhere noticed.

The vindicta or wand used in manumission, as already stated, was the rod or verge symbolizing a lance carried by the parties in a real action. The status of freedom (libertas) whether as opposed to slavery or to bondage (mancipii causa) was a real right (jus in rem), and therefore a subject to be contested in a vindicatio. Manumission by vindicta was a collusive vindicatio, in other words, an in jure cessio.

The epitomator of Gaius calls the person to whom the son was mancipated pater fiduciarius, which implies that the mancipation was accompanied by a fiducia or declaration of trust. The trust would be that the pater fiduciarius should make default or confess in the subsequent vindicatio.

§ 134. Assuming that in adoption, as in emancipation, the person to whom the son was mancipated was called pater fiduciarius, we find in adoption three fathers in the field, pater naturalis, pater fiduciarius, and pater adoptivus.

The status of paterfamilias or of filiusfamilias being, like other kinds of status, a real right, the claim of a person as filiusfamilias was a matter to be contested in a real action or vindicatio. This would seem the more obvious to the early jurists, as they probably drew no distinction between patria potestas and dominica potestas, i. e. between paternal power and absolute proprietorship. This claim was sometimes a matter of contentious (not voluntary) jurisdiction, i. e. of genuine litigation. Per hanc autem actionem liberae personae quae sunt juris nostri, utputa liberi qui sunt in potestate, non petuntur . . . . nisi forte adjecta causa quis vindicet. Unde si quis ita petit, filium suum, vel, in potestate ex jure Romano, videtur mihi et Pomponius consentire, recte eum egisse; ait enim, adjecta causa ex lege Quiritium vindicare posse, Dig. 6, 1, 2. 'If free persons, dependent on the plaintiff—for instance, children subject to his power—are sought to be recovered by vindication, the title or mode of dependence must be specified in the formula (intentio). Thus a claim of a person as son, or as subject to power by the law of Rome, even according to Pomponius, is regular: for he says that the specification of a title under a statute of the Quirites makes the vindication valid.' (The anomalous forms, ex jure Romano, ex lege Quiritium, instead of the usual, ex jure Quiritium, were perhaps peculiar to the pleadings in this kind of suit.)

Justinian simplified the formalities of emancipation and adoption. He allowed the former to be accomplished by a simple declaration before a competent magistrate, Inst. 1, 12, 6; and the latter by appearance of the parties before a competent judge and insinuatio, i. e. a memorandum of the transaction in the public records of his office (actis intervenientibus), Cod. 8, 48, 11.

In English law children are enfranchised, and the limited power of the father over their person and property is terminated, by two events which did not operate emancipation in Roman law, marriage and arrival at years of discretion, that is, attainment of majority by the completion of twenty-one years of age. At these points, under English law, the empire of the father or other guardian gives place to the empire of reason; whereas neither marriage nor majority released the Roman son or daughter from patria potestas.

§ 137. [3 *lin.*] *remancipatione desinunt* in manu esse, et *cum* ex *remancipatione manumissae fuerint*, sui *iuris efficiuntur* [3 *lin.*] nihil*o* magis *potest* cogere, q*uam* filia patrem. set filia quidem nullo modo patrem *potest* cogere, etiamsi adoptiva sit: haec autem *virum* repudio misso proinde compell*ere potest*, atque si ei numquam nupta fuisset.

§ 137. A woman subjected to hand by coemption is released therefrom by remancipation, and on subsequent manumission becomes independent. A wife subject to marital hand without dissolution of the marriage can no more compel her husband to release her from his hand than a daughter can compel her father. A daughter, however, has no means of compelling her father, even if he is only such by adoption, whereas a wife by sending a message of divorce can compel her husband to release her from his hand, just as if they had never been married.

§ 138. Ii qui in causa mancipii sunt, quia servorum loco habentur, vindicta, censu, testament*o* manumissi sui iuris fiunt.

§ 138. As persons in mancipation have the status of slaves, manumission by fictitious vindication, by entry on the censor's register, by testamentary disposition, are the modes by which they acquire independence.

§ 139. Nec tamen in hoc casu lex Aelia Sentia locum habet. itaque nihil requirimus, cuius aetatis sit is qui manumittit, et qui manumittitur: ac ne illu*d* quidem, an patronum creditoremve manumissor habeat. Ac ne numerus quidem legis Fu*r*iae Caniniae finitus in his personis locum habet.

§ 139. But to them the lex Aelia Sentia has no application: no age of the person manumitting or the person manumitted is required; the manumission is subject to no proviso against fraud on the rights of patron or creditors, nor even to the numerical limitation of the lex Furia Caninia.

§ 140. Quin etiam invito quoque eo cuius in mancipio sunt censu libertatem consequi possunt, excepto eo quem pater ea lege mancipio dedit, ut sibi remancipetur: nam quodammodo tunc pater potestatem propriam reservare sibi videtur eo ipso, quo*d* mancipio recipit. Ac ne i*s* quidem dicitur invito eo cuiu*s* in mancipio est censu libertatem consequi, quem pater ex noxali causa mancipio dedit, velut qui furti eius nomine damnatus est, et *eum* mancipio actori dedit: nam hunc actor pro pecunia habet.

§ 140. The assent of the holder in mancipation is not required for manumission by entry on the register of the censor, except when a son has been mancipated by a father with a condition of remancipation, for by such a condition the father is deemed to have reserved a certain amount of parental power: the assent of the holder in mancipation is also necessary to manumission by entry on the censor's register when a delinquent son has been surrendered by his father in consequence of a noxal suit; when, for instance, the father has been condemned in an action for a theft committed by the son, and has by mancipation surrendered his son to the plaintiff in lieu of pecuniary damages.

§ 141. In summa admonendi sumus, adversus eos quos in mancipio habemus nihil nobis contumeliose facere licere: alioquin iniuriarum *actione tenebimur*. Ac ne diu quidem in eo iure detinentur homines, set plerumque hoc fit dicis gratia uno momento; nisi scilicet ex noxali causa manciparentur.

§ 141. Finally, it is to be observed that contumelious treatment of a person held in mancipation is not permitted, but renders liable to an action of outrage; and the status generally is not persistent, but merely formal and momentary, except when it is the consequence of surrender in lieu of damages in an action of trespass.

§. 137. Dissolution of marriage was either by the consent of both parties (divortium) or by the act of one (repudium). The message of repudiation contained the formula, Tuas res tibi habeto, 'Take away thy property.' Mimam illam suam suas res sibi habere jussit, claves ademit, exegit, Cic. Phil. 2, 28. 'The actress was ordered to pack, deprived of the keys, turned out of the house.' The lex Julia de adulteriis prescribed a form for repudium, and required the message to be delivered by a freedman of the family, in the presence of seven witnesses above the age of puberty and citizens of Rome. The party who made a causeless repudium, or whose misconduct justified a repudium, was punished by pecuniary losses in respect of dos and propternuptial donations. After much veering legislation in later times, Justinian enacted that a man or woman who divorced without a cause should retire to a cloister and forfeit all his or her estate, one moiety to his or her successors, and the other moiety to the cloister. Nov. 134, 11.

DE TUTELIS.

§ 142. Transeamus nunc ad aliam divisionem. nam ex his personis, quae neque in potestate neque in manu neque in mancipio sunt, quaedam vel in tutela sunt vel in curatione, quaedam neutro iure tenentur. videamus igitur quae in tutela vel in curatione sint: ita enim intellegamus ceteras personas quae neutro iure tenentur.

§ 142. Let us now proceed to another classification: persons not subject to power, nor to hand, nor held in mancipation, may still be subject either to guardianship or to administration, or may be exempt from both forms of control. We will first examine what persons are subject to guardianship and administration, and thus we shall know who are exempt from both kinds of control.

§ 143. Ac prius dispiciamus de his quae in tutela sunt.

§ 143. And first of persons subject to guardianship or tutelage.

§ 144. Permissum est itaque parentibus liberis quos in potestate sua habent testamento *tut*ores dare: masculini quidem sexus inpuberibus *dumtaxat, feminini autem tam inpuberibus quam nubilibus.* veteres enim voluerunt feminas, etiamsi per*f*ectae aetatis sint, propter animi levitatem in tutela esse.

§ 144. The law allows a parent to appoint guardians in his will for the children in his power, below the age of puberty, if they are males, above the age of puberty, if they are females; for, according to our ancestors, women even after the age of puberty, from their intellectual weakness, require to be kept in tutelage.

§ 145. Itaque si quis filio filiaeque testamento tutorem dederit, et ambo ad pubertatem pervenerint, filius quidem desinit habere tutorem, filia vero nihilominus in tutela permanet: tantum enim ex leg*e* Iulia et Papia Pop*pae*a iure liberorum a tutela liberantur feminae. loquimur autem exceptis virginibus vestalibus quas etiam veteres in honore*m* sacerdotii liberas esse voluerunt: itaque etiam leg*e* XII Tabularum cautum est.

§ 145. Accordingly, when a brother and sister have a testamentary guardian, on attaining the age of puberty the brother ceases to be a ward, but the sister continues, for it is only under the lex Julia and Papia Poppaea and by title of maternity that females are emancipated from tutelage; except in the case of vestal virgins, for these, even in our ancestors' opinion, are entitled by their sacerdotal function to be free from control, and so the law of the Twelve Tables enacted.

§ 146. Nepotibus autem neptibusque ita demum possumus testa*mento* tutores dare, si post mortem nostram in patris sui potestatem iure recasuri non sint. itaque si filius meus mortis meae tempore in potestate mea sit, nepotes quos ex eo *habeo* non pot*e*rint ex testamento meo habere tutorem, quamvis in potestate mea fuerint: scilicet quia mortuo me in patris sui potestate futuri sunt.

§ 146. A grandson or granddaughter can only receive a testamentary guardian provided the death of the testator does not bring them under parental power. Accordingly, if before the grandfather's death the father was in the grandfather's power, the grandchildren, though in the grandfather's power, cannot have a testamentary guardian, because his death leaves them in the power of the father.

§ 147. Cum tamen in compluribus aliis causis postumi pro iam natis habeantur, et in hac causa placuit non minus postumis, quam iam natis testamento tutores dari posse: si modo in ea causa sint, ut si vivis nobis nasc*an*tur, in potestate nostra fiant. hos etiam heredes instituere possumus, cum extraneos postumos heredes instituere permissum non sit.

§ 147. As in many other matters, after-born children are treated on the footing of children born before the execution of the will, so it is ruled that after-born children, as well as children born before the will was made, may have guardians therein appointed, provided that if born in the testator's lifetime they would be subject to his power [and immediate successors], for the inheritance may be devised to such after-born children, but not to after-born strangers.

§ 148. *Uxori* quae in manu est proinde acsi filiae, item nurui quae in fili*i* manu est proinde ac nepti tutor dari potest.

§ 149. Rectissime autem tutor sic dari potest: LUCIUM TITIUM LIBERIS MEIS TUTOREM DO. sed et si ita scriptum sit: LIBERIS MEIS vel UXORI MEAE TITIUS TUTOR ESTO, recte datus intellegitur.

§ 150. In persona tamen uxoris quae in manu est rece*p*ta est etiam tutoris optio, id est, ut liceat ei permittere quem velit ipsa tutorem sibi optare, hoc modo: TITIAE UXORI MEAE TUTORIS OPTIONEM DO. quo casu licet uxori *eligere tutorem* vel in omnes res vel in unam fort*e* aut duas.

§ 151. Ceterum aut plena optio datur aut angusta.

§ 152. Plena ita dari solet, ut proxum*e* supra diximus. angusta ita dari solet: TITIAE UXORI MEAE DUMTAXAT TUTOR*IS* OPTIONEM SEMEL DO, aut DUMTAXAT BIS DO.

§ 153. Quae optiones plurimum inter se differ*u*nt. nam quae plenam optionem habet potest semel et bis et ter et saepius tutorem optare. quae vero angus*tam* habet optionem, si dumtaxat semel data est optio, amplius quam semel optare non potest: si tantum bis, amplius quam bis optandi facultatem non habet.

§ 154. Vocantur autem hi qui nominatim testamento tutores dantur, dativi; qui ex optione sumuntur, optivi.

§ 148. A wife in the testator's hand may receive a testamentary guardian as if she were a daughter, and a son's wife in the son's hand as if she were a granddaughter.

§ 149. The most regular form of appointing a guardian is in the following terms: 'I APPOINT'—or, 'I DEVISE AND APPOINT—LUCIUS TITIUS GUARDIAN TO MY CHILDREN;' the form, 'BE LUCIUS TITIUS GUARDIAN TO MY CHILDREN'—or, 'TO MY WIFE'—is also valid.

§ 150. To a wife in his hand a testator is permitted to devise the selection of her guardian, that is, he may authorize her to choose whom she pleases, in the following terms: 'TO TITIA MY WIFE I DEVISE THE SELECTION OF HER GUARDIAN;' whereupon she may nominate either a general guardian or a guardian for certain specified matters.

§ 151. The option of a guardian may be limited or unlimited.

§ 152. Unlimited option is usually devised in the form above mentioned; limited option in the following terms: 'TO TITIA MY WIFE I DEVISE NOT MORE THAN ONE OPTION'—or, 'NOT MORE THAN TWO OPTIONS—OF A GUARDIAN.'

§ 153. The effect of these forms is very different: unlimited option is a power of changing the guardian an indefinite number of times; limited option is the right of a single choice, or of two choices, as may happen.

§ 154. A guardian nominated by the testator is called a dative guardian; one selected by the widow is called an optative guardian.

Having examined those inferiorities of legal capacity which constituted a status, we now proceed to examine certain cases of incapacity which, though analogous to the former as belonging to the sphere of unequal rights, were not included by the Romans under the denomination of status. The inferiorities of capacity in infancy, minority, wardship, curatel, were not so considerable as those which we have hitherto examined. The diminution of rights in a lapse from independence to curatel was less than the least capitis minutio, and accordingly a prodigal who was interdicted from the administration of his estate and subjected to the control of a curator, was not said to undergo a status mutatio: his patrimony still vested in him, though he was deprived of its administration; whereas adrogatio and in manum conventio divested a person of the capacity of ownership and contractual right: inferior status, in a word, is incapacity of right; wardship and curatel are only incapacities of action.

Guardianship is thus defined: Est autem tutela jus ac potestas in capite libero, ad tuendum eum qui propter aetatem se defendere nequit, jure civili data ac permissa, Inst. 1, 13, 1. 'Guardianship is a right and power over an independent person conferred or authorized by the civil law for the protection of one who is incapacitated by age for self-defence.' The duties of the guardian related both to the person and to the property of the ward. In respect of his person, the guardian was charged with the care of his nurture and education: in respect of his property, the guardian's function was distinguished as either exclusive administration or concurrent interposition of authority. Up to the age of seven the ward was called infans, and during this period the guardian acted alone (administratio, negotiorum gestio); after the completion of seven years until the age of puberty (fourteen for males, twelve for females) the ward acted, and the guardian concurrently gave his sanction (auctoritas). Even in the latter period the guardian might act alone or concurrently according to his discretion: he probably gave his sanction in proceedings governed by the Civil law [Nemo alieno nomine lege agere potest, Dig. 50, 17, 123. 'No appearance in another person's name, i. e. no representation or agency, is admissible in the old actions of law'], and simply administered in proceedings governed by the law of nations. In the time of Gaius, women continued subject to guardianship after the age of puberty: the functions of the guardian were then confined to auctoritas, which in most cases was a mere formality: the power of administration vested in the woman, § 190.

§ 147. Postumus (afterborn) has no etymological connection with humus, and no reference to the death of the testator, but simply denotes a person born after the execution of a will, whether after the death or in the lifetime of the testator. The law, however, originally made a distinction between the two cases. The institution or disinherison of a postumus born after the death of a testator was valid at Civil law, and availed to save the will from rupture by afterbirth (agnatio) of an immediate successor (suus heres): the same institution or disinherison would have been invalid and unavailing if the postumus had been born in the lifetime of the testator, before the enactment of the lex Junia Velleia in the reign of Augustus, 2 § 130, commentary. A grandson was postumus alienus if born in the lifetime of his father; he was postumus suus, i. e. immediate lineal successor to his grandfather, if born after the death of his father, 2 § 241, and only in this event could he receive a guardian by the will of his grandfather. Aquillius Gallus invented a form for the conditional institution or disinherison of a grandson, and, doubtless, also for the nomination of his guardian, by a will executed in the lifetime of his father: conditioned, that is, to take effect in the event of the decease of the father before the death of the grandfather. It appears, then, that the statement of Gaius, § 147, is inaccurate, unless we complete it by words taken from the parallel passage in the Institutes, and read: Si modo in ea causa sint ut, si vivis nobis nascantur, [sui et] in potestate nostra fiant.

§ 148. In filii manu must be regarded as an inaccurate expression: for filiusfamilias was incapable of all civil rights, including manus, and could only serve as a conduit-pipe by which the right of manus vested in his father.

DE LEGITIMA AGNATORUM TUTELA.

§ 155. Quibus testamento quidem tutor datus non sit, iis ex lege XII agnati sunt tutores, qui vocantur legitimi.

§ 155. In default of a testamentary guardian the statute of the Twelve Tables assigns the guardianship to the nearest agnates, who are hence called statutory guardians.

§ 156. Sunt autem agnati per virilis sexus personas cognatione iuncti, quasi a patre cognati: veluti frater eodem patre natus, fratris filius neposve ex eo, item patruus et patrui filius *et nepos* ex

§ 156. Agnates (3 § 10) are cognates through males, that is, through their male ascendents: as a brother by the same father, such brother's son or son's son; a father's brother, his son or son's son. Cognates

eo. At hi qui per feminini sexus *personas cognatione iunguntur non sunt agnati, sed alias* naturali iure cognati. *itaque* inter avunculum et sororis filium non agnatio est, sed cognatio. item amitae, materterae filius non est mihi agnatus, set cognatus, et invicem scilicet ego illi eodem iure coniun*gor*: quia qui nascuntur patris, non matris familiam sequuntur.

through female ascendents are merely natural kinsmen. Thus, between a man and his sister's son there is not agnation, but cognation: so my father's sister's son or my mother's sister's son is not my agnate, but my cognate, and vice-versa, for children are member's of their father's family, but not of their mother's.

§ 157. Sed olim quidem, quantum ad legem XII tabularum atti*net*, etiam feminae agnatos habebant tutores. set postea lex Claud*ia* lata est quae, quod ad feminas atti*net*, tutelas *illas* sustulit. itaque masculus quidem inpubes fratrem puberem aut patruum habet tutorem; feminae vero talem habere tutorem non *intelleguntur*.

§ 157. In former times, the statute of the Twelve Tables made females as well as males wards of their agnates: subsequently a law of the Emperor Claudius abolished this wardship in the case of females: accordingly, a male below the age of puberty has his brother above the age of puberty or his paternal uncle for guardian, but females are not in the wardship of their agnates.

§ 158. Set agnationis quidem ius capitis diminutione perimitur, cognationis vero ius non commutatur: quia civilis ratio civilia qu*idem* iura corrumpere potest, naturalia vero non potest.

§ 158. Loss of status extinguishes rights by agnation, while it leaves unaffected rights by cognation, because civil changes can affect rights annexed to a civil title, but not rights annexed to a natural title.

The maxim of the Civil law is stated by Justinian: Plerumque ubi successionis est emolumentum, ibi et tutelae onus esse debet, Inst. 1, 17. 'As a general rule, those that have the emolument of succession should bear the burden of guardianship.' Feudal law, and its daughter, the Common law, in respect of guardianship in socage, was guided by the opposite policy. Guardianship in socage occurs when lands descend upon a minor, and devolves by the Common law upon those of his next of blood upon whom the inheritance cannot descend. Thus, if the lands descend to the heir from the paternal line, the mother or other nearest maternal relative shall have the guardianship; and, vice-versa, the father or other nearest paternal relative, if the lands descend from the maternal line. While recognizing that proximity of blood is a natural recommendation to this office, the Feudal law judges it improper to trust the person of the infant into the hands of a possible heir, for fear he should be tempted to abuse his trust. The law of Scotland and the ancient law of France took a middle course, and committed the pupil's estate to the person entitled to the legal succession, because he is most interested in preserving it from waste, but excluded him from the custody of the pupil's person, because his interest is placed in opposition to the life of the pupil. Coke and Blackstone triumph in the superior wisdom of the Common law compared with the Romon law. Kent, the American jurist, is inclined to believe that the English, the Scotch, and the French law equally proceed on too great a distrust of the ordinary integrity of mankind. It is to be observed that the fears and precautions of Feudal law, though not imitated by the Roman legislator, were paralleled by Roman testators when they made a substitution, that is, a devise to a second successor, in the event of the first successor dying before attaining to years of puberty (pupillaris substitutio), 2 § 181. It is perhaps less remarkable that a legislator should seek by a general rule to guard against occasional depravity, than that a testator, exercising an individual choice, should select for the successor of his fortunes a person whom he believes capable of the blackest crime.

§ 158. The maxim here enunciated is calculated to give a false idea of the relation of the institutes of Gentile law to those of Civil law. Title by cognation is just as much an institute of Positive law as title by agnation. The synthesis of title and right in Civil law may be freakish and capricious, while that in Gentile law is reasonable and expedient; but both are equally positive institutions, and both are equally mutable and liable to be overruled. Accordingly, the specious-sounding maxim, that revolutions in status or civil condition cannot affect such rights as are annexed to natural titles, crumbles away as soon as we examine it, for we find that it only holds good of the most insignificant change, the minima capitis minutio, and that maxima and media capitis minutio extinguish gentile title by cognation as well as civil title by agnation, Inst. 1, 16, 6.

The truth is, that the effects of a collision of Civil and Natural law fall under two very different classes, which it is important to distinguish.

1. If the command of the civil lawgiver, under the sway of motives financial, political, ethical, or religious, is highly imperious and absolutely compulsive, all natural titles with which it may come in conflict are absolutely void and inoperative; e. g. the Sc. Velleianum, prohibiting suretyship of women, allowed no naturalis

obligatio to be produced by any such suretyship: and so with the laws prohibiting gambling and usury.

2. If the command of the civil law is less peremptory and absolute, it may deprive any conflicting natural title of plenary force, and yet leave to it a naturalis obligatio capable of acquiring efficacy by some machinery of Positive law; e.g. the Sc. Macedonianum, prohibiting money loans to a filiusfamilias without the sanction of his father, made them irrecoverable by action, and yet the courts recognized in the borrowing filiusfamilias a naturalis obligatio, which was capable of novation, Dig. 46, 2, 19, and a bar to recovery back (condictio indebiti) in case of actual repayment, Dig. 14, 6, 10.

When Justinian revolutionized the law of intestate succession and made the right of succession depend on cognation instead of agnation, he made a corresponding change in the obligation of guardianship, which henceforth devolved on cognates instead of agnates, women as formerly, with the exception of mothers and grandmothers, being excluded from the office, Nov. 118, 5.

DE CAPITIS MINUTIONE.

§ 159. Est autem capitis diminutio prioris *capitis* permutat*io*. *ea*que tribus modis accidit: nam aut maxima est capitis dimi*nutio*, aut minor quam quidam mediam vocant, aut minima.

§ 159. Loss of status, in other words, civil degradation or diminution of civil rights, is of three orders, greatest, minor or mediate, and least.

§ 160. Maxima est *ca*pitis diminutio, cum aliquis simul et civitatem et libertatem amittit; quae.... qui ex patria [3½ *lin.*]; *item feminae liberae ex senatusconsulto* Claudiano ancillae fiunt eorum dominorum, *qui*bus invitis et denunciantibus *nihilo* min*us* cum servis *eorum* coierint.

§ 160. The greatest loss of status is the simultaneous loss of citizenship and freedom, which is the consequence of .... or under the Sc. Claudianum of persistent intercourse on the part of a freewoman with another person's slave in spite of the prohibition and denunciation of the owner.

§ 161. Minor capi*tis* dim*inutio est, cum civitas quidem ami*ttitur, libertas vero retinetur. *quod accidit ei cui a*qua et igni interdictum *fuerit*.

§ 161. Minor loss of status is loss of citizenship unaccompanied by loss of liberty, and is incident to interdiction of fire and water.

§ 162. Minima *capitis* diminutio est, *cum et ci*vitas et libertas reti*netur, sed status hominis commutatur. quod accidit* in his qui adoptantur, item in his qui coemp-

§ 162. The least loss of status is descent in domestic rights without loss of citizenship or freedom, and occurs in adoption, coemption, noxal surrender, and manumission

tionem faciunt, et in his qui mancipio dantur, quique ex mancipatione manumittuntur; adeo quidem, ut quotiens quisque mancipetur, *aut remancipetur*, totiens capite diminuatur.

by mancipation, and so inseparably that each successive mancipation by the natural father, and every remancipation by a coemptionator, is a fall in domestic status.

§ 163. Nec solum maior*ibus* diminutionibus ius adgnationis corrumpitur, sed etiam minima. et ideo si ex duobus liberis alterum pater emancipaverit, *post* obi*tum* eius neuter alteri agnationis iure *tutor esse* poterit.

§ 163. Not only by the two greater losses of status are rights of agnation extinguished, but also by the least: accordingly, if one of two children is emancipated, the elder cannot on the father's decease be guardian to the younger by right of agnation.

§ 164. Cum autem ad agnatos tutela *pertinet, non* simul ad omnes pertinet, set ad eos tantum qui proximo gradu sunt. [*desunt lin.* 24.]

§ 164. When agnates are entitled to be guardians, it is not all who are so entitled, but only those of the nearest degree.

§ 160. In the lines now illegible, Gaius may have mentioned, as causes reducing to slavery, surrender by the pater patratus to a foreign state for an offence against international law, Livy, 5, 36, or non-inscription on the censorial register (cum incensus aliquis venierit, Ulp. 11, 11), or evasion of military service (populus quum eum vendidit qui miles factus non est, Cic. Pro Caec. 34), or capture by the enemy, § 129, or condemnation for a capital crime, which made the convict a slave of punishment (servus poenae, Inst. 1, 16, 1), i.e. reduced him to penal servitude, or condemnation of a freedman for ingratitude towards his patron (libertus ingratus circa patronum condemnatus, ibid.), whereupon he forfeited his freedom, or collusion of a freeman in consenting to be sold as a slave on condition of sharing the purchase-money (cum liber homo, major viginti annis, ad pretium participandum sese venundari passus est, Inst. 1, 3, 4). After the price had been paid, the vendor disappeared, the supposed slave recovered his liberty by a liberalis causa, and the purchaser was left without his slave and without his money. To check this fraud a statute enacted, that if the person sold was twenty years old at the time of the sale or partition of the price, he should really become the slave of the purchaser, Dig. 40, 12, 7.

The libertus ingratus would exemplify a fall from the condition of libertinus to that of servus; any of the other instances might be a case of a fall from ingenuus to servus; the fall from ingenuus to libertinus would also by the definition (a descent from a higher to a lower grade in the category of liberty) be a case of capitis minutio maxima, and occurred by the operation of the Sc. Claudianum. A freewoman (ingenua) who had commerce with a slave with the consent of his proprietor procreated slaves without forfeiting her own freedom, § 84; she lost status, however, for she became the freedwoman of the proprietor, Paulus, 4, 10, 2; Tac. Ann. 12, 53.

§ 161. Under the category of Civitas, as there are three classes, civis, latinus, peregrinus, so there are three possible degradations, the fall from civis to Latinus, instanced in the emigrant to a Latin colony, § 131; the fall from civis to peregrinus, instanced in the interdiction or deportation of a civis; and the fall from Latinus to peregrinus, instanced when the same events happened to Latinus. A lapse from liber to servus was a dissolution of marriage, for servus was incapable of matrimony: a lapse from civis to peregrinus was a dissolution of civil wedlock (connubium), for this could only subsist between cives; but if both parties consented, they might continue in gentile wedlock, Cod. 5, 17. The confiscation of property or universal succession of the fiscus, which accompanied greatest and minor loss of status, was not a necessary incident of capitis minutio (it did not happen when civis became Latinus by emigration; and an alien, which a citizen became by deportation, was capable of holding property), but was a special provision of the criminal code.

The political elements of civitas, suffragium and honores, were forfeited by infamy (infamia) or loss of civic honour (existimatio); and hence arises the question whether infamia is to be regarded as a capitis minutio.

In the commencement of this commentary we alluded to the law of honour to illustrate the difference of positive law from all law not positive; but in Rome the law of honour, as the law of religion in most modern states, was partially taken up into positive legislation. The public sentiments of esteem and disesteem, that is to say, were armed with political sanctions, and thus certain proceedings were discouraged which were not otherwise prohibited by positive law, and the due application of these sanctions was the function of a special organ appointed by the legislator. This organ was the censor, who had both a discretionary power of branding a man with ignominy by an annotation against his name in the civic register (notatio, subscriptio censoria), and, as revisor of the lists of the senate, the knights, and the tribes, enforced the disabilities of infamy by removing the infamous person from any of those bodies. As the Comitia Centuriata, as well as the Comitia Tributa, had in later times been connected with the division into tribes, the tribeless man (aerarius) forfeited his vote and became incapable of military service, Livy, 7, 2. These graver consequences of infamy were not in the discretion of the censor, but governed by strict rules of consuetudinary law (jus moribus introductum). Infamy was the consequence of condemnation in any criminal trial (publicum judicium); in certain civil actions founded on delict, theft, rapine, outrage, fraud; or on certain contracts, such as partnership, agency (mandatum), deposit; or on quasi contract, such as guardianship; or of insolvency (bona possessa, proscripta, vendita); or, without any judicial condemnation, was annexed to certain violations of the marriage laws, such as bigamy or the marriage of a widow before the termination of her year of mourning, and to the pursuit of certain professions, such as that of stage-player or gladiator. In some of these latter instances consuetudinary law, as above intimated, inflicted positive sanctions on acts that originally had only been prohibited by the sanctionless law of honour. In view of these consequences, infamia may at one time have been regarded as capitis minutio. Cicero pro Quinctio speaks of a suit involving existimatio as a causa capitis, and Tertullian, the father of the Church, who was noted for his knowledge of Roman law, and possibly was identical with the jurist of that name, of whom five fragments are preserved in the Digest, speaks of infamia as capitis minutio, De Spectaculis, 22. But the political rights of civitas had ceased to be of importance under the emperors, and we are expressly told in the Digest that infamy did not constitute a status mutatio, Dig. 50, 16, 103.

Besides extinguishing the political or publicistic elements of civitas, infamia affected to a certain extent its private elements, both commercium and connubium; the former, as we shall see, in respect of the office of procurator, 4 § 124, and the latter in respect of the disabilities of celibacy under the lex Julia, which were not removed by marriage with an infamis. Both these classes of disability had practically vanished even before they were abolished in the time of Justinian.

This seems the proper place to notice certain inequalities of condition, analogous to the old distinctions of status, which grew up in the later ages of Rome, and some of which survived the fall of the Roman empire. From the establishment of the empire the army was caressed by each succeeding despot, and privileges of various kinds were so accumulated on the military service, that the relation of the soldiery to the rest of the world very much resembled the ancient relation of Romanus to peregrinus. The preeminence of the military caste was the result of elevation; other unprivileged castes were created by depression. As the new religion grew to political power, zealous legislators were eager to promote its ascendency by the means of political sanctions. Pagans, Jews, heretics, apostates, protestants, papists, were successively frowned upon by the legislator, and for a long season subjected to incapacities and disabilities as great as, or greater than, those which weighed upon infamis: until by a change in political conceptions these inequalities of right have been again levelled and almost obliterated in most of the codes of modern Europe. See also the remarks on Colonatus, 3 § 145.

§ 162. In the category of domestic position there are three classes, (1) sui juris, or paterfamilias and materfamilias; (2) filiusfamilias and filiafamilias; and (3) mancipium: but there are only two possible degradations, (1) from sui juris to filius- or filiafamilias, which occurs in adrogation and the in manum conventio of a woman previously independent; and (2) from filius- or filiafamilias to mancipium, which occurs in noxal surrender, in emancipation, in adoption as implying mancipation, and in the remancipation of a woman by her husband or the person who held her in manu in virtue of a fiduciary coemption. The descent from sui juris to mancipium cannot occur, because the only persons capable of passing into the condition of mancipium by the process of mancipation were filius- and filiafamilias and women in manu, i. e. persons already alieni juris. If remancipation is mentioned in § 162 it cannot mean remancipation to the natural father after the third mancipation of a child in the process of emancipation or adoption, § 134, for this remancipation involves no descent in status: by the effect of the third mancipation the child is already in the state of bondage, and after remancipation he continues in the same state, without having descended to any lower stage in the hierarchy of status. The remancipation which operates a degradation must be remancipation by the husband or coemptionator, whereby a filiafamilias or woman in manu is reduced from that rank to the lower standing of mancipium, §§ 115, 137, 195.

In the translation of the text, and in the exposition of capitis minutio, and particularly of the third and last kind, I have adopted the theory of Savigny as being the most tenable, and forming the most harmonious system of legal conceptions. I must now briefly notice an opposing theory, and the objections that may be raised against that of Savigny. Some expositors hold that capitis minutio minima did not necessarily and essentially involve any degradation, any downward step on the ladder of status, but might be merely a horizontal movement on the same platform, a transit from family to family, a disruption of the ties of agnation, a cessation of membership in a given civil group. This opinion is founded on the authority of Paulus, undeniably an eminent juris auctor, who defines the least diminution of head as follows: Capitis deminutionis tria genera sunt, maxima, media, minima; tria enim sunt quae habemus, libertatem, civitatem, familiam. Igitur cum omnia haec amittimus, hoc est, libertatem et civitatem et familiam, maximam esse capitis deminutionem; cum vero amittimus civitatem, libertatem retinemus, mediam esse capitis deminutionem; cum et libertas et civitas retinetur, familia tantum mutatur, minimam esse capitis deminutionem, constat, Dig. 4, 5, 11. 'Capital diminution is of three orders, greatest, minor, least; as there are three things that we have, liberty, citizenship, family. The universal loss of freedom, citizenship, family, is the greatest capital diminution: loss of citizenship while liberty is retained is minor capital diminution: when liberty and citizenship are retained, and family only is changed, there is the least capital diminution.' Consistently with this definition Paulus affirms that the children of adrogatus suffer capitis minutio minima: Liberos qui arrogatum parentem sequuntur, placet minui capite, quum in aliena potestate sint et familiam mutaverint, Dig. 4, 5, 3. 'The children who follow an adrogated parent suffer diminution of head, as they are dependent and have changed family.' Here, then, if Paulus is right, we have capitis minutio without any degradation, any loss of rank; for the children of adrogatus have the same status of filiifamilias after their father's adrogation as they had before, although in a different family. The proposition, however, that the children of adrogatus suffer capitis minutio is not confirmed by any other jurist, and Savigny supposes that the doctrine was peculiar to Paulus, and was in fact inaccurate. Another objection to the theory of Savigny, though not so serious as the opposing authority of Paulus, is presented by the operation of in manum conventio.

When an independent woman made a coemption she undoubtedly declined in status, as before coemption she was sui juris, and after coemption she is filiafamilias. But a filiafamilias who made a coemption apparently suffered no degradation: the definitive result of the coemption leaves her, as before, filiafamilias, and that, apparently, without having passed through any lower stage; for Gaius expressly says that the lex mancipii, or formula of mancipation in coemption, was not calculated to reduce the woman to a servile condition, § 123. Gaius tells us, however, that coemption operates a capitis minutio, § 162, without limiting the effect to the case of a woman sui juris. The operation of coemption to produce capitis minutio is also mentioned by Ulpian, and again without any express limitation to the case of an independent woman: Minima capitis diminutio est per quam, et civitate et libertate salva, status dumtaxat hominis mutatur; quod fit adoptione et in manum conventione, 11, 13. 'There is least capital diminution when both franchise and freedom are unimpaired, and only position in household life is changed, as occurs in adoption and subjection to hand.' If filiafamilias underwent capitis minutio when she made a coemption, her case disproves our theory that all capitis minutio requires degradation: but Savigny assumes that, though in these passages there is no express limitation to the case of independent women, yet this limitation must be understood; and there is nothing outrageous in this supposition.

While, however, these objections to the hypothesis of Savigny are doubtless serious, on the other hand they are compensated by legal facts which are absolutely irreconcilable with the adverse hypothesis, the cases of Flamen Dialis and Virgo Vestalis. Virgo autem Vestalis simul est capta atque in atrium Vestae deducta et pontificibus tradita, eo statim tempore sine emancipatione ac sine capitis minutione e patris potestate exit et jus testamenti faciendi adipiscitur .... Praeterea in commentariis Labeonis quae ad duodecim tabulas composuit ita scriptum est: Virgo Vestalis neque heres est cuiquam intestato, neque intestatae quisquam, sed bona ejus in publicum redigi aiunt, Gellius, 1, 12. 'As soon as a vestal virgin is selected and conducted to the shrine of Vesta and delivered to the pontifices, she instantaneously, without emancipation and without capital diminution, is freed from parental power and acquires testamentary capacity. . . . . Moreover, in the commentary of Labeo on the Twelve Tables it is stated that a vestal virgin is neither heir-at-law to any one who dies intestate nor, if she herself die intestate, leaves any heir-at-law, and that in this event her property lapses to the state.' For Flamen Dialis, see 3 § 114. If mere transit from a family and ceasing to belong to a given group of agnates constituted capitis minutio, and was its definition, then the vestal virgin must inevitably have suffered capitis minutio; the fact that she did not, in spite of leaving her family and snapping the agnatic tie, is at once conceivable, on the supposition that there is no capitis minutio without degradation.

Unless capitis minutio minima involved a downward step on the stair of status, it has no analogy to the other forms of capitis minutio, and it is not obvious why it should have the same generic appellation, or why it should be handled in the same department of the code. The rupture of the ties of agnation, extinguishing rights of intestate succession, might be a loss, but it was not a loss from inferiority of privilege; it was a loss of an equal among equals; it resembled the loss which a husband incurred by divorce of his wife, or a father by emancipation of his son, or a devisee or heir by neglecting to accept a succession within the appointed period, 2 § 164; none of which persons were said to undergo capitis minutio, because none of them suffered a reduction of the universitas juris called status.

On the whole, then, Savigny seems justified in considering the definition given by Paulus and his statement respecting the children of adrogatus as inexact. Paulus himself, in speaking of emancipation, implies the true conditions of capitis minutio: Emancipato filio et ceteris personis capitis minutio manifeste accidit, quum emancipari nemo possit nisi in imaginariam servilem causam deductus, Dig. 4, 5, 3. 'An emancipated son or other descendant clearly has his head diminished, as emancipation necessarily involves an imaginary descent into a servile condition.'

Although rupture of the ties, and forfeiture of the rights, or release from the duties, of agnation, were not the essence of capitis minutio minima, yet they were among its principal consequences. The capite minutus lost his claim as suus heres at civil law, that is, his right to succeed to an intestate ascendent, or to be instituted heir in his will or formally disinherited. These effects of capitis minutio were, however, counteracted by jus praetorium or the legislation of the praetor. He also lost his right as legitimus heres at civil law, that is, his right to succeed to an intestate collateral; and here the praetor only so far interposed to assist the capite minutus, as, in default of all persons entitled as agnates, to call him to the succession in the inferior order of cognates. The collateral successor was called legitimus heres (statutory successor) because his title was founded on the statutes of the Twelve Tables, which, in default of lineal descendants, called collateral agnates to the succession. Subsequent statutes created certain quasi agnates or persons entitled to succeed in the same order as if they were agnates, who hence were also called legitimi heredes; e. g. children entitled to succeed to an intestate mother under the Sc. Orphitianum, and mothers entitled to succeed to intestate children under the Sc. Tertullianum. The effect of capitis minutio in extinguishing title to succeed was confined to legitimus heres created by the Twelve Tables, and did not extend to the legitimus heres created by these subsequent statutes.

Besides the effects of capitis minutio which followed logically from its consisting in a degradation or fall in status, and from its involving elimination from a given family or a certain circle of agnates, it had certain other anomalous or arbitrary consequences—consequences, that is, which may have once been explicable on known maxims of the civil law, but which are now inexplicable, whose rationale had perhaps been lost even in the classical period, and is certainly now past conjecture. Such is the rule, that capitis minutio minima extinguished the debts of capite minutus. It is true that the injustice operated by this rule of civil law in the case of adrogatio was counteracted by the interposition of the praetor, 3 § 84, but, as at civil law filiusfamilias, though incapable of rights, was capable of obligations, it is not obvious why even at civil law a man's debts should have been cancelled by his degradation from the status of paterfamilias to that of filiusfamilias.

DE LEGITIMA PATRONORUM TUTELA.

§ 165. *Ex eadem lege duodecim tabularum libertorum et libertarum tutela ad patronos liberosque eorum pertinet, quae et ipsa legitima tutela*

§ 165. The same statute of the Twelve Tables assigns the guardianship of freedmen and freedwomen to the patron and the patron's chil-

vocatur: non quia nominatim ea lege de hac tutela cavetur, sed quia perinde accepta est per interpretationem, atque si verbis legis introducta esset. eo enim ipso, quod hereditates libertorum libertarumque, si intestati decessissent, *iusserat lex ad patronos* liberosve eorum pertinere, crediderunt veteres voluisse legem etiam tutelas ad eos pertinere, cum et agnatos quos ad hereditatem vocavit, eosdem et tutores esse iusserat.

dren, and this guardianship, like that of agnates, is called statutory guardianship, not that it is anywhere expressly enacted in that body of statutes, but because their interpretation by the jurists has procured for it as much reception as it could have obtained from express enactment; for the fact that the succession of a freedman or freedwoman, when they die intestate, was given by the legislator to the patron and patron's children, was deemed a proof of his intention to give them the wardship, because when he was dealing with agnates he had coupled wardship with succession.

DE FIDUCIARIA TUTELA.

§ 166. Exemplo patronorum *etiam* fiduciariae *tutelae* receptae sunt. *eae enim tutelae scilicet* fiduciariae vo*cantur* proprie, quae ideo nobis competunt, quia *liberum* caput mancipatum nobis vel a parente vel a coemptionatore manumiserimus.

§ 166. The analogy of the patron guardian led in its turn to fiduciary guardianship. Fiduciary guardianship arises when a free person, mancipated by a parent or by the party to a coemption, is manumitted by the alienee.

§ 167. Set Latinarum et Latino*rum* inpuberum *tutela non omni modo* ad *manumissores, sicut bona eorum,* pertinet, sed ad eos quorum *ante manu*missionem ex iure Quiritium *fuerunt: unde si ancilla ex iure Quiritium* tua sit, in bonis mea, a me quidem solo, non etiam a te manumissa, Latina fieri potest, et bona eius *ad me pertinent, sed eius tutela* tibi competit: nam ita lege Iunia cavetur. itaque si ab eo cuius et in bonis et ex iure Quiritium ancilla fuerit facta sit Latina, ad eundem et bona et tutela pertinet.

§ 167. The guardianship of Latins, male or female, below the age of puberty, does not necessarily devolve on their manumitter, like their succession, but on whoever before manumission was their quiritary owner. Accordingly, a female slave belonging to you as quiritary owner, to me as bonitary owner, if manumitted by me without your joining in the manumission, becomes a Latin, and her succession devolves on me, her guardianship on you, by the enactment of the lex Junia. If, on manumission by one who combines the characters of bonitary and quiritary owner, she becomes a Latin, he becomes both her successor and her guardian.

DE CESSICIA TUTELA.

§ 168. *Agnatis, qui legitimi tutores sunt, item manu*missoribus per-

§ 168. Statutory guardians, whether agnates or patrons, are per-

missum est feminarum tutelam alii in iure cedere: pupillorum autem tutelam non est permissum cedere, quia . . n *videtur* . . osa, cum tempore pubertatis finiatur.

mitted to transfer the guardianship of a female ward by surrender before a magistrate; the guardianship of a male ward is not allowed to be transferred, because it is not considered onerous, being terminated by the ward's attaining the age of puberty.

§ 169. Is autem cui ceditur tutela cessicius *tut*or vocatur.

§ 169. The surrenderee of a guardianship is called a cessionary guardian.

§ 170. Quo mortuo aut capite diminuto revertitur ad eum tutorem tutela qui cessit. ipse quoque qui cessit, si mortuus a*ut* capite d*iminutus* sit, a cessic*i*o tutela discedit et revertitur ad eum, qui post eum qui cesserat secundum gradum in tutela habueri*t*.

§ 170. On his death or loss of status the guardianship reverts to the surrenderor, and on the surrenderor's death or loss of status it is devested from the cessionary and devolves on the person next entitled after the surrenderor.

§ 171. Set quantum ad agnatos pertinet, nihil hoc tempore de cessicia tutela quaeritur, cum agnatorum tutelae in feminis lege Claudia sublatae sint.

§ 171. As far, however, as agnates are concerned, in the present day there is no such thing as cessionary guardianship, for agnatic guardianship over female wards was abolished by the lex Claudia.

§ 172. Sed fiduciarios quoque quidam putaverunt cedendae tutelae ius non habere, cum ipsi se oneri subiecerint. quod etsi placeat, in parente tamen qui filiam neptemve aut proneptem alteri ea lege mancipio dedit, ut sibi remanciparetur, remancipatamque manumisit, idem dici non debet, cum is et legitimus tutor habeatur; et non minus huic quam patronis honor praestandus est.

§ 172. Fiduciary guardians, according to some, are also disabled from transferring their guardianship, having voluntarily undertaken the burden; but although this is the better opinion, yet a parent who has mancipated a daughter, granddaughter, or great-granddaughter, with a condition of remancipation to himself, and manumitted her after remancipation, should be excepted from the rule, for he is ranked with statutory guardians, and has the same privilege as the patron of a manumitted slave.

§ 167. It seems anomalous that a Latin, i.e. a non-civis, should have been a subject of wardship: for as tutela is an institute of jus civile (§ 142, commentary), i.e. jus civium, we should have expected that, as in the case of patria potestas, both pater and filius must be cives Romani, § 128, so here both parties, the ward as well as the guardian, must of necessity be cives Romani. The anomaly, however, was expressly enacted by the lex Junia: which further departed from the law of the Twelve Tables by separating the guardianship from the right of succession; for it gave the guardianship to the quiritary owner, but the right of succession to the bonitary owner. Latinus was not only capable of being a ward, but also of being a guardian, Fragmenta Vaticana, 193; that is, though he was incapable of being a testamentary guardian, § 23, he could be made a tutor dativus, or appointed by a magistrate, § 185. This magisterial disregard of the spirit of the lex Junia is similar to the praetor's behaviour in respect of another of its dispositions. The law disabled Latins from taking as devisees or legatees under a will; the praetor allowed them to take by means of a declaration of trust, § 24.

§ 168. The reason given for the non-assignability of guardianship of infants will vary according as we read, Quia non videtur lucrosa, or, Quia non videtur onerosa. In English jurisprudence guardianship is said not to be capable of assignment or transfer, because it is not a right but a duty.

§ 172. It is clear that the natural father was statutory, not fiduciary, guardian, for it is incredible that the remancipation to the natural father, § 134, was accompanied by a fiducia. The sons of the natural father ought also to have been statutory guardians, like the sons of any other patronus, but we find that they were only deemed to be fiduciary guardians, § 175. The question whether a guardian was statutory or fiduciary might be of importance, as it affected the rights of the ward, § 194. Justinian attempts to give a reason in the nature of the case why the sons were only fiduciary guardians, Inst. 1, 19, but it breaks down. He says that a slave, if not manumitted by the father, would have become the slave of the sons; but the same, as far as we know, was true of the mancipium, who on the death of his father would have become the bondsman of his brothers. It must have been, then, by some positive enactment that the sons of the emancipating father were deemed to be merely fiduciary guardians of their brother or sister.

DE PETENDO ALIO TUTORE.

§ 173. Praeterea senatusconsulto mu*li*eribus permissum est in absentis tutoris locum alium petere: quo petito prior desinit. nec interest quam longe aberit is tutor.

§ 173. Moreover, a decree of the senate permits female wards to demand a substitute in the place of an absent guardian, and the appointment of a substitute supersedes the previous guardian, and the length of his absence is immaterial.

§ 174. Set excipitur, ne in absentis patroni locum liceat libert*ae* tutorem petere.

§ 174. But an exception is made in favour of an absent patron, who cannot be superseded on the application of a freedwoman.

§ 175. Patroni *au*tem loco habemus *etiam* paren*tem* qui i*n e mancipio* sibi remancipatam filiam neptemve aut proneptem manumissione legitimam tutelam nanctus est. huius quidem liberi fiduciarii tutoris loco numerantur: patroni autem liber*i* eandem tutelam adipiscuntur, quam et pater eorum habuit.

§ 175. Ranked with patrons is the parent who by mancipation, remancipation, and manumission of a daughter, granddaughter, or great-granddaughter, has become her statutory guardian. His sons only rank as fiduciary guardians, unlike a patron's sons, who succeed to the same form of guardianship as vested in their father.

§ 176. *Sed ad certam quidem causam* etiam in patroni absentis locum *permisit senatus* tutorem petere, veluti ad hereditatem adeundam.

§ 176. For a special and limited purpose the senate permits even a patron in his absence to be superseded by a substitute; for instance, to authorize the acceptance of an inheritance.

§ 177. Idem senatus censuit et in persona pupilli patroni filii.

§ 177. The senatusconsult gives similar permission when a patron's son is himself a ward.

§ 178. I*temque* lege Iulia de maritandis ordinibus ei quae in legitima tutela pupilli sit permittitur dotis constituendae gratia a praetore urbano tutorem petere.

§ 178. Before the senatusconsult the lex Julia regulating the marriages of the various orders, when a patron's son who was statutory guardian of a woman was himself a ward, permitted the woman to apply to the praetor of the city to substitute a guardian for the purpose of effecting a settlement of her dower.

§ 179. Sa*ne* patroni filius etiamsi inpubes sit, liber*tae efficietur* tu*t*or, *at* i*n* n*u*lla r*e* a*uct*or fieri potest, cum ipsi nihil permissum sit sine tutoris auctoritate agere.

§ 179. For a patron's son even before the age of puberty is a freedwoman's guardian, but unable to authorize any proceeding, being himself disabled from acting without his guardian's authorization.

§ 180. Item si qua in tutela legitima furiosi aut muti sit, permittitur et senatusconsulto dotis constituendae gratia tutorem petere.

§ 180. Also, a woman whose statutory guardian is a lunatic or dumb is permitted by the senatusconsult, for the purpose of settling her dower, to apply for a substitutive guardian.

§ 181. Quibus casibus salvam manere tutelam patrono patronique filio manifestum est.

§ 181. In which cases the continued guardianship of the patron or patron's son is undisputed.

§ 182. Praeterea senatus censuit, ut si tutor pupilli pu*pillae*ve suspectus a tutela remotus sit, sive ex

§ 182. The senate further decreed that if the guardian of a male or female ward is suspected of mis-

iusta causa fuerit excusatus, in locum eius alius tutor *detur*, quo *dato prior tutor* amit*tit* tutelam.

conduct and removed from office, or if he alleges valid grounds for declining to act and is relieved of his functions, a substitute shall be appointed by the magistrate, and on his appointment the office of the former guardian shall determine.

§ 183. Ha*ec omnia* similiter *et* Roma*e et in* provinc*iis solent observari* .... si vero ....

§ 183. These rules are in force both in Rome and in the provinces.

§ 184. Olim cum legis actiones in usu erant, etiam ex illa causa tutor dabatur, si inter tutorem et mulierem pupillumve legis actione agendum erat: *nam* qu*ia ipse* qui*dem tutor* in re sua auctor esse non pot*erat*, *alius dabatur*, q*uo* a*uctor*e *illa legis act*io perager*etur*: qui dicebatur praetoriu*s tutor*, quia a praetore urbano dabatur. post sublatas legis actiones quidam putant hanc speciem dandi t*utoris non esse necessariam*; sed *adhuc dari* in *usu est*, *si legiti*mo iudic*io agat*ur.

§ 184. In former days, when actions of law were a legal process, another cause of appointing a substitute was the imminence of an action of law between the guardian and the female or ward; for as the guardian could not give his authority in respect of his own suit, another guardian was appointed to authorize the proceedings in the action, who was called a praetorian guardian, because he was appointed by the praetor of the city. Since the abolition of the actions of the law some hold this kind of guardian to be unnecessary, but the appointment is still customary on the occasion of a statutory suit. (4 § 103.)

§ 179. The law was changed by Justinian, who enacted that no one could become guardian who had not attained his majority, i. e. completed twenty-five years of age, Cod. 5, 30, 5.

DE ATILIANO TUTORE, ET EO QUI EX LEGE IULIA ET TITIA DATUR.

§ 185. Si cui nullus omnino tutor sit, ei datur in urbe Roma ex lege Atilia a praetore u*r*bano et maiore parte Tribunorum *p*lebis, qui Atilianus tutor vocatur; in provinciis vero a praesidibus provinciarum ex lege Iulia et Titia.

§ 185. Failing every other form of guardian, at Rome a guardian is appointed under the lex Atilia by the praetor of the city and the major part of the tribunes of the people, called an Atilian guardian: in the provinces, a guardian is appointed by the president of the province under the lex Julia and Titia.

§ 186. Et ideo si cui testamento tutor sub condicione aut ex die certo datus sit, quamdiu condicio aut dies pendet, tutor dari po*test*; item si pure datus fuerit, quamdiu nemo heres existat, tamdiu ex iis

§ 186. Accordingly, on the appointment of a testamentary guardian subject to a condition, or, on an appointment limited to take effect after a certain time, during the pendency of the condition and be-

legibus tutor petendus est: qui desinit *tutor* esse postea q*uam* quis ex testamento tutor esse coeperit.

fore the expiration of the term, a substitute is appointed by these magistrates; also, when the appointment of a testamentary guardian is not subject to a condition, so long as the succession has not vested, a temporary guardian may be obtained under those statutes, whose office will determine as soon as the testamentary guardianship has vested.

§ 187. Ab hostibus quoque tutore capto ex his legibus tu*tor* dat*ur*, qui desinit tutor esse, si is qui captus est in civitatem reversus fuerit: nam reversus recipit tutelam iure postliminii.

§ 187. On the hostile capture of a guardian the same statutes regulate the appointment of a substitute to continue in office until the return of the captive; for if the captive returns he recovers the guardianship in virtue of his rehabilitation.

§ 188. Ex *h*is apparet quot sint species tutelarum. si vero quaeramus, in quot genera hae species deducantur, lo*nga* erit disputatio: nam de ea re valde veteres dubitaverunt, nosque diligentius hunc tractatum exsecuti sumus et in edicti interpretatione, et in his libris quos ex Quinto Mucio fecimus. hoc *so*lum tantisper sufficit admonuisse, quod quidam quinque genera esse dixerunt, ut Quintus Mucius; alii tria, ut Servius Sulpicius: alii duo, ut Labeo; alii tot genera esse crediderunt, quot etiam species essent.

§ 188. The foregoing statement shows the various forms of guardian: the question of the number of orders to which these forms may be reduced involves a long discussion, for it is a point on which the ancient jurists differed greatly; and as I have examined it at length, both in my interpretation of the edict and in my commentary on Quintus Mucius, for the present occasion it may suffice to observe that some, as Quintus Mucius, make five orders; others, as Servius Sulpicius, three; others, as Labeo, two; others make as many orders as there are forms of guardian.

A magisterially appointed guardian is called by modern commentators tutor dativus, a name used by Gaius in another sense, § 154; by the Romans he was called tutor Atilianus or Juliotitianus (*see* Theophilus), in memory of the statutes from whence the magistrates derived their power of nominating to the office of guardian. This power was not a portion of their inherent or immemorial attributions (imperium, jurisdictio): Tutoris datio neque imperii est neque jurisdictionis, sed ei soli competit cui nominatim hoc dedit vel lex vel senatusconsultum vel princeps, Dig. 26, 1, 6, 2. It was conferred on the praetor by the lex Atilia; on the praeses provinciae by the lex Julia et Titia. The lex Atilia

is of uncertain date, but from Livy (post patroni mortem, quia nullius in manu esset, tutore a tribunis et praetore petito, 39, 9) it appears to have been older than 197 B.C. As there were ten tribunes, and the lex Atilia required the concurrence of the majority, the tutor Atilianus was nominated by the praetor and six tribunes. The lex Julia et Titia empowering the praeses provinciae to nominate a guardian is placed in the year 31 B.C.

In the time of Justinian the Atilian and Juliotitian guardian, not being compellable to act or to give security for the due discharge of their office, had fallen into desuetude, and in their stead guardians were appointed by the consul or praetor or praeses provinciae, after a special investigation (ex inquisitione). Justinian empowered the municipal magistrate called defensor civitatis, with the assistance of the bishop, to appoint guardians, taking securities for the due discharge of their office, whenever the fortune of the ward was under 500 golden solidi; a golden solidus being between a sovereign and a napoleon, i. e. 22½ francs, in value. Guardians appointed after inquest (ex inquisitione) were not required to give security for due administration, Inst. 1, 20, 3.

§ 188. In the time of Justinian there were three forms of guardian,—testamentary, or appointed by will; statutory, or prescribed by the law in case of intestacy; and magisterial (dativus), or appointed by the magistrate, in default of a testamentary or statutory guardian. The other forms of guardian had become obsolete in consequence of the changes in legislation.

DE MULIERUM TUTELA.

§ 189. Sed inpuberes quidem in tutela esse omnium civitatium iure contingit; quia id naturali rationi conveniens est, ut is qui perfectae aetatis non sit alterius tutela regatur. nec fere ulla civitas est, in qua non licet parentibus liberis suis inpuberibus *testamento* tutorem dare; quamvis, ut supra diximus, soli cives Romani videantur tantum liberos in potestate habere.

§ 189. The wardship of children under the age of puberty is prescribed by every legislation, for it is a dictate of natural reason that persons of immature years should be under foreign guidance and control, and almost all states permit a parent to nominate a testamentary guardian for his children under the age of puberty, though, as we have before stated, only citizens of Rome appear to be invested with parental power.

§ 190. Feminas vero perfectae aetatis in tutela esse fere nulla pre-

§ 190. But why women of mature years should contiue in ward-

tiosa ratio suasisse videtur. nam quae vulgo creditur, quia levitate animi plerumque decipiuntur, et *aequum* erat eas tutorum auctoritate regi, magis speciosa videtur quam vera. mulieres enim quae perfectae aetatis sunt ips*ae* sibi negotia tractant, et in quibusdam causis dici*s* gratia tut*or* interponit auctoritatem suam; saepe etiam invitus auctor fieri a praetore cogitur.

ship there appears to be no valid reason; for the common allegation, that their weakness of judgment exposes them to the danger of miscarriage, and that humanity requires them to be put under the control and authority of a guardian, seems rather specious than true, for women above the age of puberty administer their own property, and in some circumstances it is a mere formality that their guardian interposes his assent; in many others, if he refuses, he may be compelled to withdraw his opposition by an appeal to the praetor.

§ 191. Unde cum tutore nullum ex tutel*a* iudicium mulieri datu*r*: at ubi pupillorum pupillarumve negotia tutores tracta*nt*, *eis* post pubertatem tutelae iudici*o* rationem reddunt.

§ 191. Accordingly, a guardian is not suable on account of administration by a woman in wardship; whereas the guardian of an infant, male or female, is liable to be sued on account of his administration as soon as the ward attains to the age of puberty.

§ 192. Sane patronorum et parentum legitimae tutelae vim aliquam habere intelleguntur eo, quod hi neque ad testamentum faciendum, neque ad res mancipi alienandas, neque ad obligationes suscipiendas auctores fieri coguntur, praeterquam si magna causa alienandarum rerum mancipi obligationisque suscipiendae interveniat. eaque omnia ipsorum causa constituta sunt, ut quia ad eos intest*ata*rum mortuarum hereditates pertinent, neque per testamentum excludantur ab hereditate, neque alienatis pretiosioribus rebus susceptoqu*e* aere alieno minus loc*u*ples *ad eos* heredita*s* *per*veniat.

§ 192. The statutory guardianship of patrons and parents is not purely illusory, as they cannot be compelled to give their sanction to a will or to the alienation of mancipable property, or to the completion of a contract, unless there are very weighty reasons for the contract or the alienation; but this rule is in their own interest as heirs in intestacy, and is designed to prevent their loss of the estate by testamentary disposition, or the diminution of its value by debt or by alienation of a considerable portion.

§ 193. Aput peregrinos non similiter, ut aput nos, in tutela sunt feminae: set tamen plerumque quasi in tutela sunt: u*t* ecce lex Bithynorum, si qui*d* mulier *contra*hat, maritum auctorem esse iu*b*et aut filiu*m* eius puberem.

§ 193. In other countries women are not under the same tutelage as at Rome, but are generally subject to a quasi tutelage: for instance, the law of Bithynia requires the contract of a woman to be sanctioned by her husband or by a son above the age of puberty.

As women were capable of administration, the functions of the guardian, which in the case of infants were either administrative or sanctionative, in the case of women were confined to sanctioning. Pupillorum pupillarumque tutores et negotia gerunt et auctoritatem interponunt: mulierum autem tutores auctoritatem dumtaxat interponunt, Ulp. 11, 25. It is transparent that the wardship of women after the years of puberty was not designed to protect their own interests, but those of their heirs apparent, their agnates. Originally the authorization of the guardian was not sufficient to validate the will of an independent woman: it was necessary that she should first break the ties of agnation, and separate from her family by means of a coemption (with her guardian's sanction) and subsequent remancipation and manumission. She then, with the sanction of the manumissor, in his character of fiduciary guardian, could make a valid will. In the time of Gaius, Hadrian having abolished the necessity of coemption, to make a valid will an independent woman only required the sanction of her guardian, 2 § 112. In the time of Justinian the tutelage of women above the age of puberty had ceased, and no sanction was requisite.

It is to be observed, that as women were gradually enfranchised from their disabilities, they also forfeited some of their original privileges. It was a rule of the administration of justice that while error of fact might be pleaded to defend a person against the consequences of his own acts or omissions, no one should be allowed to allege an error of law, Dig. 22, 6, 9. An exception however was made in favour of minors, of soldiers, of the utterly uneducated (rustici), and of women. Against their ignorance of rules of law, particularly those rules of Civil law which are not, like rules of Gentile law, the almost self-evident dictates of reason and common sense, they were relieved by a branch of the praetor's equitable jurisdiction, called integri restitutio, a power of cancellation and rescission, in cases of manifest collision between law and equity. This privilege of women was partially abrogated by a constitution of the Emperor Leo, A.D. 469: Ne passim liceat mulieribus omnes suos contractus retractare, in his quae praetermiserint vel ignoraverint: statuimus si per ignorantiam juris damnum aliquod circa jus vel substantiam suam patiantur, in his tantum casibus in quibus praeteritarum legum auctoritas eis suffragatur, subveniri, Cod. 1, 18, 13. 'To prevent the indiscriminate revocation by women of all their contracts on the ground of omission or error, be it enacted, that ignorance of law, whereby a woman is damnified in her right or property, shall only be a title to relief in those cases where women are expressly excepted from the provisions of any statute.'

QUIBUS MODIS TUTELA FINIATUR.

§ 194. Tutela autem liberantur ingenuae quidem trium *liberorum iure, libertinae vero quattuor, si in patroni*, liberorumve eius legitima *tutela sint.* nam et ceterae quae alterius generis tutores habent, velut Atilianos aut fiduciarios, trium liberorum iure *liberantur.*

§ 194. Guardianship terminates for a freeborn woman by title of maternity of three children, for a freedwoman under statutory guardianship by maternity of four children: those who have other kinds of guardians, Atilian, for instance, or fiduciary, are released from wardship by title of three children.

§ 195. *Potest* autem pluribus modis *libertina* alterius generis habere, veluti si a femina manumissa sit: tunc enim e lege Atilia petere debet tutorem, vel in provincia *e lege Iulia et Titia*: *nam* patronae *tutelam libertorum suorum libertarumve gerere non possunt. Sed et si sit a masculo* manumissa, et auctore eo coemptionem fecerit, deinde remancipata et manumissa sit, patronum quidem habere tutorem desinit, incipit autem habere eum tutorem a quo manumissa est, qui fiduciarius dicitur. Item si patron*us sive filius eius* in adoptionem se dedit, debet sibi *e lege Atilia vel Titia* tutorem petere. Similiter ex iisdem legibus petere debet tutorem *liberta*, si patronus decedit nec ullum virilis sexus liberorum in familia re*lin*quit.

§ 195. There are various modes by which a freedwoman may have the other kinds of guardian: for instance, on manumission by a woman, when she must request a guardian under the lex Atilia, or in the provinces under the lex Julia and Titia, as a female patron cannot be guardian to a freedman or freedwoman: also on manumission by a male, if with his sanction she makes a coemption, and then is remancipated and manumitted, for the patron then ceases to be guardian, and is replaced by the second manumitter, who is called a fiduciary guardian. Also on the adrogation of her patron or his son she must demand a guardian under the lex Atilia or Titia, and in compliance with the same laws she must demand a guardian on the decease of her patron without leaving any son in the family.

§ 196. *Masculi quando* puberes esse coeperint, tutela liberantur. *Puberem autem Sabinus* quidem *et Cassius ceterique nostri praeceptores eum* esse putant qui habitu corporis pubertatem ostendit, *hoc est* qui generare potest; sed in his qui pubescere non possunt, quales sunt spadones, eam aetatem esse spectandam, cuius aetatis puberes fiunt. sed diversae sc*h*olae auctores

§ 196. For males the attainment of the age of puberty is a release from wardship. Puberty, according to Sabinus and Cassius and the other authorities of my school, depends on physical development, that is, on capacity of generation; or in case of impotence on the completion of eighteen years, or the age which even in the latest constitutions usually implies capacity of

annis putant pubertatem aestimandam, id est eum puberem esse existimandum, *qui* XIIII. *annos explevit*—[24 *lineae.*]

generation. The other school hold that puberty is to be exclusively measured by age, that is to say, that it should be deemed to be attained on the completion by a male of his fourteenth year.

§ 196. All jurists agreed that in the case of the spado (natural impotence) some fixed date must be assumed as the conventional period of puberty. The Sabinian rule appears to be preserved in a passage of Paulus: Spadones eo tempore testamentum facere possunt quo plerique pubescunt, id est, anno decimo octavo, 3, 4 *a*, 2. 'In cases of natural impotence testamentary capacity is acquired at the age which almost always (even in the tardiest developments) marks generative capacity, namely, eighteen years completed.' Fourteen was assumed to be the average age of puberty; but it was too early, even in the southern climes subject to Roman legislation, for a minority of constitutions which advance more slowly to maturity. Eighteen was supposed to be sufficiently postponed to include most of these cases of retarded development. We have already, in treating of adrogation, § 106, commentary, met with the phrase, plena pubertas, denoting eighteen years of age. We may suspect that in Paulus we should read, quo plerique pubescunt qui tardius pubescunt; and in Gaius, cujus aetatis puberes fiunt qui tardius puberes fiunt; the similarity of ending having caused the omission of the clauses by the transcribers.

This paragraph is the first which refers to the existence of rival schools among the Roman juris auctores, to which we shall find frequent allusions in the remainder of the treatise. This divergence of the schools dates from the first elevation of the jurist to a species of public functionary, namely, from the reign of Augustus, in whose time, as we have seen, § 7, commentary, certain jurists began to be invested by imperial diploma with a quasi legislative authority. In his reign the rival oracles were Antistius Labeo and Caius Ateius Capito: Hi duo primum veluti diversas sectas fecerunt, Dig. 1, 2, 47. 'The first founders of the two opposing sects.' From Labeo's works there are 63 extracts in the Digest, and Labeo is cited as an authority in the extracts from other jurists oftener than any one else except Salvius Julianus. From Sempronius Proculus, a disciple of Labeo, and of whom 37 fragments are preserved in the Digest, the school derived its name of Proculiani. Other noted jurists of this school were Pegasus, in the time of Vespasian; Celsus, in the time of Domitian, who gave rise to the proverb, responsio Celsina, a discourteous answer, and of whom 142 fragments are preserved; and Neratius, of whom 64 fragments are preserved. To the other school belonged Masurius Sabinus, who flourished under Nero, and from whom the sect were called Sabiniani. Sabinus is mentioned by Persius:—

Vindicta postquam meus a praetore recessi,
Cur mihi non liceat jussit quodcunque voluntas,
Excepto si quid Masuri rubrica vetavit?—5, 90.

'Touched by the enfranchising wand, I came my own master from the praetor's court. What hinders me to follow the dictates of my will, except where the Masurian rubric has forbidden?' To the same school belonged Caius Cassius Longinus, who flourished under Nero and Vespasian, and from whom the sect are sometimes called Cassiani: Javolenus Priscus, of whom 206 fragments are preserved: Salvius Julianus, who reduced the praetorian edict to a permanent form in the reign of Hadrian, and of whom 457 fragments are preserved: Pomponius, of whom 585 fragments are preserved: Sextus Caecilius Africanus, celebrated for his obscurity, so that Africani lex in the language of lawyers meant lex difficilis, of whom 131 fragments are preserved: and, lastly, our author, Gaius, who flourished under Hadrian, Antoninus Pius, and Marcus Aurelius, and from whose writings 535 extracts are to be found in the Digest.

If we now inquire whether this divergence of schools was based on any difference of principle, the answer is, No: on none, at least, that modern commentators have succeeded in discovering: it was merely a difference on a multitude of isolated points of detail. We are told indeed that the founders were men of dissimilar characters and intellectual dispositions: that Labeo was characterized by boldness of logic and a spirit of innovation; while Capito rested on tradition and authority, and inclined to conservatism, Dig. 1, 2, 47; but it is altogether impossible to trace their opposing tendencies in the writings of their successors: and we must suppose that the intellectual impulse given by Labeo was communicated to the followers of both schools of jurisprudence. But though, as we have stated, no difference of principle was involved, each school was accustomed to follow its leaders with much servility; and it is quite an exception to find, on a certain question, Cassius, a member of the Sabinian school, following the opinion of Labeo; while Proculus, who gave his name to Labeo's school, preferred the opinion of Ofilius, the teacher of Capito, 3 § 140.

We may briefly mention some of the most illustrious jurists who flourished subsequently to the era of Gaius. Aemilius Papinianus flourished under Marcus Aurelius and Septimius Severus, and was murdered by the order of Caracalla: 595 extracts from his writings are contained in the Digest. It was perhaps due to the transcendent genius, or at least to the extraordinary reputation, of Papinian, which made him seem too great to be reckoned any man's follower, that we cease henceforth to hear of opposing schools of jurisprudence. Papinian appears to have been stationed at York, with the function of praefectus praetorio, so that England may claim some slight connection with the brightest luminary of Roman law.

A disciple and colleague of Papinian was Domitius Ulpianus, murdered by the praetorian soldiery, whose domination he resisted, in the presence of the Emperor Severus Alexander: 2462 fragments, composing about a third of the whole Digest, are taken from his writings. An epitome of his Liber Singularis Regularum is still extant in a manuscript of the Vatican Library, and is the work referred to when, without mentioning the Digest, we cite the authority of Ulpian.

Another disciple and colleague of Papinian was Julius Paulus, of whose writings 2080 fragments are preserved in the Digest, forming about a sixth of its mass. An epitome of his treatise called Sententiae Receptae is found in the code of Alaric, king of the Visigoths; and it is to this book that we refer when we simply cite the authority of Paulus.

A disciple of Ulpian's was Herennius Modestinus, of whom 345 extracts are contained in the Digest. After Modestinus the lustre of Roman jurisprudence began to decline.

In what did the relation of disciple and teacher (praeceptor) consist? Principally in this, that a jurist of eminence allowed youths who aspired to a knowledge of the law to attend in his chambers and hear the advice which he gave to his clients. Jus civile dicere semper pulchrum fuit, hominumque clarissimorum discipulis floruerunt domus, Cic. Orator. 41. 'To instruct in law was always honorable, and eminent jurists have ever had crowds of disciples to grace their chambers.' Cicero himself had been introduced in his youth to Qu. Mucius the augur, and learnt law in his auditory, Laelius, 1. Three terms are used to indicate three stages of legal education: instituere, audire, instruere: Servius plurimum eos de quibus locuti sumus audivit, institutus a Balbo Lucilio, instructus autem maxime a Gallo Aquilio, Dig. 1, 2, 43. 'Servius was long an auditor of all these jurists: his education was commenced by Lucilius, and completed by Aquilius.' Instituere is to initiate in the elements of law, to lay the foundations of juridical knowledge. After completing this stage, the student was allowed to attend in the auditorium of a jurist and hear the oracles he delivered on consultation. Instruere denoted a closer intimacy and longer communication, and gave the learner the name of the praeceptor's studiosus. The first two processes seem contrasted in the following passage of Cicero: Qu. Scaevola quanquam nemini se ad docendum dabat, tamen consulentibus respondendo studiosos audiendi docebat, Brutus, 89. 'Scaevola gave no lessons in jurisprudence, but his answers to clients were instructive to his auditors.' Ulpian calls Modestinus, studiosus meus, Dig. 47, 2, 52, 20. That studiosus was not a mere student appears from many passages: Divus Antoninus Pius rescripsit: juris studiosos, qui salaria petant, haec exigere posse, Dig. 50, 13, 4. 'The Emperor Pius ruled that barristers (apprentiees) can recover their fees (by the praetor's cognitio extraordinaria).' Deinde instituit ut ingratorum in principem testamenta ad fiscum pertinerent, ac ne impune esset studiosis juris, qui scripsissent vel dictassent ea, Suetonius, Nero, 32. 'Nero enacted that the successions of persons ungrateful to the emperor should be confiscated, and made it penal in a lawyer to write or dictate an ungrateful will.' Cur, inquit, hoc me potius rogas, quam ex istis aliquem peritis studiosisque juris, quos adhibere in consilium judicaturi soletis? Gellius, 12, 13. 'Why do you not consult one of the lawyers who would sit as your assessor if you were judex?' Probably every lawyer was called a juris studiosus until by imperial diploma he had received the jus respondendi which made him a juris auctor.

At a later period we find that institution or preparatory tuition in law was undertaken by private teachers, who made this a special occupation. They are alluded to by Ulpian under the name of juris civilis professores, Dig. 50, 13, 1, 5. They were called professors because they were required to declare (profiteri) their intention before some competent authority, from whom they received permission to pursue their vocation, and they became thereupon entitled to certain privileges accorded to the professors of a liberal art. They appear to be distinguished from the practising lawyers in the following passage from Gellius, a contemporary of Gaius: Quaesitum esse memini in plerisque Romae stationibus jus publice docentium aut respondentium, an quaestor populi Romani a praetore in jus vocari posset, 13, 13. 'The question was canvassed in nearly all the rooms of the law professors, and nearly all the chambers of the jurists at Rome, whether a quaestor could be summoned by a praetor to his court:' where the stationes or standing places of the professors and jurists may remind us of the ancient custom of the English sergeants of meeting their pupils and clients at certain pillars in the church of St. Paul's.

In the time of Justinian we find professors in the modern sense, and academic instruction in three public schools of law at Rome, Constantinople, and Berytus. In a constitution addressed to the professors (antecessores), and prefixed to the Digest, Justinian modifies the existing plan of studies, and prescribes what portion of the Institutions, Digest, and Code is to be studied in each year of the quinquennial course.

DE CURATORIBUS.

§ 197. . . . . . aetatem pervenerit in qua res suas tueri possit. *idem* aput peregrinas gentes custodiri superius indicavimus.

§ 197. After release from wardship the estate of a minor is managed by a curator until he reaches the age at which he is competent to administer his own affairs, and the same rule obtains in other nations, as we have already mentioned.

§ 198. Ex iisdem causis et in provinciis a praesidibus earum curatores dari voluit.

§ 198. Under similar circumstances the president of a province appoints a curator by the constitution of Marcus Antoninus.

DE SATISDATIONE TUTORUM VEL CURATORUM.

§ 199. Ne tamen et pupillorum et eorum qui in curatione sunt negotia *a* tutoribus curatoribusque consumantur aut deminuantur, curat praetor, ut et tutores et *curatores* eo nomine satisdent.

§ 199. To protect wards and minors from the destruction or waste of their property by guardians and curators, it is the function of the praetor to require guardians and curators to give security for due administration.

§ 200. Set hoc non est perpetuum. nam et tutores testamento dati satisdare non coguntur, quia fides eorum et diligentia ab ipso testatore probata est; *et curatores* ad quos non e lege curatio pertinet, *set qui* vel a consule vel a praetore vel a praeside provinciae *dan*tur, plerumque non coguntur satisdare, scilicet quia satis i*donei electi* sunt.

§ 200. But this is not without exception, for testamentary guardians are not compelled to give security, as their integrity and vigilance have been approved by the testator; and curators who have not been appointed by any statute, but by the nomination of a consul or praetor or president of a province, are generally not required to give security, their selection being deemed sufficient evidence of their trustworthiness.

In English jurisprudence there is no distinction corresponding to that between tutor and curator, infant (impubes) and minor (adolescens). Infant and minor are in English synonymous: guardianship continues to the attainment of majority, i. e. to the completion of 21 years of age; and after that the young of both sexes are considered to be capable of taking care of themselves, and are free from further control. At Rome wardship (tutela) ceased at the age of 14 for males and 12 for females, ages at which the young manifestly continue to stand in need of guidance and protection.

Such protection was provided for them partly by two statutes, partly by praetorian legislation. (1) The lex Plaetoria was as old as Plautus, who makes a youth exclaim: Tum lex me perdit quinavicenaria; metuunt credere omnes, Pseudolus, 1, 3, 69. 'The statute with its five and twenty years prevents my getting credit.' It made a criminal offence, and subject to a criminal prosecution (judicium publicum, Cic. De Nat. Deor. 3, 30), what Cicero calls circumscriptio adolescentium, De Off. 3, 15; i. e. overreaching and circumventing persons below the age of 25. The circumscription of a minor, like maladministration by a guardian, rendered the person convicted thereof infamis. The statute provided, apparently, that a contractor with a minor might secure himself against the penalties of the law, if a curator were nominated by the praetor to advise the minor in respect of the special transaction. (2) As the lex Plaetoria was only applicable in cases of fraud (dolus malus, Cic. De Off. 3, 15), the protection it gave to minors was inadequate: accordingly, the praetor proclaimed in his edict that he would relieve minors who had been damaged in consequence of inexperience and improvidence by rescission and cancellation of the proceeding (in integrum restitutio). To obtain this relief it was not necessary to prove any fraud on the part of the person who contracted with the minor. (3) A person who wished to bring an action against a minor could compel him to obtain from the praetor a curator for the purpose of defending the particular suit; whose office ceased as soon as the special litigation terminated. Marcus Aurelius, under whom Gaius flourished, enacted that any minor who chose should be able to obtain from the praetor a general curator (generalis curator), who then should be charged with the general administration (generalis administratio) of his estate, Capitolinus, 10. In view of this option of the minor, Justinian could still say: Inviti adolescentes curatores non accipiunt praeterquam ad litem, Inst. 1, 23, 2. 'Unless they choose, minors need not have a curator, except for a suit.' A minor who had a curator could not aliene without the consent of his curator: he could incur an obligation without the consent of his curator, subject to his right of in integrum restitutio. Even the existence of a curator did not deprive the minor of his right of restitution, but of course it could not be obtained so readily as when he acted without the advice of a curator.

The tutor and curator were entirely separate functionaries: when women were under perpetual tutelage, a woman might have both a tutor and a curator. The curator of a minor must be distinguished from an agent (procurator), a person invested with certain rights and duties, which will be explained when we examine the different kinds of contract. An agent is governed by the instructions (mandatum) of his principal: a minor is under the direction of his curator: the employment of an agent is a private matter, purely voluntary on the part of the principal; the curator is a public functionary, and to a certain extent imposed on the minor.

Besides minors, lunatics and prodigals of whatever age were committed to the charge of curators. The curatio of lunatics and prodigals is, indeed, older than that of minors, being regulated by the Twelve Tables, which directed that the nearest agnate should be committee of a lunatic, and manage the estate of an interdicted prodigal. In later times it was usual for the praetor or praeses provinciae to appoint a curator after inquest (ex inquisitione). Paulus has preserved the form of words in which the prodigal was interdicted: Moribus per praetorem bonis interdicitur hoc modo: Quando tu bona paterna avitaque nequitia tua disperdis, liberosque tuos ad egestatem perducis, ob eam rem tibi ea re commercioque interdico, 3, 4*a*, 7. 'By customary law the praetor interdicts a prodigal from the administration of his property in the following terms: As thy profligacy is wasting the estate of thy father and ancestors, and bringing thy children to destitution, I therefore interdict thee from the control of thy patrimony, and from all disposition of property.'

From § 189 it might appear that Gaius referred the institution of guardianship to the code of Jus Gentium. We have, however, quoted from the Digest, § 142, a passage which ascribes it to Jus Civile: and, indeed, no institution containing numerical definitions (fixing, for example, on 12 and 14 for the years of puberty of the two sexes, and 25 for the year of majority of both sexes, without regard to individual development of intelligence) can be supposed to belong to natural law, if natural law is the less arbitrary element of the positive code. Moreover, the law of guardianship has been most variable, not only if we look to different countries, but also if we look at different periods in the same country; and the praetor or chancellor or other authority that has had the supervision of guardians has always exercised a great latitude of discretion; features which again forbid us to ascribe the rules of wardship to any comparatively immutable code of nature. A striking illustration and proof of the civil character of the rules of wardship in Roman law is furnished by the fact that though a promise by a ward without his guardian's authority has no binding force, i. e. produces no civilis obligatio, in other terms is not actionable, except so far as he is thereby enriched; yet, irrespectively of the gain or loss of the ward, Roman jurisprudence recognized that his promise produced a naturalis obligatio, for it ruled that such promise might be the basis of a suretyship, 3 § 119, and might extinguish a previous debt by novation, 3 § 176; and both suretyship and novation are institutions which are essentially accessary; that is to say, each implies the existence of two distinct obligations, either civil or natural, one assuring and the other assured, or one transforming and the other transformed.

In integrum restitutio, a branch of the praetor's equitable jurisdiction, and one of the most remarkable cases of his cognitio extraordinaria, has been mentioned more than once, and deserves here a brief explanation. Restituere in a general sense denotes any undoing of a wrong, any replacement of a person or his right in his or its original condition, whether by the voluntary act of the wrongdoer, or after action brought, and then either at the invitation of the judge (in virtue of the clause, ni restituat, 4 § 47), or in execution of a judicial sentence. But in the phrase we are examining it denotes the act, not of a private party, but of a judicial authority. In integrum restitutio is the restitution by the praetor of a person or his right to his or its original uninjured condition, in cases when no remedy is to be obtained either from the rigorous rules of the civil law or jus strictum (e. g. by civilis actio), or even from equity as administered by the ordinary judges in the ordinary forms (e. g. by exceptio or bonae fidei actio). The interposition in such cases of the highest Roman minister of justice resembles that of the English chancellor when a suitor is unable to obtain redress by the rules and forms of the courts of common law. The delicate function of overruling the ordinary course of law where it collided with equity was, as intimated, only confided to the highest judicial authority, and even in his hands was governed, at all events in later times, by precise rules of positive law. Five grounds or titles (justae causae) to extraordinary relief (extraordinarium auxilium) were recognized and enumerated in the edict, Dig. 4, 1: intimidation (metus), fraud (dolus malus), absence, error, minority (aetatis infirmitas). In process of time, as the rules by which relief was granted became precisely determined, two of these titles, fraud and intimidation, were transferred from the extraordinary to the ordinary course of procedure (ordo judiciorum); and, in cases of intimidation or fraud, restitution by the praetor was almost superseded by the actio quod metus causa and exceptio metus, or the actio doli and exceptio doli.

Originally capitis minutio of a defendant was ground for a restitution, 3 § 84; but this ceased at an early period to be a genuine case of restitution, for rescission of the adrogation, adoption, emancipation, whereby a person's debts were extinguished, was granted as a matter of course without any previous investigation (causae cognitio), and without any period of prescription like that which limited the right to pray for restitution, namely, originally, annus utilis, and in the time of Justinian, quadriennium continuum (3 § 117, commentary).

Of the five titles to restitution that we have enumerated, four, namely, intimidation, fraud, absence, error, implying equality of rights in all parties, belong to the law of Things; title by minority, implying a privileged class or inequality of rights, belongs to the law of Persons.

BOOK II.

DE REBUS SINGULIS ET DE RERUM UNIVERSITATIBUS.

DE RERUM DIVISIONE.

§ 1. *Superiore commentario de iure personarum* exposuimus; modo videamus de rebus: *quae vel* in nostro patrimonio sunt, vel extra nostrum patrimonium habentur.

§ 1. In the preceding book the law of persons was expounded; now let us proceed to the law of things, which are either subject to private dominion or not subject to private dominion.

§ 2. Summa itaque rerum divisio *in duos articulos deducitur: nam aliae sunt divini iuris*, aliae humani.

§ 2. The first division of things is into two classes: things subject to divine dominion, and things subject to human dominion.

§ 3. Divini iu*ris* su*nt* velu*ti* res sac*rae* et religiosae.

§ 3. Subject to divine dominion are things sacred and things religious.

§ 4. Sacrae sunt quae Diis superis consecratae sunt; religiosae, quae Diis manibus relictae sunt.

§ 4. Sacred things are those consecrated to the gods above; religious, those devoted to the gods below.

§ 5. *Sed* sacrum *quidem* so*lum* exi*stumatur* auctoritate p*opuli Romani fieri; consecratur enim lege de* ea re lata aut senatusconsulto fa*cto*.

§ 5. Sacred things can only become so with the authority of the people of Rome, by consecration in pursuance of a law or a decree of the senate.

§ 6. Religiosum vero nostra voluntate facimus mortuum inferentes in locum nostrum, si modo eius mortui funus ad nos pertineat.

§ 6. A religious thing becomes so by private will, when an individual buries a dead body in his own ground, if the burial is his proper business.

§ 7. Set in provinciali solo placet plerisque solum religiosum non fieri,

§ 7. On provincial soil, according to most authorities, as the dominion

quia in *eo solo* dominium populi Romani est vel Caesaris, nos autem possessionem tantum *et usumfructum* habere videmur. utique tamen *eiusmodi locus, licet non sit* religiosus, pro *religioso habetur*, quia etiam quod in provinciis non ex auctoritate populi Romani consecratum est, proprie sacrum non est, tamen pro sacro habetur.

belongs to the people of Rome or the emperor, and individuals only have possession or usufruct, such places, though not properly religious, are quasi-religious; just as provincial soil, in default of the authorization of the people of Rome, is rendered by consecration not sacred, but quasi-sacred.

§ 8. Sanctae quoque res, velut muri et portae, quodammodo divini iuris sunt.

§ 8. Sanctioned places are to a certain extent under divine dominion, such as city gates and city walls.

§ 9. Quod autem *divini* iuris est, id nullius in bonis est: id vero quod humani *iuris est plerumque alicuius in bonis est: potest autem et nullius in bonis esse. nam res hereditariae, antequam aliquis heres existat, nullius in bonis sunt.*

§ 9. Things subject to divine dominion are exempt from private dominion; things subject to human dominion are generally subject to private dominion, but may be otherwise: for an inheritance before a successor is ascertained has no actual proprietor.

§ 10. *Hae autem res quae humani iuris sunt, aut publicae sunt aut privatae.*

§ 10. Things subject to human dominion are either public or private.

§ 11. *Quae publicae sunt, nullius in bonis esse creduntur; ipsius enim universitatis esse creduntur. privatae autem sunt, quae singulorum sunt.*

§ 11. Things public belong to no individual, but to a society or corporation; things private are subject to individual dominion.

DE REBUS INCORPORALIBUS.

§ 12. *Quaedam praeterea res corporales sunt, quaedam incorporales.*

§ 12. Again, things are either corporeal or incorporeal.

§ 13. *Corporales hae sunt quae tangi possunt, veluti* fundus, homo, vestis, *aurum, argentum et denique* aliae res *innumerabiles.*

§ 13. Things corporeal are tangible, as land, a slave, clothing, gold, silver, and innumerable others.

§ 14. *Incorporales sunt quae tangi* non *possunt: qualia sunt ea quae in iure consistunt, sicut hereditas, ususfructus, obligationes quoquo modo contractae. nec ad rem pertinet, quod in hereditate res corporales continentur; nam et fructus qui ex fundo percipiuntur corporales sunt, et id quod ex aliqua obligatione nobis debetur plerumque corporale est, veluti fundus, homo, pecunia: nam ipsum ius successionis, et ipsum ius utendi* fruendi, *et ipsum ius*

§ 14. Things incorporeal are intangible; rights, for instance, such as inheritance, usufruct, obligation, however contracted. For though an inheritance relates to things corporeal, and the fruits of land enjoyed by a usufructuary are corporeal, and obligations generally relate to the conveyance of something corporeal: land, slaves, money; yet the right of succession, the right of usufructuary enjoyment, and the right of the contractor, are incor-

obligationis incorporale est. eodem numero sunt et iura praediorum urbanorum et rusticorum, quae etiam servitutes vocantur. [13 *fere lineae desunt.*]

poreal. So are the rights attached to property in houses and land, denominated servitudes or easements.

Having treated of the law of Persons (unequal rights), we proceed to the law of Things (equal rights), and the first right which Gaius intends to discuss is the right called Dominion. Seduced, however, by an ambiguity of the word Res, which signifies either a right or the subject of a right, his opening statements (§§ 12, 13, 14) are deplorably confused.

In order to see our way, let us first examine Res as denoting the Subject of a right. Every right implies, as we have stated, an obligation; and every right or obligation implies at least two persons, one of whom has the right while the other has the obligation. The immediate OBJECT of every right is an act or forbearance of the person who has the obligation. But the act or forbearance generally relates to some body, that is, to some tangible portion of the external world, whether a thing or a person. This body, accordingly, may be called the mediate, indirect, or secondary Object of the right, or, in the nomenclature we have adopted, its SUBJECT. The subject of a right, however, is not always a body; it may be corporeal or incorporeal. For instance, dominion over land is a right to forbearance on the part of all the world from molestation of the owner in dealing with the land. A servitude, say a right of way, is a right to forbearance on the part of all the world from molestation of the person entitled in passing over certain land. A contractual right is a right to a positive act or performance on the part of a determinate person, say, to the conveyance or delivery of a certain piece of land. In these cases, land, the subject or secondary object of the right is something corporeal. So, too, when a third person is the subject of a right; for instance, a child or a gladiator, 3 § 199, in the possession (detention or custody) of the parent or employer, and whose removal from such possession engenders in the removing party an obligation ex delicto. But in primordial rights, the subject, at least as distinguished from the two parties in whom the right and obligation respectively vest, is something incorporeal. A man has a right to forbearance on the part of all the world from molestation in his life, health, locomotion, honour. These subjects of the right are incorporeal. Other rights, apparently, have no determinate subject, corporeal or incorporeal, to which they are correlated. In a right to the services of a menial or gladiator, for instance, it would be hard to indicate any subject or secondary object to which the obligation of the menial or gladiator relates.

It is clear that no division of subjects of right will coincide with a classification of rights, and that if we divide Res in the metaphysical sense of the World, or Being, or Existence (a sense suggested by the differentiae, corporalis, and incorporalis), Dominion, like all other rights, will be a member of the branch res incorporalis. Gaius, however, wishes us to identify Dominion with res corporalis, while we make Obligation and the fractions of Dominion (servitutes), and even some forms of Dominion (e.g. hereditas), members of the contra-distinguished branch, res incorporalis. (Cf. 3 § 83, omnes ejus res incorporales et corporales quaeque ei debita sunt.)

Gaius was probably not entirely responsible for this confusion of thought, which, perhaps, was too deeply inwoven in the formulae of Roman jurisprudence to be easily eliminated by an institutional writer. E.g. the declaration (intentio) of a real action (in rem actio) was of the form: Si paret (1) illum fundum—(2) illam hereditatem—actoris esse. (Cf. 4 § 3. In rem actio est cum aut corporalem rem intendimus nostram esse aut jus aliquod nobis competere.) Now as hereditas is a jus successionis (2 § 14), it is clear that, if the second formula is correct, the first formula ought to be, not, Si paret illum fundum—but, Si paret illius fundi proprietatem—actoris esse. To meet this and similar inaccuracies of the framers of the formularies, Gaius is misled into identifying in res corporalis two things completely disparate, Right and the Subject of a right. (There is a similar confusion in English law, chattels, tenements, and hereditaments being sometimes used to denote the subjects, movable or immovable, of certain rights, sometimes the rights over those subjects.)

In order to distribute the world of rights minus the rights of status, and to indicate the position held by Dominion in the system and the method substantially followed by Gaius, we may adopt the following division:—

Equal rights are either SANCTIONED, primary, final; or SANCTIONING, secondary, instrumental.

SANCTIONED rights are either—

REAL: rights availing against all the world (JUS IN REM), or

PERSONAL: rights availing against certain determinate persons (JUS IN PERSONAM).

Sanctioned rights against the world are either—

Unrelated to the external material universe, or
Related to the material universe.

Sanctioned rights unrelated to the material universe are PRIMORDIAL, or inborn rights. (These are not examined separately by Gaius, but are implied in obligatio EX DELICTO.)

Sanctioned rights related to the material universe are POSSESSION, DOMINION, SERVITUDE.

Sanctioned rights availing exclusively against certain persons, correlate to obligations EX CONTRACTU: that is, to the duties immediately produced by contract and before its violation.

SANCTIONING rights are capable of the same subdivision as SANCTIONED rights. They are not examined separately by Gaius, but partly under the head of obligatio EX DELICTO (founded on violation of PRIMORDIAL or other REAL right), partly under the head of obligatio EX CONTRACTU (obligation produced indirectly by contract, that is, by its violation), partly under the head of ACTIONES (procedure), personal actions prosecuting obligation EX DELICTO and EX CONTRACTU; and real actions being the remedy for violations of POSSESSION, DOMINION, SERVITUDE.

We shall find hereafter that the position of POSSESSION in Roman jurisprudence—whether it belongs to the department of JUS IN REM or of OBLIGATIO EX DELICTO is a moot question; but at present we need do no more than notice the existence of the controversy. We need also only to indicate a further division of rights and obligations into SINGLE rights and obligations, such as those of which we have just given a classification, and AGGREGATES of rights and obligations (UNIVERSITAS JURIS), such as Hereditas. A UNIVERSITAS JURIS includes Obligations as well as Rights, Jus in personam as well as Jus in rem, and Sanctioning rights as well as Sanctioned rights. But in spite of the diverse character of these elements of which it is composed, the JURIS UNIVERSITAS itself, or the ideal whole of these various elements, is regarded, e. g. in Hereditatis petitio, as a Right, not an Obligation; as a Jus in rem, not a Jus in personam; as a Sanctioned right, not a Sanctioning right. (As Res includes Obligation (res incorporalis) as well as Dominion (res corporalis), I have used the term RERUM UNIVERSITAS to denominate the subject of Books II and III, as marking more clearly than JURIS UNIVERSITAS an antithesis to RES SINGULAE; though I am aware that Rerum universitas has generally a more insignificant acceptation, denoting an artificial whole—a flock, herd, or library—in opposition to the ingredients—the single sheep, horses, books—of which it is composed.)

As Gaius thought that he could obtain the idea of Dominion by a division of Res into corporalis and incorporalis, so he seems to have thought that he could distinguish private dominion, the special department which he intends to examine, from other forms of dominion by a further division of Res. The phrases res divinae, res humanae, res communes, res publicae, res privatae, do, indeed, suggest the notion that res privatae is a specific member of the genus Res; but the appearance is fallacious. Very little reflection will convince us that res divinae, res publicae, res privatae are not a division of the SUBJECTS of property (res); for the same thing, a piece of ground, for instance, may be the subject of divine or public or private dominion; but merely a division of proprietors. In res divinae, the only doubtful case, the gods were deemed to be proprietors. Sed et illa interdicta quae de locis sacris et de religiosis proponuntur veluti proprietatis causam continent, Dig. 43, 1, 2, 2. 'The interdicts respecting sacred and religious places protect a quasi-property.'

The division of the subjects of right by their physical differences, the only way in which they can be divided, though only of subordinate importance, and though it cannot furnish the distinctions of Dominion and Obligation, nor of Public and Private dominion, yet has a considerable influence on jurisprudence, and demands a certain amount of attention. Thus ocean, air, and light, as opposed to the earth, are by their nature essentially res communes. Being incapable of appropriation, they have not been appropriated and are held in communism. Again, the distinction of res corporales and res incorporales may ground the distinction between Dominion and Primordial rights. Again, in wild animals, as opposed to tame, property is only coextensive with detention. On the difference between specific and generic things, or things consumed by use, quae pondere numero mensurave constant, and things not consumed by use, is founded the distinction between the contracts of mutuum and commodatum. On the same difference of specific and generic things are founded in English law different rules for the transmutation of property in the contract of sale, 3 § 139; and the distinction of movables and immovables founds a still more important difference in the English forms of alienation and rules of succession.

The phrases in nostro patrimonio and extra nostrum patrimonium, § 1, are apparently equivalent to alicujus in bonis and nullius in bonis, § 9, and to the expressions we meet elsewhere, in commercio and extra commercium.

Of res communes, or the dominion of mankind, which sometimes comes under discussion but is not mentioned by Gaius, we may observe, that it scarcely falls within the scope of our present province, namely, positive law, for all positive law is confined to the territory of the particular sovereign state by which it is enacted.

All the things within the territory of a given state are subject to its dominion, that is, are res publicae in a general sense of the term. Of these things it allows the dominion over some to vest in private individuals for their own advantage, while it retains the dominion over others in itself as a corporation or collective person (personarum universitas). This gives us a division of all things into res privatae and res publicae in a narrower sense of the term. We must note, however, that the dominion of the state is not exactly similar to private dominion, that is to say, is not dominion in the proper sense or the sense in which the word is used in civil law. For the civil dominion of private persons is a right protected and sanctioned by a political superior, whereas a sovereign state is by hypothesis in subjection to no superior. A state, then, can only be said to have dominion in a modified sense of the word, that is, so far as it is not restrained by any positive law of any superior from using and dealing with certain things as it may please.

Of things subject to public dominion, some are vested immediately in the state, others in subordinate persons, single or corporate, magistrates, for instance, and municipalities, to be held by such persons for various public purposes. Among these we may reckon res divinae which are portions of public dominion vested in certain corporations in trust for religious purposes.

Another division of res publicae is into res in patrimonio populi and res non in patrimonio populi. Under the former are included the public treasury, the public domain, public slaves, escheats (caduca) or res privatae that relapse to the state by forfeiture, or as ultimus heres; in other words, all things of which the state as universitas retains not only the property but also the use and disposition (quasi propriae et privatae res universitatis, Dig. 43, 8, 2, 4). The other class includes, high roads, public rivers, public buildings, &c., that is, all things of which the property is in the community and the use in the members of the community. Or we may say that the property is in the universitas, but it is subject to a personal servitude (usus) vested in all the private members of that universitas (singuli, universi).

Not only res publicae but res privatae may be subject to this sort of personal servitude. For instance, the banks of public rivers and the trees thereupon are the property of the adjacent proprietors: but the navigators of these rivers have the right of mooring, landing, unlading, and using the banks in various other ways, Inst. 2, 1, 4.

Property absolute or pre-eminently so called, may be defined as a right of unlimited duration, imparting to the owner a power of indefinite use, and a power of aliening from all who in default of alienation by him might succeed by descent; or, in other words, from all successors interposed between himself and the sovereign as ultimus heres. It is accordingly sometimes said to consist of jus utendi, fruendi, abutendi; where abusus includes the power of consumption or destruction and alienation.

Besides absolute property Roman law recognizes various kinds of partial property, real rights over a subject of which the dominion is in another person, called jura in re or jura in re aliena, rights which fall short of absolute property but approximate to it in various degrees. Such are servitudes, mortgage (pignus), superficies, and emphyteusis. These may all be regarded as detached fractions of property, portions of the right of dominion taken from the proprietor and vested in another person. They are explained by Justinian in the parallel passage of his Institutes, and, though not mentioned by Gaius, demand here a brief notice.

Servitudes are (1) praedial or real (praediorum), that is, belong to a person as owner of a certain house or land (praedium dominans) in respect of a house or land belonging to another proprietor (praedium serviens), or (2) personal (personarum), that is, are vested in a person without relation to his ownership of praedium dominans. (Compare in English law the division of easements into easements appurtenant to land and easements in gross.)

Praedial servitudes are servitudes properly so called and are contrasted with property by their precise and definite circumscription. Property is a right against the world which gives to the party in whom it resides a power of dealing with the subject which is not capable of exact definition. Servitude is such a right against the world as gives to the party in whom it resides a power of using the subject which is susceptible of precise description. It is a definite subtraction from the indefinite powers of use and exclusion which reside in the proprietor; or a right against the owner and the rest of the world to put a thing to uses of a definite class.

Praedial servitudes are (1) rustic, or relating to land, or (2) urban, or relating to houses. Instances of rustic servitudes are iter, or jus eundi, right of way for beast and man on foot or on horseback over praedium serviens to praedium dominans; actus, or jus agendi, right of way for ordinary carriages (not for heavy laden waggons): via, or jus vehendi, right of paved way (for heavy laden waggons): aquaeductus, right of conveying water over praedium serviens.

Instances of urban servitudes are jus tigni immittendi, the right of resting a beam on a neighbour's wall; jus stillicidii recipiendi, the right of directing the rainfall from a roof on to a neighbour's roof or ground: jus altius non tollendi, the right of having access of light to one's windows free from obstruction.

Personal servitudes are rights of a less limited character: instances are Habitatio, the right of occupying a house, Usus, the right of using a thing and consuming its immediate fruits or products, without the right of letting the thing or selling its products, of acquiring, in other words, its rent and profits, which may be regarded as its mediate or secondary fruits. Fructus, usually called Ususfructus, the further right of leasing the thing and selling its fruits. Habitatio, Usus, Ususfructus were usually estates for life, and, unlike real servitudes, implied Detention of the subject; Possession of the subject, as opposed to Detention, remaining in the proprietor.

For pignus, see 3 § 90, commentary.

Superficies is the right of a person who has bought a house without the ground on which it stands, or who has built a house on another's ground with his permission, a house, that is, which at civil law, by the rule of Accession, is the property of the proprietor of the soil. The Praetor, however, recognized in the superficiarius a jus in re which he protected by an interdict de superficie and an actio in rem utilis.

For emphyteusis, see 3 § 145. Although an emphyteusis might be of unlimited duration, and was alienable without the consent of the proprietor, yet the proprietor had a reversion on failure of the heirs of the emphyteuta, just as the feudal lord of a fee has the reversion on failure of the heirs of the tenant in fee. Accordingly, emphyteusis is regarded as the model on which feudal tenure was instituted. This reversion or escheat to the lord of the fee makes property in land theoretically imperfect, and, like emphyteusis, rather a jus in re aliena than plenary dominion. Property in chattels, on the contrary, has no reversioner interposed between the proprietor and the sovereign as ultimus heres, and, therefore, is absolute.

RERUM CORPORALIUM ADQUISITIONES CIVILES.

§ 15. Item [2 *lin.*] *Ea autem animalia nostri quidem praeceptores* statim ut nata sunt mancipi esse putant: *Nerva vero, Proculus* et ceteri diversae scholae auctores non aliter ea mancipi esse putant, quam si domita sunt; et si propter nimiam feritatem domari non possunt, tunc videri mancipi esse, *cum ad eam aetatem pervenerint, cuius aetatis domari solent.*

[See p. 142.] § 15. These, according to my school, are mancipable as soon as born; according to Nerva and Proculus and their followers, are not mancipable until tamed, or if too wild to be tamed, until they attain the age at which other individuals of the species are tamed.

§ 16. *Ex diverso bestiae nec* mancipi sunt, velut ursi, leones, item ea animalia quae fere bestiarum numero sunt, velut elefantes et cameli: et ideo ad rem non pertinet, quod haec animalia etiam

§ 16. Things not mancipable include wild beasts, as bears, lions, and semi-wild beasts, as elephants and camels, though sometimes employed for draught or carriage.

collo dorsove domantur . . . . . . quorum . . . mancipi esse; quaedam non mancipi sunt.

§ 17. Item *fere* omnia *quae incorpor*alia sunt nec mancipi sunt, exceptis servi*tutibus* prae*diorum rusticorum in Italico solo, quae mancipi sunt*, quamvis sint ex numero *rerum* incorpor*alium*.

§ 17. Also things incorporeal, except rustic servitudes on Italian soil.

§ 18. Magna autem differentia est mancipi *rerum et* nec mancipi.

§ 18. There is an important difference between things mancipable and things not mancipable.

§ 19. Nam res nec *mancipi nuda traditione alienari possunt*, si modo corporales sunt et ob id recipiunt traditionem.

§ 19. Property in things not mancipable is transferred by mere delivery of possession, if they are corporeal and capable of delivery.

§ 20. Itaque si tibi vestem vel aurum vel argentum tradidero, *s*ive ex venditionis causa sive *ex donationis* sive qua*v*is alia ex *causa*, *t*ua fit ea res *sine ulla iuris solemnitate*.

§ 20. Thus when possession of clothes or gold or silver is delivered to a vendee or donee or a person otherwise entitled, the property passes by the mere act of prehension.

§ 21. *In eadem* causa sunt *provincialia* praedia, quorum *alia stipen*diaria, alia tributaria vocamus. Stipendiaria sunt ea quae in his provinciis sunt, quae propriae populi Romani esse intelleguntur. Tributaria sunt ea quae in his provinciis sunt, quae propriae *Caesaris esse cre*duntur.

§ 21. Similarly transferrible are estates in provincial lands, whether stipendiary or tributary; stipendiary being lands in provinces subject to the dominion of the people of Rome, tributary, lands in the provinces subject to the dominion of the Emperor.

§ 22. Mancipi vero res *ae*que per mancipationem ad alium transferuntur; unde *scilicet* mancipi res sunt dictae. quod autem valet manci*patio, idem valet et in iure cessio*.

§ 22. Property in things mancipable, on the contrary, is conveyed by mancipation, whence their name, or—a universally applicable mode of transfer—by surrender before a magistrate in a fictitious vindication.

§ 23. *Et manci*patio quidem quemadmodum fiat, superiore commentario tradidimus.

§ 23. The process of mancipation was described in the preceding book.

§ 24. In iure cessio autem hoc modo fit. aput ma*gistratum* populi Romani, vel*ut* Praetorem, vel aput Praesidem provinciae is cui res in iure ceditur, rem tenens ita dicit: HUNC EGO HOMINEM EX IURE QUIRITIUM MEUM ESSE AIO. deinde postquam hic vindicaver*it*, *Praetor interro*gat eum qui cedit, an contra

§ 24. Surrender in a fictitious vindication is in the following form: in the presence of a magistrate of the people of Rome, such as a praetor or the president of a province of the people, the surrenderee grasping the subject says: I CLAIM THIS SLAVE AS MY PROPERTY BY TITLE QUIRITARY. Then the praetor inter-

vindicet. quo negante aut tacente, tunc ei qui vindicaverit eam rem addicit. idque legis actio vocatur, quae fieri potest etiam in provinciis *aput Praesides earum.*

rogates the surrenderor whether he makes a counterclaim, and upon his disclaimer or silence awards the thing to the demandant. This proceeding is called an action of the law, and can be performed before the president of a province of the Emperor.

§ 25. *Plerum*que *tamen et* fere semper mancipationibus utimur. quod enim ipsi per nos praesentibus amicis agere possumus, hoc *non est necesse* cum maiore difficultate aput Praetorem aut aput Praesidem provinciae *quaerere.*

§ 25. Generally, however, and almost always the process of mancipation is preferred; for why should a result that can be accomplished in private with the assistance of our friends be prosecuted with greater trouble in the court of the praetor or president of the province?

§ 26. *At si* neque mancipata, neque in iure cessa sit res man*cipi* [*desunt* 31 *lin.*].

§ 26. If neither mancipation nor surrender in court is employed in the conveyance of a mancipable thing . . . .

§ 27. *In summa adm*onendi sumus *nexum Italici soli proprium* esse, provincialis soli nex*um* non *esse: recipit enim nexus* significationem solum non aliter, *quam si* mancipi *est*, provincial*e vero* nec mancipi *est.* —enim vero provincia . . . . . de mancipa—.

§ 27. Finally, we must observe that alienation by bronze and balance is peculiar to Italian soil, and inapplicable to provincial soil. It exclusively applies to things subject to private or quiritary dominion, whereas provincial soil is only subject to public dominion.

Having described the various kinds of real right (jus in rem), i.e. dominion and its fractions (jura in re), we proceed to the TITLES of real rights, that is to say, the events to which these rights are annexed by the legislator; in other words, the modes prescribed by the legislator by which such rights may be acquired; in other words, the legislative definitions of the classes of persons in whom such rights are declared to be vested.

The Titles of real rights are divisible into Titles by which single real rights are acquired and Titles by which aggregates of rights (universitates jurum) are acquired.

Titles by which single real rights are acquired are divisible into Titles sanctioned by the civil law and Titles sanctioned by natural (gentile) law (jus gentium), natural law denoting the rules introduced by praetors and jurists as consonant to the general reason of mankind.

Titles by civil law are in jure cessio, usucapio, mancipatio, traditio, and others which will be mentioned. Titles by natural law are traditio, occupatio, accessio, and others which will be mentioned. We commence with Titles by civil law, and the introductory propositions which are now illegible in the manuscript of Gaius may be supplied from Ulpian, Regulae, 19, 1.

Things are either mancipable or not mancipable. Things mancipable are land and houses on Italian soil, slaves, tame animals employed for draught and carriage, as oxen, horses, mules, and asses.

Of civil Titles the oldest were probably in jure cessio and usucapio, the one public the other private, the one containing an act of a political authority, the other subordinate and supplementary to this, and though equally effectual where it applied, yet not quite so extensive in its application.

In jure cessio or surrender before a magistrate cannot fail to recal to an English lawyer two similar modes of alienation that recently existed in English jurisprudence, alienation by Fine and alienation by Recovery, both of which, like in jure cessio, were based on a fictitious action; in both of which, that is to say, although the parties did not really stand in the relation of adverse litigants, the alienee was supposed to recover an estate by process of law. By a Fine, an action commenced against the alienor and at once terminated by his acknowledging the right of the alienee, a tenant in tail could aliene the fee simple, so far at least as to bar his own issue. By a Recovery, a tenant in tail could convey an absolute estate in fee. This was an action supposed to be, not like a Fine immediately compromised, but carried on through every regular stage to the conclusion; whereby the alienee recovered judgment against the alienor, who in his turn recovered judgment against an imaginary warrantor whom he vouched to warranty (cf. laudat auctorem, 3 § 139, commentary). Another employment of fictitious action in English law as a solemn form, not of alienation but of contract, a title, consequently, not of jus in rem but of jus in personam, namely, the Judgment Debt (see 3 § 134, commentary), has no parallel in Roman jurisprudence of the classical period: though in earlier times the Nexum, expressing the obligation of the promisor by the term Damnas, i.e. condemnatus, apparently placed him in the position of a judgment debtor (pro judicato), and rendered him liable to the most rigorous form of execution (manus injectio).

In jure cessio to a late period was the principal mode of manumitting slaves, and a part of the process of emancipation, that is, the release of a son from the patria potestas.

To relieve the magistrate and the parties from the troublesome process of in jure cessio, a new mode of conveyance, by bronze and balance (nexum, mancipium, per aes et libram), which did not require the intervention of a public functionary, was introduced at some subsequent period, but confined to the alienation of certain specific subjects of property. The things capable of this mode of alienation were at first, probably, only the ordinary booty of a predatory tribe, slaves and the larger kinds of cattle; but afterwards included land, rustic servitudes, and the familia or universitas jurum of a testator, 2 § 103. Not only slaves, but liberae personae of an inferior domestic status, filiusfamilias and filiafamilias, were subject to conveyance by mancipation. By this process, a genuine sale for a valuable consideration, a father could sell his son into domestic bondage (mancipium): by this process, reduced to the state of a fiction, a woman became subject to the manus of a husband (coemptio), and a filiusfamilias was adopted (adoptio) or emancipated (emancipatio).

Mancipation, as conveying property without possession, 4 § 131, may be compared to a Deed in English law; and, like the corresponding English solemnity, might be used as a formality either of alienation or of contract, 3 § 173; or, if we take contract in a wider sense, of contract either translative or obligative. After the introduction of mancipation mancipable things were the most easily alienable: they could be aliened by mancipation as well as by surrender in court and usucapion, whereas not-mancipable things were only alienable by the two latter modes of transfer.

At a later period, however, in order to facilitate the transfer of property in those cases where it was most difficult, a new and still simpler process was introduced, namely, tradition or the delivery of possession. In such not-mancipable things as were corporeal, the transfer of possession or physical dominion, that is, the exclusive power of acting corporeally on a given body, a title in gentile law, was declared by the legislator to be a title in civil law, to operate a transfer of legal or civil dominion, dominion ex jure Quiritium. Thus the tables were now turned: things, which formerly were most difficult, were now most easy to aliene: the term mancipable, which before denoted an enlargement of the powers of alienation, now denoted a restriction; for mancipable things were things alienable either by surrender or by usucapion or by the cumbrous process of mancipation, but not by tradition: not-mancipable things were things alienable (such of them at least as were corporeal) either by surrender or by usucapion or by the simple process of tradition, though not by mancipation.

In respect of land the title in English law corresponding to tradition is Feoffment. The essence of a feoffment is livery of seisin (delivery of possession) and, though subsequently a deed was always added, yet, originally, livery of seisin was a valid transfer of property without an accompanying deed. There is this, however, to be observed, that in English law conveyance by livery was an older title than conveyance by deed, whereas in Roman law mancipation, which we have assimilated to conveyance by deed, was older than tradition; and property in land, the great subject of transfer by feoffment, was in Rome originally conveyed not by tradition but by mancipation, tradition being, however, a further requisite to effect the transfer of possession.

We proceed to notice minor points in the text of Gaius. We have hitherto spoken of tradition as a title whereby property was acquired. Tradition, however, was only an element, usually the final element, of the complex mode of acquisition to which it gives its name. To be capable of passing property, tradition must be accompanied by another element, usually an antecedent element, some contract or other source of obligation, or some evidence of intention to aliene. The same was true of usucapion. Besides possession for a certain term it was requisite that possession should have had an innocent inception or belief of the possessor that he had a right to take possession (bona fides). This second condition of acquisition was indicated by the preposition pro governing a noun or participle; the bona fide possessor was said to possess pro emptore, pro donato, pro legato, pro derelicto, &c. The condition itself was called the causa, (§ 20) or justa causa, or titulus, of the tradition or usucapion; and we now may notice the exact relation of the word Title as used in this commentary to the Titulus of the classical jurists. Title, as used by Austin and as used in this commentary, denotes the totality of the complex conditions to which the law annexes any right, in rem or in personam: titulus as used by the classical jurists is only one portion of the modes of acquisition called Tradition and Usucapion.

Instead of denoting the whole of a complex investitive fact, it denotes in their writings only a constituent part of this fact: it merely denotes the fact by which the acquisition begins, as contradistinguished from the fact by which the acquisition is completed.

§ 21. The system of taxation which Rome imposed on her provinces demands a brief notice. Under the Republic different provinces were subject to different systems, but with the Empire a tendency to uniformity of taxation commenced: the distinction of tributary and stipendiary provinces was merely nominal in the time of Gaius, and it ceased entirely in the time of Pomponius and Ulpian. As early, probably, as from the time of Marcus Aurelius, under whom Gaius flourished, the following system of direct taxation was uniformly established throughout the Roman world.

Direct taxation was of two kinds: it embraced (1) a poll tax or capitation tax, i. e. a tax on persons (capitis tributum), and (2) a tax on land (agri tributum). The tax on persons (capitatio humana) was a fixed sum, probably of small amount, that was only levied on persons who were not liable to the land tax, on tributarii as opposed to possessores. It was chiefly contributed by three classes, (1) tenant farmers of a semi-servile condition (coloni), (2) artisans and labourers, (3) slaves. From this capitation tax were exempted all who had the rank of municipal senators (decuriones, curiales, ordo), even though they were not possessores. From the classes on whom it was levied, capitatio humana was sometimes called capitatio plebeia.

The tax on landholders (possessores) was also called capitation (capitatio terrena). The reason of this will appear when we explain the mode in which it was levied. The whole territory was ideally divided into units of taxation (capita, juga) districts varying in size according to the nature of the soil, each having an estimated capital value of 1000 solidi or aurei, and hence called millena. From these capita or juga the land tax derived its name of capitatio or jugatio. The list of capita was called a Cadastre (capitastrum), and was revised every fifteen years (one of the earliest land valuations, made by order of Augustus, is mentioned by St. Luke, 2, 1). Every year, as soon as the Minister of Finance had settled the budget of expenditure, proclamation (indictio, delegatio) was made of the amount of taxes required, or rather, the total being divided by the number of capita, of the amount to be paid by each caput.

Each caput paid the same sum. The financial year commenced on 1st of September; and the tax was payable in three instalments, on the 1st days of the following January, May, and September. Besides the money tax, and proportioned to it, landowners had to pay a certain tax in raw produce (annona).

Italy and the privileged towns that enjoyed Jus Italicum were exempt from both these forms of direct taxation; jus Italicum consisting, as we have stated, of three elements, (1) free municipal constitution, (2) capacity of the soil of quiritary ownership, and (3) immunity from both kinds of direct taxation, jugatio humana and jugatio terrena. Italy, however, with the exception of the district about Rome, was subject to certain payments in kind (annona), whence its division into Italia annonaria and Italia urbicaria. According to others, Italia urbicaria contributed to the use of the metropolis payments similar to those which Italia annonaria paid to the imperial household. Moreover, to compensate for her immunity from other taxation, Italy paid 5 per cent. on all testamentary successions (vicesima hereditatum) and 5 per cent. on the value of all manumitted slaves, Livy, 7, 16. Under Diocletian Italy lost her immunities and was reduced to the condition of a province. Savigny, Vermischte Schriften, 16.

§ 24. The legati Caesaris or Presidents of imperial provinces had originally no jurisdiction to preside over legis actio, but this was afterwards conferred upon them, Tac. Ann. 12, 60.

RERUM INCORPORALIUM ADQUISITIONES CIVILES.

§ 28. Incorporales *res* traditionem non recipere manifestum est.

§ 28. Incorporeal things are obviously incapable of transfer by delivery of possession.

§ 29. Sed iura praediorum urbanorum in iure ta*ntum ce*di possunt; rusticorum vero etiam mancipari possunt.

§ 29. Urban servitudes can only be created by surrender in a fictitious vindication; rustic servitudes may either be acquired by this method or by mancipation.

§ 30. Ususfructus in iure cessionem tantum recipit. Nam dominus proprietatis alii usumfructum in iure cedere potest, ut ille usumfructum habeat, et ipse nudam proprietatem *retineat*. Ipse usufructuarius in iure cedendo domino proprietatis usumfructum *efficit*, ut a se discedat et convertatur in proprietatem. alii

§ 30. Usufruct can only be created by surrender in a fictitious vindication. A usufruct surrendered by the owner of the property passes to the surrenderee, leaving the naked property in the surrenderor. A usufruct surrendered by the usufructuary to the owner of the property passes to the sur-

vero in iure cedendo nihilominus ius suum retinet: creditur enim ea cessione nihil agi.

renderee and is reannexed to the property. Surrendered to a stranger it continues in the usufructuary, for the surrender is deemed inoperative.

§ 31. Sed haec scilicet in Italicis praediis ita sunt, quia et ipsa praedia mancipationem et in iure cessionem *recipiunt*. alioquin in provincialibus praediis sive qu*is* usumfructum sive ius eundi, agendi, aquamve ducendi, vel altius tollendi aedes, aut non tollendi, ne luminibus vicini officiatur, ceteraque similia iura constituere velit, pactionibus et *s*tipulationibus id efficere potest; quia ne ipsa quidem praedia mancipationem aut *in* iure cessionem recipiunt.

§ 31. These modes of creating usufruct are confined to estates in Italian soil, just as only these estates can be conveyed by mancipation or surrender. On provincial soil, usufructs and servitudes of cattle way, carriage way, watercourse, obstructing lights, not obstructing lights, and the like, must be created by convention and stipulation; for the estates themselves, the subject of these servitudes, are incapable of conveyance by mancipation or surrender.

§ 32. Et cum ususfructus et hominum et ceterorum animalium constitui possit, intellegere debemus horum usumfructum etiam in provinciis per in iure cessionem constitui posse.

§ 32. In slaves and other animals usufruct can be created even on provincial soil by surrender before a magistrate.

§ 33. Quod autem diximus usumfructum in iure cessionem tantum recipere, non est temere dictum, quamvis etiam per mancipationem constitui possit eo quod in mancipanda proprietate detrahi potest: non enim ipse ususfructus mancipatur, sed cum in mancipanda proprietate deducatur, eo fit, ut aput alium ususfructus, aput alium proprietas sit.

§ 33. My recent statement that usufruct was only conveyed by surrender was not inaccurate, although it may to this extent be created by mancipation that we may mancipate the property and reserve the usufruct; for the usufruct itself is not mancipated, although the mancipation of the property and reservation of the usufruct separates the holder of the usufruct from the holder of the property.

§ 34. Hereditas quoque in iure cessionem tantum recipit.

§ 34. Inheritances also are only alienable by surrender.

§ 35. Nam si is ad quem ab intestato legitimo iure pertinet hereditas in iure eam alii ante aditionem cedat, id est ante quam heres extiterit, perinde fit heres is cui in iure cesserit, ac si ipse per legem ad hereditatem vocatus esset: post obligationem vero si ce*ss*erit, nihilominus ips*e* heres permanet et ob id creditoribus tenebitur, debita vero pereunt, eoque modo debitores he-

§ 35. If the person entitled in intestacy by agnation surrender the inheritance before acceptance, that is to say, before his heirship is consummated, the surrenderee becomes heir just as if he was entitled by agnation; but if the agnate surrenders after acceptance, in spite of the surrender he continues heir and answerable to the creditors, his rights of action are extinguished

reditarii lucrum faciunt; corpora vero eius hereditatis perinde transeunt ad eum cui cessa est hereditas, ac si ei singula in iure cessa fuissent.

and thus the debtors to the estate are discharged of liability without payment, while the property in the corporeal subjects of the inheritance passes to the surrenderee just as if they were separately surrendered.

§ 36. Testamento autem scriptus heres ante aditam quidem hereditatem in iure cedendo eam alii nihil agi*t*; postea vero quam adierit si cedat, ea accidunt quae proxime diximus de eo ad quem ab intestato legitimo iure pertinet hereditas, si post obligationem *in* iure cedat.

§ 36. A devisee's surrender before acceptance is inoperative: after acceptance it has the operation just ascribed to the agnate's surrender of an intestate succession after acceptance.

§ 37. Idem et de necessariis heredibus diversae scholae auctores existimant, quod nihil videtur interesse utrum *aliquis* adeundo hereditatem fiat heres, an invitus existat: quod quale sit, suo loco appare*b*it. sed nostri praeceptores putant nihil agere necessarium heredem, cum in iure cedat hereditatem.

§ 37. So has a surrender by a necessary successor according to the other school, because it seems immaterial whether a man is a voluntary or an involuntary successor (a distinction that will be explained hereafter): according to my school a necessary heir's surrender of the inheritance is inoperative.

§ 38. Obligationes quoquo modo contractae nihil eorum recipiunt. nam quod mihi ab aliquo debetur, id si velim tibi deberi, nullo eorum modo quibus res corporales ad alium transferuntur id efficere possum; sed opus est, ut iubente me tu ab eo stipuleris: quae res efficit, ut a me liberetur et incipiat tibi teneri: quae dicitur novatio obligationis.

§ 38. Obligations, in whatever way contracted, are incapable of transmission by either method. If I wish to transfer my claim against a third person, none of the modes whereby corporeal things are transferred is effective: but I must order the alienee to bind the debtor by stipulation: whereupon my debtor is discharged of his debt to me and becomes liable to the alienee; which transformation of a debt is called novation.

§ 39. Sine hac vero novatione non poteris tuo nomine agere, sed debes ex persona mea quasi cognitor aut procurator meus experiri.

§ 39. In default of such novation he cannot sue in his own name, but must sue in my name as my cognitor or procurator.

§ 31. It appears that convention (pactio) alone unaccompanied by tradition or quasi tradition was capable of creating a servitude, in opposition to the general rule of Roman law, that convention can only create at the utmost an obligation (jus in personam), and in order to create a jus in rem must be accompanied by delivery of possession. Other exceptional instances in which convention without any further accompaniment creates a jus in rem, that is, transfers either property or jus in re, are hypotheca (see 3 § 91) and societas omnium bonorum (see 3 § 148).

The nature of the servitude altius tollendi is not explained in our sources and is not easy to conjecture. My right of increasing the height of my building, and thus obstructing the lights of my neighbour, would seem to be part and parcel of my unlimited rights of dominion: and, if a dispute arose, one would think that the burden of proof would be on my neighbour, who would have to prove a special limitation of my rights as owner of a praedium serviens and a special right residing in himself as owner of a praedium dominans: that is to say, that instead of my having to prove a servitude or jus altius tollendi, my neighbour would have to prove a servitude or jus altius non tollendi. Cum eo qui tollendo obscurat vicini aedes quibus non serviat nulla competit actio, Dig. 8, 2, 9. 'A man who by building obscures his neighbour's lights, unless subject to a servitude, is not actionable.' Altius aedificia tollere, si domus servitutem non debeat, dominus ejus minime prohibetur, Cod. 3, 34, 8. 'A man cannot be prevented from raising the height of his house unless it is subject to a servitude.' None of the explanations that have been proposed is satisfactory, and we must content ourselves with quoting from the Digest one instance in which the necessity of proving a jus altius tollendi is intelligible. If my neighbour asserted against me a servitude altius non tollendi, i. e. sought by action to prevent my exercising my indefinite powers of dominion, I might decline to defend the action and thus avoid a judicial decision; but as a penalty for this I was not allowed afterwards to exercise my alleged right without first proving judicially in the form of a servitude a jus altius tollendi, Dig. 39, 1, 15. This was a particular application of the general rule of procedure in real actions, that if the defendant or person in possession of the contested right declined to defend himself in the course prescribed by law, by giving securities, &c., he was put out of possession; and, if he afterwards wished to exercise his right, must first recover possession of it as plaintiff in a suit, 4 § 88.

§ 34. The statement that an inheritance is not mancipable may seem inconsistent with what we are afterwards told of the testament by bronze and balance, § 102. There is, however, no real inconsistency. The subject mancipated in the will by bronze and balance, though a universitas, was not an inheritance—there was no inheritance to mancipate, for nemo est heres viventis—but the collective rights—familia, patrimonium—of the testator.

§ 38. The mode of transferring obligations may be more properly considered hereafter, when we examine the titles by which Jus in personam originates or terminates.

DE USUCAPIONIBUS.

§ 40. Sequitur ut admoneamus aput peregrinos quidem unum esse dominium: ita *a*ut dominus quisque est, aut dominus non intellegitur. Quo iure etiam populus Romanus olim utebatur: aut enim ex iure Quiritium unusquisque dominus erat, aut non intellegebatur dominus. set postea divisionem accepit dominium, ut alius possit esse ex iure Quiritium dominus, alius in bonis habere.

§ 40. We must next observe that for aliens there is only one dominion and only one definition of a proprietor, and so it was in ancient times with the people of Rome, for a man had either quiritary dominion or none at all. They afterwards decomposed dominion so that one person might have quiritary dominion over a subject over which another person had bonitary dominion.

§ 41. Nam si tibi rem mancipi neque mancipavero neque in iure cessero, sed tantum tradidero, in bonis quidem tuis ea res efficitur, ex iure Quiritium vero mea permanebit, donec tu eam possidendo usucapias: *s*emel enim impleta usucapione proinde pleno iure incipit, id est et in bonis et ex iure Quiritium tua res esse, ac si ea mancipata vel in iure cessa *esset*.

§ 41. If a mancipable thing is neither mancipated nor surrendered by default in a fictitious vindication but simply delivered, the bonitary dominion passes to the alienee, but the quiritary dominion remains in the alienor until the alienee acquires it by usucapion; for as soon as usucapion is completed, plenary dominion, that is, the union of bonitary and quiritary dominion, vests in the alienee just as if he had taken by mancipation or surrender before a magistrate.

§ 42. *Usucapio autem* mobilium quidem rerum anno completur, fundi vero et aedium biennio; et ita lege XII tabularum cautum est.

§ 42. Usucapion of movables requires a year's possession for its completion, of land and houses, two years' possession, a rule which dates from the law of the Twelve Tables.

§ 43. Ceterum etiam earum rerum usucapio nobis competit quae non a domino nobis traditae fuerint, sive mancipi sint *e*ae res sive nec mancipi, si modo ea bona fide acceperimus, cum crederemus eum qui tra*di*derit dominum esse.

§ 43. Quiritary dominion may also be acquired by usucapion even on a non-proprietor's delivery of possession, and in things either mancipable or not mancipable, if they are delivered to an innocent alienee who believes the deliverer to be proprietor.

§ 44. Quod ideo receptum videtur, ne rerum dominia diutius in incerto essent: cum sufficeret domino ad inquirendam rem suam anni aut biennii spatium, quod tempus ad usucapionem possessori tributum est.

§ 44. The reason of the law appears to be the inexpediency of allowing dominion to be long unascertained, the original proprietor having ample time to look after his property in the year or two years which must elapse before usucapion is complete.

§ 45. Set aliquando etiamsi maxime quis bona fide alienam rem possideat, numquam tamen illi usucapio procedit, velut si qui rem furtivam aut vi possessam possideat; nam furtivam lex XII tabularum usucapi prohibet, vi possessam lex Iulia et Plautia.

§ 45. Some things, however, notwithstanding the good faith of the possessor, cannot be acquired by usucapion, things, for instance, of which the owner lost possession by theft or violence, stolen things being declared incapable of usucapion by the law of the Twelve Tables, and things taken with violence by the lex Julia and Plautia.

§ 46. Item provincialia praedia usucapionem *non* recipiunt.

§ 46. So, too, provincial land and houses are incapable of usucapion.

§ 47. *Item olim* mulieris quae in agnatorum tutela erat res mancipi usucapi non poterant, praeterquam si ab ipsa tutore *auctore* traditae essent: id*que* ita lege XII tabularum cau*tum erat.*

§ 47. Formerly, when a woman was under her agnate's guardianship, her mancipable things were not subject to usucapion, unless she herself delivered possession of them with her guardian's authority, and this was an ordinance of the Twelve Tables.

§ 48. Item liberos homines et res sacras et religiosas usucapi non posse manifestum est.

§ 48. Free men, also, and things sacred or religious, are obviously not susceptible of usucapion.

§ 49. Quod ergo vulgo dicitur furtivarum rerum et vi possessarum usucapionem per legem XII tabularum prohibitam esse, non eo pertinet, ut *ne ipse* fur *quive per* vim *possidet*, usucapere *pos*sit (nam huic ali*a* ratione usucapio non competit, quia scilicet mala fide possidet): sed nec ullus alius, quamquam ab eo bona fide emerit, usucapiendi ius habeat.

§ 49. The common statement that in things stolen or violently possessed, usucapion is barred by the law of the Twelve Tables, means, not that the thief or violent dispossessor is incapable of usucapion, for he is barred by another cause, his guilty knowledge; but that even an innocent purchaser from him is incapable of acquiring by usucapion.

§ 50. Unde in rebus mobilibus non facile *procedit, ut bonae fidei possessori usucapio com*petat, quia qui alienam rem vendidit et tradidit furtum committit: idemque accidit, etiam si ex ali*a* causa tradatur. Set tamen hoc aliquando aliter se habet.

§ 50. Accordingly, in things movable an innocent possessor can seldom acquire dominion by usucapion, because he that sells and delivers, or otherwise bargains and delivers, possession of a thing belonging to another, is guilty of theft.

nam si heres rem defuncto commodatam aut locatam *vel* aput eu*m* depositam, existimans eam esse hereditariam, vendiderit aut donaverit, furtum non committit. item si is ad quem ancillae ususfructus pertinet, partum et*iam* suum esse credens vendiderit aut donaverit, furtum non committit; *f*urtum enim sine affectu furandi non committitur. aliis quoque modis accidere potest, ut quis sine vitio furti rem alienam ad aliquem transferat et efficiat, ut a possessore usucapiatur.

However, this admits of exception, for an heir who believes a thing lent or let to, or deposited with, his ancestor to be a portion of the inheritance, and sells it or gives it away, is not guilty of theft: again, the usufructuary of a female slave who believes her offspring to be his property and sells it or gives it away, is not guilty of theft; for theft implies unlawful intention: and similarly other circumstances may prevent the crime of theft from attaching to the delivery of a thing belonging to another, and enable the receiver to acquire by usucapion.

§ 51. Fundi quoque alieni potest aliquis *s*ine *vi* possessionem nancisci, quae vel ex negligentia domini vacet, vel qu*ia* dominus sine successore decesserit vel longo tempore afuerit. nam si ad alium bona fide accipientem transtulerit, po*t*erit usucapere possessor; et quamvis ipse qui vacantem possessionem nactus est, intellegat alienum esse fun*d*um, *tamen* nihil hoc *bonae fidei* possessori ad *us*ucapionem nocet, *cum* inprobata sit eorum *sen*tentia qui putaverint furti*vum* fundum fieri po*ss*e.

§ 51. Land belonging to another may be entered without violence, when vacant by neglect of the owner, or by his death without leaving a successor, or his long absence from the country, and an innocent person to whom the possession is transferred may acquire the property by usucapion; for though the original seizer of the vacant possession knew that the land belongs to another, yet his knowledge is no bar to the usucapion of the innocent alienee, as it is no longer held that theft can be committed of land.

§ 52. Ru*rs*us ex contrario accidit, ut qui sciat alienam r*em* se possidere usucapiat: velut si rem hereditariam cuius po*ss*essionem heres nondum nactus est, aliquis pos*se*derit; nam ei concessum *est usucapere*, si modo ea res est quae recipit usucapionem. quae species possessionis et usucapionis pro herede vocatur.

§ 52. On the other hand, knowledge of the existence of a proprietor does not always prevent usucapion, for any one may seize a portion of an inheritance of which the heir has not yet taken possession and acquire it by usucapion, provided it is susceptible of usucapion, and he is said to acquire by title of quasi successor.

§ 53. Et in tantum haec usucapio concessa est, ut et res quae solo continentur anno usucapiantur.

§ 53. With such facility is this usucapion permitted that even land may be thus acquired in a year.

§ 54. Quare autem etiam hoc casu soli rerum annua constituta sit usucapio, illa ratio est, quod o*l*im rerum hereditariarum posses-

§ 54. The reason why even land in these circumstances demands only a year for usucapion is, that in ancient times the possession of portions

sione *velut* ipsae hereditates usucapi credebantur, scilicet anno. lex enim XII tabularum soli quidem res biennio usucapi iussit, ceteras vero anno. ergo hereditas in ceteris rebus videbatur esse, quia soli non est, quia neque corporalis est: *et* quamvis postea creditum sit ipsas hereditates usucapi non posse, tamen in omnibus rebus hereditariis, etiam quae solo tenentur, annua usucapio remansit.

of the inheritance was held to be a means of acquiring the inheritance itself, and that, of course, in a year: for while the law of the Twelve Tables fixed two years for the usucapion of land, and one year for the usucapion of other things, an inheritance was held to fall under the category of 'other things,' as it is neither land nor corporeal: and though it was afterwards held that the universal succession was not acquirable by usucapion, yet the component hereditaments, including land, continued acquirable by a year's possession.

§ 55. Quare autem omnino tam inproba possessio et usucapio concessa sit, illa ratio est, quod voluerunt veteres maturius hereditates adiri, ut essent qui sacra facerent, quorum illis temporibus summa observatio fuit, et ut creditores haberent a quo suum consequerentur.

§ 55. The motive for permitting at all so unscrupulous an acquisition was the wish of the ancient legislator to accelerate the acceptance of successions, and thus provide persons to perform the sacred rites, to which in those days the highest importance was attached, and to ascertain the persons whom creditors might sue for payment of their claims.

§ 56. Haec autem species possessionis et usucapionis etiam lucrativa vocatur: nam sciens quisque rem alienam lucrifacit.

§ 56. This mode of acquisition is sometimes called gratuitous usucapion, for the possessor has notice of another's ownership.

§ 57. Sed hoc tempore etiam non est lucrativa. nam ex auctoritate Hadriani senatusconsultum factum est, ut tales usucapiones revocarentur; et ideo potest heres ab eo qui rem usucepit, hereditatem petendo perinde eam rem consequi, atque si usucapta non esset.

§ 57. In the present day, however, it is ineffectual, for the Senate on the motion of Hadrian decreed that such usucapions are revocable, and the heir by suing for the inheritance may recover possession just as if the property had never been transmuted.

§ 58. Et necessario tamen herede extante ipso iure pro herede usucapi potest.

§ 58. Even a necessary heir, however, by the civil law may lose portions of his inheritance by this usucapion.

§ 59. *Ad*huc etiam ex aliis causis sciens quisque rem alienam usucapit. nam qui rem alicui fiduciae causa mancipio dederit vel in iure cesserit, si eandem ipse possederit, potest usucapere, anno scilicet, et*iam* soli si sit. quae species usucapionis di-

§ 59. There are other conditions under which a knowledge of another's ownership is no bar to usucapion. After a fiduciary mancipation or surrender of his property, if the owner subsequently has possession of it, he recovers his do-

citur usureceptio, quia id quod aliquando habuimus recipimus per usucapionem.

minion even over land in the period of a year, by what is called a possessive recovery, because a foregoing dominion is thereby reacquired.

§ 60. Sed cum fiducia contrahitur aut cum creditore pignoris iure, aut cum amico, quod tutius nostrae res aput eum essent, si quidem cum amico contracta sit fiducia, sane omni modo conpetit usus receptio; si vero cum creditore, soluta quidem pecunia omni modo conpetit, nondum vero soluta ita demum competit, si neque conduxerit eam rem a creditore debitor, neque precario rogaverit, ut eam rem possidere liceret; quo casu lucratiua usucapio conpetit.

§ 60. The fiduciary alienee is either a creditor in the position of mortgagee or a friend and protector of the alienor's property in the character of depositary: in the latter case the owner is always capable of possessive recovery: if the alienee is a creditor, the owner can always re-acquire after payment of the debt; but before payment of the debt he can only re-acquire provided he has not hired the thing of his creditor nor possessed it in consequence of request and licence, and thus he re-acquires without giving a consideration.

§ 61. Item si rem obligatam sibi populus vendiderit, *eamque* dominus possederit, concessa est usus receptio: sed hoc casu praedium biennio usurecipitur. et hoc est quod volgo dicitur ex praediatura possessionem usurecipi. nam qui mercatur a populo praediator appellatur.

§ 61. Again, the owner of a thing mortgaged to the state and sold for non-payment of the mortgage debt may re-acquire it by possession, but in this case, if it is land, usucapion is biennial: and this is the meaning of the saying, that after praediatura (a public sale) land is recoverable by (biennial) possession, a purchaser from the state being called praediator.

Roman law originally only recognized one kind of dominion, called emphatically, quiritary dominion. Gradually, however, certain real rights arose which though they failed to satisfy all the elements of the definition of quiritary dominion, were practically its equivalent, and received from the courts a similar protection. These real rights might fall short of quiritary dominion in three respects, (1) either in respect of the persons in whom they resided, (2) or of the subjects to which they related, (3) or of the title by which they were acquired.

(1.) To be capable of quiritary dominion a man must have one of the elements of a Roman citizenship. Jus quiritium, right quiritary, sometimes, indeed, denotes all the elements of civitas Romana, Roman citizenship: see 3 § 72. Beneficio principali Latinus civitatem Romanam accipit si ab imperatore jus quiritium impetraverit, Ulpian 3, 2. But the only element of citizenship required for quiritary dominion was commercium, and as we have seen that the Latinus possessed commercium without connubium, the Latinus was capable of quiritary dominion. The alien (peregrinus) on the contrary was incapable: yet he had an equivalent real right, called by Gaius dominion, § 40, which he acquired by titles of natural law (jus gentium), e. g. tradition, occupation, accession, praescriptio, &c., and could maintain by a real action in the court of the praetor peregrinus or praeses provinciae.

(2.) Provincial land was not capable of quiritary dominion. Originally, indeed, private dominion appears to have been confined to movables; and immovables, at least lands, were only subject to the other kind of dominion, public dominion or communism. Private dominion, however, first invaded a portion of the land, to which it was confined within the historic period, and finally superseded public dominion over all the ancient Roman territory; and ager publicus, as opposed to ager privatus, ceased to exist on Italian soil. But in the provinces subsequently conquered, land continued to the end subject exclusively to public dominion; and thus the essential feature of feudal tenure, the exclusive vesting of absolute or ultimate dominion over land in the sovereign, a principle commonly supposed to have been first introduced into Europe by the invading German hordes, had already existed in full force over by far the greater portion of the Roman world. It is true that the provinces were divided into so-called ager publicus and ager privatus; but ager privatus, as well as ager publicus, was subject to a vectigal, and the tenant of the one and lessee of the other were equally devoid of absolute ownership. An estate in ager privatus was acquirable by titles of natural law (jus gentium) and recoverable by real action (vindicatio), and was sometimes called dominion; but was theoretically only possessio or ususfructus, § 7.

(3.) Bonitary dominion was distinct both from alien dominion and from dominion over provincial land: it may be defined as the property of a Roman citizen in a subject capable of quiritary property, acquired by a title not known to the civil law, but introduced by the praetor, and protected by his imperium or supreme executive power. Thus: we have seen that only non-mancipable things were capable at civil law of transfer by tradition; suppose, now, that a mancipable thing were conveyed to a vendee by tradition; the process would not make him proprietor; he would be merely a bona fide possessor, until by the lapse of a year or of two years he acquired quiritary property by usucapion. The praetor, however, assisted the less cumbrous mode of alienation by treating the vendee as proprietor; by giving him, if in possession, the exceptio rei venditae et traditae against the vendor who sought to recover as quiritary proprietor, and enabling the vendee, if dispossessed, to recover against the world by a vindication based on a fiction of usucapion (actio in rem publiciana, 4 § 36). Bonitary proprietorship, or proprietorship acquired by titles unknown to the civil law, when once invented, was employed by the praetor in other legislative innovations, particularly, as we shall see hereafter, in creating universal successions (bonorum possessio) in bankruptcy, and universal successors unknown to the civil law in testamentary and intestate devolution. These bonitary proprietors could assert their rights by an action, real or personal, based on a fiction of inheritance (formula Serviana, 4 § 35), or an action, real or personal, not based on fiction, but in which they appeared as procurators of the original proprietor (formula Rutiliana, 4 § 35).

The barbarous term Bonitary (formed from the classical, in bonis esse, in bonis habere), has the authority of Theophilus, who speaks of δεσπότης βονιτάριος, 1, 5, 4; he also calls bonitary dominion natural dominion (φυσικὴ δεσποτεία), as opposed to statutory, civil, or quiritary dominion (ἔννομος δεσποτεία).

The only substantial inferiority in later times of the bonitary to the quiritary proprietor was that the former was incapable of giving by manumission more than latina libertas, 1 § 213, so that after Latinitas was abolished Justinian could truly say that the difference between the two kinds of ownership was merely nominal, Cod. 7, 25.

§ 43. Quiritary dominion, as separated from bonitary dominion, was called nudum jus quiritium. After Justinian had abolished the nudum jus quiritium, Cod. 7, 25, and the distinction of things mancipable and things not mancipable, Cod. 7, 31, and, consequently, the distinction between bonitary and quiritary dominion, we might have expected that the actio Publiciana, which, as we have just seen, originated in the distinction between things mancipable and things not mancipable, would have become obsolete. We find it, however, still treated as an important remedy in Justinian's legislation. The reason is, that this remedy was not only applicable to the alienation by tradition of a mancipable thing, the application we have hitherto considered, but to the alienation of anything whatever by a non-proprietor to an innocent alienee. Usucapion, as in the former case, would in the lapse of time have given the alienee plenary dominion, and, with it, vindication in the event of a loss of possession; but if he lost possession while usucapion was still incomplete, he would have had no remedy (for, not being owner, he could not vindicate), if the praetor had not allowed him to sue by the actio Publiciana, which treated bona fide possession, that is, usucapion possession, or the inception of usucapion, as if it were plenary dominion. In the Digest this circumstance is mentioned as the sole ground on which Publiciana was maintainable, as indeed it was, after the abolition of mancipation. Si quis id quod traditur (we should probably read, Si quis quid traditum) ex justa causa non a domino, et nondum usucaptum petet, judicium dabo, Dig. 6, 2, pr. 'On delivery for a just consideration by a non-proprietor, and before usucapion, the alienee shall have an action to recover possession.' In the intentio of this action the plaintiff set out the contract or other justa causa which preceded tradition, 4 § 36, whereas, in an ordinary vindication, he merely asserted his ownership in general terms.

§ 45. Lex Plautia was passed by the tribune Marcus Plautius after the Social war, B.C. 59. Lex Julia de vi publica seu privata is supposed to have been enacted about the middle of the reign of Augustus.

§§ 52—58. A successor (heres) was either voluntarius, empowered to accept or reject the succession, or necessarius, designated without any such power of election. Heres voluntarius was either an agnate entitled to succeed an intestate, or any devisee, not being a child of the testator, entitled under a will. Heres necessarius was either a manumitted slave, or a self-successor (suus heres), that is, a child under power of the testator or intestate, § 152. In every case but that of the suus heres, so long as the heir had not taken possession, any stranger was permitted to seize parts of the inheritance and acquire property therein by usucapion. The only title (causa, titulus) required for this acquisition was the overture or delation of the inheritance and vacancy of possession. The possession which Gaius (§ 52) calls pro herede (see Dig. 5, 3, 9) is more properly called pro possessore. Pro possessore vero possidet praedo, qui interrogatus cur possideat, responsurus sit, quia possideo, nec contendit se heredem vel per mendacium, nec ullam causam possessionis possit dicere, ibid. 'Possessor, as possessor, is the robber, who, asked why he possesses, answers, "Because I possess," and does not claim to be heir even mendaciously, and has no title of possession to allege.' The constitution of Hadrian (Sc. Juventianum) did not prevent the usucapion, but made it nugatory by allowing the heir to recover the hereditaments by real action (hereditatis petitio, or the interdict Quorum bonorum), just as if the usucapion had never been completed. The word 'however,' § 58, appears to be an admission of Gaius, that the reason he has suggested for this eccentric rule, the wish to ascertain speedily the person bound to perform the sacred rites and to satisfy the creditors, is inadequate, as the seizure and usucapion was permitted even when an enfranchised slave was heir, when, that is to say, the alleged motive could not operate, as a manumitted slave is a necessary and immediate successor. Indeed, in 3 § 201, Gaius speaks as if it were exclusively against the enfranchised slave, and not against the voluntarius heres, that this mode of acquisition was permitted by the law; but his language admits of explanation. Gaius is there illustrating the proposition that a man may acquire by usucapion a thing which he is aware already has a proprietor. Now in the interval before a heres voluntarius has accepted the succession, the interval during which strangers would be most likely to seize portions of the inheritance, these portions would be res nullius, § 9, would have no proprietor, and therefore could not illustrate the proposition that res aliena, i.e. res alicujus, was capable of usucapion in spite of the acquirer's knowledge of existing ownership. Gaius, therefore, takes no notice of usucapion against heres voluntarius, and only quotes the usucapion against the enfranchised slave.

The only successor who was not liable to be thus plundered was the suus heres. Nihil pro herede posse usucapi, suis heredibus existentibus, magis obtinuit, Cod. 7, 29, 2. 'That no stranger can acquire as quasi-heir by usucapion against a self-successor, is an established rule of law.'

The person who seized possession of the vacant hereditament, as we see in the last-quoted passage, was said to possess as quasi-heir (pro herede). Possession pro herede is probably the explanation of an enigmatical rule in Roman law: ipsum sibi causam possessionis mutare non posse, Dig. 41, 3, 33, 1; causam possessionis neminem sibi mutare posse, Dig. 41, 5, 2, 1. 'No man can change at pleasure his title of possession.' With the intention, apparently, of limiting the operation of possessio pro herede, an anomalous institution of questionable expediency, the rule declares that a person who commences his possession or detention of a thing in the character of a vendee from a non-proprietor, or as lessee, borrower, depositary, or even thief, shall not be able, on the death of the true proprietor, to accelerate or initiate usucapion by merely professing that he ceases to hold in his former character and proceeds to hold as possessor pro herede.

Possession pro herede was perhaps the germ of the intestate succession of next of kin or cognati, a succession, as we shall see, not originally recognized in Roman law; at least, the family or next of kin of an intestate would generally have the best chance of seizing any movables or immovables that he left; and perhaps it was this equitable result, no less than the object mentioned by Gaius, that, in the absence of a regular succession of cognati, led the public to look on possessio pro herede as a rational and salutary institution.

The institution of possessio lucrativa pro herede, or rather the Sc. Juventianum by which it was defeated, has left its traces in the formula, still to be found in the Digest, of the interdict Quorum bonorum, 4 § 144, the remedy whereby a person who claimed not as civil heir (heres), but as praetorian successor (bonorum possessor), established his right to succeed and recovered possession of the hereditaments. To leave these traces in the wording of the interdict was an oversight on the part of Justinian, as in his legislation the last remnants of the institution of usucapio pro herede had been definitively abolished.

§ 61. The circumstances contemplated seem to be as follows: A proprietor is debtor to the state, and his lands are mortgaged as security for the debt. On default of payment, the state exercises the power of sale: if the debtor is not turned out of possession by the purchaser (praediator) in two years he recovers his proprietorship by usureception.

Provincial lands were not subject to Usucapion: they might however be acquired by an analogous title, longi temporis praescriptio, i. e. possession for ten years during the presence of the former proprietor (inter praesentes), and for twenty years during his absence (inter absentes).

Usucapion required something beyond mere possession for a certain period; and something beyond what we hereafter call Interdict possession, 4 § 148. The conditions of possession which entitled a possessor to appeal for the protection of his possession to the praetor's interdict were merely that it should be adverse (with the knowledge of the other party and without his permission), and, in respect of the other party, commenced without violence (nec vi nec clam nec precario). To produce Usucapion, possession must be based on a justa causa or titulus, such as contract or bequest; and commenced with bona fides on the part of the possessor, e. g. ignorance of the alienor's want of title, if the subject had been delivered to him by a non-proprietor; and the thing itself must be capable of Usucapion, e. g. not taken by theft or violence from the former proprietor.

Justinian remodelled the law of Usucapion. For movables he extended the period from one year to three years: for immovables he abolished the distinction between Italian and provincial land, and in every case required ten years' possession if the parties were domiciled in the same province, and twenty years possession if they were not domiciled in the same province. Further, he introduced a new usucapion (longissimi temporis praescriptio), which was governed by less stringent conditions than the ordinary usucapion (longi temporis praescriptio). It applied both to movables and immovables, was not vitiated by certain flaws in the subject (furtiva, violenta), and needed no support of any titulus, but only required bona fides in its inception on the part of the possessor, Cod. 7, 39, 8. It was completed in thirty years.

Usucapion, particularly in this its later form, requires to be carefully distinguished from the Limitation of actions (temporalis praescriptio) with which it has been coordinated by some civilians under the name of Acquisitive, as opposed to Extinctive, Prescription. We shall see, 4 § 110, that all actions were originally divided into temporales and perpetuae, temporales being such as could only be brought within a certain period (e. g. in the case of penal actions, a year) from the time when the right of action accrued, perpetuae such as were subject to no such limitation. Subsequently, however, even the latter were limited, and no action could be brought after thirty years from the nativity of the action or the time when the right of action accrued (actio nata). In the case of personal actions there is no danger of confusing Usucapion and Limitation. Usucapion implies possession, and in the case of personal actions, or jus in personam, no such thing as possession is conceivable, for possession only relates to the subjects of jus in rem. Usucapion and the Limitation of real actions are more similar, but even here a distinction may be recognized. Limitation is the extinction of a right by neglect of the person entitled, by his omission to enforce his remedy: Usucapion is the acquisition of a right by something positive on the part of the acquirer, his strictly defined possession during a certain number of years. Even extraordinary Usucapion requires, as we have seen, bona fides in the commencement of possession: no such condition is attached to Limitation or temporalis praescriptio.

English law originally only recognized Usucapion in the case of incorporeal hereditaments or servitudes, e. g. rights of way; for the acquisition of which the Prescription Act, 2 and 3 Will. 4, c. 71, requires possession during twenty years. But since the Act for the limitation of real actions, 3 and 4 Will. 4, c. 27, deprives a proprietor of land of his right as well as his remedy if he omit to bring his action to recover it within twenty years after the right accrued, Usucapion (Acquisitive prescription) in corporeal as well as incorporeal hereditaments may be said to be recognized in English law.

Besides the civil titles which we have examined, two others are mentioned by Ulpian: Singularum rerum dominia nobis adquiruntur mancipatione, traditione, in jure cessione, usucapione, adjudicatione, lege, 19, 2.

Adjudication (for the nature of which see 4 § 42), whereby property might be taken from one individual and vested in another without any of the ordinary methods of conveyance, may be compared in its operation to the vesting orders made by the Court of Chancery under the Trustee acts. When trustees are disabled by lunacy or infancy from dealing with the estates vested in them, the Court of Chancery is empowered to make orders the effect of which is that the estate becomes immediately vested in the substituted trustees as effectually as if a conveyance had been duly made by the person previously entitled to the legal estate. Another parallel is to be found in the awards of certain commissioners acting under powers given by act of parliament. Thus the order of the Inclosure commissioners for exchange and partition of land closely resembles in subject and effect the adjudicatio of a judex in the actio finium regundorum.

Lex is an ambiguous and miscellaneous title. It includes title by escheat or forfeiture (caducum) under the lex Papia Poppia, and bequest or legacy (legatum), a title deriving its validity from the lex of the Twelve Tables, Ulpian, 19, 17. Extending our view from res singulae, to which Ulpian confines himself, to universitates, lex was an apt denomination of title by will at the period when wills required the ratification of the Comitia Calata, 2 § 101, as at that time testamentary dispositions were really acts of the legislature. Title by lex in this case may be compared to conveyances by private act of parliament in English jurisprudence.

It may assist to clear our conception of title if we observe that the title 'Lege' is ambiguous, and that (1) while one of its meanings implies an absence of all title, (2) another denotes a miscellaneous group of heterogeneous titles.

(1) The only case in which Law can be said in any distinctive sense to be a cause of acquisition is privilegium or private law. The acquisition of a right by immediate grant from the sovereign (private act of the legislature, private act of parliament) is unlike the acquisition of a person entitled under some general disposition of a universal law. Acquisition by bequest or escheat is not an acquisition by law in any pre-eminent manner, but only in the same degree as is acquisition by mancipation or usucapion or any other title, for all these acquisitions are equally founded on law or the general disposition of the legislator. But in acquisition by privilegium there is properly speaking neither title nor law. Law is properly speaking a universal proposition, annexing a right or duty to a title: it knows nothing of individual persons, but stops short at classes of persons, classes, that is, defined by the title. Again, title is properly speaking a contingent fact distinct from a corresponding law: a fact which may occur an indefinite number of times, and entitle, that is, invest with rights or duties, an indefinite number of persons, in accordance with the dispositions of one and the same unchanging law. Title, loosely and inaccurately defined as a fact investing a person with a right, would include a privilege, i. e. a law conferring a right immediately on a given individual without the intervention of a fact distinguishable from the law: but title, properly defined as an intervening fact through which a law confers a right mediately, excludes privilege.

Whenever there is a genuine title and genuine law, the title is interposed between the right or duty and the person therewith invested, just as the middle term is interposed between the major and minor terms of a syllogism. E.g. All persons marked, stamped, characterized by a certain fact (B), are invested with a certain right or duty (A); a given individual person (C) bears the badge, mark, or stamp of this fact (B); therefore this individual (C) is invested with these rights or duties (A). A genuine law is only the major premiss, the universal proposition, all B is A. The conclusion, C is A, stating the rights or obligations of the individual, is a mediate or dependent proposition, depending partly on the law and partly on an independent fact, the minor premiss C is B, which often requires to be ascertained by judicial investigation. The condition, represented by the middle term, which connects or disconnects the right or duty, represented by the major term, with a person, represented by the minor term, is the title. In a privilegium we have no such premisses and no such middle term. The conjunction of C with A, the investment of an individual with rights (or the disjunction of C from A, the spoliation of his rights), is here an ungrounded proposition, unwarranted by any recognized title; in other words, unsupported by any subsumption of fact under law. (The syllogism we have indicated affords a convenient means of distinguishing an Institution from a Right or Obligation. An Institution (e. g. Property, Slavery, Tithe, Advowson) is the same thing as a Right or Obligation, but the one is abstract, the other concrete. The same major term A which as predicate of the major premiss represents an Institution, as predicate of the conclusion represents a Right or Obligation.)

(2) In Bequest and Escheat and the succession of necessarius heres there is a genuine law and a genuine title, but the law is not the title, any more than it is in any other mode of acquisition. Either because these modes include fewer voluntary acts than some closely allied modes (for instance, the necessarius heres acquires without aditio, which is a parcel of the title of voluntarius heres), or for some other reason, divers modes are lumped together under the head of acquisition by lex. The name, however, besides being a misnomer, is merely a sink or receptacle of miscellaneous unrelated titles, just as we shall find in the doctrine of obligations that miscellaneous titles (variae causarum figurae) are lumped together under the denomination of quasi-contract.

QUIBUS ALIENARE LICEAT VEL NON.

§ 62. Accidit aliquando, ut qui dominus sit aliena*ndae* rei potestatem non habeat, et qui dominus non sit *alienare* possit.

§ 62. It sometimes occurs that a proprietor has not a power of alienation, and that a non-proprietor has a power of alienation.

§ 63. Nam dotale praedium maritus invita mulier*e* per legem Iuliam

§ 63. The alienation of dower land by the husband, without the

prohibetur alienare, quamvis ipsius *sit* vel mancipatum ei dotis causa vel in iure cessum vel usucaptum. quod quidem ius utrum ad Italica tantum praedia, an etiam ad provincialia pertineat, *dubitatur*.

consent of the wife, is prohibited by the lex Julia, although, the husband is proprietor of the land by its mancipation as dower, or by surrender before a magistrate, or by usucapion. Whether this disability is confined to Italian soil, or extends to the provinces, authorities differ.

§ 64. Ex diverso agnatus furiosi curator rem furiosi alienare potest ex lege XII tabularum; item procurator, *id est cui libera administratio permissa est;* item creditor pignus ex pactione, quamvis eius ea res non sit. sed hoc forsitan ideo videatur fieri, quod voluntate debitoris intellegitur pignus alienari, qui olim pactus est, ut liceret creditori pignus vendere, si pecunia non solvatur.

§ 64. Contrariwise, an agnate, as a lunatic's committee, is empowered to aliene his property by the law of the Twelve Tables; and so is an agent, when invested by his principal with free power of administration (Inst. 2, 1, 43). Again, a pledgee, in pursuance of his convention, may aliene the pledge, though not proprietor; this, however, may be said to rest on the assent of the pledgor previously given in the contract of pledge, which empowered the pledgee to sell in default of payment.

§§ 62–64. It is conjectured that by some accidental displacement these three paragraphs have been transposed, and that in their proper order they should follow § 79 and precede § 80. There seems no good reason why they should be interposed between the titles of civil law and the titles of natural law.

§ 63. The lex Julia, relating only to Italian soil, permitted the husband to aliene the dotal land, with the consent of the wife, but prohibited its hypothecation, even with her consent. Justinian extended the prohibition to provincial soil, and to alienation with the wife's consent, Inst. 2, 8, pr.

ADQUISITIONES DOMINII NATURALES.

§ 65. Ergo ex his quae diximus adparet quaedam naturali iure alienari, qualia sunt ea quae traditione alienantur; quaedam ciuili, nam mancipationis et in iure cessionis et usucapionis ius proprium est civium Romanorum.

§ 65. Thus it appears that some modes of alienation are titles of natural law, as delivery of possession, and others of civil law, as mancipation, surrender, usucapion, for these are titles confined to citizens of Rome.

§ 66. Nec tamen ea tantum quae traditione nostra fiunt naturali nobis ratione adquiruntur, sed etiam

§ 66. Another title of natural law, besides Tradition, is Occupation, whereby things not already

quae occupando ideo *adquisierimus*, quia antea nullius essent: qualia sunt omnia quae terra, mari, coelo capiuntur.

subjects of property become the property of the first occupant, as the wild inhabitants of earth, air, and water, as soon as they are captured.

§ 67. Itaque si *feram* bestiam aut volucrem aut piscem *ceperimus*, *quidquid ita* captum *fuerit*, *id statim nostrum fit*, *et eo usque* nostrum esse intellegitur, donec nostra custodia coerceatur. cum vero custodiam nostram evaserit et in naturalem libertatem se receperit, rursus occupantis fit, quia nostr*um* esse desinit. naturalem autem libertatem recipere videtur, cum aut oculos nostros evaserit, aut licet *in* conspectu sit nostro, difficilis tamen *eius* rei persecutio sit.

§ 67. For wild beasts, birds, and fishes, as soon as they are captured, become, by natural law, the property of the captor, but only continue such so long as they continue in his power; after breaking from his custody and recovering their natural liberty, they may become the property of the next occupant; for the ownership of the first captor is terminated. Their natural liberty is deemed to be recovered when they have escaped from his sight, or, though they continue in his sight, when they are difficult to recapture.

§ 68. In iis autem animalibus quae ex consuetudine abire et redire solent, veluti columbis et apibus, item cervis qui in silvas ire et redire solent, talem habemus regulam traditam, ut si revertendi animum habere desierint, etiam nostra esse desinant et fiant occupantium. revertendi autem animum videntur desinere habere, cum revertendi consuetudinem deseruerint.

§ 68. In those wild animals, however, which are habituated to go away and return, as pigeons, and bees, and deer, which habitually visit the forests and return, the rule has been handed down, that only the cessation of the instinct of returning is the termination of ownership, and then the property in them is acquired by the next occupant; the instinct of returning is held to be lost when the habit of returning is discontinued.

§ 69. Ea quoque quae ex hostibus capiuntur naturali ratione nostra fiunt.

§ 69. Capture from an enemy is another title of property by natural law.

§ 70. Sed et id quod per alluvionem nobis adicitur eodem iure nostrum fit. per alluvionem autem *id* videtur adici quod ita paulatim flumen agro nostro *adicit*, ut aestimare non possimus quantum quoquo momento temporis adiciatur. hoc est quod volgo dicitur, per adluvionem id adici videri quod ita paulatim adicitur, ut oculos nostros fallat.

§ 70. Alluvion is another mode of acquisition by the same code. Alluvion is an addition of soil to land by a river, so gradual that in short periods the change is imperceptible; or, to use the common expression, a latent addition.

§ 71. Quod si flumen partem aliquam ex tuo praedio de*traxe*rit et ad meum praedium *a*ttulerit, haec pars tua manet.

§ 71. But a parcel of your land swept away by a river, and carried down to mine, continues your property.

§ 72. At si in medio flumine insula nata sit, haec eorum omnium communis est qui ab utraque parte fluminis prope ripam praedia possident. si vero non sit in medio flumine, ad eos pertinet qui ab ea parte quae proxuma est iuxta ripam praedia habent.

§ 72. An island that rises in the middle of a river is the common property of the proprietors on both banks of the river; if it is not in the middle of the stream, it belongs to the proprietors of the nearer bank.

§ 73. Praeterea id quod in solo nostro ab aliquo aedificatum est, quamvis ille suo nomine aedificaverit, iure naturali nostrum fit, quia superficies solo cedit.

§ 73. Again, a building erected on my soil, though in the name and for the use of the builder, belongs to me; for the ownership of a superstructure follows the ownership of the soil.

§ 74. Multoque magis id accidit et in planta quam quis in solo nostro posuerit, si modo radicibus terram complexa fuerit.

§ 74. The same occurs a fortiori when trees are planted on my land, as soon as they strike root.

§ 75. Idem contingit et in *frumento* quod in solo nostro ab aliquo satum fuerit.

§ 75. Similarly, when corn is sown on my land.

§ 76. Sed si ab eo petamus fructum vel aedificium, et inpensas in aedificium vel in seminaria vel in sementem factas ei solvere nolimus, poterit nos per exceptionem doli repellere; utique si bonae fidei possessor fuerit.

§ 76. But if I bring an action to recover the produce or the building, and refuse to compensate the other party for his outlay on the building or the plantation or the cornfield, he will defeat my action by the plea of fraud, if he was an innocent possessor.

§ 77. Eadem ratione probatum est, quod in *ch*artulis sive membranis meis aliquis scripserit, licet aureis litteris, meum esse, quia litter*ae* *ch*artulis sive membranis cedunt. itaque si ego eos libr*o*s easque membranas petam, nec inpensam scripturae solvam, per exceptionem doli mali summoveri potero.

§ 77. Similarly, the writing inscribed on my paper or parchment, even in letters of gold, is acquired to me, for the property in the letters follows the property in the paper or parchment; but if I sue for the books or parchment without offering compensation for the writing, my action will be defeated by the plea of fraud.

§ 78. Sed si in tabula mea aliquis pinxerit velut imaginem, contra probatur: magis enim dicitur tabulam pictur*ae* cedere. cuius diversitatis vix idonea ratio redditur. ce*r*te secundum hanc regulam si me possidente petas imaginem tuam esse, nec solvas pretium tabulae, poteris per exceptionem doli mali summoveri. at si tu possideas, consequens est, ut utilis mihi actio ad-

§ 78. The canvas belonging to me, on which another man has painted a picture, is subject to a different rule, for the ownership of the canvas is held to follow the ownership of the painting: a difference which scarcely rests on a sufficient reason. By this rule, if I am in possession, and you claim the painting without offering the price of the canvas, I may defeat your

versum te dari debeat: quo casu nisi solvam impensam picturae, poteris me per exceptionem doli mali repellere, utique si bona fide possessor fueris. illud palam est, quod sive tu subripuisses tabulam sive alius, conpetit mihi furti actio.

claim by the plea of fraud. If you are in possession, I may claim the reconveyance of the canvas in a modified action, but unless I offer the price of the painting, you defeat me by pleading fraud, if you are an innocent possessor. It is certain, that, if you or another purloined the canvas, I can bring an action of theft.

§ 79. In aliis quoque speciebus naturalis ratio requiritur: proinde si ex uvis *aut olivis aut spicis* meis vinum aut oleum aut frumentum feceris, quaeritur utrum meum sit id vinum aut oleum aut frumentum, an tuum. item si ex auro aut argento meo vas aliquod feceris, aut ex meis tabulis navem aut armarium aut subsellium fabricaveris; item si ex lana mea vestimentum feceris, vel si ex vino et melle meo mulsum feceris, sive ex medicamentis meis emplastrum aut collyrium feceris: *quaeritur, utrum tuum sit id quod ex meo effeceris,* an meum. quidam materiam et substantiam spectandam esse putant, id est, ut cuius materia sit, illius et res quae facta sit videatur esse; idque maxime placuit Sabino et Cassio. alii vero *eius rem* esse putant qui fecerit; idque maxime diversae scholae auctoribus visum est: sed eum quoque cuius materia et substantia fuerit, furti adversus eum qui subripuerit habere actionem; nec minus adversus eundem condictionem ei competere, quia extinctae res, licet vindicari non possint, condici tamen furibus et quibusdam aliis possessoribus possunt.

§ 79. On a change of species, also, we have recourse to natural law to determine the proprietor. Thus, if grapes, or olives, or sheaves, belonging to me, are converted by another into wine, or oil, or corn, a question arises whether the property in the corn, wine, or oil, is in me, or in the author of the conversion; or if my gold or silver is manufactured into a vessel, or a ship, chest, or chair is constructed from my timber, or my wool is made into cloth, or my wine and honey are made into mead, or my drugs into a plaster or eye-salve, it becomes a question whether the property in the new product is vested in me or in the manufacturer. According to some, the material or substance is the criterion; that is to say, the owner of the material is to be deemed the owner of the product; and this was the doctrine of Sabinus and Cassius; according to others, the ownership of the product is in the manufacturer, and this was the doctrine of the opposite school; who also held that the owner of the substance or material could maintain an action of theft against the purloiner, or an action for reconveyance, because, though the destruction of property is a bar to a vindication, it is no bar to a personal action against the thief and certain other possessors.

§ 65. Tradition or transfer of possession, as we have seen, was admitted in the civil law as a mode of transferring quiritary property in such non-mancipable things as were corporeal: in mancipable things it could only transfer bonitary property. In Justinian's time Tradition had superseded Surrender in court and Mancipation; and transfer of possession was the universal solemnity for transfer of dominion.

If we consider Surrender, Mancipation, Tradition, we shall see that they are only three forms of one identical title, Alienation. The substance or essence of the title, the intention on the one side to transfer property, on the other to accept it, is the same in all three; it is only the adventitious or accidental or evidentiary (3 § 92) portion of the title in which they differ.

Although delivery of possession, like the solemnities of mancipation and surrender, is, as compared with the will or intention of the parties, only an evidentiary and symbolic part of the title, yet both parcels, the external as well as the internal act, are indispensable in the transfer of dominion. Traditionibus et usucapionibus dominia rerum, non nudis pactis, transferuntur, Cod. 2, 3, 20. 'Tradition and usucapion, not naked convention, operate a transfer of dominion.' We have already noticed exceptions to this rule in the case of servitus, hypotheca, societas, 1 § 31. Again, Nunquam nuda traditio transfert dominium sed ita si venditio vel aliqua justa causa praecesserit propter quam traditio sequeretur, Dig. 41, 1, 31. 'Naked delivery does not transfer property, but must be based on contract of sale or some other sufficient inducement.' It is clear that mere Tradition, or transfer of physical control, without any further element of Title, cannot pass Dominion, for in Loan for use (commodatum) tradition merely passes Detention without Possession; in Pledge (pignus), it passes Possession without Property; in Deposit, it sometimes passes Detention and sometimes Possession. The cases in which Property is passed by Tradition may be reduced to three classes, traditio donandi animo, traditio credendi animo, and traditio solvendi animo. In the first, it simply confers property on the donee; in the second, it confers property on the transferee, and subjects him to an obligation; in the third, it confers property on the transferee, and discharges the transferror of an obligation. In the two latter cases, i. e. tradition by way of loan (mutui datio) and tradition by way of payment (solutio), the titulus, or justa causa accompanying tradition, contains much that is unessential to the transfer of dominion, the only absolutely essential element being the intention of the parties to give and take dominion. In Donation, the justa causa traditionis consists solely of this essential element.

The justa causa, then, which must accompany tradition, is the animus or voluntas transferendi dominii, and this, apparently, is given as the whole of the matter in a passage of Gaius quoted in the Digest: Hae quoque res, quae traditione nostrae fiunt, jure gentium nobis acquiruntur; nihil enim tam conveniens est naturali aequitati, quam voluntatem domini volentis rem suam in alium transferre ratam haberi, Dig. 41, 1, 9, 3. 'Tradition is a natural mode of acquisition, for it is a plain dictate of reason that the will of an owner to transfer his ownership to another should be allowed to take effect.'

Delivery sometimes precedes the intention to transfer, for instance, in a conditional sale: in which case the transfer of property is suspended until the condition is fulfilled.

The transferee may be an incerta persona; for instance, when money is scattered among a mob by a praetor or consul (missilium jactus), Inst. 2, 1, 46.

Herein Dominion (jus in rem) differs from Obligation (jus in personam). When an Obligation is created, the payee or creditor or person on whom a right is conferred, cannot be incerta persona; at least jurisprudence had not recognized an obligation or personal right vested in incerta persona before the invention of papers payable to the holder or bearer: and here the admissibility of incerta persona as creditor is effected by the introduction of jus in rem into jus in personam. The incorporeal obligation (jus in personam), is, as it were, incorporated in a document, a subject of ownership (jus in rem), and ownership of the document is deemed to be investiture with the obligation. The emission of the Obligations (papers) now resembles the jactus missilium; the bank, company, or government, that issues the obligations, treats detention of the document as presumptive evidence of ownership, and discharges its obligation by paying whoever presents the paper for payment. In these contracts the payee, promisee, or creditor, is only defined by the class term 'bearer' or 'holder,' i. e. is an incerta persona, individually unknown to the debtor before the moment of presentation.

One act of assent may suffice as the antecedent to many acts of prehension; for instance, in the severance and consequent acquisition (perceptio) of fruits by a lessee (colonus) or usufructuary. Here the delivery (apprehension) occurs from time to time; the will or intention of the original proprietor was manifested once for all when he created the usufruct or lease.

In one case the operation, even of contract and delivery combined, is limited by the Twelve Tables, namely, in Sale. Here it is provided that tradition shall not operate a transmutation of property without a further condition—payment of the purchase money, unless the sale is intended to be a sale on credit, Inst. 2, 1, 41.

Tradition in Roman law was never fictitious; it was always an actual delivery of a power of physical or corporeal control. In English law, indeed, conveyance by a deed under the Statute of Uses is said to transfer possession; but this is impossible: the physical fact of possession can no more be produced by writing on a parchment, than ignition, or explosion, or chemical decomposition can be produced by writing on a parchment, or by any other than its appropriate antecedent. The possession conveyed by assurance under the Statute of Uses is merely a fictitious possession; and instead of saying that the deed passes possession, it would be nearer the truth to say that, in respect of a conveyance under the Statute of Uses, all those parts of the law are deemed to be expunged which make the rights and duties of the alienee dependent on possession.

For a further examination of the nature of Possession, see 4 § 149.

§ 66–69. Occupation gives property in a thing which previously has no proprietor. Quod enim ante nullius est, id naturali ratione occupanti conceditur, Inst. 2, 1, 12. If a thing had already an owner, it is only after dereliction by him that it can be appropriated by occupation. Dereliction, or renunciation of property, requires both the intention to abandon it and an external action. Thus the casting overboard of articles in a tempest to lighten a ship is not dereliction, as there is no intention of abandoning the property in the event of salvage, Inst. 2, 1, 48. Nor does the mere intention of abandonment constitute dereliction of property without a throwing away or removal or some other external act; and herein dereliction of property differs from dereliction of possession, which does not require this second element. Differentia inter dominium et possessionem haec est quod dominium nihilo minus ejus manet qui dominus esse non vult, possessio autem recedit ut quisque constituit nolle possidere, Dig. 41, 2, 17. 'There is this difference between dominion and possession, that dominion continues after the will to own has ceased, whereas possession ceases with the cessation of the will to possess.'

§ 68. Among wild animals (ferae naturae) a distinction is to be drawn. In those of them that are half tamed (mansuefactae), among which are mentioned deer, peacocks, pigeons, bees, property is not limited by detention, as in other wild animals, but by animus revertendi. A migrating swarm (examen) of bees, accordingly, would only continue to belong to the owner of the hive as long as it continues in his sight and is easy to recapture, as it has no intention of returning. In tame animals, e. g. dogs or geese, the rights of the owner are not extinguished by their straying without an intention to return.

§ 70–78. The intimate conjunction of two things, so that they are no longer separable and restorable to their former condition, produces a transmutation of property. A separable junction (commixtio), as when two flocks of sheep are intermingled, or when a stone is set in a ring, or when two metals are soldered together (plumbatura) or are fused but may be chemically separated, produces no change of property. In one case, however, namely, when material has been used in building a house or cultivating a vineyard, although the property of the owner continues, the Twelve Tables deprive him of the right to demand its separation by real action (vindicatio), and only allow him to bring the action de tigno juncto aedibus vel vineae and recover double the value.

An inseparable union sometimes produces co-ownership in the whole (condominium or communio), sometimes the exclusive ownership of one of the parties (accessio).

When two things belonging to different owners are mixed without producing a new species (confusio), nor the relation of principal and accessory, e. g. when two similar wines or metals are mixed, or when a new species is produced with the consent of both owners, as when mead is produced by mixing honey and wine, electrum by mixing gold and silver, then each owner loses his separate ownership of a part, and becomes joint owner of the whole.

When a new species is produced by one owner without the consent of the other, then the exclusive ownership is vested in the producer, and the other can only obtain redress for loss of his ownership.

Further, when the mixture establishes the relation of principal and accessory, that is, when one thing loses its independent existence and becomes a part of the other (accessio), then the property in the whole is vested in the proprietor of the dominant part;

e. g. the property in the ship follows the property in the keel, proprietas totius navis carinae causam sequitur, Dig. 6, 1, 61. It will sometimes be a question which part is to be regarded as principal and which as accessory, and the solution does not always depend on their comparative value. Sometimes the relation of substance and accident prevails, for instance, in a tapestry the property in the embroidery follows the property in the wool. Sometimes the comparative value decides; for instance, the property in the canvas follows the property in the painting: and this seems more rational, though Gaius appears to think that a picture ought to be governed by the analogy of a manuscript, where the property in the writing follows the property in the paper.

§ 78. The remedy of the ex-proprietor of the accessory is an in factum actio (4 § 46), Dig. 6, 1, 33, 5. Ulpian, Dig. 6, 1, 5, 3, speaks of a real action (utilis in rem actio), which, as a real action implies that the plaintiff is proprietor, seems to mean a Fictitious action, 4 § 34, i. e. one whose formula feigns that the property was never devested by Accession. This may be what Gaius means by utilis actio.

§ 79. Specification or labour is a title distinct from Accession, though similar. Here one person contributes only his labour, whereby he transforms the material or materials belonging to another into a new product (nova species). The Sabinians held that the product belonged to the owner of the matter, the Proculeians to the producer of the form. Justinian adopts an intermediate opinion, which Gaius mentions, Dig. 41, 1, 7, 7, that the product belongs to the producer, provided that it cannot be reduced to the original substance, in which case it belongs to the owner of that substance; e. g. a vessel belongs to the owner of the gold or silver out of which it was made: and provided further that the change is a genuine fabrication or manufacture; for instance, the mere thrashing out of corn is not sufficient to change the ownership, and therefore the corn belongs to the owner of the sheaves.

DE PUPILLIS AN ALIQUID A SE ALIENARE POSSUNT.

§ 80. Nunc admonendi sumus neque feminam neque pupillum sine tutoris auctoritate rem mancipi alienare posse; nec mancipi

WHETHER WARDS CAN ALIENE.

§ 80. We must next observe, that neither a woman nor a ward can aliene a mancipable thing without their guardian's authority: a

vero feminam quidem posse, pupillum non posse.

ward cannot aliene a non-mancipable thing without the guardian's authority, a woman can.

§ 81. Ideoque si quando mulier mutuam pecuniam alicui sine tutoris auctoritate dederit, quia facit eam accipientis, cum scilicet ea pecunia res nec mancipi sit, contrahit obligationem.

§ 81. Thus a woman lending money without the guardian's authority passes the property therein to the borrower, money being a non-mancipable thing, and imposes a contractual obligation.

§ 82. At si pupillus idem fecerit, quia *eam pecuniam non facit accipientis*, null*am* contr*ah*it obligationem. unde pupillus vindicare qui*d*em nummos suos potest, sicubi extent, id est *intendere suos ex iure Quiritium esse; mala fide consumtos vero ab eodem* repetere potest *quasi possideret. unde* de pupillo quidem quaeritur, an num*mos quoque* quo*s* mutuos dedit, ab eo qui accepit *bona fide* alienat*os* p*etere* possit, quoniam *is scilicet accipientis eos nummos facere videtur.*

§ 82. But a ward lending money without his guardian's authority does not pass the property, and does not impose a contractual obligation, and therefore he can recover back the money, if it exists, by real action, that is, by claiming it as quiritary proprietor; if it has been fraudulently consumed, he can claim it as if it were still in the possession of the borrower; whether he can if it has been innocently aliened by the borrower, who thus has passed the property to the alienee, is a controversy.

§ 83. *At ex contrario res tam mancipi quam* nec mancipi mulie*ribus* et pupillis *sine* tutoris auctoritate solvi possunt, quoniam meliorem condicionem suam facere iis etiam sine tutoris auctoritate concessum est.

§ 83. On the contrary, both mancipable and non-mancipable things can be conveyed to women and wards without their guardian's authority, because they do not require his authority to better their position.

§ 84. Itaque si debitor pecuniam pupillo solvat, facit quidem pecuniam pupilli, sed ipse non liberatur, quia nullam obligationem pupillus sine tutoris auctoritate dissolvere potest, quia nullius rei alienatio ei sine tutoris auctoritate concessa est. set tamen si ex ea pecunia locupletior factus sit, et adhuc petat, per exceptionem doli mali summoveri potest.

§ 84. Accordingly, a debtor who pays money to a ward passes the property therein to the ward, but is not discharged of his obligation, because a ward cannot release from any liability without his guardian's authority, as without such authority he cannot aliene any right: if, however, he profits by the money, and yet demands further payment, he may be barred by plea of fraud.

§ 85. Mulieri vero etiam sine tutoris auctoritate recte solvi potest: nam qui solvit, liberatur obligatione, quia res nec mancipi, ut proxume diximus, a se dimittere mulier et sine tutoris auctoritate potest: quamquam hoc ita est, si accipiat pecuniam; at si non acci-

§ 85. A woman may be lawfully paid without her guardian's authority, and the payer is discharged of liability, because, as we lately mentioned, a woman does not need her guardian's authority for the alienation of a non-mancipable right, provided always that she receives

piat, *sed* habere se dicat, et per acceptilationem velit debitorem sine tutoris auctoritate liberare, non potest.

actual payment: for if she is not actually paid, she cannot feign receipt and release her debtor by fictitious acknowledgment (3 § 169) without her guardian's authority.

§ 82. For mutuum, see 3 § 90. If the money delivered by a ward could be traced it was recoverable by real action (vindicatio): if it had been consumed in bona fides a personal action, condictio certi, would lie to recover an equivalent sum: if it had been consumed in mala fides a personal action, ad exhibendum, would lie to recover an equivalent sum and damages, Inst. 2, 8, 2.

§ 85. The pupilage of women after attaining the age of twelve, i. e. the age of puberty, had become obsolete before the time of Justinian, and with it their incapacities of alienation.

PER QUAS PERSONAS NOBIS ADQUIRATUR.

§ 86. Adquiritur autem nobis non solum per nosmet ipsos, sed etiam per eos quos in potestate manu mancipiove habemus; item per eos servos in quibus usumfructum habemus; item per homines liberos et servos alienos quos bona fide possidemus. de quibus singulis diligenter dispiciamus.

§ 86. We may acquire property not only by our own acts but also by the acts of persons in our power, hand, or mancipation; further, by slaves in whom we have a usufruct; further, by freemen or slaves belonging to another if we are innocent possessors: and let us now examine these cases in detail.

§ 87. Igitur *quod* liberi nostri quos in potestate habemus, item quod servi *nostri* mancipio accipiunt, vel ex traditione nanciscuntur, sive quid stipulentur, vel ex aliqualibet causa adquirunt, id nobis adquiritur: ipse enim qui in potestate nostra est nihil suum habere potest, et ideo si heres institutus sit, nisi nostro iussu, hereditatem adire non potest; et si iubentibus nobis adierit, hereditatem nobis adquirit proinde atque si nos ipsi heredes instituti essemus. et convenienter scilicet legatum per eos nobis adquiritur.

§ 87. The rights of property which children under power or slaves acquire by mancipation or tradition, the rights to a service they acquire by stipulation, and all rights they acquire by any other title, are acquired for their superior; for an inferior is incapable of holding property, and if instituted heir he must have the command of his superior to be capable of accepting the inheritance, and if he has the command of the superior and accepts the inheritance, it is acquired for the superior just as if he himself had been instituted heir: and the same occurs in the case of a legacy.

§ 88. Dum tamen sciamus, si alterius in bonis sit servus, alterius

§ 88. When one man is bonitary proprietor of a slave and another

ex iure Quiritium, ex omnibus causis ei soli *per* eum adquiri cuius in bonis est.

§ 89. Non solum autem proprietas per eos quos in potestate habemus adquiritur nobis, sed etiam possessio: cuius enim rei possessionem adepti fuerint, id nos possidere videmur: unde etiam per eos usucapio procedit.

§ 90. Per eas vero personas quas in manu mancipiove habemus, proprietas quidem adquiritur nobis ex omnibus causis, sicut per eos qui in potestate nostra sunt: an autem possessio adquiratur, quaeri solet, quia ipsa*s* non possidemus.

§ 91. De his autem servis in quibus tantum usumfructum habemus ita placuit, ut qui*d*quid ex re nostra vel ex operis suis adquirunt, id nobis adquiratur; quod vero extra eas causas, id ad dominum proprietatis pertineat. itaque si iste *servus* heres institutus sit legatumve quod ei datum fuerit, non mihi, sed domino proprietatis adquiritur.

§ 92. Idem placet de eo qui a nobis bona fide possidetur, sive liber sit sive alienus servus. quod enim placuit de usufructuario, idem probatur etiam de bona fide possessore. itaque quod extra duas istas causas adquiritur, id vel ad ipsum pertinet, si liber est, vel ad dominum, si servus sit.

§ 93. Sed si bonae fidei p*ossessor usuceperit servum*, quia eo modo dominus fit, *ex* omni causa per eum sibi adquirere potest: usufructuarius vero usucapere non potest, primum quia non possidet, *sed* habet ius utendi et fruendi; deinde quia scit alienum servum e*sse*.

quiritary proprietor, whatever the mode of acquisition, it enures exclusively to the bonitary proprietor.

§ 89. Not only property is acquired for the superior but also possession, for the detention of the inferior is deemed to be the possession of the superior, and thus the former is to the latter an instrument of usucapion.

§ 90. Persons in the hand or mancipation of a superior acquire dominion for him just as persons in his power; whether they acquire possession for him, is a controversy, not being themselves in his possession.

§ 91. Respecting slaves in whom a person has only a usufruct, the rule is, that what they acquire by administering the property of the usufructuary or by their own labour is acquired for the usufructuary; but what they acquire by any other means belongs to their proprietor (the reversioner). Accordingly, if such a slave is instituted heir or made legatee, the succession or legacy is acquired, not to the usufructuary, but to the proprietor.

§ 92. The innocent possessor of a freeman or a slave belonging to another has the same rights as a usufructuary; what they acquire by any other title than the two we mentioned, belonging in the one case to the freeman in the other to the true proprietor.

§ 93. After a bona fide possessor has acquired the ownership of a slave by usucapion, all acquisitions by the slave enure to his benefit. A usufructuary cannot acquire a slave by usucapion, for, in the first place, he has no true possession, but only a quasi possession of a servitude; in the second place, he is aware of the existence of another proprietor.

§ 94. De illo quaeritur, an per eum servum in quo usumfructum habemus possidere aliquam rem et usucapere possumus, quia ipsum non possidemus. Per eum vero quem bona fide possidemus sine dubio et possidere et usucapere possumus. loquimur autem in utriusque persona secundum *distinctionem* quam proxume exposuimus, id est si quid ex re nostra vel ex operis suis adquirant, id nobis adquiritur.

§ 94. It is a question whether a slave can be an instrument of possession and usucapion to a usufructuary, not being himself in his possession. A slave, undoubtedly, can be the instrument of possession and usucapion to a bona fide possessor. Both cases are limited by the distinction recently drawn, that is, the proposition is confined to the things acquired by the slave in the administration of a party's property or by his own labour.

§ 95. Ex his apparet per liberos homines, quos neque iuri nostro subiectos habemus neque bona fide possidemus, item per alienos servos, in quibus neque usumfructum habemus neque iustam possessionem, nulla ex causa nobis adquiri *posse*. *et hoc est quod dicitur* per extraneam personam nihil adquiri *posse, excepta possessione, de ea enim* quaeritur, anne *per liberam personam* nobis adquiratur.

§ 95. It appears that freemen not subject to my power nor in my innocent possession, and my neighbour's slave of whom I am neither usufructuary nor just possessor, cannot under any circumstances be instruments of my acquisition, and this is the import of the dictum that a stranger cannot be an instrument in the acquisition of anything except, perhaps, possession; for in respect of possession there is a controversy whether an independent person can be instrumental in its acquisition.

§ 96. In summa sciendum *est* iis *qui in* potestate manu mancipiove sunt nihil in iure cedi posse. cum enim *istarum* personarum nihil suum esse possit, conveniens est scilicet, ut nihil *suum esse* per se in iure vindicare possint.

§ 96. Finally, it is to be observed that persons under power, in hand, or in bondage, cannot acquire by surrender before a magistrate, for, being incapable of ownership, they are incompetent to bring a claim of ownership before a tribunal.

§ 87. Manus and mancipium had ceased to exist before the time of Justinian, and patria potestas was much reduced. Originally, the filiusfamilias was incapable of property: in the peculium, the goods he was allowed to administer, he had no property nor even possession, 4 § 148, but merely detention. The military profession were the first to emerge from this position of inferiority, and in respect of peculium castrense the filiusfamilias was deemed to have the status of paterfamilias. By the introduction of peculium quasi castrense this privilege was extended to certain civil functionaries and liberal professions: and by inventing peculium adventitium Justinian still further emancipated the filiusfamilias. Peculium adventitium, as opposed to peculium profectitium, was what came to the son from any other source than the estate and permission of the father: in respect of peculium profectitium the old law continued in force; the paterfamilias remained absolute proprietor: but in respect of peculium adventitium the right of the father was reduced to a life estate or usufruct: in respect of the fee or reversion in remainder after this life estate the filiusfamilias was proprietor, Inst. 2, 9, 1. The reduction of patria potestas, and the abolition of the dependent law of Agnation, may be almost regarded (so fundamental were these institutions in jus civile) as the abrogation of the civil law, and the substitution in its stead of what the Romans called jus gentium or the law of nature.

§ 94. The question whether an usufructuary slave may be an instrument of acquiring possession is decided in the affirmative, Dig. 41, 2, 1, 8.

§ 95. All voluntary titles or modes of acquiring either rights against one (jus in personam), or rights against the world (jus in rem) are divisible, as we have before mentioned, into two parcels; an essential portion, some mental or internal act, the Intention of the parties; and an evidentiary portion, the Execution of this intention, its incorporation in some external act. Can these elements of title be contributed by different persons? Can the Intention of disposing, that is, of acquiring or aliening, reside in one, and can its Execution, its external manifestation, be delegated to a representative?

Originally, that is, under the ancient civil law, representation was only admitted when the representative was in an inferior status to the principal, was his slave, or subject to his potestas, manus, or mancipium. This limitation was found to be inconvenient, when, in the progress of Roman conquest, Roman citizens became proprietors in remote parts of the world; and Possession was allowed to be acquirable by the instrumentality of libera persona, that is, of a person who stood in no relation of inferiority to the acquirer. In a civil solemnity, like mancipation, a man could not be represented by an independent agent; but when, subsequently, the transfer of possession became the universal mode of transferring dominion, it followed that Property, as well as Possession, could be acquired by the agency of libera persona. Si procurator rem mihi emerit ex mandato meo, eique sit tradita meo nomine, dominium mihi et proprietas acquiritur etiam ignoranti, Dig. 41, 1, 13. 'If an agent buys a thing by my instructions, and receives possession thereof in my name, the dominion and property is acquired for me even without notice of his act.' Per liberam personam ignoranti quoque adquiri possessionem et, postquam scientia intervenerit, usucapionis conditionem inchoari posse, tam ratione utilitatis quam jurisprudentia receptum est, Cod. 7, 32, 1. 'An independent person may be an instrument whereby, without notice, a principal may acquire possession, and, after notice, may commence usucapion; as is established both by motives of convenience and principles of jurisprudence.' Notice was required for usucapion, because, as we have seen, usucapion requires bona fides.

The acquisition of Obligations or personal rights by brokerage of an independent agent was less perfectly developed. Originally, the process employed was a duplication of the relation of agency (mandatum). A as principal (dominus) appointed B his agent (procurator). B then contracted with a third party in his own name, and, in order to transfer the benefit of his contract to A, he ceded to him his right of action, that is to say, B, as principal, in his turn made A his agent (procurator in rem suam), whereby A was able to sue in the name of B, and obtain judgment in the name of A. Finally, the praetor allowed the principal to sue immediately, without this cession of actions, by bringing a utilis actio, i. e. a fictitious action, or action which feigned that the cession had taken place, or rather, that the principal had been the immediate contractor, not represented by an agent. But this fiction was only required in respect of contracts governed by principles of civil law, i. e. the Formal contracts, of which at last the only instance was Stipulatio. In Formless contracts, or contracts governed by jus gentium, the agent was a mere conduit pipe; the principal acquired an immediate right or obligation, without Cession and without Fiction. Ea quae civiliter adquiruntur, per eos qui in potestate nostra sunt adquirimus, veluti stipulationem; quod naturaliter adquiritur, sicuti est possessio, per quemlibet, volentibus nobis possidere, adquirimus, Dig. 41, 1, 53. 'Rights obtained by civil titles can only be acquired by the mediation of persons in our power; for instance, rights by stipulation: rights obtained by natural titles, such as the right of possession, are acquirable through any agent that we choose to employ.' See 3 § 163, to which place this topic more properly belongs.

As a Rerum universitas includes Obligations (res incorporalis), active and passive, as well as Dominion (res corporalis), the consideration of Obligation should, theoretically speaking, precede the consideration of Rerum universitas; in an elementary exposition like the present, however, no practical inconvenience is occasioned by postponing the consideration of Obligations, the remaining branch of Res singulae, while we gain by exhausting the subject of jus in rem before proceeding to the examination of jus in personam.

We may remember that Rerum universitas, as well as Servitudes and Obligations, was included by the Romans under the term Res incorporalis, 2 § 14. The whole division of rights, however, into Res corporalis and Res incorporalis is unsatisfactory; for, as we have already noticed, it was only from confusion of thought that Dominion was held to be Res corporalis; and all Rights are, really, Res incorporales.

QUIBUS MODIS PER UNIVERSITATEM RES ADQUIRANTUR.

§ 97. *Hactenus* tantisper admonuisse sufficit quemadmodum SINGULAE res nobis adquirantur. nam legatorum iura, quo et ipso singulas res adquirimus, opportunius alio loco referemus. Videamus itaque nunc quibus modis per UNIVERSITATEM res nobis adquirantur.

§ 97. So much at present respecting the modes of acquiring SINGLE rights; for bequest, another title whereby single rights are acquired, will find a more suitable place in a later portion of our treatise. We proceed to the titles whereby an AGGREGATE of rights is acquired.

§ 98. Si cui heredes facti sumus, sive cuius bonorum possessionem petierimus, sive cuius bona emerimus, sive quem adrogaverimus, sive quam in manum ut uxorem receperimus, eius res ad nos transeunt.

§ 98. If we become the successors, legal or praetorian, of a person deceased, or purchase the estate of an insolvent, or adopt a person sui juris, or receive a wife into our hand, the whole estate of those persons is transferred to us in an aggregate mass.

§ 99. Ac prius de hereditatibus dispiciamus, quarum duplex condicio est: nam vel ex testamento, vel ab intestato ad nos pertinent.

§ 99. Let us begin with inheritances, whose mode of devolution is twofold, according as a person dies testate or intestate.

§ 100. Et prius est, ut de his dispiciamus quae nobis ex testamento obveniunt.

§ 100. And we first treat of acquisition by will.

DE TESTAMENTIS ORDINANDIS.

§ 101. Testamentorum autem genera initio duo fuerunt. nam aut calatis comitiis faciebant, quae

§ 101. Wills were originally of two kinds, being made either at the comitia calata, which were held

comitia bis in anno testamentis faciendis destinata erant, aut in procinctu, id est cum belli causa *ad* pu*gn*am ibant: procinctus est enim expeditus et armatus exercitus. alterum itaque in pace et in otio faciebant, alterum in proelium exituri.

twice a year for making wills, or in martial array, that is to say, in the field before the enemy, martial array denoting an army clad and armed for battle. One kind, then, was used in time of peace, the other in time of war.

§ 102. Accessit deinde tertium genus testamenti, quod per aes et libram agitur. qui neque calatis comitiis neque in procinctu testamentum fecerat, is si subita morte urgebatur, amico familiam suam [id est patrimonium suum] mancipio dabat, eumque rogabat quid cuique post mortem suam dari vellet. quod testamentum dicitur per aes et libram, scilicet quia per mancipation*e*m peragitur.

§ 102. More recently, a third kind was introduced, effected by bronze and balance. A man who had not made his will, either in the comitia calata or in martial array, being in apprehension of approaching death, used to convey his estate by mancipation to a friend, whom he requested to distribute it to certain persons in a certain manner after his death. This mode of testamentary disposition is called the will by bronze and balance, because it involves the process of mancipation.

§ 103. Sed ill*a* quidem duo genera testamentorum in desuetudinem abierunt; hoc vero solum quod per aes et libram fit in usu retentum est. sane nunc al*i*ter ordinatur atque olim solebat. namque olim familiae emptor, id est qui a testatore familiam accipiebat mancipio, heredis locum optinebat, et ob id ei mandabat testator, quid cuique post mortem suam dari vellet. nunc vero alius heres testamento instituitur, a quo etiam leg*a*ta relinquuntur, alius dicis gratia propter veteris iuris *i*mitationem familiae emp*t*or *ad*hibetur.

§ 103. The first two modes have fallen into desuetude, and that by bronze and balance, which alone survives, has undergone a transformation. In former times the vendee of the estate, the alienee by mancipation from the testator, was the successor, and received the testator's instructions respecting the disposition of his property after his death. At the present day, the person who is instituted successor, and who is charged with the execution of the bequests, is different from the person who, for form's sake, and in imitation of the ancient process, represents the purchaser.

§ 104. Eaq*ue* res ita agitur. Qui facit *testamentum*, *ad*hibitis, sicut in ceteris *m*ancipationibus, v testibus civibus Romanis pu*be*ribus et libripende, postquam tabulas testamenti scrips*erit*, *m*ancipat alicui dicis gratia familiam suam; in qua re his verbis familiae emptor utitur: FAM*ILIA*M PECUNIAMQUE TUAM ENDO MANDATELA TUTELA

§ 104. The proceedings are as follows: The testator having summoned, as is done in other mancipations, five witnesses, all Roman citizens of the age of puberty, and a holder of the balance, and having already reduced his will to writing, makes a fictitious mancipation of his estate to a certain vendee, who thereupon utters these words:

CUSTODELAQUE MEA *ESSE AIO EAQUE*, QUO TU IURE TESTAMENTUM FACERE POSSIS SECUNDUM LEGEM PUBLICAM, HOC AERE, et ut quidam adiciunt, AENEAQUE LIBRA ESTO MIHI EMPTA. deinde aere percutit libram, idque aes dat testatori velut pretii loco. deinde testator tabulas testamenti tenens ita dicit: HAEC ITA UT IN HIS TABULIS CERISQUE SCRIPTA SUNT ITA DO, ITA LEGO, ITA TESTOR, ITAQUE VOS QUIRITES TESTIMONIUM MIHI PERHIBETOTE. et hoc dicitur nuncupatio. nuncupare est enim palam nominare; et sane quae testator specialiter in tabulis testamenti scri*p*serit, ea videtur generali sermone nominare atque confirmare.

'Thy family and thy money into my charge, ward, and custody I receive, and, in order to validate thy will conformably to Roman law, with this ingot, and'—as some continue—'with this scale of bronze, unto me be it purchased.' Then with the ingot he strikes the scale, and delivers the ingot to the testator, as by way of purchase-money. Thereupon the testator, holding the tablets of his will, says as follows: 'This estate, as in these tablets and in this wax is written, I so grant, so devise, so dispose; and do you, Quirites, so give me your attestation.' These words are called the nuncupation, for nuncupation signifies public declaration, and by these general words the specific written dispositions of the testator are published and confirmed.

§ 105. In testibus autem non debet is esse qui in potestate est aut familiae emptoris aut ipsius testatoris, quia propter veteris iuris imitationem totum hoc negotium quod agitur testament*i* or*d*inandi gratia creditur inter familiae emptorem agi et testatorem: quippe olim, ut proxime diximus, is qui familiam testatoris mancipio accipiebat, heredis loco erat. itaque reprobatum est in ea re domesticum testimonium.

§ 105. For the part of witness, it is a disqualification to be in the power of the fictitious vendee or of the testator, because, the old proceeding furnishing the model, the whole testamentary process is supposed to be a transaction between the vendee and the testator; and in old times, as was just observed, the vendee was the testamentary successor; wherefore no person in the power of the vendee was a competent witness.

§ 106. Unde et si is qui in potestate patris est familiae emptor adhibitus sit, pater eius testis esse non potest: at ne is quidem qui in eadem potestate est, velut frater eius. Sed si filiusfamilias ex castrensi peculio post missionem faciat testamentum, nec pater eius recte testis adhibetur, nec is qui in potestate patris sit.

§ 106. Hence, if the vendee is a filiusfamilias, neither his father nor any one in his father's power, his brother, for instance, is competent to attest; and if a filiusfamilias, after his discharge from service, make a will of his military peculium, neither his father nor any one in his father's power is qualified to be a witness.

§ 107. De libripende eadem quae et de testibus dicta esse intellegemus; nam et is testium numero est.

§ 107. The same rules apply to the balance-holder, for the balance-holder is a witness.

§ 108. Is vero qui in potestate heredis aut legatarii est, cuiusve heres ipse aut legatarius in potestate est, quique in eiusdem potestate est, *adeo* testis et libripens *ad*hiberi potest, ut ipse quoque heres *aut* legatarius iure adhibeantur. sed tamen quod ad heredem pertinet quique in eius potestate est, cuiusve is in potestate erit, minime hoc i*u*re uti debemus.

§ 108. Not only is a person who is in the power of the heir or legatee, or a person who has power over the heir or legatee, or a person in the same power as the heir or legatee, capable of being witness or balance-holder, but the heir or legatee himself can act in this character. However, it is advisable that the heir, and those in his power, and the person in whose power he is, should not exercise their qualification.

§ 101. A will is thus defined by Ulpian: Testamentum est mentis nostrae justa contestatio, in id sollemniter facta, ut post mortem nostram valeat, 20, 1. 'A will is our intention, duly attested and solemnly declared, to take effect after our death.' So important is the institution of a heres to the validity of a will in Roman law, that a Roman testament might be simply defined the institution of a heres.

Testamentary disposition was an interference with the more ancient law of succession by descent or intestate devolution, and the diversion of property from the legal course of transmission seemed at first so great an innovation as to require legislative sanction. Accordingly, the will executed in the Comitia Calata, or convocation of the curiae, was really a private law; and even the will in procinctu, when we remember the original identity at Rome of the civil and military organization, may be regarded as a legislative act of the people in military convocation.

The latter form was familiar to the contemporaries of Cicero: Reprehendebat igitur Galbam Rutilius quod is . . . . duos filios suos parvos tutelae populi commendasset ac se, tanquam in procinctu testamentum faceret sine libra atque tabulis, populum Romanum tutorem instituere dixisset illorum orbitati, De Orat. 1, 53. 'Rutilius blamed the abject artifice of Galba in commending his children to the protection of the people, and, as if he was making a will on the eve of battle, without bronze ingot and scale or written tablets, exclaiming that he named the Roman people guardian of their orphanage.'

§ 102. The mancipative will, or will by bronze and scale, probably began to supersede the older form as soon as the Twelve Tables had given legal force to the nuncupative part of mancipation (Cum nexum faciet mancipiumque, uti lingua nuncupassit, ita jus esto, Festus. 'In contract or conveyance by bronze and balance, the oral declaration shall have legal force,') and had expressly recognized in every paterfamilias a power of testamentary disposition (Uti legassit super familia, pecunia, tutelave suae rei, ita jus esto, Ulpian, 11, 14. 'The directions of a testator respecting his family, property, and the guardianship of his children, shall be carried into effect).'

§ 103. The introduction of writing marks an era in mancipative wills. Originally, the testator gave oral instructions to the familiae emptor in the presence of the witnesses respecting the distribution of his estate. These oral instructions, forming the lex mancipii, or conditions of the conveyance, were called the nuncupatio. Afterwards, for the sake of secresy, the testator committed his intentions to writing, and the nuncupation became a mere form of publication, or general ratification of the directions contained in the tablets which the testator held in his hand. It was probably in part, as Theophilus says, with the same view of concealing the testator's intentions, that the familiae emptor was separated from the heres, but in part also to enable the testator to institute as heres a person who from infancy or any other disability was incapable of co-operating in a mancipation.

§ 105. It is an intelligible rule, that a person interested in the validity of a will should be incompetent as a witness; and, when the familiae emptor was the heir, it was reasonable to disqualify for attestation any one united in interest to the familiae emptor. But when the mancipation was purely fictitious (imaginaria mancipatio, Ulpian, 20, 3; imaginaria venditio, Inst. 2, 10, 1), and the imaginary vendee distinct from the heir, the continuance of this disqualification shows the tendency of the Romans to venerate rules after the principles on which they were founded had ceased to operate. In the meantime the heir, who was really interested, was competent to be a witness. Cicero, for instance, mentions that he and Clodius were both witnesses to a will in which they were appointed heirs, Pro Milone, 18, 48. Justinian converted the advice of Gaius into a rule of law, and disabled the heir and persons united to him by the bond of potestas from giving attestation, Inst. 2, 10, 10. Legatees retained their competency to attest.

By English law, 1 Vict. c. 26, any devise or legacy to an attesting witness is void, and the evidence of the witness admissible, and no person is incompetent to attest on account of being appointed executor.

In another form of will deriving its validity from the authority of the praetor, the form of mancipation was dropped, and the only authentication required was the apposition of the seals of seven attesting witnesses. Under such a will, however, the devisee could not take the legal estate or hereditas, but only the equitable estate or bonorum possessio.

Before the time of Justinian, a form of will had been established deriving its validity from three orders of legislation (jus tripertitum), the civil law, the praetorian edict, and the imperial constitutions. In accordance with the last, the witnesses were required to sign or subscribe their names; in accordance with the praetorian edict they were required to attach their seals (signacula); and in accordance with the civil law, their number was required to be seven (a number obtained by adding the libripens and familiae emptor to the five witnesses of the mancipation), and the whole formality of attestation and publication was required to be continuous, that is, to proceed from beginning to end without interruption or interposition of any other business.

Another form of will is mentioned by Justinian as perfectly valid at civil law, the Nuncupative will, consisting solely of an oral declaration in the presence of seven witnesses, Inst. 2, 10, 14. A modification of this produced one of the most solemn forms of testament. The nuncupation was made before the Praeses provinciae, or magistrates of the municipal senate (curia); and thereupon a memorandum or protocol (insinuatio) of the testator's dispositions was made at length in the public records (acta or gesta) of the proceedings of the governor or senate. This was called a public testament.

By English law, 1 Vict. c. 26, only two witnesses are required to a will, whether of real or personal estate. The will must be in writing, signed at the end by the testator, or by some other person in his presence and by his direction; and such signature must be made or acknowledged by the testator in the presence of the two witnesses, who must be present at the same time, and who must attest and subscribe the will in the presence of the testator.

DE TESTAMENTIS MILITUM.

§ 109. Sed haec diligens observatio in ordinandis testamentis militibus propter nimiam inperitiam *const*itutionibus Principum remissa est. nam quamvis neque legitimum numerum testium a*d*hibuerint, neque vendiderint familiam, neque nuncupaverint testamentum, recte nihilominus testantur.

§ 110. Praeterea permissum est iis et peregrinos et Latinos instituere heredes vel iis legare: cum alioquin peregrini quidem ratione civili prohibeantur capere hereditatem legataque, Latini vero per legem Iuniam.

§ 111. Caelibes quoque qui lege Iulia hereditatem legataque capere vetantur, item orbi, id est qui liberos non habent, quos lex *Papia plus quam semissem capere* prohibet (23 *lin.*).

§ 109. But from these strict rules in the execution of a will soldiers, in consideration of their extreme ignorance of law, have by imperial constitutions a dispensation. For neither the legal number of witnesses, nor the ceremony of mancipation or of nuncupation, is necessary to give force to their will.

§ 110. Moreover, they may make aliens and Latini Juniani their heirs or legatees, whereas under other wills an alien is disqualified from taking a succession or legacy by the civil law, and Latini Juniani by the lex Junia.

§ 111. Celibates also, whom the lex Julia disqualifies for taking successions or legacies, and childless persons whom the lex Papia prohibits from taking more than half a succession or legacy (see § 286, are exempt from these incapacities under the will of a soldier).

§ 109. The military will, which superseded the old testament in procinctu, could only be executed during actual service, and in this period only when the soldier was in camp, not when he was at home or on leave of absence. A will made after the soldier's discharge from service or during his absence from camp was governed by the same rules as the will of a civilian (paganus). A military will, executed without the ordinary formalities, only remained valid during a year after discharge from service. Inst. 2, 11, 3.

TESTAMENTIFACTIO.

§ 112. S*ed senatus divo Hadriano auctore, ut supra quoque significavimus, mulieribus etiam coemptione non facta* testamentum facer*e permisit, si modo maiores facerent* annorum XII tutore auctore; scilicet ut quae tutela liberatae non essent ita testari deber*e*nt.

§ 112. But the senate, on Hadrian's proposition, as already mentioned (1 § 115*a*), made coemption, remancipation, manumission, unnecessary, and permitted women to make a will on attaining 12 years of age, only requiring their guardian's authority if they were still in a state of pupilage.

§ 113. Videntur ergo melioris condicionis esse feminae quam masculi: nam masculus minor annorum XIIII testamentum facere non potest, etiamsi tutore auctore testamentum facere velit; femina vero post XII ann*um* testamenti faciundi ius nanci*s*citur.

§ 114. Igitur si quaeramus an valeat testamentum, inprimis advertere debemus an is qui id fecerit habuerit testamenti factionem: deinde si habuerit, requiremus an secundum iuris civilis regulam *testa*tus sit; exceptis militibus, qui*bus* propter nimiam *inp*eritiam, ut diximus, quomodo velint vel quomo*do poss*int, permittitur testamentum facere.

§ 113. Women, then, are in a better legal position than men, for a male under 14 years of age cannot make a will, even with his guardian's sanction, but a female acquires the capacity of devising as soon as she is 12 years old.

§ 114. Accordingly, to determine the validity of a will, we must first ascertain whether the testator had testamentary capacity; next, if he had, whether he conformed to the requisitions of the civil law in its execution, with this reservation, that soldiers, on account of their extreme ignorance of law, as was mentioned, are allowed to make their wills in any way they like and in any way they can.

§ 112. On the lost leaf of the Veronese codex Gaius proceeded to mention the classes who were incompetent to make a will. Among these would be the filiusfamilias, who could only dispose of his peculium castrense and quasi castrense.

§ 113. By English law, the age at which a person was competent to make a will was formerly the same as by Roman law, namely, 12 years for females, 14 years for males; but now, by 1 Vict. c. 26, no one is competent to make a will before attaining 21 years of age.

BONORUM POSSESSIO SECUNDUM TABULAS.

§ 115. Non tamen, ut iure civili *val*eat testamentum, sufficit ea observatio quam supra expo*su*imus de familiae venditione et de testibus et de nuncupationibus.

§ 116. Ante omnia requirendum est an institutio heredis sollemni more facta sit: nam aliter facta institutione nihil proficit familiam testatoris ita venire, teste*ve* ita *ad*hibere, aut nuncupare testamentum, ut supra diximus.

§ 117. Sollemnis autem institutio haec est: TIT*I*US HERES ESTO. sed et illa iam conprobata videtur:

§ 115. The civil law, however, is not satisfied by observing the requisitions hereinbefore explained respecting mancipation, attestation, and nuncupation.

§ 116. Above all things, we must observe whether the institution of an heir was in the sacramental terms; for if the institution of an heir was not in the traditional form, it is unavailing that the mancipation, attestation, nuncupation, were regular.

§ 117. The solemn form of institution is this: 'Be Titius my successor.' The following also seems

TITIUM HEREDEM ESSE IUBEO. at illa non est conprobata: TITIUM HEREDEM ESSE VOLO. set et illae a plerisque inprobatae sunt: HEREDEM INSTITUO item HEREDEM FACIO.

now to be recognized: 'I order that Titius be my successor.' 'I wish Titius to be my successor' is not admitted; and most reject the following: 'I institute Titius my successor,' 'I make Titius my successor.'

§ 118. Observandum praeterea est, ut si mulier quae in tutela sit faciat testamentum, tutoris *auctoritate* facere debeat: alioquin inutiliter iure *civili* testabitur.

§ 118. It is also to be remembered that a woman who has a guardian must have her guardian's authority to devise, or her will is invalid at civil law.

§ 119. Praetor tamen, si septem signis testium signatum sit testamentum, scriptis heredibus secundum tabulas testamenti *bonorum possessionem* pollicetur: *et* si nemo sit ad quem ab intestato iure legitimo pertineat hereditas, velut frater eodem patre natus aut patruus aut fratris filius, ita poterunt scripti heredes retinere hereditatem. nam idem iuris est et si alia ex *causa* testamentum non valeat, velut quod familia non venierit aut nuncupationis verba testator locutus non sit.

§ 119. The praetor, however, if the will is attested by the seals of seven witnesses, promises to give the devisees the praetorian succession, and if there is no one to take the legal inheritance by descent, a brother by the same father, for instance, a father's brother, or a brother's son, the devisees are secure from eviction; for the same rule obtains if the will is invalid from any other cause, such as the absence of mancipation or nuncupation.

§ 120. Sed videamus an *non*, etiamsi frater aut patruus extent, potiores scriptis heredibus habeantur. rescri*pto* enim Imperatoris Antonini significatur, eos qui secundum tabulas testamenti non iure factas bonorum possessionem petierint, posse adversus eos qui ab intestato vindicant hereditatem defendere se per exceptionem doli mali.

§ 120. But are not even a brother and paternal uncle postponed to the devisees? for the rescript of the emperor Marcus Aurelius Antoninus Philosophus permits the devisee under an informal will to repel the claimants in intestacy by the plea of fraud.

§ 121. Quod sane quidem ad masculorum testamenta pertinere certum est; item ad feminarum quae ideo *non* utiliter testat*ae* sunt, quod verbi gratia familiam non vendiderint aut nuncupationis verba locutae non sint: an autem et ad ea testamenta feminarum quae sine tutoris auctoritate fecerint haec constitutio pertineat, videbimus.

§ 121. This applies to the wills of males and females which are informal for such faults as want of mancipation or nuncupation: whether also to wills of females who devise without their guardian's authority, is the question.

§ 122. Loquimur autem de his scilicet feminis quae non in legitima parentium aut patronorum tutela sunt, sed de his quae alteriu*s* generis

§ 122. We are not speaking of females who are the statutory wards of their parent or patron, but of those who are wards of the

tutores habent, qui etiam inviti coguntur auctores fieri: alioquin parentem et patronum sine auctoritate eius facto testamento non summoveri palam est.

other sort of guardian, whose guardians are compellable to lend their authorization; for a parent or patron can certainly not be disinherited by an unauthorised will.

§ 117. The necessity of using formal words in the institution of an heir was abolished by a constitution of Constantine, Constantius, and Constans, A.D. 339, Cod. 6, 23, 15.

As to the nomenclature employed in the following exposition of Roman testamentary law, it must be observed that Heres corresponds sometimes to the Heir, sometimes to the Devisee, sometimes to the Executor, of English jurisprudence. In the language of English jurisprudence, Heir denotes a successor to real estate, while Executor denotes a successor to personal property. Again, Heir denotes a successor to real estate by descent, Devisee denotes a successor to real estate under a will. Accordingly, to avoid misleading an English reader by false associations, in translating the word Heres, Successor has generally been employed instead of Heir, without, however, entirely renouncing the use of the shorter word, which is often convenient from its relation to the indispensable terms disinherit and disinheritance.

Devisee has generally been employed, in preference to Executor, as a translation of scriptus heres, but it must then be stripped of any reference to the distinction between property in money and property in land. The word Executor is not available as a translation of heres. The executor of English law, unless also a legatee, holds a merely onerous office; whereas the heres of Roman law was always a beneficiary. The Roman heres, in fact, united the characters of the English executor and residuary legatee: and the lex Falcidia provided that the residue should always amount to at least a fourth of the testator's property.

Bequest (which in English law is related to personalty as devise to realty) has been used in connection with legacies, i. e. with dispositions in favour of legatarius as opposed to heres; in favour, that is, of a person who takes a single thing belonging to the testator, not his familia, or the Universitas of his rights and obligations, or even a fraction of this Universitas.

§ 120. The praetorian succession, or right of succession introduced by the praetor under the name of Bonorum possessio, sometimes beside, and sometimes instead of, civilis hereditas, may be divided into testate succession and intestate succession. The latter branch (bonorum possessio intestati) was firmly established at an earlier period than the former (bonorum possessio secundum tabulas). The rescript of Marcus Aurelius, mentioned by Gaius, may be regarded as having definitively established the validity of the praetorian testament; in other words, as having raised in respect of validity bonorum possessio testati to the level of bonorum possessio intestati.

§ 122. In ancient Rome, females, even after attaining their majority, were subject to perpetual guardianship. In the time of Gaius, the only effectual guardianship to which they continued subject appears to have been that of ascendents and patrons. By the time of Justinian even this had ceased, for he mentions without any reservation that the tutelage of women ceases on their attaining the age of 12, Inst. 1, 22.

DE EXHEREDATIONE LIBERORUM.

§ 123. Item qui filium in potestate habet curare debet, ut eum vel heredem instituat vel nominatim exheredet; alioquin si eum silentio praeterierit, inutiliter testabitur: adeo quidem, ut nostri praeceptores existiment, etiamsi vivo patre filius defunctus sit, neminem heredem ex eo testamento existere posse, scilicet quia statim ab initio non constiterit institutio. sed diversae scholae auctores, siquidem fili*us* mortis patris tempore vivat, sane impedimento eum esse scriptis heredibus et illum ab intestato heredem fieri confitentur: si vero ante mortem patris interceptus sit, posse ex testamento hered*ita*tem adiri putant, nullo iam filio impedimento; quia scilicet existimant *non* statim ab initio inutiliter fieri testamentum filio praeterito.

§ 123. Moreover, a testator who has a son in his power must take care either to institute him heir or to disinherit him, for passing him over in silence vacates the will. So much so, that according to the Sabinians, even if the son die in the lifetime of the father, no devisee can take under the will because of its original nullity. But, according to the Proculeians, although the son, if alive at the time of his father's death, bars the devisees and takes as self-successor by intestacy, yet, if the son die before the father, the devisees may succeed, being no longer barred by the son, assuming that the will was not absolutely vacated by his silent pretermission.

§ 124. Ceteras vero liberorum personas si praeterierit testator, valet testamentum. praeteritae istae personae scriptis heredibus in partem ad*crescunt : si sui instituti sint* in virilem; si extranei, in dimidiam.

§ 124. But if other issue is passed over in silence the will is not avoided, but the omitted persons come in to share with the devisees, taking an aliquot part if the latter are self-successors, a moiety if they

id est si quis tres verbi gratia filios heredes instituerit et filiam praeterierit, filia adcrescendo pro quarta parte fit heres; *placuit enim eam tuendam esse pro ea parte, quia etiam ab intestato eam partem* habitura esset. at si extraneos ille heredes instituerit et filiam praeterierit, filia adcrescendo ex dimidia parte fit heres. Quae de filia diximus, eadem *et* de n*e*pot*e* deq*ue* omnibus liberorum personis, si*ve* masculini *sive* feminini sexus, dicta intellegemus.

are strangers. Thus if a man has three sons and makes them his successors, saying nothing of his daughter, the daughter comes in as co-successor and takes a fourth of the estate, being deemed entitled to the portion which would have devolved to her by intestacy: but when the devisees are strangers, the daughter, if passed over, comes in and takes a moiety. What has been said of the daughter applies to the son's children, male and female.

§ 125. Quid ergo est? licet *feminae* secundum *ea quae* diximus scriptis heredibus dimidiam partem ta*ntum* detrahant, tamen Praetor eis contra tabulas bonorum possessionem promittit, qua ratione extranei heredes a tota hereditate repelluntur: et efficeretur s*a*ne *per hanc* bonorum possessi*onem*, *ut* nihil inter femin*as* et masculos interesset.

§ 125. But though a female according to this statement of the law only deprives the devisees of a moiety, the praetor promises her the whole praetorian succession, so that the devisees, if strangers, lose the whole, and the effect of this praetorian succession would be to efface the distinction between males and females.

§ 126. Se*d* nuper Imperator Antoninus significavit rescri*p*to su*as* non plus nancisci feminas per bonorum possessionem, quam quod iure adcrescendi consequerentur. quod in emancipatis f*eminis similiter obtinet, scilicet ut quod* adcrescendi iure habitur*ae* essent, *si suae* fuissent, id ipsum etiam per bonorum possessionem habeant.

§ 126. But the emperor Antonine has recently decided that female self-successors shall not take more by praetorian succession than they would by coming in as coheirs at civil law. And the same rule applies to emancipated daughters, namely, that the shares they would have had as coheirs had they not been emancipated shall be the measure of what they obtain by praetorian succession.

§ 127. Sed si qui*dem* filius a patre exheredetur, nominatim ex*her*edari ante . . . . potest exheredari. nominatim autem exheredari videtur sive ita exheredetur: *TITIUS FILIUS MEUS EXHERES ESTO*, *sive ita*: *FILIUS MEUS* EXHERES ESTO, non adiecto proprio nomine.

§ 127. A son must be disinherited individually. Individual disherison may be expressed in these terms: Be Titius my son disinherited: or in these: Be my son disinherited, without inserting his name.

§ 128. *Masculorum ceter*orum personae vel feminini sexus *aut nominatim exheredari possunt, aut inter ceteros, velut hoc modo*: *CETERI EXHEREDES SUNTO*: *quae verba*

§ 128. Other males and all female issue may be either individually or collectively disinherited thus: Be the remainder disinherited, which words usually follow the institution

post institutionem heredum adici solent. sed *haec ita sunt iure civili.*

§ 129. Nam Praetor omnes virilis sexus, tam *filios quam ceteros*, id est nepotes quoque et pronepotes *nominatim exheredari iubet, feminini vero inter ceteros: qui nisi fuerint ita exheredati, promittit eis contra tabulas bonorum possessionem.*

§ 130. Postumi quoque liberi *vel heredes institui debent vel* exheredari.

§ 131. Et *in eo par omnium condicio est, quod et in filio postumo et in quolibet ex ceteris liberis, sive feminini sexus sive masculini, praeterito, valet quidem testamentum, sed postea adgnatione postumi sive postumae rumpitur, et ea ratione totum infirmatur: ideoque si mulier ex qua postumus aut postuma sperabatur abortum fecerit, nihil impedimento est scriptis heredibus ad hereditatem adeundam.*

§ 132. *Sed feminini quidem sexus postumae vel nominatim vel inter ceteros exheredari solent. dum tamen si inter ceteros exheredentur, aliquid eis legetur, ne videantur per oblivionem praeteritae esse: masculos vero postumos, id est filium et deinceps, placuit non aliter recte exheredari, nisi nominatim exheredentur, hoc scilicet modo:* QUICUMQUE MIHI FILIUS GENITUS FUERIT, EXHERES ESTO.

§ 133. *Postumorum loco sunt et hi qui in sui heredis locum succedendo quasi adgnascendo fiunt parentibus sui heredes. ut ecce si filium et ex eo nepotem neptemve in potestate habeam, quia filius gradu praecedit, is solus iura sui heredis habet, quamvis nepos quoque et neptis ex eo in eadem potestate sint; sed si filius meus me vivo moriatur, aut qualibet ratione exeat de potestate*

of the heir: this, however, is only the rule of the civil law.

§ 129. For the Praetor requires all male issue, sons, grandsons, greatgrandsons, to be disinherited individually, although he permits female issue to be disinherited in an aggregate, and, failing such disherison, promises them the praetorian succession.

§ 130. Children born after the making of the will must either be instituted heirs or disinherited:

§ 131. and in this respect are similarly privileged that whether a son or any other issue, male or female, born after the making of the will, be passed over in silence, the will is originally valid, but subsequently rescinded and avoided by the birth of the child; so that if the woman from whom a child was expected have an abortive delivery, there is nothing to prevent the devisees from taking the succession.

§ 132. Female issue born after the making of the will may be either individually or generally disinherited, with this proviso, that if they are generally disinherited, some legacy must be left them in order that they may not seem to have been forgotten when they were passed over. But male issue, sons and further lineal descendants, are held not to be duly disinherited unless they are disinherited individually, thus: Be any son that shall be born to me disinherited.

§ 133. With issue born after the making of the will are classed children who succeed to the place of a self-successor, and thus become self-successors to an ancestor. For instance, if a testator have a son, and by him a grandson or granddaughter under his power, the son being nearer in degree alone has the rights of self-successor, although the grandson and granddaughter are equally

mea, incipit nepos neptisve in eius locum succedere, et eo modo iura suorum heredum quasi adgnatione nancisci.

in the ancestor's power. But if the son die in the lifetime of the testator, or by any other means pass out of the testator's power, the grandson and granddaughter succeed to his place, and thus acquire the rights of self-successors to the testator just as if they were children born after the making of the will.

§ 134. *Ne ergo eo modo rumpat mihi testamentum, sicut ipsum filium vel heredem instituere vel exheredare nominatim debeo, ne non iure faciam testamentum, ita et nepotem neptemve ex eo necesse est mihi vel heredem instituere vel exheredare, ne forte, me vivo filio mortuo, succedendo in locum eius nepos neptisve* quasi adgnatione rumpat test*amentum : idque lege Iunia Velleia provisum est ; qua simul cavetur, ut illi tanquam postumi, id est* virilis sexus nominatim, feminini vel nominatim vel inter ceteros exheredentur, dum tamen iis qui inter ceteros exheredantur *aliquid legetur.*

§ 134. To prevent this subsequent avoidance of my will, just as a son must be either instituted heir or disinherited individually to make a will originally valid, so a grandson or granddaughter by a son must be either instituted heir or disinherited, for if the son die in the testator's lifetime the grandson and granddaughter take his place and vacate the will just as if they were children born after its execution. Accordingly the lex Junia Velleia allows them to be disinherited just like children born after a will is executed, that is to say, males individually, females either individually or collectively, provided that those who are disinherited collectively receive a legacy.

§ 135. *E*mancipatos liberos *iure civili neque heredes instituere neque exheredare necesse est, quia* non sunt sui heredes. sed Praetor omnes, tam feminini quam masculini sexus, si heredes non instituantur, exheredari iubet, virilis sexus *filios et ulterioris gradus nominatim, feminini* vero inter ceteros. q*uod*si neque heredes instituti fuerint, neque *ita*, ut supra diximus, exheredati, Praetor promittit eis contra tabulas bonorum possessionem.

§ 135. Emancipated children by civil law need neither be appointed heirs nor disinherited because they are not self-successors. But the Praetor requires all, females as well as males, unless appointed heirs, to be disinherited, males separately, females collectively, and if they are neither appointed heirs nor disinherited as described, the Praetor promises to give them the praetorian succession.

§ 135*a*. In potestate patr*e constituto, qui* inde nati sunt, nec in accipienda *bonorum possessione* patri *concurrunt qui possit* eos in potestate habere ; aut si petitur, non impetra*bitur.* namqu*e* per *ipsum* patre*m suum* pro*hib*entur. nec differu*nt emancipati et sui.*

§ 135*a*. Grandchildren by an unemancipated son are excluded from the succession by the prior right of their father ; and, therefore, their pretermission is immaterial if the father survive the grandfather, whether they are emancipated or unemancipated.

§ 136. *Adoptivi*, quamdiu tenentur in adoptionem, naturalium loco sunt: emancipati vero *a* patre adoptivo neque iure civili, neque quod ad edictum Praetoris pertinet, *inter liberos numerantur*.

§ 136. Adoptive children, so long as they continue in the power of the adoptive father, have the rights of natural children: but when emancipated by the adoptive father they neither at civil law nor in the Praetor's edict are regarded as his children.

§ 137. Qua ratione accidit, ut ex diverso, quod ad naturalem parentem pertinet, quamdiu quidem sint in adoptiva familia, extraneorum numero habeantur. *cum vero emancipati fuerint ab adoptivo patre, tunc incipiant* in ea causa esse qua futuri essent, si ab ipso naturali patre *emancipati* fuissent.

§ 137. And conversely in respect of their natural father as long as they continue in the adoptive family they are strangers: but when emancipated by the adoptive father they have the same rights in their natural family as they would have had if emancipated by their natural father (that is, unless either instituted heirs or disinherited by him, may claim the praetorian succession against his will).

§ 123. Justinian confirms the doctrine of Sabinus that the birth of a suus heres after the making of a will invalidates the will even though the child die before the testator, Inst. 2, 13, pr. The necessity of disinheriting a suus heres is grounded on the principle of primitive law, that the child is co-proprietor with the parent: hence, unless something occurs to divest the child of his property, he will simply become sole proprietor by survivorship on the death of his father. In suis heredibus evidentius apparet, continuationem dominii eo rem perducere, ut nulla videatur hereditas fuisse, quasi olim hi domini essent, qui etiam vivo patre quodammodo domini existimabantur. Unde etiam filiusfamilias appellatur, sicut paterfamilias, sola nota hac adjecta, per quam distinguitur genitor ab eo qui genitus sit. Itaque post mortem patris non hereditatem percipere videntur, sed magis liberam bonorum administrationem consequuntur. Hac ex causa, licet non sint heredes instituti, tamen domini sunt, nec obstat, quod licet eos exheredare, quos et occidere licebat, Dig. 38, 2, 11. 'In self-succession we have a still more striking instance of an unbroken continuity of dominion, for there appears to be no vesting of new property by descent, but the heir is deemed to have been previously proprietor even during the lifetime of the father. Hence the names filiusfamilias and paterfamilias, implying a similar legal relation to the patrimony, though one is parent and the other child. Therefore the death of the parent occasions no acquisition of new property by descent, but only an increased freedom in the administration of already existing property. Hence, even in the absence of testamentary institution, a self-successor is proprietor: and it is no objection to this, that a parent has the power of disinheriting a self-successor, for he also had the power of putting him to death.'

§ 124. Justinian abolished accretion and equalized the sexes, enacting that the pretermission of any suus heres or sua heres should absolutely vacate a will by civil law, and entitle to bonorum possessio contra tabulas by praetorian law, like the pretermission of the son, Cod. 6, 28, 4.

§ 127. Justinian abolished this distinction and required that all sui heredes should be disinherited individually like the son. Ibid.

§ 130. Afterborn children (postumi), that is, children born after the making of a will, are uncertain persons, and by the general rule that uncertain persons cannot be instituted or disinherited (incerta persona heres institui non potest, Ulpian 22, 4.), ought to be incapable of institution or disinheritance, and, therefore, if they are sui heredes, would necessarily invalidate a will, because every will is informal when there exists a suus heres who is neither instituted nor disinherited. If the suus heres was born in the lifetime of the testator, the revocation of the will would not be an irremediable evil, because the testator would still have it in his power to make another will, and accordingly in this case the civil law left the general rule to operate. But if the suus heres were born after the death of the testator, the evil would be irreparable, and the testator would die intestate. To prevent this, the civil law made an exception to the rule that an uncertain person cannot be instituted or disinherited, and permitted the institution or disinheritance of any suus heres who should be born after the death of the testator: and on the authority of the celebrated jurist Aquilius Gallus, the inventor of a form of acceptilation (3 § 169), this power was extended to the institution or disinheritance of any afterborn grandchild of the testator whose father should die in the interval between the making of the will and the death of the testator. Gallus Aquilius sic posse institui postumos nepotes induxit: Si filius meus vivo me morietur, tunc si quis mihi ex eo nepos sive quae neptis post mortem meam in decem mensibus proximis, quibus filius meus moreretur, natus nata erit, heredes sunto, Dig. 28, 2, 29, pr. 'Gallus Aquilius introduced the institution of after-

born grandchildren in the following manner: If my son die in my lifetime, then let any grandson or granddaughter by him who may be born after my death within ten months after the death of my son, be my successor.'

In respect of the suus heres born after the making of the will but in the lifetime of the testator, the case which the civil law left to the operation of the general rule, it might certainly be sometimes possible to make a new will after his birth, but it might sometimes be impossible or highly inconvenient, and accordingly the lex Junia Velleia passed A.D. 10, at the close of the reign of Augustus, in its first chapter permitted such children also of the testator to be instituted or disinherited. In its second chapter it permitted the institution or disinheritance of another class of uncertain persons, viz. quasi-afterborn children (postumorum loco); grandchildren, for instance, who were born before the making of the will but whose acquisition of the character of sui heredes is subsequent to the making of the will.

The afterborn stranger, though incapable at civil law of being appointed heir (§ 242), was relieved by the praetor who gave him the praetorian succession (bonorum possessio). Justinian allowed him to take the legal estate, Inst. 3, 9, pr.

§ 132. To the necessity of leaving some legacy to the disinherited afterborn sua heres (and not, as Blackstone suggests, to the querela inofficiosi) we must attribute the vulgar error in England of the necessity of leaving the heir one shilling in order to cut him off effectually. The querela inofficiosi was not barred by any legacy, however slight, being left to the heir, but only by giving him one fourth of his intestate portion. See 2 § 151. It seems that even a legacy left to an afterborn sua heres might be unavailing to save the will from avoidance, unless it amounted to one fourth of her share by descent. If no legacy at all were left, the will would be informal from want of proper disinheritance of the sua heres, and absolutely void; if less than a fourth of her share were left, the will would not be absolutely void but voidable, i.e. liable to be overthrown if the aggrieved party chose to impeach it as inofficiosum.

QUIBUS MODIS TESTAMENTA INFIRMENTUR.

§ 138. Si quis post factum testamentum adoptaverit sibi filium, aut per populum eum qui sui iuris

§ 138. If after making his will a man adopts as son either a paterfamilias by a lex curiata or a filius-

est, aut per Praetorem eum qui in potestate parentis fuerit, omnimodo testamentum eius rumpitur quasi agnatione sui heredis.

§ 139. Idem iuris est si cui post factum testamentum uxor in manum conveniat, vel quae in manu fuit nubat: nam eo modo filiae loco esse incipit et quasi sua *est*.

§ 140. Nec prodest *si*ve haec, *si*ve ille qui adoptatus est, in eo testamento sit institu*tu*s institutave. nam de exheredatione eius supervac*uu*m videtur quaerere, cum testamenti faciundi *te*mpore suorum heredum numero non fueri*t*.

§ 141. Filius quoque qui ex prima secundave mancipatione manumittitur, quia revertitur in potestatem patriam, rumpit ante factum testamentum. nec prodest si in eo testamento heres institutus vel exheredatus fuerit.

§ 142. Simile ius olim fuit in eius persona cuius nomine ex senatusconsulto erroris causa pro*b*atur, quia forte ex peregrina vel Latina, quae per errorem quasi civis Romana uxor ducta esset, natus esset. nam sive heres institutus esset a parente sive exheredatus, sive vivo patre causa probata sive post mortem eius, omnimodo quasi adgnatione rumpebat testamentum.

§ 143. Nunc vero ex novo senatusconsulto quod auctore divo Hadriano factum est, si quidem vivo patre causa probatur, aeque ut olim omnimodo rumpit testamentum: si vero post mortem patris, p*rae*teritus quidem rumpit testamentum, si vero heres in eo scriptus est vel exheredatus, non rumpit testamentum; ne scilicet diligente*r* facta testamenta rescinderentur *eo te*mpore *quo* renovari non possent.

familias by mancipation and fictitious vindication, his will is inevitably vacated as it would be by the subsequent birth of a self-successor.

§ 139. The same happens if after making his will the testator receives a wife into his hand, or marries a person who is in his hand, as she thereby acquires the rights of a daughter and becomes his self-successor.

§ 140. And it is unavailing that such a wife or adopted son was in that will appointed heir, for not having been self-successors when the will was made they clearly cannot have been therein disinherited.

§ 141. So a son manumitted after the first or second sale reverts into the power of his father and vacates a previous will, nor does it avail that he is therein appointed heir or disinherited.

§ 142. The same rule formerly held of the son in whose behalf the decree of the senate allows proof of error, if he was born of an alien or Latin mother who was married in the mistaken belief that she was a Roman [see 1 § 67]: for whether he was appointed heir by his father or disinherited, and whether the error was proved in his father's life or after his death, in every case the will was avoided as by the subsequent birth of a self-successor.

§ 143. Now, however, by a recent decree of the senate, made on the proposition of the late emperor Hadrian, if the father is alive when the error is proved, the old rule obtains and the will is in every case avoided; but when the error is proved after the father's death, if the son was passed over in silence, the will is vacated; but if he was appointed heir or disinherited the will is valid; so that carefully executed wills shall not be rescinded at a period when re-execution is impossible.

§ 144. Posteriore quoque testamento quod iure factum *fuerit* superius rumpitur. nec interest an extiterit aliquis ex eo heres, an non extiterit: hoc enim solum spectatur, an existere potuerit. ideoque si quis ex posteriore testamento quod iure factum est, aut noluerit heres esse, aut vivo testatore, aut post mortem eius antequam hereditatem adiret decesserit, aut per *cre*tionem exclusus fuerit, aut condicione sub qua heres institutus est defectus sit, aut propter caelibatum ex lege Iulia summotus fuerit ab hereditate: quibus casibus paterfamilias intestatus moritur: nam et prius testamentum non valet, ruptum a posteriore, et posterius aeque nullas vires habet, cum ex eo nemo heres extiterit.

§ 144. A subsequent will duly executed is a revocation of a prior will, and it makes no difference whether a successor ever actually takes under it or no; the only question is, whether one might. Accordingly, whether the successor instituted in a subsequent will duly executed declines to be successor, or dies in the lifetime of the testator, or after his death before accepting the succession, or is excluded by expiration of the time allowed for deliberation, or by failure of the condition under which he was instituted, or by celibacy as the lex Julia provides; in all these cases the testator dies intestate, for the earlier will is revoked by the later one, and the later one is inoperative, as it creates no actual successor.

§ 145. Alio quoque modo testamenta iure facta infirmantur, velut *cum* is qui fecerit testamentum capite diminutus sit. quod quibus modis accidat, primo commentario relatum est.

§ 145. There is another event whereby a will duly executed may be invalidated, namely, the testator's undergoing a loss of status: how this may happen was explained in the preceding book.

§ 146. Hoc autem casu *in*rita fieri testamenta dicemus, cum alioquin et quae rumpuntur inrita fiant; *et quae statim ab initio non iure fiunt inrita sunt; sed et ea quae iure facta sunt et postea propter capitis diminutionem inrita fiunt*, possunt nihilominus rupta dici. sed quia sane commodius erat singulas causas singulis appellationibus distingui, ideo quaedam non iure fieri dicuntur, quaedam iure facta rumpi, vel inrita fieri.

§ 146. In this case the will may be said to be null; for although both those that are rescinded and those that are not duly executed may be said to be null, and those that are duly executed but subsequently annulled by loss of status may be said to be vacated, yet as it is convenient that different grounds of invalidity should have different names to distinguish them, we will say that some wills are unduly executed, others duly executed but subsequently vacated or subsequently annulled.

§ 138. The innovations of Justinian changed the effects of adoption. Under his enactment, if a child is adopted by an ascendant the old rules obtain; but a person adopted by a stranger only acquires rights in the adoptive family in case of the adopter's intestacy, and therefore need not be instituted or disinherited by the adopter; he retains, however, his rights in his natural family, and therefore must be instituted or disinherited in the will of his natural parent.

§ 139. By English law the only circumstance by which a will is avoided (besides revocation, cancellation, execution of a later will), is the marriage of the testator, and this operates universally, irrespectively of the birth of children.

BONORUM POSSESSIO SECUNDUM TABULAS.

§ 147. Non tamen per omnia inutilia sunt ea testamenta, quae vel ab initio non iure facta sunt, vel iure facta postea inrita facta *aut* rupta sunt. nam si septem testium signis signata sint testamenta, potest scriptus heres secundum tabulas bonorum possessionem petere, si modo defunctus testator et civis Romanus et suae potestatis mortis tempore fuerit: nam si ideo inritum fit testamentum, quod postea civitatem vel etiam libertatem testator amisit, *a*ut is in adoptionem se dedit *et* mortis tempore in adoptivi patris potestate fuit, non potest scriptus heres secundum tabulas bonorum possessionem petere.

§ 147. Wills are not altogether inoperative either when originally informal or when at first valid and subsequently vacated or annulled; for if the seals of seven witnesses are attached, the testamentary heir is entitled to demand the praetorian succession, in accordance with the written dispositions, if the testator was a citizen of Rome and in his own power at the time of his death; but if the cause of nullity was the testator's subsequent loss of citizenship, or loss of liberty, or adoption and decease in his adoptive father's power, the devisee is barred from demanding the praetorian succession in accordance with the written dispositions.

§ 148. *Qui autem* secundum tabulas testamenti, quae aut statim ab initio non iure factae sint, aut iure factae postea *r*uptae vel inritae erunt, bonorum possessionem accipiunt, si modo possunt hereditatem optinere, habebunt bonorum possessionem cum re: si vero ab *i*is avocari hereditas potest, habebunt bonorum possessionem sine re.

§ 148. Praetorian succession according to a will either originally irregular or originally regular and subsequently vacated or annulled, if tenable without molestation, is effective; if defeasible by an adverse claimant, is ineffective [see 3 § 36].

§ 149. Nam si quis heres iure civili institutus sit vel ex primo vel ex posteriore testamento, vel ab intestato iure legitimo heres sit, is potest ab *i*is hereditatem *a*vocare. si vero nemo sit alius iure civili heres, ipsi retinere hereditatem

§ 149. For a successor duly appointed by an earlier or later will, or a statutory successor by intestacy, can evict the praetorian successor from the inheritance [see, however, § 120]; though in default of such claim the praetorian successor can

possunt, *si possident, aut interdictum* adversus eos habent q*ui bona possident eorum bonorum adipiscendae possessionis causa. interdum tamen, quanquam testamento* iure civili *instituus, vel* legitimus quoque *heres sit, potiores* scrip*ti* habentur, velut *si testamentum* ideo *non iure* factum sit au*t* quod familia non venierit, aut nuncupationis verba testator locutus non sit.

retain possession, if he already has it, and if he has it not, can obtain it by the interdict quorum bonorum. Sometimes, however, a duly instituted or statutory successor is postponed to an irregularly appointed successor; for instance, if the irregularity was only the absence of mancipation or nuncupatory publication.

§ 150. A*lia causa est eorum,* qu*i herede non extante bona possiderint, nec tamen a Praetore bonorum possessionem acceperint: etiam hi* possessores *tamen* res olim *obtinebant ante legem Iuliam,* qua lege bona caduca fiunt et ad populum deferri iubentur, si defuncto nemo *successor extiterit.*

§ 150. The praetorian succession is sometimes defeated by the lex Julia caducaria; in pursuance of which the succession may become vacant, and escheat to the treasury [Ulpian, 28, 7].

§ 151. . . . . potest, ut iure facta testamenta . . . . infirme*n*tur apparet posse . . . . testator . . . . eius . . . . iure civili valeat qui . . . . tabulas testame*nti* [2 *lin.*] quidem . . . . si quis ab i*ntestato* bonorum possessionem petieri*t* [3 *lin.*] perveniat hereditas. et hoc ita *re*scripto Imperatoris Antonini significatur.

§ 151. [This paragraph apparently mentioned certain cases where, after the confirmation of the praetorian testament by the constitution of Marcus Aurelius, § 120, the praetorian succession secundum tabulas was no longer, as formerly, defeasible by the heir at civil law].

§ 148. There was no ipso jure, or necessarius, bonorum possessor, corresponding to the heres necessarius, § 152, with whom delatio and acquisitio hereditatis were coincident: all bonorum possessores corresponded to the other class of heres, the heres extraneus or voluntarius, with whom acquisitio was distinct from delatio hereditatis, and required a voluntary act (aditio). That is to say, the person called (vocatus) by the praetorian edict to the succession forfeited his right to succeed unless he made his claim (agnitio, petitio, admissio, bonorum possessionis), within a certain period, usually 100 dies utiles from the date of the vocatio (delatio). On the claim being made, the grant (datio) of bonorum possessio followed as a matter of course without any judicial investigation (causae cognitio). It was a mere formality, a certificate of the magistrate, the praetor or praeses provinciae, that the agnitio had been made within the allotted period, before the expiration of the term allowed for deliberation. If any real controversy arose, it was decided by one of two actions, hereditatis petitio, or the Interdict Quorum bonorum. If the claimant relied on his title at civil law, he sued by hereditatis petitio; if he relied on the title given him by the praetorian edict, he sued by the Interdict Quorum bonorum. If defeated in either of these proceedings, he gained nothing by having obtained the formal grant of praetorian succession—he had only bonorum possessio sine re.

§ 150. Escheat (from excidere) is etymologically the same word as caducum and denotes to a certain extent a similar destination of property.

By English law, if a man dies intestate, and without kindred, the devolution of his property follows different rules according as it is real or personal. By feudal law, if a vassal holding a transmissible feud died without heirs, his feud escheated or reverted to the lord. So in England if a tenant in fee die without leaving lawful heirs, for instance, if he leave no relations but aliens (who are incapable of holding land), his land escheats to the lord of the fee. But the personal property of a man who dies intestate and without kindred, goes to the crown, subject always to the widow's right to a moiety in case she survive.

DE HEREDUM QUALITATE ET DIFFERENTIA.

§ 152. Heredes autem aut necessarii dicuntur aut sui et necessarii aut extranei.

§ 153. Necessarius heres est servus cum libertate heres institutus; ideo sic appellatus, quia, sive velit sive nolit, omnimodo post mortem testatoris protinus liber et heres est.

§ 154. Unde qui facultates suas suspectas habet, solet servum primo aut secundo vel etiam ulteriore gradu liberum et heredem instituere, ut si creditoribus satis non fiat, potius huius heredis quam ipsius testatoris bona veneant, id est ut ignominia quae accidit ex venditione bonorum hunc potius heredem quam ipsum testatorem contingat; inquamquam aput *Fu*fidium Sabino placeat eximendum eum esse igno-

§ 152. Successors are necessary, self-successors and necessary, or external.

§ 153. A necessary successor is a slave enfranchised and instituted heir, so called because, willing or unwilling, without any alternative, on the death of the testator he immediately has his freedom and the succession.

§ 154. For when a man's affairs are embarrassed, it is common for a slave, either in the first place or as a substitute in the second or any inferior place, to be enfranchised and appointed heir, so that, if the creditors are not paid in full, the heir is insolvent instead of the testator, and the ignominy of insolvency attaches to the heir instead of the testator; though, as Fufidius relates, Sabinus held that

minia, quia non suo vitio, sed necessitate iuris bonorum venditionem pateretur: sed alio iure utimur.

he ought to be exempted from ignominy, as it is not his own fault, but legal compulsion, that makes him insolvent; this, however, is not the law.

§ 155. Pro hoc tamen incommodo illud ei commodum praestatur, ut ea quae post mortem patroni sibi adquisierit, sive ante bonorum venditionem sive postea, ipsi reserventur. et quamvis *pro portione* bona venierint, iterum ex hereditaria causa bona eius non venient, nisi si quid ei ex hereditaria causa fuerit adquisitum, velut si *ex eo quod* Latinus adquisierit, locupletior factus sit; cum ceterorum hominum quorum bona venierint pro portione, si quid postea adquirant, etiam saepius eorum bona veniri solent.

§ 155. To compensate this disadvantage he has the advantage that his acquisitions after the death of his patron, and whether before or after the sale, are for his own benefit, and although a portion only of the debts is satisfied by the sale, he is not liable to a second sale of his after-acquired property for the debts of the testator, unless he gain anything as heir, if he inherit, for instance, the property of a Latinus Junianus, another freedman of the testator; whereas other persons, who only pay a dividend, on subsequently acquiring any property, are liable to repeated sales.

§ 156. Sui autem et necessarii heredes sunt velut filius filiave, nepos neptisve ex filio, deinceps ceteri, qui modo in potestate morientis fuerunt. sed uti nepos neptisve suus heres sit, non sufficit eum in potestate avi mortis tempore fuisse, sed opus est, ut pater quoque eius vivo patre suo desierit suus heres esse, aut morte interceptus aut qualibet ratione liberatus potestate: tum enim nepos neptisve in locum sui patris succedunt.

§ 156. Self-successors and necessary are such as a son or daughter, a grandson or granddaughter by the son, and further similar lineal descendants, provided that they are under the power of the ancestor when he dies. To make a grandson or granddaughter self-successor it is, however, not sufficient that they were in the power of the grandfather at the time of his death, but it is further requisite that their father in the life of the grandfather shall have ceased to be self-successor, whether by death or by any other mode of liberation from parental power, as the grandson and granddaughter then succeed to the place of the father.

§ 157. Sed sui quidem heredes ideo appellantur, quia domestici heredes sunt, et vivo quoque parente quodam modo domini existimantur. unde etiam si quis intestatus mortuus sit, prima causa est in successione liberorum. necessarii vero ideo dicuntur, quia omnimodo, *sive* velint *sive nolint*, *tam* ab in-

§ 157. They are called self-successors because they are members of the family, and even in the lifetime of the parent are deemed to a certain extent co-proprietors; wherefore in intestacy the first right of succession belongs to the children. They are called necessary, because they have no alternative,

testato quam ex testamento heredes fiunt.

but, willing or unwilling, both in testacy and intestacy, they become successors.

§ 158. Sed his Praetor permittit abstinere se ab heredi*tate*, ut potius parentis bona veneant.

§ 158. The praetor, however, permits them to abstain from the succession, and leave the ancestor to be declared insolvent.

§ 159. Idem iuris est et *in* uxoris persona quae in manu est, quia filiae loco est, et in nurus quae in manu filii est, quia neptis loco est.

§ 159. The same rule governs a wife in the hand of a husband, for she is on the footing of a daughter, and a son's wife in the hand of the son, for she is on the footing of a granddaughter.

§ 160. Quin etiam similiter abstinendi po*te*statem facit Praetor etiam [mancipato, id est] ei qui in causa mancipi*i* est, cum liber et heres institutus sit; cum necessarius, non etiam suus heres sit, tamquam servus.

§ 160. A similar power of abstention is granted by the praetor to a person held in mancipation when enfranchised and made successor, although he is a necessary successor and not a self-successor, mancipation being assimilated to servitude.

§ 161. Ceteri qui testatoris iuri subiecti non sunt extranei heredes appellantur. itaque liberi quoque nostri qui in potestate nostra non sunt, heredes a nobis instituti sicut extranei videntur. qua de causa et qui a matre heredes instituuntur eodem numero sunt, quia feminae liberos in potestate non habent. servi quoque qui cum liber*tate* heredes instituti sunt et postea a domino manumissi, eodem numero habentur.

§ 161. Those who were not subject to the testator's power are called strangers, or external successors. Thus children not in our power, if instituted successors, are deemed strangers; and children instituted by their mother belong to this class, because women are not invested with power over their children. Slaves instituted heirs with freedom annexed, and subsequently manumitted, belong to the same class.

§ 162. Extraneis autem heredibus deliberandi potestas data est de adeunda hereditate vel non adeunda.

§ 162. External or voluntary successors have the right of deliberating whether they will accept or disclaim a succession.

§ 163. Sed sive is cui a*b*stinendi potestas e*s*t immiscuerit se bonis hereditariis, sive is *c*ui de adeunda *hereditate* deliberare licet, adierit, postea relinquendae hereditatis facultatem non habet, nisi si minor sit annorum XXV. nam huius aetatis hominibus, sicut in ceteris omnibus causis, deceptis, ita etiam si temere damnosa*m* hereditatem susceperint, Praetor succurrit. scio quidem divum Hadrianum etiam maiori XXV annorum veniam dedisse, cum

§ 163. But if a person who has the power of abstention interferes with the succession, or a person who has the power of deliberation accepts, he has no longer the power of relinquishing the inheritance, unless he is a minor under twenty-five years of age; for minors, both when they take any other injudicious step, and when they incautiously accept a disadvantageous inheritance, obtain relief from the praetor. The late Emperor Ha-

post aditam hereditatem grande aes alienum quod aditae hereditatis tempore latebat apparuisset.

drian even relieved a person who had attained his majority, when, after his acceptance of a succession, a great debt, unknown at the time of acceptance, had come to light.

§ 164. Extraneis heredibus solet cretio dari, id est finis deliberandi, ut intra certum tempus vel adeant hereditatem, vel si non adeant, temporis fine summoveantur. ideo autem cretio appellata est, quia cernere est quasi decernere et constituere.

§ 164. External heirs are commonly allowed an interval for decision, that is, a definite delay for deliberation, within which time they must accept, and in default of acceptance are barred. It is a term for decision, because it is a term within which the heir must come to a determination and resolution.

§ 165. Cum ergo ita scri*p*tum sit: HERES TITIUS ESTO: adicere debemus; CERNITOQUE IN CENTUM DIEBUS PROXUMIS QUIBUS SCIES POTERISQUE. QUOD NI ITA CREVERIS, EXHERES ESTO.

§ 165. Accordingly, after the words, 'Titius, be thou my heir,' we ought to add, 'and declare whether thou accept within a hundred days on which thou hast power to declare after the day on which thou hast notice; or in default of so declaring be thou disinherited.'

§ 166. Et qui ita heres institutus est si velit heres esse, debebit intra diem cretionis cernere, id est haec verba dicere: QUOD ME PUBLIUS MAEVIUS TESTAMENTO SUO HEREDEM INSTITUIT, EAM HEREDITATEM ADEO CERNOQUE. Quodsi ita non creverit, finito tempore cretionis excluditur: nec quicquam proficit, si pro herede gerat, id est si rebus hereditariis tamquam heres utatur.

§ 166. And the successor thus appointed, if he wish to inherit, must within the term prescribed declare his decision in the following words: 'Whereas Publius Mevius in his will has made me his successor, that succession I hereby accept and undertake.' In default of such declaration, the elapsing of the period allowed shuts him out from the inheritance, and it is of no avail that he behave as successor, that is, deal with the estate of the deceased as proprietor.

§ 167. At is qui sine cretione heres institu*tus* sit, aut qui ab intestato legitimo iure ad hereditatem vocatur, potest aut cernendo aut pro herede gerendo vel etiam nuda voluntate suscipiendae hereditatis heres fieri: eique liberum est, quocumque tempore voluerit, adire hereditatem. *sed* solet Praetor postulantibus hereditariis creditoribus tempus constituere, intra quod si velit adeat hereditatem: si minus, ut liceat creditoribus bona defuncti vendere.

§ 167. In the absence of a prescribed term for deliberation, and in intestate succession at civil law, a man takes the inheritance either by declaration, or by acts of ownership, or by naked intention, and is not barred from accepting by any lapse of time; but it is usual for the praetor, at the demand of the creditors of the deceased, to appoint a period, on the expiration of which without his acceptance the creditors are permitted to put up the estate of the deceased for sale.

§ 168. Sic*ut* autem cum cretione heres institutus, nisi creverit hereditatem, non fit heres, ita non aliter excluditur, quam si non creverit intra id tempus quo cretio finita si*t*. itaque licet ante diem cretionis constituerit hereditatem non adire, tamen paenitentia actus superante die cretionis cernendo heres esse potest.

§ 169. At hic qui sine cretione heres institutus est, quique ab intestato per legem vocatur, sicut voluntate nuda heres fit, ita et contraria destinatione statim ab hereditate repellitur.

§ 170. Omnis autem cretio certo tempore constringitur. in quam rem tolerabile tempus visum est centum dierum: potest tamen nihilominus iure civili aut longius aut brevius tempus dari: longius tamen interdum Praetor coartat.

§ 171. Et quamvis omnis cretio certis diebus constringatur, tamen alia cretio vulgaris vocatur, alia certorum dierum: vulgaris illa, quam supra exposuimus, id est in qua *a*dic*i*untur haec verba: QUIBUS SCIET POTERITQUE; certorum dierum, in qua detractis his verbis cetera scribuntur.

§ 172. Quarum cretionum magna differentia est. nam vulgari cretione data nulli dies conputantur, nisi quibus scierit quisque se heredem esse institutum et possit cernere. certorum vero dierum cretio*ne* data etiam nescient*i* se heredem institutum esse numerantur dies continui; item ei quoque qui aliqua ex causa cernere prohibetur, et eo amplius ei qui sub condicione heres institutus est, tempus numeratur. unde melius et aptius est vulgari cretione uti.

§ 168. When a term is prescribed for declaring, a man is barred by not declaring, but only by not declaring within the last day of the appointed term; and though, pending the term, he may have elected to disclaim, yet if he change his mind before the time is expired and declare his acceptance, he takes the estate.

§ 169. If no term is prescribed in the institution, or if a man is entitled by intestacy at civil law, just as a mere intention makes him heir, so the contrary intention immediately bars him from the succession.

§ 170. Every period of deliberation has a certain limit, and a reasonable limit is held to be a hundred days, yet by the civil law a longer or shorter period is allowed to be fixed, though a longer period is sometimes shortened by the praetor.

§ 171. Although, however, the time of deliberation is always limited to certain days, yet one mode of limitation is called ordinary, the other determinate; the ordinary being that above indicated, namely, with the addition of the words, 'after notice of institution and available for declaration;' determinate that in which these words are omitted.

§ 172. These modes are very different in effect, for when the ordinary period is allowed no days are computed until the heir has notice and is in a position to decide, but when a determinate period is allowed, notwithstanding the heir's want of notice of his institution, the days begin to be counted without intermission, and notwithstanding his inability from any cause to declare, or any condition annexed to his institution, nevertheless the days begin to be reckoned.

Accordingly, it is better and more considerate to employ the ordinary mode of limitation.

§ 173. Continua haec cretio vocatur, quia continui dies numerantur. sed quia tamen dura est haec cretio, altera in usu habetur: unde etiam vulgaris dicta est.

§ 173. The determinate period is called continuous, because the days are reckoned without intermission. Because of the harshness of this condition the other is commonly employed, and hence is called ordinary.

§ 152. The rules of institution and disinheritance were restrictions of the unlimited power of testamentary disposition conferred by the Twelve Tables. The general tendency and purpose of these restrictions are to protect children against the caprice of parents, and to be fully comprehended they should be viewed in connection with three other branches of law, the rules respecting testamentum inofficiosum, the provisions of the lex Falcidia and those of the senatusconsultum Pegasianum. All these limitations of testamentary power may be considered as correlations and compensations of the patria potestas. An English testator has unlimited power to dispose of his property, and natural feeling is supposed to be a sufficient guaranty that none of his children will be left without suitable provision. Of Roman testators Justinian says rather crudely: Plerumque parentes sine causa liberos suos vel exheredant vel omittunt, Inst. 2, 18, pr. 'Most parents disinherit or pretermit their children without any cause.' In spite of this expression, we may conjecture that parental caprice was not greater in Rome than in England, but the monstrous development of the patria potestas, whereby the person and fortunes of the child were entirely at the mercy of the father during his lifetime, made any instance of testamentary caprice seem more iniquitous, more intolerable, in Rome than it would in England. The restrictions were as follows:—

(1) We have seen that a suus heres must either be instituted or disinherited. This secured him against being simply forgotten.

(2) If he was disinherited without a cause, or received less than one fourth of his share by descent (quarta legitimae) he could by impeaching the will as immoral or unnatural (querela inofficiosi testamenti) have it set aside on the fictitious presumption of the testator's insanity. The presumption, at least, was

so far fictitious that it was not allowed to be rebutted by any other proof of his sanity except proof of the adequacy of the motives for which the child was disinherited. The querela inofficiosi was a form of petitio hereditatis, that is, a real action, and fell under the jurisdiction of the centumviral court. The amount which must be devised to a suus heres to save a will from avoidance for inofficiositas was probably fixed by the lex Falcidia, for it is identical with the amount which that law secures to the child when instituted heir. The querela inofficiosi could not only be brought by suus heres but by certain other near relatives, namely, parents, brothers, and sisters, and by children against their mothers' will; in which cases, it must be confessed, the alleged motive, compensation for the patria potestas, is wanting.

(3) Although a suus heres were instituted heir, yet the institution might be made illusory by the exhaustion of the whole inheritance in legacies, leaving nothing to the heir but the burden of administration. To meet this, the lex Falcidia provided that when more than three fourths of an inheritance is absorbed in legacies, all the legacies should abate proportionably so as to leave the heir a clear fourth of the portion in which he was instituted (quarta Falcidiae).

(4) The senatus consultum Pegasianum provided against the inheritance being similarly exhausted by fideicommissa.

We may add that an infant adopted by adrogation, if disinherited or without cause emancipated, was entitled to one fourth of the inheritance of his adoptive father (quarta Antonini) 1 § 102.

§ 157. Communism or co-ownership appears to be an older institution than divided or individual ownership. Even after the rights of the paterfamilias had been enormously developed at the expense of the rest of the household, a vestige of the times when property vested rather in the family than in the chief was preserved in the rules respecting the suus heres. Suus heres appears equivalent to sibi heres, and implies that he who now enters on proprietary rights in the character of paterfamilias had already possessed proprietary rights over the same subject matter in the character of filiusfamilias.

Less barbarous than self-successor (the term chosen to represent suus heres as expressing sibi heres) but too long for perpetual use, would have been the circumlocution, immediate lineal successor.

Suus heres is a lineal descendant as opposed to the legitimus heres or agnate, who is a collateral relation: and he is an immediate successor as opposed to an eventual successor. For instance, a grandson by an unemancipated son is in the grandfather's power, and may eventually be his successor, but is not his suus heres during the life of the son.

§ 162. After accepting an inheritance the heir became liable to the testator's creditors for the full amount of the testator's debts. To avoid the danger of accepting an inheritance more onerous than lucrative he might by application to the praetor obtain a delay of a hundred days for deliberation.

Justinian introduced the benefice of Inventory, reducing the liability of an heir who made the required inventory to the extent of the assets that came to his hands. The inventory must be commenced within thirty days from notice of the inheritance and completed in sixty other days. It must be executed in the presence of a notary (tabellarius) and the persons interested or three witnesses.

By English law the executor in every case is bound to make an inventory, and in no case is he answerable to the testator's creditors beyond the assets that come to his hands, unless for a sufficient consideration he make his own estate chargeable by a written engagement, as provided by the Statute of Frauds.

§ 173. The formularies of cretio, after being dispensed with in certain cases by other emperors, were totally abrogated by Justinian: Cretionum scrupulosam sollennitatem hac lege penitus amputari decernimus, Cod. 6. 30. 17. 'Declaration with its embarrassing formalities is hereby decreed to be absolutely abolished.' When it became customary for the praetor to grant to any devisee who desired it a hundred days for deliberation, the designation of such a period by the testator became unnecessary.

DE VULGARI SUBSTITUTIONE.

§ 174. Interdum duos pluresve gradus heredum facimus, hoc modo: LUCIUS TITIUS HERES ESTO CERNITOQUE IN DIEBUS *CENTUM* PROXIMIS QUIBUS SCIES POTERISQUE. QUOD NI ITA CREVERIS, EXHERES ESTO. TUM MAEVIUS HERES ESTO CERNITOQUE IN DIEBUS CENTUM et

§ 174. Sometimes two or more degrees of heirs are instituted, as follows: 'Lucius Titius, be thou my successor, and declare within a hundred available days after notice: or, in default of so declaring, be disinherited. Then, Mevius, be thou my successor, and declare

reliqua: et deinceps in quantum velimus substituere possumus.

within a hundred days,' &c.; and in this way we can make as many substitutions as we like.

§ 175. Et licet nobis vel unum in unius locum substituere pluresve, et contra in plurium locum vel unum vel plures substituere.

§ 175. We may substitute in place of one either one or several, and, conversely, in the place of several we may substitute either several or one.

§ 176. Primo itaque gradu scriptus heres hereditatem cernendo fit heres et substitutus excluditur; non cernendo summovetur, etiam si pro herede gerat, et in locum eius substitutus succedit. et deinceps si plures gradus sint, in singulis simili ratione idem contingit.

§ 176. Accordingly, if the person instituted in the first degree accepts the inheritance, he is heir, and the substitutes are excluded: if he fail to declare, he is barred in spite of acts of ownership, and his place is taken by the substitute; and if there are several degrees, in every one a similar result occurs.

§ 177. Sed si cretio sine exheredatione sit data, id est *in* haec verba: SI NON CREVERIS TUM PUBLIUS MAEVIUS HERES ESTO, illud diversum invenitur, quia si prior omissa cretione pro herede gerat, substitutus in partem admittitur, et fiunt ambo aequis partibus heredes. *quod* si neque cernat neque pro herede gerat, sane in univers*um* summovetur, et substitutus in totam hereditatem succedit.

§ 177. If power of deliberation is conferred without a clause of disherison, that is, in these words: 'If thou fail to declare, be Publius Mevius my heir,' the result is herein different, that, if the person first instituted, though he omit the declaration, act as heir, the substitute is only admitted to a portion, and both take a moiety: if he neither declare nor act as heir, he is entirely excluded, and the substitute takes the whole.

§ 178. Sed dudum quidem placuit, quamdiu cernere et eo modo heres fieri possit prior, etiam si pro herede gesserit, non tamen admitti substitutum: cum vero cretio finita sit, tum pro herede gerente*m* admittere substitutum: *olim* vero placuit, etiam superante cretione posse eum pro herede gerendo in partem substitutum admittere et amplius ad cretionem reverti non posse.

§ 178. It is a well-established rule that, as long as a term prefixed for declaring and taking the succession subsists, if a person in a higher grade act as heir, he does not let in the substitute, and that even after the expiration of the term his acts of heirship make him coheir with the substitute. It once was held that, even pending the allotted term, acts of heirship let in the substitute and bar the prior heir from reverting to his right of formal declaration.

DE PUPILLARI SUBSTITUTIONE.

§ 179. Liberis nostris inpuberibus quos in potestate habemus non solum ita, ut supra diximus, substituere poss*umus*, id est ut *si* here-

§ 179. To children below the age of puberty in the power of the testator, not only can such a substitute as we have described be ap-

des non extiterint, alius nobis heres sit; sed eo amplius, ut etiam si heredes nobis extiterint et adhuc impuberes mortui fuerint, sit iis aliquis heres, velut hoc modo: TITIUS FILIUS MEUS MIHI HERES ESTO. SI FILIUS MEUS MIHI *HERES NON ERIT SIVE HERES* ERIT ET *PRIUS* MORIATUR QUAM IN SUAM TUTELAM VENERIT, SEIUS HERES ESTO.

pointed, that is, one who shall take the succession on their failure to inherit, but also one who, if after inheriting they die before attaining the age of puberty, shall be their successor; which may be done in the following terms: 'Be my son Titius my successor, and if my son does not become my successor, or after becoming my successor die before attaining the age of puberty, then be Seius the successor.'

§ 180. Quo casu si quidem non extiterit heres filius, substitutus patri fit heres: *si vero* heres extiterit filius et ante pubertatem decesserit, ipsi filio fit heres substitutus. quamobrem duo quodammodo sunt testamenta: aliud patris, aliud filii, tamquam si ipse filius sibi heredem instituisset; aut certe unum est testamentum duarum hereditatum.

§ 180. In which case, if the son fail to inherit, the substitute is the heir of the testator, but if the son die after inheriting and without attaining the age of puberty, the substitute is heir to the son. Thus there are two wills, so to speak, the father's and the son's, just as if the son had made a successor; or at any rate there is one will dealing with two inheritances.

§ 181. Ceterum ne post obitum parentis periculo insidiarum subiectus videatur pupillus, in usu est vulgarem quidem substitutionem palam facere, id est eo loco quo pupillum heredem instituimus: *nam* vulgaris substitutio ita vocat ad hereditatem substitutum, si omnino pupillus heres non extiterit; quod accidit cum vivo parente moritur, quo casu nullum substituti maleficium suspicari possumus, cum scilicet vivo testatore omnia quae in testamento scripta sint ignorentur. illam autem substitutionem per quam, etiamsi heres extiterit pupillus et intra pubertatem decesserit, substitutum vocamus, separatim in inferioribus tabulis scribimus, easque tabulas proprio lino propriaque cera consignamus; et in prioribus tabulis cavemus, ne inferiores tabulae vivo filio et adhuc inpubere aperiantur. Sed longe tutius est utrumque genus substitutionis separatim in inferioribus tabulis consignari, quod si ita con-

§ 181. However, to save the ward from the danger of foul play after the death of the parent, it is common for the ordinary substitution to be made openly, that is, in the clause wherein the ward is instituted, for as the ordinary substitution only calls a man to the succession in case of the ward altogether failing to inherit, and this can only occur by his death in the lifetime of his parent, the substitute in this case is open to no suspicion of crime, because while the testator is alive the contents of the will are a secret. But the substitution wherein a man is named heir on the succession and death of the ward is written separately on later tablets, tied with their own cords and sealed with their own wax, and prohibited in the prior tablets to be opened in the lifetime of the son before he attains the age of puberty. Indeed it is far safer that both kinds of substitution should be sealed up separately in two subse-

signatae vel separatae fuerint substitutiones, ut diximus, *ex* priore potest intellegi in altera [alter] quoque idem esse substitutus.

§ 182. Non solum autem heredibus institutis inpuberibus liberis ita substituere poss*u*mus, ut si ante pubertatem mortui fuerint, sit is heres quem nos voluerimus, sed etiam exheredatis. itaque eo casu si quid pupillo ex hereditatibus legatisve aut donationibus propinquorum adquisitum fuerit, id omne a*d* substitutum pertinet.

§ 183. Quaecumque diximus de substitutione inpuberum libe*ro*rum, vel heredum institutorum vel exheredatorum, eadem etiam de postumis intellegemus.

§ 184. Extraneo vero heredi instituto ita substituere non possumus, ut si heres extiterit et intra aliquod tempus decesserit, alius ei heres sit: sed hoc solum nobis permissum est, ut eum per fideicommissum obligemus, ut hereditatem nost*ra*m vel totam vel *pro* parte restituat; quod ius quale sit, suo loco trademus.

quent tablets, for if the ordinary substitution is contained in the first tablets it is easy to conjecture that the same substitute is appointed in the second.

§ 182. Not only when we leave our succession to children under the age of puberty can we make such a substitution that if they die before puberty the substitute is their successor, but we can do it when we disinherit them, so that whatever the ward acquires by devises, legacies, donations of his relatives, all passes to the substitute.

§ 183. What has been said of substitution to children below the age of puberty, whether appointed heirs or disinherited, is true of substitution to afterborn children.

§ 184. To a stranger instituted heir we cannot appoint a substitute who, if the stranger inherit and die within a certain time, shall be his successor: we have only the power to bind him by a trust to convey the inheritance to another, in part or in whole, a right which shall be explained in the proper place.

§ 177. A constitution of Marcus Aurelius changing this rule, and mentioned by Ulpian: Sed postea divus Marcus constituit, ut et pro herede gerendo ex asse fiat heres, 22, 34: 'Subsequently Marcus Aurelius enacted that acts of heirship should make him exclusive heir,' was clearly not enacted when this paragraph was written by Gaius, and furnishes an indication of the date at which this book of his Institutions was published. Marcus Aurelius was sole emperor A.D. 169–176.

§ 179. Cicero frequently mentions a great case in which the question arose whether a vulgaris substitutio may be implied from a pupillaris substitutio. The centumviral court decided that the intention rather than the words of the testator should prevail, and that the heir appointed to succeed the son in case the son died before puberty should be deemed appointed to succeed the testator in case no son was born: Malim mihi L. Crassi unam pro M'. Curio dictionem quam castellanos triumphos duos, Brutus, 73. 'I would rather have made the single speech of Lucius Crassus for Manius Curius than have had two triumphs for the capture of fortresses.' The other passages are worth referring to, De Orat. 1, 39, 57; 2, 6, 32; Brutus, 39, 52; Pro Caecina, 18; Topica, 10. Marcus Aurelius enacted that in every case pupillaris substitutio should be implied in vulgaris substitutio and vice versâ, unless the contrary intention was expressed, Dig. 28, 6, 4.

DE HEREDIBUS INSTITUENDIS.

§ 185. Sicut autem liberi homines, ita et servi, tam nostri quam alieni, heredes scribi possunt.

§ 185. Not only freemen but slaves, whether belonging to the testator or to another person, may be instituted heirs.

§ 186. *Sed* noster servus simul et liber et heres esse iuberi debet, id est hoc modo: STICHUS SERVUS MEUS LIBER HERESQUE ESTO, vel HERES LIBERQUE ESTO.

§ 186. A slave belonging to the testator must be simultaneously instituted and enfranchised in the following manner: 'Stichus, my slave, be free and be my heir;' or, 'Be my heir and be free.'

§ 187. Nam si sine libertate heres institutus sit, etiam si postea manumissus fuerit a domino, heres esse non potest, quia institutio in persona eius non consti*tit*; ideoque licet alienatus sit, non potest iussu domini cernere hereditatem.

§ 187. If he is not enfranchised at the same time that he is instituted, no subsequent manumission by his owner enables him to take the succession, because the institution is originally void, and if aliened he cannot declare his acceptance by the order of the alienee.

§ 188. Cum libertate vero heres institutus, si *quidem in eadem causa manserit, fit* ex testamento liber *idemque* necessarius heres. si vero ab ipso testatore manumissus fuerit, suo arbitrio hereditatem adire potest. quodsi alienatus sit, iussu novi domini *adire hereditatem debet, et ea* ratione per eum dominus fit heres: *nam ipse alienatus neque* heres neque liber esse potest.

§ 188. When a slave is simultaneously instituted and enfranchised, if he continue in the same condition, the will converts him into a freeman and a necessary heir: if the testator himself manumits him in his lifetime, he may use his own discretion about acceptance: if he is aliened he must have the order of his new master to accept, and then his master through him becomes successor, the alienated slave himself becoming neither successor nor free.

§ 189. Alienus quoque servus heres institutus, *si in* eadem causa duraverit, iussu domini here*di*tatem

§ 189. When another person's slave is instituted heir, if he continue in the same position, he must

adire debet; si vero alienatus fu*erit ab eo, aut vivo* testatore aut post mortem eius ante*quam adeat, debet iussu novi* domini cernere. si *manumissus est antequam adeat*, suo arbitrio adire hereditatem potest.

have the order of his master to accept the succession: if aliened by him in the lifetime of the testator, or before acceptance, he must have the order of the alienee to accept: if manumitted before acceptance, he may follow his own judgment as to accepting.

§ 190. *Si* autem servus alienus heres institutu*s est* vulgari cretione data, ita i*ntelle*gitur dies cretionis ceder*e, si* ipse servus scierit se heredem institutum esse, nec ullum impedimentum sit, quominus certiorem dominum faceret, ut illius iussu cernere possit.

§ 190. When a slave of another person is instituted heir with the ordinary term allowed for deliberation, the term only begins to run when the slave has notice of his appointment, and is not disabled from informing his master so that he may obtain his order for acceptance.

§ 187. This rule was abolished by Justinian, who enacted that the enfranchisement of the testator's slave, though unexpressed, should always be implied in his institution as heir.

§ 188. Justinian explains why the slave lost his liberty: Destitisse enim a libertatis datione videtur dominus qui eum alienavit, Inst. 2, 14, 1. 'A revocation of the bequest of liberty is inferred from the fact of his alienation.' If we ask why the implied intention that suffices to revoke the enfranchisement does not suffice to revoke the institution, the answer is, that a bequest can be revoked by implied intention, whereas an institution requires a more solemn revocation, by cancellation of the will, or execution of a later will, or some other means.

§ 190. In the corresponding title of the Institutes, Justinian mentions that an heir might either be appointed to take the whole of an inheritance or to share it with other coheirs in any proportions. We may briefly state the technical terms and rules of interpretation by which different shares were allotted. An inheritance was commonly regarded as a pound (as) consisting of twelve ounces (unciae). The different fractions were thus denominated: uncia, a twelfth of an as, or an ounce; sextans, a sixth of an as, or two ounces; quadrans, a fourth of an as, or three ounces; triens, a third of an as, or four ounces; quincunx, five ounces; semis, half an as, or six ounces; septunx, seven ounces; bes (bis triens), two thirds of an as, or eight ounces; dodrans (deme quadrantem) an as minus a fourth, or nine ounces; dextans (deme sextantem), an as minus a sixth, or ten ounces; deunx (deme uncian), an as minus an ounce, or eleven ounces; as, twelve ounces.

An heir instituted in twelve ounces (ex asse) took the whole: but it was a rule that no one could be partly testate and partly intestate, and therefore if an heir were instituted in a part (ex parte) and no other coheir instituted, that part represented a pound, and the heir took the whole. So if the shares allotted to several coheirs amounted to more than twelve ounces, then, if no other heir was appointed with an unexpressed share, the as was deemed to consist of more than twelve ounces, and each coheir took a ratable part of the inheritance. If one heir were instituted in a part, say ex besse, and a coheir were instituted for whom no part was expressed, then the coheir would take the residue of the as, that is, would be deemed to be instituted ex triente. But if the parts expressed for certain heirs exhausted or exceeded the as and another heir or heirs were named without express shares, then the whole inheritance was supposed to consist of two asses (dupondius) and the expressed shares were reduced to so many ounces out of twenty-four, the heir or heirs with unexpressed parts taking the residue. Similarly, if necessary, the inheritance was supposed to consist of thirty-six ounces.

If the institution of one coheir lapsed, the shares of the remaining coheirs were ratably augmented (accretio) just as, if originally less than twelve ounces had been distributed, the expressed shares of each would be ratably augmented so as to exhaust the inheritance.

This rule, however, was modified by the leges caducariae, passed chiefly to discourage celibacy, namely the lex Julia de maritandis ordinibus, A.D. 4, and the lex Papia Poppaea, on marriage and succession, A.D. 9, in which the provisions of the lex Julia were incorporated, for which reason both laws are sometimes referred to as lex Julia et Papia.

Caducum is a devise or bequest, valid at Civil law, but vacated by some particular statute: Quod quis sibi testamento relictum ita ut jure civili capere possit, aliqua ex causa non ceperit, caducum appellatur, veluti ceciderit ab eo: verbi gratia si coelibi vel Latino Juniano legatum fuerit, nec intra dies centum vel coelebs legi paruerit vel Latinus jus Quiritium consecutus sit: aut si ex parte heres scriptus vel legatarius ante apertas tabulas decesserit vel pereger factus sit, Ulpian, 17, 1. 'A vacant devise or bequest is one valid at civil law, but lapsed by some statute, such as a legacy to a celibate or Latinus Junianus, who fails within a hundred days to comply with the law, or acquire full citizenship; or a devise to a coheir, or bequest to a legatee who dies or becomes an alien before the will is opened.' [By the Civil law, unconditional devises and bequests vested (dies cedit) at the death of the testator (though still defeasible by the failure of the will); by the lex Papia Poppaea not before the opening of the will.]

The leges caducariae, which fixed the conditions of caducity, were aimed against the coelebs and the orbus. Coelebs is defined to be an unmarried man between the age of twenty and sixty, or an unmarried woman between the age of twenty and fifty. Orbus is a man between fifty and sixty without children, natural or adoptive.

A celibate could take nothing as heres extraneus or legatee; an orbus could only take half of the devise or bequest intended for him. The devises thus vacant were allotted by the leges caducariae in the first place to conjoint legatees of the same specific thing with children; in the second place to heirs with children; in the third place to other legatees with children; and in last remainder to the treasury (aerarium). Caracalla, A.D. 212–217, made them lapse immediately to the treasury: Hodie ex constitutione imperatoris Antonini omnia caduca fisco vindicantur, sed servato jure antiquo liberis et parentibus, Ulpian, 17, 2. 'At present by a constitution of Caracalla, all vacant devises are confiscated, saving the rights of parents and children.' From the rules of caducity ascendants and descendants of the testator to the third degree were excepted both by the lex Papia and by the constitution of Caracalla. Constantine, A.D. 320, abolished the pains and penalties of celibacy and childlessness, Cod. 8, 58, and Justinian formally and finally abrogated the leges caducariae.

By substitutions or alternative institutions testators were able to modify the course of accrual by Civil law (jus accrescendi), and what perhaps was still more interesting, to escape from the operation of the laws of caducity, by which sometimes a whole inheritance might fall into the clutches of the treasury.

DE LEGATIS.

§ 191. Post haec videamus de legatis. Quae pars iuris extra propositam quidem materiam videtur; nam loquimur de his iuris figuris quibus per universitatem res nobis adquiruntur. sed cum omnimodo de testamentis deque heredibus qui testamento instituuntur locuti sumus, non sine causa sequenti loco poterat haec iuris materia tractari.

§ 191. Let us now examine legacies, a kind of title which seems foreign to the matter in hand, for we are expounding titles whereby aggregates of rights are acquired; but we had at any rate to treat of wills and heirs appointed by will, and it was natural in close connection therewith to consider this species of title [for a legacy is an accessory of a will].

§ 192. Legatorum utique genera *sunt* quattuor: aut enim per vindicationem legamus, aut per damnationem, aut sinendi modo, aut per praeceptionem.

§ 192. Legacies are of four kinds; by vindication, by condemnation, by permission, by preception.

§ 193. Per vindicationem *hoc modo legamus*: *LUCIO TITIO* verbi gratia HOMINEM STICHUM DO LEGO. sed *et* si *alterutrum* verbum positum sit, velut: *hominem Stichum do, per* vindicationem legatum est. si *vero etiam aliis verbis velut* ita legatum fuerit: su*mito, vel ita*: *sibi habeto*, *vel* ita: CAPITO, aeque per vindicationem *legatum est*.

§ 193. A legacy by vindication is in the following form: 'To Lucius Titius I give and bequeath, say, my slave Stichus,' or only one word need be used as, 'I give my slave Stichus;' and other terms such as: 'Let him take,' 'Let him have,' 'Let him seize,' equally confer a legacy by vindication.

§ 194. *Ideo au*tem per vindicationem legat*um* a*ppellatur*, q*uia* po*st* aditam hereditatem statim ex iure Quiritium res legatarii fit; et si eam rem legatarius vel ab herede vel ab alio quocumque qui eam possidet petat, vindicare debet, id est intendere *eam rem suam* ex iure Quiritium esse.

§ 194. It is so called, because immediately on the acceptance of the succession the thing becomes the Quiritarian property of the legatee, and if he claims it from the heir or any other possessor, he ought to bring a real action, that is, declare himself proprietor thereof by law of the Quirites.

§ 195. In eo *vero* dissentiunt prud*entes, quod Sabinus* quidem et Cassius ceterique nostri praeceptores quod ita legatum sit statim post aditam hereditatem putant fieri legatarii, etiamsi ignoret sibi legatum esse dimissum, et postea quam scierit et *repudiaverit*, tum perinde esse atque si legatum non esset: Nerva vero et Proculus ceterique illius *sch*olae auctores non aliter putant rem legatarii fieri, quam si voluerit eam ad se pertinere. Sed hodie ex divi Pii Antonini constitu-

§ 195. However, there is a controversy on this matter between jurists, for, according to Sabinus and Cassius and the other authorities of my school, what is thus left becomes the property of the legatee immediately on the acceptance of the succession, even before he has notice of the legacy, and on notice and repudiation by the legatee, the legacy is cancelled. Nerva and Proculus and the jurists of that school make the passing of the property to the legatee depend on his

tione hoc magis iure uti videmur quod Proculo placuit. nam cum legatus fuisset Latinus per vindicationem coloniae: deliberent, inquit, decuriones an ad se velint pertinere, proinde ac si uni legatus esset.

accepting the legacy; and now a constitution of the late emperor Pius Antoninus seems to have established the doctrine of Proculus as the rule, for in the case of a Latinus Junianus bequeathed by vindication to a colony, he said, 'The senate must deliberate whether they wish to become proprietors just as if the bequest was to an individual.'

§ 196. *Eas* autem solae res per vindicationem legantur recte quae ex iure Quiritium ipsius testatoris sunt. sed eas quidem *res* quae pondere, numero, mensura constant, placuit sufficere si mortis tempore sint ex iure Quiritium testatoris, veluti vinum, oleum, frumentum, pecuniam numeratam. ceteras res vero placuit utroque tempore testatoris ex iure Quiritium esse debere, id est et quo faceret *t*estamentum et quo moreretur: alioquin inutile est legatum.

§ 196. Only those things are properly bequeathed by vindication which are the Quiritarian property of the testator; things, however, estimated by weight, number, or measure, need only be the Quiritarian property of the testator at the time of his death, for instance, wine, oil, corn, ready-money: other things are required to be the testator's Quiritarian property at both periods, both at the time of his death and at the time of making his will, or the legacy is void.

§ 197. Sed sane hoc ita est iure civili. Postea vero auctore Nerone Caesare senatusconsultum factum est, quo cautum est, ut si eam rem quisque legaverit quae eius numquam fuerit, perinde utile sit legatum, atque si optimo iure relictum esset. optumum autem ius est per damnationem legatum; quo genere etiam aliena res legari potest, sicut inferius apparebit.

§ 197. However, this is only the civil law. In later times, on the proposition of Nero, a senatusconsult was passed, providing that if a testator bequeathed a thing which never belonged to him, the bequest should be as valid as if it were made in the most favourable form; the most favourable form being by condemnation, whereby the property of another person may be bequeathed, as will presently appear.

§ 198. Sed si quis rem suam legaverit, deinde post testamentum factum eam alienaverit, plerique putant non solum iure civili inutile esse legatum, sed nec ex senatusconsulto confirmari. quod ideo dictum est, quia etsi per damnationem aliquis rem suam legaverit eamque postea alienaverit, plerique putant, licet ipso iure debeatur legatum, tamen legatarium petentem per exceptionem doli mali repe*l*li quasi contra voluntatem defuncti petat.

§ 198. If a man bequeath a thing belonging to him, and afterwards aliene it, most jurists agree that the bequest is not only avoided at civil law, but recovers no validity by the senatusconsult, because, even when a thing is bequeathed by condemnation and afterwards aliened, although the bequest is valid at civil law, it is generally agreed that the claim of the legatee would be repelled by the plea of fraud, as contravening the testator's intention.

§ 199. Illud constat, si duobus pluribusve per vindicationem eadem res legata sit, sive coniunctim sive disiunctim, si omnes veniant ad legatum, partes ad singulos pertinere, et deficientis portionem collegatario adcrescere. coniunctim autem ita legatur: TITIO ET SEIO HOMINEM STICHUM DO LEGO; d*is*iunctim ita: LUCIO TITIO HOMINEM STICHUM DO LEGO. SEIO EUNDEM HOMINEM DO LEGO.

§ 199. It is a settled rule, that if the same thing be bequeathed by vindication to two or more persons, whether jointly or severally, and all claim the legacy, each is only entitled to a ratable part, and a lapsed portion accrues to the colegatees. A joint bequest is as follows: 'To Titius and Seius I give and bequeath my slave Stichus;' a several bequest as follows: 'To Lucius Titius I give and bequeath my slave Stichus. To Seius I give and bequeath the same slave.'

§ 200. Illu*d* quaeritur, quod sub condicione per vindicationem legatum est, pendente condicione cuius esset. Nostri praeceptores heredis esse putant exemplo statuliberi, id est eius servi qui testamento sub aliqua condicione liber esse iussus est, quem constat interea heredis servum esse. sed divers*ae* scholae auctores putant nullius interim eam rem esse; quod multo magis dicunt de eo quod sine condicione pure legatum est, antequam legatarius *ad*mittat legatum.

§ 200. When a condition is annexed to a bequest by vindication, it is a question who, pending the condition, is the owner: my school say, the heir, as in the case of the slave conditionally enfranchised by will, who is admitted to be in the interim the property of the heir: the other school assert that there is no interim proprietor, and they insist still more strongly that this is so in the case of an unconditional simple bequest before the acceptance by the legatee.

§ 201. Per damnationem hoc modo legamus: HERES MEUS STICHUM SERVUM MEUM DARE DAMNAS ESTO. sed et si DATO scriptum sit, per damnationem legatum est.

§ 201. A legacy by condemnation is in the following form: 'Be my heir condemned to give my slave Stichus,' or simply, 'Let my heir give my slave Stichus.'

§ 202. *Quo* genere legati etiam aliena res legari potest, ita ut heres redimere et praestare aut aestimationem eius dare debeat.

§ 202. By this form a testator may bequeath a thing belonging to another person, binding the heir to purchase and deliver the specific thing, or pay its value.

§ 203. Ea quoque res quae in rerum natura non est, si modo futura est, per damnationem legari potest, velut fructus qui in illo fundo nati erunt, aut quod ex illa ancilla natum erit.

§ 203. A thing which does not exist but will exist, may be bequeathed by condemnation, as the produce of such and such land, or the child of such and such female slave.

§ 204. Quod autem ita legatum est, post aditam hereditatem, etiamsi pure legatum est, non ut per vindicationem legatum continuo legatario adquiritur, sed nihilominus heredis est ideo legatarius in per-

§ 204. Bequests in this form, even though no condition is annexed, unlike bequests by vindication, are not forthwith on the acceptance of the succession the property of the legatee, but continue

sonam agere debet, id est intendere heredem sibi dare oportere: et tum heres *rem*, si mancipi sit, mancipio dare aut in iure cedere possessionemque tradere debet; si nec mancipi sit, sufficit si tradiderit. nam si mancipi rem tantam tradiderit, nec mancipaverit, usucapione *dumtaxat* pleno iure fit legatarii: *finitur* autem *usucapio ut supra quoque* diximus, mobilium quidem rerum anno, earum vero quae solo tenentur, biennio.

the property of the heir, and the legatee must sue for them by personal action, that is, declare that the heir is bound to convey, and the heir, if the thing is mancipable, must convey it by mancipation or default in a fictitious vindication and livery of seisin; if not mancipable, by mere delivery of possession: for if a mancipable thing is merely delivered without mancipation, usucapion is required to give plenary dominion to the legatee, and usucapion, as before mentioned, in the case of movables requires a year's possession, in the case of immovables two years' possession.

§ 205. Est et *alia differentia inter legatum per vindicationem et per damnationem: si enim eadem res* duobus pluribusve per damn*ati*onem legata sit, si quidem coniunctim, plane singulis partes debentur *sicut in per vindicationem legato. si vero* disiunctim, singulis solida res de*betur*, ut scilicet heres alteri rem, alteri aestimationem eius praestare debeat. et in coniunctis deficientis portio non ad collegatarium pertinet, sed in hereditate remanet.

§ 205. There is another difference between bequest by vindication and bequest by condemnation herein, that if the same thing is bequeathed to two or more by condemnation, if they are named jointly, each is entitled to a ratable part, as in legacy by vindication; if severally, each is entitled to the whole, and the heir is bound to convey the specific thing to one, and the value to the other; and in a joint bequest a lapsed portion does not accrue to the colegatee, but belongs to the heir.

§ 206. Quod autem diximus deficientis portionem *in* per damnationem quidem legato in hereditate retineri, in per vindicationem vero collegatario accrescere, admonendi sumus ante legem Papiam iure civili ita fuisse: post legem vero Papiam deficientis portio caduca fit et ad eos pertinet qui in eo testamento liberos habent.

§ 206. The statement that a lapsed portion in legacy by condemnation falls to the heir, and in legacy by vindication accrues to the colegatee, be it observed, gives the rule of the civil law before the lex Papia; but since the lex Papia, a lapsed portion becomes vacant, and belongs to the devisees who have children.

§ 207. Et quamvis prima causa sit in caducis vindicandis heredum liberos habentium, deinde, si heredes liberos non habeant, legatariorum liberos habentium, tamen ipsa lege Papia significatur, ut collegatarius coniunctus, si liberos habeat, potior

§ 207. And although the first title to a vacant legacy is that of heirs with children, and the second, if the heirs are childless, of legatees with children, yet the lex Papia itself declares that in a joint bequest a legatee with children

sit heredibus, etiamsi liberos habebunt.

is to be preferred to heirs with children.

§ 208. *Sed* plerisque placuit, quantum ad hoc ius quod lege Papia coniunctis constituitur, nihil interesse utrum per vindicationem an per damnationem legatum sit.

§ 208. And it is generally agreed that as to the rights which the lex Papia gives to joint legatees, it makes no difference whether the bequest is by vindication or by condemnation.

§ 209. Sinendi modo ita legamus: HERES MEUS DAMNAS ESTO SINERE LUCIUM TITIUM HOMINEM STICHUM SUMERE SIBIQUE HABERE.

§ 209. A bequest by permission is in the following form: 'Be my heir condemned to permit Lucius Titius to take and to have to himself my slave Stichus.'

§ 210. Quod genus legati plus quidem habet *quam* per vindicationem legatum, minus autem quam per damnationem. nam eo modo non solum suam rem testator utiliter legare potest, sed etiam heredis sui: cum alioquin per vindicationem nisi suam rem legare non potest; per damnationem autem cuiuslibet extranei rem legare potest.

210. A bequest in this form has more latitude than one in the form of vindication, but less than one in the form of condemnation, for hereby not only can the testator's property be effectively bequeathed, but also that of the heir, whereas by the form of vindication the testator can only bequeath his own property, and by the form of condemnation he can bequeath the property of any stranger.

§ 211. Sed si quidem mortis testatoris tempore res ipsius testatoris sit vel heredis, plane utile legatum est, etiamsi testamenti faciundi tempore neutrius fuerit.

§ 211. If at the time of the testator's death a thing belong to the testator or the heir, the bequest is valid, even though at the time of making the will it belonged to neither.

§ 212. Quodsi post mortem testatoris ea res heredis esse coeperit, quaeritur an utile sit legatum. *et* plerique putant inutile esse: qui*d* ergo est? licet aliquis eam rem legaverit quae neque eius *u*mquam fuerit, neque postea heredis eius umquam esse coeperit, ex senatusconsulto Neroniano proinde videtur ac si per damnationem relicta esset.

§ 212. If it first belong to the heir after the death of the testator it is a question whether the bequest is valid, and it is generally held to be invalid. However, even though a thing bequeathed never belonged either to the testator or to the heir, by the senatusconsult of Nero all bequests are put on the same footing as a bequest by condemnation.

§ 213. Sicut autem per damnationem legata res non statim post aditam hereditatem legatarii efficitur, sed manet heredis eo usque, donec is heres tradendo vel mancipando vel in iure cedendo legatarii eam fecerit; ita et in sinendi modo legato iuris est: et ideo huius quoque legati nomine in personam actio

§ 213. Just as a thing bequeathed by condemnation does not immediately on the acceptance of the succession belong to the legatee, but continues to belong to the heir until by delivery, or mancipation, or default in a fictitious vindication, he makes it the property of the legatee; so it happens in bequest

est QUIDQUID HEREDEM EX TESTAMENTO DARE FACERE OPORTET.

by permission, and accordingly this form of bequest is ground to support a personal action in the terms: 'Whatever the heir is bound by the will to convey or perform.'

§ 214. Sunt tamen qui putant ex hoc legato non videri obligatum heredem, ut mancipet aut in iure cedat aut tradat, sed sufficere, ut legatarium rem sumere patiatur; quia nihil ultra ei testator imperavit, quam ut sinat, id est patiatur legatarium rem sibi habere.

§ 214. Although some hold that a bequest in this form does not bind the heir to mancipate or cede by fictitious action, or deliver, but is satisfied by the legatee being permitted to take the thing, as the testator only enjoined the heir to let him have it.

§ 215. Maior illa dissensio in hoc legato intervenit, si eandem rem duobus pluribusve disiunctim legasti: quidam putant utrisque solidum deberi, sicut per *damnationem*: nonnulli occupantis esse meliorem condicionem aestimant, quia cum in eo genere legati damnetur heres patientiam praestare, ut legatarius rem habeat, sequitur, ut si priori patientiam praestiterit, et is rem sumpserit, securus sit adversus eum qui postea legatum petierit, quia neque habe*t* rem, ut patiatur eam ab eo sumi, neque dolo malo fecit quominus eam rem haberet.

§ 215. A more serious question arises in another point respecting this form of bequest: if the same thing is bequeathed severally to two or more, some hold that each is entitled to the whole, as in bequest by condemnation; others hold that the first occupant is alone entitled, because as this form of bequest only condemns the heir to suffer the legatee to have the thing, as soon as the first occupant has been suffered to take it, the heir is safe against any subsequent claimant, as he neither has possession of the thing, so as to let it again be taken, nor has fraudulently parted with possession.

§ 216. Per praeceptionem hoc modo legamus: LUCIUS TITIUS HOMINEM STICHUM PRAECIPITO.

§ 216. A bequest by preception is in the following form: 'Let Lucius Titius take my slave Stichus by preception [before partition].'

§ 217. Sed nostri quidem praeceptores nulli alii eo modo legari posse putant, nisi ei qui aliqua ex parte heres scri*p*tus esse*t*: praecipere enim esse praecipuum sumere; quod tantum in eius personam procedit qui aliqua ex parte heres institutus est, quod is extra portionem hereditatis praecip*uum* legatum habiturus sit.

§ 217. My school hold that such a bequest can only be made to one of several coheirs, because preception, or previous taking, can only be attributed to a person who, taking as heir, over and above his portion as heir, and before partition of the inheritance between the coheirs, takes something as legatee.

§ 218. Ideoque si extraneo legatum fuerit, inutile est legatum, adeo ut Sabinus existimaverit ne quidem ex *senatusconsulto* Neroniano posse convalescere: nam eo, inquit, sena-

§ 218. Therefore, if a stranger have a legacy in this form it is void, and Sabinus held that the flaw is not remedied by the senatusconsult of Nero, for that senatusconsult

tusconsulto ea tantum confirmantur quae verborum vitio iure civili non valent, non quae propter ipsam personam legatarii non deberentur. sed Iuliano ex Sexto placuit etiam hoc casu ex senatusconsulto confirmari legatum: nam ex verbis etiam hoc casu accidere, ut iure civili inutile sit legatum, *inde* manifestum *esse*, quod eidem aliis verbis recte legatur, velut [*per* vindicationem et per damnationem], sinendi modo: tunc autem vitio personae legatum non valere, cum ei legatum sit cui nullo modo legari possit, velut peregrino cum quo testamenti factio non sit; quo plane casu senatusconsulto locus non est.

only cures verbal flaws which make a bequest informal at civil law, not personal disabilities of the legatee. Julian, however, and Sextus held that this bequest also is made valid by the senatusconsult, as only being avoided at civil law by a verbal informality, as appears from the fact that the very same person might take by a bequest in another form, for instance, the form of permission, whereas personal disability of a legatee implies inability to take under any form, as that of an alien, who cannot be a party to a will, and is not relieved by the senatusconsult.

§ 219. Item nostri praeceptores quod ita legatum est nulla ratione putant posse consequi eum cui ita fuerit legatum, *praeter*qu*am* iudicio familiae erciscundae quod inter heredes de hereditate erciscunda, id est dividunda, accipi solet: officio enim iudicis id contineri, ut et quod per praeceptionem legatum est adiudicetur.

§ 219. Again, my school hold that in this form of bequest, the only action by which a legatee can recover is the action for partition of an inheritance, the judge's commission including a power of adjudicating a thing bequeathed by preception.

§ 220. Unde intellegimus nihil aliu*d* secundum nostrorum praeceptorum opinionem per praeceptionem legari posse, nisi quod testatoris sit: nulla enim alia res quam hereditaria deducitur in hoc iudicium. itaque si non suam rem eo modo testator legaverit, iure quidem civili inutile erit legatum; sed ex senatusconsulto confirmabitur. aliquo tamen casu etiam alienam rem *per* praeceptionem legari posse fatentur: veluti si quis eam rem legaverit quam creditori fiduciae causa mancipio dederit; nam officio iudicis coheredes cogi posse existimant soluta pecunia solvere eam rem, ut possit *prae*cipere *is* cui ita legatum sit.

§ 220. From this it follows that, according to my school, nothing can be bequeathed by preception but what belongs to the testator, for nothing but the inheritance forms the subject of this action. If, then, a thing that does not belong to the testator is bequeathed in this form, the bequest is void at civil law, but made valid by the senatusconsult. In one case they admit that another person's property may be bequeathed by preception, for instance, if a man bequeath a thing which he has conveyed by fiduciary mancipation to a mortgagee, as it is within the powers of the judge to order the coheirs to redeem the property by payment of the mortgage debt, and thus enable the legatee to exercise his right of preception.

§ 221. *S*ed diver*sae* sc*h*olae auc-

§ 221. The other school hold that

tores putant etiam extraneo per praeceptionem legari posse proinde ac si ita scribatur: TITIUS HOMINEM STICHUM CAPITO, supervacuo adiecta PRAE syllaba; ideoque per *vindicationem eam rem* legatam videri. quae sententia dicitur divi Hadriani constitutione confirmata esse.

a stranger may take a bequest in the form of preception just as if it were in the form: 'Let Titius take my slave Stichus,' the addition [by preception, or, before partition] being mere surplusage, and the bequest being in effect in the form of vindication; and this opinion is said to be confirmed by a constitution of the late emperor Hadrian.

§ 222. Secundum hanc igitur opinionem, si ea res *ex* iure Quiritium defuncti fuerit, po*test* a legatario vindicari, sive is unus ex heredibus sit sive extraneus: et si in bonis tantum testatoris fuerit, extraneo quidem ex senatusconsulto utile erit legatum, heredi vero familiae herciscundae iudicis officio praestabitur. quod si nullo iure fuerit testatoris, tam heredi quam extraneo ex senatusconsulto utile erit.

§ 222. According to this view, if the thing was the Quiritarian property of the defunct, it can be recovered in a real action by the legatee, whether an heir or a stranger, and if it was only the bonitarian property of the testator, a stranger will recover the bequest under the senatusconsult, an heir by the authority of the judge in an action for partition of inheritance. If it was in no sense the property of the testator, either an heir or a stranger may recover it under the senatusconsult.

§ 223. Sive tamen heredibus, secundum nostrorum opinionem, sive etiam extraneis, secundum illorum opinionem, duobus pluribusve eadem res coniunctim aut disiunctim legata fuerit, singul*i* partes ha*b*ere debent.

§ 223. Whether heirs, according to my school, or strangers, according to the other, if two or more legatees have the same thing bequeathed to them, each legatee is only entitled to a ratable portion.

§ 197. Senatusconsulto Neroniano cautum est ut quod minus pactis (aptis?) verbis legatum est perinde sit acsi optimo jure legatum esset: optimum autem jus legati per damnationem est, Ulpian, 24, 11. 'The senatusconsult of Nero provided that every inaptly worded bequest should be deemed to be expressed in the most favourable form: the most favourable form being by condemnation.'

By this senatusconsult, A.D. 64, the four forms of legacy are not entirely abolished, but the importance of their distinctions is very much diminished. A legacy, by whatever form bequeathed, is henceforth always recoverable, provided it could have been effectively bequeathed in any form.

Subsequently a constitution of Constantine, Constantinus, and Constans, A.D. 339, which, as we have already seen, abolished the necessity of sacramental terms in instituting an heir, dispensed with them also in the remaining testamentary dispositions: Et in postremis ergo judiciis ordinandis amota erit sollennium verborum necessitas, Cod. 6, 23, 15. In legatis vel fidei commissis necessaria non sit verborum observantia, ita ut nihil prorsus intersit, quis talem voluntatem verborum casus exceperit aut quis loquendi usus effuderit, Cod. 6, 37, 21. 'Legacies and trusts need no verbal formulas, and it is utterly immaterial, given the intention, in what grammatical form it is clothed, or in what idiom it is enounced:' apparently a part of the same constitution.

Three years afterwards, a constitution of Constantius and Constans abolished all legal formulas in the following terms: Juris formulae, aucupatione syllabarum insidiantes, cunctorum actibus penitus amputentur, Cod. 2, 58, 1. 'Legal formulas, with snares in every syllable to make them treacherous, in every occasion are to be utterly abolished.'

Finally, Justinian enacted ut omnibus legatis una sit natura, Inst. 2, 20, 2, that all bequests should be one of nature; and allowed them to be recovered by personal or real action, at the option of the legatee; or, perhaps we should say, according to the exigences of the case: for some subjects are essentially incapable of recovery by real action; e. g. if a determinate quantity of anything estimated by number, measure, or weight, were bequeathed by a testator who had none in his possession at the time of his death, the heir would be bound to procure and convey it or its value to the legatee, but there would be no specific thing in existence which the legatee could recover by real action.

§ 215. A passage in the Digest, 33, 2, 14, makes this depend on the intention of the testator.

§ 218. Juliano ex Sexto. If this is equivalent to Juliano libris ex Sexto, it would mean 'Julian in his abbreviation of Sextus Pomponius.' Von Savigny proposes Juliano et Sexto; Boecking, Juliano libro sexto Digestorum.

AD LEGEM FALCIDIAM.

§ 224. Sed olim quidem licebat totum patrimonium legatis atque libertatibus erogare, nec quicquam heredi relinquere praeterquam inane nomen heredis; idque lex XII tabularum permittere videbatur, qua ca-

§ 224. By the ancient law a testator's whole estate, between legacies and enfranchisements, could be bequeathed away, and nothing left to the heir but an empty title; and this privilege seemed granted by

vetur, ut quod quisque de re sua testatus esset, id ratum haberetur, his verbis: UTI LEGASSIT SUAE REI, ITA IUS ESTO. quare qui scripti heredes erant, ab hereditate se abstinebant; et idcirco plerique intestati moriebantur.

the Twelve Tables, which concede an unlimited power of testamentary disposition, in these terms: 'A man's last directions respecting his property shall be enforced by the power of the state:' hence the persons who were appointed heirs declined to accept the inheritance, and people commonly died intestate.

§ 225. Itaque lata est lex Furia, qua, exceptis personis quibusdam, ceteris plus mille assibus legatorum nomine mortisve causa capere permissum non est. sed et haec lex non perfecit quod voluit. qui enim verbi gratia quinque milium aeris patrimonium habebat, poterat quinque hominibus singulis millenos asses legando totum patrimonium erogare.

§ 225. This led to the enactment of the lex Furia, whereby, excepting certain specified classes, a thousand asses was made the maximum that a legatee or donee in contemplation of death, was permitted to take. This law, however, failed to accomplish its purpose, for a testator with an estate of, say, five thousand asses, might leave to five legatees a thousand asses apiece, and strip the heir of the whole.

§ 226. Ideo postea lata est lex Voconia, qua cautum est, ne cui plus legatorum nomine mortisve causa capere liceret quam heredes caperent. ex qua lege plane quidem aliquid utique heredes habere videbantur; *sed* tamen fere vitium simile nascebatur: nam in multas legatariorum personas distributo patrimonio poterant adeo heredi minimum relinquere, ut non expediret heredi huius lucri gratia totius hereditatis onera sustinere.

§ 226. This occasioned the enactment of the lex Voconia, providing that no legatee or donee in contemplation of death should take more than the heir. By this law, some portion at all events was secured to the heir, but, like the former, it could be defeated, for the multitude of legatees between whom a man distributed his estate might leave so little to the heir as to make it not worth his while to undertake the whole burden of the succession.

§ 227. Lata est itaque lex Falcidia, qua cautum est, ne plus ei legare liceat quam dodrantem. itaque necesse est, ut heres quartam partem hereditatis habeat. et hoc n*unc* iure utimur.

§ 227. At last, the lex Falcidia was enacted, prohibiting to bequeath away more than three fourths of an estate, in other words, securing for the heir one fourth of the inheritance, and this is the rule of law now in force.

§ 228. In libertatibus quoque dandis nimiam licentiam conpescuit lex Furia Caninia, sicut in primo commentario rettulimus.

§ 228. The enfranchisement of slaves was likewise kept within limits by the lex Furia Caninia, as mentioned in the first volume of these Institutions.

§ 224. A slightly different form of this celebrated ordinance is given by the Auctor ad Herennium: Paterfamilias uti super familia pecuniave sua legaverit ita jus esto, 1, 13, 23; also Cic. De Invent. 2, 50. 14, 8.

§ 225. The lex Furia testamentaria, supposed to have been passed 183 B.C., although it imposed on the legatee who took more than a thousand asses a penalty of four times the amount of the excess, which was recoverable by manus injectio pura, 3 § 33, yet is instanced by Ulpian as a minus quam perfecta lex, because, though it imposed a penalty on the legatee, it did not invalidate the prohibited bequest, Ulpian, 1, 2.

§ 226. The lex Voconia, supposed to have been passed by the tribune Quintus Voconius Saxa, 169 B.C., contained a provision to the effect that a woman could not be instituted heiress to a classicus, or person scheduled in the first class of the census, i.e. registered as owner of property to the amount of a hundred thousand sesterces and upward, 2 § 274; and another, mentioned in the text, whereby the utmost amount that any one, male or female, could take as legatee, would be limited to half the value of the inheritance. This disposition of the lex Voconia was probably the origin of the form of legacy called partitio, 2 § 254, whereby a testator bequeathed as legacy an aliquot part of his inheritance. A testator with one heres would leave to a female legatee one half, with two heredes one third, of the inheritance, and so on, if he wished to leave her the utmost the law permitted.

The result of the lex Voconia, coupled with the rules of pretermission and intestacy, is the following: a daughter might take half her father's estate either as legatee (partiaria, 2 § 254) or, if pretermitted (praeterita), as heiress, 2 § 124. If she was filia unica, she might take the whole estate as heiress, if her father died intestate: but Romans were very averse to dying intestate; and in this event she would not have the free disposition of her property, as she would be the ward of her agnates.

§ 227. The terms of the principal clause of the lex Falcidia, passed B.C. 40, are given in the Digest: Quicunque civis Romanus post hanc legem rogatam testamentum faciet, is quantam cuique civi Romano pecuniam jure publico dare legare volet, jus potestasque esto, dum ita detur legatum, ne minus quam partem quartam hereditatis ex eo testamento heredes capiant. Eis quibus quid ita datum legatumve erit, eam pecuniam sine fraude sua capere liceto, isque heres qui eam pecuniam dare jussus damnatus erit, eam pecuniam debeto dare quam damnatus est, Dig. 35, 2, 1, pr. 'Every Roman citizen who, after this law passes, makes a will, is entitled and empowered to give and bequeath whatever money to whatever citizen of Rome he desires in accordance with the laws of Rome, provided that such bequest leave at least one fourth of the inheritance to be taken under that will by the heirs. Such bequests the legatees are permitted to accept without penalty (an allusion to the penalty of the lex Furia), and the heir therewith charged is bound to pay.'

The words limiting the operation of the lex Falcidia to wills executed after the date of its enactment take this law out of the general rule respecting the temporal limits of the application of laws in the event of legislative innovations. The general rule for determining, on any change of the law, whether a given right is to be governed by the older or the newer law, is the principle that a new law has no retroactive influence on vested rights (acquired rights), but governs all that have yet to vest. Now under a will no one has vested rights, whatever his expectations, before the death of the testator. This date fixes the overture of the succession (vocatio heredis, delatio hereditatis), the vesting of the rights of the successor and also of the legatee (legatorum dies cedens, § 244), and determines the law by which they are governed. By the general rule, then, the lex Falcidia would have applied to all wills whose testators died after its enactment, at whatever date they were executed. The legislator wished to disarm the opposition of those who had made their wills by excepting them from its operation; though in many cases the lex Falcidia would be less rigorous than the lex Furia and lex Voconia, which it superseded, and testators would be glad to revise their testamentary dispositions. Savigny, System, § 394.

DE INUTILITER RELICTIS LEGATIS.

§ 229. Ante *h*eredis institutionem *in*utiliter legatur, scilicet quia testamenta vim ex institutione heredis accipiunt, et ob id velut caput et fundamentum intellegitur totius testamenti heredis institutio.

§ 229. A legacy bequeathed before a successor is appointed is void, because a will derives its operation from the appointment of a successor, and accordingly the appointment of a successor is deemed the beginning and foundation of a will.

§ 230. Pari ratio*ne* nec libertas ante heredis institutionem dari potest.

§ 230. For the same reason a slave cannot be enfranchised before a successor is appointed.

§ 231. Nostri praeceptores nec tutorem eo loco dari posse existimant: se*d* Labeo et Proculus tutorem posse dari, quod nihil ex

§ 231. Nor, according to my school, can a guardian be nominated before an heir is appointed: according to Labeo and Proculus he

hereditate erogatur tutoris datione.

may, because no part of the inheritance is bequeathed away by the nomination of a guardian.

§ 232. Post mortem quoque heredis inutiliter legatur; id est hoc modo: CUM HERES MEUS MORTUUS ERIT, DO LEGO, aut DATO. Ita autem recte legatur: CUM HERES MORIETUR: quia non post mortem heredis relinquitur, sed ultimo vitae eius tempore. Rursum ita non potest legari: PRIDIE QUAM HERES MEUS MORIETUR. quod non pretiosa ratione receptum videtur.

§ 232. A bequest to take effect after the death of the heir is void, that is to say, if limited in the following terms: 'After my successor's death I give and dispose,' or, 'let my successor give.' The following limitation is valid: 'When my heir dies,' because the legacy is not to take effect after his death, but at the last moments of his life. A bequest to take effect on the day preceding the death of the successor is void. This distinction reposes on no valid reason.

§ 233. Eadem et de libertatibus dicta intellegemus.

§ 233. The same rules apply to enfranchisements.

§ 234. Tutor vero an post mortem heredis dari possit quaerentibus eadem forsitan poterit esse quaestio, quae de *eo* agitatur qui ante heredum institutionem datur.

§ 234. Whether a guardian can be nominated to begin his functions after the death of the heir, probably admits of the same divergence of opinion as whether he can be nominated before the appointment of the heir.

DE POENAE CAUSA RELICTIS LEGATIS.

§ 235. Poenae quoque nomine inutiliter legatur. poenae autem nomine legari videtur quod coercendi heredis causa relinquitur, quo magis heres aliqui*d* faciat aut non faciat; velut quod ita legatur: SI HERES MEUS FILIAM *SUAM* TITIO IN MATRIMONIUM COLLOCAVERIT, X *MILIA* SEIO DATO; vel ita: SI FILIAM TITIO IN MATRIMONIUM NON COLLOCAVERIS, X MILIA TITIO DATO. sed et [*si quis*] si heres verbi gratia intra biennium monumentum sibi non fecerit, X Titio dari iusserit, poenae nomine legatu*m est. et de*nique ex ipsa definitione multas similes species *prop*rias fingere possumus.

§ 235. Penal bequests are void. A penal bequest is one intended to coerce the heir to some performance or forbearance. For instance, the following: 'If my heir give his daughter in marriage to Titius, let him pay ten thousand sesterces to Seius:' and the following: 'If thou do not give thy daughter in marriage to Titius, do thou pay ten thousand sesterces to Titius:' and the following: 'If my heir does not, say, within two years build me a monument, I order him to pay ten thousand sesterces to Titius;' all these are penal bequests, and many similar instances may be imagined in accordance with the definition.

§ 236. Nec libertas quidem poenae nomine dari potest; quamvis de ea re fuerit quaesitum.

§ 236. Freedom cannot be left as a penal bequest, although the point has been disputed.

§ 237. De tutore vero nihil pos-

§ 237. The nomination of a guar-

sumus quaerere, quia non potest datione tutoris heres conpelli quidquam facere aut non facere; ideoque nec datur poenae no*mi*ne tutor; *et si* datus fuerit, magis sub condicione quam po*e*nae nomine datus videbitur.

dian cannot give rise to the question, because the nomination of a guardian cannot be a means of compelling an heir to any performance or forbearance, and a penal nomination of a guardian is inconceivable: if, however, a nomination were made with this design, it would be deemed rather conditional than penal.

§ 238. Incertae personae legatum inutiliter relinquitur. incerta autem videtur persona quam per incertam opinionem animo suo testator subicit, v*elut si* ita legatum sit: QUI PRIMUS AD FUNUS MEUM VEN*ERIT*, *EI HERES* MEUS X *MILIA* DATO. idem iuris est, si generaliter omnibus legaverit: QUICUMQUE AD FUNUS MEUM VENERIT. i*n ea*dem causa est quod ita relinquitur: QUICUMQUE FILIO MEO IN MATRIMONIUM FILIAM SUAM CONLOCAVERIT, EI HERES MEUS X MILIA DATO. illu*d* quoque in eadem causa est quod ita r*e*linquitur: QUI POST TESTAMENTUN CONSULES DESIGNATI ERUNT, aeque incertis personis legari videtur. et denique aliae multae huiusmodi species sunt. Sub certa vero demonstratione incertae personae recte legatur, velut: EX COGNATIS MEIS QUI NUNC *S*UNT QUI PRIMUS AD FUNUS MEUM VENERIT, EI X MILIA HERES MEUS DATO.

§ 238. A bequest to an uncertain person is void. An uncertain person is one of whom the testator has no certain conception, as the legatee in the following bequest: 'Whoever comes first to my funeral, do thou, my heir, pay him ten thousand sesterces:' or a whole class thus defined: 'Whoever comes to my funeral:' or a person thus defined: 'Whoever gives his daughter in marriage to my son, do thou, my heir, pay him ten thousand sesterces:' or persons thus defined: 'Whoever after my will is made are the first consuls designate:' all these persons are uncertain, and many others that might be instanced. A bequest to an uncertain member of a certain class is valid, as the following: 'Of all my kindred now alive whoever first comes to my funeral, do thou, my heir, pay him ten thousand sesterces.'

§ 239. Libertas quoque non videtur incertae personae dari posse, quia lex Furia Caninia iubet nominatim servos liberari.

§ 239. Freedom cannot be bequeathed to an uncertain person because the lex Furia Caninia requires slaves to be enfranchised by name.

§ 240. Tutor quoque certus dari debet.

§ 240. An uncertain person cannot be nominated guardian.

§ 241. Postumo quoque alieno inutiliter legatur. *est autem* alienus postumus, qui natus inter suos heredes testatori futurus non est. ideoque ex emancipato *quo*que filio conceptus nepos extraneus *est postumus avo; item qui in ute*ro est eius *quae conubio non interveniente ducta est* uxor, extraneus postumus patri contingit.

§ 241. An afterborn stranger cannot take a bequest: an afterborn stranger is one who on his birth will not be a self-successor to the testator: thus a grandson by an emancipated son is an afterborn stranger to his grandfather, and a child in the womb of one who is not a wife by civil wedlock is an afterborn stranger to his father.

§ 242. Ac ne heres quidem potest institui postumus alienus: est enim incerta persona.

§ 243. Cetera vero quae supra diximus ad legata proprie pertinent; quamquam non inmerito quibusdam placeat poenae nomine heredem institui non posse: nihil enim intererit, utrum legatum dare iubeatur heres, si fecerit aliquid aut non fecerit, an coheres ei adiciatur; quia tam *co*heredis adiectione quam legati datione conpellitur, ut aliquid contra propositum suum faciat.

§ 244. An ei qui in potestate sit eius quem heredem instituimus recte legemus, quaeritur. Servius recte legari probat, sed evanescere legatum, si quo tempore dies legatorum cedere solet, adhuc in potestate *sit*; ideoque sive pure legatum sit et vivo testatore in potestate heredis esse desierit, sive sub condicione et ante condicionem id acciderit, deberi legatum. Sabinus et Cassius sub condicione recte legari, pure non recte, putant: licet enim vivo testatore possit desinere in potestate heredis esse, ideo tamen inutile legatum intellegi oportere, quia quod nullas vires habiturum foret, si statim post testamentum factum decessisset testator, hoc ideo valere quia vitam longius traxerit, absurdum esse*t*. diversae scholae auctores nec sub condicione recte legari *putant*, quia quos in potestate habemus, eis non magis sub condicione quam pure debere possumus.

§ 245. Ex diverso constat ab eo qui in potestate *tua* est, herede instituto, recte tibi legari: sed si tu per eum heres extiteris, evanescere

§ 242. An afterborn stranger cannot even be appointed heir, because he is an uncertain person.

§ 243. Though what was said above of penal dispositions refers properly to bequests, yet a penal appointment of an heir is justly considered to be void, for it makes no difference whether a legacy is left away from an heir on his doing or failing to do something, or a coheir is appointed, as the addition of a coheir is just as effective a means of coercion to force an heir to take some step against his will.

§ 244. Whether a person in the power of an heir can be the donee of a legacy is a question. Servius holds that the bequest is valid, though it lapses if he continue under power at the date when the legacies vest; and whether the bequest is absolute and the legatee ceases to be subject to the power of the heir in the lifetime of the testator, or whether it is conditional and he is liberated before the condition is accomplished, in either case he holds the legatee entitled to the legacy. Sabinus and Cassius hold that a conditional bequest is valid, an absolute bequest invalid, because though the legatee may cease to be subject to the heir in the lifetime of the testator, yet the bequest must be deemed invalid because a disposition which would be void if the testator died immediately after making his will, cannot acquire validity by the mere prolongation of his life. The other school of jurists hold that even a conditional bequest is invalid because a person under power is as incapable of conditional as of absolute rights against his superior.

§ 245. Conversely it is certain that if a person in your power is appointed heir, he can be charged with payment of a legacy to you;

legatum, quia ipse tibi legatum debere non possis; si vero filius emancipatus aut servus manumissus erit vel in alium translatus, et ipse heres extiterit aut alium fecerit, deberi legatum.

though if you inherit by his means the legacy fails, because you cannot be bound to pay yourself; but if your son is emancipated, or your slave manumitted or aliened, and himself becomes successor or makes the alienee successor, you are entitled to the legacy.

§ 237. The rules requiring that bequests should follow the institution of the heir, and should be limited to take effect in the lifetime of the heir, and prohibiting penal bequests, were abolished by Justinian.

§ 238. Justinian abolished the rule prohibiting bequests to uncertain persons, and permitted bequests to corporations, classes, and pious or charitable uses, Cod. 6, 48.

§ 242. Although an after-born stranger could not be appointed heir by the civil law, yet the praetor sustained such an appointment, and gave him the bonorum possessio. Justinian permitted him to take the legal estate, Inst. 3, 9, pr.

§ 244. Cedere diem significat incipere deberi pecuniam; venire diem significat eum diem venisse quo pecunia peti possit, Dig. 50, 16, 213. 'Cedit dies denotes the moment when a right to receive payment vests; venit dies denotes the moment when payment may be exacted.'

A right to a conditional legacy vested when the condition was accomplished. Though an unconditional legacy was liable to be defeated by the heres declining the inheritance, or the will from any other cause failing of operation, yet, as soon as the validity of the will was ascertained by the aditio of the heres, the vesting of an unconditional legacy dated back from the death of the testator.

One of the Catos was the author of a maxim, that to test the validity of a legacy we must examine whether it would be valid if the testator died immediately after executing his will. This was called regula Catoniana, Dig. 37, 4, 1. The retroactive effect of the removal of an original impediment to the validity of a title is called the Convalescence of the title. Accordingly, Cato's rule may be described as a rule denying the Convalescence of legacies. Cato's rule, however, was only a criterion of the validity of unconditional bequests; the validity of conditional bequests can only be tested when the condition is accomplished. Accordingly, of the three opinions mentioned in this paragraph, that of Sabinus is to be regarded as sound, and is so treated by Justinian, Inst. 2, 20, 32.

DE FIDEICOMMISSARIIS HEREDITATIBUS.

§ 246. Hinc transeamus ad fideicommissa.

§ 246. We now proceed to trusts.

§ 247. Et prius de hereditatibus videamus.

§ 247. And to begin with trust successions:

§ 248. Inprimis igitur sciendum est opus esse, ut aliquis heres recto iure instituatur, eiusque fidei committatur, ut eam hereditatem alii restituat: alioquin inutile est testamentum in quo nemo recto iure heres instituitur.

§ 248. The first requisite is a legal successor in the first instance in trust to transfer the succession to another, for the will is void without a legal successor in the first instance.

§ 249. Verba autem utilia fideicommissorum haec recte maxime in usu esse videntur: PETO, ROGO, VOLO, FIDEICOMMITTO: quae proinde firma singula sunt, atque si omnia in unum congesta sint.

§ 249. The words properly and commonly used to create a trust are: 'I beg, I request, I wish, I intrust;' and they are just as binding separately as united.

§ 250. Cum igitur scri*p*serimus: *LUCIUS* TITIUS HERES ESTO, possumus adicere: ROGO TE, LUCI TITI, PETOQUE A TE, UT CUM PRIMUM POSSIS HEREDITATEM MEAM ADIRE, GAIO SEIO REDDAS RESTI*T*UAS. possumus autem et de parte restituenda rogare; et liberum est vel sub condicione vel pure relinquere fideicommissa, vel ex die certa.

§ 250. Accordingly, when we have written: 'Lucius Titius, be thou my heir,' we may add: 'I request and beg thee, Lucius Titius, as soon as thou canst accept my inheritance, to convey and transfer it to Gaius Seius;' or we may request him to transfer a part. So a trust may be either conditional or absolute, and to be performed either immediately or on a future day.

§ 251. Restituta autem hereditate is qui restituit nihilominus heres permanet; is vero qui recipit hereditatem, aliquando heredis loco est, aliquando legatarii.

§ 251. After the transfer of the inheritance the transferror continues heir, the transferree being sometimes quasi heir, sometimes quasi legatee.

§ 252. *Olim autem* nec heredis loco erat nec legatarii, sed potius emptoris. tunc enim in *usu* erat ei cui restituebatur hereditas nummo uno eam hereditatem dicis causa venire; et quae stipulationes inter *venditorem hereditatis et emptorem interponi solent, eaedem interponebantur inter* heredem et eum cui restituebatur hereditas, id est hoc modo: heres quidem stipulabatur

§ 252. Formerly he became neither quasi heir nor quasi legatee but quasi purchaser. In those times it was customary for the transferree to pay a sesterce as fictitious purchaser of the inheritance, and the stipulations appropriate to a vendor and purchaser of an inheritance were entered into by the heir and transferree, that is to say, the heir stipulated from the transferree to be

ab eo cui restituebatur hereditas, ut quicquid hereditario nomine condemnatus fuisset, sive quid alias bona fide dedisset, eo nomine indemnis esset, et omnino si quis cum eo hereditario nomine ageret, ut recte defenderetur: ille vero qui recipiebat hereditatem invicem stipulabatur, ut si quid ex hereditate ad heredem pervenisset, id sibi restitueretur; ut etiam pateretur eum hereditarias actiones procuratorio aut cognitorio nomine exequi.

indemnified for any sums he should be condemned to pay or should in good faith pay on account of the inheritance, and to be adequately defended in any suit on account of the inheritance; and the transferree on the other hand stipulated to receive from the heir all profits arising from the inheritance and to be permitted to sue as cognitor or procurator of the heir.

§ 253. Sed posterioribus temporibus Trebellio Maximo et Annaeo Seneca Consulibus senatusconsultum factum est, quo cautum est, ut si cui hereditas ex fideicommissi causa restituta sit, actiones quae iure civili heredi et in heredem conpeterent ei et in eum darentur cui ex fideicommisso restituta esset hereditas. post quod senatusconsultum desierunt illae cautiones in usu haberi. Praetor enim utiles actiones ei et in eum qui recepit hereditatem, quasi heredi et in heredem dare coepit, eaeque in edicto proponuntur.

§ 253. In more recent times, in the consulate of Trebellius Maximus and Annaeus Seneca, a senatusconsult was passed providing that, when an inheritance is transferred in pursuance of a trust, the actions which the civil law allows to be brought by the heir or against the heir shall be maintainable by the transferree and against the transferree. Henceforth the old covenants were discontinued, and the Praetor used to give to and against the transferree the modified actions which are formulated in the album.

§ 254. Sed rursus quia heredes scripti, cum aut totam hereditatem aut paene totam plerumque restituere rogabantur, adire hereditatem ob nullum aut minimum lucrum recusabant, atque ob id extinguebantur fideicommissa, Pegaso et Pusione *Consulibus* senatus censuit, ut ei qui rogatus esset hereditatem restituere perinde liceret quartam partem retinere, atque e lege Falcidia in legatis retinendi ius conceditur. ex singulis quoque rebus quae per fideicommissum relinquuntur eadem retentio permissa est. per quod senatusconsultum ipse onera hereditaria sustinet; ille autem qui ex fideicommisso reliquam partem hereditatis recipit, legatarii partiarii loco est, id est eius legatarii cui pars bonorum legatur. quae species legati partitio

§ 254. However as heirs, when made trustees to transfer the whole or nearly the whole of a succession, declined for a small benefice or no benefice to accept the succession, and this caused a failure of the trusts, the senate in the consulship of Pegasus and Pusio decreed, that a devisee in trust to transfer a succession should have the same right to retain a fourth of the succession as the lex Falcidia gives to an heir charged with the payment of legacies; and gave a similar right of retaining the fourth of any specific thing left in trust. When this senatusconsult comes into operation, the heir is sole administrator and the transferree of the residue is on the footing of a partiary legatee, that is, of a legatee of a certain part of the estate under the kind of legacy

vocatur, quia cum herede legatarius partitur hereditatem. unde effectum est, ut quae solent stipulationes inter heredem et partiarium legatarium interponi, eaedem interponantur inter eum qui ex fideicommissi causa recipit hereditatem et heredem, id est ut et lucrum et damnum hereditarium pro rata parte inter eos commune sit.

called participation. Accordingly the stipulations appropriate between an heir and partiary legatee are entered into by the heir and transferree, in order to secure a ratable division of the gains and losses arising out of the succession.

§ 255. Ergo si quidem non plus quam dodrantem hereditatis scriptus heres rogatus sit restituere, tum ex Trebelliano senatusconsulto restituitur hereditas, et in utrumque actiones hereditariae pro rata parte dantur: in heredem quidem iure civili, in eum vero qui recipit hereditatem ex senatusconsulto Trebelliano. quamquam heres etiam pro ea parte quam restituit heres permanet, eique et in eum solidae actiones competunt: sed non ulterius oneratur, nec ulterius illi dantur actiones, quam apud eum commodum hereditatis remanet.

§ 255. But if no more than three fourths of the inheritance is in trust to be transferred, then the Sc. Trebellianum governs the transfer, and both are liable to be sued for the debts of the inheritance in ratable portions, the heir by civil law, the transferree by the Sc. Trebellianum: for though the heir even as to the transferred portion continues heir, and can sue or be sued for the totality of a debt, in practice the praetor only allows him to sue or be sued in the proportion of his beneficial interest in the inheritance.

§ 256. At si quis plus quam dodrantem vel etiam totam hereditatem restituere rogatus sit, locus est Pegasiano senatusconsulto.

§ 256. If more than three fourths or the whole is devised in trust to be transferred, the Sc. Pegasianum comes into operation.

§ 257. Sed is qui semel adierit hereditatem, si modo sua voluntate adierit, sive retinuerit quartam partem sive noluerit retinere, ipse universa onera hereditaria sustinet: sed quarta quidem retenta quasi partis et pro parte stipulationes interponi debent tamquam inter partiarium legatarium et heredem: si vero totam hereditatem restituerit, ad exemplum emptae et venditae hereditatis stipulationes interponendae sunt.

§ 257. And when once the heir has accepted, that is to say, voluntarily, whether he retains one fourth or declines to retain it, he is sole administrator: but, if he retains a fourth, he should covenant with the transferree as quasi partiary legatee; if he transfers the whole, he should covenant with him as quasi vendee.

§ 258. Sed si recuset scriptus heres adire hereditatem, ob id quod dicat eam sibi suspectam esse quasi damnosam, cavetur *Pegasiano* senatusconsulto, ut desiderante eo cui restituere rogatus est, iussu Praetoris adeat et restituat, perindeque

§ 258. If an heir refuse to accept a succession from a suspicion that the liabilities exceed the assets, it is provided by the Sc. Pegasianum, that on the request of the transferree he shall be ordered by the Praetor to accept and transfer; whereupon the

ei et in eum qui receperit actiones dentur, ac iuris est ex senatusconsulto Trebelliano. quo casu nullis stipulationibus opus est, quia simul et huic qui restituit securitas datur, et actiones hereditariae ei et in eum transferuntur qui receperit hereditatem.

§ 259. Nihil autem interest utrum aliquis ex asse heres institutus aut totam hereditatem aut pro parte restituere rogetur, an ex parte heres institutus aut totam eam partem aut partis partem restituere rogetur: nam et hoc casu de quarta parte eius partis ratio ex Pegasiano senatusconsulto haberi solet.

transferree shall be just as capable of suing and being sued as the transferree under the Sc. Trebellianum. In this case no stipulations are necessary, because the transferror is protected, and the hereditary actions pass to and against the transferree.

§ 259. It makes no difference whether a sole heir or a part heir is under a trust to transfer, for a part heir is entitled under the Sc. Pegasianum to retain a fourth of his part.

§ 246. The dispositions of a testator which have been hitherto considered were directions addressed to his successor, resembling the orders of a father to his son or of a master to his slave, or the commands of a magistrate to his subordinate or of the state to its members. Hence the importance of the regular institution of a successor, of finding a person who, being a mere creature of the testator's, shall be compelled to execute his commands.

Fideicommissa, to which we now proceed, are not commands, but requests. Legatum est quod legis modo, id est, imperative, testamento relinquitur, nam ea quae precativo modo relinquuntur fideicommissa vocantur, Ulpian, 24, 1. 'A legacy is a legislative or imperative testamentary disposition: a precative disposition (a disposition in the form of entreaty) is a trust.'

The original object of trusts was to extend the testator's bounty to those who were legally incapacitated to be legatees; for instance, aliens and Latini Juniani; for though Hadrian subsequently incapacitated aliens for taking the benefit of a trust, yet, as declarations of trust were exempt from many other restrictions which hampered direct devises, they survived the circumstance which was the principal motive of their introduction.

Trusts had originally no legal validity, and we see from Cicero, Verres, 2, 1, 47, that it was usual for the testator to make the successor take an oath to perform the testator's wishes, thus supplying by religious motives the want of a political sanction. But Augustus, as we are informed by Justinian, in some individual cases of breach of trust directed the consuls to interpose their authority and compel trustees to execute their charge; and trusts soon became an ordinary mode of testamentary disposition, and, in process of time, a permanent fiduciary jurisdiction was established, the court of the praetor fideicommissarius.

The conversion of a moral into a political obligation by the legalization of trusts, was similar to what occurred when the Twelve Tables gave legal force to the nuncupation declaring the conditions and purposes of a mancipation; and, remembering the celebrated ordinance, Cum nexum faxit mancipiumque, uti lingua nuncupassit, ita jus esto, it may occur to us to wonder why Augustus did not imitate the energetic brevity of the ancient legislator, and simply enact, Cum testamentum faxit codicillosve, uti fideicommiserit, ita jus esto. There would then have been no need of the cumbrous machinery of fictitious sales and stipulations between quasi vendor and quasi vendee; but a little reflection will show that such an enactment would have operated very inconveniently, and have defeated the very purposes for which trusts were instituted. Such an enactment would have made trusts, like nuncupations, a matter of civil law; and the jus strictum of the civil law was far from elastic or rational even in the time of Augustus; so that, if it was intended to enlarge the powers of testators and the discretion of the fiduciary tribunal, it was absolutely necessary to make trusts a province not of legal but of equitable jurisdiction.

§ 251. The transferree, it will be seen, was quasi heir when the Sc. Trebellianum applied: when the Sc. Pegasianum applied he was either quasi legatee or quasi vendee.

§ 253. The terms of the Sc. Trebellianum, passed in the reign of Nero, A. D. 62, are given in the Digest: Quum esset aequissimum in omnibus fideicommissariis hereditatibus, si qua de his bonis judicia penderent, ex his eos subire, in quos jus fructusque transferretur, potius quam cuique periculosam esse fidem suam, placuit et actiones, quae in heredes heredibusque dari solent, eas neque in eos neque his dari, qui fidei suae commissum, sicuti rogati essent, restituissent, sed his et in eos quibus ex testamento fideicommissum restitutum fuisset, quo magis in reliquum confirmentur supremae defunctorum voluntates, Dig. 31, 1, 2. 'Forasmuch as equity requires that whenever a succession is devised in trust, any actions arising thereout should be brought against the transferree of the succession and its benefits, and that the devisee should incur no risk in consequence of his trust; it is decreed that the actions of and against an heir, shall not be granted to or against an heir who transfers a succession in pursuance of a trust, but to and against the testamentary transferree, in order that in future the last wishes of testators may have more effect.'

§ 254. By the Sc. Trebellianum, if the whole beneficial interest in an inheritance was transferred, the whole right of suing and being sued passed to the transferree: if only a portion of the beneficial interest was transferred, both the transferror and the transferree could sue and be sued in the same proportion. The Sc. Pegasianum, passed in the reign of Vespasian, A. D. 70–76, apparently provided that when less than a fourth of the inheritance is left to the benefit of the heir, the Sc. Trebellianum should be inoperative, that is to say, that in such a case the actions by or against the inheritance shall not be maintainable by or against both the heir and transferree in the proportion of their interests, but should be exclusively maintainable by or against the heir. In fact, having subjected the transferree to the liability of abatement which the lex Falcidia imposed on the legatee, it seemed logical to put him in all other respects on the footing of a legatee, including the immunity from being sued and incapacity of suing for the debts of the succession. Having thus made the heir sole administrator, in order to secure a just and ratable division of the gains and losses of administration, the Sc. Pegasianum directed the heir and transferree to enter into the covenants usual between an heir and a partiary legatee. A partiary legatee is a legatee by partition, which Theophilus calls a fifth form of legacy, and of which Ulpian gives the formula: Sicut singulae res legari possunt, ita universarum quoque summa legari potest, ut puta hoc modo: Heres meus cum Titio hereditatem meam partito dividito, quo casu dimidia pars bonorum legata videtur: potest autem et alia pars veluti tertia vel quarta legari: quae species partitio appellatur, Ulpian 24, 25. 'As single things can be bequeathed, so can a universality, for instance thus: Do thou, my heir, partition and divide my inheritance with Titius; in which case a moiety is deemed to be bequeathed, but any other part, a third or fourth, may be bequeathed, and this form of bequest is called partition.' This form of legacy probably owed its origin to the lex Voconia, § 226.

§ 257. It is therefore not true, as might be inferred from § 254, that the stipulations between quasi vendor and quasi vendee were entirely discontinued. The reason why these obsolete covenants again became necessary is probably because the Sc. Pegasianum, having abrogated the Sc. Trebellianum in all cases where less than a fourth of the inheritance is left to the heir, had omitted to declare what mutual securities were proper to be taken by the heir and transferree, in case the heir declined to avail himself of his right to retain a fourth.

Modestinus suggested another course. He held that if the heir declined to avail himself of his right, and transferred the whole inheritance, there was no need of any stipulations, as the Sc. Trebellianum would then apply. However he thought the point doubtful, for he recommended that the heir should feign unwillingness to accept a damnosa hereditas, and should make a compulsory acceptance by the order of the praetor, in which case the actions are transferred in totality to the transferree by the express provision of the Sc. Pegasianum, Dig. 36, 1, 45. The sequence of §§ 257, 258 seems to indicate an intention of Gaius to suggest that this course might be adopted.

§ 259. The stipulations of the transferree as quasi vendee or quasi partiary legatee introduced by the Sc. Pegasianum were not only a cumbrous machinery, but after all afforded an insufficient security to the parties. The heir and transferree were always in mutual danger of one another's insolvency, and an heir after transferring the whole inheritance, though not fairly liable to any molestation or vexation on account of it, might find himself with two lawsuits on his hands: he might first be sued by the creditors of the estate, and then have to recover back what he is condemned to pay them from the transferree by suing him on the covenants of quasi vendor and quasi vendee.

It is not surprising, therefore, that Justinian abolished these provisions of the Sc. Pegasianum, and enacted that in every case there shall be a transfer or division of actions as contemplated by the Sc. Trebellianum, i.e. that the actions by or against the inheritance shall either be transferred in totality to the transferree, or be maintainable by or against both the heir and the transferree in the proportion of their interests.

The following observations may serve to complete the explanation of the Sc. Trebellianum and the Sc. Pegasianum.

Succession is the transfer of a right from one person (auctor) to another person (successor), such as occurs, for instance, in the voluntary alienation of property. Here the same dominion that was previously exercised by the alienor is subsequently exercised by the alienee. The right continues the same; the person invested therewith is changed. It was characteristic of jus in personam or obligation (before, at least, the invention of papers payable to the holder and transferable by delivery) that it was not capable of a similar alienation. All that could be done to accomplish a similar result was to employ one of two cumbrous processes, Novation or Cession of Action (Procuration), 2 § 38. In these procedures there is no Succession, for in Novation the transferree is not invested with the same right that previously vested in the transferror, but a new right is created in the transferree while the old right of the transferror is extinguished: and in Procuration or Cession the right still continues vested in the transferror, who allows the transferree to recover it or enforce it by action and retain the fruits of the recovery.

This inalienability of obligations, however, was confined to SINGULAR successions (in singularum rerum dominium successio). UNIVERSAL succession (per universitatem successio) or the transmission of the ideal whole of a patrimony, of which we have an example in hereditas testamentary or intestate, differed from SINGULAR succession by the capacity of passing obligation as well as Dominion. The heres of the testator or intestate sued and was sued in his own name on the obligations, active or passive, that originally vested in the deceased. But UNIVERSAL succession was an institution only recognised by Roman jurisprudence in certain definite cases. It was a formidable operation and rigorously circumscribed. It was not a transaction that the law allowed to be accomplished at the discretion of individual parties in pursuance of private convention. It was only admitted in the cases enumerated by Gaius, 2 § 98, and, without legislative interference, the list could not be augmented.

These difficulties in the transfer of obligation opposed a great obstacle to the transfer (restitutio) of trust successions: and these difficulties were partially removed by the Sc. Trebellianum and Sc. Pegasianum, and more completely by Justinian, by investing the Restitutio with the character of successio per universitatem, in other words, by the legislative sanction of a new instance of UNIVERSAL succession.

DE SINGULIS REBUS PER FIDEICOMMISSUM RELICTIS.

§ 260. Potest autem quisque etiam res singulas per fideicommissum relinquere, velut fundum, hominem, *vestem*, argentum, pecuniam; et vel ipsum heredem rogare, ut alicui restituat, vel legatarium, quamvis a legatario legari non possit.

§ 260. Not only aggregates of right, but single rights, may be left in trust, as property in land, in a slave, in a garment, in plate, in money; and the trust may be imposed either on an heir or on a legatee, although a legatee cannot be charged with a legacy.

§ 261. Item potest non solum propria testatoris res per fideicommissum relinqui, sed etiam heredis aut legatarii aut cuiuslibet alterius. itaque et legatarius non solum de ea re rogari potest, ut eam alicui restituat, quae ei legata sit, sed etiam de alia, sive ipsius legatarii sive aliena sit. sed hoc solum observandum est, ne plus quisquam rogetur alicui restituere, quam ipse ex testamento ce*per*it: nam quod amplius est inutiliter relinquitur.

§ 261. Not only the testator's property, but that of an heir, or legatee, or stranger, may be left in trust. Thus a legatee may be charged with a trust to transfer either a thing bequeathed to him, or any other thing belonging to himself or to a stranger; provided always that he is not charged with a trust to transfer more than he takes under the will, for in respect of such excess the trust would be void.

§ 262. Cum autem aliena res per fideicommissum relinquitur, necesse est ei qui rogatus est, aut ips*am* redimere et praestare, aut aestimationem *eius* solvere. *sicut iuris est, si* per damnationem aliena res legata sit. sunt tamen qui putant, si rem per fideicommissum relictam dominus non vendat, extingui fideicommissum: sed aliam esse causam per damnationem legati.

§ 262. When a stranger's property is left by trust, the trustee must either procure and convey the specific thing or pay its valuation, like an heir charged under a bequest by condemnation; though some hold that the owner's refusal to sell avoids a trust to convey while it does not avoid a bequest by condemnation.

§ 263. Libertas quoque servo per fideicommissum dari potest, ut vel heres rogetur manumittere, vel legatarius.

§ 263. Liberty can be left to a slave by a trust charging either an heir or a legatee with his manumission.

§ 264. N*ec interest utrum de suo proprio servo testator* roget, an de eo qui ipsius heredis *aut lega*tarii vel etiam extranei sit.

§ 264. And it makes no difference whether the slave is the property of the testator, of the heir, of the legatee, or of a stranger.

§ 265. Itaque et alienus ser*v*us redimi et manumitti debet. quod *si dominus eum non ven*dat, sane *extinguitur libertas, quia pro libertate preti*i computatio nulla intervenit.

§ 265. A stranger's slave, therefore, must be purchased and manumitted, but his owner's refusal to sell extinguishes the gift of liberty, because liberty admits of no pecuniary compensation.

§ 266. Qui autem ex fideicommisso manumittitur, non testatoris

§ 266. A trust of manumission makes the slave the freedman, not

fit *libertus, etiamsi testatoris servus sit, sed eius qui manumittit.*

§ 267. At qui directo, testamento, liber esse iubetur, *velut* hoc *modo :* *STICHUS SERVUS MEUS LIBER ESTO,* *vel STICHUM SERVUM MEUM LIBERUM ESSE IUBEO, is ipsius testatoris* fit libertus. Nec alius ullus directo, ex testamento, libertatem habere potest, quam qui utroque tempore testatoris *ex iure Quiritium fuerit, et quo faceret* testamentum et quo moreretur.

§ 268. Multum autem *differunt* quae per fideicommissum relinquuntur ab his quae directo iure legantur.

§ 269. Nam ecce per fideicommissum etiam *nutu* hereditas relinqui potest: cum alioquin legatum nisi testamento facto inutile sit.

§ 270. Item intestatus moriturus potest ab eo ad quem bona eius pertinent *fideicommissum* alicui relinquere: cum alioquin ab eo legari non possit.

§ 270 *a. Item legatum codicillis* relictum non aliter valet, quam si a testatore confirmati fuerint, id est nisi in testamento caverit testator, ut quidquid in codicillis scripserit id ratum sit: fideicommissum vero etiam non confirmatis codicillis relinqui potest.

§ 271. Item a legatario legari non potest: sed fideicommissum relinqui potest. quin etiam ab eo quoque cui per fideicommissum relinquimus rursus alii per fideicommissum relinquere possumus.

§ 272. Item servo alieno directo libertas dari non potest: sed per fideicommissum potest.

§ 273. Item codicillis nemo heres institui potest neque exheredari, quamvis testamento confirmati sint. at hic qui testamento heres institutus est potest codicillis rogari, ut eam hereditatem alii totam vel ex

of the testator, though he may have been the owner of the slave, but of the manumitter.

§ 267. A direct bequest of liberty, such as: 'Be my slave Stichus free,' or, 'I order that my slave Stichus be free,' makes the slave the freedman of the testator. A direct bequest of liberty can only be made to a slave who is the testator's quiritarian property at both periods, both at the time of making his will and at the time of his decease.

§ 268. There are many differences between fiduciary devises and direct bequests.

§ 269. In a fiduciary devise a nod of the head is sufficient to pass the succession, while a bequest not contained in a testament is void.

§ 270. Again, a man going to die intestate can charge his heir with a trust, but cannot charge him with a legacy.

§ 270 *a*. Again, a legacy left by codicil is not valid, unless the codicil is ratified, that is, unless the testator has provided in his will that any codicil should be valid: whereas a trust requires no ratification of the codicil.

§ 271. A legatee cannot be charged with a legacy, but can be charged with a trust, and the beneficiary of a trust may himself be charged with a further trust.

§ 272. A slave of a stranger cannot be enfranchised by direct bequest but may by the interposition of a trust.

§ 273. A codicil is not a valid instrument for the institution of an heir or his disinheritance, though ratified by will: but an heir instituted by will may be charged by a codicil to convey the estate in whole

parte restituat, quamvis testamento codicilli confirmati non sint.

or in part to another person without any previous ratification by will.

§ 274. Item mulier quae ab eo qui centum milia aeris census est per legem Voconiam heres institui non potest, tamen fideicommisso relictam sibi hereditatem capere potest.

§ 274. A woman, whom a testator registered in the census as owning a hundred thousand sesterces is forbidden by the lex Voconia to institute heiress, can take the succession by the intervention of a trustee.

§ 275. Latini quoque qui hereditates legataque directo iure lege Iunia capere prohibentur ex fideicommisso capere possunt.

§ 275. Latin Juniani, who are disabled by the lex Junia from taking an inheritance or legacy by direct devise, can take it by means of a declaration of trust.

§ 276. Item cum senatusconsulto prohibitum sit proprium servum minorem annis XXX liberum et heredem instituere, plerisque placet posse nos iubere liberum esse, cum annorum XXX erit, et rogare, ut tunc illi restituatur hereditas.

§ 276. A decree of the senate (rather, the lex Aelia Sentia 1 § 18) incapacitates a testator's slave under thirty years of age for being enfranchised and instituted heir; but, according to the prevalent opinion, he can be ordered to be free on attaining the age of thirty, and the heir may be bound by a declaration of trust to then convey the inheritance to him.

§ 277. Item quamvis non *possimus* post mortem eius qui nobis heres extiterit, alium in locum eius heredem instituere, tamen possumus eum rogare, ut cum morietur, alii eam hereditatem totam vel ex parte restituat. et quia post mortem quoque heredis fideicommissum dari potest, idem efficere possumus et si ita scripserimus: CUM TITIUS HERES MEUS MORTUUS ERIT, VOLO HEREDITATEM MEAM AD PUBLIUM MAEVIUM PERTINERE. utroque autem modo, tam hoc quam illo, Titius heredem suum obligatum relinquit de fideicommisso restituendo.

§ 277. An heir in remainder after the death of a prior heir cannot be instituted, but an heir may be bound by a declaration of trust to convey the estate, when he dies, in whole or in part to another person; or, as a trust may be limited to take effect after the death of the trustee, the same purpose may be accomplished in these terms: 'When my heir is dead, I wish my inheritance to go to Publius Mevius;' and whichever terms are employed, the heir of my heir is bound by a trust to convey the inheritance to the person designated.

§ 278. Praeterea legata *per* formulam petimus: fideicommissa vero Romae quidem aput Consulem vel aput eum Praetorem qui praecipue *de* fideicommissis ius dicit persequimur; in provinciis vero aput Praesidem provinciae.

§ 278. Legacies are recovered by judex and formula; trusts are enforced by the extraordinary jurisdiction of the consul or praetor fideicommissarius at Rome; in the provinces by the extraordinary jurisdiction of the president.

§ 279. Item de fideicommissis semper in urbe ius dicitur: de legatis vero, cum res aguntur.

§ 279. Cases of trust are heard and determined at Rome at all times of the year; cases of legacy can only be litigated during term.

§ 280. Fideicommissorum usurae et fructus debentur, si modo moram solutionis fecerit qui fideicommissum debebit: legatorum vero usurae non debentur; idque rescripto divi Hadriani significatur. scio tamen Iuliano placuisse in eo legato quod sinendi modo relinquitur idem iuris esse quod in fideicommissis: quam sententiam et his temporibus magis optinere video.

§ 280. Trusts entitle to payment of interest and interim profits on delay of performance by the trustee; legatees are not entitled to interest, as a rescript of Hadrian declares. Julianus, however, held that a legacy bequeathed in the form of permission is on the same footing as a trust, and this is now the prevalent doctrine.

§ 281. Item legata Graece scripta non valent: fideicommissa vero valent.

§ 281. Bequests expressed in Greek are invalid; trusts expressed in Greek are valid.

§ 282. Item si legatum per damnationem relictum heres infitietur, in duplum *cum eo* agitur: fideicommissi vero nomine semper in simplum persecutio est.

§ 282. An heir who disputes a legacy in the form of condemnation is sued for double the sum bequeathed; a trustee is only suable for the simple amount of the subject of trust.

§ 283. Item *quod* quisque ex fideicommisso plus debito per errorem solverit, repetere potest: at id quod ex causa falsa per damnationem legati plus debito solutum sit, repeti non potest. idem scilicet iuris est de eo [legato] quod non debitum vel ex hac vel ex illa causa per errorem solutum fuerit.

§ 283. On overpayment by mistake in the case of a trust, the excess can be recovered back by the trustee; on overpayment by mistake of a bequest by condemnation, the excess cannot be recovered back by the heir; so, on total failure of a disposition and payment by mistake, a trust sum can, a legacy by condemnation cannot, be recovered back.

§ 284. Erant etiam aliae differentiae, quae nunc non sunt.

§ 284. There formerly were other differences which are now abolished.

§ 285. Ut ecce peregrini poterant fide*i*commissa *ca*pere: et fere haec fuit origo fide*i*commiss*orum*. sed postea id prohibitum est; et nunc ex oratione divi Hadriani senatusconsultu*m* factum est, ut ea fide*i*commissa fisco vindicarentur.

§ 285. Thus aliens could be benefited by a declaration of trust, and this was the principal motive in which trusts originated, but afterwards they were incapacitated; and now, by a decree of the senate passed on the proposition of Hadrian, property devised in trust for the benefit of aliens is confiscated.

§ 286. Caeli*b*es quoque qui per legem Iuliam hereditates legataque capere prohibentur, olim fideicommissa videbantur capere posse. Item orbi qui per legem Papiam, ob id quod liberos non habent, dimidias partes hereditatum legatorumque perdunt, olim solida fideicommissa

§ 286. Celibates, who are disabled by the lex Julia from taking successions or legacies, were formerly deemed capable of benefiting by a declaration of trust. And childless persons, who forfeit by the lex Papia half the successions and legacies destined for

videbantur capere posse. sed postea senatusconsulto Pegasiano perinde fideicommissa quoque, ac legata hereditatesque capere posse prohibiti sunt. eaque translata sunt ad eos qui testamento liberos habent, aut si nullus liberos habebit, ad populum, sicuti iuris est in legatis et in hereditatibus.

them, were formerly deemed capable of taking the whole as beneficiaries of a trust. But at a later period the Sc. Pegasianum extended to trust dispositions the disabilities which attach to legacies and successions, and made the trust fund escheat to the devisees and legatees who have children, and, failing devisees and legatees with children, to the state, in the same way as legacies and successions.

§ 287. Eadem aut simili ex causa autem olim incertae personae vel postumo alieno per fideicommissum relinqui poterat, quamvis neque heres institui neque legari ei possit. sed senatusconsulto quod auctore divo Hadriano factum est idem in fideicommissis quod in legatis hereditatibusque constitutum est.

§ 287. From the same or a similar reason an uncertain person or an afterborn stranger could formerly take the benefit of a trust, though he could neither take as heir nor as legatee, until a decree of the senate, passed on the proposition of the emperor Hadrian, extended to trust funds the disabilities relating to legacies and successions.

§ 288. Item poenae nomine iam non dubitatur nec per fideicommissum quidem relinqui posse.

§ 288. Penal dispositions are at last decided to obtain no validity by being clothed in a fiduciary form.

§ 289. Sed quamvis in multis iuris partibus longe latior causa sit fideicommissorum, quam eorum quae directo relinquuntur, in quibusdam tantumdem valeant: tamen tutor non aliter testamento dari potest quam directo, veluti hoc modo: LIBERIS MEIS TITIUS TUTOR ESTO, vel ita: LIBERIS MEIS TITIUM TUTOREM DO: per fideicommissum vero dari non potest.

§ 289. Although in many circumstances declarations of trust have an ampler scope than direct dispositions, and in some respects are on a par, yet a testamentary guardian can only be appointed by direct nomination, as thus: 'Be Titius guardian to my children;' or thus: 'I nominate Titius guardian to my children;' he cannot be appointed indirectly by the intermediation of a trustee.

§ 264. Justinian declares that the heir is not forthwith released from his obligation by the owner's refusal to sell, but will be bound to seize any opportunity that may subsequently offer of purchasing and manumitting the slave in pursuance of the trust, Inst. 2, 24, 2.

§ 270. Codicils, according to Justinian, first acquired legal validity in the time of Augustus, who being trustee under a codicil set the example of performing the trust. The jurist Trebatius being consulted by Augustus, whether it was possible to give legal force to codicils without defeating the policy of testamentary law, gave a decided opinion in the affirmative; and all scruples respecting the validity of codicils vanished when it became known that codicils had been left by the eminent jurist Labeo.

Codicillus is the diminutive of codex, and denotes the less important and solemn documents or instruments of a man of business, a pocket-book, an agenda, a codicil; as codex denotes the more important and formal documents, a journal, a ledger, a will. A codicil enabled a testator who had solemnly executed a will to add to or modify its dispositions without the necessity of re-execution. It was usual in a will to ratify any prior or subsequent codicils; a codicil, however, might exist without any will. An informal will could only take effect as a codicil if such was the expressed intention of the testator. A codicil could not contain an institution or disinheritance or substitution; but it might contain a trust for the transfer of the whole of an inheritance. A testator could only leave a single will, for a later will revoked a former; but he might leave many codicils. A codicil needed no formalities, though Justinian required the attestation of five witnesses, not, however, as an essential solemnity, but as a means of proof: for, in the absence of five witnesses, the heir might be required to deny the existence of a declaration of trust upon his oath, Inst. 2, 23, 12.

§ 278. Fideicommissa were enforced by persecutio, or the praetor's extraordinaria cognitio. (See 4 § 187, commentary.)

§ 279. The law terms at Rome during the greater part of the formulary period, were of two different kinds: (1) the juridical term or term for jurisdictio, and (2) the judicial term or term for trials.

(1) The term for jurisdiction, that is, for the solemn acts of the praetor sitting on the tribunal in his court in the comitium, was that originally prescribed for the ancient leges actiones. The year was divided into forty dies fasti, unconditionally allotted to juridical proceedings, one hundred and ninety dies comitiales, available for juridical purposes unless required for the legislative assemblies, dies intercisi, of which certain hours were available for jurisdiction, and sixty dies nefasti, which were absolutely unavailable for juridical proceedings.

(2) Judicia, or trials before a judex in the forum, were unaffected by dies fasti and nefasti, but dependent on another division, dies festi and profesti; dies festi (days devoted to feriae, ludi, epulae, sacrificia) being exempted from litigation. Besides these occasional

interruptions of litigation, there were longer set vacations, which we find rearranged on several occasions. Thus at one time we find two judicial terms (rerum actus, cum res aguntur) in the year, a winter and a summer term, and two vacations, one in spring and another in autumn. Claudius substituted a single vacation at the close of the year, and made the law term continuous. Rerum actum, divisum antea in hibernos aestivosque menses, conjunxit, Suetonius, Claudius, 23. Galba abolished this vacation, and confined the intervals of litigation to dies feriati. Marcus Aurelius, in the time of Gaius, abolished the distinction between the jurisdiction term (dies fasti) and the trial term (rerum actus). He devoted two hundred and thirty days (adding the number of dies fasti to the number of dies comitiales) to forensic proceedings, under the name of dies juridici or dies judiciarii, and allowed even the rest of the year, dies feriati, to be used for litigation with the consent of the parties. Judiciariae rei singularem diligentiam adhibuit: fastis dies judiciarios addidit, ita ut ducentos triginta dies annuos rebus agendis litibusque disceptandis constitueret, Capitolinus, Marcus, 10. 'He also regulated the administration of justice, noting forensic days in the calendar, and allotting two hundred and thirty to litigation and civil suits.'

Subsequently to the time of Gaius, a law of Valentinian, Theodosius, and Arcadius, A.D. 389, while it declared the principle that all days are dies juridici, excepted, besides Sundays and certain other holidays, two months for harvest and vintage, and two weeks at Easter. Justinian further appointed, by way of interpolation in this law, certain vacations at Christmas, Epiphany, and Pentecost, Cod. 3, 12, 7, thus furnishing the model on which the four English law terms were regulated by Edward the Confessor. Subsequently, the Statute of Westminster, 3, Edward I, permitted assizes, i.e. trials by jury of issues of fact, to be held in the vacations, re-establishing a distinction corresponding to that of jurisdictional (dies fasti) and judicial terms (rerum actus): with this difference, however, that as the same judicial authorities preside over proceedings in banco, or issues of law, and proceedings at nisi prius, or issues of fact, the seasons set apart for the latter, that is, the trial terms, are merely the vacations of the former, that is, of the sittings in banco. See Puchta, Institutionen, § 158.

§ 283. Money paid by mistake was not recoverable when the payor was liable to be sued for double damages, Inst. 3, 27, 7, because then the payment is not deemed to be a mistake, but a compromise, in order to avoid the chance of condemnation in double damages.

§ 285. So by English law aliens were not, till recently, allowed to purchase land or to take land by devise. Land purchased by an alien or devised to an alien was forfeited to the crown. An alien, however, could hold personal property and take bequests of personal property. In France, formerly, an alien was not allowed to make a will, but all his property at his death escheated to the crown by the droit d'aubaîne (aubaine = alibi natus).

§ 289. Justinian abolished the distinction between legacies and trusts, enacting that legacies should no longer be governed by the rigours of the civil law, but subject to the same rules and construed with the same liberality as trusts, Inst. 2, 20, 3.

By English law, a will of lands operates as a mode of conveyance requiring no extrinsic sanction to render it available as a document of title. A will of personalty requires for its authentication to be proved before a court by the oath of the executor and, unless the attestation clause is in a certain form, by the affidavit of one of the subscribing witnesses; or, if the validity of the will is disputed, by examination of the witnesses on oath in the presence of the parties interested. The will itself is deposited in the registry of the Court of Probate; a copy of it in parchment, under the seal of the Court of Probate, delivered to the executor along with a certificate of proof, is the only proper evidence of his right to intermeddle with the personal estate of the testator.

The following were the corresponding formalities of Roman law:—

Tabulae testamenti aperiuntur hoc modo, ut testes vel maxima pars eorum adhibeatur qui signaverint testamentum; ita ut, agnitis signis, rupto lino, aperiatur et recitetur, atque ita describendi exempli fiat potestas, ac deinde signo publico obsignatum in archium redigatur, ut si quando exemplum ejus interciderit, sit unde peti possit.

Testamenta in municipiis, coloniis, oppidis, praefectura, vico, castello, conciliabulo facta, in foro vel basilica praesentibus testibus vel honestis viris inter horam secundam et decimam diei recitari debebunt, exemploque sublato ab iisdem rursus magistratibus obsignari quorum praesentiâ constat aperta.

Testamentum lex statim post mortem testatoris aperiri voluit, et ideo, quamvis sit rescriptis variatum, tamen a praesentibus intra triduum vel quinque dies aperiendae sunt tabulae; ab absentibus quoque intra eos dies cum supervenerint: nec enim oportet tam heredibus aut legatariis aut libertatibus quam necessario vectigali moram fieri, Paulus, Sent. Rec. 4, 6.

'A will is opened in the following manner: the witnesses, or the majority, who affixed their seals, are summoned and acknowledge their seals, the cord is broken, the tablets are opened, the will is read, a copy is taken, a public seal is affixed to the original, and it is deposited in the archives, so that if the copy is ever lost there may be a means of making another.

'In municipalities, colonies, towns, prefectures, wicks, castles, staples, a will must be read in the forum or basilica, in the presence of the attesting witnesses or of respectable persons, between eight o'clock in the morning and four o'clock in the afternoon; and, as soon as a copy has been made, must be sealed up again by the magistrate in whose presence it was opened.

'A will is intended by the law to be opened immediately after the death of the testator; accordingly, though rescripts have varied, it is now the rule that, if all the parties are present, three or five days is the interval within which the tablets must be opened; if they are absent, the same number of days after they are assembled; in order that heirs, legatees, manumitted slaves, and the military treasury (entitled, 3 § 125, to vicesima hereditatum, i. e. 5 per cent. on the value of Roman citizens' testamentary successions), may come into their rights without unnecessary delay.'

In cases of urgency, when the will was opened in the absence of the attesting witnesses in the presence of respectable persons, it was afterwards forwarded to the witnesses for the verification of their seals, Dig. 29, 3, 7. Every one who desired it had the power of inspecting a will and taking a copy, Dig. 29, 3, 8.

BOOK III.

DE RERUM UNIVERSITATIBUS ET DE OBLIGATIONIBUS.

DE HEREDITATIBUS QUAE AB INTESTATO DEFERUNTUR.

§ 1. *Intestatorum hereditates lege XII tabularum primum ad suos heredes pertinent.*

§ 2. *Sui autem heredes existimantur liberi qui in potestate morientis fuerint, veluti filius filiave, nepos neptisve ex filio, pronepos proneptisve ex nepote filio nato prognatus prognatave. nec interest utrum naturales sint liberi, an adoptivi. Ita demum tamen nepos neptisve et pronepos proneptisve suorum heredum numero sunt, si praecedens persona desierit in potestate parentis esse, sive morte id acciderit sive alia ratione, veluti emancipatione: nam si per id tempus quo quis moritur filius in potestate eius sit, nepos ex eo suus heres esse non potest. idem et in ceteris deinceps liberorum personis dictum intellegemus.*

§ 3. *Uxor quoque quae in manu est sua heres est, quia filiae loco est; item nurus quae in filii manu est, nam et haec neptis loco est. sed ita demum erit sua heres, si filius cuius in manu erit, cum pater moritur, in potestate eius non sit. idemque dicemus et de ea quae in nepotis*

§ 1. Intestate successions by the law of the Twelve Tables devolve first to self-successors.

§ 2. Self-successors are children in the power of the deceased at the time of his death, such as a son or a daughter, a grandchild by a son, a great-grandchild by a grandson by a son, whether such children are natural or adoptive: subject, however, to this reservation, that a grandchild or great-grandchild is only self-successor when the person in the preceding degree has ceased to be in the power of the parent either by death or some other means, such as emancipation; for instance, if a son was in the power of the deceased at the time of his death, a grandson by that son cannot be a self-successor, and the same proviso applies to the subsequent degrees.

§ 3. A wife in the hand of the deceased is a self-successor, for she is a quasi daughter; also a son's wife in the hand of the son, for she is a quasi granddaughter; subject, however, to the proviso that she is not self-successor if her husband is in the power of his father at the

manu matrimonii causa sit, quia proneptis loco est.

time of his father's death. A wife in the hand of a grandson is a self-successor, subject to the same proviso, because she is a quasi great-granddaughter.

§ 4. *Postumi quoque, qui si vivo parente nati essent, in potestate eius futuri forent, sui heredes sunt.*

§ 4. After-born children, who, if born in the lifetime of the parent, would have been subject to his power, are self-successors.

§ 5. *Idem iuris est de his quorum nomine ex lege Aelia Sentia vel ex senatusconsulto post* mortem patris causa probatur: nam et hi vivo patre causa probata in potestate eius futuri essent.

§ 5. Also those in whose behalf the provisions of the lex Aelia Sentia (1 § 32) or the senatusconsult have been satisfied by proof of excusable error subsequently to the death of the parent, for if the error had been proved in the lifetime of the parent they would have been subject to his power.

§ 6. Quod etiam de eo filio, qui ex prima secundave mancipatione post mortem patris manumittitur, *in*tellegemus.

§ 6. Also, a son, who has undergone a first or second mancipation and is manumitted after the death of the father, is a self-successor.

§ 7. Igitur cum filius filiave, et ex altero filio nepotes neptesve extant, pariter ad hereditatem vocantur; nec qui gradu proximior est ulteriorem excludit: ae*qu*um enim videbatur nepotes neptesve in patris sui locum portionemque succeder*e*. pari ratione et si nepos neptisve sit ex filio et ex nepote pronepos *pro*neptisve, simul omnes vocantur ad hereditatem.

§ 7. Accordingly, a son or daughter and grandchildren by another son are called contemporaneously to the succession; nor does the nearer grade exclude the more remote, for justice seemed to dictate that grandchildren should succeed to their father's place and portion. Similarly, a grandchild by a son and a great-grandchild by a grandson by a son are called contemporaneously to the succession.

§ 8. Et quia placebat nepotes nep*tes*ve, item pronepotes proneptesve in parentis suo locum succedere: conveniens esse visum est non in capita, sed *in* stirpes hereditates dividi, ita ut filius partem dimidiam hereditatis ferat, et ex altero filio duo pluresve nepotes alteram dimidiam; item si ex duobus filiis nep*otes* extent, et ex altero filio unus forte vel duo, ex altero tres aut quattuor, ad unum aut ad duos dimidia pars pertineat, et ad tres aut quattuor altera dimidia.

§ 8. And as it was deemed to be just that grandchildren and great-grandchildren should succeed to their father's place, it seemed consistent that the number of stems, and not the number of individuals, should be the divisor of the succession; so that a son should take a moiety, and grandchildren by another son the other moiety; or if two sons left children, that a single grandchild or two grandchildren by one son should take one moiety, and three or four grandchildren by the other son the other moiety.

§ 1. The words 'testate' and 'intestate,' in the language of English lawyers, are only applicable, I believe, to a deceased person. The awkwardness of having no corresponding adjectives to couple with succession must be my apology for sometimes speaking of testate or intestate succession.

For the meaning of suus heres, see commentary on 2 § 157 and 2 § 123.

DE LEGITIMA AGNATORUM SUCCESSIONE.

§ 9. Si nul*lus sit* suorum heredum, tunc hereditas *pertinet* ex eadem lege XII tabularum ad *adgnatos*.

§ 10. *Vocantur autem* adgnati qui legitima cognatione iuncti sunt: legitima autem cognatio est ea quae per virilis sexus personas *coniungitur. itaque eodem patre nati* fratres agna*ti sibi sunt, qui etiam consanguinei* vocantur, nec requiritur an *etiam matrem eandem habuerint.* item patruus fratris filio et invicem *is illi* agnatus est. eodem numero *sunt fratres* patrueles *inter se, id est* qui ex duobus f*ratribus progene*rati sunt, quo*s* plerique *etiam consobrinos vacant. qua ratione scilicet etiam ad plures gradus agnationis pervenire poterimus.*

§ 11. *Non tamen omnibus simul agnat*is d*at* lex XII tabularum hereditatem, sed his q*ui tunc, cum certum est aliquem intestato decessisse, proximo* gradu sunt.

§ 12. Nec in eo iure successio *est: ideoque si a*gnatus proximus hereditat*em* omiserit, *vel antequam adierit*, decesserit, sequentibus nihil iuris ex *lege com*petit.

§ 13. Ideo autem non mortis tempore, *quis proximus sit requirimus, sed eo* tempore *quo certum fuerit aliquem intestatum decessisse*,

§ 9. If there is no self-successor, the succession devolves by the same law of the Twelve Tables to the agnates.

§ 10. Agnates are statutory cognates. Statutory cognates are kindred related through males. Thus brothers by the same father are agnates, though by different mothers, and are called consanguineous; and a father's consanguineous brother is agnate to the nephew, and vice versâ; and the sons of consanguineous brothers, who are called consobrini, are mutual agnates; so that there are various degrees of agnation.

§ 11. Agnates are not called all contemporaneously to the succession by the law of the Twelve Tables, but only those of the nearest degree at the moment when it is certain that the deceased is intestate.

§ 12. And in title by agnation there is no advancement of grades; that is to say, if an agnate of the nearest grade decline the succession, or die before acceptance, the agnates of the next grade do not become entitled under the statute.

§ 13. The date for determining the nearest agnate is not the moment of death, but the moment when intestacy is certain, because

*quia si quis testamento fa*cto decesserit, melius *esse* visum est tunc ex iis requiri proximum, cum certum esse coeperit neminem ex eo testamento fore heredem.

it seemed better, when a will is left, to take the nearest agnate at the moment when it is ascertained that there will be no testamentary successor.

§ 14. Quod ad feminas tamen attinet, in hoc iure aliu*d* in ipsarum hereditatibus capiendis placuit, aliu*d* in ceterorum bonis ab his capiendis. nam feminarum *heredi*tates perinde ad nos a*g*nationis iure redeunt atque masculorum: nostrae vero hereditates ad feminas ultra consanguineorum gradum non pertinent. itaque soror fratri sororive legitima heres est; amita vero et fra*tris* filia legitima heres esse *non potest. sororis autem nobis loco est* etiam mater aut noverca quae *per in ma*num conventionem aput patrem nostrum iura filiae con*secu*ta est.

§ 14. As to females, the rules of title by descent are not the same in respect of the successions which they leave and in respect of the successions which they take. An inheritance left by a female is acquired by a male by the same title of agnation as an inheritance left by a male, but an inheritance left by a male does not devolve to females beyond sisters born of the same father. Thus a sister succeeds to a sister or brother by the same father, but the sister of a father and daughter of a brother have no statutory title by descent. The rights of quasi sister belong to a mother or stepmother who passes into the hand of a father by marriage and acquires the position of a quasi daughter.

§ 15. Si ei qui defunctus erit *sit* frater et alterius fratris filius, sicut ex superioribus intellegitur, frater prior est, quia gradu praecedit. sed alia facta est iuris interpretatio inter suos heredes.

§ 15. If the deceased leaves a brother and another brother's son, as observed above (§ 11), the brother has priority, because he is nearer in degree, which differs from the rule applied to self-successors.

§ 16. Quodsi defuncti nullus frater extet, *sed* sint liberi fratrum, ad omnes quidem hereditas pertinet: sed quaesitum est, si dispari forte numero sint nati, ut ex uno unus vel duo, ex altero tres vel quattuor, utrum in stirpes dividenda sit hereditas, sicut inter suos heredes iuris est an potius in capita. ia*m*dudum tamen placuit in capita dividendam esse hereditatem. itaque quotquot erunt ab utraque parte personae, in tot portiones hereditas dividetur, ita ut singuli singulas portiones ferant.

§ 16. If the deceased leaves no brother, but children of more than one brother, they are all entitled to the succession; and it was once a question, in case the brothers left an unequal number of children, whether the number of stems was to be the divisor of the inheritance, as among self-successors, or the number of individuals; however, it has long been settled that the divisor is the number of individuals. Accordingly, the total number of persons determines the number of parts into which the inheritance must be divided, and each individual takes an equal portion.

§ 17. Si nullus agnatus sit, eadem

§ 17. In the absence of agnates the

lex XII tabularum gentiles ad hereditatem vocat. qui sint autem gentiles, primo commentario rettulimus. et cum illic admonuerimus totum gentilicium ius in desuetudinem abisse, supervacuum est hoc quoque loco de ea re curiosius tractare.

same law of the Twelve Tables calls the gentiles to the succession. Who are gentiles was explained in the first book, and as we then stated that the whole law relating to gentiles is obsolete, it is unnecessary to go into details on the present occasion.

§ 9. The term agnatio has already occurred (2 § 131) in the exposition of testacy, where it denoted the birth of a suus heres, and in the doctrine of intestacy it has the same signification. The same persons who in relation to a common ancestor are sui heredes, in relation to one another are agnati. Agnates, accordingly, may be described as all the members of a family; but then we must add that the family may either be actual or ideal, meaning by ideal either a family once actual but disintegrated by the death of the ancestor, or a family purely imaginary. While the common ancestor survives, the bonds of agnation are close, and the family is actual; after his death, when his descendants have formed separate families, all the members of those families are still agnates, because they are members of an ideal family which once was actual; and the descendants of those descendants are more remotely agnates, because, though never members of an actual family, they would have been so if the common ancestor had lived for, say, a hundred or a thousand years.

The words of the Twelve Tables creating title by agnation are as follow: Si intestato moritur cui suus heres nec escit, adgnatus proximus familiam habeto. 'If a man die intestate leaving no self-successor, his nearest agnate (the nearest self-successor of one of his ancestors) shall have the succession.'

§ 10. Consanguinei, brothers or sisters by the same father, opposed to uterini, brothers or sisters by the same mother, are properly included among agnates, being agnates of the first degree; but sometimes the word 'agnates' specifically denotes the subsequent degrees, and as females were only entitled to inherit by the first degree of agnation, § 14, the word 'agnates' was further limited to denote male agnates. Agnati autem sunt cognati virilis sexus per virilem descendentes, Paulus, Sent. Rec. 4, 8, 13. 'Agnates are male cognates related through males.'

§ 12. If the nearest degree of agnates in existence repudiated the succession, or died before acceptance, the succession did not devolve to the next degree of agnates, but passed by a different title to a different order of claimants, namely, to cognates, or next of kin, Ulpian, 26, 5. This rule was a scrupulous interpretation of the exact words of the Twelve Tables: Si intestato moritur cui suus heres nec escit, adgnatus *proximus* familiam habeto. No innovation in this respect was introduced by the praetors, whose policy was to prefer the natural title of cognation to the civil title of agnation. Justinian, however, abolished the rule, and allowed a devolution through the degrees of agnation, on the ground that, as the burden of tutela devolved through the degrees of agnation, there ought to be a corresponding and compensating devolution of the advantages of inheritance, Inst. 3, 2, 7. This change, however, was deprived of importance by the subsequent Novella 118, which introduced an entirely new system of succession, governed solely by cognatio.

§ 13. The moment at which it is ascertained that the deceased is intestate will be separated by an interval from the moment of his decease, when the intestacy is caused by the repudiation or incapacitation of the devisee, or the failure of the condition on which he was instituted. In this interval the nearest agnate may die, and a remoter agnate become the nearest agnate. It therefore was necessary to determine whether the title of nearest agnate is acquired at the moment of decease or of ascertained intestacy; and the latter moment was selected.

§ 14. The limitation, in respect of females, of title by agnation to females who were agnates in the first degree (consanguineae) was not contained in the Twelve Tables, but introduced by the jurists as an interpretation of the lex Voconia (B.C. 168), Paulus Sent. Rec. 4, 8, 22. The harshness of this limitation was mitigated by the praetors, who introduced title by cognation, and allowed females of remoter degrees of agnation to succeed in the order of cognates in default of successors by title of agnation; but Justinian totally abolished the limitation, and restored the rule of the Twelve Tables, allowing females to succeed in the order of agnates, however remote might be their degree of agnation, provided that no nearer degree was in existence.

The celebrated Novella, 118, as above stated, totally abolished title by agnation, and made succession by intestacy entirely dependent on the degrees of cognation or natural relationship.

§ 17. A fragment of Ulpian contains the provision of the Twelve Tables: Si agnatus nec escit, gentilis familiam nancitor. 'In the absence of an agnate, the gentile shall have the succession.' Gaius probably gave the definition of Gentiles after 1 § 164, where there is now an hiatus in the MS. Cicero gives the following account: Gentiles sunt qui inter se eodem nomine sunt: non est satis; qui ab ingenuis oriundi sunt: ne id quidem satis est; quorum majorum nemo servitutem servivit: abest etiam nunc; qui capite non sunt deminuti: hoc fortasse satis est, Topica, 6. 'Gentiles are those who bear a common name—this is inadequate; who are born of freemen—this is still insufficient; none of whose ancestors were slaves—something still is wanting; who have never suffered a loss of status. This perhaps is a complete definition.' This definition explains why gentility in modern languages implies pure blood, good extraction, noble genealogy; but it leaves the subject wrapped in obscurity. As many of the plebeians were the descendants of manumitted slaves, title by gentility would often imply the devolution of plebeian successions into the hands of patricians, a mode of transmission which would be less and less tolerated as Rome became more and more republican. Cicero, however, mentions a cause founded on title by gentility: Quid, qua de re inter Marcellos et Claudios patricios centumviri judicarunt? Cum Marcelli ab liberti filio stirpe, Claudii patricii ejusdem nominis hereditatem gente ad se redisse dicerent: nonne in ea causa fuit oratoribus de toto stirpis ac gentilitatis jure dicendum? De Orat. 1, 39. 'In the cause between the [plebeian Claudii] Marcelli and the patrician Claudii before the centumviral court, wherein the plebeian Claudii claimed the succession to a freedman's son by title of race, the patrician Claudii by title of gentility, had not the advocates to discuss the whole law of title by race and title by gentility?'

Of the technical meaning of 'stirps' we have no information, but we may conjecture that the question litigated was this: supposing a patron died without any lineal descendants, and without any agnates; in the succession to the estate of his freedman's son was priority to be given to the gens of the patron, or to the persons entitled under the clause in the edict called (see § 76, commentary) unde cognati manumissoris? It seems that the succession to a freedman's son might ascend to the patron or his relatives (agnates, gentiles, cognates); and that the patrician Claudii were the gentiles of the patron, the plebeian Claudii were his cognates, but not his gentiles.

BONORUM POSSESSIO INTESTATI.

§ 18. Hactenus lege XII tabularum finitae sunt intestatorum hereditates: quod ius quemadmodum strictum fuerit, palam est intellegere.

§ 18. These are all the provisions in the law of the Twelve Tables for intestate devolution, and how harshly they operated is patent.

§ 19. Statim enim emancipati liberi nullum ius in hereditatem parentis ex ea lege habent, cum desierint sui heredes esse.

§ 19. For instance, emancipated children forfeit all title to the succession of their parent by being divested of the character of self-successors.

§ 20. Idem iuris est, si ideo liberi non sint in potestate patris, quia sint cum eo civitate Romana donati, nec ab Imperatore in potestatem redacti fuerint.

§ 20. So do children whose freedom from the power of their parent only resulted from their receiving jointly with their father a donation of Roman citizenship (1 § 94), without a fiat of the emperor subjecting them to parental power.

§ 21. Item agnati capite diminuti non admittuntur ex ea lege ad hereditatem, quia nomen agnationis capitis deminutione perimitur.

§ 21. Again, agnates who have descended in status are barred from the succession under the statute, title by agnation being extinguished by descent in status.

§ 22. Item proximo agnato non adeunte hereditatem, nihilo magis sequens iure legitimo admittitur.

§ 22. And if the nearest agnate renounces a succession, the next degree, according to the statute, is not a whit the more entitled to succeed.

§ 23. Item feminae agnat*ae* quaecumque consanguineorum gradum excedunt, nihil iuris ex lege habent.

§ 23. Female agnates beyond the degree of sisters by the same father have no title to succeed under the statute.

§ 24. Similiter non admittuntur cognati qui per feminini sexus personas necessitudine iunguntur; adeo quidem, ut nec inter matrem et filium filiamve ultro citroque hereditatis capiendae ius conpetat, praeter quam si per in manum conventionem consanguinitatis iura inter eos constiterint.

§ 24. Cognates who trace their kin through females are similarly barred, so that even a mother and a son or daughter have no reciprocal right of succession, unless by subjection to the hand of the husband the mother has become a quasi sister to her children.

§ 25. Sed hae iuris iniquitates edicto Praetoris emendatae sunt.

§ 25. But to these legal inequalities the edict of the praetor administers a corrective.

§ 26. Nam *liberos* omnes qui legitimo iure deficiuntur vocat ad hereditatem proinde ac si in potestate parentum mortis tempore fuissent, sive soli sint sive etiam sui heredes, id est qui in potestate patris fuerunt, concurrant.

§ 26. All children whose statutory title fails are called by the praetor to the succession, just as if they had been in the power of their parent at the time of his decease, whether they come alone or in concurrence with self-successors, that is, with

other children who were subject to the power of the parent.

§ 27. Adgnatos autem capite deminutos non secundo gradu post suos heredes vocat, id est non eo gradu vocat quo per legem vocarentur, si capite minuti non essent; sed tertio, proximitatis nomine: licet enim capitis deminutione ius legitimum perdiderint, certe cognationis iura retinent. itaque si quis alius sit qui integrum ius agnationis habebit, is potior erit, etiam si longiore gradu fuerit.

§ 27. Agnates who have descended in status are called by the praetor, not indeed in the next degree to self-successors, that is, in the order in which the statute would have called them but for their loss of status, but in the third rank under the designation of cognates (next of kin); for though their descent in status has blotted out their statutory title, they nevertheless are still entitled as cognates; but if another person exists with unimpaired title by agnation, he is called in preference, although he may be an agnate in a remoter degree.

§ 28. Idem iuris est, ut quidam putant, in eius agnati persona, qui proximo agnato omittente hereditatem, nihilo magis iure legitimo admittitur. sed sunt qui putant hunc eodem gradu a Praetore vocari, quo etiam per legem agnatis hereditas datur.

§ 28. The rule is similar, according to some, in respect of the remoter agnate who has no statutory title to succeed on the renunciation of a nearer agnate; according to others, the praetor calls him to the succession in the order allotted by the statute to agnates.

§ 29. Feminae certe agnatae quae consanguineorum gradum excedunt tertio gradu vocantur, id est si neque suus heres neque agnatus ullus erit.

§ 29. Female agnates, at all events, beyond the degree of sisters are called in the third degree, that is to say, after self-successors and other agnates.

§ 30. Eodem gradu vocantur etiam eae personae quae per feminini sexus personas copulatae sunt.

§ 30. So are those persons who trace their kindred through females.

§ 31. Liberi quoque qui in adoptiva familia sunt ad naturalium parentum hereditatem hoc eodem gradu vocantur.

§ 31. Children in an adoptive family are called to succeed their natural parents in the same order.

§ 32. Quos autem Praetor vocat ad hereditatem, hi heredes ipso quidem iure non *fiunt. nam* Praetor heredes facere non potest: *per legem enim tantum vel similem iuris constitutionem heredes fiunt, veluti per senatusconsultum et constitutionem principalem:* sed *eis si quidem* Praetor d*et bonorum possessionem, loco* heredum *constituuntur.*

§ 32. Those whom the praetor calls to a succession do not become successors at civil law, for the praetor cannot make a successor; only a law or similar ordinance can constitute a successor, such as a decree of the senate or an imperial constitution: the praetor's grant of possession only makes the grantee a quasi successor.

§ 33. A*dhuc autem* alios *etiam complures gradus Praetor facit in bonorum possessione danda,* dum id

§ 33. Several additional grades of grantees of possession are recognized by the praetor in his desire

agit, ne quis sine successore moriatur. de quibus in his commentariis *copiose non agimus ideo, quia* hoc ius totum propriis commentariis *quoque* al*ias explicavimus. Hoc* solum admonuisse sufficit [*desunt lin.* 36].

§ 34. *Item ab intestato* heredes suos et agn*atos* ad bonorum possessionem vocat. quibus casibus beneficium eius in eo solo videtur aliquam utilitatem *habere, quod* is qui ita bonorum possessionem *petit*, interdicto cuius principium est QUORUM BONORUM uti possit. cuius interdicti q*uae* sit utilitas, suo loco proponemus. alioquin remota quoque bonorum possessione ad eos hereditas pertinet iure civili.

§ 35. Ceterum saepe quibusdam ita datur bonorum possessio, ut is cui data sit, *non* optineat hereditatem: quae bonorum possessio dicitur sine re.

§ 36. *N*am si verbi gratia iure facto testamento heres insti*t*utus creverit hereditatem, sed bonorum possessionem secundum tabulas testamenti petere noluerit, contentus eo, quod iure civil*i* heres sit, nihilo minus ii qui nullo facto testamento ad intestati bona vocantur possunt petere bonorum possessionem: sed sine re ad eos hereditas pertinet, cum testamento scriptus heres e*v*incere hereditatem possit.

§ 37. Idem iuris est, si intestato aliquo mortuo suus heres nol*uerit petere bonorum possessionem*, con*tentus* l*egitimo iure. nam* et agnato competit quidem bonorum possessio, sed sine r*e*, cum evinci hereditas a*b suo* herede potest. et illud convenient*er*, si ad agnatum iure civili pertinet hereditas et hic adierit hereditatem, sed *bonorum possessionem* petere noluerit, et si quis ex proximis cognatus petierit, sine re habebit bonorum possessionem propter eandem rationem.

that no one may die without a successor; but I forbear to examine them on the present occasion, because I have handled the whole subject of title by descent in a separate treatise devoted to this matter.

§ 34. Besides these grantees, when a man dies intestate, the praetor grants possession to self-successors or agnates, the only advantage they derive from the grant being that it entitles them to the interdict beginning with the words: 'Whatsoever portion of the goods' (the use of which will be explained in due time and place, 4 § 144), for independently of the grant of possession, they are entitled to the inheritance by the civil law.

§ 35. Possession is often granted to a person who will not have quiet enjoyment, and is then said to be ineffective.

§ 36. For instance, if an heir appointed by a duly executed will accepts the inheritance, but omits to demand possession in conformity with the will, contenting himself with his title at civil law, those who without a will would be entitled by descent may nevertheless obtain possession, but the grant will be ineffective, because they can be evicted by the testamentary heir.

§ 37. The same happens when a man dies intestate and a self-successor omits to demand possession, contenting himself with his statutory title; for an agnate may obtain the possession, but it will be ineffective, because he can be evicted by the self-successor. Similarly, if an agnate entitled by civil law accepts the succession but omits to demand possession, a cognate can obtain possession, but only ineffectively, for the same reason.

§ 38. Sunt et alii quidam similes casus, quorum *aliquos* superiore commentario tradidimus.

§ 38. There are other similar cases, some of which were mentioned in the preceding book.

§ 28. There is no other trace of a difference of opinion as to the order in which a remoter agnate was entitled on the renunciation of a nearer. Justinian states that before his time such an agnate was only entitled to succeed in the order of cognates, but altered the rule and allowed him to succeed in the order of agnates; that is to say, introduced a devolution of title from nearer to remoter agnate on the renunciation of the former, Inst. 3, 2, 7.

§ 32. The praetor, as executive power:

(1) Gave possession to the person entitled by law, that is, enforced the rights conferred on persons by the law; e.g. he gave possession secundum tabulas testamenti to the testamentary heir, § 36, or contra tabulas testamenti to praetermitted children, 2 § 125, or in intestacy to the suus heres or the agnate, § 37.

(2) He also gave possession to persons on whom the law had conferred no rights, that is, he supplemented the law; e.g. in default of sui heredes and agnates he granted possession to cognates; he gave possession secundum tabulas to the devisee under a will invalid at Civil law, because the testator had been incapacitated at some period between the execution of his will and his decease: this possession, however, was ineffective (sine re) against any person entitled in intestacy by the Civil law, 2 § 149, and Ulpian, 23, 6.

(3) He sometimes gave possession adverse to rights which the law had conferred on other persons, that is, he contradicted or corrected the law; e.g. he gave possession secundum tabulas to the devisee under a will invalid at Civil law, from want of mancipation or nuncupation, 2 § 149. He gave possession secundum tabulas to the afterborn stranger (postumus alienus), Inst. 3, 9, pr. who, as an uncertain person, could not be instituted by the Civil law, 2 § 242; and he gave possession contra tabulas to the emancipated child passed over in silence by a testator, 2 § 135.

As in the two latter functions of supplementing and correcting the law, the praetor did what is elsewhere performed by courts of equity, we have sometimes translated the contrasted terms heres and bonorum possessor by the terms 'legal successor' and 'equitable successor.'

The equitable or praetorian successor could not sue or be sued by the direct actions of the Civil law, but only by fictitious actions, 4 § 34. The claim of a succession founded on a title at Civil law was called hereditatis petitio; a claim founded on a purely praetorian title, e.g. cognation, was pursued by the Interdict Quorum bonorum, or, in the latest period, by possessoria hereditatis petitio, Dig. 5, 5, 1.

§ 33. The orders or grades or classes to whom the praetor successively granted bonorum possessio in intestacy were as follow:

(1) Children (liberi), including not only sui heredes, but also emancipated children, § 26, on condition that the latter brought their goods into hotchpot (collatio bonorum), Dig. 37, 6. Children given in adoption were not admitted in this order, but in the third order of cognates, § 31.

(2) Statutory heirs (legitimi), i. e. all who were entitled to inherit under any statute, e. g. agnates who were entitled under the Twelve Tables, mothers, who were entitled to succeed their children under the Sc. Tertullianum, children, who were entitled to succeed their mothers under the Sc. Orphitianum, and sui heredes who had repudiated or omitted to demand possession as members of the first order within the interval allowed, namely, a year.

(3) Next of kin (proximi cognati) including those who had neglected to claim in the first or second order.

(4) Husband and wife, when the wife is not in manu. A wife in manu would be quasi daughter and therefore sua heres and entitled to succeed with liberi in the first order.

These various grades of title are called unde liberi, unde legitimi, unde cognati, unde vir et uxor, phrases which properly denote those articles of the edict in which these classes are summoned to the succession: ea pars edicti unde liberi vocantur, &c., but are used by Roman lawyers as epithets of bonorum possessio.

The degrees of cognation in a direct line are the number of generations that separate a descendant from an ascendant: to compute the degrees of collateral cognation we must add the degrees of direct cognation. Thus a man is one degree from his father, and therefore two from his brother and three from his nephew. He is two degrees from his grandfather, and therefore three from his uncle and four from his first cousin or cousin german (consobrinus). He is three degrees from his great-grandfather, and therefore four from his great-uncle and five from his great-uncle's son (propior sobrino) and six from his second cousin (sobrinus), that is, his great-uncle's grandson, for second cousins are the children of first cousins. He is seven degrees from his second cousin's children, and this is the only case in which the seventh degree of cognation was recognized as giving a title to succeed in intestacy, the law only recognizing in other lines the sixth degree of cognation.

§ 36. Originally the person entitled to the praetorian succession was required to address a formal demand to the magistrate: but under Justinian any signification of intention to accept the succession was sufficient without a demand. The interval allowed for this signification of intention (agnitio) to a parent or child of the defunct was a year, to other claimants a hundred days. If a person in a superior order or degree omitted to signify his acceptance in the interval allowed, the succession then devolved to the next order or degree. If the person who thus omitted to signify acceptance had only a praetorian title to the succession, his right was entirely forfeited by the omission; but if he was entitled at civil law he could evict the bonorum possessor, who accordingly was said to have only a nugatory or ineffective possession (sine re).

§ 38. We have already seen that the devisee under an unauthorized will of a female, though he obtained bonorum possessio, might be evicted by the person entitled as agnate, 2 § 119, and that a devisee under a praetorian will might be evicted by a devisee under a prior civil will or by a person entitled as agnate, unless the sole informality of the praetorian will, which rendered it invalid as a civil will, was the omission of mancipation or nuncupation, 2 § 149.

DE SUCCESSIONE LIBERTORUM CIVIUM ROMANORUM.

§ 39. Nunc de libertorum bonis videamus.

§ 40. Olim itaque licebat liberto patronum suum in testamento praeterire: nam ita demum lex XII tabularum ad hereditatem liberti vocabat patro*nu*m, si intestatus mortuus esset libertus nullo suo herede *re*licto. itaque intestato quoque mortuo liberto, si is suum heredem reliquerat, nihil in bonis eius patrono iuris erat. et si quidem ex naturalibus liberis aliquem suum heredem reliquisset, nulla videbatur

§ 39. Succession to freedmen next demands our notice.

§ 40. Freedmen were originally allowed to pass over their patron in their testamentary dispositions. By the law of the Twelve Tables the inheritance of a freedman only devolved on his patron when he died intestate and without leaving a self-successor. If he died intestate but left a self-successor, the patron was excluded, and if the self-successor was a natural child, this was no grievance; but if the

esse querella; si vero vel adoptivus filius filiave, vel uxor quae in manu esset sua heres esset, aperte iniquum erat nihil iuris patrono superesse.

self-successor was an adoptive child or a wife in the hand, it was hard that they should bar all claim of the patron.

§ 41. Qua de causa postea Praetoris edicto haec iuris iniquitas emendata est. sive enim faciat testamentum libertus, iubetur ita testari, ut patrono suo partem dimidiam bonorum suorum relinquat; et si aut nihil aut minus quam partem dimidiam reliquerit, datur patrono contra tabulas testamenti partis dimidiae bonorum possessio. si vero intestatus moriatur, suo herede relicto adoptivo filio, *vel* uxore quae in manu ipsius esset, vel nuru quae in manu filii eius fuerit, datur aeque patrono adversus hos suos heredes partis dimidiae bonorum possessio. prosunt autem liberto ad excludendum patronum naturales liberi, non solum quos in potestate mortis tempore habet, se*d* etiam emancipati et in adoptionem dati, *si* modo aliqua ex parte heredes scripti *sint, aut praeteriti con*tra tabulas testamenti bonorum possessionem ex edicto petierint: nam exheredati nullo modo repellunt patronum.

§ 41. Accordingly, at a later period the praetor's edict corrected this injustice of the law. If a freedman makes a will, he is commanded to leave a moiety of his fortune to his patron; and if he leaves him nothing, or less than a moiety, the patron in derogation of the will can obtain possession of a moiety from the praetor. If he die intestate, leaving as self-successor an adoptive son or a wife in his hand or a son's wife in the hand of his son, the patron can obtain even against these self-successors possession of a moiety from the praetor. The freedman is enabled to exclude the patron if he leaves natural children, whether in his power at the time of his death or emancipated or given in adoption, provided he leaves them any portion of the succession, or that, being passed over in silence, they impeach the will and demand possession in pursuance of the edict; for, if they are disinherited, they do not avail to bar the patron.

§ 42. Postea lege Papia aucta sunt iura patronorum quod ad locupletiores libertos pertinet. Cautum est enim ea lege, ut ex bonis eius qui sestertiorum *nummorum centum* mili*um plurisve* patrimon*ium reliqu*erit, et pauciores quam tres liberos habebit, sive is testamento facto sive intestato mortuus erit, virilis pars patrono debeatur. itaque cum unum filium unamve filiam heredem reliquerit libertus, perinde pars dimidia patrono debetur, *ac si* sine ullo filio filiave moreretur; cum vero d*uos* duasve heredes reliquerit, tertia pars debetur; si tres relinquat, repellitur patronus. [*linea vacua.*]

§ 42. At a still later period the lex Papia Poppaea augmented the rights of the patron against the estate of more opulent freedmen. By the provisions of this law whenever a freedman leaves property of the value of a hundred thousand sesterces and upwards, and not so many as three children, whether he dies testate or intestate, a portion equal to that of a single child is due to the patron. Accordingly, if a single son or daughter survives, half the estate is claimable by the patron, just as if the freedman had died childless; if two children inherit, a third of the property belongs to the patron; if three children survive, the patron is excluded.

§ 43. In bonis libertinarum nullam iniuriam antiquo iure patiebantur patroni. cum enim hae in patronorum legitima tutela essent, non aliter scilicet testamentum facere poterant quam patrono auctore. itaque sive auctor ad testamentum faciendum factus *erat, neque tantum, quantum vellet, testamento sibi* relic*tum erat, de se queri debebat, qui id a liber*ta impe*trare potuerat.* si *vero* auctor *ei factus* non erat, *etiam tut*ius *hereditatem* morte *eius capie*bat; *nam neque suum heredem liberta relinquebat qui* posset patronum a bonis *eius vindicandis re*pellere.

§ 43. In successions to freedwomen no wrong could possibly be done the patron under the primitive law: for, as the patron was statutory guardian of the freedwoman, her will was not valid without his authorization, so that, if he authorized a will under which he did not take as much as he chose, he had only himself to blame, for he might have imposed his own terms on the woman; if he did not authorize a will, he was assured of the whole succession, for a woman could have no self-successor to bar the claim of the patron.

§ 44. Sed postea lex Papia *cum* quattuor liberorum iure libertinas tutela patronorum liberaret et eo modo *inferret, ut iam sine patroni tut*oris auctor*itate testari possent, prospexit, ut pro numero liberorum quos superstites liberta* habuerit virilis pars patrono debeatur . . . ex bonis eius, quae omnia . . . . iuris [2 *lin.*] ad patronum pertinet.

§ 44. But when at a subsequent period, by the enactment of the lex Papia, four children were a title that released a freedwoman from the guardianship of her patron, so that his authorization ceased to be necessary to the validity of her will, the same law enacted that a portion of her estate equal to that of a single child should always be due to the patron.

§ 45. *Quae* autem diximus de patrono, eadem intellegemus et de *filio patroni, item de* nep*ote ex filio, et de* prone*pote ex nepote filio nato* pro*g*nato.

§ 45. What has been said of the patron applies to a son of the patron, a grandson by a son, a great-grandson by a grandson by a son.

§ 46. *Fil*ia vero patron*i, item neptis ex filio, et* pron*eptis ex* nepot*e f*ilio n*ato prognata*, quamvis ide*m ius habeant, quod lege* XII tabularum patron*o* datum est, *Praetor tamen vocat tantum masculini sexus* patron*orum* lib*eros : sed filia, ut contra tabulas* testamenti liberti *vel* ab *intestato contra filium* adoptivum *vel uxorem nurumve dimidiae partis* bonorum possessionem petat, trium liberorum iure lege Papia consequitur: aliter hoc ius non habet.

§ 46. Although a daughter of a patron, a granddaughter by a son, a great-granddaughter by a grandson by a son have identical rights under the statute of the Twelve Tables with the patron, the praetorian edict only calls the male issue to the succession: but a daughter of the patron can override a will or the intestate claim of an adoptive child, or a wife, or a son's wife, and demand possession of a moiety under the title of mother of three children by the provisions of the lex Papia; otherwise she has no title.

§ 47. Se*d* ut ex bonis libert*ae suae* quattuor liberos haben*tis vir*ilis

§ 47. In the succession to a freedwoman mother of four chil-

pars ei deberetur, liberorum *quidem iure non est conprehensum*, ut quidam putant. sed tamen intestata liberta mortua, verba legis Papiae faciunt, ut ei virilis pars debeatur. si vero testamento facto mortua sit liberta, tale ius ei datur, quale datum est *patronae tribus liberis honoratae*, ut proinde *bonorum possessionem habeat, quam patronus* liberique contra tabulas testa*menti* liberti habent: quamvis parum diligenter ea pars legis scripta sit.

dren, a patron's daughter is not always entitled as mother of three children to the portion of a child, as some suppose: but, if the freedwoman die intestate, the words of the lex Papia give her the portion of a child; if the freedwoman die testate, the patron's daughter only has the same title as a freeborn patroness mother of two children; the same rights, that is, as the praetorian edict confers on a patron and his son in derogation of a freedman's will, though this portion of the law is carelessly written.

§ 48. Ex *h*is apparet *ex*traneos heredes patronorum longe remot*um ab omni eo* iure iri, quod *vel* in *in*testatorum bonis *vel contra* tab*ulas* testamenti patrono competit.

§ 48. It is apparent that the external heir of a patron is utterly destitute of title by patronage, whether a freedman die testate or intestate.

§ 49. Patronae olim ante legem Papiam hoc solum ius habebant in bonis libertor*um*, quod etiam patronis *ex* lege XII tabularum datum est. nec *enim* ut contra tabulas tes*ta*menti, in *quo* p*raeteritae* eran*t*, vel ab intestato contra filium adoptivum vel uxorem nurumve bonorum possessionem par*tis* d*imidiae* pe*t*erent, Praetor sim*i*liter *ut patrono* lib*erisque eius concessit*.

§ 49. Patronesses, before the lex Papia was passed, had only the same rights as patrons under the statute of the Twelve Tables: neither in derogation of a will in which they are omitted, nor against the intestate claim of an adoptive child or a wife or a son's wife could they, like the patron or the patron's son, obtain possession of a moiety from the praetor.

§ 50. *Sed postea lex Papia* duob*us liberis* honora*t*ae ingenuae patronae, libertinae tribus, eadem fere iura dedit quae ex edicto Praetoris patroni habent. trium vero liberorum iure honoratae ingenuae patronae ea iura dedit quae per eandem legem patrono data sunt: libertinae autem patronae non idem iuris praestitit.

§ 50. But subsequently by the lex Papia two children entitle a freeborn patroness, three children an emancipated patroness, to nearly the same rights as the edict confers on a patron; and three children entitle a freeborn patroness to the rights which the lex Papia confers on a patron: an emancipated patroness is never so entitled.

§ 51. Quod autem ad libertinarum bona pertinet, si quidem intestatae decesserint, nihil novi patronae liberis honoratae lex Papia praestat. itaque si neque ipsa patrona, neque liberta *capite deminuta* sit, ex lege XII tabularum ad eam hereditas pertinet, et excluduntur libertae liberi; quod iuris est etiamsi

§ 51. As to the successions of freedwomen who die intestate, no new right is conferred on a patroness through the title of children by the lex Papia; accordingly, if neither the patroness nor the freedwoman has descended in status, the law of the Twelve Tables transmits the succession to the patroness, and

liberis honorata non sit patrona: numquam enim, sicut supra diximus, feminae suum heredem habere possunt. si vero vel huius vel illius capitis deminutio interveniat, rursus liberi libertae excludunt patronam. quia legitimo iure *capitis deminutione* perempto evenit, ut liberi libertae cognationis iure potiores habeantur.

excludes the freedwoman's children, even when the patroness is childless; for a woman, as before remarked, can never have a self-successor: but if either of them has descended in status, the children of the freedwoman exclude the patroness, because her statutory title is obliterated by the descent in status, and the children are admitted as next of kin.

§ 52. Cum autem testamento facto moritur liberta, ea quidem patrona quae liberis honorata non est nihil iuris habet contra libertae testamentum: *ei* vero quae liberis honorata sit, hoc ius tribuitur per legem Papiam quod habet ex edicto patronus contra tabulas liberti.

§ 52. When a freedwoman dies testate, a patroness not entitled by children has no right in derogation of the will: but a patroness entitled by children has the same right conferred upon her by the lex Papia as the praetorian edict confers on the patron.

§ 53. Eadem lex patronae filiae liberis honoratae .... patroni iura dedit; sed in huius persona etiam unius filii filiaeve ius sufficit.

§ 53. By the same law a patroness's daughter duly entitled by children has the rights of .... but in this case one son or daughter is a sufficient title.

§ 54. Hactenus omnia *ea* iura quasi per indicem tetigisse satis est: alioquin diligentior interpretatio propriis commentariis exposita est.

§ 54. This summary indication of the rules of succession to freedmen who have enjoyed the plenary franchise may suffice for the present occasion: a more detailed exposition is to be found in my separate treatise on this branch of law.

§ 54. The provisions of the lex Papia Poppaea respecting the rights of patroni filia and patrona are very intricate and obscure and require to be examined in detail.

Against the estate of a libertus the lex Papia Poppaea gave to patroni filia mother of three children the same rights as the praetorian edict had given to patronus; that is to say, whether libertus die testate or intestate, unless his devisees or heirs are sui heredes naturales (not a wife nor an adoptive child), filia patroni mother of three children is entitled to a moiety of the estate.

Against the estate of liberta who dies testate, filia patroni mother of three children has the edictal rights of patronus against the estate of libertus. This improved the position of filia patroni, for, not having the tutela libertae like patronus, 1 § 195, she could not under the Twelve Tables exercise any control over the testamentary dispositions of liberta by withholding her auctoritas. Filia patroni has this right even against the estate of a testate liberta mother of four children, but in this case it would amount to little, being merely the right to a moiety in the improbable contingency of the freedwoman devising her estate away from her children.

Against the estate of liberta mother of four children who dies intestate filia patroni has the Papian rights of the patronus in the same case (assuming, what is not certain, that the Papian rights of patronus were the same whether the freedwoman died testate or intestate), i. e. a right to the share of a child. In this solitary case the Papian rights of filia patroni would be measured not by the edictal but by the Papian rights of patronus.

Patrona mother of three children had against the estate of libertus the Papian rights of patronus; patrona mother of two children had the same rights as filia patroni, i. e. the edictal rights of patronus.

Against the estate of liberta who dies testate patrona mother of (two?) children has the same rights as filia patroni, i. e. the edictal rights of patronus against the estate of libertus. It is not stated whether patrona mother of three children had the Papian rights of patronus against the estate of liberta mother of four children who dies testate, though we might have conjectured this from her rights against the estate of libertus.

The rights of patrona mother of children against the estate of intestate liberta mother of four children was a casus omissus in the lex Papia Poppaea, apparently, from the inadvertence of the legislator, and accordingly was governed by the provisions of the Twelve Tables. Except on this point the rights of patrona mother of two children were the same as the rights of filia patroni mother of three children. On this point, then, it appears that patrona had greater rights against the estate of intestate liberta mother of four children than patronus, for patronus (assuming, as above, that he had the same rights in testacy and intestacy) was only entitled to the share of a child, whereas patrona was entitled to the whole inheritance. The right, however, of patrona was more precarious, for, descending from the Twelve Tables, it might be extinguished by change of status, whereas the rights of patronus and filia patroni, being derived from the lex Papia Poppaea, were unaffected by change of status. Novae hereditates legitimae capitis deminutione non pereunt, sed illae solae quae ex lege duodecim tabularum deferuntur, Inst. 3, 4, 2. 'The newly introduced rights of succession of the statutory class are not extinguished by change of status like those conferred by the law of the Twelve Tables.'

§ 54. Gaius wrote a treatise in fifteen books, Ad leges Juliam et Papiam, from which there are thirty extracts in the Digest; another in ten books, Ad edictum urbicum; and another in three books, De manumissionibus: to any of which he may allude.

DE BONIS LIBERTORUM LATINORUM.

§ 55. Sequitur ut de bonis Latinorum libertinorum dispiciamus.

§ 56. Quae pars iuris ut manifestior fiat, admonendi sumus, de quo alio loco diximus, eos qui nunc Latini Iuniani dicuntur olim ex iure Quiritium servos fuisse, sed auxilio Praetoris in libertatis forma servari solitos; unde etiam res eorum peculii iure ad patronos pertinere solita est: postea vero per legem Iuniam eos omnes quos Praetor in libertatem tuebatur liberos esse coepisse et appellatos esse Latinos Iunianos: Latinos ideo, quia lex eos liberos perinde esse voluit, atque si essent cives Romani ingenui qui ex urbe Roma in Latinas colonias deducti Latini coloniarii esse coeperunt: Iunianos ideo, quia per legem Iuniam liberi facti sunt, etiamsi non cives Romani. *qua*re legis Iuniae lator, cum intellegeret futurum, ut ea fictione res Latinorum defunctorum ad patronos pertinere desinerent, ob *id quod neque ut* servi *d*ecederent, ut possent *iure peculii* res eorum ad patronos pertinere, neque liberti Latini hominis bona possent manumissionis iure ad patronos pertinere, necessariu*m existimavit*, ne beneficium istis datum in iniuriam *patrono*rum converteretur, cavere, u*t bona horum liberto*rum proinde ad manumissores pertinerent, ac si lex lata non esset. itaque iure quodammodo peculii bona Latinorum ad manumissores *eorum* pertinent.

§ 55. We proceed to the successions of Latini Juniani.

§ 56. To understand this branch of law we must recollect what has been already mentioned (1 § 22), that those who are called Latini Juniani were originally slaves by law of the Quirites, though maintained by the praetor's protection in a condition of quasi freedom, so that their possessions devolved to their patrons by the title of peculium. At a more recent period [A.D. 19], when the lex Junia Norbana was enacted, those whom the praetor had protected in quasi freedom became legally free, and were called Latini Juniani: Latini, because the law assimilated their freedom to that of freeborn citizens of Rome who, on quitting Rome for a Latin colony, became Latin colonists; Juniani, because the lex Junia gave them liberty without citizenship: and as the author of the lex Junia foresaw that the effect of this fiction would be that the goods of deceased Latini Juniani would cease to belong to the patron, as they would not be slaves at the time of their death, so that their goods should belong to the patron by the title of peculium, and they would not escheat to him by title of manumission; he deemed it necessary, to prevent the favour to these freedmen from becoming a wrong to the patron, to provide that their goods should belong to the manumitter in the same way as if the law had not been enacted. Consequently the goods of Latini Juniani belong to their manumitters by the title of quasi peculium.

§ 57. *Unde evenit, ut multum differant ea* iura quae in bonis Latinorum ex lege Iunia constituta sunt, ab his quae in hereditate civium Romanorum libertorum observantur.

§ 57. Accordingly there are wide differences between the title to the goods of Latini Juniani under the lex Junia and the title to the successions of freedmen possessed of the plenary franchise.

§ 58. Nam civis Romani liberti hereditas ad extraneos heredes patroni nullo modo pertinet: ad filium autem patroni nepotesque ex filio et pronepotes ex nepote *filio nato prognatos* omnimodo pertinet, etiamsi *a* parente fuerint exheredati: Latinorum autem bona tamquam pecula servorum etiam ad extraneos heredes pertinent, et ad liberos manumissoris exheredatos non pertinent.

§ 58. When a freedman possessed of the full franchise dies, an external heir of the patron has no claim on his succession, while a son of the patron, a grandson by a son, a great-grandson by a grandson by a son, have an indefeasible claim even after disinheritance; whereas, when a Latinus Junianus dies, his goods are transmitted to his patron's external heir, and the claim of the patron's children is barred by disinheritance.

§ 59. Item *civis Romani liberti* hereditas ad duos pluresve patronos aequaliter pertinet, licet dispar in eo servo dominium habuerint: bona vero Latinorum pro ea parte pertinent pro qua parte quisque eorum dominus fueri*t*.

§ 59. A freedman with the plenary franchise leaves several patrons his cosuccessors in equal portions, in however unequal proportions they had been his proprietors; whereas the goods of a Latinus Junianus belong to his patrons in the ratio of the property which they had in him when he was a slave.

§ 60. Item in hereditate civis Romani liberti patronus alterius patroni filium excludit, et filius patroni alterius patroni nepotem repellit: bona autem Latinorum et ad ipsum patronum et ad alterius patroni heredem simul pertinent quo qua parte ad ipsum manumissorem pertinerent.

§ 60. In the succession to a freedman who had the plenary franchise, one patron bars another patron's son, and a son of one patron bars another patron's grandson; whereas the goods of a Latinus Junianus belong to a patron and another patron's heir in the same proportions in which they would have belonged to the two patrons.

§ 61. Item si unius patroni tres forte liberi sunt, et alterius unus, hereditas civis Romani liberti in capita dividitur, id est tres fratres tres portiones ferunt et unus quartam: bona vero Latinorum pro ea parte ad successores pertinent pro

§ 61. If one patron leave three sons, and another patron one, the succession of a freedman who had the plenary franchise is divided by the number of individuals; that is to say, every one takes an equal portion; whereas the goods of a

qua parte ad ipsum manumissorem pertinerent.

Latinus Junianus belong to the sons of the patrons, not in their own right, but in right of representation; that is to say, in the proportion in which they would have belonged to the original manumitters.

§ 62. Item si alter ex iis patronis suam partem in hereditatem civis Romani liberti spernat, vel ante moriatur quam cernat, tota hereditas ad alterum pertinet: bona autem Latini pro parte decedentis patroni caduca fiunt et ad populum pertinent.

§ 62. If one patron renounce his part in the inheritance of a freedman who had the plenary franchise, or die before acceptance, the whole inheritance belongs to the other; but the goods of a Latinus Junianus that would have descended to a deceased patron are vacant and escheated to the state.

§ 63. Postea Lupo et Largo Consulibus senatus censuit, ut bona Latinorum primum ad eum pertinerent qui eos liberasset; deinde ad liberos eorum non nominatim exheredatos, uti quisque proximus esset; tunc antiquo iure ad heredes eorum qui liberassent pertinerent.

§ 63. At a later period, when Lupus and Largus were consuls, the senate decreed that the goods of a Latinus Junianus should belong in the first place to the manumitter, in the next to such issue of the patron as are not individually disinherited in the order of their proximity, and, in default of these, should belong by the ancient rule of devolution to the external heir of the manumitter.

§ 64. Quo senatusconsulto quidam *id* actum esse putant, ut in bonis Latinorum eodem iure utamur, quo utimur in hereditate civium Romanorum libertinorum; idemque maxime Pegaso placuit. quae sententia aperte falsa est. nam civis Romani liberti hereditas numquam ad extraneos patroni heredes *pertinet: bona autem* Latinorum etiam hoc ipso senatusconsulto non obstantibus liberis manumissoris etiam ad extraneos heredes pertinent. item in hereditate civis Romani liberti liberis manumissoris nulla exheredatio nocet: in bonis Latinorum *autem nocere* nominatim factam exheredationem *ipso* senatusconsulto significatur. Verius est ergo hoc solum eo senatusconsulto actum esse, ut manumissoris liberi qui nominatim exheredati non sint praeferantur extraneis heredibus.

§ 64. The effect of this senatusconsult is, according to some authorities, that the goods of a Latinus Junianus are acquired by the same title as the succession of a freedman who has enjoyed the full franchise, and this was the doctrine of Pegasus: but this opinion is clearly erroneous, for a freedman who has the full franchise never transmits his succession to an external heir of his patron; whereas the goods of a Latinus Junianus, by the express terms of the senatusconsult, in default of children of the manumitter devolve on his external heir. Again, in the succession of a freedman who had the full franchise, the children of the manumitter are not barred by any form of disinheritance; whereas, in respect of the goods of a Latinus Junianus, they are barred by individual disinheritance by the express terms of the senatusconsult. The only true effect, then, of the senatusconsult is, that the manumitter's children in the absence of individual disinheritance take precedence of external heirs.

§ 65. *Itaque* et emancipatus filius patroni praeteritus, quamvis contra tabulas testamenti parentis sui bonorum possessionem non petierit, tamen extraneis heredibus in bonis Latinorum potior habetur.

§ 65. Accordingly, an emancipated son of the patron who is passed over in silence by his father, though he omits to impeach his father's will and demand possession, takes precedence of an external heir in respect of the goods of a Latinus Junianus.

§ 66. Item filia ceteri*que* quos exheredes licet iure civili *facere inter ceteros, quamvis id suff*iciat, *ut* ab omni *hereditate patris* sui summove*antur*, tamen in bonis Latinorum, nisi nominatim a parente fuerint exheredati, potiores erunt extraneis heredibus.

§ 66. Again, a daughter and other issue who can be disinherited at civil law in a mass and thereby effectively barred from all the succession of their parent, in respect of the goods of a Latinus Junianus, in default of individual disinheritance, have priority over an external heir.

§ 67. Item ad *l*iberos qui *ab* hereditate parentis se abstinuerunt, *bona Latinorum pertinent, quamvis alieni habeantur a paterna hereditate, quia ab* hereditate exheredati nullo modo dici possunt, non magis quam qui testamento silentio praeteriti sunt.

§ 67. Children who abstain from the succession of their parent are entitled to the goods of his Latinus Junianus in spite of their abstention, because they cannot be said to be disinherited any more than children who are passed over by a testator in silence.

§ 68. *Ex his* omnibus satis illu*d* apparet, si is qui Latinum fecerit, ... [*desunt* 25 *lin.*]

§ 68. From all these points it is sufficiently apparent that he who makes a Latinus Junianus. . . .

§ 69. .... *pu*tant ad eos pertinere, qui*a* nullo interveniente extraneo herede senatusconsulto loc*us* non est.

§ 69. .... hold them entitled in unequal portions, because in the absence of an external heir the senatusconsult has no application.

§ 70. *Sed* si cum liberis suis etiam extraneum heredem patronus reliquerit, *Ca*elius Sabinus ait tota bona pro virilibus partibus ad liberos defuncti pertinere, quia cum extrane*us* heres intervenit, non habet lex Iunia locum, sed senatusconsultum. Iavolenus autem ait tantum eam partem ex senatusconsulto liberos patroni *p*ro virilibus partibus habituros esse, quam extranei here-

§ 70. If the children of the patron are joint heirs with a stranger, Caelius Sabinus holds, that the totality of the goods of a Latinus Junianus devolves in equal portions to the children, because the existence of an external heir brings them within the senatusconsult instead of the lex Junia. According to Javolenus, only that part will devolve under the senatusconsult in equal

des ante senatusconsultum lege Iunia habituri essent, reliquas vero partes pro hereditariis partibus ad eos pertinere.

portions to the children of the patron to which, before the senatusconsult was passed, the external heir would have been entitled under the lex Junia, and the residue will devolve to them in the proportion of their shares in their father's succession.

§ 71. Item quaeritur, an hoc senatusconsultum ad eos patroni liberos pertineat qui ex filia nep*te*ve procreantur, id est ut nepos meus ex filia potior sit in bonis Latini mei quam extraneus heres. item *an* ad maternos Latinos hoc senatusconsultum pertineat, quaeritur, id est ut in bonis Latini materni potior sit patronae filius quam heres extraneus matris. Cassio placuit utroque casu locum esse senatusconsulto. sed huius sententiam plerique inprobant, quia senatus de his liberis patronarum nihil sentiat, qui aliam familiam sequerentur. idque ex eo adparet, quod nominatim exheredatos summovet: nam videtur de his sentire qui ex*h*eredari a parente solent, si heredes non instituantur; neque autem matri filium filiamve, neque avo materno nepotem neptemve, si eum eamve heredem non instituat, exheredare necesse est, sive de iure civili quaeramus, sive de edicto Praetoris quo praeteritis liberis contra tabulas testamenti bonorum possessio promittitur.

§ 71. It is a further question, whether this senatusconsult extends to children born of a daughter or granddaughter of a patron, so that in respect of the goods of a Latinus Junianus a grandson by a daughter will take precedence of an external heir. Again, whether a maternal Latinus Junianus is within the senatusconsult, so that in respect of a Latinus Junianus, manumitted by a mother, precedence is given to the patroness' son over an external heir of the mother. Cassius held that both cases are within the scope of the senatusconsult; but his opinion is generally rejected on the ground that the senate did not intend to benefit patronesses' sons; persons, that is, who are members of a different family; as appears from its making individual disinheritance a bar; for herein the senate appears to contemplate those who must be disinherited by their parent in default of institution. Now a mother need not disinherit her child, nor a grandmother a grandchild, in default of institution, either by the civil law or by that part of the praetorian edict which promises possession in spite of a will to children passed over by a testator in silence.

§ 72. Aliquando tamen civis Romanus libertus tamquam Latinus moritur, veluti si Latinus salvo iure patroni ab Imperatore ius Quiritium consecutus fuerit: nam *ita* divus Tr*a*ianus constituit, si Latinus invito vel ignorante patrono ius Quiritium ab Imperatore consecutus

§ 72. Sometimes a freedman who has enjoyed the full franchise dies as a Latinus Junianus; for instance, a Latinus Junianus who has obtained an imperial grant of Quiritary status without prejudice to the rights of his patron: for by a constitution of the emperor Trajan

sit. quibus casibus dum vivit iste libertus, ceteris civibus Romanis libertis similis est et iustos liberos procreat, moritur autem Latini iure, nec ei liberi eius heredes *esse* possunt; et in hoc tantum habet testamenti factionem, uti patronum, heredem instituat, eiqu*e*, si heres esse noluerit, alium substituere possit.

a Latinus Junianus who obtains an imperial grant of Quiritary status without the consent or knowledge of his patron resembles during his lifetime other fully enfranchised freedmen, and procreates lawful children, but dies with the status of a Latinus Junianus, leaving no children that can inherit; and has only this amount of testamentary capacity that he may institute his patron heir, and name a substitute to him in case of his renouncing the inheritance.

§ 73. Et quia hac constitutione videbatur effectum, ut numquam isti homines tamquam cives Romani morerentur, quamvis eo iure postea usi essent, quo vel ex lege *Aelia* Sentia vel ex senatusconsulto cives Romani essent: divus Hadrianus iniquitate rei motus auctor fuit senatusconsulti *f*aciundi, ut qui ignorante vel recusante patrono ab Imperatore ius Quiritium consecuti essent, si eo iure postea usi essent, quo ex lege Aelia Sentia vel ex senatusconsulto, si Latini mansissent, civitatem Romanam consequerentur, proinde ipsi haberentur, ac si lege Aelia Sentia vel senatusconsulto ad civitatem Romanam pervenissent.

§ 73. But as the effect of this constitution seemed to be, that such a person could never die in possession of the plenary franchise, even though he subsequently acquired the title to which the lex Aelia Sentia or the senatusconsult (1 § 31) annexes the right of Roman citizenship, the emperor Hadrian, to mitigate the harshness of the law, passed a senatusconsult, that a freedman, who obtained from the emperor a grant of Quiritary status without the knowledge or consent of his patron, on subsequently acquiring the title to which the lex Aelia Sentia or the senatusconsult, if he had remained a Latinus Junianus, would have annexed the rights of Roman citizenship, should be deemed to have originally acquired Quiritary status by the title of the lex Aelia Sentia or the senatusconsult.

DE BONIS LIBERTORUM DEDITICIORUM.

§ 74. Eorum autem quos lex Aelia Sentia dediticiorum numero facit, bona modo quasi *civium Romanorum* libertorum, modo quasi Latinorum ad patronos pertinent.

§ 74. Those who under the lex Aelia Sentia are quasi surrendered leave their goods to their patrons sometimes like freedmen fully enfranchised, sometimes like Latini Juniani.

§ 75. Nam eorum bona qui, si in aliquo vitio non essent, manumissi cives Romani futuri essent, quasi civium Romanorum patronis eadem

§ 75. Those of them who, but for some offence, would have obtained on manumission the plenary franchise leave their goods to their

lege tribuuntur. non tamen hi habent etiam testamenti factionem; nam id plerisque placuit, nec immerito: nam incredibile videbatur pessimae condicionis hominibus voluisse legis latorem testamenti faciundi ius concedere.

patrons like fully enfranchised freedmen by the provision of the above mentioned statute; but, according to the prevalent and better opinion, they cannot make a will; for it seems incredible that the most abject order of freedmen should have been intended by the legislator to enjoy the power of testamentary disposition.

§ 76. Eorum vero bona qui, si non in aliquo vitio essent, manumissi futuri Latini essent, proinde tribuuntur patronis, ac si Latini decessissent. nec me praeterit non satis in ea re legis latorem voluntatem suam verbis expressisse.

§ 76. The goods of those who, but for some offence, would have become on manumission Latini Juniani devolve to their patrons as the goods of Latini Juniani, though, as I am aware, the legislator has not expressed his intention in this matter in terms as unequivocal as might be desired.

§ 59. It was an arbitrary rule of Roman jurisprudence that rights of patronage were not divisible in unequal portions (placuit nullam esse libertorum divisionem, Dig. 37, 14, 24), that is, that several joint proprietors of a slave in unequal portions acquired by his manumission equal rights as joint patrons against his succession.

§ 60. The rights of patrons were modelled on those of agnates, and we know that only the nearest agnate was entitled to succeed. Therefore on the decease of one of several joint patrons his rights accrued to the remainder by survivorship. But the peculium of a slave belongs to his coproprietors in the ratio of their property, and on the decease of one, his rights do not accrue to the coproprietors, but are transmitted to the representatives of the deceased.

§ 63. The Sc. Largianum was passed under the emperor Claudius, A.D. 42.

§ 69. The Sc. Largianum giving a successoral right to the children of the patron, put them all on a footing of equality like manumitting joint proprietors, § 59, but it only took effect when a stranger was appointed heir or coheir; if then a patron left his whole inheritance to his children, but in unequal portions, their rights to the succession of a Latinus Junianus would be governed by the older law, and would be proportionate to their shares in their father's succession.

§ 76. The third class of freedmanship (dedititia libertas) had long been obsolete when it was formally abolished by Justinian, A.D. 530, Cod. 7, 5.

The second class (latinitas), under which the freedman relapsed into servitude at the moment of death, was also offensive to Roman feelings in the time of Justinian, and was by him formally abolished, the principal modes of creating latinitas being transformed into modes of acquiring quiritary status or civitas Romana, and the remainder being declared inoperative, Cod. 7, 6.

The rules of succession to intestate freedmen of the first class, the only class henceforth recognized, were immensely simplified by Justinian. He abolished all distinction between freedman and freedwoman, between patron and patroness, children of patron and children of patroness of either sex, treated adoptive children of the patron or freedman as strangers, and deprived patrons of their right to succeed before the children of a freedwoman; that is, he eliminated from the title to succession all the doctrines of agnation or the civil family: deprived patrons of their right of succession concurrently with the children of opulent freedmen; that is, reduced them to the rank of agnates, where they had been placed by the Twelve Tables, from that of sui heredes, to which they had been virtually promoted by subsequent legislation: and changed the remaining series of titles by patronage as defined by the praetorian edict in default of patrons and their children.

The praetorian edict had contained the following series of titles to bonorum possessio, or classes of successors to the estate of intestate freedmen:

(1) Unde liberi. The children of the deceased, whether under power, or emancipated, or given in adoption, had the first and highest title to succeed to the estate of their father.

(2) Unde legitimi. Patrons and their children occupy the second rank. As a freedman could have no agnates or cognates (agnation and cognation being only traceable through a common ancestor, and Roman law taking no notice of servile relationship, Inst. 3, 6, 10) the Twelve Tables in default of sui heredes of the freedman, that is to say, in the rank corresponding to that which they gave to agnates in other successions, conferred the right of succeeding to the estate of a freedman on the patron and such children of the patron as continued in the civil family of their father.

(3) Tum quem ex familia (patroni proximum inveniam?). Fail-

ing the patron and the patron's children, the nearest agnates of the patron were entitled to succeed.

(4) Unde liberi patroni patronaeque et parentes eorum. Failing agnates of the patron, his cognates in an ascending or descending line were summoned to the succession.

(5) Unde vir et uxor.

(6) Unde cognati manumissoris. Failing the preceding titles, the patron's collateral cognates succeeded.

If no one succeeded under any of these titles, the estate of the deceased escheated to the treasury.

For this series of titles Justinian substituted one far simpler, the same nominally as that which governs succession to freemen, though with some necessary modifications of signification, and consisting of the following groups: (1) Unde liberi; (2) Unde legitimi; (3) Unde cognati; (4) Unde vir et uxor.

The first head includes all the natural descendants of the freedman or freedwoman, and excludes their adoptive children.

The second head entitles patrons and their natural children, whether in their civil family or not; that is to say, it entitles the patron and his children not, as formerly, in their character of supposed agnates of the freedman, but in the character of his supposed cognates.

The third head summons to the succession all the collateral cognates of the patron, but only to the fifth degree. The freedman himself, from the law's disregard of servile relationship, could no more have cognates than he could agnates.

The augmented rights which the lex Papia conferred on patrons against the estate of more opulent freedmen were abolished by Justinian, except in the case of their testacy. If a freedman possessed of a hundred aurei and upwards (this sum Justinian considered equivalent to the hundred thousand sesterces and upwards of the lex Papia) institutes a stranger as his heir (adoptive children being regarded as strangers) the patron and his descendants to the fifth degree are entitled to a clear third of the inheritance. This third to which the patron is entitled against the external devisee of an opulent freedman, Justinian calls his Falcidia, and says that the Falcidia of the devisees, instead of being one fourth of the estate as in other cases, will in this case be only a fourth of two thirds, that is, a sixth of the estate, Cod. 6, 4. In fact the praetorian edict giving the patron in the absence of sui heredes naturales of the freedman a right to a moiety of his estate, and the lex Papia giving him a right to a half or a third, even concurrently with sui heredes naturales, had really pro tanto promoted the patron from the order of agnates, assigned to him by the Twelve Tables to that of sui heredes; at least, they gave him indefeasible rights similar to those of suus heres, both against intestate successions and against testamentum inofficiosum. Justinian cut down the rights of the patron and reduced him, except in this instance, to his old rank of agnate: still, by calling his portion his Falcidia, he recognizes that he has to this extent treated him as a suus heres.

A remarkable feature which pervades these new rules of succession to intestate freedmen is their disregard of agnation or civil relationship, wherein they are an anticipation of Novella, 118, which, A.D. 543, eliminated agnation from title by descent in the succession of ingenui. It had taken eight or nine hundred years to rid Roman jurisprudence of a barbarian caprice which had filled it with intricacy and, as irrational laws cannot be supposed to be generally comprehended, must have often caused cruel disappointments as to the devolution of property among blood relations.

SUCCESSIO PER BONORUM VENDITIONEM.

§ 77. Videamus autem et de ea successione quae nobis ex emptione bonorum competit.

§ 78. Bona autem veneunt aut vivorum aut mortuorum. vivorum, velut eorum qui fraudationis causa latitant, nec absentes defenduntur; item eorum qui ex lege Iulia bonis cedunt; item iudicatorum post tempus, quod eis partim lege XII tabularum, partim edicto Praetoris ad expediendam pecuniam tribuitur. mortuorum bona veneunt velut eorum, quibus certum est neque heredes neque bonorum possessores neque ullum alium iustum successorem existere.

§ 79. Si quidem vivi bona ve-

§ 77. We next proceed to succession of a vendee to the estate of a bankrupt.

§ 78. The estate of a bankrupt may be sold either in his lifetime or after his death. It is sold in his lifetime when, for instance, he defrauds his creditors by absconding, or when he is absent and undefended, or when he avails himself of the lex Julia and surrenders his estate, or when, after judgment recovered against him, he has suffered the term to expire that is prescribed, partly by the Twelve Tables, partly by the edict of the praetor, for the satisfaction of a judgment debt. A bankrupt's estate is sold after his death when it is certain that he has left neither an heir, nor a praetorian representative, nor any other lawful successor.

§ 79. If the bankrupt whose

neant, iubet ea Praetor per dies continuos XXX possideri *et* proscribi; si vero mortui, p*er* dies XV. postea iubet convenire creditores, et ex eo numero magistrum creari, id est eum per quem bona veneant. itaque si vivi bona veneant, in diebus *x legem bonorum vendendorum fieri* iubet, si mortui, in *diebus v. a quibus tandem* vivi bona *die* XX, mortui vero *die* X emptori addici iubet. quare autem tardius viventium bonorum venditio compleri iubet*ur*, illa ratio est, quia de vivis curandum erat, ne facile bonorum venditiones paterentur.

estate is to be sold is alive, an order issues from the praetor, and his estate is possessed and advertised for sale for thirty continuous days; if the bankrupt is dead, it is possessed and advertised for fifteen days. After this delay a second order issues from the praetor, directing the creditors to hold a meeting and elect out of their number a liquidator, by whom the estate may be sold. And after the expiration of the ten (?) days next following, if the bankrupt is alive, or of five (?) if he is dead, a third order issues from the praetor, and the conditions of sale are published. Finally, after the expiration of the twenty (?) days next following, if the bankrupt is alive, after the expiration of ten (?) if he is dead, a decree of the praetor transfers the universal estate of the bankrupt to the purchaser. The longer delay prescribed for the sale of the estate of a living bankrupt is founded on the greater consideration due to the living than to the dead, and is designed to protect a living debtor from unnecessary bankruptcy.

§ 80. Neque a*utem* bonorum possesso*rum*, *neque bonorum emptorum res* pleno iure fiunt, sed in bonis efficiunt*ur*; *ex iure* Quiritium autem ita demum adquiruntur, si usuceperunt. interdum quidem bonorum empto*rum idem plane i*us quod est m*a*ncipum *esse intelle*gitur, si per eos *scilicet* bonorum emptori*bus addicitur qui publice sub hasta vendunt* [*deest* 1 *lin*].

§ 80. Neither a praetorian successor to an intestate, nor a purchaser in bankruptcy acquires plenary dominion, but only bonitarian ownership. Quiritarian ownership is only acquired by usucapion, though sometimes the purchaser of an universitas acquires at once quiritarian ownership [namely, when he purchases the estate of a bankrupt who has made cessio bonorum under the lex Julia (?)].

§ 81. Item quae de*bita sunt ei cuius fuerunt bona*, aut ipse debuit, neque bonorum possessore*s neque* bon*o*rum emptore*s* ipso iure debe*nt aut ipsis debentur : sed* de omnibus rebus *utilibus actionibus et conveniuntur et experiuntur, quas inferius pro*ponemus.

§ 81. Debts owed to or by an intestate or a bankrupt are not at civil law owed to or by the praetorian successor or vendee in bankruptcy, but are recoverable by modified forms of action, which will be explained hereafter [4 § 34].

§ 77. Missio in possessionem and the subsequent bonorum venditio correspond in their essential character to the adjudication of bankruptcy and the concomitant transfer of the debtor's estate to the creditor's trustee of English jurisprudence.

Roman law never established any distinction between traders and non-traders, in other words, between bankruptcy and insolvency, a distinction once important in English law, and which even at the present day is not entirely effaced. Formerly, in consideration of the hazardous nature of trade, and the necessity of large credits to sustain an extensive commerce, the trader was treated with greater indulgence than the non-trader; and bankruptcy operated as a discharge of obligations, whereas insolvency only discharged the person of the debtor, and left his obligation to pay out of his after acquired estate in full force. This distinction is now abolished, and traders and non-traders are placed on the same footing. Roman law in respect of the continuing obligation of the bankrupt resembled the English law of insolvency.

In order to form a clear conception of this branch of the law, it is necessary to distinguish between an ordinary judgment execution in a personal action, that is to say, the enforcement by the power of the state of a judgment debt against a debtor who contumaciously omits to satisfy the judgment by voluntary payment, from an adjudication of bankruptcy, which is the process when a debtor is not only unwilling but also unable to fulfil his obligations. The English process in an ordinary execution is either a writ of fieri facias, commanding the sheriff to satisfy the debt by seizure and sale of the personal goods of the debtor; or a writ of levari facias, now disused, directing him to levy the debt out of the personal goods of the debtor, and the rents and profits of his land; or a writ of elegit, commanding him to deliver the debtor's goods to the creditor at an appraisement, and to put the creditor in possession of the debtor's land, to hold until out of the rents and profits thereof the debt is levied; or formerly, before imprisonment for debt was abolished, a writ of capias ad satisfaciendum, commanding him to imprison the body of the debtor until satisfaction was made for the debt. After a man's body was taken in execution, no other process could be sued out against his lands or his goods, and after his lands were seized by elegit, his body could not be taken, but if part only of the debt was levied on a fieri facias, the creditor might have a capias ad satisfaciendum for the residue. So that body and goods might be taken in execution, or land and goods, but not both body and land. None of these remedies, we may observe, includes the sale of the debtor's land. In bankruptcy, on the contrary, the whole real as well as personal estate of the debtor is transferred to the creditor's trustee, to be sold or otherwise disposed of, at the discretion of the creditors.

We find a corresponding difference between execution and bankruptcy in Roman law, at all events in its later period. The proceeding in an ordinary execution, as opposed to proceedings in insolvency, was called pignoris capio, Dig. 4, 2, 1. A portion of the debtor's estate was seized, not by the plaintiff, as in the old legis actio called pignoris capio, but by public officers (the officiales, viatores, apparitores, executores of the magistrate), and after being detained for two months to enforce payment by way of pledge, were sold in satisfaction of the debt. Movables were to be seized and sold in the first instance, but, if these were insufficient, lands might be seized and sold, Dig. 42, 1, 15. If a purchaser could not be found the property might be delivered to the creditor at an appraisement, ibid. In pignoris capio there was only a conveyance of a portion of the debtor's estate, there was no transfer of his juris universitas as in insolvency.

We have said that it was necessary to distinguish proceedings in bankruptcy from execution in a personal action. There is not the same danger of confusion between bankruptcy and execution in a real action. The judgment in a real action declares the plaintiff proprietor, if it passes in his favour, and possession of the thing in dispute is delivered to him by the sovereign power. The judgment in a personal action only declares the plaintiff creditor, and some payment or conveyance has still to be performed by the debtor.

As the levy of an execution by seizure and sale of a trader's goods for a debt of fifty pounds is an act of bankruptcy, it is evident that in English law execution will often involve bankruptcy; that is to say, when one creditor has obtained payment of a debt by an ordinary execution, other creditors will proceed by petition for an adjudication of bankruptcy.

In order to understand the proceedings in bonorum emptio, or execution against the property of an insolvent debtor, the principal sanction of the Roman civil code in its later periods, we must study the earlier mode of execution by manus injectio, or process against the body of the debtor, which was one of the old legis actiones regulated by the Twelve Tables, and which was the model on which proceedings in missio in possessionem, or process against an insolvent's estate, were regulated by subsequent praetorian legislation. These proceedings are known to us by the statements of Aulus Gellius, who has given us the very terms of the Twelve Tables. Confessi igitur aeris ac debiti judicatis triginta dies sunt dati conquirendae pecuniae causâ quam dissolverent, eosque dies decemviri justos appellaverunt velut quoddam justitium, id est juris inter eos quasi interstitionem quandam et cessationem, quibus diebus nihil cum his agi jure posset. Post deinde nisi dissolverent, ad praetorem vocabantur, et ab eo quibus erant judicati addicebantur, nervo quoque aut compedibus vinciebantur. Sic enim sunt opinor verba legis: Aeris confessi rebusque jure judicatis triginta dies justi sunto. Post deinde manus injectio esto, in jus ducito. Ni judicatum facit, aut quis endo eom jure vindicit, secum ducito, vincito aut nervo aut compedibus. . . . Erat autem jus interea paciscendi, ac nisi pacti forent habebantur in vinculis dies sexaginta. Inter eos dies trinis nundinis continuis ad praetorem in comitium producebantur, quantaeque pecuniae judicati essent praedicabatur. Tertiis autem nundinis capite poenas dabant aut trans Tiberim peregre venum ibant. . . . Tertiis, inquit, nundinis partis secanto. Si plus minusve secuerunt, se fraude esto, Gellius, 20, 1. 'After an admission of debt or a judgment the debtor was allowed thirty days for payment. This delay is called a lawful interval by the decemvirs, and interposed a stay of legal proceedings. After its expiration, in default of payment, the debtor was summoned before the praetor and delivered to the custody of the creditor, to be confined in stocks or chains. The following are the expressions of the law: Admitted debts and judgment debts must be satisfied within a lawful term of thirty days. When these are elapsed the debtor may be apprehended and taken before the magistrate. In default of satisfying the judgment, or of finding bail in the court who will bind himself to defend an action for the debt, he shall be delivered into the hands of the creditor, to be forcibly removed and confined in stocks or fetters. . . . During a subsequent interval the debtor might effect a compromise, but in default of a compromise was detained in chains for sixty days. During this period, on three continuous ninth or market-days he was taken before the praetor in the comitium, where the amount of the judgment debt was proclaimed. On the third market-day he was put to death, or sold into slavery beyond the Tiber. . . . On the third market-day, say the Twelve Tables, the creditors may cut their portions of his body, and no creditor who cuts too little or too much shall be therefore called to account.'

In close imitation of this execution against the body, a process of execution against the property of an insolvent was introduced by a praetor named Publius Rutilius, upwards of a century before the Christian era. It is from an assumption of the parallelism of these proceedings that we conjecture that in missio in possessionem an interval of two months was required to elapse between the first seizure and the ultimate sale (addictio) of the insolvent's estate. [We may notice that the magisterial award (addictio) of the insolvent's body took place, according to Gellius, at the commencement of the sixty days of his detention; whereas the transfer (addictio) of the insolvent's estate to the vendee takes place at the end of sixty days from the original seizure.] In confirmation of the opinion that the period of sixty days was observed in both forms of execution (corporeal and proprietary) against the insolvent, we may remember that in ordinary execution (pignoris capio), as above mentioned, a period of sixty days elapsed between the seizure and sale of the distress.

Some of the details of the proceedings in a missio in possessionem which are omitted by Gaius may be supplied from Theophilus. Before the final transfer of the debtor's estate (addictio) three decrees of the praetor were necessary :—

(1) A decree authorizing the seizure of the debtor's estate and its advertisement for sale (proscriptio). Theophilus gives the form of this advertisement : *ὁ δεῖνα, χρεωστὴς ἡμέτερος ὑπάρχων, εἰς αἰτίαν ἐνέπεσε διαπράσεως. ἡμεῖς, κρεδίτωρες ὄντες, τὴν τούτου διαπιπράσκομεν περιουσίαν. ὠνητὴς ὁ βουλόμενος προσίτω*, 3, 12. 'So-and-so, our debtor, is bankrupt ; we, his creditors, are about to sell his estate ; whoever wishes to purchase is invited to attend.' In the old system of manus injectio, the judgment debtor (judicatus), after the expiration of the thirty dies justi, was no longer allowed to defend an action in person, but might, as we see by the above-quoted fragment of the Twelve Tables, be defended by a vindex. In the formulary system, the equivalent of the vindex was satisdatio judicatum solvi, security with two sureties for the payment of the judgment to be recovered, and the judgment recoverable in an actio judicati was for twice the amount of the disputed judgment debt,

Gaius, 4 § 9, 4 § 102. Supposing, however, the missio in possessionem was not founded on a previous judgment, but on the debtor's absconding or keeping house, then the period at which he was disabled from defending an action, unless he gave security (judicatum solvi), was the expiration of thirty days after his estate had been seized and advertized for sale, Cicero, Pro Flacco.

(2) After the possession and proscription of the estate for thirty days, a second decree of the praetor empowered the creditors to hold a meeting and elect a magister to manage the sale, corresponding to the creditor's assignee or, at the present day, the creditor's trustee of English law.

(3) After a certain period, a third decree authorized the publication of the conditions of sale, which were appended to the original advertisement.

After another period, completing, in all probability, sixty days from the first missio in possessionem, the sale took place by public auction, the universitas juris of the debtor being transferred to the bidder who offered the creditors the highest dividend, that is, the greatest amount in the pound on their respective claims.

The periods prescribed for these successive stages of the proceedings are not decipherable in the manuscript of Gaius. In the translation they are assumed, in the case of a deceased bankrupt, to have been half the periods prescribed in the case of a living debtor.

The principal acts or defaults which entitled a Roman creditor to bonorum venditio, may be compared with those which entitle an English creditor to petition for an adjudication in bankruptcy, i.e. to the so-called acts of bankruptcy of English jurisprudence.

(1) As manus injectio might be founded on a previous judgment or an admission of debt (res judicata or aes confessum), and missio in possessionem might be granted instead of pignoris capio against judicatus who makes default, so in English law non-payment of an admitted or a judgment debt after service of a debtor's summons is an act of bankruptcy, and instead of suing out a writ of execution the creditor may petition for adjudication of bankruptcy.

(2) When there is no previous judgment or admission of debt, a debtor who absconds or secretes himself, with intent to defraud his creditors, commits an act of bankruptcy in both systems of law. In English law, for instance, if a debtor makes an appointment with a creditor to meet at the debtor's place of business, and avoids the meeting with the intention of delaying the creditor; or if he

withdraws from his usual counting-house to a room upstairs, to avoid the rightful and personal solicitation of his creditors for payment, he commits an act of bankruptcy. So in Roman law: Praetor ait: In bona ejus qui judicio sistendi causâ fidejussorem dedit, si neque potestatem sui faciet neque defendetur, iri jubebo, Dig. 42, 4, 2. 'The praetor says in the edict: If a man enter into a bond with suretyship to appear at a trial, and neither appears in person nor by procurator, I will permit the plaintiff to seize his goods.' Again: Praetor ait: Qui fraudationis causâ latitabit, si boni viri arbitratu non defendetur, ejus bona possideri vendique jubebo, Dig. 42, 7, 1. 'The praetor says in the edict: If a man secrete himself with intent to defraud his creditors, and is not defended by a procurator who gives security approved by an arbitrator, I will order his property to be seized and sold.'

There is no adjudication of bankruptcy against a deceased debtor in English law, but there may be a transfer of his universitas juris as in Roman law; for creditors, in default of other administrators, may take out letters of administration against the estate of a deceased debtor.

Cessio bonorum was introduced by a lex Julia, enacted either by Julius or Augustus Caesar, and if by the latter, in imitation of a measure of the former which he himself has recorded. In the year 48 B.C. when Caesar was consul, credit having collapsed in consequence of the civil war, debtors being generally insolvent, and money having disappeared, Caesar allowed them to discharge their obligations by the transfer of their estates, movable and immovable, to their creditors, at the value, appraised by arbitrators, which they would have borne before the commencement of the war, De Bello Civili, 3, 1. Cessio bonorum conferred three benefits on the debtor: exemption from arrest and imprisonment, exemption from infamy, exemption of his after-acquired property from liability beyond a certain amount. Of these in order.

(*a*) After the abolition of the legis actiones, and the introduction of execution against the estate, execution against the body of the debtor still remained as one of the remedies of the civil code. The insolvent debtor was incarcerated and compelled to labour for the benefit of the creditor, although he could no longer be sold as a slave. Of this there are many proofs. Praetor eos duci, bona eorum possideri, proscribique venireque jubeto. Lex Galliae Cisalpinae. 'The praetor shall order the body of the insolvent to be delivered to the creditor and imprisoned, and his estate to be possessed, proscribed, and sold.' Quum judicatum non faceret, addictus Hermippo et ab hoc ductus est, Cicero, Pro Flacco, 20. 'On failing to pay the judgment debt, his body was delivered to the creditor, and removed to prison.' The Twelve Tables allowed the debtor to be chained and put in stocks, but this was abolished by the lex Poetelia, B.C. 322, which declared that no one should be kept in stocks or bonds except for crime. As, however, we hear of insolvent debtors in bonds at a later period (B.C. 216. Qui pecuniae judicati in vinculis essent, Livy, 23, 14), it has been supposed that the lex Poetelia only prohibited the detention of a debtor in stocks or fetters after the expiration of sixty days. As personal execution was one of the ultimate sanctions of the civil code, Livy speaks of the prohibition of stocks and chains as the destruction of one of the principal pillars of credit: Victum eo die ob impotentem injuriam unius ingens vinculum fidei, 8, 28. From this personal execution a debtor was exempted by cessio bonorum. In eo tantummodo hoc beneficium eis prodest ne judicati detrahantur in carcerem, Cod. 7, 71, 1. 'The principal benefit of bonorum cessio is, that it exempts the insolvent from incarceration.'

(*b*) The assignment (addictio) of the insolvent debtor reduced him to a state of partial servitude. But the Roman lawyers distinguished between partial slavery (servire) and complete slavery (servum esse), Quintilian, 7, 3. For instance, the addictus retained his praenomen, nomen, cognomen, tribe, could by payment of his debt recover his liberty at any time without the consent of the creditor, and on recovery of his liberty was not libertinus but ingenuus. As, then, addictio did not reduce a freeman to slavery, it did not operate a degradation of status (capitis minutio).

Insolvency, however, deeply affected another branch of status, namely, civitas, although even here, as it only partially destroyed the privileges of civitas, it was not considered to operate a capitis minutio. Civitas, as we have seen, consisted of two portions, certain political or public rights, jus suffragii and jus honorum, and certain civil or private rights, collectively denominated commercium and connubium. The political half of civitas was destroyed by insolvency, which deprived a man of his electoral powers and his capacity for office, and reduced him to the condition of aerarius; and even the civil half was seriously impaired, and principally in respect of commercium. Of the aggregate of capacities called commercium the privilege forfeited by insolvency was the capacity of appointing or being appointed procurator, Inst. 4, 43, 11. By being disabled from appointing a procurator a man might be seriously hampered in his commercial proceedings, as he would be unable to cede a right of action; by being disqualified for acting as procurator he would be unable to acquire by cession a right of action, and would be unable to sue for a penalty as an informer in a popularis actio, 4 § 82, for the prosecutor in such an action was considered to be the procurator of the people. The various privileges enjoyed by a citizen of untarnished credit, and liable to be forfeited by insolvency, were called his existimatio, and the disabilities of insolvency were summed up in the word 'infamia' or 'ignominia.' From this loss of existimatio the insolvent was exempted by bonorum cessio. Debitores qui bonis cesserint licet ex eâ causâ bona eorum venierint, infames non fiunt, Cod. 2, 12, 11. 'The surrender of a debtor's estate, though followed by a sale, does not involve infamy.'

(c) Proceedings in bankruptcy or insolvency, particularly in modern days, may be looked upon in two lights: either as a mode of execution, that is, as assisting the creditor to recover as much as may be of his rightful claims, or as a mode of liberation, that is, as a relief of an unfortunate debtor, releasing him of his debts without payment, and enabling him to 'begin the world again' without the overwhelming pressure of his past obligations. By the present English law, a bankrupt is discharged of his obligations by payment of a dividend of ten shillings in the pound, or, failing this, by a resolution of his creditors that his bankruptcy has arisen from circumstances for which he cannot justly be held responsible, and an expression of their desire that he should receive an order of discharge. Roman law only admitted this in one case, the case of a slave instituted heres necessarius, 2 § 155, in order to save the credit of an insolvent testator. After once undergoing bankruptcy, such a person was not liable to further molestation. But the after-acquired property of other insolvents remained liable to successive sales until plenary satisfaction of their debts. Accordingly, bankruptcy is not enumerated, 3 § 168, as one of the modes of extinguishing obligation.

To encourage the bankrupt, however, to make a bonorum cessio, in order that as much as possible might be saved from the wreck of his fortunes for the benefit of his creditors, bonorum cessio not only discharged him, as we have seen, from personal execution, but discharged from liability such portion of his after-acquired property as was necessary for his subsistence. Qui bonis cesserint nisi solidum creditor receperit non sunt liberati, Cod. 7, 71, 1. Is qui bonis cesserit, si quid postea acquisierit, in quantum facere potest convenitur, Dig. 42, 3, 4. 'Bonorum cessio does not discharge the insolvent's estate until he makes full satisfaction, but exempts him from subsequent pursuit for more than he can afford to pay.'

Both in Roman and in English law there is a transfer of the insolvent's juris universitas, but with this difference—in English law the bankrupt's estate is vested in the creditor's trustee, in Roman law it vested not in the magister but in the vendee, the emptor bonorum.

In the last period of Roman law, such as we find in the time of Justinian, venditio bonorum was superseded by distractio bonorum, which involved no transfer of the juris universitas. A curator was appointed by the praetor, and instead of selling the active and passive universality of the insolvent's estate to a purchaser who became liable to the insolvent's creditors, merely sold the active residue of his estate in detail. Justinian attributes this change to the abolition of the formulary procedure and generalization of cognitio extraordinaria; Theophilus, to the abolition of the conventus, assizes, sessions, or brief law terms of the provinces, and the erection of permanent provincial tribunals. But it is not easy to see in what respect the changes were correlated.

In § 80 Gaius apparently mentioned that one case of bonorum emptio vested quiritary property in the vendee, and some expositors have conjectured that he alluded to bonorum sectio. Some criminal condemnations involved confiscation, and the sale of the criminal's estate was conducted not by a magister but by a quaestor of the treasury, who sold under the spear, the symbol of quiritary dominion. Sectio bonorum passed quiritary property and transferred the juris universitas of the criminal. It is alluded to, 3 § 154, 4 § 146. But it is not likely that in this passage Gaius should have spoken of an institution of the criminal code, and it seems more probable that he spoke of bonorum cessio. At all events there seems no reason for doubting that when the bankrupt joined in the conveyance the vendee acquired quiritary dominion.

DE ACQUISITIONE PER ARROGATIONEM ET PER IN MANUM CONVENTIONEM.

§ 82. Sunt autem etiam alterius generis successiones, *quae* neque lege XII tabularum neque Praetoris edicto, sed eo iure *quod* consensu receptum est introductae sunt.

§ 83. *Ecce enim* cum paterfamilias se in adoptionem d*edit*, mulierve in manum convenit, *omnes eius* res incorporales et corporales quaeque ei debitae sunt, patri ado*ptivo* coemptionatorive adquiruntur, exceptis iis quae per capitis deminutionem pereunt, quales sunt ususfructus, operarum obligatio *libertorum* quae per iusiurandum contracta est, et *quae continentur* legitimo iudicio.

§ 84. *Sed ex div*erso q*uod debet is qui se in* adoptionem dedit, v*el quae in manum convenit, ad* ips*um quidem* coemptionatorem aut at patrem adoptivum *pertinet* hereditarium aes alienum, *proque eo, quia suo* nom*ine* ipse pater adoptivus *aut coemptionator* heres fit, directo tenetur iure, *non vero is qui* se adoptandum dedit, qua*e*ve *in manum convenit, quia* desinit *iure civili* here*s esse*. de eo vero quod pri*us suo nomine eae* personae debuerint, licet neque pater ado*ptivus* teneatur neque coemptionator, *neque* ipse quidem qui se in adoptionem ded*it vel* quae in manum convenit, maneat obligatus obliga*tave*, quia *scilicet* per capitis diminutionem *liber*etur, tamen in eum eamve *ut*ilis actio datur r*escissa* capitis deminutione: et si adversus hanc actionem non defendantur, quae bona eorum futura fuissent, si se alieno iuri non subiecissent, universa vendere creditoribus Praetor permittit.

§ 82. There are other kinds of universal succession not governed by the law of the Twelve Tables nor by the praetor's edict, but by rules of consuetudinary law.

§ 83. When a paterfamilias gives himself in adoption, or a woman subjects herself to a fictitious purchaser, all their property, incorporeal and corporeal, and all debts due to them, are acquired by the adoptive father and the fictitious purchaser, excepting such rights as are extinguished by loss of status—usufruct, for instance, bounden services of freedmen secured by oath, and claims disputed in a pending statutory trial.

§ 84. Conversely, as to what is owed by the person adopted or the woman subjected to hand, if it is a debt of an ancestor or testator, the fictitious purchaser or adoptive father, by acquiring the succession, becomes directly liable, while the person adopted and woman sold into subjection are released from liability by ceasing to be successors at civil law; but if the debt was owed in their own name, their adoptive father or fictitious purchaser incurs no liability, while the person adopted and woman sold into subjection cease to be liable at civil law, their liability being extinguished by their loss of status: they are liable, however, in a praetorian action based on a feigned restoration of their status (4 § 38), and if the action is not defended the goods which would have belonged to them but for their degradation may be all sold by their creditors on obtaining the requisite permission of the praetor.

§ 84. By arrogation a man descended from the superior status of paterfamilias to the inferior status of filiusfamilias, from domestic independence to domestic dependence. It operated, that is to say, a degradation (capitis minutio minima). Capitis minutio minima had various effects on a man's rights and obligations:—

(*a*) As it implied a change of family, it entailed a loss of rights founded on agnation, including the sworn services of a freedman.

(*b*) It involved some forfeiture of rights contested in a legitimum judicium (3 § 181), but on this point the state of the MS. of Gaius leaves us in the dark.

(*c*) It had further effects which perhaps we must be contented at the present day to regard as merely positive and inexplicable. Thus it extinguished any ususfructus or usus vested in the arrogatus. This effect was abrogated by Justinian.

(*d*) It extinguished debts owed by the arrogatus. As a filiusfamilias was just as capable at civil law of incurring debts as a paterfamilias, it is hard to say why the passage from one condition to the other should operate an extinction of debt. This effect, as we see, was counteracted by the quasi legislative action of the praetor.

Arrogatio in the legislation of Justinian ceased to operate a transfer of the universitas juris. It only conveyed to the arrogator a life estate (ususfructus) in the property of the arrogatus. The reversion or fee (dominium) remained in the arrogatus, Inst. 3, 10, 2.

Coemptio is not noticed by Justinian, as the in manum conventio of the wife was obsolete long before his time.

DE HEREDITATIS IN JURE CESSIONE.

§ 85. *Item si is ad quem ab intestato legitimo iure pertinet hereditas eam hereditatem, antequam cernat* aut pro herede gerat, alii in iure cedat, plen*o* iur*e heres fit is cui eam cesserit, perinde ac si ipse per* legem ad hereditatem vocaretur. quodsi posteaquam heres extiterit, cesserit, adhuc heres manet et ob id creditoribus ipse tenebitur: sed res corporales transferet proinde ac si singulas in iure cessisset; debita

§ 85. If a person entitled to succeed as agnate to an intestate, before declaring his acceptance or acting as heir, surrender the inheritance in a fictitious vindication, the plenary right of succession passes to the surrenderee exactly as if he were entitled by agnation. If the agnate first accepts and then surrenders, he continues heir, and is liable to the creditors for the debts of the deceased: the corporeal subjects of

vero pereunt, eoque modo debitores hereditarii lucrum faciunt.

the inheritance pass just as if they were separately surrendered, but the debts to the inheritance are extinguished and the debtors are discharged of liability.

§ 86. Idem iuris est, si testamento scriptus heres, posteaquam heres extiterit, in iure cesserit hereditatem. ante aditam vero hereditatem cedendo nihil agit.

§ 86. The same happens when a devisee accepts and then surrenders, but before acceptance his surrender is inoperative.

§ 87. Suus autem et necessarius heres an aliquid agant in iure cedendo, quaeritur. nostri praeceptores nihil eos agere existimant: diversae scholae auctores idem eos agere putant, quod ceteri post aditam hereditatem; nihil enim interest, utrum aliquis cernendo aut pro herede gerendo heres fiat, an iuris necessitate hereditati adstringatur. [*lin. vacua.*]

§ 87. Whether a self-successor or a necessary successor passes the succession by surrender to a fictitious vindicator, is a question. According to my school they have not the power: the other school think that the effect is the same as when the other heirs surrender after acceptance, and that it makes no difference whether a man is heir by legal compulsion or by voluntary acceptance or by acts of heirship.

§ 87. Gaius now proceeds to another mode of conveying a juris universitas, the conveyance by an agnate of a delated but not accepted inheritance. We must bear in mind the distinction between heres and vocatus ad hereditatem, the offer (delatio) of an inheritance by the law or by a testator, and its final acquisition (aditio, acquisitio) by the delatee (2 § 152). In the case of the heres necessarius, the self-successor and the testator's manumitted slave, delatio and acquisitio coincide; but in the case of the voluntarius heres, the agnate or the extraneus scriptus, they are two distinct events. An explanation of the causes of the different effects of an in jure cessio by these different classes might have thrown some light on this branch of early Roman law, but the reasons are not given by Gaius, and perhaps we must now be content to regard these distinctions as merely positive and inexplicable rules.

Successio per universitatem, as already mentioned, was an institution only recognized by the legislator in a limited number of cases: one individual could not make another, in pursuance of private convention, his universal successor. In respect of the voluntary transfer, inter vivos, of an inheritance, universal succession was only admitted in two cases: transfer by an agnate of delata hereditas (of his right to acquire an intestate succession) in the interval between delatio and aditio, and transfer (restitutio) by a devisee of a fideicommissaria hereditas in pursuance of a testamentary trust.

The usual conveyance of an inheritance was not by in jure cessio, but by emptio venditio accompanied with tradition and stipulations respecting the debts to or from the inheritance, 2 § 252.

DE OBLIGATIONIBUS.

§ 88. *Nunc transeamus* ad obligationes. quarum summa divisio in duas species deducitur: omnis enim obligatio vel ex contractu nascitur vel ex delicto.

§ 89. Et prius videamus de his quae ex contractu nascuntur. harum quattuor genera sunt: aut enim re *con*trahitur obligatio, aut verbis, aut litteris, aut consensu.

§ 88. We proceed to treat of obligations, which fall into two principal classes, obligations created by contract and obligations created by delict.

§ 89. We first treat of those which are founded on contract, which are of four orders, for contract is concluded by performance, by words, by writing, or by consent.

Having examined Unequal primary real rights (status) and a portion of Equal primary real rights, namely, property and servitudes, and omitting the detailed examination of another portion of Equal primary real rights, namely, Primordial rights, we quit the subject of real rights, jura in rem, negative rights, or rights to forbearances binding indifferently all the world, and proceed to Obligations, jura in personam, positive rights, that is to say, rights to certain acts or performances binding exclusively certain individuals.

The law of Obligation, at least of obligation founded on contract, differs from other branches of law in that its function is rather auxiliary to human freedom than restrictive or coercive. While the law of Status and the law of Property are imperious and peremptory and felt by the fetters they impose on human volition, the law of Contract is ministerial to manifestations of will, and fosters and protects the most diversified activity and enterprize. The law of Contract is the most plastic part of the code and the part most susceptible of development: it is the portion of Roman jurisprudence which has survived with least alteration in modern Europe; and of all modern codes it is the portion whose relative importance is already the greatest and is continually increasing.

The Obligation which is a subject of jurisprudence implies compulsion: Debitor intelligitur is a quo invito pecunia exigi potest, Dig. 50, 16, 108. 'Debtor (obliged) denotes a person from whom money may be extorted against his will:' i. e. it excludes merely moral duties (officia) because the sovereign applies no coercion to enforce their performance.

Obligation, in the narrower sense in which we proceed to use the term, also excludes those duties which the legislator imposes on all the world alike towards a person invested with a Real right, whether a Primordial right or a right of Dominion. These duties are mainly negative, duties of forbearance or abstention; whereas Obligations in the narrower sense, the sense in which the word is used by the classical jurists, are mainly positive, duties of action or performance. The former, that is, negative obligations, obligations correlative to jus in rem, have scarcely received a distinctive appellation in the Latin language: for the sake of distinction they may be called, in a specific sense, Necessitas.

Justinian defines Obligation as follows: Obligatio est juris vinculum quo necessitate astringimur alicujus solvendae rei secundum nostrae civitatis jura, Inst. 3, 13. 'Obligation is a legal bond, that is, the being compelled to some performance by the law of the state (power of the sovereign).'

Having formerly divided Obligations into Primary and Secondary, we may inquire which of these classes is more directly contemplated in this definition. Apparently the class of Secondary obligations: at least the definition is not applicable to all cases of Primary obligation. In Obligations ex contractu the necessitas both of the Primary and the Secondary obligation is a necessitas solvendi: but in Obligation ex delicto the necessitas of the Secondary obligation is necessitas solvendi; the necessitas of the Primary obligation (there is no Obligation in the classical sense of the term) is not so much necessitas solvendi as necessitas abstinendi.

The performance (solutio) of which the law imposes a necessity when it imposes an obligation is sometimes decomposed into three elements, expressed by three terms, datio, factio, praestatio. In personam actio est quotiens cum aliquo agimus qui nobis ex contractu vel ex delicto obligatus est, id est, cum intendimus dare, facere, praestare oportere, 4 § 2. 'A personal action pursues an obligation arising from contract or delict, and declares that the defendant is bound to convey, perform, or indemnify.' Obligationum substantia non in eo consistit ut aliquod corpus nostrum aut servitutem nostram faciat, sed ut alium nobis obstringat ad dandum aliquid vel faciendum vel praestandum, Dig.

44, 7, 3. 'An obligation does not subject a thing corporeal or incorporeal to our dominion, but compels a person to convey some dominion, or render some service, or repair some loss.' Datio denotes the transfer of quiritarian dominion in a certain thing or sum of money: Factio any service (traditio, restitutio, exhibitio, &c.) other than the transfer of quiritary dominion in a certain thing: and Praestatio, apparently, the discharge of any obligation engendered by maleficium.

However diversified may be the Object of an obligation, it is always transformable, in the eye of the law, into the payment of a certain sum of money. Ea enim in obligatione consistere quae pecunia lui praestarique possunt, Dig. 40, 7, 9, 2. 'Obligation can only have for its Object something redeemable and replaceable by money.' Hence if it is desired to bind to the performance of some act not in its nature susceptible of pecuniary appreciation, it is necessary to make the direct Object of stipulation the payment of a certain penal sum, and the non-performance of the act desired the title or condition whereupon the penal sum shall be forfeited; for then the obligation, having a pecuniary value, is a civil obligation enforceable by the tribunals. The performance of the act desired is thus practically enforced, although nominally it is removed from the position of Object of the stipulation to that of Condition.

In speaking of the right of Dominion, we have already noticed (2 § 1, commentary) that besides the primary OBJECT of the right (abstention from molestation), there is always a secondary object or SUBJECT, land, house, slave, or the like, to which such molestation relates. So, in view of this transformability of all Objects of obligation into money payments, we may say that the OBJECT of every obligation is an Alienation, or transfer of property; and the SUBJECT is always a certain amount of Pecuniary value.

The primary and most comprehensive division of Obligatio is one that has already been noticed, 1 § 1, into (A) CIVILIS obligatio, and (B) NATURALIS obligatio.

(A) CIVILIS obligatio is obligation enforceable by action, whether it derives its origin from Jus civile, as the obligation engendered by Formal contracts or the obligation enforceable by bilaterally penal suits, or from such portion of Jus gentium as had been completely naturalized in the civil law and protected by all its remedies; such as the obligation engendered by Formless contracts, and obligation to indemnify engendered by delict.

(B) Obligatio NATURALIS is obligation not immediately enforceable by action, or obligation imposed by that portion of Jus gentium which is only imperfectly recognized by Civil law; obligation, however, which is recognized by Positive law in various operations, e. g. as founding an equitable defence or Exceptio, as giving a right of Retention (barring condictio indebiti soluti) and Compensation; and as forming a basis of various Accessory institutes of Civil law, such as Novatio, Pignus, Fidejussio, Constitutum.

Naturalis obligatio, with its partial and occasional protection, may seem a singular and anomalous institute of Roman law, but it is paralleled by the recognition, though perhaps to a minor extent, of Imperfect obligations in English jurisprudence. Imperfect obligations are so called, not because they are less binding in the forum of conscience than those which are perfect, but because they are not directly enforced by political sanctions, because various motives induce the political legislator to exempt the debtor from positive coercion. Instances of imperfect obligation are, debts contracted in infancy, debts barred by a statute of limitations, debts discharged by adjudication of bankruptcy. A ratification in writing after the attainment of majority, or a written promise to pay by the bankrupt or debtor discharged by limitation, perfects and revives the imperfect obligation, and makes it ground to support an action: a ratification and revival which may be assimilated to the Novation or transformation of naturalis into civilis obligatio operated by the Roman contract of Constitutum. As in English law a merely moral duty is an inadequate consideration to support and validate a promise to pay, the validity of such ratificatory promises shows conclusively that the obligation of the infant, the insolvent, the debtor discharged by limitation, is regarded in English jurisprudence as something more than a moral obligation, as, to a certain extent, a legal obligation; that is, is viewed by English tribunals in the light in which naturalis obligatio was viewed by Roman tribunals.

Civil obligations fall under two principal classes: (1) those to which the title or investitive fact is a CONTRACT; and (2) those to which the title or investitive fact is a DELICT. In obligation created by CONTRACT there are two stages: there is first a primary or sanctioned Personal right antecedent to wrong, and afterwards a secondary or sanctioning Personal right consequent on a wrong. In obligation founded on DELICT there is the second stage, a secondary or sanctioning Personal right consequent on a wrong, but the first stage is not a Personal right (jus in personam), but a Real right (jus in rem), whether a Primordial right, right of Status, or of Property.

These two typical classes, however, fail to comprehend all the obligations enforceable by action, and two supplementary classes have to be added: (3) obligations similar to those founded on contract; and (4) obligations similar to those founded on delict.

A Contract is a convention or agreement (conventio, pactio, pactum) enforceable by appeal to a court of judicature. Et est pactio duorum pluriumve in idem placitum consensus, Dig. 2, 14, 1, 2. 'A convention is the consent of two or more parties that a party shall do or not do some particular thing.'

Consensus, the essence of convention, will be found on close examination to consist not, as might at first sight appear, of two precisely similar elements contributed by the two consenting parties, but of two dissimilar elements, an intention signified by a promisor, and a corresponding expectation signified by a promisee. The promisor promises that he will do or perform some given act or acts, or that he will forbear or abstain from some given act or acts; that is, he signifies to the promisee that he intends to do the acts or to observe the forbearances which form the object of his promise: and the promisee accepts the promise; that is, signifies to the promisor his belief or expectation that the latter will do or forbear agreeably to the intention which he has expressed. Every convention, then, consists of a promise proffered and accepted; that is, (1) of a signification by the promising party of his intention to do the acts or to observe the forbearances which he promises to do or observe, and (2) a signification by the promisee that he expects that the promising party will fulfil the proffered promise. Without signification of the intention there is no promise; without signification of the expectation there is no reason for enforcing the promise. The consensus of the parties is the chiming or going together of this intention with this expectation; their direction to a common object, the acts or forbearances contemplated by the convention. Pollicitation is the offer of the one party before it is accepted by the other. Pactum est duorum consensus atque conventio; pollicitatio vero offerentis solius promissum, Dig. 50, 12, 3.

A leading division of contracts or conventions enforceable by action is into FORMAL contracts, or contracts of civil law (legitimi, Dig. 2, 14, 5), and FORMLESS contracts, or contracts of Jus gentium. Formal contracts are Nexum, Verbal contract or Stipulatio, and Literal contract or Expensilatio. Formless contracts are Real (Mutuum, Commodatum, Depositum, Pignus, Innominate contract), or Consensual (Emptio, Locatio, Societas, Mandatum). Formal contracts derive their validity from the observance of a symbolic form prescribed by positive law, and calculated to inspire by its solemnity serious reflection in the negotiators, and to distinguish definitive resolution from preparatory negotiation and debate. In Real contract the earnestness and definitiveness of the resolution is proved by one contractor parting with property or possession. The obligation, too, contracted by the other party is perfectly plain, being in most cases simply restitution. In Exchange (permutatio), an Innominate contract, the duty of the promisor is not quite so simple; it is not restitution, but the transfer of an equivalent; and, accordingly, the validity of the contract of Exchange was not established till a comparatively late period of Roman jurisprudence. The daily and hourly employment of the Consensual contracts of Purchase and Hiring, while it would make the requirement of any formality intolerably inconvenient, also renders the nature of these contracts perfectly familiar to all the world, so that the mere mention of their Names awakens as vivid a picture of their consequences as could the observance of the most ceremonious Form. In the remaining Consensual contracts, Agency and Partnership, the position of the Agent or Partner who is called to account for property that has passed into his hands or that has been lost by his negligence is so similar to that of a party to a Real contract that there could be no hesitation in extending to these contracts the protection of the public tribunals.

A convention that was neither valid by its Form, nor was one of the four Consensual contracts with their familiar Names, nor was a Real contract, that is, a convention where on one side the consideration (causa praeter conventionem, Dig. 2, 14, 7, 4) was executed, nor was made valid by the edict or any special statute, was not directly enforceable at law, and was called a Nudum pactum. A Nude pact, though ineffectual to produce civilis obligatio, produces naturalis obligatio. Igitur nuda pactio obligationem non parit, sed parit exceptionem, Dig. 2, 14, 7, 4. 'A nude pact creates no (civil) obligation, but creates a defence.' Interest on a loan could only be secured by the Formal contract of Stipulatio: but a nude pact to pay interest could be confirmed by pignus, Dig. 13, 7, 11, 3, and could be pleaded in bar to a suit for recovering back the interest when actually paid (condictio indebiti soluti): and we have seen that exceptio, pignus, solutum non repeti, are some of the criteria which indicate the existence of naturalis obligatio, Dig. 46, 3, 5, 2.

Another important division of contracts is into UNILATERAL and BILATERAL. Wherever mutual promises are proffered and accepted there are in strictness two or more conventions; but where the performance of either of the promises is made to depend on the performance of the other, the several conventions are cross or implicated conventions, and therefore are commonly deemed one convention. Where one only of the agreeing parties gives a promise, the proffered and accepted promise is called a Unilateral convention; where each gives a promise, and the performance of either is made to depend on the performance of the other, the several proffered and accepted promises are called a Bilateral or Synallagmatic convention. But strictly speaking, as before stated, every convention is Unilateral, and every Bilateral convention is formed by the implication of several Unilateral conventions. The sole Unilateral conventions are Expensilatio, Stipulatio, Mutuum. Venditio, Locatio, Societas, are examples of Bilateral conventions. Depositum, Commodatum, Pignus, Mandatum, are called imperfectly Bilateral conventions, because they do not necessarily and originally produce any reciprocal obligation, but only ex postfacto, i.e. in consequence of some occurrence subsequent to the convention. The action founded on the original obligation of a semi-bilateral convention, i.e. the action of the depositor, lender for use, pawnor, principal, is called judicium directum: the action founded on the accidental or ex postfacto obligation, i.e. the action of the depositary, borrower for use, pawnee, agent, is called judicium contrarium. Unilateral conventions, even though, like Mutuum, institutions of Jus gentium, give rise to condictiones or actions of strict civil law (stricti juris actiones); bilateral and semi-bilateral conventions give rise to equitable actions (bonae fidei actiones).

The classification of contracts by Gaius does not include what was perhaps originally the sole form of contract, the Nexum, although it appears to have been in existence in his time. Si quid eo nomine debeatur quod per aes et libram gestum est, 3 § 173. Nexum, Mucius Scaevola scribit, quae per aes et libram fiant ut obligentur praeterquam quae mancipio dentur, Varro 6, 5. 'Nexum, according to Scaevola, includes the proceeding with the bronze ingot and balance, either to conclude a contract or to operate a transfer.' Nexum est, ut ait Gallus Aelius, quodcunque per aes et libram geritur, idque necti dicitur; quo in genere sunt haec, testamenti factio, nexi datio, nexi liberatio, Festus, under the word 'Nexum.' 'Nexum, according to Aelius, is any proceeding with the bronze ingot and balance, including testamentary disposition, formation of contract, discharge of contract.' Quod si in iis rebus repetendis quae mancipi sunt, is periculum judicii praestare debet qui se nexu obligavit, profecto etiam rectius in judicio consulis designati is potissimum, consul qui consulem declaravit, auctor beneficii populi romani defensorque periculi esse debebit, Cicero pro Muraena, 2. 'As against eviction from an estate conveyed by nexum the vendor is vouched by the vendee to bear him harmless, so against impeachment a consul designate should have his official predecessor, who declared him consul, as warrantor and defender of the honour the people have conferred.' Cum nexum faciet mancipiumque, uti lingua nuncupassit, ita jus esto, Twelve Tables. 'In a contract or conveyance by ingot and scale the spoken words shall determine the rights and duties of the parties.'

Contract by Nexum seems to have been partly Real, partly Verbal. Before the weighing of the ingots was a mere fiction, the contract was Real; after the Twelve Tables gave binding force to the nuncupation, it became Verbal.

The effect of Nexum seems to have been to place the borrower in the position of a judgment debtor (pro judicato): in default of payment within thirty days after the appointed time, he was probably subject to proceedings in bankruptcy (Manus injectio), and forfeited, though not freedom (libertas), the possession of freedom: he became a slave, to use a modern expression, de facto, though not de jure: to use the Roman expression, though he was not servus but liber, yet he was in servitute, not in libertate.

When the lex Poetelia (?), Livy 8, 28 (confer Gaius, 4 § 25), prohibited this pignoration or pledging of the body of the borrower, Nexum, being no longer armed with special remedies, ceased to be a form of contract, though it continued to be a form of alienation.

The subsequent modes of Formal contract, Verbal, and Literal, are derivatives and modifications of the Nexum. Stipulation, or Verbal contract, dropped the pantomime and retained only the spoken words, or nuncupatory part of the Nexum. Expensilation, or Literal contract, treats as alone essential the written evidence in the Ledger by which the Nexum is recorded. Real contracts are institutes of Jus gentium, and are Formless; they contain nothing symbolical or evidentiary, and are perfected by traditio, numeratio, or delivery.

The arrangement adopted by Gaius is not to be commended. He begins with a kind of Formless contract (Real), proceeds to Formal contracts (Verbal and Literal), and then returns to the Formless (Consensual). It would have been better to follow the chronological order; to have first examined the Formal contracts, and then have proceeded to the Formless.

QUIBUS MODIS RE CONTRAHATUR OBLIGATIO.

§ 90. Re contrahitur obligatio velut mutui datione. *quae* proprie in his fere rebus contingit qua*e* [res] pondere, numero, mensura consta*nt*: qualis est pecunia numerata, vinum, oleum, frumentum, aes, argentum, aurum. quas res aut numerando aut metiendo aut pendendo in hoc damus, ut accipientium fiant et quandoque nobis non eadem, sed alia eiusdem naturae reddantur: unde etiam mutuum appellatum est, quia quod ita *ti*bi a me datum est ex meo t*u*um fit.

§ 90. Of real contracts, or contracts created by performance, we have an example in loan for consumption, or loan whereby property is transferred. This chiefly relates to things which are estimated by weight, number, or measure, such as money, wine, oil, corn, bronze, silver, gold. We transfer our property in these on condition that the receiver shall transfer back to us at a future time, not the same things, but other things of the same nature: and this contract is called Mutuum, because thereby meum becomes tuum.

§ 91. Is quoque qui non debitum accepit ab eo qui per errorem solvit re obligatur. nam proinde ei condici potest SI PARET EUM DARE OPORTERE, ac si mutuum accepisset. unde quidam putant pupillum aut mulierem cui sine *tu*toris auctoritate non debitum per errorem datum est non teneri condictione, non magis quam mutui datione. sed hae*c* species obligationis non videtur ex contractu consistere, quia is qui solvendi animo dat magis distrahere vult negotium quam contrahere.

§ 91. The receiver of what was not owed from a person who pays in error is also under a real obligation, for he may be sued by Condictio with the formula: 'If it be proved that he ought to convey,' just as if he had received the property in pursuance of a loan. And, accordingly, some have held that a ward or female, if their guardian has not authorized them to receive a payment, are not liable to be sued for money paid in error any more than they are for money received as a loan. This, however, is a mistake, as the liability is not founded on contract, for a payment in order to discharge a debt is intended to extinguish an obligation, not to establish one.

The thing to be restored by the borrower in a loan for consumption was not the specific thing that was borrowed, but some other thing of the same genus. Such members of a genus as are naturally capable of mutual substitution (quae vice mutua funguntur) received from modern civilians the barbarous name of res fungibiles. A more significant barbarism, if any was necessary, would have been res vicariae, from the principal word of the definition. The classical name was neither res fungibilis, nor res vicaria, but Quantitas, Dig. 44, 2, 7, pr.

The liability to refund money had and received by mistake, though enforced like a loan by condictio, is not an obligation ex contractu, but quasi ex contractu, and as such will be noticed hereafter.

The obligation arising by a contract of mutuum is only an obligation to repay the principal of the debt. The loan is regarded as gratuitous; if any interest is intended to be paid, it requires to be secured by an accompanying verbal contract, or stipulation. The repayment of the principal was enforced by the general personal action of condictio.

Connected with the contract of mutuum was the senatusconsultum Macedonianum, named, according to Theophilus, after a parricide, according to some commentators, after a money-lender. This decree passed, according to Tacitus, under Claudius (Annales, 11, 13), according to Suetonius, under Vespasian (Suet. Vesp. 11), prohibited lending money to a person under power (filiusfamilias) without the consent of the father. Verba senatusconsulti Macedoniani haec sunt: Quum inter ceteras sceleris causas Macedo quas illi natura administrabat etiam aes alienum adhibuisset, et saepe materiam peccandi malis moribus praestaret qui pecuniam, ne quid amplius diceretur, incertis nominibus crederet; placere, ne cui qui filiofamilias mutuam pecuniam dedisset etiam post mortem parentis ejus, cujus in potestate fuisset, actio petitioque daretur; ut scirent qui pessimo exemplo foenerarent, nullius posse filiifamilias bonum nomen expectata patris morte fieri, Dig. 14, 6, 1. 'Whereas to his natural temptations Macedo added indebtedness, and facilities for profligacy are often provided by money-lenders, who, fearing an express prohibition, advance money to sons without asking the consent of the father; be it enacted that no loan of money to a filiusfamilias shall be recoverable by action even after the death of the father, in order that unprincipled usurers may despair of acquiring under any circumstances a legal claim.' Neither the age nor the rank of a filiusfamilias affected his incapacity to contract a pecuniary loan. In filiofamilias nihil dignitas facit quominus senatusconsultum Macedonianum locum habeat; nam etiam si consul sit vel cujusvis dignitatis, senatusconsulto locus est, nisi forte castrense peculium habeat, tunc enim senatusconsultum cessabit usque ad quantitatem castrensis peculii, quum filiifamilias in castrensi peculio vice patrumfamiliarum fungantur, Dig. 14, 6, 2. 'No rank takes a person out of the law, nor does even the consulship or any other office remove the disability; but it does not extend to the castrense peculium, for in respect of this a person under power has all the capacities of a paterfamilias.' Julianus scribit, exceptionem senatusconsulti Macedoniani nulli obstare nisi qui sciret aut scire potuisset filiumfamilias esse eum cui credebat, Dig. 14, 6, 19. 'The law can only be pleaded against a lender who knew or might have known that the borrower was a filiusfamilias.' Si tantum sciente patre creditum sit filio, dicendum est cessare senatusconsultum, Dig. 14, 6, 12. 'The mere knowledge (and silent acquiescence) of the father takes a case out of the law.' The disability of the filiusfamilias did not extend to any contract other than a pecuniary loan. Is autem solus senatusconsultum offendit qui mutuam pecuniam filiofamilias dedit, non qui alias contraxit, puta vendidit, locavit, vel alio modo contraxit; nam pecuniae datio perniciosa parentibus eorum visa est, Dig. 14, 6, 3, 3. 'The law only incapacitates the filiusfamilias for receiving a loan of money, not for forming any other contract; for it is the loan of money that was deemed to be dangerous to the parent.'

By the English law bargains made with expectant heirs and remaindermen, during the lifetime and without the knowledge of the parent, may be set aside by a court of equity on the ground of unfairness or inadequacy. The object of this rule, however, is rather to protect a necessitous borrower against his own improvidence than, as in the senatusconsultum Macedonianum, to remove temptations to parricide.

Besides the mutuum there are four other Real contracts, Commodatum, Depositum, Pignus, Innominate contract; each of which requires a brief notice.

Commodatum, a loan for use, is the gratuitous lending of an article to be used by the borrower. It must be gratuitous, for, if any compensation is to be paid, the transaction ceases to be a commodatum, and becomes a letting and hiring (locatio conductio). A loan for use differs from a mutuum, or loan for consumption, in that it passes no property to the borrower. Accordingly, in a loan for use the specific thing that was lent is to be returned, whereas in a loan for consumption it is only to be returned in kind. Again, in case of destruction by an inevitable accident, as fire, shipwreck, or invasion, in a mutuum the loss falls on the borrower, in a commodatum on the lender. The commentators have expressed this by the formula, res perit domino, 'the loss from destruction falls on the proprietor,' but the maxim only applies to contracts of mutuum and commodatum; for in a sale (emptio venditio), as soon as the obligation is complete, before the property has passed by delivery to the buyer, if the thing is destroyed without the fault of the vendor, the loss falls on the buyer, and he can be compelled to pay the purchase-money, although the subject of sale has never been in his possession. We must not identify the borrower's right to use, which consists in an obligation, with the servitude (jus in re) or fraction of proprietorship called Usus, which is created by other methods and governed by different rules.

Depositum is the delivery of a thing for custody, to be redelivered on demand, without compensation. It must be gratuitous, for if a compensation is to be given it is a contract of hiring and letting, and not a deposit. The property remains in the depositor; the depositary has sometimes Possession, but, as a rule, merely Detention. The identical thing that was deposited is to be returned, not an equivalent of the same kind or quality, as in mutuum. A depositary who uses a deposit is guilty of theft. Furtum autem fit non solum cum quis intercipiendi causa rem alienam amovet sed generaliter cum quis alienam rem invito domino contrectat. Itaque si is apud quem res deposita est ea re utatur . . . furtum committit, Inst. 4, 1, 6. 'Theft is not only the appropriation of what belongs to another by taking it away, but any dealing with a thing without the permission of the owner. Therefore a depositary who uses a deposit for his own purposes is guilty of theft.' An involuntary depositor, that is, one under stress of shipwreck, fire, civil commotion, the fall of a house, can sue in penal damages for twice the value of the deposit. Praetor ait: Quod neque tumultus neque incendii, neque ruinae, neque naufragii causa depositum sit, in simplum, earum autem rerum quae supra comprehensae sunt in duplum judicium dabo, Dig. 16, 3, 1. 'The praetor says in his edict: When neither tumult, fire, the fall of a house, nor shipwreck is the occasion of a deposit, the simple value, otherwise, twice the value, of the deposit shall be recoverable by action.' Sequestration is the deposit of a subject of litigation by consent of parties or order of the court in the hands of a stake-holder (sequester) to abide the result of the trial. If a husband wasted the dower of a lunatic wife, it might be sequestered for her benefit. Sin vero dotem ita eum dissipare manifestum est ut non hominem frugi, oportet tunc dotem sequestrari, quatenus ex ea mulier competens habeat solatium una cum sua familia, Dig. 24, 3; 22, 8. 'If the dower is scandalously wasted, it must be sequestered to secure a competent sustentation for the wife and her household.' Sequestration could not be demanded in an action on contract. Quoties ex quolibet contractu pecunia postulatur, sequestrationis necessitas conquiescat; oportet enim debitorem primo convinci, et sic deinde ad solutionem pulsari, Cod. 4, 4. 'When money is sued for on a contract, sequestration cannot be demanded, for a debt must be proved before payment is enforced.' The sequester was sometimes the officer of the court. Si satisdatum pro re mobili non sit et persona suspecta sit ex qua satis desideratur, apud officium deponi debebit, si hoc judici sederit, donec vel satisdatio detur, vel lis finem accipiat, Dig. 2, 8, 7, 2. 'In the absence of sureties, if the defendant is suspected, movable goods may be deposited in the office of the court at the discretion of the judge, until sureties are given, or the trial concluded.'

Pignus, pledge, pawn, or mortgage, is the transfer of a qualified property (jus in re aliena) in a thing, movable or immovable, to be held as a security for a debt, and to be retransferred when the debt is satisfied.

There are three forms of Pignus, corresponding to three eras in the development of Roman law, which must be separately examined.

(1) The earliest form of pledge was effected by a nexum, accompanied with a fiducia, or contract for reconveyance. This

ceremony was employed in the contract of pledging, in the contract of deposit, and as we have seen, 1 § 132, in the emancipation of children. Fiduciam vero accepit cuicunque res aliqua mancipatur ut eam mancipanti remancipet; velut si quis tempus dubium timens amico potentiori fundum mancipet, ut ei, quum tempus quod suspectum est praeterierit, reddat: haec mancipatio fiduciaria nominatur idcirco quod restituendi fides interponitur, Boethius ad Cic. Top. 10, § 41. 'Fiducia is a thing mancipated under an agreement for remancipation, as when land in a time of danger is conveyed to a powerful friend in trust to be reconveyed when the danger is past. Such mancipation is called fiduciary, from the trust or promise of remancipation.' Fiducia est cum res aliqua sumendae mutuae pecuniae gratia vel mancipatur vel in jure ceditur, Isidor. Orig. V. 25, 23. 'Fiducia is the transfer of a thing by mancipation or surrender in court as a security for a loan.' Pecuniam adolescentulo grandi foenore, fiducia tamen accepta, occupavisti. Hanc fiduciam commissam tibi dicis, tenes hodie ac possides, Cic. Pro Flacco, 21. 'You lent the youth money at an enormous interest, although secured by mortgage. This mortgage you say is forfeited, and you have taken possession.' The creditor's right of forfeiture or foreclosure (commissio) was gradually limited. A power of sale was inherent in such a mortgage. Si inter creditorem et debitorem convenerit ut fiduciam sibi vendere non liceat, non solvente debitore creditor denuntiare ei sollenniter potest et distrahere: nec enim ex tali conventione fiduciae actio nasci potest, Pauli Sent. 2, 13, 5. 'Notwithstanding an agreement that the pawnee shall have no power to sell the pawn, on default of the pawnor to pay, and after formal notice the pawnee may proceed to sale, nor would such an agreement give the pawnor an action of fiducia.' But the pawnee could not become the purchaser. Debitor creditori fiduciam vendere non potest sed aliis si velit vendere potest, ita ut ex pretio ejusdem pecuniam offerat creditori atque ita remancipatam sibi rem emptori praestet. Si per suppositam personam creditor pignus suum invito debitore comparaverit, emptio non videtur et ideo quandoque lui potest, ex hoc enim causa pignoris vel fiduciae finiri non potest, Pauli Sent. 2, 13, § 3, 4. 'The debtor may sell the pawn to any but the creditor, and paying the creditor with the purchase-money may have the pawn remancipated to himself and convey it to the purchaser. If the pawnee buy in the pawn by means of a collusive bidder, the sale is void, and the pawn may be redeemed at any time, for such a proceeding cannot extinguish the right of the pawnor.'

(2) Pignus was effected by delivery of possession without the solemnities of mancipatio. The mortgagor continued to be proprietor of the thing pledged. Pignus, manente proprietate debitoris, solam possessionem transfert ad creditorem, Dig. 13, 7, 5, 1. Qui pignori dedit, ad usucapionem tantum possidet; quod ad reliquas omnes causas pertinet, qui accepit possidet, Dig. 41, 3, 16. 'The mortgagor only possesses for usucapion, for all other intents and purposes the mortgagee has possession.'

(3) Hypothecation was effected by mere convention without delivery of possession. It, therefore, was not a real but a consensual contract. The mortgagee, however, acquired the same rights by hypothecation as by pignoration.

In hypotheca, then, and pignus, the property remained in the mortgagor. But when a praetor, Servius, before the time of Cicero, gave a landlord the right of recovering against all the world, by a real action called actio Serviana, the farming stock of a tenant mortgaged as a security for rent, and the actio quasi Serviana gave a similar right to all mortgagees, the mortgagee clearly acquired not only an obligation or jus in personam against the mortgagor, but also a modified property or jus in rem against all the world. The right, that is, of the mortgagee was not purely a jus in rem, nor purely a jus in personam, but a combination of jus in rem and jus in personam. An instance of a far more complex combination of jura in rem and jura in personam, transferred by a single event, is to be found in inheritance, where rights of dominion, rights against debtors, obligations to creditors, the juris universitas of the deceased, pass in a body to the successor.

The action of the mortgagee to recover the thing pledged, called quasi Serviana, hypothecaria, or pignoraticia contraria, was a real action or vindicatio. In vindicatione pignoris quaeritur an rem de qua actum est possideat is cum quo actum est. Nam si non possideat nec dolo fecerit quo minus possideat, absolvi debet: si vero possideat et aut pecuniam solvat aut rem restituat, aeque absolvendus est; si vero neutrum horum faciat, condemnatio sequetur, Dig. 20, 1, 16, 3. 'In the vindication of a pledge the question is whether the pledge is in the possession of the defendant. If it is not in his possession, and if he has not fraudulently parted with possession, or if he pays the mortgage debt, or if he restores the pledge, he is absolved; otherwise he is condemned.' It would be interesting to know what were the precise terms of the formula in this action. As the property in the pledge remained in the pledgor, the formula could not allege the proprietorship of the pledgee: so that the formula must either have resembled the formula in vindication of a servitus (jus petitori competere, 4 § 3), or have been a formula of fact (in factum concepta, 4 § 46), i.e. have consisted solely of an allegation of fact and a condemnatio, without any definition of the right (jus) which the claimant affirmed; e.g. 'If it be proved that such and such land was mortgaged by the defendant to the plaintiff as security for the payment of such and such a debt, and that such debt has not been paid, do thou, Judex, condemn the defendant to pay the amount of such debt to the plaintiff, unless at thy order he deliver such land to the plaintiff; in absence of such proof, pronounce the defendant's absolution.'

Innominate or unnamed contract is a convention followed by execution or a commencement of execution on the part of one of the parties. Pacts which are transformed into contracts by partial execution fall into four classes. Aut enim do tibi ut des, aut do ut facias, aut facio ut des, aut facio ut facias, Dig. 19, 5, 5, pr. 'There may be conveyance in consideration of conveyance, or conveyance in consideration of performance, or performance in consideration of conveyance, or performance in consideration of performance.' Some of such conventions would give rise to Named consensual contracts, such as sale, letting, mandate. Those which fail to satisfy the definitions of the named contracts, and yet are obligatory, are thrown into a miscellaneous class, called Innominate contracts. Those of the category, facio ut des, were enforced by the praetorian action de dolo. Quodsi faciam ut des, et postea quam feci cesses dare, nulla erit civilis actio et ideo de dolo dabitur, Dig. 19, 5, 5, 3. The remainder were enforced by a civil action, called actio praescriptis verbis. This was an equitable action (ex fide bona) to recover not merely the value conveyed, but also damages for the loss sustained by the plaintiff from default of specific performance. When the executed part of the convention was a conveyance, if restitution was a sufficient compensation, the thing conveyed might be recovered back by condictio causâ datâ, causâ non secutâ, i.e. a suit to recover property conveyed for a consideration which has failed. In qua actione (i.e. si rem do ut rem accipiam) id venit, non ut reddas quod acceperis, sed ut damneris mihi quanti interest meâ illud de quo convenit accipere; vel si meum recipere velim, repetam quod datum est, quasi ob rem datum, re non secuta, Dig. 19, 5, 5, 1. 'Praescriptis verbis is brought to recover, not restitution, but damages equal to the plaintiff's interest in a specific performance. Restitution may be enforced by a suit for reconveyance upon failure of consideration.'

Examples of Innominate contract are Exchange (permutatio), Dig. 19, 4; Compromise (transactio), Dig. 2, 15; Cod. 2, 4; Conditional sale (aestimatum), that is to say, a promise to pay a certain price for an article if the promisor succeeds in reselling it at a profit, with a power, in the opposite event, of returning the article to the promisee, Dig. 19, 3; and Permissive occupancy (precarium), or permission, at the request (precibus) of the grantee, to use an article without compensation, with a proviso for redelivery on demand. The precarious grantee (precario rogans), as a rule, has Possession, but by special agreement may have mere Detention; whereas the borrower for use (commodatarius) in every case has only Detention. Itaque cum quid precario rogatum est, non solum hoc interdicto uti possumus, sed etiam praescriptis verbis actione quae ex bona fide oritur, Dig. 43, 16. 'The grantor can recover possession either by the interdict de precario or by the equitable action praescriptis verbis. This action is so denominated because, in the absence of a generic name for the contract, the fact begetting the obligation was detailed at length in the demonstratio of the formula. Actio quae praescriptis verbis rem gestam demonstrat, Cod. 2, 4, 6. Hence it is often called actio in factum praescriptis verbis. This, however, is a misleading name, because it might lead us to suppose that the formula had an intentio in factum. But it is a civil action, and the formula contains the word 'oportet' (quidquid ob eam rem illum illi dare facere oportet), that is to say, has an intentio in jus. It is better, therefore, to call it simply actio praescriptis verbis. The name of this Roman action ex contractu may be illustrated by a comparison with the name of an English action ex delicto, trespass on the case, so named from the comparative particularity with which the circumstances of the plaintiff's case are detailed in the written allegations.

DE VERBORUM OBLIGATIONE.

§ 92. Verbis obligatio fit ex interrogatione et responsione, velut: DARI SPONDES? SPONDEO; DABIS? DABO; PROMITTIS; PROMITTO; FIDE PROMITTIS? FIDE PROMITTO; FIDE IUBES? FIDE IUBEO; FACIES? FACIAM.

§ 92. A verbal contract is formed by question and answer, thus: 'Art thou sponsor to me for the conveyance?' 'I am sponsor to thee for the conveyance.' 'Wilt thou convey?' 'I will convey.' 'Dost thou pledge thy credit?' 'I pledge my credit.' 'Dost thou bid me trust thee as guarantor?' 'I bid thee trust me as guarantor.' 'Wilt thou perform?' 'I will perform.'

§ 93. Sed haec quidem verborum obligatio: DARI SPONDES? SPONDEO, propria civium Romanorum est, ceterae vero iuris gentium sunt; itaque inter omnes homines, sive cives Romanos sive peregrinos, valent. et quamvis ad *Graecam* vocem expressae fuerint, velut hoc modo: [δώσεις; δώσω· ὁμολογεῖς; ὁμολογῶ· πίστει κελεύεις; πίστει κελεύω· ποιήσεις; ποιήσω]; etiam haec tamen inter cives Romanos valent, si modo Graeci sermonis intellect*u*m habeant. et e contrario quamvis Latine enuntientur, tamen etiam inter peregrinos valent, si modo Latini sermonis intellectum habeant. at illa verborum obligatio: DARI SPONDES? SPONDEO, adeo propria civium Romanorum est, ut ne quidem in Graecum sermonem per interpretationem proprie transf*er*ri possit; quamvis dicatur a Graeca voce figurata esse.

§ 93. The formula: "'Art thou sponsor?' 'I am sponsor,'" is only valid between Roman citizens; the others belong to gentile law, and bind all parties, whether Romans or aliens, and, if understood, bind Romans when expressed in Greek, and aliens when expressed in Latin. The formula, 'Art thou sponsor?' is so peculiarly Roman that it cannot be expressed in Greek, though the word 'sponsor' is said to have a Greek origin.

§ 94. Unde dicitur uno casu hoc verbo peregrinum quoque obligari posse, velut si Imperator noster principem alicuiu*s* peregrini populi de pace ita interroget: PACEM FUTURAM SPONDES? vel ipse eodem modo interrogetur. quod nimium subtiliter dictum est; quia si quid adversus pactionem fiat, non ex stipulat*u* agitur, sed iure belli res vindicatur.

§ 94. According to some, there is one case in which an alien may be bound by this word, namely, when a Roman emperor in concluding a treaty thus interrogates a foreign sovereign: 'Art thou sponsor for peace?' and a Roman, they hold, may similarly be bound to an alien. But this is a misconception, for the violation of a treaty between sovereign states is not redressed by legal process, but by the sword.

§ 95. Illu*d* dubitari potest, si quis [*desunt* 24 *lin.*]

§ 95. . . . .

§ 96. .... obligentur: utique *cum* quaeritur de iure Romanorum. nam aput peregrinos quod iuris sit, singularum civitatium iura requirentes aliud in *alia* lege *reperimus*.

§ 96. [Gaius perhaps observed that the FORMS prescribed by law, under pain of nullification, for Contracts, Wills, and any other Titles, belong to the Civil, National, or Local, as opposed to the Gentile, Cosmopolitan, or Universal, ingredients of each particular code].

§ 92. Before we proceed to examine Formal, that is to say, Verbal and Literal contracts, it is desirable, at the risk of some repetition, to review the general nature of Title.

A Title is a fact, incident, or event, to which the law annexes a right or obligation; or it is a fact by which the law confers a right or imposes an obligation on a person; or it is an incident through which the law invests a person with a right or obligation; or, extending its function, it is an event which gives a beginning or puts an end to a right or obligation; it is a fact, incident, or event, whereby the law invests with a right or divests of a right; or a fact, incident, or event, whereby the law burdens us with an obligation or exonerates from an obligation.

The rights conferred through a title may be jura in rem, available against all the world; or jura in personam, available only against a determinate person. It is with the latter that we are at present concerned.

The facts called Titles, whether they confer a jus in rem or a jus in personam, are never absolutely elementary,—are always decomposable into a bundle of more elementary facts. Nevertheless, and with this reservation, Titles may be divided into such as are comparatively simple, and such as are comparatively complex.

The bundle of facts composing a comparatively complex Title can usually be divided into two portions, one of which may be called principal or essential, the other secondary or adventitious.

For instance, in the bundle of facts composing an alienation, or creating a jus in rem, the essential or principal portion is the free will and intention of the alienor to divest himself of a right and invest the alienee with it, and the acceptance of the proffered right by the alienee: the accessory and adventitious portion is the signification of these intentions by the execution of a certain written instrument or deed, and their completion by the solemn delivery and acceptance of seisin or possession.

These accessory formalities and solemnities are ancillary to the essential purpose of the transaction, being destined partly to prevent rash and inconsiderate engagements, partly to furnish evidence and proof of the convention or principal part of the transaction.

Indeed, the accessory portion of the Title may contain an element still more remotely and casually connected with the principal transaction, such as the stamp affixed to the document executed by the parties. The stamp in no way contributes to the purpose and intention of the parties, but the legislator makes it necessary to the validity of the transaction from financial motives, for the sake, namely, of the public revenue.

Setting aside this purely arbitrary addition to the Title, we may say that the function of the Title is not only to be the antecedent to which the law annexes as a consequent a certain right or obligation, but also to be a sign, badge, or manifestation, to denote to the world the person in whom a right has vested, or on whom an obligation has become incumbent.

The peculiar characteristic of Formal, that is to say, Verbal and Literal contracts, is this: evidentiary solemnities compose in these contracts an indispensable part of the title to a jus in personam. The Formless contracts, namely, the Real contracts, of which we have already treated, and the Consensual contracts, of which we shall treat hereafter, cannot, indeed, be enforced in a court of law unless they are proved to have been concluded, unless, that is, evidence be given of their existence. But the contract and the evidence of the contract are distinct and independent. In Formal contracts a preappointed evidence of the essential portion of the contract, that is, of the intention of the promisor and expectation of the promisee, is made by the legislator a constituent accessory element of the contract or title itself. It is not perfect or complete without this evidence. If the transaction did not include certain preappointed evidentiary formalities, the Verbal or Literal contract has never been formed and does not exist.

§ 94. The obligation of an independent sovereign state to another independent sovereign state does not resemble the obligation of one subject to another subject of the same sovereign or political superior. If a contract between two subjects is broken, it is enforced by the power of the common sovereign. But if a treaty between two sovereigns is violated, there is, by hypothesis, no common superior by whom it may be enforced. The

treaties of sovereign states correspond to the moral obligations of individuals. They may be binding in the forum of conscience or of heaven, but, if these are disregarded, are not enforced by any earthly tribunal. The moral obligation is not secured by any legal sanction; and the sovereign whose treaty rights are violated can obtain no redress except from his own power of inflicting evil on the violator.

The necessity of employing any consecrated terms in a stipulation was abrogated by a constitution of Leo, dated the calends of January, A.D. 469. Omnes stipulationes, etiamsi non solennibus vel directis sed quibuscunque verbis consensu contrahentium compositae sunt [vel], legibus cognitae suum habeant firmitatem, Cod. 8, 38, 10. 'Stipulations, though not in consecrated formulas or direct terms, in whatever words the agreement of the parties is expressed, if otherwise legal, shall have binding force.'

It appears from the epitome of Gaius, contained in the laws of the Visigoths (Breviarium Alarici), that Gaius proceeded to mention two modes of verbal obligation without previous interrogation, the dotis dictio, and the jurata promissio liberti. Dotis dictio was the declaration of a wife, or her father, or her debtor, settling a dotal estate, movable or immovable, on the husband. Jurata promissio liberti was the sworn promise of a freedman, immediately after his manumission, to render certain services (operae) to his patron. It was usual to bind the conscience of the slave by a similar promise before manumission; but such a promise had no legal operation.

DE INUTILIBUS STIPULATIONIBUS.

§ 97. Si id quod dari stipulamur tale sit, ut dari non possit, inutilis est stipulatio: velut si quis hominem liberum quem servum esse credebat, aut mortuum quem vivum esse credebat, aut locum sacrum vel religiosum quem putabat *esse* humani iuris *sibi dari* stipuletur.

§ 97*a*. *item si quis rem quae in rerum natura non est aut esse non potest, velut hippocentaurum stipuletur*, aeque inutilis est stipulatio.

§ 98. Item si quis sub ea condicione stipuletur quae existere non

§ 97. The impossibility of a stipulated conveyance vacates the stipulation; for instance, if a man stipulates for the conveyance of a freeman whom he supposes to be a slave, or of a dead slave whom he supposes to be alive, or of ground devoted to the celestial or infernal gods which he supposes to be a subject of commerce, or of a non-existent thing, such as a hippocentaur, the stipulation is void.

§ 98. An impossible condition, that the promisee, for instance,

potest, *vel*uti si digito caelum tetigerit, inutilis est stipula*ti*o. sed legatum sub inpossibili condicione relictum nostri praeceptores proin*de valere* putant, ac si *ea condicio adiecta non* esset: divers*ae* sc*h*olae auctores non minus legatum inutile existimant, quam stipulationem. et sane vi*x* idonea diversitatis ratio reddi potest.

should touch the sky, makes the stipulation void, although a devise with an impossible condition, according to the authorities of my school, has the same effect as if the condition were not annexed. According to the other school it is as null and void as if it were a stipulation, and in truth no satisfactory reason can be alleged for making a distinction.

§ 99. Praeterea inutilis *est stipulatio, si quis* ignor*ans rem suam esse eam sibi dari stipuletur; nam* id quod al*i*cu*i*us est, id ei dari non potest.

§ 99. So a stipulation to convey the promisee's property to the promisee is null and void, for the conveyance is impossible.

§ 100. Denique inutilis est talis stipulatio, si quis ita dari stipuletur: POST MORTEM MEAM DARI SPONDES? vel ita: *POST MORTEM TUAM DARI SPONDES? valet autem, si quis ita dari stipuletur: CUM MORIAR DARI SPONDES? vel ita:* CUM MORIERIS DARI SPONDES? id est ut in novissimum vitae tempus stipulatoris aut promissoris obligatio conferatur. nam inelegans esse visum est ex heredis persona incipere obligationem. rursu*s* ita stipulari non possumus: PRIDIE QUAM MORIAR, aut: PRIDIE QUAM MORIERIS, DARI SPONDES? quia non potest aliter intellegi pridie quam aliquis morietur, quam si mors secuta sit; rursus morte secuta in praeteritum redducitur stipulatio et quodammodo talis est: HEREDI MEO DARI SPONDES? quae sane inutilis est.

§ 100. A stipulation to convey after the death of the promisee or promisor is invalid, but a stipulation to convey at the death, that is, at the last moment of the life of the promisee or promisor, is valid. For it has been held anomalous to make the successor of either of the contracting parties the first subject of the obligation. Again, a stipulation to convey on the day before the death of the promisee or promisor is invalid, for the day before the death cannot be ascertained till after death, and after death the time is past for performance to the promisee, and the stipulation amounts to a promise to convey to the promisee's successor, which is void.

§ 101. Quaecumque de morte diximus, eadem et de capitis diminutione dicta intellegemus.

§ 101. What is said of death must also be understood of loss of status.

§ 102. Adhuc inutilis est stipulatio, si quis ad id quod interrogatus erit non responderit: velut si sestertia X a te dari stipuler, et tu *nummum* sestert*ium* V mi*lia* promittas; aut si ego pu*r*e stipuler, tu sub condicione promittas.

§ 102. Another cause of nullity is the want of correspondence between the question and answer; if I stipulate, for instance, for ten thousand sesterces and you promise five thousand, or if you meet my absolute stipulation by a conditional promise.

§ 103. Praeterea inutilis est stipulatio, si ei dari stipulemur cuius iuri subiecti non sumus: unde illud quaesitum est, si quis sibi et ei cuius iuri subiectus non est dari stipuletur, in quantum valeat stipulatio. nostri praeceptores putant in universum valere, et proinde ei soli qui stipulatus sit solidum deberi, atque si extranei nomen non adiecisset. sed diversae *scholae* auctores *dimidium ei deberi* existimant, pro alie*na* . . . [*desunt* 4 *lin.*]

§ 104. *Item inutilis est* stipulatio, *si* ab *eo stipuler qui iuri meo subiectus* est, *vel si* is a me *stipuletur. sed de servis et de his qui* in mancipio *sunt illud praeterea ius observatur, ut* non solum ipsi *cuius in potestate mancipiove* sunt obligari non pos*sint*, *s*ed ne alii quide*m* ull*i*.

§ 105. Mutum neque stipulari neque promittere posse palam *est. Quod et* in surdo receptum est: quia et is *qui stipulatur* verba promittentis, et qui promittit, *verba stipulantis* exaudire debet.

§ 106. Furiosus nullum ne*gotium gerere potest*, quia non intellegit quid agat.

§ 107. Pupillus omne negotium recte gerit: ita tamen ut *tutor*, sicubi tutoris auctori*tas ne*cessaria sit, *ad*hibeatur, velut si ipse obligetur; nam alium sibi obligare etiam sine tutoris auctoritate potest.

§ 108. Idem iuris est in feminis quae in tutela sunt.

§ 109. Se*d* quod diximus de pupilli*s*, utique de eo verum est qui iam aliquem intellectum habet: nam infans et qui infanti proximus est non multum a *furioso* differt, quia huius aetatis pupilli nullum intellectum habent: sed in his pupillis per utilitatem benignior iuris interpretatio facta est.

§ 103. No valid stipulation can be made to convey to a person who has not power over the stipulator, whence the question has been mooted to what extent a stipulation for payment to the stipulator and a stranger is valid. My school hold that it is valid for the whole sum stipulated, and that the stipulator is entitled to the whole, just as if the stranger had not been mentioned. The other school hold that he is only entitled to the moiety.

§ 104. No valid stipulation can be made between a person under power and the person to whom he is subject. A slave and a person in mancipation can incur an obligation neither to the person in whose power or mancipation they are, nor to any other person.

§ 105. The dumb cannot stipulate or promise, nor can the deaf, for the promisee in stipulation must hear the answer, and the promisor must hear the question.

§ 106. A lunatic cannot enter into any contract because he has no judgment of consequences.

§ 107. A ward can enter into any contract provided that he has his guardian's authority when necessary, as it is for incurring an obligation, although not for imposing an obligation.

§ 108. The same rule applies to women who are wards.

§ 109. This concession of legal capacity to wards is manifestly reasonable in respect of children approaching the age of twelve or fourteen; and children who have only just completed their seventh year, though resembling lunatics in point of intelligence, are permitted, with a view to their interests, to have the same capacity as those approaching twelve or fourteen.

§ 97. When a stipulation was inutilis, i.e. null and void by the civil law, no action could be brought. Sed et officio quoque praetoris continetur ex hujusmodi obligationibus actionem denegari, Dig. 45, 1, 27. 'It is the duty of the praetor to refuse an action to an immoral stipulation.' A penal clause would generally (see note to § 103 for an exception) give no validity to a stipulation otherwise void. Si homo mortuus sisti non potest, nec poena rei impossibilis committetur, quemadmodum si quis Stichum mortuum dari stipulatus, si datus non esset, poenam stipularetur, Dig. 45, 1, 69. 'A slave deceased cannot be produced, and a penal sum annexed to the breach of an impossible condition, for instance, the conveyance of a deceased slave, is not forfeited.'

§ 98. A Condition is an incident common to Contracts and to Testamentary dispositions, i. e. to all declarations of will, and demands a brief examination. A Condition is a species of Title; it is a certain contingent occurrence or non-occurrence, performance or non-performance, by arbitrary appointment conferring on a certain person a certain right, or imposing on him a certain obligation. It may be defined as the middle term (B) of a syllogism of which the minor term (C) represents a person, and the major term (A) a right or obligation, and of which both the premisses are Contingent. It is the last feature that we shall proceed to consider.

The major premiss must be contingent; it must be an arbitrary determination that makes the right or obligation (A) depend on the given title (B); the nexus between the middle and major terms must be solely the will of the testator or contractors, not the will of the legislator; the title must not be in its own nature the Necessary presupposition of the right. E.g. in the following cases: the institution of a person as heir, *if he survive the testator*, *if he accept the inheritance;* the bequest of a legacy, *if the heir accept the inheritance;* the promise of a dower, *if the marriage is celebrated;* the seeming condition is required by the law, and its expression is superfluous: such an event, therefore, is not a genuine condition. Again, the nexus between the minor and middle terms may be either the will of the person entitled (conditio potestativa, Cod. 6, 51, 7), or chance (conditio casualis); but one way or other the minor premiss must be contingent; the fulfilment of the condition must be neither Necessary nor Impossible: it must be a future and uncertain contingency whether the title (B) shall be realized or fulfilled in respect of a given person (C). The condition, accordingly, must not be a past or present event, e.g. *if Titius was consul last year, if Titius is now consul;* such a fact is now certain and Necessary, and any disposition contingent thereon is really unconditional.

The effect of an Impossible condition is different in Contracts and Testamentary dispositions; it invalidates contract; whereas in a testament it is deemed unwritten (pro non scripto habetur), and the disposition is regarded as unconditional. This was the rule that finally prevailed: Obtinuit, impossibiles conditiones testamento adscriptas pro nullis habendas, Dig. 35, 1, 1, 3. 'It has been finally decided that impossible conditions to testamentary dispositions are mere surplusage.' This was the doctrine of the Sabinians, and was confirmed by Justinian, Inst. 2, 14, 10. Illegal and immoral conditions followed the same rule as impossible conditions. The question why Contracts and Wills were governed by different rules, which Gaius admits to be obscure, may receive some light from the following considerations. Testamentary dispositions in their nature are acts of liberality on the part of the testator. Even when he employs them as inducements to an illegal or immoral act, it is not quite certain that the refusal to perform the act would deprive the devisee of his liberality. At all events, the devisee is innocent of unlawful intention, and the same cannot be said of the contractor who is guilty of an agreement to violate the law. Accordingly, the law aids the devisee but not the contractor; and the rule, once established for immoral conditions, was extended to impossible conditions.

On this point the French code agrees with the Roman law. In the Austrian code the Proculeian doctrine is followed: i. e. testamentary dispositions as well as contracts are invalidated by immoral or impossible conditions. The Prussian code follows a middle course: impossible conditions invalidate a testamentary disposition; immoral conditions are deemed unwritten and the disposition is construed as unconditional.

§ 100. These distinctions were abrogated by Justinian, who enacted that an act could be stipulated to be performed either before or after the death of either of the contractors, Inst. 3, 19, 13.

§ 103. A slave or filiusfamilias who stipulated a payment to himself acquired an obligation for the master or paterfamilias. He could also stipulate directly a payment to the master or parent. Except in these relations, it was the rule that a man could not stipulate for payment to a third person, for in case of breach of stipulation, how could damages for non-performance be assessed? The rule, however, was subject to various exceptions. Payment to a third party might be secured by a penal clause, stipulating, in default of performance, payment of a penal sum to the promisee, Inst. 3, 19, 19. If the promisee had a pecuniary interest in the payment to the third person, the stipulation was valid without a penal clause, Inst. 3, 19, 20. Again, in the adoption of an infant sui juris as regulated by Antoninus Pius, the promisee to whom the adrogator promised to perform the conditions of the adrogation was a public slave or free man in charge of the records (tabularius), Inst. 1, 11, 3. And in the covenant by a guardian for the due administration of the estate of an infant ward (rem pupilli salvam fore) the promisee might be a public slave, or a person appointed by the praetor, or the praetor himself, Dig. 27, 8, 1, 15. Moreover, certain procurators could stipulate for payment to their principals, as, for instance, the procurator of a tutor, curator, soldier, representative of a municipality (actor municipum), and any procurator in a stipulation directed by the praetor, as, for example, a stipulation for indemnity against damage apprehended (stipulatio damni infecti), Dig. 46, 5, 5.

With these exceptions, it was the inflexible rule of the Civil law that a Verbal contract could only be concluded between principals—between persons covenanting in their own names. This impediment in the way of commerce was met, as we have already stated, by a double use of a Consensual contract, which will presently be examined, the contract of Agency (mandatum). An Agent or mandatary stipulated in his own name with a third person, and then ceded his right of action to his principal; that is, made his principal his mandatary: the principal then sued and recovered on the Stipulation as cessionary of the action, that is, as mandatary of his mandatary. In the latest period the actual Cession of the action was unnecessary: the praetor allowed the principal to sue by an actio Utilis, i. e. an action whose formula contained a Fiction, with whose precise nature we are unacquainted, but perhaps to the effect that the principal was the universal successor of the agent. In respect of Formless contracts, or contracts governed by Jus Gentium, the institute of Agency was more completely recognized. If an Agent merely acted as emissary (nuncius) and instrument (minister) of his principal, that is, contracted in the name of his principal, the principal acquired an immediate right against the third contractor and incurred a direct obligation to him: he could sue him or be sued by him in an actio Directa—he was not driven to an actio Utilis or Fictitia. In this respect the distinction between Formal and Formless contracts may be thus expressed: in Formal contracts the Civil law requires both elements of Title, the essential element (intention to create an obligation) and the evidentiary element (the question or answer) to be acts of the same person: in Formless contracts Gentile law allows these elements to be sundered; allows the essential part (intention) to be the act of one person, the Principal, and the evidentiary part (the external manifestation of this intention) to be the act of another person, the Agent.

The controversy between the Sabinians and Proculeians is decided in favour of the latter by Justinian, who enacts that a stipulation for payment of a sum to the promisee and a stranger entitles the promisee to payment of half the sum and is void as to the remainder, Inst. 3, 19, 4.

§ 109. The age of puberty, as we have seen, was 14 for males, 12 for females. Before this period the child was called impubes: up to the age of 7 he was called infans. In the interval between 7 and 14 he was described either as infantiae proximus or as pubertati proximus. According to some commentators the interval was equally divided between these appellations, so that from 7 to 10½ a boy was infantiae proximus, and from 10½ to 14 pubertati proximus. According to Savigny these names only covered the space of a year measured from each limit, so that from 7 to 8 a child was infanti proximus, from 13 to 14 puberi proximus, and from 8 to 13 without any distinctive appellation.

The principal peculiarity that results from the nature of verbal and literal contracts and distinguishes them from other conventions is, that other conventions are not legally valid unless the promisor be shown to get a quid pro quo, that is, unless an adequate consideration be proved: whereas verbal and literal contracts, securing by the solemnity of their formalities due deliberation on the part of the contractors, are valid in the eye of the civil law without proof of consideration.

Although, however, the want of consideration did not invalidate a stipulation by the civil law, yet it was a good defence in equity, and might be pleaded by the exceptio doli mali or non numeratae pecuniae. Si quis sine causa ab aliquo fuerit stipulatus, deinde ex ea stipulatione experiatur, exceptio utique doli mali ei nocebit. Licet enim eo tempore quo stipulabatur nihil dolo malo admiserit, tamen dicendum est eum, cum litem contestatur, dolo facere qui perseveret ex ea stipulatione petere, Dig. 44, 4, 2, 3. 'The absence of consideration renders an action on a stipulation liable to be barred by a plea of fraudulent intention. For though originally the stipulation was not tainted with fraud, yet to sue on such a stipulation is fraudulent.' The exception of dolus malus was allowed by Marcus Aurelius (A. D. 169–176) to be pleaded in all actions of civil law. Sed et in strictis judiciis, ex rescripto divi Marci, opposita doli mali exceptione, compensatio inducebatur, Inst. 4, 6, 30. 'Even in actions of civil law, after the rescript of Marcus Aurelius, the plea of dolus malus forced the plaintiff to recognize any set-off to his claim.'

If instead of generally alleging fraud (Si in ea re nihil dolo malo Auli Agerii factum est neque fit), the plea alleged the particular fact of non-payment (exceptio in factum composita), it was called exceptio pecuniae non numeratae. Compare Gaius, 4 § 116: Si stipulatus sim a te pecuniam, tanquam credendi causa numeraturus, nec numeraverim . . . . placet per exceptionem doli mali te defendi debere, with Just. Inst. 4, 13, 2: Si quis, quasi credendi causa, pecuniam stipulatus fuerit, neque numeraverit . . . . placet per exceptionem pecuniae non numeratae te defendi debere.

An important peculiarity of these exceptions was that the burden of proof was not, as in other exceptions, on the defendant, but on the plaintiff. Si ex cautione tua, licet hypotheca data, conveniri coeperis, exceptione opposita seu doli seu non numeratae pecuniae, compellitur petitor probare, pecuniam tibi esse numeratam; quo non impleto absolutio sequetur, Cod. 4, 30, 3. 'If you are sued on your stipulation (or written admission) confirmed by a mortgage, the plea of fraud or money not received will force the claimant to prove that the money was lent, or you will be acquitted.' A rescript of Diocletian and Maximian (A. D. 286–305) expressly states that this plea was admissible in an action founded on stipulation. Si stipulatione interposita placita creditor non dederit, in factum esse dandam exceptionem convenit, Cod. 4, 30, 9. 'If, after a stipulation, the contemplated loan was not advanced by the promisee, this fact may be pleaded in an exception.'

It is clear that when these rules were established the whole nature of verbal and literal contracts was changed: Formal contracts were abolished, so far as the rules extended, or transformed into real contracts, the obligation of the promisor depending on the performance of the promisee (re), that is, on the execution by the promisee of his part of the consideration, not on the solemnity of the spoken words (verbis) or written document (literis).

This transformation of a verbal or literal into a real contract was, however, confined to contracts contemplating a loan of money. Ignorare autem non debes non numeratae pecuniae exceptionem ibi locum habere ubi quasi credita pecunia petitur, Cod. 4, 30, 5. 'The exception of money not received is confined to actions brought to recover money lent.' Moreover, by a constitution of Marcus Aurelius, the exception could only be pleaded within five years from the date of the contract, which delay was reduced to two years by Justinian, Inst. 3, 21. After this interval, accordingly, stipulation resumed, or rather, for the first time assumed, its proper character of a Formal contract.

STIPULATIONES ACCESSORIAE.

§ 110. Possumus tamen ad id quod *stipulamur* alium *ad*hibere *qui* idem *stipuletur*, quem vulgo adstipulatorem vocamus.

§ 110. Although another person cannot stipulate for us, yet in our stipulations we can associate with ourselves another person who stipulates for the same performance, and is called an adstipulator.

§ 111. Sed huic proinde actio *com*petit, proindeque ei recte solvitur ac nobis. sed quidquid consecutus erit, mandati *iu*dicio nobis restituere cogetur.

§ 111. He can sue as well as the stipulator, and payment to him discharges the debtor as well as payment to the stipulator, but whatever he recovers, the action of mandate compels him to hand over to the stipulator.

§ 112. Ceterum potest etiam aliis verbis uti adstipulator, quam quibus nos usi sumus. itaque si verbi gratia ego ita stipulatus sim: DARI SPONDES? ille sic adstipulari potest: IDEM FIDE TUA PROMITTIS? vel IDEM FIDE IUBES? vel contra.

§ 112. The adstipulator need not employ the same terms as the stipulator; if the one says, 'Art thou sponsor for the conveyance?' the adstipulator may say, 'Dost thou for the same pledge thy credit?' or, 'Dost thou for the same bid me trust thee?' or vice versa.

§ 113. *Item minus* adstipulari potest, plus non potest. itaque si ego sestertia X stipulatus sum, ille sestertia V stipulari potest; contra vero plus non potest. item si ego

§ 113. He may contract for less than the stipulator, but not for more. Thus, if I stipulate for ten thousand sesterces he may stipulate for five thousand, or if I stipulate

pure stipulatus sim, ille sub condicione stipulari potest; contra vero non potest. non solum autem in quantitate, sed etiam in tempore minus et plus intellegitur: plus est enim statim aliquid dare, minus est post *tempus*.

absolutely he may stipulate conditionally, but not vice versa. More and less is to be understood of time as well as of quantity, immediate payment being regarded as more, and future payment as less.

§ 114. In hoc autem iure quaedam singulari iure observantur. nam adstipulatoris heres non habet actionem. item servus adstipulando nihil agit, qui ex ceteris omnibus causis stipulatione domino adquirit. idem de eo qui in mancipio est magis pl*acu*it; nam et is servi loco est. is autem qui in potestate patris est, agit aliquid, sed parenti non adquirit; qu*amvis* ex omnibus ceteris causis stipulando ei adquirat. ac ne ipsi quidem aliter acti*o* c*om*petit, quam si sine capitis diminutione exierit de potestate parentis, veluti morte eius, aut quod ipse flamen Dialis inauguratus est. eadem de filia familias, et quae in manu est, dicta intellegemus.

§ 114. In this matter there are some exceptional rules. The successor of the adstipulator cannot sue; a slave cannot be adstipulator, though in any other circumstance his stipulation acquires a right for his master; a person in domestic bondage cannot be adstipulator, because he is likened to a slave; a son in the power of his father can be adstipulator, but does not acquire a right for his father, as in all other stipulations, and he himself has no right of action until, without loss of status, he ceases to be subject to his father, by his father's death, for instance, or by being inaugurated priest of Jupiter. The same is true of a filiafamilias and a wife in the power of her husband.

§ 115. Pro eo quoque qui promittit solent alii obligari, quorum alios sponsores, alios fidepromissores, alios fideiussores appellamus.

§ 115. For the promisor, similarly, other persons are bound, who are called sponsors or fidepromissors or fidejussors.

§ 116. Sponsor ita interrogatur: IDEM DARI SPONDES? fidepromissor: IDEM FIDEPROMITTIS? fideiussor ita: IDEM FIDE TUA ESSE IUBES? videbimus de his autem, quo nomine possint proprie adpellari, qui ita interrogantur: IDEM DABIS? IDEM PROMITTIS? IDEM FACIES?

§ 116. A sponsor is thus interrogated: 'Art thou for the same payment sponsor?' a fidepromissor thus: 'Dost thou for the same pledge thy credit?' a fidejussor thus: 'Dost thou the same guarantee?' We shall have to consider the question what is the proper name for those who are thus interrogated: 'Wilt thou the same convey? Dost thou the same promise? Wilt thou the same perform?'

§ 117. Sponsores q*uidem* et fidepromissores et fideiussores saepe solemus accipere, dum curamus ut diligentius nobis cautum sit. adstipulatorem vero fere tunc solum a*d*hibemus, cum ita stipulamur, ut aliquid post mortem nostram detur:

§ 117. Sponsors and fidepromissors are often employed for additional security; an adstipulator is only employed to secure payment after our death. Our own stipulation to this is void, and therefore we associate with ourselves an ad-

quod cum stipulando nihil agimus, *ad*hibetur *ad*stipulator, ut is post mortem nostram agat: qui si quid fuerit consecutus, d*e* *restitu*endo eo mandati iudicio heredi *nostro* tenetur.

stipulator, who sues after our death, and is compelled by an action of mandate to hand over to our successor whatever he recovers.

§ 118. Sponsoris *vero* et fidepromissoris similis condicio *est*, fideiussoris va*l*de *d*issimilis.

§ 118. The rules which govern the sponsor and fidepromissor are similar, and very unlike those which govern the fidejussor.

§ 119. Nam illi quidem nullis obligationibus accedere possunt nisi verborum; quamvis interdum ipse qui promiserit non fuerit obligatus, velut *si femina* aut pupillus sine tutoris auctoritate, aut quilibet pos*t* mortem suam dari promiserit. at illu*d* quaeritur, si *servus* aut peregrinus spoponderit, an pro eo sponsor aut fidepromissor obligetur. fideiussor vero omnibus obligationibus, id est sive re sive verbis sive litteris sive consens*u* contractae fuerint obligationes, adici potest. a*t* ne illu*d* quidem interest, utrum civilis an naturalis obligatio sit cui adiciatur; adeo quidem, ut pro servo quoque obligetur, sive extraneus sit qui a servo fideiussorem accipiat, sive dominus in id quod sibi debeatur.

§ 119. The former are adjuncts of none but verbal contracts, though (like fidejussions) they are sometimes effective when the principal promisor is not validly bound, as, for instance, when a female or ward contracts without the guardian's authority, or a person promises a payment after his death. It is a moot question when a slave or alien promises by the term spondeo, whether his sponsor or fidepromissor is effectively bound. A fidejussor may accompany any obligations, whether real, verbal, literal, or consensual, and whether civil or natural. Accordingly, he may be bound for the obligation of a slave either to a stranger or to his master.

§ 120. Praeterea sponsoris et fidepromissoris heres non tenetur, nisi si de peregrino fidepromissore quaeramus, et alio iure civitas eius utatur: fideiussoris autem etiam heres tenetur.

§ 120. Again, no successor of the sponsor or fidepromissor is bound, except the successor of an alien fidepromissor in whose country such a rule prevails; but the fidejussor's successor is always bound.

§ 121. Item sponsor et fidepromissor *per* legem Furiam biennio liberantur; et quotquot erunt numero eo tempore quo pecunia peti potest, in tot partes deducitur inter eos obligatio, et singuli viriles partes *dare iu*bentur. fideiussore*s* vero perpetuo tenentur; et quotquot erunt numero, singuli in solidum obligantur. *itaque liberum est creditori a quo velit s*olidum petere. *Sed ex epistula divi Hadriani compellitur* creditor a singulis, qui modo sol-

§ 121. Again, a sponsor and fidepromissor, by the lex Furia, at the end of two years are discharged of obligation, and the total obligation is divided into as many parts as there are sponsors or fidepromissors at the time when the payment is due; and each is only liable for a single part. Fidejussors are liable for ever, and, however many there are, each is liable for the whole amount, and the creditor may sue whichever he chooses for the whole.

vendo *sint, partes petere.* eo igitur distat haec epistula a lege Furia, quod si quis ex sponsoribus aut fidepromissoribus solvendo non sit, *non augetur onus ceterorum*, quotquot erunt. *Cum autem lex Furia tantum in* Italia locum habeat, *consequens est, ut in provinciis* sponsores quoque et fidepromissores proinde ac fideiussores in perpetuo teneantur et singuli in solidum obligentur, nisi ex epistula divi Hadriani hi *quoque adiuvari videantur.*

But by the letter of Hadrian he is compellable to sue only for an aliquot part, determined by the number of the solvent. Herein the letter of Hadrian differs from the lex Furia, for the insolvency of one sponsor or fidepromissor does not increase the liability of the remainder. As the lex Furia only applies to Italy, in the provinces, sponsors and fidepromissors, like fidejussors, are liable for ever, and each would be liable for the whole amount, if they were not held to be relieved by the letter of Hadrian.

§ 122. Praeterea inter sponsores et fidepromissores lex Apuleia quandam societatem introduxit. nam si quis horum plus sua portione solverit, de eo quod amplius dederit *adversus ceteros actionem habet. Lex autem Apuleia ante* legem Furiam lata est, quo tempore in solidum obligabantur: unde quaeritur, an post legem Furiam adhuc legis Apuleiae beneficium supersit. et utique extra *Italiam* superest; nam *lex* quidem Furia tantum in *Italia* valet, Apuleia vero etiam in *ceteris praeter Italiam regionibus. Alia sane est fideiussorum condicio; nam ad hos lex* Apuleia non pertinet. itaque si creditor ab uno totum *consecutus* fuerit, huius solius detrimentum *erit, scilicet* si is pro quo fideiussit solvendo non *sit. sed ut ex* supradictis appar*et*, is a quo creditor totum petit, poterit ex epistula divi Hadriani desiderare, ut pro parte in se detur actio.

§ 122. Moreover, between sponsors and fidepromissors the lex Apuleia introduced a sort of partnership, for any one of them who has paid more than his share can recover the excess from the others. The lex Apuleia was passed before the lex Furia, when each sponsor and fidepromissor was liable for the whole amount; and accordingly it is questioned whether, since the lex Furia, the sponsor and fidepromissor still enjoy the benefit of the lex Apuleia. It is undoubtedly available in the provinces, for the lex Furia does not extend beyond Italy; whereas the lex Apuleia extends to the whole empire. A different rule applies to fidejussors, for they do not come within the lex Apuleia; accordingly, if one fidejussor pay the whole amount, he alone suffers by the insolvency of the principal; but it is his own fault; for, as was said above, a fidejussor sued for the whole amount is entitled by the letter of Hadrian to require the claim to be reduced to his ratable portion.

§ 123. Praeterea lege . . . . cautum est, ut is qui sponsores aut fidepromissores accipiat praedicat palam et declaret, et de qua re satis accipiat, et quot sponsores aut fidepromissores in eam obligationem accep-

§ 123. Further, the lex . . . . provides that a creditor who obtains the guaranty of sponsors and fidepromissors shall previously announce and declare to them the amount of the debt to be guaran-

turus sit: et nisi praedixerit, permittitur sponsoribus et fidepromissoribus intra diem xxx. praeiudicium postulare, quo quaeratur, an ex ea lege praedictum sit; et si iudicatum fuerit praedictum *non* esse, liberantur. Qua lege fideiussorum menti*o* nulla fit: sed in usu est, etiam si fideiussores accipiamus, praedicere.

teed and the number of sponsors or fidepromissors by whom it is to be guaranteed; and in the absence of such declaration the sponsors or fidepromissors are permitted within thirty days to demand a trial of the issue, whether the requisite declaration was made; and on judgment that it was not made are discharged of liability. The law makes no mention of fidejussors, but it is usual in a guaranty by fidejussors to make a similar declaration.

§ 124. Sed beneficium legi*s* Corneliae omnibus commune est. qua lege idem pro eodem aput eundem eodem anno vetatur in ampliorem summam obligari creditae pecuniae quam in xx mili*a*; et quamvis sponsor vel fidepromissor in amplam pecuniam, velut si sestertium C milia *se obligaverit, non tamen tenebitur*. Pecuniam autem creditam dicimus non solum eam quam credendi causa damus, se*d* omnem quam tunc, *cum* contrahitur obligatio, certum est debitum iri, id est *quae* sine ulla condicione deducitur in obligationem. itaque et ea pecunia quam in diem certum dari stipulamur eodem numero est, quia certum es*t* eam debitum iri, licet post tempus petatur. Appellatione autem pecuniae omnes res in ea lege significantur. itaque si vinum vel frumentum, et si fundum vel hominem stipulemur, haec lex observanda est.

§ 124. The benefit of the lex Cornelia is available for all sureties, forbidding the same person to be surety for the same debtor to the same creditor in the same year for more than twenty thousand sesterces of liquidated debt; and if a sponsor or fidepromissor guarantees a larger sum, for instance, one hundred thousand sesterces, he can only be condemned in twenty thousand sesterces. Liquidated debt includes, besides money advanced, all money which at the time of contracting is certain to be due, that is, which depends on no condition. Accordingly, it includes money stipulated to be paid on a future day; for this is certain to be due, although at a future period. Money in this law includes everything, so that, if we stipulate for the conveyance of wine, or corn, or land, or a slave, the lex Cornelia applies.

§ 125. Ex quibusdam tamen causis permittit ea lex in infinitum satis accipere, veluti si do*t*is nomine, vel eius quod ex testamento tibi debeatur, aut iussu iudicis satis accipiatur. et adhuc lege vicesima hereditatium cavetur, ut ad eas satisdationes quae ex ea lege proponuntur lex Cornelia non pertineat.

§ 125. In some circumstances, however, the law permits a surety to be bound for an indefinite amount, as security for dower, for instance, or for a legacy, or by judicial order. Also the lex Julia imposing a duty of one twentieth on testamentary successions provides that the securities therein required shall be excepted from the scope of the lex Cornelia.

§ 126. In eo iure quoque iuris par condicio est omnium, sponso-

§ 126. The rights of sponsors, fidepromissors, and fidejussors are

rum, fidepromissorum, fideiussorum, quod ita obligari non possunt, ut plus debeant quam debet is pro quo obligantur. at ex diverso ut minus debeant, obligari possunt, sicut in adstipulatoris persona diximus. nam ut astipulatoris, ita et horum obligatio accessio est principalis obligationis, nec plus in accessione esse potest quam in principali re.

§ 127. In eo quoque par omnium causa est, quod si qui pro reo solverit, eius reciperandi causa habet cum eo mandati iudicium. et hoc amplius sponsores ex lege Publilia propriam habent actionem in duplum, quae appellatur depensi.

also identical in this respect, that they cannot be bound for more than their principal. They may, however, be bound for less, just as the adstipulator may stipulate for less. For their obligation, like that of the adstipulator, is an accessory of the principal obligation, and the accessory cannot be greater than the principal.

§ 127. They further resemble in this, that whoever pays for the principal can recover the amount from him by action of mandate. Sponsors by the lex Publilia have an additional remedy, being able, unless reimbursed in six months, to recover twice the sum advanced by the action on money paid by a sponsor.

§ 110. If there are several promisees who all interrogate, or several promisors who are all interrogated, before any answer is returned, there is only a single stipulation and a single obligation, though existing alternatively between different promisors and promisees. Each promisee is entitled to receive the whole (in solidum) and each promisor is bound to pay the whole, but the receipt of one promisee extinguishes the rights of the rest, and payment by one promisor exonerates the rest of liability. Under the old law an action brought against one promisor probably barred an action against the others, if the action was statutable, by novatio, if it was imperio continens, by exceptio (see 4 § 108): but Justinian enacted that co-promisors shall not be discharged by action brought against one unless complete satisfaction of the debt be recovered, Cod. 8, 41, 28. The promisee in a stipulation was called reus stipulandi, the promisor, reus promittendi. A plurality of promisees or promisors in a single stipulation were called conrei stipulandi or conrei promittendi.

But if a plurality of promisees receive separate answers or a plurality of promisors return separate answers, there is a plurality of stipulations and obligations, of which one is principal and the remainder accessory. An accessory promisee is called adstipulator, an accessory promisor is called adpromissor.

§ 114. The peculiarity of the rules respecting the adstipulator arise from the fact that he was a mandatary, agent, or trustee, the repositary of a special personal confidence. Hence his rights did not pass to his heres nor to his paterfamilias. Ordinary rules, however, obtained so far, that he could not sue so long as he remained a filiusfamilias, nor after his rights had been extinguished by a capitis diminutio. When the development of the law of mandate led to the frequent appointment of a procurator, the adstipulator ceased to be necessary except for securing performance of an act after the death of the principal promisee, § 117. He ceased to be necessary even for this purpose when a stipulation for an act after the death of the stipulant was decided to be valid, and accordingly the adstipulator has disappeared from the legislation of Justinian.

§ 115. The adpromissor at different epochs of the law appears as sponsor, fidepromissor, fidejussor. A sponsor could only intervene when both parties were Roman citizens, a fidepromissor was used when either party was a peregrinus, § 120. There is a striking parallelism between the rules relating to a sponsor or fidepromissor and those relating to an adstipulator. The obligation does not pass to the heres, and the stipulation of the sponsor or fidepromissor may be valid when that of the principal, though valid by Jus gentium, is by Civil law invalid; for instance, for a performance after the death of the principal promisee. The sponsor and fidepromissor can only be adjuncts to a stipulation, the fidejussor may be employed to guaranty any obligation.

§ 121. The lex Furia discharging the sponsor and fidepromissor of liability in two years and limiting the liability of each to a proportionate part, is supposed to have been enacted B.C. 95.

The epistle of Hadrian (A.D. 117–138) left the fidejussor liable by civil law to the whole debt, but allowed him to reduce his liability to a proportional part by an exceptio, of which the following passage appears to give the form: Si contendat fidejussor caeteros solvendo esse, etiam exceptionem ei dandam: Si non et illi solvendo sint, Dig. 46, 1, 28. 'The contention of a fidejussor that his co-fidejussors are solvent may be expressed in an exception: Unless such and such co-guarantors are solvent.'

§ 122. The lex Apuleia, which gave the sponsor or fidepromissor the action pro socio whereby he could recover by contribution from his co-guarantors whatever he had paid in excess of his proportionate share, was passed B.C. 102.

§ 123. For the illegible name of the law requiring the principal to give information of the amount of the debt and the number of co-sureties various guesses have been made by different critics—Porcia, Petreia, Cornelia, Pompeia, Apuleia.

§ 124. The lex Cornelia, the first which mentions the fidejussor as well as the sponsor and fidepromissor, limiting the amount for which the same guarantor could be bound in the same year for the same principal to the same guarantee, was passed in the dictatorship of Sylla, B.C. 81, and seems to show that the stringency of the lex Furia had led to a more frequent employment of the fidejussor in place of the sponsor and fidepromissor. The sponsor and fidepromissor have vanished from the legislation of Justinian.

§ 125. Perhaps for vicesima we should read vicesimaria or vicesimae. The lex Julia vicesimaria was a law of Augustus, imposing, in support of the military treasury, a succession duty of one twentieth of the value on the testamentary succession of all cives Romani.

§ 127. The lex Publilia, which enabled a sponsor who had paid the debt of his principal, unless reimbursed within six months, to recover by actio depensi, a form of manus injectio pro judicato (Gaius, 4 § 22), twice the amount of the original debt, is of uncertain date.

If a fidejussor, instead of claiming the reduction of his liability by division among the co-fidejussors under the epistle of Hadrian, was prepared to pay the whole debt, he could require the creditor to cede to him his actions against the principal debtor and the co-fidejussors, and then paying the creditor, not as surety (for then the debt and right of action would be extinguished), but as purchaser of the debt, he could be appointed procurator of the creditor (receive a power of attorney), and would be able to sue in the name of the creditor for his own benefit. Fidejussoribus succurri solet, ut stipulator compellatur ei qui solidum solvere paratus est, vendere ceterorum nomina, Dig. 46, 1, 17. 'Guarantors are relieved by the guarantee being compelled, if one is ready to pay the whole, to sell him the debt of the others.' Cum quis, et reum et fidejussores habens, ab uno ex fidejussoribus accepta pecunia, praestat actiones, poterit quidem dici nullas jam esse, quum suum perceperit et perceptione omnes liberati sint; sed non ita est; non enim in solutum accepit, sed quodammodo nomen debitoris vendidit, et ideo habet actiones, quia tenetur ad id ipsum ut praestet actiones, Dig.

46, 1, 36. 'When a creditor secured by guarantors receives the whole sum from one and cedes him his rights of action, it may be argued that the rights are extinguished because the claim of the creditor is satisfied and the satisfaction discharges the debtor and co-guarantors: but it is not so; for it is not in satisfaction but in purchase of the debt that the payment is made, and therefore the creditor retains the right of action and is bound to let the purchaser sue in his name.'

By the English law, if there be several co-guarantors, and one of them on the default of the principal pay the whole debt or more than his proportion of it, he may claim contribution against his co-guarantors, and recover for such excess above his proper share. But if there be three sureties, and one of them be insolvent, and a second pay the whole debt, at law he can only recover from the third his proportional share, that is, one third of the debt; but in equity he would recover one moiety.

The surety or guarantor, after payment of the debt, had formerly no right to insist that the debt or instrument by which the debt was evidenced should be assigned to him; for such assignment was held to be utterly useless, inasmuch as the debt was extinguished, and the instrument was worthless as an evidence of debt because proof of payment would be a conclusive answer to any claim depending thereupon. (The emptio nominis conceded to the Roman surety was not recognized.) Co-guarantors, however, were entitled in equity to all collateral securities which the guarantee or creditor might have taken. But by a recent enactment every surety who pays a debt is entitled to stand in the place of the creditor, and to have all the creditor's securities assigned to him; and no action upon them against the debtor or co-sureties can be barred by plea of payment by the surety.

A surety or guarantor of a debt may require the creditor to proceed against the principal first, provided he offer to indemnify him in such proceedings, and to pay any deficiency in the sum which he may recover.

The most noticeable rule of English law respecting the contract of guaranty is that it must be in writing. No action shall be brought whereby to charge the defendant upon any special promise to answer for the debt, default, or miscarriage of another person, unless the agreement upon which such action shall be brought, or some memorandum or note thereof, shall be in writing and signed by the party to be charged therewith, or some other person thereunto by him lawfully authorized, Statute of Frauds, 29 Charles II.

The general name of a stipulation by way of security for a debt is cautio. If the debtor alone was bound, it was called nuda repromissio. If sureties were also bound, it was called satisdatio or satisacceptio. Security might be given, not by stipulation, but by mandate, in which case the surety was called mandator, or by a convention called constitutum or pecunia constituta. A general name embracing all these kinds of surety was intercessor.

Before quitting the subject of suretyship we must observe a peculiar feature of Roman law, the incapacity of women to play the part of guarantors. This was enacted by the senatusconsultum Velleianum passed in the reign of Claudius, A.D. 46: Cujus senatusconsulti verba haec sunt: Quod Marcus Silanus et Velleius Tutor, consules, verba fecerunt de obligationibus feminarum quae pro aliis reae fierent, quid de ea re fieri oporteret, de ea re ita consuluerunt: Quod ad fidejussiones et mutui dationes pro aliis pro quibus intercesserint feminae pertinet [we should probably read, omitting the former pro, Quod ad fidejussiones et mutui dationes aliis, pro quibus intercesserint feminae, pertinet] tametsi ante videtur ita jus dictum esse, ne eo nomine ab his petitio neve in eas actio detur, quum eas virilibus officiis fungi et ejus generis obligationibus obstringi non sit aequum: arbitrari senatum, recte atque ordine facturos ad quos de ea re in jure aditum erit, si dederint operam ut in ea re senatus voluntas servetur, Dig. 16, 1, 2. 'On the question of the consuls Marcus Silanus and Velleius Tutor, how the liabilities of women who undertake to be responsible for the debts of others should be dealt with by the tribunals, it was resolved that guaranties of women and loans to others for whom women assume responsibility, though formerly held to be valid, shall not henceforth be valid to support any actions or suits against female guarantors, as manly functions and liabilities are not fairly chargeable on women, [and] the senate deem it incumbent on the judicature to see that their will in this matter is enforced.'

Though the senatusconsultum seems to say that no action shall be brought against a female guarantor, yet the frequent occurrence of the phrase, exceptio senatusconsulti Velleiani, shows that an action might be brought, but was barrable by an exception pleading the senatusconsult. This was probably owing to the doubt once entertained whether a senatusconsult had the force of a statute,

1 § 4, whether, that is to say, after the Sc. Velleianum, an intercessio by a woman was null and void at civil law.

DE LITTERARUM OBLIGATIONE.

§ 128. Litteris obligatio fit veluti in no*mini*bus transcripticiis. fit a*utem* nomen transcripticium duplici modo, vel a re in personam, vel a persona in person*am*.

§ 128. Literal contracts, or obligations created by writing, are exemplified by transcriptive entries of debit or credit in a journal. Transcriptive entries are of two kinds, either from thing to person or from person to person.

§ 129. *A re in personam tran*scriptio fit, veluti si id quod *tu* ex emptionis causa aut conductionis aut societatis mihi debeas, id expensum tibi tulero.

§ 129. Transcription from thing to person is exemplified when the sum which you owe me on a contract of sale or letting or partnership is debited to you in my journal as if you had received it as a loan.

§ 130. A persona in person*am* transcriptio fit, veluti si id quod mihi Titius debet tibi id expensum tulero, id est si Titius te delegaverit mihi.

§ 130. Of transcription from person to person we have an example when the sum which Titius owes me is entered in my journal as advanced to you, assuming that you are indebted to Titius and that Titius has substituted me for himself as your creditor.

§ 131. Alia causa est eorum nominum quae arcaria vocantur. in his enim re*i*, non litterarum obligatio consistit: quippe non aliter vale*nt*, quam si numerata sit pecunia; numeratio autem pecuniae rei, non *litterarum* facit obligationem. qua de causa recte dicemus arcaria nomina nullam facere obligationem, sed obligationis factae testimonium praebere.

§ 131. Transcriptive entries differ from mere entries of a person as debtor to cash; here the obligation is not Literal but Real, for money must have been actually paid, and payment of money constitutes a real not a Literal obligation. Consequently the entry of a person as debtor to cash does not constitute an obligation, but is evidence of an obligation.

§ 132. Unde proprie dicitur arcariis nominibus etiam peregrinos obligari, quia non ipso nomine, sed n*u*meratione pecuniae obligantur: quod genus obligationis iuris gentium est.

§ 132. Accordingly, debits to cash bind aliens as well as citizens, because it is not the entry in the journal but the payment of money that constitutes the contract, and this mode of obligation is common to all the world.

§ 133. tra*n*scripticiis vero nominibus an obligentur peregrini, merito quaeritur, quia quodammodo iuris civilis est talis obligatio: quod Nervae placuit. Sabino autem et Cassio

§ 133. Whether transcriptive debits form a contract binding on aliens has been doubted with some reason, for this contract is an institution of civil law, as Nerva held.

visum est, si a re in personam fiat nomen transcripticium, etiam peregrinos obligari: si vero a persona in personam, non obligari.

Sabinus and Cassius, however, held that transcription from thing to person forms a contract binding on an alien, though not transcription from person to person.

§ 134. Praeterea litterarum obligatio fieri videtur chirografis et syngrafis, id est si quis debere se aut daturum se scribat; ita scilicet, si eo nomine stipulatio non fiat. quod genus obligationis proprium peregrinorum est.

§ 134. Another Literal obligation is that created by chirographa and syngraphae, or written acknowledgments of debt or promises to pay, unaccompanied by stipulation. This mode of contract is proper to aliens.

One of the account books kept by the Romans, a nation of book-keepers, was a waste or day book, called Adversaria, into which all transactions were entered as they occurred. At the end of each month the contents of the Adversaria were posted into the more formal journal, the Tabulae, or Codex accepti et expensi. One page of this, as appears from Pliny, was devoted to the incomings, the other to the outgoings. Huic (Fortunae) omnia expensa, huic omnia feruntur accepta, et in tota ratione mortalium sola utramque paginam facit, Hist. Nat. 2, 7. 'Fortune is debited with everything and credited with everything, and, in the book-keeping of mortals, Fortune alone occupies both the pages.' According to Dionysius of Halicarnassus every Roman had to take an oath once in five years before the Censors that his book-keeping was honest and accurate.

One species of Literal obligation, namely Expensilation, in the nature of a novation or transformation of a pre-existing debt into one of a stricter form, was effected by an entry in these domestic registers, and from Cicero, Pro Roscio Comoedo, we may infer that the entry was binding even though it had not been transferred from the Adversaria to the Codex. The creditor, apparently, with the consent and by the order of the debtor, debited the latter with a certain sum in the books of the creditor (expensilatio). Afterwards a corresponding entry was made by the debtor in the books of the debtor (acceptilatio). The literal contract, however, appears to have been complete without the latter entry. Quod si ille suas proferet tabulas, proferet suas quoque Roscius. Erit in illius tabulis hoc nomen. At in hujus non erit. Cur potius illius quam hujus credetur? Scripsisset ille si non jussu hujus expensum tulisset? Non scripsisset hic quod sibi expensum ferri jussisset? Nam quemadmodum turpe est scribere quod non debeatur, sic improbum est non

referre quod debeas, Pro Roscio Comoedo, 1. 'If the plaintiff produces his journal, the defendant will produce his. The plaintiff's will contain the debt, the defendant's will not. Why should the plaintiff's be believed rather than the defendant's? Would the plaintiff, it may be said, have made the entry without the authority of the defendant? Would the defendant, it may be answered, have omitted to make a corresponding entry if he had given the authority? For as it is dishonest to make a false debit, so it is to suppress a true credit.' Deinde in codicis extrema cera nomen infimum in flagitiosa litura fecit: expensa Chrysogono servo H.S. sexcenta millia accepta pupillo Malleolo retulit, In Verrem, 2, 1, 36. 'At the bottom of the last page of the codex, over a damning erasure, Verres entered himself as debtor to his ward, Malleolus, in the sum of six hundred thousand sesterces, received by Chrysogonus, slave of Verres.'

The lender dictated to the borrower the entry to be made in the books of the borrower.

Scribe decem a Nerio. Non est satis. Adde Cicutae
Nodosi tabulas centum: mille adde catenas:
Effugiet tamen haec sceleratus vincula Proteus.
. . . Putidius multo cerebrum est, mihi crede Perilli
Dictantis quod tu nunquam rescribere possis.—Horace.

'Enter ten sestertia to the credit of Nerius. 'Tis not enough. Add covenants of Cicuta the knot-tier on a hundred pages; add a thousand chains: yet the wily Proteus will escape these bonds. . . . Greater far is the madness of Perillius [Nerius] to dictate credits which your debits can never balance.'

Apparently, the true contract was the entry in the creditor's book. The consent (jussus) of the debtor to this entry was necessary, but not restricted to any particular form. The entry in the debtor's book was evidence, but not the only admissible evidence, that he had assented to the entry in the creditor's book.

Theophilus, in his Greek version of the Institutes, gives the following account of the process: ἡ δὲ literis [ἐνοχὴ] ἐστὶ τὸ παλαιὸν χρέος εἰς καινὸν δάνειον μετασχηματιζόμενον ῥήμασι καὶ γράμμασι τυπικοῖς. . . . ἦν δὲ ταῦτα τὰ ῥήματα, ἅτινα καὶ ἐλέγετο καὶ ἐγράφετο· τοὺς ἑκατὸν χρυσοῦς, οὓς ἐμοὶ ἐξ αἰτίας μισθώσεως χρεωστεῖς, σὺ ἐκ συνθήκης καὶ ὁμολογίας δώσεις τῶν οἰκείων γραμμάτων; εἶτα ἐνεγράφετο, ὡς ἀπὸ τοῦ ἐνόχου ἤδη γενομένου ἐκ τῆς μισθώσεως, ταῦτα τὰ ῥήματα· Ἐκ τῆς συνθήκης ὀφείλω τῶν οἰκείων γραμμάτων. Καὶ ἡ μὲν προτέρα ἐνοχὴ ἀπεσβέννυτο, καινοτέρα δὲ ἐτίκτετο, Theophilus, 3, 21. 'A literal obligation was an old debt transformed into a new loan by certain solemn words and writings. The words which were spoken and written in the register were as follows: "The hundred aurei which you owe me on account of rent will you pay me on the convention and acknowledgment of your own journal?" Then followed, as if written by the person indebted for rent, these words: "I owe you that sum by the admission of my own journal." Whereby the pre-existing obligation was extinguished and a new one created.'

The account of Theophilus clearly only applies to one form of expensilation, the transcriptio a re in personam. The use of this kind of transcriptio is obvious: it was a mode of converting Formless contracts into Formal contracts—equitable obligations into civil obligations: of metamorphosing claims recoverable by actions ex bona fide, e.g. conducti locati, empti venditi, which in many points favoured the defendant, into debts recoverable by the short and sharp remedy of the civil action of Condictio, which, when brought for certa pecunia credita, was the more formidable to a dishonest litigant, as it was accompanied by sponsio poenalis, whereby the vanquished party forfeited a third of the sum in litigation, in addition, if he was the defendant, to the original claim, 4 § 171.

A narrative of Cicero shows the employment and possible misemployment of this transcriptio. He relates how a purchaser was defrauded by a vendor, and in consequence of the form of contract had no redress. Stomachari Canius. Sed quid faceret? Nondum enim Aquilius collega et familiaris meus protulerat de dolo malo formulas, De Off. 3, 14. 'The purchaser was indignant, but he was helpless, for my colleague Aquilius had not then invented the action of Fraud.' It may occur to us, on hearing the story, that as the actio Empti was an action ex bona fide, that is, one in which the judex was empowered to consider allegations of bad faith, the defrauded purchaser would not have been without a remedy. But, as Savigny points out, Cicero had guarded against this objection by a certain feature which he gives to the narrative. Emit homo cupidus et locuples tanti quanti Pythius voluit, et emit instructos. *Nomina facit*, negotium conficit. 'The purchaser was eager and rich, he bought at the price the seller named, and he bought the gardens ready furnished. The contract is by expensilatio; the business is concluded.' Nomen, which sometimes signifies any debt, is here used, in a specific sense, for a debt created by Literal contract; accordingly, nomina facit implies that the purchase, as soon as concluded, had been novated, § 176, i. e. extinguished by metamorphosis into a ledger debt; so that the transaction was removed from the domain of equity to that of civil law, which in its primitive simplicity had no provision for dolus malus.

Transcription a persona in personam was the substitution or exchange of a debt owed by C to B, in discharge of a debt owed by B to A; or, at all events, the substitution of C in lieu of B as debtor to A. It is impossible to form an exact conception of the mode in which these transcriptions were operated without a greater knowledge than we possess of the Roman method of book-keeping. A passage in the Digest implies that transcriptio a persona in personam was performed by the substituted debtor. Aliquando licet alienam obligationem suscipiat mulier, non adjuvatur hoc senatusconsulto. Quod tum accidit . . . . si hereditatem emerit et aes alienum hereditarium in se transcribat, Dig. 16, 1, 13. 'Some obligations of another may be assumed by a woman, notwithstanding the Sc. Velleianum, as, for instance, if she purchase a succession and debit herself with the sums due from the deceased.' Nomen facere, as we have just stated, is to contract a debt by literal obligation. Nomen signifies the name of the debtor, as in the line of Horace: Scriptos nominibus certis expendere nummos; 'Recorded on his ledger to lend moneys to solvent borrowers;' and in the following passage of the Digest: Si plures sint rei stipulandi, vel plures argentarii, quorum nomina simul facta sunt, unius loco numerabuntur, quia unum debitum est, Dig. 2, 14, 9. 'Several joint promisees in a stipulation, or several bankers in whose respective books the same debtor is contemporaneously debited with the same sum, count as one creditor in insolvency, because there is but one debt.' In the business of bankers (argentarii), whose book-keeping of course was extremely regular, the Literal contract appears to have survived when it had fallen into desuetude in other quarters.

In the time of Justinian both of the modes of Expensilatio, properly confined to Roman citizens, had become obsolete; but another form of Literal contract, the Syngrapha or Chirographum, available where either of the parties was an alien, was still in use. Syngrapha and Chirographum, apparently, are synonymous, and signify any contract in writing, such contract in Greece being always ground to support an action, whatever its subject or form.

The desuetude of Nomina transcriptitia was probably due to the invention of Constitutum, a Consensual contract, which answered the same purpose of converting an equitable obligation into an obligation of jus strictum, and which with its excessively penal sponsio, 4 § 171, gave the creditor even a more effective remedy than the action on Expensilatio (Condictio for pecunia certa credita).

Arcarium nomen was the record, not of a fictitious loan, like nomen transcripticium, but of the counting out of money from the cash-box (arca), that is, of a genuine loan, and was, accordingly, a memorandum of a Real obligation. The origin of the name is illustrated by the following passage: Quidam ad creditorem literas ejusmodi fecit: Decem quae Lucius Titius ex arca tua mutua acceperat, salva ratione usurarum, habes penes me, domine. Respondi, secundum ea quae proponerentur actione de constituta pecunia eum teneri, Dig. 13, 5, 26. 'A man wrote to a creditor as follows: "The ten sestertia which Lucius Titius received from your cash-box as a loan, and the interest thereupon, you have, my lord, in my hands. I advised that, upon the facts proposed, the action of guaranty, called constituta pecunia, would lie against the writer."'

The coexistence of Nomina Arcaria with Nomina Transcriptitia shows that entry in a Ledger did not operate a novation and convert a debt into a ledger debt, unless such effect was intended.

A stipulatio, unlike the entry in the journal or ledger, was not an invariable accompaniment of an advance of money (mutui datio, annumeratio); and, when it was employed simultaneously with annumeratio, unlike expensilatio, it always constituted the sole contract: there were not two contracts, a Real contract and a Verbal contract, but only a Verbal contract, and this without the intervention of Novation, Dig. 46, 2, 6, 1, and Dig. 46, 2, 7. Nam quoties, pecuniam mutuam dantes, eandem stipulamur, non duae obligationes nascuntur sed una verborum, Dig. 45, 126, 2. 'An advance accompanied by Stipulation does not produce two contracts, but one, a Verbal contract.'

Savigny thinks that personal execution (incarceration) of a judgment debtor (judicatus) was confined to actions brought on loans of money (annumeratio). This, if true, would account for a debt being sometimes left in its original form of a Real contract (mutuum), sometimes being converted into a Verbal contract (stipulatio) or Literal contract (expensilatio). When the interest of the borrower prevailed, the contract would take the form of stipulatio or expensilatio, with a milder remedy; when the interest of the lender predominated, the contract would retain the form of mutui datio, with its more stringent execution. But the doctrine of Savigny is not commonly adopted.

The exceptio doli mali or pecuniae non numeratae, throwing the burden of proof on the plaintiff, as we have stated in respect of verbal contracts, destroyed the effect of literal contracts for the five years or two years during which the exceptio could be pleaded. After this time, however, not only were formal Literal contracts binding, but any written admission of debt in whatever terms was conclusive against the writer. Sin autem cautio indebite exposita esse dicatur, et indiscrete loquatur, tunc eum in quem cautio exposita est compelli debitum esse ostendere quod in cautionem deduxit; nisi ipse specialiter qui cautionem exposuit causas explanavit pro quibus eandem conscripsit. Tunc enim stare eum oportet suae confessioni, nisi evidentissimis probationibus in scriptis habitis ostendere paratus sit, sese haec indebite promisisse, Dig. 22, 3, 25, 4. 'When a written acknowledgment of debt is alleged to be without consideration, if it does not specify the origin of the debt, the burden of proof is on the plaintiff; but if it specify the cause of debt, the defendant must stand by his admission, unless he has the clearest documentary evidence to prove the failure of consideration.'

The change in the law accounts for the changed meaning of cautio as we find it in Justinian's legislation. It originally signified a probative or evidentiary document, as opposed to a literal contract, and denoted the written memorandum which usually accompanied every contract, whether real, verbal, or consensual. It is often named, for instance, in connection with deposit, sale, stipulation, and other contracts. But in the Code and Digest we often also find it apparently equivalent to chirographum or some other kind of literal contract, binding simply by its form; e. g. Si quasi accepturi mutuam pecuniam adversario cavistis quae numerata non est, per condictionem obligationem repetere, etsi actor non petat, vel exceptione non numeratae pecuniae adversus agentem uti potestis, Cod. 4, 30, 7. 'If you gave your adversary an acknowledgment of debt in contemplation of a loan which was not advanced, you may force him by action to deliver up the obligation if he delays to sue upon it, or may bar his claim by exception of money not advanced if he sues.' It would be necessary to have the instrument surrendered, because after two years it would be conclusive evidence of debt.

It may assist us in understanding the distinction of Formless and Formal contracts, Verbal and Literal, if, before we quit this subject, we cast a hasty glance at the corresponding institutions of English law.

In the eye of the English law, contracts are either Simple (parol), that is, enforceable only on proof of consideration, or Special, that is, binding by the solemnity of their form. Special contracts are either contracts under Seal or contracts of Record. A common species of Deed, or written contract under seal, is the Bond or Obligation, which, like Stipulatio, is used to secure the payment of money or performance of any other act, and, like Stipulatio, either binds the debtor alone or the debtor and sureties. It consists of an obligatory part or penal clause, and a condition added, that if the obligor does some particular act the obligation shall be void, but else shall remain in full force.

Contracts of Record are either Recognizances or Judgment debts.

A Recognizance is an acknowledgment before a court or magistrate that a man owes the Queen or a private plaintiff (as the case may be) a certain sum of money, with a condition avoiding the obligation to pay if he shall do some particular act, as, if he shall appear at the assizes, keep the peace, pay a certain debt, or the like. A Recognizance resembles Stipulation in its form, being entered into by oral interrogation and answer, but differs in that it can only be taken before a court or magistrate duly authorized, whereas stipulatio was transacted between private parties.

A Judgment debt, or debt due by the judgment of a court of record, is sometimes the result of a judgment in an adverse suit, but sometimes it is merely a form of written contract, and may be entered into in various ways. A fictitious action is brought, and the party to be bound either makes no reply, or fails to instruct his attorney, or confesses the action and suffers judgment to be at once entered up; or the party to be bound consents to a judge's order authorizing the plaintiff to enter up judgment and issue execution against him, either at once and unconditionally, or on a future day conditionally on non-payment of whatever amount may be agreed upon; or the party to be bound gives a warrant of attorney, that is, authority to an attorney to confess an action of debt or suffer judgment to go by default, the warrant being accompanied by a defeazance declaring it to be merely a security for payment of a certain sum and interest, and providing that no execution shall issue unless default in the payment shall have been made.

The conjunction of a penal clause and a condition avoiding it is common to the judgment debt, recognizance, bond, and stipulation. The Roman Nexum, as we have stated, had apparently the effect of a Judgment debt.

DE CONSENSU OBLIGATIONE.

§ 135. Consensu fiunt obligationes in emptionibus et venditionibus, locationibus conductionibus, societatibus, mandatis.

§ 135. Consent creates a contract in purchase and sale, letting and hiring, partnership, agency.

§ 136. Ideo autem *istis* modis consensu dicimus obligationes contrahi, *quia* neque verborum neque scripturae ulla proprietas desideratur, sed sufficit eos qui negotium gerunt consensisse. unde inter absentes quoque talia negotia contrahuntur, veluti per epistulam aut per internuntium, cum alioquin verborum obligatio inter absentes fieri non possit.

§ 136. In these contracts consent is said to create the obligation, because no form of words or of writing (nor any delivery) is required, but the consent of the parties is sufficient. Absent parties, therefore, can form these contracts; for instance, by letter or messenger; whereas in Verbal contracts presence is necessary.

§ 137. Item in his contractibus alter alteri obligatur de *eo* quod alterum alteri ex bono et aequo praestare oportet, cum alioquin in verborum obligationibus alius stipuletur, alius promittat, et in nominibus alius expensum ferendo obliget, alius obligetur.

§ 137. Further, these contracts are bilateral, that is, both parties incur a reciprocal obligation to perform whatever is fair and equal; whereas Verbal and Literal contracts (and the Real contract of mutuum) are unilateral, that is, confer only a right on one party, and impose only an obligation on the other.

§ 138. Sed absenti expensum ferri potest, etsi verbis obligatio cum absente contrahi non possit.

§ 138. Absence is no impediment to Literal contracts, though it is to Verbal.

Besides the four Consensual contracts which are named in the text, certain praetorian and statutory conventions, though not denominated contracts, were enforceable by action. Examples of praetorian pacts, or pacts enforced by the praetor, are hypotheca, which we have already mentioned in connection with pignus, and constituta pecunia, which we mentioned when treating of stipulation, as a form of consensual guaranty. An instance of statutory pact, or pact made valid by statute, is donatio inter vivos. It was irrevocable, and the donor could be forced by action to perform his promise. Perficiuntur autem [donationes inter vivos] cum donator suam voluntatem scriptis aut sine scriptis manifestaverit. Et ad exemplum venditionis nostra constitutio eas etiam in se habere necessitatem traditionis voluit, ut etiamsi non tradantur, habeant plenissimum robur et perfectum, et traditionis necessitas incumbat donatori, Inst. 2, 7, 2. 'Donations inter vivos are complete when the donor's intention, whether written or unwritten, has been signified. And, like a sale, they involve the necessity of delivery, so that before delivery they are perfectly valid, and delivery can be recovered by action from the donor.'

We have stated above that conventions are either unilateral or bilateral. The only unilateral conventions are mutuum, stipulatio, expensilatio. The actions founded on these were actions stricti juris, of strict civil law; for, though Mutuum was an institute of Jus gentium, it was an institute which the civil law protected with all its rigour. Examples of bilateral, otherwise called synallagmatic, conventions, are venditio, locatio, societas. Certain other contracts, namely, depositum, commodatum, pignus, mandatum, are called imperfectly bilateral, because they do not originally and necessarily produce any reciprocal (ultro citroque) obligation, but only ex postfacto, i. e. in consequence of some event subsequent to the convention. Bilateral and imperfectly bilateral conventions give rise to equitable actions, or actions ex fide bona. The action founded on the original obligation of an imperfectly bilateral contract, i. e. the action of the depositor, lender for use, pawnor, principal, is called judicium directum; the action founded on the accidental and subsequent obligation, i. e. the action of the depositary, borrower for use, pawnee, agent, is called judicium contrarium.

The form of an intentio in an equitable suit is given by Gaius, 4 § 47. Quidquid ob eam rem Numerium Negidium Aulo Agerio dare facere oportet EX FIDE BONA, ejus judex Numerium Negidium Aulo Agerio condemnato. From 3 § 137 we may infer that instead of ex fide bona we might substitute the words ex bono et aequo.

DE EMPTIONE ET VENDITIONE.

§ 139. *Emptio et venditio contrahitur* cum de pretio convenerit, quamvis nondum pretium numeratum sit, ac ne arra quidem data

§ 139. The contract of purchase and sale is complete as soon as the price is agreed upon and before the price or any earnest money is paid. The

fuerit. nam quod arrae nomine datur argumentum est emptionis et venditionis contractae.

earnest money is merely evidence of the completion of the contract.

§ 140. Pretium autem certum esse debet: alioquin si ita inter eos convenerit, ut quanti Titius rem aestimaverit, tanti sit em*pt*a, Labeo negavit ullam vim hoc negotium habere; *quam sententiam* Cassius probat: Ofilius et eam empt*ionem putat et ven*ditionem; cuius opinionem Proculus secutus est.

§ 140. The price must be certain. If there is an agreement to purchase at a price to be fixed by Titius, Labeo and Cassius say the contract is invalid, Ofilius and Proculus say it is valid.

§ 141. *Item* pretium in numerata pecunia consistere debet. *nam* in ceteris rebus an pretium esse possit, veluti homo aut toga aut fundus alterius rei *pretium esse possit*, valde quaeritur. nostri praeceptores putant etiam in alia re posse consistere pretium; unde illu*d* est quod vulgo putant per permutationem rerum emptionem et venditionem contrahi, eamque speciem emptionis e*t* venditioni*s* vetustissimam esse; argumentoque utuntur Graeco poeta Homero qui aliqua parte sic ai*t*:

Ἔνθεν ἄρ' οἰνίζοντο καρηκομόωντες Ἀχαιοί,
Ἄλλοι μὲν χαλκῷ, ἄλλοι δ' αἴθωνι σιδήρῳ,
Ἄλλοι δὲ ῥινοῖς, ἄλλοι δ' αὐτῇσι βόεσσιν,
Ἄλλοι δ' ἀνδραπόδεσσιν.

Diversae scholae auctores dissentiunt, aliu*d*que esse existimant permutationem rerum, aliu*d* emptionem et venditionem: alioquin *non posse* rem expediri permutatis rebus, quae videatur res venisse e*t quae* pretii nomine data esse; sed rursus utramque videri et venisse et utramque pretii nomine datam esse absurdum videri. Se*d ai*t Caelius Sabinus, si rem Ti*tio* venalem habent*e*, veluti fundum, acceperim, et pretii nomine hominem forte dederim, fundum quidem videri venisse, hominem autem pretii nomine datum esse, *ut* fund*us* acciperetur.

§ 141. The price should be in money, for it is much disputed whether anything but money, such as a slave, a robe, a piece of land, can be treated as price. My school hold the affirmative, and regard exchange as a species, and the oldest species, of purchase and sale; in support of which they quote the lines of Homer:

'Here touched Achaean barks in quest of wine.
They purchased it with copper and with steel,
With hides, with horned cattle, and with slaves.'

The other school maintain the negative, and distinguish between exchange and purchase and sale, because in exchange we cannot determine which is the thing sold and which is the price, and both things cannot be regarded as both the thing sold and the price. Caelius Sabinus says that if Titius offers, say, land for sale, and I give him a slave for it, the thing sold is the land and the price is the slave.

It is necessary to distinguish clearly between the completion of a contract of sale and the subsequent transmutation of property; between the creation of a jus in personam and the creation of a jus in rem; between the acquisition of an obligation and the acquisition of ownership.

The contract is complete as soon as the price is agreed upon, but no property passes until the price is paid and possession is delivered, or, in the case of a sale on credit, until possession is delivered. Quod vendidi et tradidi non aliter fit accipientis quam si, aut pretium nobis solutum sit, aut satis eo nomine factum, vel etiam fidem habuerimus emptori sine ulla satisfactione, Dig. 18, 1, 19. 'Sale and delivery do not pass property unless the price is paid, or security is given for the price, or credit is given without security.' Venditae vero et traditae res non aliter emptori acquiruntur quam si is venditori pretium solverit, vel alio modo ei satisfecerit, velut expromissore aut pignore dato . . . sed si is qui vendidit fidem emptoris secutus fuerit, dicendum est statim rem emptoris fieri, Inst. 2, 1, 41. 'Sale and delivery do not pass property, unless the vendee pays the price, or gives the vendor security; for instance, by a guarantor discharging the vendee, or by mortgage. If, however, the sale is on credit, ownership immediately passes.'

By English law, if the contract is for the sale of SPECIFIC goods, ready for delivery, there is no distinction between the jus in personam and the jus in rem; the contract is complete and the property passes at one and the same moment.

If the sale is on credit, property passes immediately upon the striking of the bargain or understanding as to terms, even before delivery of the goods.

If the sale is for ready money, there must be a delivery or tender of the whole of the goods or price, or delivery and acceptance of part of the goods or price, before there is any contract, and at the same moment the property is transmuted from the vendor to the vendee.

If the contract is not for the purchase of *specific* goods, but of goods of a certain nature or class, there arises a distinction between property and obligation; for, though the contract is complete, no property passes until the particular goods are ascertained by delivery.

In the sale of land the equitable estate is conveyed by the contract to convey; the legal estate is only passed by the subsequent deed. Formerly the deed was a Feoffment which was inoperative without livery of seisin, that is, delivery of possession; but now the deed of Grant passes property without delivery of possession.

By the Code Napoleon delivery is requisite for the transfer of property in movables, but property in immovables is transferred as soon as the contract is complete.

By Roman law, the goods are at the risks of the purchaser as soon as the contract is complete, and before the property is transmuted. The formula, res perit domino, therefore, does not apply to the contract of purchase and sale, but only to the contracts of mutuum and commodatum.

In English law, the risk always belongs to the person in whom the property resides, and the maxim, res perit domino, is applicable to sales.

§ 139. Arrha, as a general rule, was evidence of the completion of contract, but not always, at least in the time of Justinian. If the parties so agreed, arrha was only a penal sum, whose forfeiture entitled either negotiator to recede from a negotiation or rescind a completed contract, Cod. 4, 21, 17. In the absence of such special agreement, in default of voluntary performance, performance could be enforced by action, and forfeiture of the arrha was cumulative upon and additional to specific performance: the vendee, if he was in default, could not reckon the arrha as part of the purchase-money; and the vendor, if in default, besides delivery of possession and repayment of the arrha, was compelled to pay an equal sum to the vendee.

In English law, the earnest is not an evidence of a contract, but, where it occurs, an essential part of the contract, which, therefore, is not Consensual, but Real.

§ 140. Where the price is left to be fixed by an arbitrator, Justinian enacted, in conformity with the opinion of Proculus, that the contract is binding if the arbitrator makes his valuation.

§ 141. After the time of Gaius, a constitution of Diocletian and Maximian (A.D. 286–305), conformably to the opinion of Proculus, declares exchange or barter to be a Real contract. Ex placito permutationis, nulla re secuta, constat nemini actionem competere, Cod. 4, 64, 3. 'An agreement to exchange without part execution cannot support an action.' Accordingly, we have mentioned it as belonging to the miscellaneous class of contracts Real innominate.

The obligation of the vendor was not to transfer quiritarian ownership (ut rem emptoris faciat), but merely to secure the vendee in undisturbed enjoyment (ut praestet habere licere) of the article sold, that is, to give him vacant possession and guarantee him against eviction. Accordingly, if the vendee is judicially molested in his possession, he summons his vendor to defend his title, and, if evicted, recovers against his vendor the loss he has sustained. Venditor si ejus rei quam vendiderit dominus non sit, pretio accepto, auctoritati manebit obnoxius, Paul. Sent. rec. 2, 17, 1. 'A vendor, not proprietor, on receipt of the purchase-money is liable as warrantor.' Auctoritas est actio pro evictione, Dig. 22, 2, 76. 'Auctoritas is an action on eviction against the vendor.' Caia Seia fundum a Lucio Titio emerat et, quaestione mota fisci nomine, auctorem laudaverat, et, evictione secuta, fundus ablatus et fisco adjudicatus est, venditore praesente. Quaeritur, cum emptrix non provocaverit, an venditorem possit convenire. Herennius Modestinus respondit: Sive, quod alienus fuerit quum veniret, sive, quod tunc obligatus, evictus est, nihil proponi cur emptrici adversus venditorem actio non competat, Dig. 21, 2; 73, 1. 'Caia Seia bought an estate of Lucius Titius, and being sued by the imperial treasury, vouched the vendor to warrant her title, and was evicted in his presence. Consulted, whether, by not appealing, the purchaser had lost her action for breach of warranty, Modestinus advised that, whether evicted by a proprietor or by a mortgagee, there was nothing in the facts proposed to deprive the purchaser of her remedy against the vendor.'

A sale was often accompanied by stipulations binding the vendor to repay twice the purchase-money in case of eviction, or in case the article sold was returned for unsoundness (duplae stipulatio). In the absence of express warranty the English law, applying the rule of Caveat emptor, except in the sale for a fair price of goods in the possession of the vendor, refuses to assume an implied warranty or covenant of title, or, except in certain exceptional circumstances, to assume an implied warranty of the goodness or soundness of the articles sold. But by Roman law, in the absence of such stipulations, warranty of the title and quality of the goods was held to be inherent in the contract of sale. In the case of faults of quality the purchaser could either recover part of the purchase-money by actio aestimatoria, or rescind the contract by actio redhibitoria.

By English law mere inadequacy of price affords no ground for setting aside a sale, unless it be so gross as to afford a necessary presumption of fraud and imposition, and then a court of equity will grant relief. By Roman law a vendor could rescind a contract for the sale of land on proof that the purchase-money was only half the value, Cod. 4, 44, 2.

Peculiar to the English law of sale is the provision of the Statute of Frauds, that contracts for the sale of lands must be in writing signed by the party to be charged, and contracts for the sale of goods for the price of £10 and upwards are not good unless in writing signed by the party to be charged, or unless the buyer accept and receive part of the goods, or unless he give something in part payment or in earnest to bind the bargain.

So far as delivery or payment is essential to the completion of the contract of sale, it is clear that the contract is not Consensual, but Real.

DE LOCATIONE ET CONDUCTIONE.

§ 142. Locatio autem et conductio similibus regulis constituuntur: nisi enim merces certa statuta sit, non videtur locatio et conductio contrahi.

§ 143. Unde si alieno arbitrio merces permissa sit, velut qua*n*ti Titius aestimaveri*t*, quaeritur an locatio et conductio contrahatur. qua de causa si fulloni polienda curandave, sarcinatori sarcienda vestimenta dederim, nulla statim mercede constituta, postea tantum daturus quanti inter nos convenerit, quaeritur an locatio et conductio contrahatur.

§ 144. Vel si rem tibi utendam dederim et invicem aliam rem utendam acceperim, quaeritur an locatio et conductio contrahatur.

§ 145. Adeo autem emptio et venditio et locatio et conductio familiaritatem aliquam inter se habere videntur, ut in quibusdam causis quaeri soleat utrum emptio et venditio contrahatur, an locatio et conductio. veluti si qua res in perpetuum locata sit, quod evenit in praediis municipum quae ea lege locantur, ut quamdiu id vectigal

§ 142. Letting and hiring are governed by rules like those of purchase and sale. Unless the sum to be paid as hire is fixed, the contract is not complete.

§ 143. And if the hire is to be fixed by an arbitrator, for instance, at the sum which Titius shall consider fair, it is a question whether there is a contract of letting and hiring. Accordingly, if I give clothes to a fuller to clean or finish, or to a tailor to mend, and the remuneration is not fixed at the time, but left to our subsequent agreement, it is a question whether there is a contract of letting and hiring.

§ 144. The same question arises if I lend a thing for use and receive in return the loan for use of another thing.

§ 145. Purchase and sale are so nearly akin to letting and hiring that in some cases it is a question under which category a contract falls; for instance, when land is leased in perpetuity, as occurs with the land of municipalities, which is leased on the condition that, so long as the rent is paid, the lessee and his heirs shall continue in pos-

praestetur, neque ipsi conductori neque heredi eius praedium auferatur; sed magis placuit locationem conductionemque esse.

session. But here the better opinion is that the contract is one of letting and hiring.

§ 146. Item si gladiatores ea lege tibi tradiderim, ut in singulos qui integri exierint pro sudore denarii XX mihi darentur, in eos vero singulos qui occisi aut debilitati fuerint, denarii mille: quaeritur utrum emptio et venditio, an locatio et conductio contrahatur. et magis placuit eorum qui integri exierint locationem et conductionem contractam videri, et eorum qui occisi aut debilitati sunt emptionem et venditionem esse: idque ex accidentibus apparet, tamquam sub condicione facta cuiusque venditione an locatione. iam enim non dubitatur, quin sub condicione res veniri aut locari possint.

§ 146. If a band of gladiators are delivered on the following terms, that is to say, that for the performance of every one who leaves the arena safe and sound there shall be paid twenty denarii, and for every one who is killed or disabled there shall be paid one thousand denarii, it is disputed whether the contract is one of purchase and sale or of letting and hiring; but the better opinion is that the unharmed were let and hired, the killed or disabled were bought and sold, the contracts depending on contingent events, and each gladiator being the subject of a conditional hiring and a conditional sale, for it is certain that both hiring and sale may be conditional.

§ 147. Item quaeritur, si cum aurifice mihi convenerit, ut is ex auro suo certi ponderis certaeque formae anulos mihi faceret, et acciperit verbi gratia denarios CC, utrum emptio et venditio, an locatio et conductio contrahatur. Cassius ait materiae quidem emptionem venditionem contrahi, operarum autem locationem et conductionem. sed plerisque placuit emptionem et venditionem contrahi. atqui si meum aurum ei dedero, mercede pro opera constituta, convenit locationem conductionem contrahi.

§ 147. Again, if a goldsmith agrees to make me rings of a certain weight and fashion out of his own gold for, say, two hundred denarii, it is a question whether the contract is purchase and sale or letting and hiring. Cassius says the material is bought and sold, the labour is let and hired, but most writers hold that there is only a purchase and sale. If I provide the gold and agree to pay him for his work, the contract is clearly a letting and hiring.

§ 143. Justinian decided that a hiring for a sum to be fixed by an arbitrator was valid, like a sale on similar terms, if the arbitrator made his award; but that if the sum was left to the future agreement of the parties, or, § 144, if the consideration was not pecuniary but a reciprocal service, the convention was not a Consensual one of letting and hiring, but a Real contract innominate, deriving its validity from part execution, and to be enforced by the action in factum praescriptis verbis, Inst. 3, 24, 1.

§ 145. Where Gaius speaks of ager vectigalis, Justinian speaks of ager emphyteuticus or emphyteuticarius, because in his days the rules of these two kinds of tenure had been entirely assimilated. Ager vectigalis was land leased by the Roman people, or a municipality, or a sacerdotal college, or the Vestal Virgins, for various terms of years, for a rent either in money or in produce, usually amounting to one fifth or one seventh of the profits. Emphyteusis was the grant of land in perpetuity, or for a term of years, for an annual rent, subject to forfeiture, without claim for meliorations, on non-payment of rent by the emphyteuta for three years, or for two years if the land was held of the church. Land held in emphyteusis was alienable, devisable, descendible by intestacy. The proprietor, however, had a right of pre-emption, and a fine for admission of a devisee or alienee of one fiftieth of the value, Cod. 4, 66; Novella, 120.

Emphyteusis resembled locatio in that the property remained in the grantor; it resembled venditio in that the grantee acquired not only detention of the land granted, like the hirer (colonus), but also possession, properly so called, and a proprietary right (jus in re, or, servitude) that nearly amounted to property or dominion, and could be maintained by vindicatio or real action against all the world, including the nude or nominal proprietor.

Zeno (A.D. 475–491) decided that Emphyteusis was a contract sui generis, distinct from both locatio and venditio, and requiring for its validity to be reduced to writing, Cod. 4, 66. Compare a similar provision of the English Statute of Frauds for all contracts relating to land.

Like pignus, emphyteusis is a combination of jus in personam and jus in rem, the one created by convention in writing, the other by tradition.

§ 146. Gladiators were either (1) prisoners of war, 'butchered to make a Roman holiday,' or slaves who had committed some offence, 1 § 13, or criminals under a capital sentence; or (2) freemen who voluntarily adopted the profession and hired themselves out (auctorati, 3 § 199) to persons who maintained troops or companies (ludi, familiae) of gladiators, either to make a profit, or to win the favour of the public, by their exhibition. The first gladiatorial show at Rome was exhibited B.C. 264. The passion of the populace for these exhibitions in the palmy days of Rome amounted to a mania; and a vast revolution in public sentiment was implied in their suppression, A.D. 325, by the following constitution of Constantine: Cruenta spectacula in otio civili et domestica quiete non placent; quapropter omnino gladiatores esse prohibemus, Cod. 11, 43. 'Bloody spectacles are out of place in the reign of law and the peaceful bosom of a fatherland; and gladiatorial shows, therefore, are absolutely prohibited.'

Locator denotes the person who furnishes land or a house or other article to be used by another; conductor is the person who takes the land or house (called colonus in the first case, inquilinus in the second) or other article and pays a price in money for its use. But in the case of opus faciendum, e.g. of a building to be constructed, or an article to be manufactured, the person who pays the price, that is to say, the employer or orderer, is called locator; the person who performs the work or construction and receives the price is called conductor. It may be worth inquiring how this anomaly arose, and what led to this inversion of the meanings of these correlative terms, and we shall find it in a certain incident common to these and other conventions, and which has induced the English law to regard them as composing a single class and to denote them by a common denomination.

Deposit, loan for use, pawn or pledge, letting and hiring, and mandate, are grouped together in English law under the head of Bailments. Bailment, derived from the French word bailler, 'to deliver,' is defined to be a delivery of a chattel (movable) in trust for a specific purpose; or, at greater length, a delivery of goods on a condition that they shall be restored by the bailee to the bailor, or according to his direction, as soon as the purpose for which they were bailed shall be answered. These contracts, then, all imply a delivery from the bailor to the bailee and a redelivery from the bailee to the bailor or his order. Now in locatio-conductio operis faciendi, there is usually a delivery and a redelivery: for instance, goods are delivered to an innkeeper to be kept, or to a carrier to be transported, or materials are delivered to a manufacturer to be fashioned, and these goods and materials are to be redelivered at another time, or in another place, or in an altered form. It is this delivery and redelivery to which the Latin language always looks exclusively in fixing on the persons to be denoted respectively by the words locator and conductor; and, accordingly, by locator it denotes the bailor, and by conductor the bailee, without regarding the fact that while in locatio-conductio rei or operarum the locator supplies a service for which the conductor pays the price, in locatio-conductio operis faciendi it is the locator who pays the price and the conductor who performs the service.

Colonus, or the independent person who entered into a contract of locatio-conductio respecting land, must be distinguished from the colonus who mainly composed the agricultural population under the empire. Colonatus, the condition of the latter colonus, is an institution whose origin is obscure, but which probably began to be common as early as A.D. 200. Colonatus was not a mere obligation or jus in personam, but a real right or jus in rem, and may be regarded as a new form of dependent status, a condition of subjection to a superior, which may be classified with the status of familia or domestic relations. It was a condition midway between freedom and slavery. The colonus was liber and civis, but he was called by the lawgiver servus terrae. He was inseparably bound to the soil: a fugitive colonus, like a fugitive slave, was said to commit a theft of his own body, and he could be recovered by real action (vindicatio) from any one who gave him harbour. He had property, but it was called peculium, and, though he could not be deprived of it like the slave, yet he could not aliene it without the consent of his lord. With certain exceptions, he could not maintain an action against his lord, who was called his patronus. Neither a colonus nor his descendants could divest themselves of their hereditary serfdom. The colonus, having no Real right in the soil, paid no land tax, but only a personal or capitation tax, like artisans and slaves. As having an inherited condition, the colonus or inquilinus was called originarius; as subject to the capitation tax he was called tributarius, capite censitus, adscriptitius, censibus adscriptus. He paid to his lord a certain annual rent (canon), usually in kind, and always incapable of augmentation. This fixity of his rent was the principal right which he enjoyed. See Savigny's Vermischte Schriften, 15.

DE SOCIETATE.

§ 148. Societatem coire solemus aut totorum bonorum, aut unius alicuius negotii, veluti mancipiorum emendorum aut vendendorum.

§ 148. A partnership either extends to all the goods of the partners or is confined to a single business, for instance, the purchase and sale of slaves.

§ 149. Magna autem quaestio fuit, an ita coiri possit societas, ut quis maiorem partem lucretur, mi-

§ 149. It has been much canvassed whether the law would recognize a partnership formed on

norem damni praestet. quod Quintus Mucius etiam *contra naturam societatis esse censuit; sed Servius Sulpicius, cuius* praevaluit sententia, adeo ita coiri posse societatem existimavit, ut dixerit illo quoque modo coiri posse, ut quis nihil omnino damni praestet, se*d* lucri partem capiat, si modo opera eius tam pretiosa videatur, ut ae*qu*um sit eum cum hac pactione in societatem admitti. nam et ita posse coire societatem constat, ut unus pecuniam conferat, alter non conferat, et tamen lucrum inter eos *com*mune sit; saepe enim opera alicuius pro pecunia valet.

the terms that a partner should have a greater share in the profit than he has in the loss. Quintus Mucius thought such an arrangement contrary to the nature of partnership, but Servius Sulpicius, whose opinion has prevailed, held that such a partnership was so far from invalid that a partnership might be formed on the terms that a partner should have a share in the gains and none in the losses, if the value of his services made such an arrangement fair. It is certain that a partnership may be formed on the terms that one partner shall contribute all the capital and that the gains shall be divided equally, for a man's services may be equivalent to capital.

§ 150. Et illu*d* certum est, si de partibus lucri et damni nihil inter eos convenerit, tamen aequis ex partibus commodum *e*t incommodum inter eos commune esse. sed si in altero partes expressae fuerint velut in lucro, in altero vero omissae, in eo quoque quod omissum est similes partes erunt.

§ 150. If no agreement has been made as to the division of the profit and loss, it must be in equal shares. If the shares are expressed in the event of profit but not in the event of loss, the loss must be divided in the same proportions as the profit.

§ 151. Manet autem societas eousque, donec in eodem sensu perseverant: at cum aliquis renuntiaverit societati, societas solvitur. sed plane si quis in hoc renuntiaverit societati, ut obveniens aliquod lucrum solus habeat, veluti si mihi totorum bonorum socius, cum ab aliquo heres esset relictus, in hoc ren*un*t*ia*verit *so*cietati, ut hereditatem solus lucrifaciat, cogetur hoc lucrum communicare. si quid vero aliu*d* lucri fecerit quod non captaverit, ad ipsum solum pertinet. mihi vero, quidquid omnino post renuntiatam societatem adquiritur, soli conceditur.

§ 151. The continuance of partnership depends on the continuing consent of the members: the renunciation of one dissolves the partnership. If, however, the object of a partner in renouncing the partnership is to monopolise some accruing gain; if, for instance, a partner in all goods succeeds to an inheritance and renounces the partnership in order to have exclusive possession of the inheritance, he will be compelled to divide this gain with his partners; but what he gains undesignedly he keeps to himself; and his partner always has exclusive benefit of whatever accrues to him after the renunciation.

§ 152. Solvitur adhuc societas etiam morte socii; quia qui societatem *contrahit* cert*am* personam sibi eligit.

§ 152. Dissolution of partnership is also produced by the death of a partner, for he who enters into partnership elects a determinate

person with whom he is willing to be partner.

§ 153. Dicitur et capitis diminutione solvi societatem, quia civili ratione capitis diminutio morti *aequiparari* dicitur: *sed* si *ad*huc *consentiant* in societat*em*, nova videtur incipere societas.

§ 153. Loss of status also determines partnership, because in the civil law loss of status is regarded as equivalent to death; but if the members still consent to be partners, a new partnership commences.

§ 154. Item si cuius ex sociis bona publice aut privatim venierint, solvitur societas. sed h*oc quoque casu* societas de *qua* loquimur *nova* consensu contrahitur nudo; iuris *enim* gen*tium obligationes contrahere* omnes homines naturali ratione *possunt*.

§ 154. Again, the sale of all the property of one of the partners, whether by the state or by private creditors, dissolves the partnership; but here also a new partnership may be formed by mere consent, for contracts of natural law are within the capacity of all men [even after loss of civitas, or capitis minutio media].

§ 148. In the absence of express convention a partnership is limited to gains by commercial transactions (universorum quae ex quaestu veniunt) and excludes gains by inheritance, devise, donation. A remarkable incident of unlimited partnership (universorum bonorum) was the transmutation of property operated by mere convention without delivery. In societate omnium bonorum omnes res quae coeuntium sunt continuo communicantur; quia licet specialiter traditio non interveniat, tacita tamen creditur intervenire, Dig. 17, 2, 1, 1. 'In partnership of all goods, the property of all the members becomes forthwith common, a constructive delivery being implied in the absence of actual delivery.' This rule was not applied to other forms of partnership.

§ 149. Although a partner might be exempt by the terms of the convention from any share in the losses, yet a convention that a partner should have no share in the gains was called a leonine convention, and being devoid of consideration could not be enforced. Aristo refert, Cassium respondisse, societatem talem coiri non posse, ut alter lucrum tantum, alter damnum sentiret, et hanc societatem leoninam solitum appellare, et nos consentimus, Dig. 17, 2; 29, 2. 'Aristo records the decision of Cassius that a partnership on the terms that one should take all the profits and another bear all the loss, which he called a leonine partnership, is not binding, and Ulpian concurs.'

§ 153. Of the three kinds of capitis minutio, maxima, media, and minima, that is to say, loss of libertas, loss of civitas, loss of

domestic status, only capitis minutio maxima and media operate a dissolution of partnership. Societas quemadmodum ad heredes socii non transit, ita nec ad arrogatorem, ne alioquin invitus quis socius efficiatur cui non velit; ipse autem arrogatus socius permanet; nam etsi filiusfamilias emancipatus fuerit, permanebit socius, Dig. 17, 2; 65, 11. 'Partnership passes neither to the heir nor to the adrogator of a partner, otherwise it might be involuntary; but an independent person who becomes dependent by adrogation, and a filiusfamilias who becomes independent by enfranchisement, continue partners.'

§ 154. The forced sale of a person's whole estate might be the result of either a criminal or a civil proceeding, either condemnation for crime or insolvency, and in the latter case for the benefit either of the State or of private creditors. Damnatione bona publicantur cum aut vita adimitur aut civitas aut servilis conditio irrogatur, Dig. 48, 20, 1. 'Condemnation forfeits all a criminal's goods to the treasury, if it deprives of life, or involves loss of civitas (capitis minutio media), or loss of liberty (capitis minutio maxima).'

Confiscation (publicatio) under its ancient name of sectio bonorum, has already, 3 § 80, been mentioned. The quaestors of the treasury were sent into possession; the sale, which was publicly advertised (proscriptio), took place under the spear (sub hasta), the symbol of absolute dominion, and vested in the purchaser (sector) quiritarian ownership.

DE MANDATO.

§ 155. M*andatum* consistit *sive* nostra gratia mandemus sive ali*ena*, *id est sive ut mea* negotia geras, sive u*t* alterius *mandem tibi*, *erit inter nos* obligatio, et invicem alter *a*lteri tene*b*imur, id*eoque iudicium* erit *in id quod paret te* mihi bona fide praestare oportere.

§ 156. Nam si tua gratia tibi mandem, *supervacuum* est mandatum; quod enim tu tua gratia fac*turus* sis, id ex t*ua* sententia, *non* ex meo mandatu facere *videberis*: *ita*que si otiosam pecu*niam* domi te *habere mihi dixeris*, *et* ego te hortatus fuerim, u*t eam* fenerares, quamvis *e*am ei mutuam dederis

§ 155. Agency may contemplate the benefit either of the principal or of a stranger; that is to say, your undertaking at my request to transact my business or the business of a third person will create an obligation between us, and make us mutually liable and compellable to satisfy the demands of good faith.

§ 156. But if I recommend you to perform anything for your own exclusive advantage, there is no relation of agency, for you will act on your own judgment and not by my commission. If you tell me that you have money lying in your cashbox, and, on my advice to lend it at interest, you lend it to a person from

a quo *servare non* potueris, non tamen habebis mecum man*dati actionem*. it*em* et si hortatus sim, *ut rem a*liquam emeres, q*uamvis* non expedierit tibi eam emisse, non tamen *mandati tibi tenebor*. et adeo haec ita sunt, ut quaeratur an mandati teneatur qui mandavit tibi, ut *Titio* pecuniam *fenerares* [*desunt* 2½ *lin.*], q*uia* non aliter Titio credidisses, quam si tibi mandatum esset.

whom you cannot recover it, you will have no action of mandate against me: or if I recommend you to buy, and you lose by buying, I am not liable to be sued in action of mandate. So settled is this, that it has been questioned, whether mandate can be brought on a specific recommendation to lend to Titius; but the prevalent opinion is that of Sabinus, that so specific a recommendation is sufficient to support an action of mandate.

§ 157. Illud *constat, si faciendum quid* mandet*ur* quod contra bonos mores est, non contrahi obligationem, velut si tibi mandem, ut Titio furtum aut iniuriam facias.

§ 157. It is clear that an instigation to do an unlawful act, to steal, for instance, or commit an assault, gives the agent no right of action against the instigator.

§ 158. Item si qui*d post* mortem meam faciendum *mihi* mandet*ur*, inutile mandatum est, quia generaliter placuit ab heredis persona obligationem incipere non posse.

§ 158. A commission to be executed after the death of the agent is invalid by the general rule that a successor cannot be the original subject of an obligation.

§ 159. Sed recte quoque consumma*tum* mandatum, si dum adhuc integra res sit revocatum fuerit, evanescit.

§ 159. A valid authority is annulled by revocation before a commencement of execution.

§ 160. Item si adhuc integro mandat*o* mors alterutrius alicuius interveniat, id est vel eius qui mandarit, vel eius *q*ui mandatum susceperit, solvitur mandatum. sed utilitatis causa receptum est, ut si mortuo eo qui mihi mandaverit, ignorans eum decessisse exsecutus fuero mandatum, posse me agere mandati actione: alioquin iusta et probabilis ignorantia damnum mihi *ad*feret. et h*u*ic simile est quod plerisque placuit, si debitor meus manumisso dispensatori meo per ignorantiam solverit, liberari eum: cum alioquin stricta iuris ratione non posset liberari eo quod alii solvisset quam cui solvere deberet.

§ 160. So the death of either the principal or the agent before a commencement of execution is a revocation of a power: but equity requires that, if after the death of a principal and without having notice of his decease an agent execute his commission, he may recover against the successor of the principal in an action of mandate; for otherwise an unavoidable ignorance would be visited by a legal penalty. Similar to this is the rule which is supported by the weight of authority, that a debtor who pays a manumitted steward without notice of his manumission is discharged of liability; though by the strict letter of the law he is not discharged, because he has not paid the person whom he was bound to pay.

§ 161. Cum autem is cui recte mandaverim egressus fuerit manda-

§ 161. If an agent deviates from his instructions, he may be sued for

tum, ego quidem eatenus cum eo habeo mandati actionem, quatenus mea interest implesse eum mandatum, si modo implere potuerit: at ille mecum agere non potest. itaque si mandaverim tibi, ut verbi gratia fundum mihi sestertiis C emeres, tu *sestertiis* CL emeris, non habebis mecum mandati actionem, etiamsi tanti velis mihi dare fundum quanti emendum tibi mandassem. idque maxime Sabino et Cassio placuit. Quodsi minoris emeris, habebis mecum scilicet actionem, quia qui mandat ut C milibus emeretur, is utique mandare intellegitur, ut minoris, si posset, emeretur.

the amount which his principal loses by the non-execution of the instructions, if the execution was possible; and he will have no right of action against the principal. So if I commission you to purchase an estate for, say, a hundred thousand sesterces, and you purchase for a hundred and fifty thousand, you will have no action of mandate against me although you are willing to convey to me for the price at which I authorized you to buy: so Sabinus and Cassius have decided. If you buy it for less, you will have a right of action against me, for a direction to buy for a hundred thousand sesterces is regarded as an implied direction to buy, if possible, for any smaller sum.

§ 162. In summa sciendum *est, quotiens faciendum* aliquid gratis dederim, quo nomine si mercedem statuissem, locatio et conductio contraheretur, mandati esse actionem, veluti si fulloni polienda curandave vestimenta aut sarcinatori sarcienda *dederim*.

§ 162. Finally, the delivery of material to be wrought or fashioned gratuitously, where if a remuneration had been fixed there would have been a letting and hiring, is ground for an action of mandate against the bailee; the fuller, for instance, who receives clothes to be cleaned or finished, or the tailor who receives them to be mended.

In the contract of agency (mandatum) the principal is called dominus or mandator, the agent procurator or mandatary.

We have already mentioned, when treating of the verbal contract of stipulation, that a guaranty was often given by the consensual contract of mandate. The following passage will show one of the circumstances under which a guarantor and guarantee might stand in the relation of mandant and mandatary. Tua et mandantis gratia intervenit mandatum, si mandet tibi, ut ipsius periculo stipuleris ab eo quem tibi deleget in id quod tibi debuerat, Inst. 3, 26, 2. 'Both the agent and the principal are beneficially interested in a mandate if the principal directs the agent at the risk of the principal to take a verbal bond from a debtor of the principal in discharge of a debt due from the principal to the agent.' The result of this transaction, compounded of mandate and stipulation, would be two novations, extinguishing the original debts due to and from the principal, and creating a new liability of the principal as guarantor of the substituted debtor. Delegare est vice sua alium reum dare creditori vel cui jusserit, Dig. 46, 2, 11. 'To delegate is to give in one's stead a vicarious debtor to one's creditor or his order.' Quod mihi ab aliquo debetur, id si velim tibi deberi . . . opus est ut jubente me tu ab eo stipuleris; quae res efficit ut a me liberetur et incipiat tibi teneri, quae dicitur novatio obligationis, Gaius, 2 § 38. 'The transfer of a debt requires that on the order of the transferror the transferree should stipulate payment from the debtor, whereupon the debtor is discharged of liability to the transferror and becomes bound to the transferree, which change is called novation.' In this Roman practice of discharging liabilities by substitution of another person as debtor, of which we have already had an example in the form of literal contract called transcriptio, we may see a parallel to the modern practice of discharging debts by means of bills of exchange.

A simpler instance of a guaranty given by mandate is that contained in § 156 (where the hiatus may be supplied from Justinian: sed obtinuit Sabini sententia obligatorium esse in hoc casu mandatum): he who recommends a third person as of good credit is bound to make good his representation and to indemnify another who sustains damage from giving credit on the faith of that representation. So by English law a person not interested in a transaction who makes a false and fraudulent misrepresentation which induces another to trust and contract with a third person is answerable for the loss occasioned by his misrepresentation.

As such a representation was in effect a guaranty, and to allow an action on a verbal misrepresentation would avoid the Statute of Frauds, which requires a guaranty to be reduced to writing, Lord Tenterden's Act, 9 George IV, chapter 14, enacted that no action shall be brought whereby to charge any person upon any representation or assurance concerning the character, credit, or ability of any other person, to the intent that such other person may obtain money or goods upon credit, unless such representation or assurance be made in writing, signed by the party to be charged therewith.

Mandate might be employed to operate a virtual transfer of obligation, without the intervention of novation, as in the abovementioned case, by the mere transfer of the right of action (mandare, cedere, praestare actiones). The transferror gave the transferree a procuration or power of attorney, which enabled him to sue in the name of the transferror, or, employing the formula Rutiliana, to name the transferror in the intentio and the transferree in the condemnatio, 4 § 35.

In the later period of the law the vendee or pawnee of an obligation might even sue in his own name by an equitable action called actio utilis. Postquam eo decursum est, ut cautiones quoque debitorum pignori dentur, ordinarium visum est post nominis venditionem utiles emptori vel ipsi creditori postulanti dandas actiones, Cod. 4, 39, 7. 'Since the practice of pawning promissory notes of a debtor, it is held that after a note is sold, an utilis actio can be brought upon it by the vendee, or before sale by the pawnee, in his own name.' Here we may seem to have in full bloom the institution of negotiable paper, that is, written promises to pay, transferable from person to person, and giving the transferree a right to sue in his own name.

In the Roman practice, however, we are far from a complete system of transferable obligation. The ceded or assigned obligation was never completely detached from the person and liabilities of the preceding creditor. The cessionary or assignee was open to all the exceptions that might have been opposed to the original creditor: e.g. to compensatio, or reduction by the amount of a counterclaim; to exceptio non numeratae pecuniae, or plea of want of consideration; and to exceptio of lex Anastasiana, a statute which prohibited any vendee of a debt from recovering, out of its nominal amount, more than the price at which it was actually purchased. And similar objections might be raised in respect of any creditor intermediate between the original assignor and the final assignee. The complete transferability of obligations was unknown to jurisprudence until modern legislation gave validity to contracts with an incerta persona, to a person unascertained except as member of a class; in other words, to papers payable to the Holder or Bearer.

In such papers, which are subjects of property or ownership, the incorporeal obligation is, as it were, incorporated, and Obligation is transformed into Dominion. We have instances of such papers (called negotiable) in Promissory Notes, Bills of Exchange, State obligations (documents expressing a claim against a government for a certain amount of capital debt, and having annexed to them coupons, representing claims of periodic interest), and Debentures of industrial corporations (certificates of Shares in such industrial companies, though similar to Debentures as entitling the Holder to certain dividends or shares in the profits, are foreign to our present purpose, because they essentially and originally relate to Property or jus in rem, not to Obligation or jus in personam, the Shareholders being co-proprietors). By the use of such negotiable papers the transferability of Obligation is raised to a level with the transferability of Dominion, Savigny, Obligationenrecht, 62–70.

§ 161. The doctrine of Sabinus that if an agent exceed his powers in the price at which he purchases, the principal is not bound for the purchase money even after deduction of the unauthorized excess, was overruled, as we are informed by Justinian.

§ 162. It is only in exceptional circumstances, such as those here mentioned, that the contract of mandatum can fall under the head of Bailment.

The gratuitous character of mandatum is rather nominal than real. The professor of a liberal art could recover a remuneration which, however, was disguised under the name of salarium or honorarium, and could not be sued for by action of mandate before an ordinary judge, but was a matter for the extraordinary cognizance of the praetor or chief minister of justice. Adversus eum cujus negotia gesta sunt, de pecunia quam de propriis opibus vel ab aliis mutuo acceptam erogasti, mandati actione pro sorte et usuris potes experiri. De salario autem quod promisit, apud praesidem provinciae cognitio praebebitur, Cod. 4, 25, 1. 'The employer whose business you transacted, as to the moneys out of your own pocket or taken up at loan which you spent for his use, may be forced by action of mandate to reimburse you the principal and interest. The salary which he promised must abide the decision of the president of the province.' Under the liberal professions are included advocates, physicians, oculists, aurists, dentists, copyists (librarii), short-hand writers (notarii), accountants, schoolmasters, nurses, rhetoricians, grammarians, geometers, land surveyors. The professors of philosophy and of civil law may receive fees voluntarily offered, but their functions are so exalted that it would be unseemly in them to ask for a pecuniary remuneration even at the tribunal of the praetor, Dig. 50, 13.

The law of agency or representation was only slowly developed in Roman jurisprudence. Originally the cases in which a contractor could bind a principal to his contractee or the contractee to a principal were confined to contracts by persons under power, that is to say, sons or slaves.

The right acquired by a son or slave was acquired for the father or master, 3 § 163, and if the contract was made by the order or for the use of the father or master, he was suable by the contractee, 4 §§ 70-74. But in other cases the benefit or burden of a contract was confined to the parties contracting. Accordingly, if a procurator or agent contracted with a third party, such third party could only recover his dues from the agent, and the agent would in turn recover his from the principal, and vice versa. There was no immediate relation between the third party and the principal, and any action in which the third party sued the principal or vice versa, could have only resulted from a cession of actions and transfer of obligations between the agent and principal, or the agent and the contractee. Et recte dicitur in hoc esse mandati actionem ut suscipiam obligationem quae adversus te venditori competit, nam et ego tecum agere possum ut praestes mihi adversus venditorem empti actionem, Dig. 17, 1; 45, 1. 'By the action of mandate a principal may be compelled to assume the responsibilities which his agent for purchase has incurred towards a vendor, as he may compel his agent to cede him his right of action as vendee.' Est aequum, sicut mandante aliquo actionem nacti cogimur eam praestare judicio mandati, ita ex eadem causa obligatos nos habere mandati actionem ut liberemur, Dig. 17, 45, 5. 'As an agent, if in the execution of his powers he acquires a right of action against a contractee, is compelled by action of mandate to cede it to his principal, so, if in the execution of his powers he incurs an obligation to a contractee, it is just that he should have the action of mandate to force his principal to relieve him of his responsibility.'

However, in process of time the law recognized the appointment of a cognitor or representative of a party to a suit, and such cognitor was to all intents and purposes identified with his principal, 4 § 83.

Furthermore, the manager of a shop (institor), and captain of a ship were enabled by praetorian legislation to bind the employer and shipowner (exercitor) to third parties by means of the actions institoria and exercitoria, 4 § 71. This was gradually extended so as to allow to all persons who contracted with an agent a right of action, called quasi institoria, against his employer. In eum qui mutuis accipiendis pecuniis procuratorem praeposuit, utilis ad exemplum institoriae dabitur actio, quod aeque faciendum erit etsi procurator solvendo sit qui stipulanti pecuniam promisit, Dig. 14, 4, 19. 'A person who borrowed through an agent may be sued in a modified form of action, moulded on the pattern of institoria, in spite of the solvency of his agent, who entered into the verbal bond for repayment.' Si mutuam pecuniam accipere a te Demetriano Domitianus mandavit, et hoc posse probare confidis, ad exemplum institoriae eundem Domitianum apud competentem judicem potes convenire, Cod. 4, 25, 5. 'If money was lent by you to Demetrian acting as agent for Domitian, and you can prove it, you may bring quasi institoria against Domitian.' Idem Papinianus libro eodem refert, fidejussori condemnato, qui ideo fidejussit quia dominus procuratori mandaverat ut pecuniam mutuam acciperet, utilem actionem dandam quasi institoriam, quia et hic quasi praeposuisse eum mutuae pecuniae accipiendae videatur, Dig. 17, 1; 10, 5. 'Papinian also states that a surety condemned to pay a debt, if he had been induced to become surety by the authority given by a principal to an agent to borrow, may bring a modified action, assimilated to institoria, against the principal, because the agent may be regarded as the manager of the principal's borrowing business.'

The praetors went even beyond the precedent furnished by institoria, and allowed to principals an immediate right of action against third parties who had contracted with agents. Quod procurator ex re domini, mandato non refragante, stipulatur, invito procuratore dominus petere potest, Dig. 3, 3, 68. 'When an agent, dealing with the interests of his principal and in accordance with his instructions, makes a contract, the consent of the agent is not required to entitle the principal to sue.' When the praetors, proceeding by timid and hesitating steps, had reached this point, the Roman law of agency had become identical with the system we find established in modern Europe. Under this system it is a general rule, that when an agent is duly constituted and discloses the name of his principal, so as to enable the party with whom he deals to have recourse to the principal, and contracts in his name and on his behalf, and does not exceed his authority, the principal is responsible and not the agent. The only reservation to be made is the following: In contracts governed by Jus gentium the relation of Agency was recognized in its fullest development: in Formal contracts, or contracts governed by the Civil law (of which in the last period of Roman Jurisprudence the only surviving instance was

Stipulatio), the primitive law, ignoring Agency, had so far left its traces, that the Principal could not sue or be sued on the contracts of his Agent by actio Directa, but only by actio Utilis; that is, by a formula involving, by permission of the judicature, a certain amount of Fictitious supposition. See above, § 103.

After explaining obligations founded on contract, Justinian treats of a miscellaneous group of obligations which are neither founded on contract nor on delict, and which, as the circumstances in which they arise resemble more or less the circumstances of one or other of the legal conventions, are denominated by the name of obligations quasi ex contractu. These demand from us a brief notice.

Three of them, namely, those which ground the actions by or against a tutor, by or against a curator, by or against an unauthorized agent (negotiorum gestor), clearly resemble obligations founded on the contract of mandate. The ward and minor stand to the tutor and curator nearly in the relation of principal and agent, although they are legally incompetent to give an authority (mandatum) or confer a power of administration. A person who, in the absence and without the knowledge of another, officiously interfered to protect his interests (voluntarius procurator) incurred liability and acquired rights against the person in whose affairs he interfered. English law does not recognize a title to compensation in the case of officious interference, unless we find a parallel in the rights of salvors in the case of property lost or endangered on the ocean.

Three other obligations quasi ex contractu, those that are enforced by an action for division of common property between tenants in common (communi dividundo), by action for partition of an inheritance between co-successors (familiae erciscundae), by an action for demarcation of boundaries between adjoining landowners (finium regundorum), resemble the obligations arising in partnership. These actions are distinguished from all others by the adjudicatio, a clause in the formula which empowered the judex by the mere effect of his judgment to operate a transmutation of property. They are called mixed actions by Ulpian, because both parties are equally plaintiff and defendant, Dig. 44, 7; 37, 1; by Justinian, because they are both real and personal, that is, embrace questions both of ownership and obligation; but were regarded by the jurists as properly personal actions, because they contemplate a transfer of property and condemnation of one or other of the parties, in case of inequality of apportionment, in pecuniary damages by way of compensation.

The obligation of a heres to a legatee, enforceable by actio legati (condictio ex testamento), is another case of obligation quasi ex contractu. The aditio of the hereditas may be regarded as a promise to satisfy the bequests.

Again, money paid by mistake or without consideration (indebitum solutum) created an obligation to repay, enforceable by indebiti soluti condictio, which closely resembles the obligation created by the contract of mutuum.

PER QUAS PERSONAS NOBIS OBLIGATIO ACQUIRATUR.

§ 163. Expositis generibus obligationum quae ex contractu nascuntur, admonendi sumus adquiri nobis non solum per nosmet ipsos, sed etiam per eas personas quae in nostra potestate manu mancipiove sunt.

§ 163. Having thus classified obligations produced by contract, we remark that obligations may be acquired not only by our own contracts, but also by the contracts of persons in our power, in our hand, in a state of mancipation to us.

§ 164. Per liberos quoque homines et alienos servos quos bona fide possidemus adquiritur nobis; sed tantum ex duabus causis, id est si quid ex operis suis vel ex re nostra adquirant.

§ 164. Freemen, also, and the slaves of another person, acquire for the person who possesses them in bona fides; only, however, in two circumstances, that is to say, when they acquire by their own labour, or in dealing with the property of the bona fide possessor.

§ 165. Per eum quoque servum in quo usumfructum habemus similiter ex duabus istis causis nobis adquiritur.

§ 165. A usufructuary slave acquires for the tenant for life under the same conditions.

§ 166. Sed qui nudum ius Quiritium in servo habet, licet dominus sit, minus tamen iuris in ea re habere intellegitur quam usufructuarius et bonae fidei possessor. nam placet ex nulla causa ei adquiri posse: adeo ut etsi nominatim ei dari stipulatus fuerit servus, mancipiove nom*ine* eius acceperit, quidam existim*e*nt nihil ei adqu*i*ri.

§ 166. The owner of the naked quiritary property in a slave has less right in his acquisitions than the tenant for life or bona fide possessor; for under no circumstances do the acquisitions of the slave enure to his benefit; and even when expressly named by the slave in a stipulation or mancipation, according to some authorities, the nude proprietor acquires no right.

§ 167. Co*m*munem servum pro dominica parte dominis adquirere

§ 167. A common slave acquires for all his proprietors in the propor-

certum est, excepto eo, quod uni nominatim stipulando aut mancipio accipiendo illi soli adquirit, veluti cum ita stipuletur: TITIO DOMINO MEO DARI SPONDES? aut cum ita mancipio accipiat: HANC REM EX IURE QUIRITIUM LUCII TITII DOMINI MEI ESSE AIO, EAQUE EI EMPTA ESTO HOC AERE AENEAQUE LIBRA.

tion of their property, unless he names one exclusively in a stipulation or mancipation, in which case he acquires for him alone. For instance, if he stipulates thus: 'Dost thou promise to convey to Titius, my master?' or, when he takes by mancipation, thus: 'This thing by quiritary law I declare to be the property of Lucius Titius, my master, and for him be it purchased by this bronze ingot and this scale of bronze.'

§ 167*a*. Illu*d* quaeritur *num* quod *unius* domini nomen adiectum e*ff*icit, idem faciat unius ex dominis iussum intercedens. nostri praeceptores perinde ei qui iusserit soli adquiri existimant, a*t*que si nominatim ei soli stipulatus esset servus, mancipiove accepisset. diversae scholae auctores proinde utrisque adquiri putant, ac si nulli*us* iussum intervenisset.

§ 167*a*. It is a question, whether the same effect is produced by the exclusive order of one of the masters, as by the exclusive mention of the name of one. My school maintain that the sole orderer is the sole acquirer, just as when one alone is named by the slave in a stipulation or mancipation; the other school maintain that all the owners acquire, just as if there had been no order.

§ 163. Justinian enacted, as we have seen, that while the peculium profectitium of the filiusfamilias, that is, the peculium which he derived from the grant of his father, remained the property of the father; and while in respect of peculium castrense and quasi castrense the son was paterfamilias, or absolute owner; in respect of peculium adventitium, that is, other peculium derived from any other source than the estate of the father, only the usufruct or life estate should vest in the father, the property or reversion remaining in the son. In respect of the obligations acquired by the son, the same principle was to prevail. Ut tamen quod per liberos quos in potestate habetis ex obligatione fuerit acquisitum, hoc dividatur secundum imaginem rerum proprietatis et ususfructus quam nostra discrevit constitutio: ut quod actione quoquomodo commodum perveniat, hujus usumfructum quidem habeat pater, proprietas autem filio servetur, scilicet patre actionem movente, secundum novellae nostrae constitutionis divisionem, Inst. 3, 28, pr. 'The benefit of the obligations acquired by a son shall be divided, as his property is by our constitution, into reversion and usufruct; so that the proceeds of any action shall vest in the father for life, and in the son in reversion, the whole right of action vesting in the father, according to the distinctions expressed in the statute.'

§ 167*a*. Justinian decided this question in favour of the doctrine of Sabinus, Inst. 3, 28, 13.

To the persons through whom an obligation can be acquired might be added the procurator in the later stage of the law, as soon as the principal was allowed to sue on the contracts of the agent without the agent's consent or transfer of his right of action.

QUIBUS MODIS OBLIGATIO TOLLATUR.

§ 168. Tollitur autem obligatio praecipue solutione eius quod debeatur. unde quaeritur, si quis consentiente creditore aliu*d* pro alio solverit, utrum ipso iure liberetur, quod nostris praeceptoribus placet: an ipso iure maneat obligatus, *sed* adversus petentem exceptione doli mali defendi debeat, quod divers*ae* sch*olae au*ctoribus visum est.

§ 168. Extinction of an obligation is effected chiefly by performance of the thing that is owed. It is disputed, when the creditor consents to the substitution of a different performance, whether there is a legal discharge of the obligation, as my school consider, or there is a continuance of the legal obligation, though an equitable defence against a demand may be made by the exception of fraud, as the other school maintain.

§ 169. Item per acceptilationem tollitur obligatio. acceptilatio autem est veluti imaginaria solutio. quod enim ex verborum obligatione tibi debeam, id si velis mihi remittere, poterit sic fieri, ut patiaris haec verba *me* dicere: QUOD EGO TIBI PROMISI, HABESNE ACCEPTUM? et tu respondeas: HABEO.

§ 169. Acceptilation is another mode of extinguishing an obligation. Acceptilation is an imaginary payment by a solemn form of words. If a creditor is willing to release a debt created by verbal contract, the object may be accomplished by the debtor interrogating him in these terms: 'That which I promised thee hast thou received?' and the creditor answering: 'I have received it.'

§ 170. Quo genere, ut diximus, *tantum hae obligationes solvuntur quae ex verbis consistunt*, non etiam ceterae: consentaneum enim visum est verbis factam obligationem posse aliis verbis dissolvi. *sed* et id quod ex alia causa debeatur potest in stipulationem deduci et per acceptilationem imaginaria solutione *dissolvi*.

§ 170. This process, as I said, only discharges obligations that arise from verbal contract, and no others; for logic seems to dictate that where words can bind, words may also loose. However, a debt due from any other cause may be transformed into a debt on stipulation, and released by an imaginary verbal payment or acceptilation.

§ 171. Tamen mulier sine tutoris auctore acceptum facere non potest; cum alioquin solvi ei sine tutoris auctoritate possit.

§ 171. Observe, that a woman without her guardian's authority cannot release by acceptilation, although her receipt of actual payment without her guardian's authority discharges the debtor.

§ 172. Item quod debet*ur* pro parte recte solvi *intellegitur*: an autem in partem acceptum fieri *possit, quaes*it*um* est.

§ 172. So a debt may be paid in part, but whether it can be released in part by acceptilation is a question.

§ 173. *Est* etiam alia species imaginariae solutionis per ae*s* et libram. quod et ipsum genus certis in causis receptum est, veluti si quid eo nomine debeatur quod per ae*s* et libram gestum e*s*t, sive qui*d* ex iudicati causa deb*ebi*t*ur*.

§ 173. There is another mode of imaginary payment, namely, by ingot and scale. This also is only valid in certain cases, as the release of a debt created by nexum, or of a judgment debt.

§ 174. A*d*hib*entur* autem non minus quam quinque testes et libripens. deinde is qui liberat*ur* ita oportet loquatur: QUOD EGO TIBI TOT MILIBUS EO NOMINE ... SOLVO LIBEROQ*UE* HOC AERE AENEAQUE LIBRA. HANC TIBI LIBRAM PRIMAM POSTREMA*M* ... DE LEGE *IURE* O*B*LIGATUR. deinde asse percutit libram, *e*um*que* d*a*t *ei* a quo liberatu*r*, veluti solvendi causa.

§ 174. There must be present five witnesses and a holder of the scales, and the debtor to be released must say these words: 'Whereas I am condemned to thee in so many thousand sesterces by such and such a nexum'—or, 'by such and such a judgment'—'that debt I pay and discharge by this ingot and balance of bronze. When I have struck the scale with this first, this last, ingot of bronze, no further obligation by the terms of the nexum'—or, 'by the judgment'—'remains in force.' Then he strikes the scale with the ingot, and gives it to the creditor, as if in payment.

§ 175. Similiter legatarius heredem eodem modo liberat de legato quod per damnationem relictum est, ut tamen *scilicet, sicut iudicatus sententia se damnatum* esse significat, *ita heres defuncti iudicio damnatum se* esse dicat. de eo tamen *tantum* potest hoc modo liberari quod pondere, numero constet; et ita, si certum sit, quidam et de eo quod mensura constat in*tellegendum* existimant.

§ 175. Similarly, the legatee releases the successor from a legacy left in the form of condemnation, except that whereas the other debtors recite their condemnation by the nexum or by the judgment, the successor recites his condemnation by the testament of the deceased. A debt can be thus discharged only if certain in amount and estimated by number or weight, or, according to some, by measure.

§ 176. Praeterea novatione tollitur obligatio, veluti si quod tu mihi debeas a Titio dari stipulatus sim.

§ 176. Novation is another mode of extinguishing an obligation, and takes place when you owe me a

nam interventu novae personae nova nascitur obligatio, et prima tollitur translata in posteriorem: adeo ut in*ter*dum, licet posterior stipulatio inutilis sit, tamen prima novationis iure tollatur. veluti si quod mihi debes a Titio post mortem eius vel a muliere pupillove sine tutoris auctoritate stipulatus fuero. quo casu rem amitto: nam et prior debitor liberatur, et posterior obligatio nulla est. non idem iuris est, si a servo stipulatus fuero: nam tunc proinde a*d*huc obligatus tenetur, ac si postea a nullo stipulatus fuissem.

sum and I stipulate payment thereof from Titius, for the intervention of a new person gives birth to a new obligation, and the first obligation ceases, being transformed into the second. Sometimes, even though the second stipulation is invalid, the first is avoided by novation; for instance, if you owe me a sum, and I stipulate from Titius payment thereof after his death, or if I stipulate payment thereof from a woman or ward without the guardian's authority, in this case my claim is extinguished, for the first debtor is discharged, and the second obligation is void. The same does not hold if I stipulate from a slave, for then the former debtor continues bound, just as if there was no subsequent stipulation.

§ 177. Sed si eadem persona sit a qua postea stipuler, ita demum novatio fit, si quid in posteriore stipulatione novi sit, forte si condicio vel sponsor aut dies adiciatur aut *de*trahatur.

§ 177. But when the original debtor is the promisor, a second stipulation only operates a novation if it contains something new; if a condition, for instance, or a sponsor, or a term is added or omitted.

§ 178. Sed quod de sponsore dixi, non constat. nam diversae sc*h*olae auctoribus placuit nihil ad novationem proficere sponsoris adiectionem aut detractionem.

§ 178. Respecting the sponsor, however, there is a controversy; for the other school hold that novation is not operated by a sponsor being added or omitted.

§ 179. Quod autem diximus, si condicio adiciatur, novationem fieri, sic intellegi *oportet*, ut ita dicamus factam novationem, si condicio extiterit: alioquin, si defecerit, durat prior obligatio. sed videamus, num is qui eo nomine agat doli mali aut pacti conventi exceptione possit summoveri, *et* vide*a*tur inter eos id actum, ut ita ea res peteretur, si posterioris stipulationis extiterit condicio. Servius tamen Sulpicius existimavit statim et pendente condicione novationem fieri, et si defecerit condicio, ex neutra causa agi posse, *et* eo modo rem perire. qui consequenter et illu*d* respondit, si quis id quod sibi Lucius Titius

§ 179. The statement that a condition introduced operates a novation must be restricted to mean, that a novation is produced if the condition is accomplished; if the condition fails, the prior obligation continues in force. However, it will be a question, whether the creditor who sues on that obligation cannot be repelled by the equitable plea of fraud, or of accord and agreement, and whether it was not the intention of the parties that the debt should not be recoverable unless the condition of the second stipulation were realized. Servius Sulpicius even held that novation occurs immediately, and while the

deberet, a servo fuerit stipulatus, novationem fieri et rem perire; quia cum servo agi non potest. sed in utroque casu alio iure utimur: non magis his casibus novatio fit, quam si id quod tu mihi debeas a peregrino, cum quo sponsi communio non est, SPONDES verbo stipulatus sim.

accomplishment of the condition is still uncertain; and that, if the condition fails, neither obligation can be sued upon, and the creditor's claim is extinguished; and, consistently herewith, he held that, if the debt of Lucius Titius is stipulated by the creditor from a slave, novation takes place, and the claim is extinguished, because the slave cannot be sued. But in both cases the contrary rule prevails, and no novation occurs in these cases any more than it occurs if an alien, who cannot be sponsor, promise payment of a debt by the solemn term, 'spondeo.'

§ 180. Tollitur adhuc obligatio litis contestatione, si modo legitimo iudicio fuerit actum. nam tunc obligatio quidem principalis dissolvitur, incipit autem teneri reus litis contestatione: sed si condemnatus sit, sublata litis contestatione incipit ex causa iudicati teneri. et hoc est quod aput veteres scriptum est, ante litem contestatam dare debitorem oportere, post litem contestatam condemnari oportere, post condemnationem iudicatum facere oportere.

§ 180. The extinction of an obligation is also effected by the commencement of an action, at least of a statutory action, that is to say, an action substituted by statute for certain of the legis actiones. Then the original obligation is dissolved, and a new obligation is imposed on the defendant, by the commencement of the action. If he is condemned, the second obligation is discharged, and a third obligation is imposed by the judgment. Hence the saying of the old writers, that, before action brought, a defendant is required by the law to convey; after action brought, he is required to be condemned; after condemnation passed, he is required to satisfy the judgment.

§ 181. Unde fit, ut si legitimo iudicio debitum petiero, postea de eo ipso iure agere non possim, quia inutiliter intendo DARI MIHI OPORTERE; quia litis contestatione dari oportere desiit. aliter atque si imperio continenti iudicio egerim: tunc enim nihilominus obligatio durat, et ideo ipso iure postea agere possum; sed debeo per exceptionem rei iudicatae vel in iudicium deductae summoveri. quae autem legitima sint iudicia, et quae imperio continean-

§ 181. Accordingly, after suing by statutory action, the civil law allows me no right to bring a second action, for the declaration that the defendant is bound to convey is false in law, as the commencement of the first action terminated his obligation to convey. It is otherwise if I sued at first by an action determining with the praetorship. Then the civil obligation continues, and the civil law permits me to bring a second ac-

tur, sequenti commentario referemus.

tion; but I may be repelled by the plea of previous judgment or previous litigation. What actions are statutory, and what determine with the praetorship, will be explained in the next book of these Institutions.

§ 168. Gaius only considers at present the legal modes of extinguishing an obligation, i.e. such modes as were valid by the civil law. In the next book, 4 § 115, he will treat of the exceptio, that is to say, an equitable defence to an action, which barred the plaintiff from recovering, even though an obligation were shown to be subsisting at civil law, which defence required to be alleged with the permission of the praetor in a special clause of the formula called the exceptio.

Every obligation, as we have seen, 3 § 88, commentary, refers to a certain datio, factio, or praestatio; that is to say, the fulfilment or satisfaction (solutio) of an obligation will consist in datio, factio, or praestatio.

The doctrine of Sabinus, that accord and satisfaction operate a legal extinction of an obligation, was the view that ultimately prevailed. Manifesti juris est, tam alio pro debitore solvente, quam rebus pro numerata pecunia consentiente creditore datis tolli paratam obligationem, Cod. 8, 43, 17. 'It is certain that payment by a third person, and the conveyance of goods instead of money, with the consent of the creditor, discharges an obligation.'

§ 170. Aquilius Gallus, the colleague of Cicero in his praetorship, the pupil of Quintus Mucius and teacher of Servius Sulpicius, was the inventor of formulas relating to dolus malus, Cic. de Off. 3, 14, and a mode of releasing from all obligations by a verbal ceremony. Est prodita stipulatio quae vulgo Aquiliana appellatur, per quam stipulationem contingit ut omnium rerum obligatio in stipulatum deducatur et ea per acceptilationem tollatur. Stipulatio enim Aquiliana novat omnes obligationes et a Gallo Aquilio ita composita est: Quicquid te mihi ex quacunque causa dare facere oportet, oportebit, praesens in diemve aut sub condicione; quarumcumque rerum mihi tecum actio, quaeque abs te petitio vel adversus te persecutio est, erit, quodve tu meum habes, tenes, possides, possedisti, dolove malo fecisti quominus possideas: quanti quaeque earum rerum res erit, tantam pecuniam dari stipulatus est Aulus Agerius, spopondit Numerius Negidius. Item ex diverso Numerius

Negidius interrogavit Aulum Agerium: Quicquid tibi hodierno die per Aquilianam stipulationem spopondi, id omne habesne acceptum? Respondit Aulus Agerius: Habeo acceptumque tuli, Inst. 3, 29, 2. 'There is a stipulation called Aquilian, whereby all obligations are transmuted into a verbal one, and forthwith discharged by acceptilation. For the Aquilian stipulation operates a novation of all preexisting debts, and is thus expressed: "Whatever thing, on whatever title, thou art or shalt be bound to convey to me or to perform for me now or hereafter, absolutely or conditionally; whatever thing I have or shall have an action, personal, real, or extraordinary, against thee to recover; whatever thing of mine thou hast, detainest, possessest, hast possessed, or hast fraudulently parted with possession of; whatever sum is the value of all these things, that sum dost thou to pay me promise?" so asks Aulus Agerius, and Numerius Negidius answers: "I promise." Then Numerius Negidius asks of Aulus Agerius: "Whatever I have promised thee today by the Aquilian stipulation, hast thou received it all in full?" and Aulus Agerius answers: "I have, and have given thee my release."'

The narrative form (stipulatus est, spopondit, interrogavit) in which the transaction is expressed by Justinian, properly belongs, not to the stipulation and acceptilation, but to the written memorandum (cautio) in which they are recorded.

§ 172. It was subsequently an established doctrine that a partial release by acceptilation was valid, Dig. 46, 4, 13.

§ 174. The translation follows the conjectural reading of Lachmann: Quod ego tibi tot milibus eo nomine vel eo judicio damnatus sum, eos nummos solvo liberoque hoc aere aeneaque libra. Hanc ubi libram primam postremam ferii, nihil de lege jure obligatur.

The release of a legacy would be operated per aes et libram, because the will containing the bequest was a transaction per aes et libram, on the principle that all obligations may be released by the process whereby they were contracted. Nihil tam naturale est quam eo genere quidquid dissolvere quo colligatum est, Dig. 50, 17, 35. 'Nothing more natural than the likeness of the means of binding and of unbinding.' Omnia quae jure contrahuntur, contrario jure pereunt, Dig. 50, 17, 100. 'To every legal form of charging corresponds a legal form of discharging.' Fere quibuscunque modis obligamur, iisdem in contrarium actis liberamur,

Dig. 50, 17, 153. 'To every mode of obligation there is an obverse mode of liberation.'

It is not so easy to explain why a judgment debt could only be released by the proceeding with the bronze and scales. Perhaps it was considered that a judgment being an act of the State could only be discharged by another act of the State, and that the nexum satisfied this requirement, the witnesses and balance-holder symbolizing the people in assembly, and the declaration of the lex of the nexum symbolizing a legislative enactment. We have an instance of a release from a judgment debt by nexum in Livy. Centurionem, nobilem militaribus factis, judicatum pecuniae quum duci vidisset, medio foro cum caterva sua accurrit et manum injecit. . . . Inde rem creditori palam populo solvit, libraque et aere liberatum emittit, deos atque homines obtestantem, ut M. Manlio, liberatori suo, parenti plebis Romanae, gratiam referant, 6, 14. 'A centurion famed for his valour, being condemned for debt and committed to prison, in the middle of the forum Manlius, with a crowd of followers rushing up, interposes as vindex. . . . Then he pays the creditor the debt in the presence of the people, and, after the balance and bar of bronze had completed the discharge, delivers the debtor, who called on gods and men to reward his liberator.'

As there are five modes of contracting an obligation, nexu, verbis, literis, re, consensu, there are as many corresponding modes of exoneration. Three of these, re, verbis, nexu, have been mentioned. Gaius says nothing of exoneration literis, but it is clear that as a debt could be constituted by expensilatio, so it could be cancelled by a corresponding accepti relatio.

A consensual contract, not yet followed by partial execution (re nondum secuta, Just. 3, 29, 4), could be dissolved by a contrary convention. Hae obligationes quae consensu contrahuntur contraria voluntate dissolvuntur, ibid. 'Obligations which consent creates, a contrary accord dissolves.' After a part performance, for instance, a conveyance of the consideration by one of the parties, the contract was not abandoned until the other party had made restitution, Cod. 4, 45, 1.

Not only could the obligation created by consensual contract be extinguished by consent, but obligation created by delict could by certain statutes be obliterated by convention. Legitima conventio est quae lege aliqua confirmatur, et ideo interdum ex pacto actio nascitur vel tollitur quotiens lege vel senatusconsulto adjuvatur, Dig. 47, 10, 6. 'A convention is statutory which derives validity from some statute, and grounds or destroys a right of action.' Thus the obligation and action arising out of outrage (injuriarum) and theft could be extinguished by pact, in the latter case by enactment of the Twelve Tables.

§ 176. It seems irrational that an invalid contract should be held to operate a novation, but a contract might be valid by Jus gentium though invalid at Civil law; and in respect of Novation naturalis obligatio was placed on a level with civilis obligatio. Novatio est prioris debiti in aliam obligationem, vel civilem vel naturalem, tranfusio atque translatio, hoc est cum ex praecedente causa ita nova constituitur ut prior perimatur. . . . Qualiscunque igitur obligatio est quae praecessit, novari verbis potest, dummodo sequens obligatio aut civiliter teneat aut naturaliter, ut puta si pupillus sine tutoris auctoritate promiserit, Dig. 46, 2, 1. 'Novation is the replacement and commutation of a prior debt by a subsequent obligation, civil or natural; or the destruction of a prior title by the constitution of a second. Every kind of obligation can undergo novation by verbal contract, provided that the subsequent obligation binds either by law civil or by law natural, as the promise of a ward without his guardian's authority.'

§ 177. We have already seen an instance of novation when treating of delegatio, 2 § 38, the satisfaction of a debt by substitution of a debtor. The substituted debtor who discharges the first is called expromissor, 3 § 139, commentary.

§ 178. We see by Justinian, 3, 29, 3, that the addition or omission of a fidejussor was finally held to operate a novation.

§ 179. Servius Sulpicius was wrong because novation implies a subsequent obligation, but a conditional obligation is really no obligation until the condition is realized. So if the prior obligation is conditional and the second obligation absolute, the novation is not absolute but conditional, because there is really no prior obligation until the condition is realized, at which moment novation takes place, and the prior obligation is extinguished.

Justinian enacted that no contract should operate a novation, unless the stipulating parties expressly declared their intention that such novation should be produced, Inst. 3, 29, 3.

§ 180. Litis contestatio, Joinder in issue, or the commencement of a suit, denoted, under the system of actions of the law, when pleadings were oral, the close of the proceedings in jure, when, the praetor having allowed an action, each party called those who were present to attest the nature of the issue allotted to be tried. Contestari est cum uterque reus dicit: Testes estote. Contestari litem dicuntur duo aut plures adversarii quod ordinato judicio utraque pars dicere solet: Testes estote. Festus. 'Contestation is when both parties exclaim, "Give your attestation." It marks the definitive settlement of the issue to be tried.' Under the formulary system the term was still employed, but marked the moment when the praetor delivered the written formula containing the commission of the judex. Under the third period of the law it denoted the commencement of the trial before the judex. Lis enim tunc contestata videtur, quum judex per narrationem negotii causam audire coeperit, Cod. 3, 9, 1. 'Litis contestatio is the moment when the judge begins to hear the recital of the cause of action.' By legitima judicia, 4 § 103, Gaius denotes those actions in the formulary procedure which by provision of the lex Aebutia, whereby the legis actiones were abolished, were declared to have the same effect, in respect of novation and otherwise, as the legis actiones, which they superseded. Actions terminable with the praetorship were such actions as did not derive their validity from the lex Aebutia, but from the administrative power of the praetor.

DE OBLIGATIONIBUS QUAE EX DELICTO NASCUNTUR.

§ 182. Transeamus nunc ad obligationes quae ex delicto oriuntur, veluti si quis furtum fecerit, bona rapuerit, damnum dederit, iniuriam commiserit: quarum omnium rerum uno genere consistit obligatio, cum ex contractu obligationes in IIII genera deducantur, sicut supra exposuimus.

§ 182. We proceed to obligations which originate in delict, theft, for instance, rapine, damage, or outrage, which are always Real, or incurred by some act or performance; whereas contractual obligations may be created in four different ways, as we have seen.

All actions are founded on the violation of some right, that is to say, on a wrong or delict. Even actions on contract are founded on a wrong, namely, on a breach of contract, and the plaintiff recovers not his primary right but a sanctioning right, in whatever measure it may be awarded. Delict (delictum, maleficium), however, is generally used in a more limited sense, to signify any wrong or unlawful act other than a breach of convention. Breach of contract is the violation of a jus in personam, or right available against a determinate person: delict in the narrower sense is a violation of a jus in rem, or right available against all the world. Jus in rem includes not only property and servitude but also rights of status, and what we have called primordial rights, e.g. the right to liberty, security, health, honour, reputation, for these rights can be maintained not against certain persons only but against all mankind.

Delicts or wrongs have a further division, into public and private. Public wrongs are called crimes, private wrongs are called trespasses, or torts, or civil injuries. Crimes have been defined to be such unlawful acts as are injurious in the first instance to the State; civil injuries, such as are harmful, principally or exclusively, to private individuals. But this definition is not satisfactory, because all or most crimes are injurious to private individuals, and all or most civil injuries are harmful to the community. A better definition is the following: Crimes are those unlawful acts which create an obligation (liability to punishment) which can only be remitted by the State; Civil injuries are those unlawful acts which engender an obligation remissible by the private individual whose primary rights are violated.

The following may be taken as a natural classification of actions. Every right of action arises out of a delict, i.e. a violation of some positive or negative obligation.

(1) A violation of a positive obligation, that is, an obligation to perform, is a violation of a jus in personam, and founds an action for breach of contract, called an action ex contractu.

(2) A violation of a negative obligation, that is, an obligation to abstain, is a violation of a jus in rem, and either imposes an obligation remissible by the individual aggrieved, founding a civil action real or personal, and called in the latter case an action ex delicto;

(3) Or imposes an obligation remissible by the State but irremissible by the individual, founding a criminal prosecution.

Actions ex contractu seek to enforce both the rights immediately founded on a contract and those created by a party's subsequent unlawful intention (dolus) or carelessness (culpa) in relation to the contract.

Real actions and actions ex contractu imply that a defendant HAS something which he ought not to have: withholds from the plaintiff some thing or service of pecuniary value to which the plaintiff is entitled. They do not necessarily impute unlawful disposition (dolus or culpa) to the defendant. Actions ex delicto do

not necessarily imply that the defendant has what he ought not to have; they necessarily impute unlawful disposition (dolus or culpa) to the defendant, § 211, and imply imputability, or responsibility for dolus and culpa.

In respect of contracts Culpa is distinguished as of different degrees; and sometimes a higher, sometimes a lower degree is capable of generating obligation. In respect of delicts Culpa is not distinguished by gradations; the least Culpa suffices to generate obligation.

All actions ex delicto are Penal, either bilaterally or unilaterally; that is, they tend, if not both to enrich the plaintiff and impoverish the defendant (bilaterally penal), at least to impoverish the defendant without enriching the plaintiff (unilaterally penal), as, for example, suits for indemnification. Real actions and actions ex contractu are not Penal but Conservative or Restorative; they maintain the fortunes of both parties at their original level; at the level destroyed or impeded by the defendant's wrong.

DE FURTIS.

§ 183. Furtorum autem genera Servius Sulpicius et Masurius Sabinus IIII esse dixerunt, manifestum et nec manifestum, conceptum, et oblatum: Labeo duo, manifestum, nec manifestum; nam conceptum et oblatum species potius actionis esse furto cohaerentes quam genera furtorum; quod sane verius videtur, sicut inferius apparebit.

§ 183. Thefts are divided by Servius Sulpicius and Masurius Sabinus into four kinds, theft detected in the commission, simple theft, the possession of stolen goods discovered upon search, and the introduction of stolen goods. Labeo makes only two kinds, theft detected in the commission and simple theft, because the possession and introduction of stolen goods are not thefts, but circumstances connected with theft; and this seems the better opinion, as will presently appear.

§ 184. Manifestum *furtum* quidam id esse dixerunt quod *dum fit* deprehenditur. alii *vero* ulterius, quod eo loco deprehenditur ubi fit: velut si in oliveto olivarum, in vineto uvarum furtum factum est, quamdiu in eo oliveto aut vineto fur sit; aut si in domo furtum factum sit, quamdiu in ea domo fur sit. alii adhuc ulterius, *eousque* manifestum furtum esse dixerunt, donec perferret eo quo perferre fur de-

§ 184. Theft detected in the commission is limited by some to detection in the act of taking; by others extended to detection while the thief is in the place where the theft is committed; for instance, if olives are stolen from an oliveyard, or grapes from a vineyard, while the thief is in the oliveyard or vineyard; or if a theft is committed in a house, while the thief is in the house. Others extend it

stinasset. alii adhuc ulterius, quandoque eam rem fur tenens visus fuẹrit; quae sententia non optinuit. se*d* et illorum sententia qui existimaverunt, donec perferret eo quo fur destinasset, deprehensum fur*tum manifestum esse, impro*bata *est, quod videbat*ur a*l*iquam *admittere* dubitatione*m*, u*nius* di*ei* a*n* etiam plurium dierum spatio id terminandum sit. quod eo pertinet, quia saepe in aliis civitatibus su*r*rept*as* res in alias civitates vel in alias provincias destinat fur perferre. ex duabus itaque superioribus opinionibus alterutra adprobatur: magis tamen plerique posteriorem proban*t*.

to detection before the thief has carried the goods away to the place where he intends to deposit them; others to detection while the thief has the goods in his hands. The fourth opinion has not been adopted, and the third opinion that, until the thief has carried the stolen goods to their place of destination, he may be detected in the commission, is also impugned on the ground of the uncertainty whether one day or several is the limit of the time within which he must be detected; for a thief often intends to carry the goods he has stolen in one city into another city or province. The first and second opinions are commonly adopted, and more generally the second.

§ 185. Nec manifestum furtum quod sit, ex iis quae diximus intellegitur: nam quod manifestum non est, id nec manifestum est.

§ 185. Simple theft is theft not detected in the act.

§ 186. Conceptum furtum dicitur, cum aput aliquem testibus praesentibus furtiva res quaesita et inventa est: nam in eum propria actio constituta est, quamvis fur non sit, quae appellatur concepti.

§ 186. The discovery of stolen goods, when a person's premises are searched in the presence of witnesses, makes him liable, even though innocent of theft, to a special action for receiving stolen goods.

§ 187. Oblatum furtum dicitur, cum res furtiva tibi ab aliquo oblata sit, eaque aput te concepta sit; utique si ea mente data tibi fuerit, ut aput te potius quam *aput* eum qui dederit conciperetur. nam tibi, aput quem concepta est, propria adversus eum qui optulit, quamvis fur non sit, constituta est actio, *quae* appellatur obl*a*ti.

§ 187. To introduce stolen goods is to pass them off to a man, on whose premises they are discovered, with the intent that they should be discovered on his premises rather than on those of the introducer. The man on whose premises they are found may sue the passer off, though innocent of theft, in an action for the introduction of stolen goods.

§ 188. Est et*iam* prohibiti furti adversus eum qui furtum quaerere volentem prohibuerit.

§ 188. An action for prevention of search may be brought against the man who prevents the search of his premises where stolen goods are suspected to be concealed.

§ 189. Poena manifesti furti ex lege XII tabularum capitalis erat. nam liber verberatus addicebatur ei cui furtum fecerat; (utrum autem

§ 189. The punishment provided by the law of the Twelve Tables for theft detected in the commission was capital; a freeman was first

servus efficeretur ex addictione, an adiudicati loco constitueretur, veteres quaerebant); *servum* aeque verbera*tum e saxo deiciebant*. postea i*m*probata est asperitas poenae, et tam ex servi persona quam ex liberi quadrupli actio Praetoris edicto constituta est.

scourged and then delivered, by judgment of the magistrate, to the person from whom he had stolen (whether made a slave by the delivery, or reduced to the condition of an insolvent judgment debtor, was an old question); a slave was first scourged and then flung from the Tarpeian rock. Later ages disapproved of the severity of this punishment, and theft, whether by a slave or by a freeman, was punished by the praetorian edict with fourfold damages.

§ 190. Nec manifesti furti poena per legem *XII* tabularum dupli inrogatur; quam etiam Praetor conservat.

§ 190. Simple theft is punished by the law of the Twelve Tables with double damages, which penalty the praetor has retained.

§ 191. Concepti et oblati poena ex lege XII tabularum tripli es*t*; qua*e* similite*r* a Praetore servatur.

§ 191. The possession and introduction of stolen goods are punished by the law of the Twelve Tables with triple damages, a penalty which the praetor has also adopted.

§ 192. Prohibiti actio quadrupli ex edicto Praetoris introducta *est*. lex autem eo nomine nullam poenam constituit: hoc solum praecepit, ut qui quaerere velit, n*u*dus quaerat, linteo cinctus, lancem habens; qui si quid invenerit, iubet id lex furtum manifestum esse.

§ 192. Prevention of search renders liable to fourfold damages, a penalty which the edict of the praetor first ordained. The Twelve Tables inflicted no penalty for such an offence, but directed that the subsequent searcher must be naked, only wearing a girdle, and carrying a platter in his hands, and made the ensuing discovery of stolen goods a detection of theft in the commission.

§ 193. Quid sit autem linteum, quaesitum est. *sed* verius *est* consuti genus *esse*, quo necessariae partes tegerent*ur*. quare lex tota ridicula est. nam qu*i* vestitum quaerere prohibet, is et nudum quaerere prohibit*u*rus est: eo magis quod ita quaesita res inventa maiori poenae subiciatur. deinde quod lancem sive ideo haberi iubeat, ut manibus occupantis nihil subiciatur, sive ideo, ut quod invenerit, ibi imponat: neutrum eorum procedit, si id quod *quae*ratur eius magnitudinis aut

§ 193. What the girdle was, is doubted, but it seems to have been a covering for the loins. The whole enactment of the Twelve Tables is nugatory, for he that prevents a man from searching in his clothes would prevent him from searching naked, especially as in such a search the finding of stolen goods would subject him to a heavier penalty. Besides, whether the platter is to be held by the searcher in order that his hands being engaged in holding it may not bring any-

naturae sit, ut neque subici neque ibi imponi possit. certe non dubitatur, cuiuscumque materiae sit ea lanx, satis legi fieri.

thing into the house, or in order that what is found may be placed thereupon, neither reason can be alleged when the thing searched for is of such a size or nature that it could not be brought into the house in the hand, nor placed on the platter. It is not disputed that a platter of any material satisfies the requirement of the Tables.

§ 194. Propter hoc tamen, quod lex ex ea causa manifestum furtum esse iubet, sunt qui scribunt furtum manifestum aut lege aut natura *intellegi*: lege id ipsum de quo loquimur; natura illud de quo superius exposuimus. sed verius est natura tantum manifestum furtum intellegi. neque enim lex facere potest, ut qui manifestus fur non si*t*, manifestus sit, non magis quam qui omnino fur non sit, fur sit, et qui adulter aut homicida non si*t*, adulter vel homicida sit: at illu*d* sane lex facere potest, ut perinde aliquis poena teneatur atque si furtum vel adulterium vel homicidium admi*si*sset, quamvis nihil eorum admiserit.

§ 194. On account of the enactment that a discovery in such a search is a detection of theft in the commission, some writers say that detection in the commission is of two kinds, legal and natural: legal detection being detection in such a search; natural detection, detection as recently defined. But in truth, the natural mode of detection in the commission is the only one that we can allow, for law cannot turn a thief not detected in the act into a thief detected in the act, any more than it can turn a man who is not a thief into a thief; or make an adulterer or homicide out of a man who has not killed or committed adultery. What law can accomplish is this, that a person shall be subject to a penalty just as if he had committed theft, adultery, or homicide, although he have not committed any of those offences.

§ 195. Furtum autem fit non solum cum quis intercipiendi causa rem alienam amovet, *sed* generaliter cum qui rem alienam invito domino contrectat.

§ 195. Theft is not confined to the carrying away the property of another with intent of appropriation, but embraces all corporal dealing with the property of another against the will of the owner.

§ 196. Itaque si quis re quae aput eum deposita sit utatur, furtum committit. et si quis utendam rem acceperit eamque in alium usum transtulerit, furti obligatur. veluti si quis argentum utendum acceperit, *quod* quasi amicos ad cenam invitaturus rogaverit, et id peregre secum tulerit, aut si quis e*qu*um

§ 196. Thus, to use a thing committed to one's keeping as a deposit, or to put a thing that is lent for use to a different use than that for which it was lent, is theft; to borrow plate, for instance, on the representation that the borrower is going to entertain his friends, and then to carry it away into the

gestandi gratia commodatum longius secum aliquo duxerit; quod veteres scripserunt de eo qui in aciem perduxisset.

country; or to borrow a horse for a drive, and then to take it out of the neighbourhood; or, like the man in the old case, to take it into battle.

§ 197. Placuit tamen eos qui *re*bus commodatis aliter uterentur quam utendas accepissent, ita furtum committere, si intellegant id se invito domino facere, eumque, si intellexisse*t*, non permissurum; et si permissurum crederent, extra furti crimen videri: optima sane distinctione, quia furtum sine dolo malo non committitur.

§ 197. It is held, however, that putting a thing lent for use to a different use than the lender contemplated is only theft if the borrower knows it to be contrary to the will of the owner, and that, if he had notice, he would refuse permission; but if he believes that the owner would give permission, it is not theft; and the distinction is just, for there is no theft without unlawful intention.

§ 198. Se*d et* si credat aliquis invito domino se rem *con*trectare, domino autem volente id fiat, dicitur furtum non fieri. unde illu*d* quaesitum est, cum Titius servum meum sollic*itar*it, ut quasdam res mihi subriperet et ad eum perferret, *et servus* id ad me pertul*er*it, ego, *d*um volo Titium in ipso delicto deprehendere, permiserim *ser*vo quasdam res ad eum perfe*r*re, utrum furti, an servi corrupti iudici*o* teneatur Titius mihi, an neutro: responsum, neutro eum teneri, furti ideo quod non invito me res contrectarit, servi corrupti ideo quod deterior servus factus non est.

§ 198. To deal with a thing in the belief that you are acting against the will of the owner, whereas the owner is consenting, is said not to be theft; whence a question arises, if Titius solicits my slave to steal my property, and convey it to him, and my slave informs me of it, and I, wishing to detect Titius in flagrante delicto, permit my slave to convey my goods to him; can an action of theft or for corrupting a slave be maintained against Titius? It has been held that neither action is maintainable; not theft, because I consented to his dealing with my property; not corrupting a slave, because the slave resisted the solicitation.

§ 199. Interdum autem etiam liberorum hominum furtum fit, velut si quis liberorum nostrorum qui in potestate nostra sunt, sive etiam uxor quae in manu nostra sit, sive etiam iudicatus vel auctoratus meus subreptus *f*ueri*t*.

§ 199. A freeman may be the subject of a theft; for instance, a child in my power, a wife in my hand, my insolvent debtor, or my hired gladiator, if secretly removed from my control.

§ 200. Aliquando etiam s*ua*e rei quisque furtum committit, veluti si debitor rem quam credito*r*i pignori dedit subtraxerit, vel si bonae fidei possessori rem meam possidenti subripuerim. unde placuit eum qui

§ 200. A man sometimes steals his own property; for instance, a debtor who purloins the goods which he has pledged to a creditor, or a proprietor who steals his property from a bona fide possessor; and

servum suum quem alius bona fide possidebat ad se reversum celaverit furtum committere.

accordingly it has been held, that concealment of one's slave, who, being possessed in good faith by another had returned to his owner, amounted to theft.

§ 201. Rursus ex diverso interdum *rem* alienam occupare et usucapere concessum est, nec creditur furtum fieri, velut res hereditarias quarum *non prius* nactus possessionem necessarius heres esset; *nam* necessario herede extante placuit, ut pro herede usucapi possit. *debitor quoque qui* fid*uciam quam* c*reditori* mancipaverit aut in i*u*re cesserit d*etinet*, *ut* superiore commentario rettulimus, sine furto possidere et usucapere potest.

§ 201. Conversely, property belonging to another may be seized and converted by usucapion without committing theft; hereditaments, for instance, before a necessary successor has obtained possession; for even where there is a necessary successor the first occupant may acquire by usucapion as quasi successor (2 § 58). Also a mortgagor, having detention of property mortgaged by mancipation or surrender in court, as I mentioned in the preceding book, may, without committing theft, repossess it and acquire new ownership thereof by usucapion.

§ 202. Interdum furti tenetur *qui* ipse furtum non fecerit: qualis est cuius ope consilio furtum factum est. in quo numero est qui nummos tibi excussit, ut eos alius surriperet, vel opstitit tibi, ut alius surriperet, aut *oves* aut boves tuas fugavit, ut alius eas exciperet; et hoc veteres scripserunt de eo qui panno rubro fugavit armentum. Sed si qui*d* per lasciviam, et non data opera, ut furtum committeretur, factum sit, videbimus an utilis *Aquiliae actio* dari debeat, cum per legem Aquiliam quae de damno lata *est* etiam culpa puniatur.

§ 202. Theft may be chargeable on a person who is not the perpetrator, on him, namely, by whose aid and abetment a theft is committed; to which class belongs the man who knocks out of your hand money for another to pick up, or stands in your way that another may snatch it, or scatters your sheep or oxen that another may steal them, like the man in the old books, who waved a red cloth to frighten a herd. If the same thing were done as a frolic, without the intention of assisting a theft, a modified or praetorian form of Aquilian action may be maintainable, for the Aquilian law relating to damage makes even carelessness penal.

§ 203. Furti autem a*ctio* ei c*om*petit cuius interest rem salvam esse, licet dominus non sit: itaque nec domino aliter c*om*petit, quam si *eius* in*ter*sit rem non perire.

§ 203. The action of theft is maintainable by the person interested in the preservation of the property, who need not be the owner; and even the owner cannot maintain it unless he suffers detriment from the loss.

§ 204. Unde constat creditorem de pignore subrepto furti agere

§ 204. Hence when a pawn is stolen, the pawnee can sue, and

posse; adeo quidem, ut quamvis ipse dominus, id est ipse debitor, eam rem subripuerit, nihilominus creditori competat actio furti.

even the owner or pawnor who steals a pawn is suable for theft by the pawnee.

§ 205. Item si fullo polienda curandave, aut sarcinator sarcienda vestimenta mercede certa acceperit, eaque furto amiserit, ipse furti habet actionem, non dominus; quia domini nihil *interest* ea non perisse, cum iudicio locati a fullone aut sarcinatore suum *persequi* possit, si modo is fullo aut sarcinator *ad* rem praestandam sufficiat; nam si solvendo non est, tunc quia ab eo dominus suum consequi non potest, ipsi furti actio competit, quia hoc casu ipsius interest rem salvam esse.

§ 205. So if clothes are delivered to be cleaned or finished or mended for a certain remuneration, and then are stolen, the fuller or tailor has the action, and not the owner; for the owner is not prejudiced by the loss, having his action of letting against the bailee to recover the value; supposing always, that the bailee is able to make the loss good. If the bailee is insolvent, the owner cannot recover out of him, and can maintain an action against the thief; being, in this hypothesis, interested in the loss of the property.

§ 206. Quae de fullone aut sarcinatore diximus, eadem transferemus et ad eum cui rem commodavimus: nam ut illi mercedem capiendo custodiam praestant, ita hic quoque utendi commodum percipiendo similiter necesse habet custodiam praestare.

§ 206. What has been said of the fuller and tailor applies to the borrower; for, as the remuneration they receive makes them responsible for custody, so the advantage the borrower derives from the use of an article requires him to keep it safely at his peril.

§ 207. Sed is aput quem res deposita est custodiam non praestat, tantumque in eo obnoxius est, si quid ipse dolo fecerit: qua de *causa*, *si* res ei subrepta fuerit quae restituenda est, eius nomine depositi non *tenetur*, nec ob id eius interest rem salvam esse: furti itaque agere non potest; *sed* ea actio domino competit.

§ 207. As a depositary is not answerable for the safe-keeping of the thing deposited, but only for fraud, and, if it is stolen, is not compellable to make restitution by action of deposit, he is not interested in its loss; and therefore the action of theft is only maintainable by the depositor.

§ 208. In summa sciendum est quaesitum esse, an impubes rem alienam *amovendo* furtum faciat. plerisque placet, quia furtum ex adfectu consistit, ita demum obligari eo crimine impuberem, si proximus pubertati sit, et ob id intellegat se delinquere.

§ 208. Finally, it is a question whether a child below the age of puberty, who carries away the property of another, commits a theft; and most agree that as theft depends on intention, obligation by theft is not incurred unless the child, being near to puberty, understands its delinquency.

Theft in modern systems of jurisprudence is a crime, that is, belongs to the penal or criminal code. In Roman law, as in other early systems, it is a private injury, and treated as a subject of the civil code. This was confirmed by the law of the Twelve Tables, which allowed a compromise or composition for theft, that is, allowed the obligation (liability to the legal sanction) thereby engendered to be extinguished by private convention between the party wronged and the wrongdoer, Dig. 2, 14; 7, 14.

§ 184. Aulus Gellius gives a fragment of Sabinus which combines the first and third definition of furtum manifestum. Manifestum autem furtum est, ut ait Masurius, quod deprehenditur dum fit. Faciendi finis est, cum perlatum est quo ferri coeperat, 9, 18, 1. 'Manifest theft is that which is detected in the act. The act is finished when the removal of the goods to the place intended is completed.' Justinian confirms the third definition, Inst. 4, 1, 3.

§ 189. The reason why furtum manifestum was subjected to a heavier penalty than furtum nec manifestum was not because the barbarous legislator supposed that detection in the act was an aggravation of the offence, but because he wished, by the amplitude of the legal remedy offered, to induce the aggrieved party not to take the law into his own hands and inflict summary vengeance on the offender, particularly as it was lawful to kill a nocturnal thief, or one who during the day defended himself with a weapon. In the infancy of society it is an important object to the legislator to induce an injured person to have recourse to the public tribunals instead of righting himself, that is to say, constituting himself both lawgiver and judge.

§ 193. We must distinguish between furtum conceptum and furtum lance et licio conceptum. Ea quoque furta quae per lancem liciumque concepta essent, proinde ac si manifesta forent, vindicaverunt, Gellius, 11, 18, 9. 'Possession of stolen goods discovered on search with the platter and girdle was punished as theft detected in the act.'

Traces of the word 'conceptum' occur in a fragment of the Twelve Tables: Tignum junctum aedibus vineaeque et concapet ne solvito, 'Timber built into a house or vineyard of another man and discovered there by the owner must not be severed:' where et concapet represents either et conceptum or qui concipiet.

The search with a platter and girdle was probably a custom derived from Greece, for a similar formality is described by Plato, Leges, 12, 7.

In the later period of Roman law, as in modern Europe, the search for stolen goods was not conducted by the private party but by public officers. In England the object is effected by a search warrant. Upon the information on oath that a party has probable cause to suspect that his goods have been stolen, and are concealed in a certain dwelling-house, and on his showing the cause of his suspicion, a justice of the peace may grant a warrant authorizing to enter and search for the said goods, and to attach the goods and the party in whose custody they are found, and bring them before him, that he may give an account how he came by them, and be dealt with according to law. The warrant is directed to a constable or other public officer and not to any private person, though it is proper that the party complaining should be present and assistant because he knows his goods. As touching the party that had custody of the goods, if they were stolen, but not by him but by another that sold and delivered them to him (furtum oblatum), if it appear that he was ignorant that they were stolen, he may be discharged as an offender and bound over to give evidence as a witness against him that sold them.

§ 195. The same definition of theft is given by Paulus. Fur est qui dolo malo rem alienam contrectat, Sent, R. 2, 31, 1. 'A thief is he who with evil intention handles (lifts, moves, touches,) the property of another.' Justinian gives a different definition. Furtum est contrectatio rei fraudulosa, lucri faciendi causa vel ipsius rei, vel etiam usus ejus possessionisve, Inst. 4, 1, 1. 'Theft is handling a thing with fraudulent intention to appropriate the property, use, or possession.'

It may be observed that Justinian does not say with Paulus, rei alienae, because a man may steal his own property, as when a pawnor steals from a pawnee or a proprietor from a usufructuary. So, by English law, to take a man's own goods out of the hands of a bailee, if the taking have the effect of charging the bailee, is larceny. The usus of a thing is stolen when the proprietor steals from the usufructuary, or when a pawnee unlawfully uses a pawn. Si creditor pignore utatur, furtum committit, Inst. 4, 1, 6.

Possessio is appropriated when a pawn is stolen by the pawnor, or when the depositary uses a deposit, or the borrower puts the thing borrowed to an unauthorized use. In Roman law the depositary and borrower, unlike the pawnee, have not possession but merely detention (see 4 § 153), and the same unlawful act (contrectatio) which amounts to theft converts their detention into possession.

In English law larceny is defined to be the unlawful taking and carrying away of things personal with intent to deprive the right owner of the same and to make them the property of the taker. To constitute larceny the original taking of possession must be unlawful: therefore, if the owner deliver his property to a person in trust, the subsequent conversion by the bailee, though an offence and a breach of faith, is not larceny, because the original taking was lawful. There are, however, two exceptions to this rule which deserve notice. It is larceny if the delivery was obtained by fraud, i.e. with an original design and pre-arranged plan to deprive the owner of his property and convert it to the use of the taker. The possession is then unlawful in its inception. Again, if delivery does not divest the owner of the legal possession, conversion by the taker is larceny. In this respect a servant (e.g. a shepherd, carter, porter, butler, clerk,) is to be distinguished from a bailee, for the servant is regarded as not possessing, but merely the instrument of the owner's possession.

As far as Roman law is concerned this principle would make the bailee, as well as the servant, capable of larceny, for in Roman law the bailee (except in the case of pignus) has not possession, but merely detention. The fact, however, that the pawnee, who has lawful possession, is guilty of theft if he make use of the pawn, shows that in Roman law an unlawful inception of possession is not an essential element in the definition of furtum.

§ 198. Justinian decided that the attempt to corrupt a slave was as criminal as his actual corruption, and made the offender liable to be sued both for theft and for corrupting a slave, Inst. 4, 1, 8.

§ 201. Usucapion of the property of a necessary successor, and usureceptio, or usucapion of the property of a mortgagee, have been mentioned in the preceding book. See 2 §§ 52–60.

§ 202. A person who is present aiding and abetting when an offence is committed but is not the actual perpetrator is called, in English law, a principal in the second degree. He who procures or abets another to commit an offence but is absent at the time of the commission is called an accessary before the fact. Their punishment is usually the same as that of the principal in the first degree. An accessary after the fact is one who, knowing an offence to have been committed by another, receives, harbours, or assists the offender.

§ 203. When a sale is complete, property does not, by Roman law, pass to the vendee before delivery, although the thing sold is forthwith at the risks of the vendee. If it is stolen before delivery, in spite of the rule that the action of theft is maintainable by the person interested, the vendee cannot sue in his own name, but the vendor is compellable to cede his actions and the vendee sues in the name of the vendor, Dig. 47, 2, 14, 1. From this we may infer the rule that to maintain the action of theft, besides interest in the loss, a plaintiff must have had either property or detention, both of which are wanting to the vendee in the case supposed.

The quadruple and double damages for furtum manifestum and nec manifestum were purely penal. The owner could further recover restitution of thing stolen by a real action (vindicatio) or its equivalent in a personal action (condictio furtiva), Inst. 4, 1, 20. The granting of a personal action in this case, with an intentio declaring that the thief was bound to convey the property (dare oportere), was anomalous, because the property of thing stolen was not in the thief but in the owner.

If the thing stolen had been destroyed, or if, being money, it had been spent or mixed with money of the thief, the property of the plaintiff would have been extinguished and condictio would be a suitable action. If the property existed in the hands of the thief vindicatio was the proper action. The object of the legislator in allowing the plaintiff in any case to sue by condictio was to relieve him from the necessity of ascertaining whether his property was safe or had been consumed. If we ask why, instead of using the intentio, Si paret dare oportere, 4 § 4, which might be inconsistent with the truth, the plaintiff did not use the formula, Quidquid paret dare facere oportere, which, as including compensation or simple restitution of possession, would always be consistent with truth; the answer is probably what Savigny has suggested, namely, the intention of the legislator to subject the defendant to the sponsio poenalis, the additional forfeiture of a third of the sum in litigation. It is true that this is only mentioned as incidental to a condictio for pecunia certa credita, 4 § 171, but the penalty may have also been recoverable in a claim for certain money stolen (condictio furtiva).

The plaintiff in theft had the option of proceeding by civil action or by criminal prosecution, and Ulpian informs us that the latter was the usual course, Dig. 47, 2, 94.

DE VI BONORUM RAPTORUM.

§ 209. Qui res alienas rapit tenetur etiam furti: quis enim magis alienam rem invito domino *con*trectat quam qui rapit? itaque rect*e* *dic*tum est eum improbum furem esse. *sed* propriam actionem eius *de*licti nomin*e* Praetor introduxit, quae appellatur vi bonorum raptorum; et est intra annum quadrupli actio, post annum simpli. quae actio utilis est, et si quis unam rem, licet minimam, rapuerit.

§ 209. Rapine or robbery is chargeable as theft, for who more handles the property of another against the will of the owner than the robber? who has been well denominated an audacious thief. However, as a special remedy for this offence the praetor has introduced the action for rapine with violence; which may be brought within a year for four times the value, after a year for simple damages; and which lies when only a single thing of the slightest value has been taken with violence.

The party aggrieved might either proceed by civil action or by criminal prosecution under the lex Julia de vi publica et privata. This law, enacted either by Augustus or by Julius Caesar, made the criminal guilty of public or armed violence liable to deportation; the criminal guilty of private or unarmed violence, to confiscation of a third of his goods, Inst. 4, 18, 8.

The quadruple damages in the civil action of rapine were not purely penal as in the action of furtum manifestum, but included the restitution of the property or its value. The penal damages for rapine were therefore only three times the value of the goods plundered, that is, less than the damages in furtum manifestum. If, however, the robber was taken in the act, he was chargeable, as Gaius explains, with furtum manifestum.

Robbery, like theft, requires dolus malus, that is, criminal intention. If then a man, believing himself to be rightful owner, violently invaded lands or violently seized movable goods, he was not guilty of robbery; but, by a constitution of the emperors Valentinian, Theodosius, and Arcadius, enacted A.D. 389, in order to repress violence, and deter people from taking the law into their own hands, the offender, if rightful owner, forfeited the property to the person dispossessed; if not rightful owner, was condemned, besides restitution of possession, to forfeit the value of the property, Cod. 8, 4, 7. This constitution increased the civil penalty recoverable for violent dispossession by the interdict unde vi, 4 § 154. By the interdict unde vi no penalty was originally recoverable for violent, but unarmed, dispossession of one whose own possession was tainted by an origin, violent, clandestine, or permissive: and for either armed or unarmed dispossession the penalty, as far as the property in question was concerned, was only restitution of possession. By the constitution of the three emperors the civil penalty of all violent disseisin was loss not only of possession but of property; and subsequently to this constitution the interdict unde vi ceased to make a distinction between armed and unarmed dispossession.

DE LEGE AQUILIA.

§ 210. Damni iniuriae actio constituitur per legem Aquiliam. cuius primo capite cautum est, *ut* si quis hominem alienum, eamve quadrupedem qua*e* pecudum numero sit, iniuria occiderit, quanti ea res in eo anno plurimi fu*er*it, tantum domino dare damnetur.

§ 210. Damage unlawfully caused is actionable under the lex Aquilia, whose first chapter provides, that if a slave of another man, or a quadruped of his cattle, be unlawfully slain, whatever within a year was the highest value thereof, that amount the offender shall pay to the owner.

§ 211. Is iniuria autem occidere intellegitur cuius dolo aut culpa id acciderit, nec ulla alia lege damnum quod sine iniuria datur reprehendi*tur*: itaque inpunitus est qui sine culpa et dolo malo casu quodam damnum committit.

§ 211. Unlawful slaying means slaying by intention or negligence; for it is only disobedience to law that is punished, and in the absence of intention and negligence there is no penalty for fortuitous damage.

§ 212. Nec solum corpus in actione huius legis aestimatur; sed sane *s*i servo occiso plus dominus capiat damni quam pretium servi *sit*, id quoque aestimatur: velut si servus meus ab aliquo heres institutus, ante quam iussu meo hereditatem cerneret, occis*us* fuerit; non enim tantum ipsius pretium aestimatur, sed et hereditatis amissae quantitas. item si ex gemellis vel ex comoedis vel ex sy*mph*oniacis unus occisus fuerit, non solum occisi fit aestimatio, sed eo amplius *quoque* co*m*putatur quod ceteri qui supersunt depretiati sunt. idem

§ 212. It is not only the body of the slave or animal slain that is appraised, but if the death of a slave occasion to the owner the loss of anything in addition to his price, this loss is further estimated; for instance, if my slave has been instituted somebody's heir, and before by my order he has signified his acceptance, he is slain, valuation is made not only of his body but also of the inheritance I have missed; or if one of two twins, or one of a company of players, or one of a band of musicians is slain, an estimate is made not only of his value

iuris est etiam si ex pari mularum unam, vel etiam ex quadrigis equorum unum occiderit.

but also of the extent to which the remainder are depreciated. The same holds if one of a pair of mules, or one of four chariot horses is killed.

§ 213. Cuius autem servus occisus est, is liberum arbitrium habet vel capitali crimine reum facere eum qui occiderit, vel hac lege damnum persequi.

§ 213. The owner whose slave is killed has the option of accusing the homicide of a capital crime or of suing him under this law for damages.

§ 214. Quod autem adiectum est in hac lege: QUANTI IN EO ANNO PLURIMI EA RES FUERIT, illud efficit, si clodum puta aut luscum servum occiderit, qui in eo anno integer fuerit, *ut non quanti mortis tempore, sed quanti in eo anno plurimi fuerit*, aestimatio fiat. quo fit, ut quis plus interdum consequatur quam ei damnum datum est.

§ 214. From the words of this law, 'Whatever within a year was the highest value thereof,' it follows that if a slave was lame or blind of one eye when he was slain, but had been sound within a year, as it is not his value at the time of his death but his highest value within a year that is appraised, a plaintiff will sometimes recover more than the amount of the loss he has sustained.

§ 215. Capite secundo *in* adstipulatorem qui pecuniam in fraudem stipulatoris acceptam fecerit, quanti ea res est, tanti actio constituitur.

§ 215. By the second chapter an adstipulator who defrauds a principal covenantee by releasing the covenantor can be sued for the amount of the loss occasioned.

§ 216. Qua et ipsa parte legis damni nomine actionem introduci manifestum est. sed id caveri non fuit necessarium, cum actio mandati ad eam rem sufficeret; nisi quod ea lege adversus infitiantem in duplum agitur.

§ 216. In this chapter, as well as in the others, damage is made a ground of action, though here the provision was unnecessary, because the action of Agency would give a sufficient remedy, except that the lex Aquilia, when the facts are traversed, gives double damages.

§ 217. Capite tertio de omni cetero damno cavetur. itaque si quis servum vel eam quadrupedem quae pecudum numero *est vulneraverit, sive eam quadrupedem quae pecudum numero non est*, velut canem, aut feram bestiam velut ursum leonem vulneraverit vel occiderit, ex hoc capite actio constituitur. in ceteris quoque animalibus, item in omnibus rebus quae anima carent, damnum iniuria datum hac parte vindicatur. si quid enim ustum aut ruptum aut fractum *fuerit*, actio hoc capite constituitur; quamquam

§ 217. The third chapter makes provision for all other damage. Therefore if a slave, or a quadruped included under the name of cattle, is wounded, or if a quadruped not included under the name of cattle, as a dog, or a wild beast, a bear or lion, is wounded or is killed, in this chapter an action is provided: or if other animals or things inanimate are unlawfully damaged, this chapter imposes a penalty, for all burning, breaking, crushing, is herein made actionable: and indeed the single word 'breaking' covers all these

potuerit sola rupti appellatio in omnes istas causas sufficere: ruptum *enim intellegitur quod quoquo modo corruptum* est. unde non so*lum usta aut* rupta aut fracta, se*d* et*iam* scissa et collisa et effusa et *diruta* aut perempta atque deteriora facta hoc verbo continentur.

offences, for breaking denotes every kind of injury; and not only burning, breaking, crushing, but any cutting, bruising, spilling, demolishing, destroying, or deteriorating, is hereby denominated.

§ 218. Hoc tamen capite non quanti in eo anno, sed quanti in diebus XXX proxumis ea res fuerit, damnatur is qui damnum dederit; ac ne PLURIMI quidem verbum adicitur: et ideo quidam *diversae scholae auctores* putaverunt liberum esse ius *datum, ut duntaxat* de *XXX* diebus *proxumis vel eum Praetor formulae* adiceret *quo* plurimi res fuit, vel a*lium* quo minoris fuit. sed Sabino placuit perinde habendum ac s*i* et*iam* hac parte PLURIMI verbum adiectum esset: nam legis latorem contentum fuisse, *quod prima parte eo verbo usus esset.*

§ 218. In this chapter it is not the value which the thing had within a year, but which it had within the last thirty days, that is chargeable on the author of the mischief, and it is not expressly the highest value. Hence some of the other school have held that it was left to the discretion of the praetor (judex?) whether the damages should be measured by the highest value or by any lower value which the thing may have had within the last thirty days: but Sabinus held that the law must be interpreted as if it contained the word 'highest,' the legislator having thought it sufficient to use this word in the first chapter.

§ 219. Et placuit ita demum ex ista lege actionem esse, si quis corpore suo damnum dederit. *ita*que alio modo damno dato utiles actiones dantur: velut si quis alienum hominem a*ut* pecudem incluserit et fame necaverit, aut iumentum tam vehementer egerit, ut rumperetur; *aut* si quis alieno servo persuaserit, ut in arborem ascenderet vel in puteum descenderet, et *is* ascendendo aut descendendo ceciderit, *et* aut mortuus fuerit aut aliqua parte corporis laesus sit. item si quis alienum servum de ponte a*ut* ripa in flumen proiecerit et is suffocatus fuerit, *tum* hic corpore suo damnum dedisse eo quod proiecerit, non difficiliter intellegi potest.

§ 219. It is held that an action under this statute only lies when the body of the offender is the instrument of mischief; for any other mode of occasioning loss a modified action must be brought: for instance, if a slave or quadruped is shut up and starved to death, or a horse is foundered by hard driving, or a slave is persuaded to climb a tree or descend a well, and in climbing or descending falls and is killed or hurt. But if a slave is pushed off a bridge or bank into a river and there drowned, the body of the person who pushed him may fairly be held to have caused his death.

§ 210. The lex Aquilia was a plebiscite carried by a tribune called Aquilius, according to Theophilus, at one of the secessions of the plebs, probably at the secession to the Janiculum, B.C. 285, on which same occasion the lex Hortensia was carried, making the plebiscites binding on the patricians.

The words of the first clause are preserved in the Digest: Qui servum servamve alienum alienamve, quadrupedemve pecudem injuria occiderit, quanti id in eo anno plurimi fuit, tantum aes dare domino damnas esto, Dig. 9, 2, 2. 'If a slave, male or female, of another person, or a quadruped of his cattle is unlawfully slain, whatever was the highest value it bore in the previous year, such sum shall be due as a judgment debt from the slayer to the owner.' Cattle are animals that feed in flocks or herds, and include horses, mules, asses, oxen, sheep, goats, and swine.

§ 213. The owner of a murdered slave both had a civil remedy by the lex Aquilia, and could prosecute criminally under the lex Cornelia de sicariis, passed in the dictatorship of Sylla, B.C. 80.

§ 215. The lex Aquilia, like many other Roman laws, combined heterogeneous dispositions. The first and third chapters contain remedies for destruction of property, or jus in rem, that is, the injury of a chose in possession; the second chapter contains a remedy for the destruction of an obligation, or jus in personam, that is, the injury of a chose in action.

§ 217. The terms of the third chapter are preserved in the Digest: Ceterarum rerum, praeter hominem et pecudem occisos, si quis alteri damnum faxit, quod usserit fregerit ruperit injuria, quanti ea res fuit in diebus triginta proximis, tantum aes domino dare damnas esto, Dig. 9, 2; 27, 5. 'For property, other than slave or cattle slain, damaged by burning, breaking, crushing, unlawfully, the value it bore in the thirty days preceding shall be due as a judgment debt from the offender to the owner.'

§ 219. An action founded on the text of a law was called actio directa, an action not founded on the very text of the law, but granted by the praetor in the exercise of his judicial authority in circumstances which, though different, are similar to those which founded the direct action, was called actio utilis. The direct Aquilian action could only be brought when damage was immediately caused by a body to a body. If the damage was not caused by a body, or not by immediate contact, only the actio utilis could be brought. The actio utilis was some modification of the actio directa, to which it apparently contained a reference, though the precise nature of the modification and the exact terms of the reference have not been handed down. In a case of damage where neither the agent nor the patient was a body, neither directa Aquilia nor utilis Aquilia could be maintained, but only actio in factum, Inst. 4, 3, 16. The actio in factum was a still further departure from the actio directa, to which it contained no reference, and indeed was not necessarily related to any actio directa. It was so named because the formula merely proposed a matter of fact (si paret fecisse) to be verified by the judex, and, in the event of an affirmative finding, directed a condemnation.

The mode of growth of Roman law and the relation between directa Aquilia and utilis Aquilia may be illustrated by similar phenomena in English law, and the relation between the two forms of action called Trespass and Trespass on the Case. Trespass, which lies for injury to real or personal property or to the person, accompanied with violence, has a more extensive application than directa Aquilia, but viewed only as redressing injuries to personal property, is nearly coextensive in its range. The original scheme of actions, devised in comparatively barbarous times, contained no remedy for injuries where there is no act done but only a culpable omission, or where the act is not immediately injurious, but only by consequence or collaterally, or where the idea of force is inapplicable because the subject matter is not corporeal or tangible, although the injury may be by act direct and immediate in its operation. To supply such deficiencies the statute of Westminster, 13 Edward I, had directed the clerks in chancery to frame new writs whenever the old scheme of writs contained no remedy for a wrong resembling in its features other wrongs for which a remedy was provided. Accordingly, a new writ of Trespass on the Case was framed upon the analogy of the old form of Trespass (confer, ad exemplum institoriae, § 162 com.) applying to cases where the injury is not immediate, or the subject affected is not corporeal, or the agency is not bodily force. What Edward I. directed to be done by the clerks in chancery, and what was done by the introduction of the action of Trespass on the Case, was exactly analogous to what the praetors did when, in virtue of their judicial authority, they supplemented the civil law by the introduction of actiones fictitiae and actiones in factum. In respect of torts to personal property, the latter have nearly the same sphere as Trespass on the Case. The innovations of the praetor, however, were not confined to the region of torts to personal property, but pervaded every sphere, and constituted a mass of supplementary law (jus praetorium) having to the remainder of the law (jus civile) similar relations and equal proportions to those which equity has to common law in English jurisprudence.

DE INIURIIS.

§ 220. Iniuria autem committitur non solum cum quis pugno pulsa*tus aut* fuste percussus vel etiam verberatus erit, sed et si cui convicium factum fuerit, sive quis *bona* alicuius quasi debitoris sciens eum [ipsi] nihil debere sibi proscripserit, sive quis ad infamiam alicuius libellum aut carmen scripserit, sive quis matremfamilia*s* aut praetextatum adsectatus fuerit, et denique aliis pluribus modis.

§ 220. Outrage is inflicted not only by striking with the fist or a stick or a whip, but by scandalous vociferation, or by maliciously seizing and advertising for sale under an order of the praetor the goods of a person as if he were insolvent, or an absconding debtor, or by writing defamatory prose or verse, or by constantly following a matron or youth wearing the praetexta, and by many other modes.

§ 221. Pati a*utem* iniuriam videmur non solum per nosmet ipsos, sed et*iam* per liberos nostros quos in potestate habemus; item per uxores nostras qu*amvis* in manu [nostra] *non* sint. itaque si vel*uti* filiae meae quae Titio nupta est iniuriam feceris, non solum filiae nomine tecum agi iniuriarum potest, verum etiam meo quoque et Titii nomin*e*.

§ 221. Outrage may be suffered either in one's own person, or in the person of a child in our power, or of a wife though not in our hand. So that if you insult my daughter married to Titius, but not passed out of my power into his hand, you are suable for outrage in three cumulative actions, in her name, in my name, in the name of her husband.

§ 222. Servo autem ipsi *quidem* nulla iniuria intellegitur fieri, sed domino per eum fieri videtur: non tamen iisdem modis quibus etiam per liberos nostros vel uxores, iniuriam pati videmur, sed ita, cum quid atrocius commissum fuerit, quod aperte in *con*tumeliam domini fieri videtur, veluti si quis alienum servum verberaverit; et in hunc casum formula proponitur. at si qui servo convicium fecerit vel pugno eum percusserit, non proponitur ulla formula, nec temere petenti datur.

§ 222. A slave cannot be outraged himself, but his master may be outraged in his person, not however by all the acts whereby he might be outraged in the person of a child or wife, but only by atrocious assaults, clearly tending to dishonour the master, for instance, by flogging the slave; and for this affront a formula is provided in the praetor's album: but for verbal abuse of a slave, or striking him with the fist, no formula is provided, nor would an action be readily granted.

§ 223. Poena autem iniuriarum ex leg*e* XII tabula*rum* propter membrum quidem ruptum talio erat; propter os vero fractum aut co*l*lisum trecentorum assium poena erat *statuta*, si libero os fractum erat; at

§ 223. The penalty of outrage in the Twelve Tables for a limb broken was retaliation: for a bone broken or bruised three hundred asses, if the person injured was a freeman; one hundred and fifty if he was a

si servo, CL. propter ceteras vero iniurias XXV assium poena erat constituta. et videbantur illis temporibus in magna paupertate satis idoneae istae pecuniae poenae *esse*.

slave; for other injuries twenty-five asses: and in those days of excessive poverty such sums seemed an adequate reparation.

§ 224. *Sed* nunc alio iure utimur. permittitur enim nobis a Praetore *ipsis* iniuriam aestimare; et iudex vel tanti condemnat quanti nos aestimaverimus, vel minoris, pro*ut* ill*i visum* fuerit. *sed* cum atrocem iniuriam Praetor aestimare soleat, si simul constituerit quantae pecuniae nomine fieri debeat vadimonium, hac ipsa quantitate taxamus formulam, et iudex qu*amvis* possit vel minoris damnare, plerumque tamen propter ipsius Praetoris auctoritatem non audet minuere condemnationem.

§ 224. The rule now in use is different: the plaintiff is permitted by the praetor to put his own estimate on the outrage, and the judex may either condemn the defendant in the whole of this sum, or in a lesser sum at his discretion. Atrocious outrage, however, is generally for the praetor to estimate; and when he has once fixed the sum in which the defendant must give security to appear at the trial, the plaintiff inserts the same sum in the formula; and the judex, though he has the power of condemning the plaintiff in less, generally, out of deference to the praetor, will not venture to reduce the condemnation.

§ 225. Atrox autem iniuria aestimatur vel ex facto, velut si quis ab aliquo vulneratus aut verberatus fustibusve caesus fuerit; vel ex loco, velut si cui in theatro aut in foro iniuria facta sit; vel ex persona, velut si magistratus iniuriam passus fuerit, vel senatoribus ab humili persona facta sit iniuria.

§ 225. Outrages are atrocious either by the act, as when a man is wounded, horse-whipped, or beaten with a stick; or from the place, as when an affront is offered in the theatre or the forum; or from the persons, as when a magistrate or a senator is insulted by one of inferior rank.

§ 220. Injuria in this chapter denotes not any wrongful or unlawful act, but contumelious wrong, a violation of the right to respect, honour, reputation; such as libel, malicious prosecution, assault and battery, and the like.

§ 221. If the husband were a filiusfamilias, the offender would be liable to a fourth action, on the part of the father of the husband. In each of these actions the damages might be different, being measured by the varying dignity of the party dishonoured by the outrage.

Outrage, like theft and robbery, and unlike damage under the lex Aquilia, requires dolus malus, or unlawful design. In outrage, as in other torts, the plaintiff had his option of proceeding civilly or criminally, Inst. 4, 4, 10.

In the Roman law in force at the present day, as the basis or Common Law of German jurisprudence, bilaterally penal suits appear to be obsolete, with the exception of actio Injuriarum.

After treating of obligations created by delict, Justinian proceeds to a fourth class, namely, obligations quasi ex delicto. Four instances of these are given:—(1) Si judex litem suam fecerit, i. e. if a judge makes a suit his own (or, makes a suit against himself), that is, makes himself actionable by giving a judgment contrary to law, whether from corruption or from ignorance, he was liable to be condemned in the amount recoverable in the wrongly decided suit. (2) If any thing is thrown out of a window and occasioned damage, the paterfamilias occupying the room is liable to twice the value of the damage, although the thing was thrown by some other person. (3) If any thing is suspended dangerously over a place of public resort, the paterfamilias in occupation is liable to a penalty of ten aurei. If a filiusfamilias is residing apart from his father, and the thing is thrown or suspended from his window, the filiusfamilias and not the father is liable. The last two actions are populares, that is, the damages are recoverable by a common informer. (4) If theft or malicious mischief is committed in an inn or on board a ship by a servant or sailor, the innkeeper and shipowner are liable in twice the value.

If we ask why an unskilful surgeon or physician is liable for a delict, Inst. 4, 3, 7, whereas an ignorant judge is only liable for a quasi delict, the only answer is, that an unskilful surgeon or physician comes within the terms of the lex Aquilia, for the damage is caused by a body to a body, and the ignorant judge does not. It is observable that all the quasi delicts are, rationally speaking, genuine delicts, and apparently are only excluded in Roman law from the category of delicts because they fall under no certain statute, or because they are recent additions to the code, not from any inferior degree of culpability; for even the shipowner and innkeeper are to a certain extent blameable for employing dishonest servants or for a want of supervision (aliquatenus culpae reus est quod opera malorum hominum uteretur, Inst. 4, 5, 3). There seems, then, to be no reason for retaining in a rational system of jurisprudence the class of obligations quasi ex delicto. The class of obligations quasi ex contractu is not so easy to suppress.

All quasi delicts are suable by actio in factum.

In dealing with the subject of Obligation we have frequently to use the words 'liable,' 'answerable,' 'accountable,' 'responsible.' When an agent is said to be answerable or accountable, the act is said to be imputable. The grounds or conditions of imputability are intention (dolus) and negligence (culpa), 3 § 211. It is therefore desirable to obtain a precise conception of the signification of these terms.

Desires or wishes either attain their objects immediately and instantaneously, or only by the intervention of other objects antecedently attained. The antecedent object is called a 'mean,' the consequent or mediate object is called an 'end.' If no object were immediately attainable, if every mean had to be reached by an antecedent mean, if the regression of previous conditions was unlimited, all desire would be futile and no end could ever be attained. There must be, then, some primary mean, some limit to the series of antecedent conditions, some objects of desire attained by a wish. What is the nature of these objects, and what is the name of the wish by which they are evoked?

The only objects that man can realize by a wish are the muscular movements of the bodily organs.

Greek psychology does not appear to have had a proper name for the wish which produces a movement of the limbs. Doubtless, the words ὄρεξις and ὀρεκτόν apply to these wishes and their objects, but they apply equally to ulterior ends or motives, and we want a term to signify exclusively and distinctively the primary mean. Again, προαίρεσις (resolve or resolution) denotes the desire of an original mean, but only one species thereof, namely, desire preceded by deliberation or premeditation, and we are seeking for a name of all desires that are immediately fulfilled, whether premeditated or unpremeditated, whether the counsel of reason or the impulse of unreflecting passion. For this purpose Will and Volition seem to be the most appropriate words that the English language offers. Though applicable without impropriety to distant ends, they are perhaps more commonly applied to means, and in particular to the command we exercise over our bodily frame. We say that we will a movement, that the limbs obey the will, that a bodily movement follows instantaneously upon a volition. Over whatever regions the dominion of the Will may be extended, the direct origination of motion in the limbs is its earliest manifestation, and continues its principal function to the end of life. Wanting, then, a term to denote the wish of an original mean, or rather of an object attainable without the intervention of means, we take the generic term Will or Volition and give it a specific signification, denoting thereby the desire or wish which is immediately fulfilled, whether such wish be the aimless dictate of a passing emotion or initiate the execution of a many-stepped or many-staged and long-considered plan.

Having fixed the meaning of Volition, we have materials for the definition of Intention, which is a correlative of Volition. In popular language Intention always implies the contemplation of an end. As a condition of responsibility it denotes the contemplation of the immediate consequences of those muscular movements which are the objects of Volition or determined by Will. The simplest action is a complication of a multitude of muscular movements produced by a multitude of Volitions. Suppose that certain complicated muscular movements, the lifting of a pistol, the taking aim at a man, the pulling the trigger, are the antecedents of a certain event, namely, that a man is shot. If this end was contemplated, the shooting was intentional. Intention is the contemplation of the consequence or end of bodily movements, and the belief or expectation that it will ensue. Or we may define it the combination or co-ordination of bodily movements to a contemplated and expected or anticipated end.

Intention sometimes denotes a remote or ulterior end, the ultimate motive of a series of subordinate ends; but for our present purpose it is confined to the immediate consequences of those muscular movements which are the objects of Volition. These consequences, according to our definition of Will, are not willed, but intended. The movements, being consequences of the volitions, that is, standing to them in the relation of end to mean, may be said to be both willed and intended.

Intention being defined, Negligence, the negation of intention and alternative ground of responsibility, will be more easily comprehended. An actor is negligent when he is ignorant of the consequences of his act, if his ignorance proceeds from thoughtlessness, recklessness, carelessness, want of due attention. Negligence is inadvertence to consequences to which a man might have adverted, and to which he would have adverted had he been desirous to obey the law and perform the obligations which it imposes. As obligation may either consist in performance or forbearance, so the negligent breach of obligation, which we have always spoken of hitherto as if it always consisted in commission, may be either commission or omission. The word Negligence, indeed, most properly designates inadvertence to the consequences of omission or inaction. Inadvertence to the consequences of commission may be called heedlessness. If the mischievous consequences of an act are adverted to, but on insufficient grounds are not expected to follow, the neglect of precaution is called temerity or rashness.

The foregoing definition of Intention agrees with that given by Aristotle, except that, instead of singling out one element, the consequences, as the object of consciousness, he requires that all the elements of an action, the consequences, the degree of force, the instrument, the patient or subject, the agent, the act, should be present to the mind of the actor, in order to make his conduct intentional, although of these ingredients the consequences are admitted to be one of the most important. *ὄντος δ' ἀκουσίου τοῦ βιαίου καὶ δι' ἄγνοιαν, τὸ ἑκούσιον δόξειεν ἂν εἶναι οὗ ἡ ἀρχὴ ἐν αὐτῷ, εἰδότι τὰ καθ' ἕκαστα ἐν οἷς ἡ πρᾶξις*, Ethica Nicomachea, 3, 1, 20. (So far the definition only includes the Intentional. To make it coextensive with the Imputable we must complete it by adding *καὶ ὅσα δι' ἀμέλειαν ἀγνοεῖν δοκοῦσιν*, ibid. 3, 5, 9, or, *καὶ ὅταν ἐν ἑαυτῷ ἡ ἀρχὴ ᾖ τῆς ἀγνοίας*, ibid. 5, 8, 7). 'That is involuntary (unimputable) which is caused by external compulsion or by ignorance. That is Voluntary (imputable) whose cause or beginning is internal (Will, Volition) with a knowledge of the individual ingredients which constitute the action, or without this knowledge, if the ignorance is produced by negligence—if the agent is to blame for his ignorance.' Or we may make the Voluntary inclusive of Negligence and coextensive with the Imputable by dividing Knowledge, with the writer of the Eudemian Ethics, into actual knowledge and possible knowledge. *ἐπεὶ δὲ τὸ ἐπίστασθαι καὶ τὸ εἰδέναι διττόν, ἓν μὲν τὸ ἔχειν, ἓν δὲ τὸ χρῆσθαι τῇ ἐπιστήμῃ, ὁ ἔχων μὴ χρώμενος δὲ ἔστι μὲν ὡς δικαίως ἂν ἀγνοῶν λέγοιτο, ἔστι δ' ὡς οὐ δικαίως, οἷον εἰ δι' ἀμέλειαν μὴ ἐχρῆτο . . . ταῦτ' οὖν προσδιαιρετέον*, Ethica Eudemia, 2, 9. 'To know or be aware has two meanings, to have knowledge and to use knowledge; so that a man who has knowledge and does not use it may be justly said in one sense not to know, in another sense to know, if he fails to use it from negligence. . . . This distinction, then, must be added to complete the definition of the voluntary.'

Intention (dolus) is either hasty intention (exemplified in *ἀδίκημα*), including actions impelled by any appetite or emotion, or deliberate intention (exemplified in *ἀδικία*), denominated Resolve or Resolution (προαίρεσις). προαιρετὸν τὸ ἑκούσιον τὸ προβεβουλευμένον, Ethica Nic. 3, 2, 17. 'That is resolved which is voluntary and premeditated.' ἡ προαίρεσις ἂν εἴη βουλευτικὴ ὄρεξις, ibid. 3, 3, 19. 'Resolution is deliberate volition.'

Negligent violation of the law (culpa, ἁμάρτημα) is distinguished, on the one side, from misadventure (casus, ἀτύχημα), and, on the other, from intentional violation of the law (dolus, ἀδίκημα), which again is distinguished from deliberate violation of the law (ἀδικία). τριῶν δὴ οὐσῶν βλαβῶν τῶν ἐν ταῖς κοινωνίαις, τὰ μὲν μετ' ἀγνοίας ἁμαρτήματά ἐστιν, ὅταν μήτε ὃν, μήτε ὡς, μήτε ᾧ, μήτε οὗ ἕνεκα ὑπέλαβε, ταῦτα πράξῃ . . . ὅταν μὴ παραλόγως ἡ βλαβὴ γένηται . . , ὅταν δὲ εἰδὼς μὲν μὴ προβουλεύσας δέ, ἀδίκημα . . . ὅταν δ' ἐκ προαιρέσεως, ἄδικος καὶ μοχθηρός, ibid. 5, 8. 'Of the three gradations of misconduct towards others, Fault or Negligence (culpa) is an unlawful act in ignorance of the subject, the degree, the instrument, the consequences, when it was reasonable to expect the mischief; unlawful intention (dolus) is breach of law with knowledge of these elements, but without premeditation; malice or depravity is evinced by the resolution or deliberate intention of violating law.'

The distinction between Negligence and Intention, and between hasty and deliberate intention, is not so important in the civil code as in the criminal code and in the eye of the moralist. The criminal code punishes less severely wrongs of inadvertence and crimes committed under provocation. But the thoughtless, incautious, imprudent, author of unlawful mischief, although he intended no harm, is just as accountable, chargeable, liable to the sanction of the civil law, and compellable to make reparation, as if his infraction of law was intentional.

Actions on Delict, however, differ herein from Real actions and actions on Contract, that in the former, but not in the latter, the liability of the defendant necessarily implies that he is convicted either of dolus or of culpa, 3 § 211; there is no liability for damnum absque injuria.

Dolus being defined to be knowledge or consciousness of certain facts, and culpa ignorance or unconsciousness of the same facts, are clearly two states of mind which must always be opposed. No degree of culpa will pass into dolus. Yet several expressions of the jurists imply the contrary: e.g. Magnam tamen negligentiam placuit in doli crimen cadere, Dig. 44, 7, 1, 5. 'Gross negligence is open to the charge of fraudulent intention.' But these statements only mean that dolus and culpa are often undistinguishable by a court of law. The phenomena of gross negligence are precisely similar to those of dishonest intention, and it is often impossible for a court to decide which interpretation they ought to bear. Again, as the consequences are equally mischievous, there is no reason why they should not be subject to the same legal sanction.

We have seen that ignorance of the specific constituents of an action is a ground of exculpation. This must not be extended to ignorance of the obligations to which a person is subject under certain circumstances, or of the sanctions by which these obligations are enforced. Hence the maxim that a party in a suit may allege ignorance of fact, but cannot allege ignorance of law. Regula est, juris quidem ignorantiam cuique nocere, facti vero ignorantiam non nocere, Dig. 22, 6, pr. Sciant ignorantiam facti non juris prodesse, nec stultis solere succurri sed errantibus, ibid. § 5. 'The rule is, that law is known to everybody at his own peril, facts are not known to everybody at his own peril.' 'Ignorance of fact may be pleaded, not ignorance of law; and relief is accorded to error, but not to stupidity.' The rule is founded on expediency. It would be impossible for a court to decide whether a party was really ignorant of the law, or, if this could be determined, whether his ignorance was inevitable or the effect of negligence. From the impossibility of deciding such a plea, it is not allowed to be pleaded, and ignorance of law is always assumed to be a case of Negligence. The knowledge of law, however, which everybody is presumed to possess, does not exist as a matter of fact, even among the well-disposed. All systems of law are more or less irrational, and contain many provisions which are hardly surmisable by any but professional lawyers. To mitigate the injustice that the maxim would often produce, the Roman jurists admitted an exception in favour of women, minors below the age of twenty-five, and soldiers. These classes were permitted to plead ignorance of the law, except the obvious dictates of Natural law, and were relieved against the forfeitures and obligations thereby incurred.

In its signification of deliberate intention Dolus is often used as an antithesis of violence and a synonym of Fraud. The reason of this is obvious. He who can attain his ends by force does not trouble himself with machinations and artful schemes. Wiles and plots, when their object is unlawful, usually imply an absence of violence and accompany manœuvres to surprise consent. It is in this sense that Dolus is defined by Labeo. Labeo sic definit: dolum malum esse omnem calliditatem, fallaciam, machinationem, ad circumveniendum, fallendum, decipiendum alterum adhibitam, Dig. 4, 3, 2. 'Labeo defines dolus malus as any craft, imposition, machination employed to overreach, delude, deceive, another.' There is, however, no necessary antithesis between deliberate intention and violence, and we find that the edict, Si cui dolo malo hominibus coactis damni quid factum esse dicetur, Dig. 47, 8, 2, 'Mischief with dolus malus by men assembled is subject to the same penalty as Rapine,' uses the term to signify premeditated violence.

There are three principal manifestations of Dolus, a conscious or intentional infraction of law: (1) delict, or the violation of a jus in rem, accompanied or unaccompanied with violence or intimidation, and possibly without any treachery or betrayal of confidence, e. g. theft or robbery; mala fides, involving a violation of the confidence necessary to social intercourse: and then either (2) the deliberate violation by a debtor of a jus in personam or obligation imposed by contract; in which case Dolus is opposed to Culpa and Casus: or (3) any unlawful machination or circumvention leading another person to a manifestation of Will, whether bilateral, as a contract, or unilateral, as a testamentary disposition, or the acceptance or disclaimer of a succession, &c. Dolus in this form is often called Fraud (fraus); it is ground to support an actio doli and in integrum restitutio on account of dolus.

Malice in English law appears to denote deliberate intention, or rather the depravity of disposition or badness of heart (ἀδικία) which is assumed to be evidenced by a deliberate unlawful intention. Such at least is its meaning in the definition of murder. Perhaps, however, it sometimes only denotes unlawful intention (ἀδίκημα) and, as rather belonging to the criminal than the civil code, it may be regarded as equivalent to criminal intention.

The opposite of Negligence is Diligence, activity, vigilance. These, like negligence, admit of an infinite variety of gradations, and different degrees are required of persons in different positions. In some relations a man is bound to make good losses occasioned by the slightest negligence; in others he is only compelled to indemnify for the consequences of gross negligence.

The terms, Gross and Slight, like other quantitative terms, have no positive signification until we fix upon some unit of measurement or standard of comparison to which any given instance may be referred and by which it may be measured. Two standards are frequently employed by the Roman jurists: the extraordinary care of a vigilant man of business, and the care which a given individual habitually bestows on his own interests. Although there is no necessary antithesis between these two standards, yet practically in Roman law they serve to fix the meaning of gross and slight negligence. Slight negligence is the absence of the extraordinary diligence of the most careful man of business; gross negligence is the absence of the degree of diligence which a man habitually bestows on his own concerns. The degree of diligence for which a man is held responsible depends on various principles, which may best be indicated by the following statement of the degrees of diligence exacted or of negligence imputed in the principal contracts and quasi-contracts.

Extraordinary care is required of the gratuitous borrower for use. (Is qui utendum accepit exactam diligentiam custodiae rei praestare jubetur, Inst. 3, 14, 2. In rebus commodatis talis diligentia praestanda est qualem quisque diligentissimus paterfamilias suis rebus adhibet, Dig. 13, 6, 8). The reason of this is that the contract of commodatum, being gratuitous, is solely for the advantage of the borrower. (Commodatum autem plerumque solam utilitatem continet ejus cui commodatur, et ideo verior est Quinti Mucii sententia, existimantis, et culpam praestandam et diligentiam, Dig. 13, 6, 5, 2). The same principle may be applied to the depositor and principal (Dig. 47, 2; 63, 5). Extraordinary diligence is also required of the mortgagee, (Placuit sufficere quod ad eam rem custodiendam exactam diligentiam adhiberet, Inst. 3, 14, 4. Ea igitur quae diligens paterfamilias in suis rebus praestare solet a creditore exiguntur, Dig. 13, 7, 14), the vendor, (Custodiam autem venditor talem praestare debet quam praestant hi quibus res commodata est, ut diligentiam praestet exactiorem quam in suis rebus adhiberet, Dig. 18, 6, 3), the conductor, (Culpa autem abest si omnia facta sunt quae diligentissimus quisque observaturus fuisset, Dig. 19, 2, 257), the locator, (In judicio tam locati quam conducti dolum et custodiam, non etiam casum cui resisti non potest, venire constat, Cod. 4, 6, 28). The principle appears to be that when a contract is for the interest of both parties, although their interests are rather adverse than identical, each is responsible for the least negligence. (In contractibus bonae fidei servatur, ut, si quidem utriusque contrahentis commodum versetur, etiam culpa, sin unius solius, dolus malus tantummodo praestetur, Dig. 30, 108, 12). This principle will require the same amount of diligence from the mortgagor and vendee.

Finally, extraordinary care is required of the agent, (A procuratore dolum et omnem culpam, non etiam improvisum casum, praestandum esse, juris auctoritate manifeste declaratur, Cod. 4, 35, 13. Aliena vero negotia exacto officio geruntur, nec quidquam in eorum administratione neglectum ac declinatum culpa vacuum est, Cod. 4, 35, 21), whether authorized or unauthorized, (Quo casu ad exactissimam quisque diligentiam compellitur reddere rationem, nec sufficit talem diligentiam adhibere qualem suis rebus adhibere soleret, si modo alius diligentior commodius administraturus esset negotia, Inst. 3, 27, 1).

It is not easy to say why more diligence is required of the authorized agent than of the depositary, as both are unremunerated. Perhaps it is because in agency the direct and express purpose and intent of the contract is that an experienced agent should devote more skill and vigilance to the interests of the principal than the principal himself is able to bestow; whereas in other contracts diligence is merely an implied and accessory or incidental obligation.

Moreover, Agency was not really gratuitous: the honorarium of the Agent, as we have seen, though not recoverable in an ordinary action before a judex, being recoverable at the tribunal of the praetor in the exercise of his cognitio extraordinaria.

The amount of diligence a man habitually shows in his own affairs is all that is required of the following persons: the depositary, (Quod Nerva diceret latiorem culpam dolum esse, Proculo displicebat, mihi verissimum videtur. Nam etsi quis non ad eum modum quem hominum natura desiderat diligens est, nisi tamen ad suum modum curam in deposito praestat, fraude non caret: nec enim salva fide minorem his quam suis rebus diligentiam praestabit, Dig. 16, 3, 32), the lender, (Quin etiam paulo remissius circa interpretationem doli mali debere nos versari, quoniam nulla utilitas commodantis interveniat, Dig. 47, 2; 63, 6). The reason is that the contract on their part is gratuitous, (Quia nulla utilitas ejus versatur apud quem deponitur, merito dolus praestatur solus, nisi forte merces accessit, tunc enim etiam culpa exhibetur, Dig. 13, 6, 5, 2).

The same principle applies to the tutor and curator, whose quasi-contract is moreover involuntary, (De omnibus quae fecit tutor, quum facere non deberet, item de his quae non fecit, rationem reddet hoc judicio, praestando dolum et culpam, et quantam in rebus suis diligentiam, Dig. 27, 3, 1, pr. The English law, it may be observed, appears to exact a greater amount of diligence than this from Trustees, though they are equally unremunerated). The same amount of diligence is required from the partner, (Venit autem in hoc judicium pro socio bona fides. Et Celsus scripsit socios inter se dolum et culpam praestare oportere, Dig. 17, 2; 52, 1. Socius socio etiam culpae nomine tenetur, id est, desidiae atque negligentiae. Culpa autem non ad exactissimam diligentiam dirigenda est: sufficit enim talem diligentiam communibus rebus adhibere qualem suis rebus adhibere solet, quia qui parem diligentem sibi socium acquirit, de se queri debet, Dig. 17, 2, 72), the husband in respect of the dotal estate, (In rebus dotalibus virum praestare oportet tam dolum quam culpam, quia causa sui dotem accipit; sed etiam diligentiam praestabit quam in suis rebus exhibet, Dig. 23, 3, 17), the coheir and colegatee, (Non tantum dolum sed et culpam in re hereditaria praestare debet coheres, quoniam cum coherede non contrahimus sed incidimus in eum. Non tamen diligentiam praestare debet qualem diligens paterfamilias, quoniam hic propter suam partem causam habuit gerendi .... Talem igitur diligentiam praestare debet qualem in suis rebus, Dig. 10, 2; 25, 16). In these latter relations both parties are interested and their interests are identical.

It must be observed that Ulpian, Dig. 13, 6, 5, places the husband and partner in the same category with the vendor vendee, hirer letter, mortgagor and mortgagee, whom we have put into the opposite category. This does not harmonize with the authorities we have quoted, and must be regarded as an inexactitude of Ulpian. Misled by Ulpian, Sir William Jones in his treatise on Bailments lays down the principle that, when a contract is reciprocally beneficial, only ordinary diligence is required, whereas we have shown that if the interests of the parties are not identical, the Roman law, at least, requires extraordinary diligence.

He also, in measuring diligence and negligence, introduces the conception of a mean and two extremes, making three gradations of diligence (and correspondingly of negligence), ordinary diligence, less than ordinary diligence, more than ordinary diligence: but this tripartite division produces an intricacy and complication that is not to be found in the Roman jurists.

We may observe that the investigation of Imputability is only a portion of a larger department of jurisprudence, the investigation of the general nature and import of Title.

A large proportion of Titles, i. e. facts to which Law annexes Rights and Obligations, are human Actions; and human Actions in their character of Titles to Obligations are deeply influenced and modified by certain incidents or attributes to which they are liable, such as ignorance or mistake, whether of law or of fact, motive or inducement, such as extraordinary provocation, great intimidation, overwhelming terror, and the like. It is impossible when he makes his synthesis of Title and Obligation, for the lawgiver to overlook these distinctions—if he did, law would be nugatory and could never answer its purpose, the attainment of the common weal, or whatever end the lawgiver proposes—and hence the necessity in jurisprudence of fixing, as we have attempted to do, the meanings of Volitional, Intentional, Deliberate, Culpa, Dolus, and similar Ethical terms.

A more complete theory of the Voluntary or Intentional would require us not to confine our view, as to a great extent we have done in the foregoing discussion, to delict or physical action, but to extend it to all juristic actions or manifestations of will (negotia gesta), whether bilateral, as contracts, or unilateral, as testamentary dispositions, acceptance or refusal of a succession, &c. In this wider field of view the definitions of Volition and Intention and their correlatives, Ignorance and Error, would require some modification.

Under the head of Obligatio ex delicto should be placed, in an exposition of Roman law governed by Roman views of jurisprudence, the doctrine of POSSESSION (Interdict-possession), or, rather, of Dispossession, with its remedies, the Interdicts Utrubi, Uti possidetis, and Unde vi. It should be placed here because this is the Roman arrangement.

The Roman jurists, instead of recognizing in Possession a primary right, imposing a negative obligation on all the world (jus in rem), were content with regarding Dispossession as a wrong imposing a secondary positive obligation on the individual dispossessor, and treated the possessory Interdicts as actions ex delicto. In a system of theoretic jurisprudence Possession might perhaps with equal propriety be classed with Dominion as a primary right demanding universal recognition (jus in rem), and the Interdicts allotted for its protection might be coordinated, not with Personal actions ex delicto, but with Real actions (vindicatio), the remedy whereby Dominion is protected and recovered against all the world.

BOOK IV.

DE ACTIONIBUS.

---

§ 1. *Si quaeritur*, quot genera actionum sint, verius videtur duo esse: in rem et in personam. nam qui IIII esse dixer*unt* ex sponsionum generibus, non animadverterunt quasdam species actionum inter genera se rettulisse.

§ 2. In personam actio est qua agimus quotiens cum aliquo qui nobis vel ex contractu vel ex delicto obligatus est *contendimus*, id est cum intendimus dare, facere, praestare oporter*e*.

§ 3. In *rem* actio est, cum aut corporalem rem intendimus nostram esse, *aut ius* aliquod nobis com*pe*tere, velut utend*i*, aut utendi fruend*i*, *eu*ndi, agendi aquamve ducendi, vel altius tollendi *vel pr*ospiciendi. item actio ex diverso adversario est neg*ati*va.

§ 4. Sic itaque discretis actionibus, certum est *non posse* nos rem

§ 1. We have now to treat of Actions, which fall into two classes, being either Real or Personal: for those who count four classes, including the forms of sponsio, commit the error of co-ordinating subclasses and classes.

§ 2. A Personal action seeks to enforce an obligation imposed on the defendant by his contract or delict, that is to say, is the contention that he is bound to transfer some dominion or to perform some service or to repair some loss.

§ 3. A Real action is my claim of some dominion or some fraction of dominion, as a right of use or usufruct of a thing belonging to my neighbour, a right of horseway or carriage-way through his land, of fetching water from a source in his land, of raising my house above a certain height, or of having the prospect from my windows unobstructed; or the opposite contention of my neighbour, his denial that I have any such fraction of dominion.

§ 4. Real and Personal actions being thus distinguished, it is clear

nostram ab alio ita petere, SI PARET EUM DARE OPORTERE: nec enim quod nostrum est, nobis dari potest, cum solum id dari nobis intellegatur quod *ita datur, ut* nostrum fiat; nec res quae *est nostra*, nostra amplius fieri potest. plane odio furum, quo magis pluribus actionibus teneantur, effectum est, ut extra poenam dupli aut quadrupli rei recipiendae nomine fures ex hac actione etiam teneantur, SI PARET EOS DARE OPORTERE, quamvis sit etiam adversus eos haec actio qua rem nostram esse petimus.

that I cannot demand my property from another in the following form: 'If it be proved that the defendant is bound to convey such property to me.' What is my own cannot be conveyed to me, for conveyance to me makes a thing mine, and what is already mine cannot be made more mine than it is. Yet, for the prevention of theft and multiplication of remedies against the thief, besides the penalty of twice the value of the thing stolen awarded against the thief not caught in the act, and the penalty of four times the value against the thief caught in the act, the thing itself may be recovered by a personal action in which the contention is thus worded: 'If it be proved that the defendant ought to convey the thing in question,' as well as by the real action thus formulated: 'If it be proved that the thing in question is the property of the plaintiff.'

§ 5. Appellantur autem in rem quidem actiones vindicationes; in personam vero actiones quibus dare fierive oportere intendimus, condictiones.

§ 5. A Real action is called vindicatio; a Personal action, whereby we contend that some property should be conveyed to us or some service performed for us, is called condictio.

§ 6. Agimus autem interdum, ut rem tantum consequamur, interdum ut poenam tantum, alias ut rem et poenam.

§ 6. We sue sometimes only for property to which we have a title, real or personal, sometimes only for a penalty, sometimes both for our property and for a penalty.

§ 7. Rem tantum persequimur velut actionibus *quibus* ex contractu agimus.

§ 7. We sue only for our property in (real actions and in) personal actions founded on contract.

§ 8. Poenam tantum consequimur velut actione furti et iniuriarum, et secundum quorundam opinionem *actio*ne vi bonorum raptorum; nam ipsius rei et vindicatio et condictio nobis co*m*petit.

§ 8. We sue only for a penalty in actions of Theft and Outrage, and, according to some, of Rapine; for our property itself may be recovered either by Real or by Conservative (non-penal) personal action.

§ 9. Rem vero et poenam persequimur velut ex his causis ex quibus adversus infitiantem in duplum agimus: quod accidit per actionem iudicat*i*, depensi, damni in*iuriae*

§ 9. We sue both for our property and for a penalty in those actions where the defendant who denies his obligation is condemned to pay double, as in the action to recover a

legis Aqui*liae*, *et rerum* legat*arum* nomine quae per damnationem cer*tae* relictae sunt.

judgment debt, to recover money paid by a sponsor for his principal, to recover damages for injury to property under the lex Aquilia, and to recover legacies of a definite amount bequeathed by condemnation of the successor.

§ 1. Sponsio or wager was an indirect mode of submitting questions to judicial decision, which seems to have been very commonly employed before the introduction of the formulary system. We are left to conjecture how its classification enabled any jurist to count four classes of action. Its principal division seems to be into the sponsio where the pecuniary risk was serious and the penal sum important (sponsio poenalis), and the sponsio where the penal sum was nominal and not actually exacted (sponsio praejudicialis). Adding these two divisions to real and personal actions, we should have four classes. But as every sponsio, asserting an obligation arising from stipulation, was a species of personal action, this classification would involve a co-ordination of sub-genera and genera, or subdivisions and divisions.

A Real action is one which asserts a jus in rem, a Personal action one which asserts a jus in personam. A jus in rem, we may remember, is a right to certain forbearances, or freedom from molestation, corresponding to a duty imposed on all the world; a jus in personam is a right to certain performances corresponding to a duty imposed on a determinate person. Jura in rem are Status, or Property, or Servitude, that is, some fraction of property. Jura in personam are Obligations founded on either contract or delict. Primordial rights (life, limb, liberty, honour, &c.), though jura in rem, do not give rise to real actions; their violation engenders an obligation in the violator, which is pursued by a personal action ex delicto.

A Real action, accordingly, asserts either the status or the proprietorship of the plaintiff, if we include under proprietorship the elements of property called easements or servitudes; a Personal action asserts an obligation of the defendant towards the plaintiff.

Real and Personal actions of Roman law must not be identified with those of English law. A Real action in English law may be defined with sufficient accuracy for our present purpose as an action whereby we claim property in an immovable; a claim of property in a movable is made by Personal action. In Roman law a claim of property in a movable is a Real action just as much as a claim of property in an immovable. A Personal action in Roman law asserts no property existing in the plaintiff, but an obligation or right to a conveyance or transmutation of property from the defendant to the plaintiff.

To make the English and Roman classifications coincide, Detinue and Trover (actions for the recovery of movable property) ought to be classed with real actions.

A Real action names no party but the Plaintiff in the intentio, the principal part of the formula or written instructions of the praetor to the judex, in which the plaintiff's claim is specified; a Personal action names the defendant as well as the plaintiff in the intentio. For instance, a vindicatio asserting the status of a person contained an intentio to this effect: Si paret Titium ex jure Quiritium liberum esse.

(We have no record of the precise form of the intentio in a controversy of status. We know that in a question of libertas (liberalis causa), until the time of Justinian, the person whose freedom was in dispute could not be either plaintiff or defendant, his rights were advocated by an Assertor, Cod. 7, 17, De assertione tollenda. In Justinian's time the formulary system, with its precisely framed intentio, no longer existed.)

A vindicatio asserting property in land or a slave contained an intentio in these words: Si paret illum fundum—illum hominem—ex jure Quiritium Auli Agerii (Plaintiff) esse. A vindicatio claiming not absolute property, but some element of property, for instance, a rural servitude, contained an intentio to this effect: Si paret jus eundi per illum fundum ex jure Quiritium Aulo Agerio competere.

A Personal action, on the contrary, named in the intentio the defendant, who was alleged to be under an obligation to the plaintiff. E. g. if the plaintiff alleged that the defendant lay under an obligation to pay him a certain sum of money, the intentio was in this form: Si paret Aulo Agerio Numerium Negidium (defendant) sestertium decem millia dare oportere.

The word Dare is used in the Intentio of a Condictio Certi, i. e. an action wherein the Plaintiff asserts that the Defendant is under an obligation to convey quiritary property in a determinate thing, whether a sum of money or any other subject of property, a certain slave, certain corn, certain land. E. g. Si paret Numerium Negidium Aulo Agerio sestertium decem millia—tritici Africi optimi centum modios—iter per illum fundum ad illum fundum—dare oportere.

The word Facere never appears to stand alone in an intentio, but in its stead we have Dare facere in the Intentio of Condictio Incerti, that is, of an action to enforce a claim of an uncertain amount, a claim of any service but the transfer of quiritary property in a certain thing, that is, to enforce any obligation (except those expressed by Praestare) not included under Dare as above defined. E. g. Quidquid paret Numerium Negidium Aulo Agerio dare facere oportere.

Praestare does not appear to have ever been used in the Intentio of a Formula. In its stead we find Damnum decidere, § 37. Praestare is a term of wider meaning than the two preceding, and appears specifically to denote reparation for any harm, compensation for any loss, the fulfilment, that is, of a delictual obligation. It is also used in connection with the obligation ex fide bona arising out of culpa and dolus relating to Contract.

§ 3. Negativa. An action respecting a servitude was either Confessoria or Negativa. If the plaintiff claimed a servitude over the land or house of the defendant, his action was called Confessoria; if he denied that his own land or house was subject to a servitude, his action was called Negativa (or Negatoria) in rem actio. In this action the plaintiff, probably, was not bound to prove a negative, but only the existence of his own dominion; it would then be incumbent on the defendant to prove affirmatively a limitation of this dominion.

§ 4. Gaius points out that the Roman law of his day was illogical in allowing stolen property to be recovered by Personal action. No translation of property is operated by theft. Roman law contained no disposition similar to that of English law, that property in stolen goods is transmuted by sale in market overt. Even in the hands of a third person, an innocent purchaser, the thing remained the property of the original owner, exempt from the potent chemistry of usucapion. It follows that the only action logically competent to the proprietor who still remained proprietor was a real action.

In the condictio ex causa furtiva, instead of the intentio, Si paret dare oportere, § 4, which implies that the plaintiff is not proprietor, we might have expected him to sue with the intentio, Dare facere oportere, which might be merely a form of claiming redelivery of possession, and accordingly would be consistent with his proprietorship. The following is the explanation why the other formula was allowed: A condictio certi for a certain sum of money was accompanied by a sponsio poenalis in a third of the sum in dispute, to be forfeited by the party who lost the action, 4 § 171. In order to subject the thief to this further penalty, the legislator, at the cost of an anomaly, permitted the plaintiff to sue with the formula, Si paret dare oportere.

§ 5. Condictio is an actio stricti juris. It excludes actions ex fide bona, actions ex delicto, and actions in factum. It is divided into Condictio incerti, with an intentio Quidquid paret dare facere oportere, and Condictio certi, with an intentio, Si paret dare oportere. The latter is either brought to recover a certain sum of money, and then is specially called Condictio certi, or is brought to recover land or a slave or any other certain thing, and then is called Condictio triticaria. The origin of this name is doubtful. Petitio, sometimes equivalent to vindicatio, is sometimes also equivalent to Condictio certi. In both cases it denotes the certainty and individuality of the property claimed.

§ 6. Rights may be divided into primary and secondary. Primary rights are antecedent to wrong, and may be divided into status, primordial rights, property, and obligation; the title or investitive fact which creates them being a condition defining a status or capacity of primordial rights, or one of the modes of acquiring property or of forming a contract. Secondary or sanctioning rights imply an antecedent wrong, and their title is a breach of contract or the violation of some real right, statistic, primordial, or proprietary.

Both these classes of rights and the corresponding duties are creations of the law: for every law is both imperative and punitory; that is, both by its command confers a primary right and imposes a corresponding primary duty, and sanctions its command by conferring a secondary right and imposing a secondary duty, that is, by conferring a remedy and imposing a punishment (including under punishment mere restitution or compensation) in the event of disobedience.

The sanctions of the civil law are either reparative and remedial or penal and preventive; in one case the object of the law is the

RESTORATION of the plaintiff by restitution or compensation, and then his primary right is the measure of his redress or sanctioning right; in the other case it is the repression of similar wrongs by inflicting an exemplary PUNISHMENT on the defendant which may operate as a terror to other wrong-doers; and then the sanctioning right may far exceed his primary right. See above, p. 369.

The language of Roman jurisprudence makes no distinction between a primary right and a sanctioning right when they both relate to property and the second is merely the equivalent of the first, calling both by the name of the Thing (Res). The redress directly given by the Roman law was always pecuniary compensation, and we might have expected Roman jurists above all others to distinguish between the plaintiff's primary and secondary right; but the indirect result of a real action might be the recovery of specific restitution, and it was in view of this type of redress that the Roman lawyers were led to speak of primary and sanctioning proprietary rights as identical.

If we next proceed to inquire what classes of actions are brought for reparation or the recovery of property (rei persecutio), and what for the recovery of a penalty (poenae persecutio), we shall have no difficulty in perceiving that real actions and actions on contract belong to the former class (rei persecutio); and that of actions on delict, a subdivision, which may be called Vindictive (quae ad ultionem pertinent, quae vindictam continent), such as the actio injuriarum, belong to the latter (poenae persecutio). The effect of the former is restoration: they leave the plaintiff no richer and the defendant no poorer in respect of property than he was at first; whereas the vindictive actions leave the plaintiff, in respect of property, richer, and the defendant poorer. But the remaining division of actions on delict, those brought to recover indemnification for damage to property, are more ambiguous in character. If we merely regard their effect on the plaintiff they seem to be purely reparative, for they leave the plaintiff no richer; but if we regard their effect on the defendant they seem to be penal, for if the wrong done by the defendant was a destruction of property, compensation to the plaintiff will leave the defendant poorer.

Accordingly, with respect to these semi-penal [unilaterally penal] actions, the language of the Roman jurists varies, they are sometimes regarded as rei persecutio, and sometimes as poenae persecutio; but the latter view predominated, and they have the principal incidents of penal actions: although, namely, as restorative, they are transmissible to the successor of the plaintiff, yet as penal they are only maintainable within a year, and are not maintainable against the successor of the defendant unless the suit was commenced (lis contestata) against the original wrong-doer, in which case the penal obligation is novated, 3 § 180, and becomes transmissible. These incidents are resumed in the following passage of the Digest: Si possessionis causa deterior facta esse dicetur dolo ejus qui in possessionem missus sit, actio in eum ex dolo datur, quae neque post annum neque in heredes ceterosque successores dabitur, quum ex delicto oriatur poenaeque nomine concipiatur, nisi quatenus ad eos pervenit; heredi autem dabitur quia et rei continet persecutionem, Dig. 42, 5, 11. 'If the possession is deteriorated by the fraud of the person sent to seize the estate of the judgment debtor, an action of Fraud is maintainable against him, but not after a year, nor against the successor of the defendant, as it is founded on delict and penal, except so far as the successor is enriched by the fraud of the wrong-doer; but is transmissible to the successor of the plaintiff, as its object is reparation.'

In these cases, accordingly, the plaintiff had not always an adequate remedy under the Roman law. English law originally followed the rule of Roman law, and no action of Tort, even for damage to property, would lie against the executor or administrator of the wrong-doer. But now, by 3 and 4 Will. IV, c. 42, an action for injury to property, as opposed to actions for slander and the like (vindictive actions, which die with the person), is maintainable against the executors and administrators of the wrong-doer, provided the wrong was committed within six months before his death and the action is brought within a year after his death, if it was an injury to real property, or within six months after his executors or administrators have taken on themselves administration, if it was an injury to personal property. Thus the English plaintiff has an ampler remedy than the Roman.

§ 7. One action upon contract, namely, the action against a depositary, was brought for double the value of the deposit, i. e. was partly penal, if the deposit was necessitated by fire, shipwreck, tumult, or similar distress.

§ 8. In Justinian's time the penalty of Rapine was only thrice the value of the thing taken with violence, that is, the quadruple damages were partly penal, for the actions vi bonorum raptorum and the real or personal action to recover the thing taken were not concurrent or cumulative.

§ 9. The actio judicati was brought against a defendant who denied that a judgment had been given against him or that it was still unsatisfied. He was liable to be condemned to pay twice the amount of the judgment debt, and was required to give security judicatum solvi. This security was the modern representative of the interposition of a Vindex in the old proceeding of manus injectio.

The actio depensi [see above, 3 § 127] was introduced by a lex Publilia of uncertain date, and as it was only given to the sponsor, would become obsolete when the sponsor was superseded by the fidejussor.

Justinian confined the action of the legatee against the heres for twice the value of the legacy to the case of bequests to churches and religious institutions.

LEGIS ACTIONES.

§ 10. Quaedam praeterea sunt actiones quae ad legis actionem exprimuntur, quaedam sua vi ac potestate constant. quod ut manifestum fiat, opus est ut prius de legis actionibus loquamur.

§ 10. Some actions are moulded upon, and contain a reference to, the actions of the older system; others are unrelated and independent. This requires an examination of the older system.

§ 11. Actiones quas in usu veteres habuerunt legis actiones appellabantur, vel ideo quod legibus proditae erant, quippe tunc edicta Praetoris quibus complures actiones introductae sunt nondum in usu habebantur; vel ideo quia ipsarum legum verbis accommodatae erant, et ideo immutabiles proinde atque leges observa*ba*ntur. unde *c*um qui*s* de vi*t*ibus succisis ita egisset, ut in actione vites nominaret, responsum est eum rem perdidisse, quia debuisset arbores nominare, eo quod lex XII tabularum, ex qua de vitibus succisis actio co*m*peteret, generaliter de arboribus succisis loqueretur.

§ 11. These proceedings are called Actions of the law, either because they were appointed by the law before the edict of the praetor, the source of many new actions, began to be published, or because they followed the letter of the law and in form were as immutable as law. Thus, a man who sued another for cutting his vines, and in his action called them vines, lost his right because he ought to have called them trees, as the Twelve Tables, which confer the action, speak generally of trees and not particularly of vines.

§ 12. Lege autem agebatur modis quinque: sacramento, per iudi-

§ 12. There were five actions of the law, Sacramentum, Judicis

cis postulationem, per condictionem, per manus iniectionem, per pignoris captionem.

postulatio, Condictio, Manus injectio, and Pignoris captio.

SACRAMENTUM.

§ 13. Sacramenti actio generalis erat: *de* quibu*s* enim rebus ut aliter ageretur lege cautum non erat, de h*is* sacramento agebatu*r*. eaque actio perinde periculos*a* erat falsi *nomine*, atque hoc tempore periculosa est actio certae creditae pecuniae propter sponsionem qua periclitatur reus, si temere neget, *et* restipulationem qua periclitatur actor, si non debitum petat: nam qui victus erat summam sacramenti praestabat poenae nomine: *eaque in publicum cedebat praedes*que eo nomine Praetor*i* dab*antur*, non ut nunc sponsionis et restipulationis poena lu*c*ro cedi*t* adve*rs*ari*o* qui vicerit.

§ 13. Sacramentum (Stake or Deposit) was the general action, for wherever no other mode was appointed by law, the procedure was by sacramentum. It was attended with risk to the parties, like the modern action to recover money lent, wherein the defendant and plaintiff by the sponsio and restipulatio respectively forfeit a penal sum, if unsuccessful. The praetor took securities for the stake, which the vanquished party forfeited to the treasury, not, as he forfeits the penal sum of the modern sponsio or restipulatio, to the victor in the suit.

§ 14. Poena autem sacramenti aut quingenaria erat aut quinquagenaria. *nam* de rebus mille aeris plurisve quingentis assibus, de minoris *vero* quinquaginta assibus sacramento contendeb*atur*; nam *ita* lege XII tabularum cautum erat. *sed si de libertate* hominis *contro*versia erat, etsi pretiosissimus homo esset, tamen ut L assibus sacramento contendere*tur*, ea*dem* lege cautum est favoris *causa*, *ne satis*dat*i*one o*ne*rarentur adsertores [*desunt* 23 *lin.*]

§ 14. The penal sum of the sacramentum was either five hundred asses or fifty asses; five hundred when the subject of dispute was valued at a thousand or upwards, fifty when at less than a thousand. This was provided by the law of the Twelve Tables. When, however, personal freedom was the subject of dispute, however valuable a slave the man whose status was litigated might be, the penal sum was only fifty asses. This was enacted by the Twelve Tables in favour of liberty, that the vindex or assertor of liberty might never be deterred by the magnitude of the risk.

§ 15. . . . . ad iudicem accipiundum venirent. postea v*ero* reversis dabatur *post diem* XXX. iudex: *idque* per legem Pinariam factum est; ante eam autem legem . . . dabatur iudex. illu*d* ex superioribus intellegimus, si de re minoris quam M aeris agebatur, quinquagenario sacramento, non quingenario eos

§ 15. [When the sacramentum was a personal action, that is to say, instituted to enforce an obligation, after giving securities for the stake, the parties left the praetor's court, having arranged to reappear on the thirtieth day] to receive a judex. When they appeared again on the thirtieth day the Praetor no-

contendere solitos fuisse. postea tamen quam iudex datus esset, comperendinum diem, ut ad iudicem venirent, denuntiabant. deinde cum ad iudicem venerant, antequam aput eum *causam* perorarent, solebant breviter ei et quasi per indicem rem exponere: quae dicebatur causae collectio, quasi causae suae in breve coactio.

minated a judex. This was in pursuance of the lex Pinaria, before which the judex [was named at an earlier period?]. If the subject of dispute was worth less than a thousand asses, the stake, as before mentioned, was only fifty. After the judex was named, they gave mutual notice to appear before him on the next day but one. At the appearance before the judex, before the case was fully developed, it was stated in a concise and summary form, and this summary statement was called causae collectio [or causae conjectio].

§ 16. Si in rem agebatur, mobilia quidem et moventia, quae modo in ius adferri adducive possent, in iure vindicabantur ad hunc modum. qui vindicabat festucam tenebat. deinde ipsam rem adprehendebat, velut hominem, et ita dicebat: HUNC EGO HOMINEM EX IURE QUIRITIUM MEUM ESSE AIO SECUNDUM SUAM CAUSAM SICUT DIXI. ECCE TIBI VINDICTAM INPOSUI: et simul homini festucam inponebat. adversarius eadem similiter dicebat et faciebat. cum uterque vindicasset, Praetor dicebat: MITT*IT*E AMBO HOMINEM. illi mittebant. qui prior vindica*verat*, *ita alterum interroga*bat: POSTULO ANNE DICAS QUA EX CAUSA VINDICAVERIS. ille respondebat: IUS PEREGI SICUT VINDICTAM INPOSUI. deinde qui prior vindicaverat dicebat: QUANDO TU INIURIA VINDICAVISTI, D AERIS SACRAMENTO TE PROVOCO. adversarius quoque dicebat: SIMILITER EGO TE. *seu* L asses sacramenti nominabant. deinde *eadem* sequebantur quae cum in persona*m* ageretur. Postea Praetor secundum alterum eorum vindicias dicebat, id est interim aliquem possessorem constituebat, eumque iubebat praedes adversario dare litis et vindiciarum, id est rei

§ 16. When the sacramentum was a real action, movables and animals that could be brought or led into court were claimed in presence of the praetor in the following fashion. The claimant held a wand, and grasping the slave or thing over which he claimed dominion, said: 'This man I claim, as proprietor, by the law of the Quirites, by the title which I have shown. Thus upon him I lay my lance,' whereupon he touched the man with his wand. The adversary then said the same words and performed the same acts. After both had claimed dominion, the praetor said: 'Both claimants quit your hold,' and both quitted hold. Then the first claimant said, addressing the second: 'Answer me, will you state on what title you found your claim?' and he replied: 'I stated my title before I touched him with my lance.' Then the first claimant said: 'Since you claim him in defiance of right, I challenge you to stake five hundred asses upon the issue of a trial,' to which the other answered, 'I accept the challenge.' Or else they wagered fifty asses. Then ensued the same ceremonies as in a personal action. The praetor then awarded to one of the

et fructuum: alios autem praedes ipse Praetor ab utroque accipiebat sacramenti, quod id in publicum cedebat. festuca autem utebantur quasi hastae loco, signo quodam iusti dominii: *maxime enim* sua esse credebant quae ex hostibus cepissent; unde in centumviralibus iudiciis hasta praeponitur.

claimants possession of the thing pending the suit, and made him bind himself with sureties to his adversary to restore both the subject of dispute and the mesne profits, or value of the interim possession, in the event of losing the cause. Both parties gave pledges to the praetor for the penal sum which the loser was to forfeit. The wand or straw which they wielded represented a lance, the symbol of absolute dominion, for the best title to property was held to be conquest. Accordingly the law of property is administered in the Centumviral court at the present day under the symbol of a lance.

§ 17. *Si* qua res talis erat, ut *non* sine incommodo posset in ius adferri vel adduci, velut si columna aut grex alicuius pecoris esset, pars aliqua inde sumebatur. deinde in eam partem quasi in totam rem praesentem fiebat vindicatio. itaque ex gre*g*e vel una *o*vis aut capra in ius adducebatur, vel e*tiam* pilus inde sumebatur et in ius adferebatur; ex nave vero et columna aliqua pars defringebatur. similiter si de fundo vel de aedibus sive de hereditate controversia erat, pars aliqua inde sumebatur et in ius adferebatur et in eam partem perinde atque in totam rem praesentem fiebat vindicatio: velut ex fundo gleba sumebatur et ex aedibus tegula, et si de hereditate controversia erat, aeque [*folium deperditum*].

§ 17. If the subject of dispute was such as could not conveniently be carried or led before the praetor, a portion was brought into court, and the formalities were enacted over it as if it was the whole. If it was a flock of sheep or herd of goats, a single sheep or goat, or a single tuft of hair was brought; if it was a ship or column, a fragment was broken off and brought; if it was land, a clod; if it was a house, a tile; if it was an inheritance. . . .

§ 13. The sacramentum or stake was originally deposited with the Pontifex and applied, when forfeited, to meet the expenses of the public sacrifices; whence its name. Afterwards, instead of an actual deposit, security [praedes=prae-vades] for the penal sum was given by both parties to the praetor.

In the ceremony as described by Gaius we may distinguish three stages: first, an oral pleading or altercation [secundum suam causam sicut dixi—Jus peregi sicut vindictam imposui]; secondly, a trial by battle, the original method of deciding disputed rights; and thirdly, the reference to peaceful adjudication. We may suppose that on some memorable day in the progress of civilization, before the combat had terminated fatally to one of the combatants, some Numa Pompilius, of sufficient authority to make so great an innovation, interposed and induced the parties to refer the dispute to arbitration. The case would afterwards serve as a model and precedent to future litigants; but, from a superstitious fear of losing the sanction of immemorial custom, the earlier stages of the process would still continue to be mimicked in solemn pantomime. So, in English law, trial by Wager of battle, introduced by William the Conqueror, was first partially superseded by the Grand assize, or trial by jury, an alternative substituted by Henry II, and was finally abolished in the reign of George III. 'The tenant [defendant] shall not be received to wage battle, nor shall issue be joined, nor trial had, by battle, in any writ of right,' 59 Geo. III, ch. 46.

The use of the rod or wand as representative of the spear, the symbol of dominion, may be paralleled in English law by the delivery of a staff as the symbol of power and possession in the conveyance of copyholds. 'The conveyance of copyhold estates is usually made from the seller to the lord or his steward by delivery of a rod or verge, and then from the lord to the purchaser by redelivery of the same in the presence of a jury of tenants,' Blackstone, 2, 20.

Part of the proceedings in the sacramentum was a ceremony denoted by the words manuum consertio. The Twelve Tables contained the expression, Si qui in jure manum conserunt, which is varied in a line of Ennius, Non ex jure manum consertum [vocant] sed mage ferro Rem repetunt. An explanation of the variance is given by Aulus Gellius. When land was the subject of controversy, the praetor originally repaired with the litigants to the spot, and they there performed in his presence (in jure) the ceremony of manuum consertio. But when the Roman territory was extended, the parties went without the praetor, each attended by his suit of witnesses; and finally, even the departure of the litigants was merely fictitious. This was the case in the time of Cicero, who gives the following fragments of the Sacramental procedure. He gives them disjointedly, but they perhaps form successive portions of the proceedings in a single action. Fundus qui est in agro qui

Sabinus vocatur . . . eum ego ex jure Quiritium meum esse aio . . . Inde ibi ego te ex jure manum consertum voco . . . Unde tu me ex jure manum consertum vocasti, inde ibi ego te revoco. . . . Suis utrisque superstitibus praesentibus istam viam dico. Inite viam . . . Redite viam . . . Quando te in jure conspicio . . . sed anne tu dicis qua ex causa vindicaveris, Pro Murena, 12. 'The estate in the Sabine land [between such and such boundaries] I claim as my domain by the law of the Quirites. To determine this question I challenge you to leave the court and join hands with me upon the ground. The question which you challenge me to determine by leaving the court and joining hands with you, that question I in turn challenge you to determine by a meeting on the ground. I command you both to go to the ground with your respective witnesses. Proceed. Return. Now that we meet in the presence of the praetor, will you state what is the foundation of your claim?'

What was the exact nature of the manuum consertio? The words of Aulus Gellius are as follows: Vindicia, id est, correptio manus in re atque in loco praesenti, apud Praetorem ex duodecim tabulis fiebat, in quibus ita scriptum est, Si qui in jure manum conserunt. Sed postquam praetores, propagatis Italiae finibus, . . . proficisci vindiciarum dicendarum causa in longinquas res gravabantur, institutum est . . . ut litigantes non in jure apud praetorem manum consererent, sed ex jure manum consertum vocarent, ... atque profecti simul in agrum de quo litigabatur, terrae aliquid ex eo, uti unam glebam, in jus in urbem ad praetorem deferrent, et in ea gleba tanquam in toto agro vindicarent, Aulus Gellius, 20, 10. From the conclusion of this passage we might suppose that the manuum consertio was the joint seizure of the object claimed which Gaius describes in the case of movables; but from the definition of vindicia in the commencement, manus correptio in re atque in loco praesenti, 'grasping the hand on or over the subject claimed,' the object grasped seems to have been the hand of the adversary. This interpretation is confirmed by a comparison of the process of Wager of battle in the old English law. 'When the tenant in a Writ of Right pleads that he hath more right to hold than the demandant hath to recover, and offers to prove it by the body of his champion, which tender is accepted by the demandant . . . a piece of ground is in due time set out, of sixty feet square, enclosed with lists, and on one side a court erected for the judges of the court of Common Pleas, who attend there in their scarlet robes; and also a bar is prepared for the learned sergeants at law. . . . When the champions, armed with batons, arrive within the lists or place of combat, the champion of the tenant takes his adversary by the hand [manuum consertio] and makes oath that the tenements in dispute are not the right of the demandant, and the champion of the demandant then taking the other by the hand swears in the same manner that they are: so that each champion is or ought to be thoroughly persuaded of the truth of the cause he fights for. Next, an oath against sorcery and enchantment is to be taken by both the champions. . . . The battle is then begun,' Blackstone, 3, 22. If we rely on this parallel the manuum consertio was the oath or pledge (δεξίωμα) that each party believed in the justice of his cause. The jusjurandum of the later law, which permitted either party to refer the decision of a dispute to the oath of his opponent, would be a derivative from the sacramentum or the still older process from which the sacramentum descended; consisting of one half of the process, the appeal to religious sanctions (manuum consertio), and omitting the other half, the subsequent duel. It must be confessed, however, that none of our authorities allude to the oath (jusjurandum) having formed a part of the procedure by sacramentum, and possibly manuum consertio was merely a symbolic battle.

§ 16. The specification of the title or ground of claim (expressio causae) in a real action (secundum suam causam sicut dixi) was probably limited to actions where the subject claimed was a person, and was then designed to distinguish whether the person was claimed as a son, wife, bondsman (mancipium), or slave. See p. 92.

CONDICTIO.

§ 18. Et haec quidem actio proprie *con*dictio vocabatur: nam actor adversario denunti*a*bat, ut ad iudicem capiendum die XXX. adesset. nunc vero non proprie condictionem dicimus actionem in personam *esse*, *qua* intendimus dare no*bis* oportere: nulla enim hoc tempore eo nomine denuntiatio fit.

§ 18. And this action was appropriately called condictio (notice), for the plaintiff used to give notice to the defendant to appear before the praetor on the thirtieth day to receive a judge. The name is now applied with less propriety to a personal action by which we sue for a transfer of property, for notice forms no part of the procedure.

§ 19. Haec autem legis actio constituta est per legem Siliam et Cal-

§ 19. This action of the law was created by the lex Silia and lex

purniam: lege quidem Silia certae pecuniae, lege vero Calpurnia de omni certa re.

Calpurnia, being prescribed by the lex Silia for the recovery of a certain sum, and extended by the lex Calpurnia to the recovery of a certain thing.

§ 20. Quare autem haec actio desiderata sit, cum de eo quod nobis dari oportet potuerimus sacramento aut per iudicis postulationem agere, valde quaeritur.

§ 20. Why a new action was needed, when transfer of property could be demanded either by Sacramentum or by Judicis postulatio, is canvassed.

After completing his account of Sacramentum, Gaius proceeded to explain the nature of Judicis postulatio. Of its process we have a fragment in the formula, Te, Praetor, judicem arbitrumve postulo uti des, 'I pray you, Praetor, to appoint an arbiter or judge.' It was apparently the prototype of actions ex fide bona, that is, of actions which required an equitable balancing of opposite claims, and an assessment by the judex of the damages, if any, due to the plaintiff. The actions Finium regundorum, Familiae herciscundae, Aquae pluviae arcendae, Vindiciae falsae, which are mentioned in the Twelve Tables, appear to have been tried by an arbiter or arbiters, that is, to have been forms of Judicis postulatio.

The Condictio was unknown to the Twelve Tables, having been created by the lex Silia about A.D. 510, and extended by the lex Calpurnia about A.D. 520. Its distinctive feature appears to have been the sponsio and restipulatio, § 13, a wager or verbal contract conditioned for the forfeiture by the vanquished party of one third of the sum in dispute, in addition, on the part of the defendant, to the original debt. The stake or penalty is called by Cicero legitima pars, 'statutable sum:' Pecunia petita est certa; cum tertia parte sponsio facta est. . . . Pecunia tibi debebatur certa quae nunc petitur per judicem, in qua legitimae partis sponsio facta est, Pro Roscio, 4, 5: whence we may infer that it was fixed by the lex Silia, the statute which created the procedure by condictio.

At this period the Sacramentum would be practically confined to Real actions before the Centumviral Court: Condictio would be the appropriate Personal action for recovering a certain sum or thing due upon a unilateral contract, real (mutuum), verbal (stipulatio), or literal (expensilatio); and Judicis postulatio the appropriate Personal action for recovering an uncertain sum due on a bilateral contract, and enforcing obligations to perform (facere) rather than to convey.

The gist (gîte) of the civil action of Condictio, i.e. the circumstance whereon it lay, the title or ground of action, was the increase of the defendant's fortune or patrimony by the reduction of the plaintiff's patrimony without any consideration or equivalent gain to the plaintiff. This disturbance the law restored. The simplest, and probably the earliest, instance of the principle was mutui datio. Here the defendant's wealth is increased and that of the plaintiff diminished by a voluntary act of the plaintiff; but the principle equally covers cases where the relation is not knowingly and intentionally initiated by the plaintiff, e.g. payment by mistake (solutio indebiti) and failure of consideration (causa data, causa non secuta). From mutui datio, or actual loan, the Condiction was extended to Expensilatio and Stipulatio, both of which, probably, were imaginary loans, that is, pacts solemnized and fortified by the fiction of a loan. We are expressly informed that this was the case with Expensilatio, 2 § 129, and from etymology (stips=pecunia) and the analogy of Nexum (a fictitious weighing out of bars of bronze), we may conjecture the same of Stipulatio.

The introduction of actions stricti juris is probably of more ancient date than the introduction of actions based on bona fides; the necessity, that is, of applying the power of the State to enforce the class of obligations pursued by Condictio was earlier felt than the necessity of compelling men to perform their so-called obligations ex fide bona. From the antithesis of strictum jus and bona fides it might be imagined that trust, confidence, credit, reliance on good faith, were entirely foreign to civil obligations, and were only ingredients in equitable obligations. This is the reverse of the truth. Greater confidence (fides) is involved in mutui datio, greater risk is incurred by the obligee, who starts by alienating his property and making it the property of the obligor, who denudes himself, that is, of the remedy of vindicatio, than in any other contracts, most of which leave the promisee, even before the invention of personal actions, armed, if need be, with the legal remedy of vindicatio. Other contracts we can imagine left to the protection of the moral code, to the forum of conscience, to the sanction of public opinion, at a time when it was felt that the immense confidence implied in a loan for consumption could only exist under the aegis of positive law.

When the short, sharp, and decisive remedy of a civil action had once been invented for mutui datio, the ingenuity of contracting parties and jurists would soon extend the remedy to other relations by means of a fiction of mutui datio. Expensilation, then, and Stipulation may be regarded as artifices for transferring conventions, originally perhaps, from the ethical code to the legal code; but certainly, in later times, from the laxer equitable code to the more rigorous civil code. A great part, however, of human dealings refuses to be governed by pre-determined conditions, and pre-arranged, pre-capitulated stipulations. Hence alongside of stipulatio and expensilatio existed Real and Consensual contracts; alongside of Condictio existed Judicis arbitrive postulatio; alongside of formulae stricti juris existed formulae ex fide bona.

MANUS INIECTIO.

§ 21. P*er* manus iniectionem aeque *de* his rebus agebatur, de quibus ut ita ageretur, lege ali*qua* cautum est, velut iudicati lege XII tabularum. quae actio talis erat. qui agebat sic dicebat: QUOD TU MIHI IUDICATUS SIVE DAMNATUS ES SESTERTIUM X MILIA QUAE DOLO *MALO* NON SOLVISTI, OB EAM REM EGO TIBI SESTERTIUM X MILIUM IUDICATI MANUS INICIO; et simul aliquam partem corporis eius prendebat. nec licebat iudicato manum sibi depellere et pro se lege agere; se*d* vindicem dabat, qui pro se causam agere solebat: qui vindicem non dabat, domum ducebatur ab actore et vinciebatur.

§ 21. Manus injectio (arrest) was the form of action prescribed by law in certain circumstances; as, for instance, against a judgment debtor by the law of the Twelve Tables. The procedure was as follows: the plaintiff said, 'Whereas you have been adjudged or condemned to pay me ten thousand sesterces which you fraudulently have failed to pay, therefore I arrest you as judgment debtor for ten thousand sesterces,' and at the same time laid hands on him; and the debtor was not allowed to resist the arrest, or defend himself in his own person, but gave a vindex to advocate his cause, or, in default, was taken prisoner to the plaintiff's house, and put in chains.

§ 22. Postea quaedam leges ex aliis quibusdam causis pro iudicato manus iniectionem in quosd*a*m dederunt: sicut lex Publilia in eum *pro* quo sponsor dependisset, *si* in sex mensibus proximis quam pro eo depensum esset non solvisset sponsori pecuniam; item lex Furia de sponsu adversus eum qui a sponsore plus quam virilem partem exegisset; et denique co*m*plures aliae leges in multis causis talem actionem dederunt.

§ 22. Afterwards Manus injectio was given by various laws against quasi judgment debtors, as by the lex Publilia against the principal whose debt had been paid by his sponsor, unless he indemnified his sponsor within six months from the payment of the debt; by the lex Furia de Sponsu against the creditor who had exacted from one of several sponsors more than his rateable share; and by various other laws against various other persons.

§ 23. Sed aliae leges ex quibusdam *causis* constituerunt quasdam actiones per manus iniectionem, sed puram, id est non pro iudicato: velut lex *Furia* testamentaria adversus eum qui legatorum nomine mortisve causa plus M assibus cepisset, cum ea lege non esset exceptus, ut ei plus capere liceret; item lex Marcia adversus faeneratores, ut si usuras exegissent, de his reddendis per manus iniectionem cum eis ageretur.

§ 23. Other laws gave Manus injectio simple, that is, not to quasi judgment creditors, against certain other persons; as the lex Furia testamentaria against the legatee or donee in contemplation of death who received more than a thousand asses not being included in certain privileged classes; and the lex Marcia compelled usurers to refund by this process.

§ 24. Ex quibus legibus, et si quae aliae similes essent, cum agebatur, manum sibi depellere et pro se lege agere *licebat*. nam et actor in ipsa legis actione non adiciebat hoc verbum PRO IUDICATO, sed nominata causa ex qua agebat, ita dicebat: OB EAM REM EGO TIBI MANUM INICIO; cum hi quibus pro iudicato actio data erat, nominata causa ex qua agebant, ita inferebant: OB EAM REM EGO TIBI PRO IUDICATO MANUM INICIO. nec me praeterit in forma legis Furiae testamentariae PRO IUDICATO verbum inseri, cum in ipsa lege non sit: quod videtur nulla ratione factum.

§ 24. These laws and certain others permitted the defendant to resist arrest and defend himself in person, for the plaintiff could not arrest him as quasi judgment debtor, but, after naming his cause of action, said simply, 'I therefore arrest you;' whereas, if he proceeded as quasi judgment creditor, after naming the cause he said, 'Therefore I arrest you as quasi judgment debtor.' I am aware that in proceeding under the lex Furia testamentaria the plaintiff added the words, 'As quasi judgment debtor,' though they are not inserted in the law; but I believe that this could not be justified.

§ 25. Sed postea lege . . . , excepto iudicato et eo pro quo depensum est, ceteris omnibus cum quibus per manus iniectionem agebatur permissum est sibi manum depellere et pro se agere. itaque iudicatus et is pro quo depensum est etiam post hanc legem vindicem dare debebant, et nisi darent, domum ducebantur. idque quamdiu legis actiones in usu erant semper ita observabatur; unde nostris temporibus is cum quo iudicati depensive agitur iudicat*um* solui satisdare cogitur.

§ 25. In more recent times the lex . . . permitted all defendants sued by Manus injectio, except the judgment debtor and the principal indebted to his sponsor, to resist arrest and defend themselves in person. Accordingly, the judgment debtor and principal indebted to his sponsor had to give a vindex or were taken to prison as long as the Actions of law were in force, and at the present day must give bail for the payment of the sum in which they may be condemned.

Some fragments of the law of the Twelve Tables regulating the process of Manus injectio are still preserved. Aeris confessi rebusque jure judicatis triginta dies justi sunto. Post deinde manus injectio esto. In jus ducito. Ni judicatum facit, aut quis emendo em jure vindicit, secum ducito. Vincito aut nervo aut compedibus. . . . Tertiis nundinis partes secanto. Si plus minusve secuerint, se fraude esto. 'An acknowledged or judgment debtor shall have thirty days' grace allowed. After that, he shall be arrested and taken before the magistrate, and unless he pays or is defended by a vindex, shall be taken to the creditor's house and put in chains. . . . On the third market-day the creditors shall cut his body into portions proportioned to their claims. He who cuts too large or too small a portion shall incur no risk.' This is supplemented by Aulus Gellius: Erat autem interea jus paciscendi; ac ni pacti forent, habebantur in vinculis dies sexaginta; inter eos dies trinis nundinis continuis ad praetorem in comitium producebantur quantaeque pecuniae judicati essent praedicabatur. Tertiis autem nundinis capite poenas dabant, aut trans Tiberim peregre venum ibant, 20, 1. 'The debtor, after he was delivered by the magistrate (addictus) to the creditor, might make a compromise; otherwise he was kept in chains for sixty days, during which time he was brought before the magistrate in the comitium on three successive market-days, and proclamation was made of the amount of his debt. On the third market-day he was put to death or sold into servitude beyond the Tiber.' There are many allusions in history to the private gaols of the usurers; e.g. An placeret, fenore circumventam plebem, potius quam sorte creditum solvat, corpus in nervum ac supplicia dare: et gregatim quotidie de foro addictos duci, et repleri vinctis nobiles domos, et ubicunque patricius habitet, ibi carcerem privatum esse [B.C. 366], Livy, 6, 36. 'Was it well that the commons, overwhelmed with usury, instead of paying the capital, should surrender their bodies to the stocks and torture; that herds should daily be dragged from the forum to servitude; that noble houses should be crowded with men in chains, and every patrician mansion should be a private prison?' Zeno (A.D. 490) calls the detention of a man in a private prison 'nefandissimorum hominum arrogantia'—'nefandissimum scelus,'—and says that it had long been unlawful. He makes it high treason, and punishable with death. Governors of provinces who fail to enforce the law are declared guilty of high treason, Codex, 9, 5.

§ 22. The lex Furia de sponsu (3 § 121), supposed to have been passed in B.C. 95, limited the obligation of the sponsor and fidepromissor to two years, and divided it equally among all the sponsores and fidepromissores without regard to their solvency.

§ 23. The lex Furia testamentaria (2 § 225), supposed to have been passed in B.C. 183, forbade all but certain classes to receive more than a thousand asses by way of legacy or gift to take effect at death. As, however, it did not limit the number of legatees or donees, it did not prevent the exhaustion of the inheritance; accordingly, the heres was subsequently protected by the lex Falcidia.

The lex Marcia is supposed to have been passed between B.C. 200 and B.C. 100.

Manus injectio must be regarded in two aspects, (1) as the ordinary mode of execution after a judgment, and (2) as a proceeding in bankruptcy; or rather, we must consider that in the ancient Roman law these two procedures were identical, a proceeding in bankruptcy being the only known form of a judgment execution.

Execution or proceedings in bankruptcy in the old Roman law was always directed immediately against the person of the debtor; execution against his property, under the name of Bonorum venditio, 3 § 77, was a later invention. [Savigny, however, supposes that execution against the person was confined to judgments on an actual loan of money, and that execution on other judgments was always against the estate.]

The cases, other than a judgment debt, in which the creditor might proceed by Manus injectio may be regarded, in the language of English law, as so many acts of bankruptcy. As such may be reckoned, besides those mentioned in the text, (1) Furtum manifestum, 3 § 189; (2) resistance to in jus vocatio; Si calvitur pedemve struit, manum endo jacito, Fragment of the Twelve Tables. 'If the defendant on being summoned to appear before the magistrate tergiversates or attempts to flee, the plaintiff may proceed to Manus injectio.'

We may conjecture also that avoidance of in jus vocatio by latitation or keeping house rendered a defendant liable to manus injectio. Such is the probable explanation of two fragments of the Twelve Tables: Si in jus vocat, ni it, antestator, igitur em capito.... Cui testimonium defuerit is tertiis diebus ob portum obvagulatum ito. 'On a service of summons to appear before the magistrate, if the defendant refuse obedience, the plaintiff shall obtain attestation of the fact, and then take him by force. In default of such attestation (i.e. if the defendant avoid service by keeping out of the way) the plaintiff on three market-days shall stand before the defendant's door and waul (loudly summon him to appear, and after this the defendant shall be liable to manus injectio).

(3) Forfeiture of the condition of the solemn contract called Nexum. This was of the nature of a pignus of the person of the borrower, and on forfeiture of the condition by default in repayment the debtor seems to have been in the position of a judgment debtor (pro judicato); indeed it is possible that he was in a worse condition than the judicatus, for it is not certain that his removal in custody (abductio) to the creditor's prison required a previous appearance before the magistrate.

§ 25. Puchta suggests that the law limiting the Manus injectio may have been identical with the law (called by the moderns without authority lex Poetelia) abolishing the Nexum, and with the law that introduced Condictio, that it was, in fact, the lex Silia, § 19. If it is permitted from the internal relation of things to argue to their historic connection, we might also conjecture that this law contained dispositions regulating the legal force of Stipulatio, the universally applicable form of contract which took the place of Nexum.

With liability to Manus injectio for a quasi judgment debt we may compare the arrest of an absconding debtor in the English law by a writ of capias ad respondendum. As the Roman debtor had to find a vindex or responsible representative, so the English debtor must either remain in custody or put in bail, that is, find sureties who will undertake that, if judgment is obtained against him, either he shall surrender into custody, or shall pay the debt and costs recovered, or that they themselves will pay them for him.

PIGNORIS CAPIO.

§ 26. Per pignoris capionem lege agebatur de quibusdam rebus moribus, *de quibusdam* lege.

§ 27. Introducta est moribus rei militaris. nam propter stipendium *l*icebat militi ab eo qui distr*ib*uebat, nisi daret, pignus capere: dicebatur autem ea pecunia quae stipendii nomine dabatur aes militare. item propter eam pecuniam licebat pignus capere ex qua eq*u*us emendus

§ 26. Pignoris capio (distress) was introduced in some cases by custom, in others by law.

§ 27. By custom, in obligations connected with military service; for the soldier could distrain upon his paymaster for his pay, called aes militare; for money to buy a horse, called aes equestre; and for money to buy barley for his horse, called aes hordearium.

erat: quae pecunia dicebatur aes equestre. item propter eam pecuniam ex qua hordeum equis erat conparandum; quae pecunia dicebatur aes hordiarium.

§ 28. Lege autem introducta est pignoris capio velut lege XII tabularum adversus eum qui hostiam emisset, nec pretium redderet: item adversus eum qui mercedem non redderet pro eo iumento quod quis ideo locasset, ut inde pecuniam acceptam in da*p*em, id est in sacrificium i*m*penderet. item lege . . . toria data est pignoris captio publicanis vectigal*ium* *pub*licorum populi Romani adversus eos qui aliqua lege *vectig*alia deberent.

§ 28. The law of the Twelve Tables rendered liable to distress on default of payment the buyer of a victim and the hirer of a beast of burden lent to raise money for a sacrifice. The lex praediatoria gave the power of distress to the farmers of the public revenue.

§ 29. Ex omnibus autem istis causis certis verbis pignus capiebatur; et ob id plerisque placebat hanc quoque actionem legis actionem esse. quibusdam autem *non* placebat: primum quod pignoris captio extra ius peragebatur, id est non aput Praetorem, plerumque etiam absente adversario, cum alioquin ceteris actionibus non aliter uti poss*ent* quam aput Praetorem praesente adversario: praeterea ne*fa*s*to* quoque d*ie*, id est quo non licebat lege agere, pignus capi poterat.

§ 29. As in all these cases the distreinor used a set form of words, the proceeding was generally considered an action of the law. Some, however, held otherwise, because it was performed in the absence of the praetor and generally of the debtor; whereas, the other actions of the law could only be enacted in the presence of the praetor and the adversary; besides, it could take place in the juridical vacation (2 § 279), that is, in days exempt from actions of the law.

Distress in English law bears a certain resemblance to Execution. Each is the application of constraint to a defendant's will by seizure of his goods. But making a distress is the act of a private person, and precedes the commencement of an action: execution follows after judgment obtained in an action, and is the act of the executive at the command of the sovereign. The pignoris capio of the older Roman law corresponded to distress; the pignoris captio of the formulary system generally was a mode of execution.

Pignoris capio in the older system was a remedy allowed in cases of a public character, that is, in claims relating to military service, to religion, or to the revenue. In the first case the remedy was established by custom, that is, was anterior to the Twelve Tables; in the second case it was given by the Twelve

Tables; in the third case it was created by law subsequent to the Twelve Tables.

We have mention of the aes hordearium, § 27, in Livy's account of the Servian constitution: Ad equos emendos dena millia aeris ex publico data et, quibus equos alerent, viduae attributae, quae bina millia aeris in singulos annos penderent, Livy 1, 43. 'Each soldier received ten thousand asses for the purchase of a horse, and for its maintenance a widow was assigned, who was bound to pay two thousand asses a year.'

The institution appears to have been transplanted from Greece. Cicero mentions it as in force at Corinth: Deinde equitatum ad hunc morem constituit, qui usque adhuc est retentus. Atque etiam Corinthios video publicis equis assignandis et alendis orborum et viduarum tributis fuisse quondam diligentes, De Republica, 2, 20. 'Tarquinius Priscus instituted the present organization of the cavalry. At Corinth, whence he came, there was a practice of allotting horses at the public expense and taxing the childless and widows for their maintenance.' The private persons thus appointed military paymasters appear to have been called tribuni aerarii, Gellius 7, 10. In later times soldiers were paid by the Quaestors from the public treasury.

We have something similar in the Laws of Plato: *περὶ δὲ . . . . λειτουργιῶν, ὁπόσα περὶ θυσίας εἰρηνικῆς ἢ πολεμικῶν εἰσφορῶν εἵνεκα, πάντων τῶν τοιούτων τὴν πρώτην ἀνάγκην ἰατὴν εἶναι τῆς ζημίας, τοῖς δὲ μὴ πειθομένοις ἐνεχυρασίαν τούτοις οἷς ἂν πόλις ἅμα καὶ νόμος εἰσπράττειν προστάττῃ, τῶν δὲ ἀπειθούντων ταῖς ἐνεχυρασίαις πρᾶσιν τῶν ἐνεχύρων εἶναι, τὸ δὲ νόμισμα γίγνεσθαι τῇ πόλει*, Laws, 12, 4. 'If a public duty relating to religion or war is unperformed, the first stage of penal constraint shall be defeasible by submission, and the defaulter's goods shall be merely taken in distress by the proper official; but if he continue contumacious, the distress shall be sold and the proceeds confiscated.'

A praediator is defined by Gaius, qui mercatur a populo, above, 2 § 61. Cicero speaks of jus praediatorium, Pro Balbo, 20. A lex praediatoria is mentioned by Suetonius: Ad eas rei familiaris augustias decidit, ut cum obligatam aerariis fidem liberare non posset, in vacuum lege praediatoria venalis pependerit sub edicto praefectorum, Claudius 9. 'He was so impoverished, that he could not discharge his obligation to the treasury, and his goods were declared vacant by the lex praediatoria, and advertised for sale by the edict of the prefects.'

DE FICTIONIBUS.

§ 30. Sed istae omnes legis actiones paulatim in odium venerunt. namque ex nimia subtilitate veterum qui tunc iura condiderunt eo res perducta est, ut vel qui minimum errasset *litem* perderet. itaque per legem Aebutiam et duas Iulias sublatae sunt istae legis actiones effectumque est, ut per concepta verba, id est per formulas litigaremus.

§ 31. Tantum ex duabus causis permissum est lege agere: damni infecti, et si centumvirale iudicium fit. proinde vel *hod*ie cum ad centumviros itur, ante lege agitur sacramento aput Praetorem urbanum vel peregrinum. propter damni vero infecti nemo vult lege agere, sed potius *stipulatione* quae in edicto proposita est obligat adversarium *per magistratum*, quod *et* commodius ius *et* plenius est. per pignoris [*desunt* 24 *lin.*] apparet.

§ 32. Item in ea forma quae publicano proponitur talis fictio est, ut quanta pecunia olim, si pignus captum esset, id pignus is a quo captum erat, luere deberet, tantam pecuniam condemnetur.

§ 33. Nulla autem formula ad condictionis fictionem exprimitur. sive enim pecuniam sive rem aliquam certam debitam nobis petamus, eam ipsam dari nobis oportere intendimus; nec ullam adiungimus condictionis fictionem. itaque simul intellegimus eas formulas quibus pecuniam aut rem aliquam nobis DARE OPORTERE intendimus, sua vi ac potestate valere. eiusdem naturae sunt actiones commodati, fiduciae, negotiorum gestorum et aliae innumerabiles.

§ 30. But all these actions of the law fell gradually into great discredit because the over subtlety of the ancient jurists made the slightest error fatal; and they were abolished by the lex Aebutia and the two leges Juliae, which introduced in their stead the system of formulas or written instructions of the praetor to the judex.

§ 31. Two cases only were reserved for actions of the law, apprehended damage and centumviral causes. The latter are preceded by the ceremony of sacramentum before the praetor urbanus or peregrinus, as may happen. For protection against apprehended damage a plaintiff no longer resorts to the action of the law, but stipulates to be indemnified by the defendant in the manner provided by the edict, whereby he is put to less trouble and obtains ampler redress.

§ 32. The formula provided for the farmer of the revenue directs the debtor to be condemned in the sum for which formerly, after seizure of his goods, he would have had to ransom the distress.

§ 33. No formula is moulded on a hypothetical condictio; for when we sue for a certain thing or sum of money, our intentio names the very thing or sum for which we sue, without any reference to an imagined condictio. Similarly independent of the elder system are the actions of Loan for use, Trust, Unauthorized Agency, and innumerable others.

§ 34. Habemus ad*h*uc alterius *etiam* generis fictiones *in* quibusdam formulis: velut cum is qui ex *edicto* bonorum possessionem *petiit* ficto se herede agit. cum enim praetorio iure e*t* non legiti*mo* succedat in locum defuncti, non ha*b*et direc*tas* actiones, et neque id quod defuncti fuit potest intendere suum *esse, neque id quod defuncto de*bebatur potest intendere *dare sib*i oportere; *ita*que *ficto* se herede intendit velu*ti hoc* mod*o*: IUDEX ESTO. SI AULUS AGERIUS, id est ipse actor, *LUCIO TITIO* HERES *ESSET*, TUM *SI PARET* FUNDU*M* DE QUO AGITUR EX IURE QUIRITIUM *EIUS* ESSE *OPORTERE*; vel si i*n personam* a*g*atur, praeposita simili*ter fictione illa* ita subicitur: TUM SI PARET NUMERIUM NEGIDIUM AULO *AGERIO* SESTERTIUM X MILIA DARE OPORTERE.

§ 34. The other kind of fiction is employed when the bonorum possessor or praetorian successor is feigned to be civil heir. Being only the equitable, not the legal, successor, he has no direct action, and can neither claim to be proprietor of the things belonging to the deceased, nor to be obligee of the debts due to him. Accordingly, the intentio supposes him to be civil heir, and runs as follows: 'Let C D be judex. Supposing Aulus Agerius (plaintiff) were the civil heir of Lucius Titius, if in that supposition it be proved that the land in question ought to be his by the law of the Quirites;' or, if the action is personal, 'if in that supposition it be proved that Numerius Negidius (defendant) ought to pay to Aulus Agerius ten thousand sesterces; then let the defendant be condemned,' &c.

§ 35. Similiter et bonorum emptor ficto se herede agit. se*d* interdum et alio modo agere solet. nam ex persona eius cuius bona emerit sumpta intentione convertit condemnationem in suam personam, id est ut quod illius esset vel illi dare oporteret, eo nomine adversarius huic condemnetur: quae speci*es* actionis appellatu*r* Rutiliana, quia a Praetore Publio Rutilio, qui et bonorum venditionem introduxisse dicitur, co*m*parata es*t*. superio*r* autem species actionis qua ficto se herede bonorum emptor *agit* Serviana vocatur.

§ 35. So the purchaser of a bankrupt's estate may either suppose himself to be civil heir, or may use a different form: he may name the insolvent in the intentio and himself in the condemnatio, requiring the defendant to restore or pay to himself any property that belonged or any debt that was due to the insolvent. This form of action is called Rutilian from the praetor Rutilius who invented execution in bankruptcy against the estate: the action wherein the plaintiff feigns himself civil heir is called Serviana.

§ 36. *Eiusdem generis est quae Publiciana vocatur.* datur autem haec actio ei qui ex iusta causa traditam sibi rem nondum usucepit eamque amissa possessione petit. nam quia non potest eam ex iure Quiritium suam esse intendere, fingitur rem usucepisse, et ita, quasi ex iure Quiritium dominus factus esset, inten*dit* hoc modo: IUDEX ESTO. SI

§ 36. Of the same nature is the Publician action, whereby a man claims a thing which had been delivered to him for a just consideration and of which he lost possession before he had acquired property by usucapion. Being unable to call it his property by the law of the Quirites, he is supposed to have acquired it by usucapion and his

QUEM HOMINEM AULUS AGERIUS EMIT, ET IS EI TRADITUS EST, ANNO POSSEDISSET, TUM SI EUM HOMINEM DE QUO AGITUR EIUS EX IURE QUIRITIUM ESSE OPORTERET *et reliqua*.

intentio runs as follows: 'Let C D be judex. Supposing that the slave who was sold and delivered to Aulus Agerius had continued during a year in his possession, if in that case the slave ought to have belonged to Aulus Agerius by the law of the Quirites, then condemn the defendant,' &c.

§ 37. Item civitas Romana peregrino fingitur, si eo nomine agat aut cum eo agatur, quo nomine nostris legibus actio constituta est, si modo iustum sit eam actionem etiam ad peregrinum extendi, velut si furtum *faciat* peregrinus *et* cum eo *agatur*, formula ita concipitur: IUDEX ESTO. SI PARET OPE CONSILIOVE DIONIS HERMAEI LUCIO TITIO FURTUM FACTUM ESSE PATERAE AUREAE, QUAM OB REM EUM, SI CIVIS ROMANUS ESSET, PRO FURE DAMNUM DECIDERE OPORTERET et reliqua. item si peregrinus furti agat, civitas ei Romana fingitur. similiter si ex lege Aquilia peregrinus damni iniuriae agat aut cum eo agatur, ficta civitate Romana iudicium datur.

§ 37. So an alien is feigned to be a Roman, if he sue or be sued in an action which may justly be extended to aliens. For instance, if an alien is sued for theft, the formula runs as follows: 'Let C D be judex. If it be proved that Dio Hermaeus aided and abetted in the theft of a golden cup belonging to Lucius Titius, for which, if he had been a Roman citizen he would have had to make composition for theft, then condemn Dio Hermaeus,' &c. So if an alien sue for theft or be sued under the Aquilian law for damage to property, he is feigned to be a Roman citizen.

§ 38. Praeterea *a*liquando fingimus ad*versa*rium nostrum *capite* diminutum non esse. nam si ex contractu nobis obligatus obligatave sit et capite deminutus deminutave fu*er*it, velut mulier per coemptionem, masculus per adrogationem, desinit iure civili debere nobis, nec directo intendere *possumus* dare eum eamve oportere; sed ne in potestate eius sit ius nostrum corrumpere, introducta est contra eum eamve actio *u*tilis, rescissa capitis deminutione, id est in qua fingitur capite deminutus deminutave non esse.

§ 38. Again, we may feign that the defendant has not been degraded in status: for if we make a contract with a person who afterwards is degraded in status, as an (independent) female by subjection to Hand, an independent male by adrogation, he or she ceases by the civil law to be our debtor, and we cannot directly declare in the intentio that he or she is bound to convey. To protect our rights, however, from extinction by the act of another, the praetor grants an actio utilis, rescinding or ignoring the defendant's act and feigning the continuance of his or her original status.

§ 30. The lex Aebutia is supposed to have been passed about 170 B.C. The leges Juliae are supposed to be a lex judiciaria passed by Julius Caesar about 45 B.C., and another lex judiciaria passed by Augustus about 25 B. C. After the legis actiones were abolished as modes of proceeding in civil suits their forms still survived in the ceremonies of Adoption, the manumission of a slave, the emancipation of a son, and conveyance by in jure cessio.

We may observe by anticipation that the formulary system, after an existence of nearly five hundred years, was brought by the ingenuity of lawyers into the same discredit and experienced the same fate as the system it had displaced. First Diocletian, A. D. 294, made all judicia extraordinaria, that is, required the magistrates to hear and determine all causes themselves, instead of commissioning others to hear and determine them. Placet nobis, Praesides de his causis in quibus, quod non ipsi possent cognoscere, antehac pedaneos judices dabant, notionis suae examen adhibere: ita tamen, ut, si vel propter occupationes publicas vel propter causarum multitudinem omnia hujusmodi negotia non potuerint cognoscere, judices dandi habeant potestatem, Cod. 3, 3. 'Governors of provinces shall themselves determine the causes which they used to refer to inferior judges, unless compelled by pressure of business or the number of causes to delegate their function.' Afterwards Constans, A. D. 342, abolished the necessity of using consecrated terms in any legal act. Juris formulae, aucupatione syllabarum insidiantes, cunctorum actibus radicitus amputentur, Cod. 2, 58. 'Legal formulas with their syllabic snares and pitfalls, are hereby abolished in every procedure.'

§ 31. The proceeding under the edict in Damni infecti was as follows: If A apprehended damage to his property from the downfall of a dilapidated house (aedes vitiosae, ruinosae) belonging to B, he might apply to the praetor and obtain an order that B should promise, with or without sureties according to circumstances, to indemnify A in the event of the accident. If B refused to promise, the praetor by a first decree put A in possession, that is, gave him detention or custody of B's house. If B still refused, the praetor by a second decree gave the property to A, if B was quiritarian proprietor: if B had not the quiritarian property, the praetor gave A the bonitarian property, that is, a usucapion possession which time would convert into quiritarian proprietorship. This remedy, imposing the necessity of indemnifying or surrendering the cause of damage, was an imitation of noxal actions, which compelled the father of a son or owner of a slave or of a beast that had injured a neighbour's property either to make compensation or to surrender the author of the damage.

The proceeding damni infecti nomine by action of the law, from its similarity to the proceeding in aquae pluviae arcendae, may be inferred to have been a form of judicis postulatio.

§ 34. Gaius appears to have divided Fictions into two classes, those which made a reference from the formulary system to the older system of procedure, and those which made a reference from rights protected by the praetor to rights recognized by the civil law. The former class were not an extension of the law, but only preserved to a plaintiff the remedies which he otherwise would have lost by the change of procedure when the actions of the law were abolished. For instance, the fiction of Pignoris capio was employed to preserve unimpaired the rights of the revenue contractor and as a measure for assessing the damages to which he was entitled against a defaulter.

The second class of fictions was an extension or reform of the law, protecting persons whose rights had previously not been recognized, or mitigating the rigours and liberalizing the narrow-mindedness of the ancient barbarous legislation: granting to the bonitarian proprietor by inheritance or purchase the protection enjoyed by the quiritarian proprietor; giving to the alien the redress provided for the citizen, and preserving to the creditor the remedies extinguished by the debtor's diminution of status. In their task of ameliorating the law the praetors proceeded as unobtrusively as possible, by tacit rather than by open legislation, and rather by innovations in the adjective code, to use Bentham's expression, or code of procedure, than in the substantive code. The introduction of the formulary system, giving them authority to create new actions, had virtually invested them with much legislative power. The new actions introduced by the praetor were called actiones utiles. Utiles actiones were either fictitiae or in factum. Let us examine the mode of their operation. The logic of justice as administered in the courts may be regarded as a syllogism, of which the major premiss is the substantive law annexing a certain remedy to certain conditions (to a certain title); the minor premiss the proposition that between the present plaintiff and defendant these conditions are satisfied;

and the conclusion, the enforcement of the remedy in favour of the plaintiff by the executive. Let A represent the remedy or sanctioning right, B the conditions or title, C the plaintiff. (If C represents the defendant, A will represent the sanctioning duties or obligations). The praetor proceeded in two ways, with or without the use of fiction. Without expressly asserting the major premiss, B is A, or avowedly introducing a new principle of substantive law, it is clear that he introduced it by implication if he made the conclusion, C is A, follow from the minor premiss, C is B. In granting an actio in factum, one of his most potent instruments, that is, an action whose intentio in factum concepta, of the form, Si paret . . . . fecisse, proposed a single issue of fact, the praetor tacitly introduced a new major premiss, B is A, or converted a rule of equity or public opinion into a principle of substantive law, without any fiction or reference to previous rules. When he granted a fictitious action, that is, one whose intentio in jus concepta, of the form, Si paret . . . . oportere, admitted issues both of fact and of law, the fiction furnished an exact measure of the extent to which the old law had been abandoned. If the old law is represented by the major premiss, B is A, the praetor might suppress some element, X, of the title B to which the remedy A was annexed; and make the conclusion, C is A, follow from the minor premiss, C is B minus X. The fiction would be the false assumption that C (the plaintiff's case) satisfied the abrogated condition X whenever it was proved to satisfy the remaining elements of B. By ruling that the fictitious proposition, C is X, should not be called in question, and that the defendant should not be allowed to demur to the plaintiff's claim on the ground that X was unsatisfied, the praetor would virtually abrogate the old law, B is A, and substitute for it the new law, B minus X is A. In the cases given by Gaius the condition represented by X relates to succession, usucapio, citizenship, status. It might relate to delivery, contract, alienation, or any other legal act. In the actio Pauliana, protecting creditors against fraudulent alienations, the fiction was an assumption of non-delivery (rescissa traditione). Restitutio in integrum of a minor or person who had acted under constraint of fear might assume the form of a fictitious action which treated the rescinded act as unperformed (rescissa alienatione).

§ 35. The purchaser of a bankrupt's estate, unlike the purchaser at a sectio bonorum, or sale sub hasta of the confiscated goods of a criminal, though a universal successor, only took, in the language of English law, the equitable and not the legal estate. To protect his rights the praetor allowed him to sue in the character of heres, or successor to the legal estate.

The praetor Publius Rutilius may either have been a person who was praetor in 167 B.C., or a person who was consul in 104 B.C. The formula which he introduced was used by the cognitor and procurator, 4 § 86. Before his time, apparently, the lawyers entertained a superstition about a variance between the intentio and condemnatio.

The actio Serviana here mentioned was apparently not the same as the actio Serviana whereby a lessor could recover the goods of a colonus which had been pledged as a security for the payment of rent.

§ 36. A Quintus Publicius is mentioned by Cicero, Pro Cluentio, 45, as praetor in B.C. 66 or shortly before. The actio Publiciana, 2 § 41, was used by the purchaser of a res mancipi who had taken by simple delivery what could only be conveyed by mancipation; or by a grantee from a grantor who was not proprietor. The abolition of the distinction of res mancipi and nec mancipi and of quiritarian and bonitarian property would render the action unnecessary in the first of these cases and probably in many cases of the second class. In the terms of the edict, Si quis id quod traditur ex justa causa non a domino et nondum usucaptum petet, judicium dabo, Digest, 6, 2, 1, the words 'non a domino,' which limit its application to the second class, were probably intercalated by Justinian. But the action would also be convenient to an actual proprietor who wished to be relieved of the necessity of proving his title.

The form of the actio Publiciana that we have considered proceeds on the supposition of the accomplishment of a non-accomplished usucapio. Another form, called by the commentators contraria Publicianae or Publiciana rescissoria, proceeded on the supposition that an accomplished usucapio had not been accomplished. If the goods of the plaintiff were acquired by prescription during the absence of the plaintiff in the service of his country or during his captivity in the hands of the enemy, or if they were acquired by a person in the power of an absentee defendant, in any of which cases the plaintiff would have been unable to interrupt the prescription by instituting legal proceedings, he could obtain a restitutio in integrum by a rescissory action commenced after his own or the defendant's return. As this was in direct contravention of the civil law, the action was required to be brought within a year from the removal of the disability, a period which Justinian extended for all restitutiones in integrum to four years. The other Publician action, as aiding rather than infringing the civil law, was perpetual. In the case of an absentee defendant Justinian made the Publiciana rescissoria unnecessary by giving the plaintiff a means of interrupting the usucapio (interruptionem temporis facere—usurpare). He allowed him to do so by making a protestation, in person or by writing, before the praeses provinciae, or bishop, or defensor civitatis; or, in their absence, by affixing a protestation, signed by the public notaries (tabularii) or by three witnesses, in a public place at the domicile of the possessor, Codex, 7, 40, 2.

§ 38. By a positive rule, of which we are unable to give the rationale [see page 109], the change of status produced by coemptio and adrogatio extinguished the debts of the wife or adrogatus, and the husband or adrogator acquired by manus and patria potestas their rights without their liabilities. To meet this the praetor gave the creditor an actio rescissoria: Ait praetor: qui quaeve, posteaquam quid cum his actum contractumve sit, capite deminuti deminutaeve esse dicentur, in eos easve quasi id factum non sit judicium dabo, Dig. 4, 5, 2. If the action was not defended by the husband or adrogator, the praetor gave the creditor missio in possessionem and power of sale against all the property of the wife or adrogatus, Gaius, 3 § 84.

DE PARTIBUS FORMULARUM.

§ 39. Partes autem formularum hae sunt: demonstratio, intentio, adiudicatio, condemnatio.

§ 40. Demonstratio est ea pars formulae quae praecipue ideo inseritur, ut demonstretur res de qua agitur. velut haec pars formulae: QUOD AULUS AGERIUS NUMERIO NEGIDIO HOMINEM VENDIDIT. item haec: QUOD AULUS AGERIUS *APUT* NUMERIUM NEGIDIUM *HOMINEM* DEPOSUIT.

§ 39. The formula is composed of the Demonstratio, the Intentio, the Adjudicatio, the Condemnatio.

§ 40. The principal function of the Demonstratio is to indicate the subject of dispute, as in the following example: 'Whereas Aulus Agerius sold a slave to Numerius Negidius,' or, 'Whereas Aulus Agerius deposited a slave in the hands of Numerius Negidius.'

§ 41. Intentio est ea pars formulae qua actor desiderium suum concludit. velut haec pars formulae: SI PARET NUMERIUM NEGIDIUM AULO AGERIO SESTERTIUM X MILIA DARE OPORTERE. item haec: QUIDQUID PARET NUMERIUM NEGIDIUM AULO AGERIO DARE FACERE *OPORTERE*. item haec: SI PARET HOMINEM EX IURE QUIRITIUM AULI AGERII ESSE.

§ 42. Adiudicatio est ea pars formulae qua permittitur iudici rem alicui ex litigatoribus adiudicare: velut si inter coheredes familiae erciscundae agatur, aut inter socios communi dividundo, aut inter vicinos finium regundorum. nam illic *ita est:* QUANTUM ADIUDICARI OPORTET, IUDEX TITIO ADIUDICATO.

§ 43. Condemnatio est ea pars formulae, qua iud*ici* condemnandi absolvendive potestas p*er*mittitur. velut haec pars formulae: IUDEX NUMERIUM NEGIDIUM AULO AGERIO SESTERTIUM X MILIA CONDEMNA. SI NON PARET ABSOLVE. item haec: IUDEX NUMERIUM NEGIDIUM AULO AGERIO DUMTAXAT *X MILIA* CONDEMNA. SI NON PARET ABSOLVITO. item haec: IUDEX NUMERIUM NEGIDIUM AULO AGERIO [X MILIA] CONDEMNATO et reliqua, ut non adiciatur. . . .

§ 44. Non *tamen* ist*ae* omnes par*tes* simul inveniuntur, sed quaedam inveniuntur, quaedam non inveniuntur. certe intentio aliquando sola invenitur, sicut in praeiudicialibus formulis, qualis est qua *qua*eritur aliquis libertus sit, vel quanta dos sit, et aliae complures.

§ 41. The Intentio expresses the claim of the plaintiff, thus: 'If it be proved that Numerius Negidius ought to convey ten thousand sesterces to Aulus Agerius;' or thus: 'Whatever it be proved that Numerius Negidius ought to convey or render to Aulus Agerius;' or thus: 'If it be proved that the slave in question belongs to Aulus Agerius by the law of the Quirites.'

§ 42. The Adjudicatio empowers the judex to transfer the proprietorship of a thing to one of the litigants, and occurs in the actions for partitioning an inheritance between co-successors, for dividing common property between co-proprietors, and for tracing boundaries between neighbouring landholders. In these the praetor says: 'The portion of the estate that ought to be transferred to Titius, do thou, judex, by thy award transfer to him.'

§ 43. The Condemnatio empowers the judex to condemn or absolve the defendant, thus: 'Do thou, judex, condemn Numerius Negidius to pay to Aulus Agerius ten thousand sesterces; if it be not proved, pronounce his absolution;' or thus: 'Do thou, judex, condemn Numerius Negidius to pay to Aulus Agerius a sum not exceeding ten thousand sesterces; if it be not proved, pronounce his absolution;' or thus: 'Such a sum do thou, judex, condemn Numerius Negidius to pay to Aulus Agerius,' et cetera, without naming the sum or fixing a maximum.

§ 44. These parts are not concurrent, but where some are present others are absent. Sometimes the Intentio is found alone, as in the prejudicial formula to decide whether a man is a freedman, or to ascertain the amount of a dower, or to settle other preliminary in-

demonstratio autem et adiudicatio et condemnatio nu*m*quam solae inveniuntur, nihil *enim* omnino sine intentione vel condemnatione valet; item condemnatio sine [demonstratione vel] intentione [vel adiudicatione] nullas vires habet, *et* ob id numquam solae inveniuntur.

quiries. But the Demonstratio, Adjudicatio, and Condemnatio are never found alone, for the Demonstratio is inoperative without an Intentio and Condemnatio, and the Condemnatio is inoperative without an Intentio.

§ 39. Besides the four parts mentioned by Gaius the formula always contained a nomination of a judex, and sometimes an exceptio, praescriptio, or arbitrium, accessory parts which will be presently explained.

§ 40. The demonstratio seems not to have occurred in real actions nor in personal actions in factum, but in personal actions in jus, whether founded on contract or on tort, excepting perhaps the condictio certi.

If the contract had a technical name (e. g. depositum, venditio) the demonstratio contained the name (deposuit, vendidit); if the contract was nameless, it was described in the demonstratio by a circumlocution, and the action was called actio praescriptis verbis. That a demonstratio was found in actions ex maleficio appears from Gaius, below, § 60, and from Paulus, Collatio, 2, 6. Sicut formula posita est. Quod Auli Agerii pugno mala percussa est: Illud non cogitur dicere, dextra an sinistra, nec qua manu percussa sit. Ita si dicat infamatum se esse, debet adjicere quemadmodum infamatus sit. Sic enim et formula concepta est: Quod Numerius Negidius libellum (or sibilum) immisit Aulo Agerio infamandi causa. 'As the formula is worded: Whereas Aulus Agerius was struck on the cheek by the fist: the plaintiff is not compelled to declare whether he was struck on the right or left cheek, or whether with the right or left hand. And if he sue for defamation, he must allege the means, for so the formula is framed: Whereas Numerius Negidius (hissed or) published a libel against Aulus Agerius with the purpose of defamation.'

The absence of a demonstratio in the formula of condictio certi may be inferred from the example given by Gaius, § 86, and from the assertion of Cicero, Pro Roscio Comoedo, 4, that it did not appear whether Fannius, who sued Roscius by condictio certi, founded his claim on mutui datio, expensilatio, or stipulatio. He could hardly have asserted this, if the title on which Fannius sued had been expressed in a demonstratio. On the other hand, we have a demonstratio in the condictio incerti, § 136, § 137. It is obvious that if a man sues for an indeterminate sum of money he ought to give the defendant some further information of the cause of action; but if he sues for a determinate sum or a definite thing, the defendant can scarcely be ignorant of the cause of action on which the plaintiff relies.

§ 42. The adjudicatio was only found in the three actions familiae erciscundae, communi dividundo, and finium regundorum. It was not a declaration of existing property, but a transfer of property to one of the litigants from the other. Adjudicatione dominia nanciscimur.... nam si judex uni ex heredibus aut sociis aut vicinis rem aliquam adjudicaverit, statim illi adquiritur sive mancipi sive nec mancipi sit, Ulpian, 19, 16. 'Adjudication is a transfer of dominion, for the successor, partner, landowner, to whom a thing is adjudicated by the judex, forthwith acquires property therein, whether it is mancipable or not mancipable.' In quibus tribus judiciis permittitur judici, rem alicui ex litigatoribus ex aequo et bono adjudicare, et, si unius pars praegravare videbitur, eum invicem certa pecunia alteri condemnare, Inst. 4, 6, 20. 'In these three actions the judge has the power to assign a thing on reasonable grounds to one of the litigants, and, if he thus obtain more than his share, to condemn him to make pecuniary compensation.'

§ 43. Taxatio [signified by the word 'dumtaxat'] was a limitation to the condemnatio. Besides the kind noticed by Gaius there were several others, which were probably expressed in the formula of the action. If a paterfamilias was sued for the debt of a person in his power whom he had authorized to trade, the condemnation was limited to the amount of the peculium (quatenus in peculio est); if the slave or son had traded without authority, it was limited to the amount of profit the father or master had thereby received (quatenus in rem ejus versum est); if the heir of a wrong-doer or fraudulent debtor was sued, it was limited to the amount that he gained from the wrong or fraud by his succession (dumtaxat in id quod ad eum pervenit); if a divorced wife sued her husband for her dower, an emancipated son his father, a freedman his patron, a partner his partner, a donee his donor, a creditor his debtor who after cessio bonorum had come into possession of property,—in all these cases the condemnatio was limited to the means of the defendant (quatenus facere potest). This kind of taxatio is called exceptio; e.g. Exceptio est conditio quae modo eximit reum damnatione, modo minuit damnationem, Dig. 44, 1, 22. 'An exception is a condition which either saves the defendant from condemnation, or diminishes the amount in which he is condemned.'

§ 44. A prejudicium is mentioned, 3 § 123, to try whether a creditor had openly declared to the sureties the amount of the debt and number of sureties on which would depend the several liabilities of each individual.

CONCEPTIO FORMULARUM.

§ 45. Sed eas quidem formulas in quibus de iure quaeritur *in ius* conceptas vocamus. quales sunt quibus intendimus nostrum esse aliquid ex iure Quiritium, au*t* nobis dare oportere, aut pro fure damnum *decidere oportere; in* quibus iuris civilis intentio est.

§ 45. A formula is framed to embrace an allegation of law when we declare ourselves proprietors by the law of the Quirites, or assert that the defendant is bound to convey to us or to make composition as a thief; for in these and the like cases we appeal to a principle of civil law.

§ 46. Ceteras vero in factum conceptas vocamus, id est in quibus nulla talis intentionis concept*io* est, *sed* initio formulae, nomina*to* eo quod factum *est*, adic*iun*tur ea verba per quae iudici damnandi absolvendive potestas datur. qualis est formula qua utitur patronus contra libertum qui eum contra edictum Praetoris in ius vocat; nam in ea ita est: RECUPERATORES SUNTO. SI PARET ILLUM PATRONUM AB ILLO LIBERTO CONTRA EDICTUM ILLIUS PRAETOR*IS* IN IUS VOCATUM ESSE, RECUPERATORES ILLUM LIBERTUM ILLI PATRONO SESTERTIUM X MILIA CONDEMNATE. SI NON PARET, ABSOLVITE. ceterae quoque formulae quae sub titulo de in ius vocando propositae sunt in factum conceptae sunt: velut adversus eum qui in ius vocatus neque venerit neque vindicem dederit; item contra eum qui *vi* exemerit eum qui in ius vocatur. et denique innumerabiles eiusmodi aliae formulae in albo proponuntur.

§ 46. It is framed to contain an allegation of fact when it contains no such appeal; but, after proposing a fact, proceeds at once to the Condemnatio and Absolutio; as in an action by a patron against a freedman for a summons in contravention of the edict. The formula then runs thus: 'Let M N be recuperators. If it be proved that such and such a patron was summoned to appear by such and such a freedman against the edict of such and such a praetor, do you, recuperators, condemn the said freedman to pay to the said patron ten thousand sesterces; if it be not proved, pronounce his acquittal.' The other formulas relating to summonses raise questions of fact, as the formula in an action against a defendant who on service of summons neither appears nor finds a vindex, or against a person who makes a violent rescue of a person summoned to appear, and many other formulas in the praetor's album.

§ 47. Sed ex quibusdam causis Praetor et in ius et in factum conceptas formulas proponit, vel*ut* depositi et commodati. illa enim formula quae ita concepta est : IUDEX ESTO. QUOD AULUS AGERIUS APUT NUMERUM NEGIDIUM MENSAM ARGENTEAM DEPOSUIT, QUA DE RE AGITUR, QUIDQUID OB EAM REM NUMERIUM NEGIDIUM AULO AGERIO DARE FACERE OPORTET EX FIDE BONA, EIUS IUDEX NUMERIUM NEGIDIUM AULO AGERIO CONDEMNATO, *NISI RESTITUAT*. SI NON PARET, ABSOLVITO—in ius concepta est. at illa formula quae ita concepta est : IUDEX ESTO. SI PARET AULUM AGERIUM APUT NUMERIUM NEGIDIUM MENSAM ARGENTEAM DEPOSUISSE EAMQUE DOLO MALO NUMERII NEGIDII AULO AGERIO REDDITAM NON ESSE, QUANTI EA RES ERIT, TANTAM PECUNIAM IUDEX NUMERIUM NEGIDIUM AULO AGERIO CONDEMNATO. SI NON PARET, ABSOLVITO—in factum concepta est. similes etiam commodati formulae sunt.

§ 47. Some actions may be instituted by formulas either of law or of fact, as for instance the actions of Deposit and Loan for use. The following formula: 'Let C D be judex. Whereas Aulus Agerius deposited a silver table in the hands of Numerius Negidius, whatsoever it be proved that Numerius Negidius is on that account bound by good faith to convey or render to Aulus Agerius, do thou, judex, condemn Numerius Negidius to convey or render, unless he makes restitution; if it be not proved, pronounce his acquittal :' is a formula of law. A formula thus framed : 'Let C D be judex. If it be proved that Aulus Agerius deposited a silver table in the hands of Numerius Negidius, and that by the fraud of Numerius Negidius it has not been restored to Aulus Agerius, do thou, judex, condemn Numerius Negidius to pay Aulus Agerius the value of the table; if it be not proved, pronounce his acquittal:' is a formula of fact. And there is a similar alternative in the case of Loan for use.

§ 48. Omnium autem formularum quae condemnationem habent ad pecuniariam aestimationem condemnatio concepta est. itaque etsi corpus aliquod petamus, *velut f*undum, *hominem*, vest*em*, a*urum*, *argen*tum, iudex non ipsam rem condemnat eum cum *quo* actum est, sicut olim fieri solebat, [*sed*] aestimata re pecuniam eum condemnat.

§ 48. The condemnatio is always to pay a pecuniary value. Even when we claim a corporeal thing, an estate in land, a slave, a garment, an article of gold or silver, the judex condemns the defendant to deliver not the thing itself, as in the elder system, but its value in money.

§ 49. Condemnatio autem vel certae pecuniae in for*mula* ponitur, vel incertae.

§ 49. The formula either names a certain sum in the Condemnatio or an uncertain sum.

§ 50. Certae pecuniae in ea formula qua certam *pecuniam petimus;* nam illi*c* ima parte *for*m*u*lae ita *est :* IUDEX NUMERIUM NEGIDIUM AULO AGERIO SESTERTIUM X MILIA CONDEMNA. SI NON PARET, ABSOLVE.

§ 50. In a condictio, when it names a certain sum, it concludes as follows: 'Do thou, judex, condemn Numerius Negidius to pay Aulus Agerius ten thousand sesterces; if it be not proved, absolve him.'

§ 51. Incertae vero condemnatio

§ 51. An uncertain sum is either

pecuniae duplicem significationem habet. est enim una *cum* aliqua praefinitione, quae vulgo dicitur cum taxatione, velut si inc*er*tum aliquid petamus; nam illic *ima parte for*mulae ita *est*: EIUS IUDEX NUMERIUM NEGIDIUM AULO AGERIO DU*MTAXAT* X MILIA CONDEMNA. SI NON PARET, ABSOLVE. *diver*sa est quae infini*ta est*, *vel*ut si rem aliquam a possidente nostram esse petamus, id est si in rem agamus, vel ad exhibendum; nam illic i*ta* est: QUANTI *EA* RES *ERIT TA*NTAM P*E*CUNIAM *IUDEX* NUMERIUM NEGIDIUM *AULO AGERIO* CONDEMNA. SI NON PARET, ABSOLVITO.

named with a limitation or maximum, for instance, thus: 'Do thou, judex, condemn Numerius Negidius to pay Aulus Agerius a sum not exceeding ten thousand sesterces; if it be not proved, absolve him:' or it is named without a limitation, as when we demand our property from the possessor in a real action, or demand the production of a person or thing in a personal action, where the conclusion runs as follows: 'Do thou, judex, condemn Numerius Negidius to pay Aulus Agerius whatever is the value; if it be not proved, absolve him.'

§ 52. Qui de re vero est iudex si condemnat, certam p*ecuni*am condemnare debet, etsi certa pecunia in condemnatione posita non sit. debet autem iudex attendere, *ut cum* certae pecuniae condemnatio posita sit, neque maioris neque minoris summa petita condemnet, alioquin litem suam facit. item si taxatio posita sit, ne plur*is* condemnet quam taxa*tum* sit, ali*as* enim simili*ter* litem *s*uam facit. minoris autem damnare ei per*missum* est [*desunt 7 fere lin.*]

§ 52. But whatever the claim, the judex must condemn the defendant to pay a definite sum, even though no definite sum is named in the condemnatio. When a certain sum is laid in the condemnatio, he must be careful not to condemn the defendant in a greater or lesser sum, else he makes himself liable to damages: and if there is a limitation he must be careful not to exceed the maximum, else he is similarly liable; but he may condemn him in less than the maximum.

§ 45. In the actio in jus, the intentio, Si paret oportere, is the conclusion of the judicial syllogism, coincident with the Condemnatio, and does not show whether the contested proposition was the major premiss, that is, an issue of law, or the minor premiss, that is, an issue of fact. In the actio in factum, the Intentio, Si paret fecisse, is not the conclusion, but the minor premiss of the judicial syllogism, of which the major premiss is not a law but a rule of equity reposing in the conscience of the praetor, and the conclusion the Condemnatio.

It follows that formulas in jus and in factum must not be identified with issues of law and issues of fact. The former as well as the latter might involve an issue of fact. The only difference was that the rules of law, whether admitted or controverted, to which formulas in jus appealed, were rules of civil law, not of equitable or praetorian law, which supplied the major premisses of formulas in factum. The major premiss of every judicial syllogism was a law either civil or praetorian. In actions in jus it was a principle, either acknowledged or controverted, of civil law; in actions ex bona fide and in factum it was merely an equitable rule enforced by the praetor, which in actions ex bona fide might, in actions in factum might not, be controverted.

The principles which governed equitable actions were not rules of express legislation, but opinions of the jurists, representing doubtless opinions of the public, though, like the rules administered in Chancery, they finally became as rigid and unalterable as any other portions of the law, and indeed in a special acceptation of the term were called civil law.

Some modern expositors of Roman law erroneously assume that the actio in jus always really depended on an issue in fact. In support of this opinion it may be alleged that when Cicero attempts to prove that a knowledge of the civil law is necessary to the advocate, he only instances centumviral causes, which were not tried by formula but by the older system, De Oratore, 36, 40. Again, many questions of law were undoubtedly decided at the initial stage of an action, in jure, at the appearance before the tribunal of the praetor. At this appearance the parties were attended by counsel [haerere in jure atque praetorum tribunalibus (advocatos), De Oratore, 1, 38]; and here, though the praetor would not settle a dispute of facts, many demurrers or simple issues of law might be decided, and the controversy might be terminated without ever reaching the stage of reference to a judex.

On the other hand, we have only to turn to any of Cicero's forensic orations to find issues of law argued before a judex.

Moreover, in another passage he clearly implies that the numerous class of equitable actions, at all events, involved issues of civil law. Privata enim judicia maximarum quidem rerum in juris consultorum mihi videntur esse prudentia. . . . In omnibus igitur iis judiciis in quibus EX FIDE BONA est additum; ubi vero etiam UT INTER BONOS BENE AGIER; in primisque in arbitrio rei uxoriae, in quo est, QUOD AEQUIUS MELIUS, parati esse debent. Illi enim dolum malum, illi fidem bonam, illi aequum bonum, illi quid socium socio, quid eum qui aliena negotia curasset ei cujus ea negotia fuissent; quid eum qui mandasset eumve cui mandatum esset alterum alteri praestare oporteret, quid virum

uxori, quid uxorem viro, tradiderunt, Topica, 17. 'Private suits of the highest importance turn on the doctrines of the jurist. . . . In all the actions, therefore, where the judge is instructed to look to the requirements of good faith, to the practice of honest men, or, as in the suit of a wife against her husband, to what is good and equal, the jurist should be ready to speak. For he is the authority on what constitutes fraud or good faith, what is good and equal, what are the mutual duties of partners, of principal and agent, whether authorized or unauthorized, of husband and wife.' We conclude that all complicated issues of law were referred to a judex.

§ 46. According to the Institutes, a man might not summon his patron or parent to appear in an action without the permission of the praetor, under a penalty of fifty solidi, Inst. 4, 16, 3. A solidus or aureus was a hundred sesterces, so that we must either, with Savigny, for ten thousand read five thousand sesterces in the text of Gaius, or suppose that Justinian reduced the penalty to half its original amount.

In the formulary system an appearance of the defendant before the praetor (in jure) was indispensable as the first stage of an action. In English law, after service of summons or proof that all proper means for the service of summons have been used in vain, the court will grant leave to the plaintiff to enter an appearance for the defendant. But in Roman law an original appearance of the defendant at the commencement of the action was indispensable. On service of a summons (in jus vocatio) he was bound either to obey at once and accompany the plaintiff into court, or to send a responsible representative (vindex, § 46) in his stead, or to find security, called cautio judicio sisti (to be thus interpreted: cautio sisti in jure ad judicium ordinandum), for his appearance in jure on a future day. If he took none of these steps he was liable to an actio in factum, and he might be apprehended and taken by force (duci in jus, Digest, 2, 8, 5); and any person who made a violent rescue was liable to be condemned by actio in factum to pay the amount of the plaintiff's claim, quanti ea res est ab actore aestimata, Digest, 2, 75. At the first appearance in court, after the plaintiff's indication of the action he meant to bring (editio actionis), the defendant was required to give security (vadimonium, or cautio judicio sisti) for his second appearance in court to receive a judex. At the second appearance, after the nomination (addictio) of the

judex and the joinder in issue or delivery of the formula (litis contestatio, judicium ordinatum, judicium acceptum), there was (at all events in the legis actiones) an adjournment to the next day but one (comperendinatio), and on this day the trial before the judex (judicium) proceeded. In the formulary system, then, there were two appearances in jure, one in obedience to the in jus vocatio, and a second for the assignment of a judex. In the Libellary system which prevailed in the time of Justinian the former of these appearances was suppressed, and instead thereof the plaintiff by a libellus conventionis sued out from the court a commonitio or summons to the defendant to appear before the court. On the service of this by a public officer the defendant was required to give cautio judicio sisti, security for his appearance for the arrangement of a judicium, and in default thereof was arrested.

§ 47. The lawyer's manual of practice contained alternative formulae for the same ground of action. Sed tamen non parcam operae, et ut vos in vestris formulis, sic ego in epistolis, *de eadem re alio modo*, Cicero ad Familiares, 13, 27. 'However, I will spare no trouble, and as you lawyers do in your books of formulae, I will present you in my correspondence with the same matter in another form.' Quae cum Zeno didicisset a nostris, ut in actionibus praescribi solet, *de eadem re* dixit *alio modo*, De Finibus, 5, 19. 'Zeno learnt this from the teachers of our school, and then, as the headings of the formulae say, handled the same subject in a different form.'

One great advantage of the actiones in factum was that they were available to aliens and filii familiarum. In factum actiones etiam filii familiarum possunt exercere, Digest, 44, 7, 13.

The words Nisi restituat are the clause which constitutes a formula arbitraria. In the formulary system the condemnation was always pecuniary; the defendant was always condemned by the judgment to pay the plaintiff a sum of money. By means, however, of the alternative clause in a formula arbitraria the plaintiff could recover a specific thing or enforce a specific performance. Impowered by this clause the judex made a preliminary order (jussus, arbitrium) for the restitution or performance; and if it was obeyed the defendant was absolved, if it was disobeyed the pecuniary condemnation was the penalty of disobedience.

Of the formula arbitraria in a real action we have an instance in Cicero, Lucius Octavius judex esto. Si paret fundum capenatem,

quo de agitur, ex jure Quiritium [Auli Agerii] esse, neque is fundus [Aulo Agerio] restituetur, In Verrem, 2, 2, 12. The formula might also be used in a personal action, and in an action in factum for rescinding a proceeding to which the plaintiff had been seduced by fraud or driven by fear. In an action for the production of a person or thing (ad exhibendum) the clause would be of the form nisi exhibeat, and generally some special modification of nisi actori satisfaciat. In noxal actions there was probably no clause nisi noxae dedat, but the judgment was of the form Publium Maevium Lucio Titio decem aureis condemno aut noxam dedere, Inst. 4, 17; for the defendant was intended to exercise the election of paying damages or surrendering the author of the mischief. But in other actions no such discretion was intended to be given, and the damages were meant as a penal sum to enforce obedience to the judge's order. When practicable, in later days at all events, the armed power of the state was employed to enforce compliance. Qui restituere jussus judici non paret, contendens non posse se restituere, siquidem habet rem, manu militari officio judicis ab eo possessio transfertur, et fructuum duntaxat omnisque causae nomine condemnatio fit. Si vero non potest restituere, si quidem dolo fecit quominus possit, is quantum adversarius in litem sine ulla taxatione in infinitum juraverit damnandus est. Si vero nec potest restituere, nec dolo fecit quo minus possit, non pluris quam quanti res est, id est, quanti adversarii interfuit, condemnandus est. Haec sententia generalis est, et ad omnia sive interdicta sive actiones, et sive in rem sive in personam sint, ex quibus arbitratu judicis quid restituitur, locum habet, Digest, 6, 1, 68. 'If a defendant allege inability to obey an order of restitution, if the thing exists, the judex uses the military power to put the plaintiff in possession, and only condemns the defendant for the mesne profits and appurtenances. If the defendant has maliciously disabled himself from restitution, he is condemned in the amount, subject to no taxation, at which the plaintiff on oath assesses his loss; if the inability is not maliciously produced, the judex assesses the damages. This applies to all interdicts and actions, real and personal, where the judex orders restitution.'

A parallel to the clause Ni restituat in a condemnatio may be found in the English action of Detinue for the recovery of movable goods unlawfully detained. Formerly the judgment was merely conditional that the plaintiff recover the goods, or, if they could

not be had, their value, and also damages for detaining them; so that the defendant might retain the thing by paying the value assessed. Now, however, the court has power to order execution to issue for the return of the chattel detained, without giving the defendant the option of paying its value; and if the chattel cannot be found, the defendant's lands and chattels may be distrained until it be returned. The plaintiff, however, may have its assessed value at his option. And so for a breach of contract to deliver goods for a price in money.

In the formula in jus concepta, § 47, the clause eamque dolo malo Numerii Negidii Aulo Agerio redditam non esse, which is added to the intentio, is equivalent to the clause ni restituat, which in the alternative formula is added to the condemnatio.

§ 52. A judex might make the cause his own by corruption or ignorance. Judex tunc litem suam facere intelligitur quum dolo malo in fraudem legis sententiam dixerit. Dolo malo autem videtur hoc facere si evidens arguatur ejus vel gratia vel inimicitia vel etiam sordes, ut veram aestimationem litis praestare cogatur, Digest, 5, 1, 15. 'A judex makes the cause his own when from fraud, that is, friendship, hatred, or corruption, he gives a judgment contrary to law, and he is condemned to pay the market value of the thing in dispute.' Si judex litem suam fecerit, non proprie ex maleficio obligatus videtur, sed quia neque ex contractu obligatus est, et utique peccasse aliquid intelligitur, licet per imprudentiam, ideo videtur quasi ex maleficio teneri in factum actione, et in quantum de ea re aequum religioni judicantis visum fuerit, poenam sustinebit, Digest, 50, 13, 6. 'If a judex make a cause his own, the obligation he incurs is not created by delict, nor yet by contract, but as he commits a fault, though it may be without intention, he is liable in an action in factum for a quasi-delict to such damages as may be assessed.'

PLUS PETITIO.

§ 53. Si quis intentione *plus complexus fuerit, causa cadit, id est rem* perdit, nec a Praetore in *integrum restituitur, praeterquam quibusdam* casibus in qu*ibus Praet*or *edicto succurrit* [$1\frac{3}{4}$ *lin.*]. *Plus autem quatuor* modis petitur: re, tempor*e*, *loco*, *causa* [*desunt* 11

§ 53. If the Intentio claim more than the plaintiff is entitled to, he loses the action, and is not relieved by the praetor except in a few cases mentioned in the edict. He may claim too much in amount, time, place, or specification. He may demand a larger sum than is due,

lineae]. . . . petere id *etiam* non adiecto loco.

or demand to be paid at an earlier time than he stipulated, or at a different place without confessing that the place is different from that named in the stipulation.

§ 53*a*. Causa plus petitur, velut si quis in intentione tollat electionem debitoris quam is habet obligationis iure. velut si quis ita stipulatus sit: SESTERTIUM X MILIA AUT HOMINEM STICHUM DARE SPONDES? deinde alterutrum ex his petat; nam quamvis petat quod minus est, plus tamen petere videtur, quia potest adversarius interdum facilius id praestare quod non petitur. similiter si quis genus stipulatus sit, deinde speciem petat. velut si quis *purpuram* stipulatus sit generaliter, deinde Tyriam specialiter petat: quin etiam *licet* vilissimam petat, idem iuris est propter eam rationem quam proxime diximus. idem iuris est si quis generaliter hominem stipulatus sit, deinde nominatim aliquem petat, velut Stichum, quamvis vilissimum. itaque sicut ipsa stipulatio concepta est, ita et intentio formulae concipi debet.

§ 53*a*. He claims too much by specification if he deprives the debtor of an election to which he was entitled by the contract; for instance, if he stipulated to receive alternatively either ten thousand sesterces or the slave Stichus, and makes an unconditional claim for one or the other. For though the one that he claims be of lesser value, the other may be more convenient for the debtor to convey. So if he stipulated for a genus and demands a species, stipulated, for instance, for purple and demands Tyrian purple, even though he demand the cheapest species, he claims more than his due, for the same reason. So he does if he stipulated generally for a slave and claims a certain slave, Stichus, for instance, however worthless. The Intentio, then, must exactly pursue the terms of the stipulation.

§ 54. Illud satis apparet in incertis formulis plus peti non posse, quia, cum certa quantitas non petatur, sed quidquid adversarium dare facere oporteret intenda*tur*, nemo potest plus intendere. idem iuris est, et si in rem incertae partis actio data sit; velut si heres QUANTAM PARTEM petat IN EO FUNDO, QUO DE AGITUR, *PAREAT IPSIUS* ESSE: quod genus actionis in paucissimis causis dari solet.

§ 54. It is clear that an Intentio naming an uncertain sum cannot be excessive, for it claims no certain quantity, but only whatever the defendant ought to convey or perform. The same is true of actions to recover uncertain shares, as that whereby a heres claims whatever portion of the inheritance he may be entitled to, which kind of action is seldom granted.

§ 55. Item palam est, si quis aliud pro alio intenderit, nihil eum periclitari eumque ex integro agere posse, quia *nihil in iudicium deducitur, velut si* is qui hominem Stichum petere deberet, Erotem petierit; aut si quis ex testamento dare sibi oportere intenderit, cui ex stipulatu debebatur; aut si cognitor

§ 55. It is also clear that the plaintiff who claims the wrong thing in his Intentio, runs no risk and can bring another action because his right has not been tried, if he is entitled, for instance, to Stichus and claims Eros, or if he is entitled by stipulation and claims under a will, or if a cognitor or procurator claim

aut procurator intenderit sibi dare oportere.

in his own right instead of in the right of his principal.

§ 56. Sed plus quidem intendere, sicut supra diximus, periculosum est: minus autem intendere licet; sed de reliquo intra eiusdem praeturam agere non permittitur. nam qui ita agit per exceptionem excluditur, quae exceptio appellatur litis dividuae.

§ 56. To claim too much, as I have said, is dangerous; a man who claims less than his right does not forfeit his right, but cannot sue for the remainder in the same praetorship, for he is repelled by the Exception against division of actions.

§ 57. *At* si in condemnatione plus petitum sit quam *oportet*, actoris qui*dem* periculum nullum est, sed *si* iniquam formulam acceperit, in integrum restituitur, ut minuatur condemnatio. si vero minus positum fuerit quam oportet, hoc solum consequitur quod posuit: nam tota qui*dem* res in iudicium deducitur, constringitur autem condemnationis fine, quam iudex eg*re*di non potest. nec ex ea parte Praetor in integrum restituit: facilius enim reis Praetor succurrit quam actoribus. loquimur autem exceptis minoribus XXV annorum; nam huius aetatis hominibus in omnibus rebus lapsis Praetor succurrit.

§ 57. If too much is claimed in the Condemnatio the plaintiff is not imperilled, but is relieved and allowed to reduce the Condemnatio. If less is laid in the Condemnatio than he is entitled to, he only obtains that amount, for his whole right has been brought before the judex and is reduced to the amount laid in the Condemnatio, a limit which the judex cannot exceed; and in this case the praetor gives no relief, for he is less ready to relieve the plaintiff than the defendant, excepting always minors, whom he invariably relieves.

§ 58. Si in demonstratione plus aut minus positum sit, nihil in iudicium deducitur, et ideo res in integro manet: et hoc est quod dicitur falsa demonstratione rem non perimi.

§ 58. If more or less is laid in the Demonstratio, the plaintiff's right is not tried and therefore remains intact, and this is the meaning of the saying that a false Demonstration does not extinguish a right.

§ 59. Sed sunt qui putant minus recte *com*prehendi. nam qui forte Stichum et Erot*em* emerit, recte videtur ita demonstrare: QUOD EGO DE TE HOMINEM EROTEM EMI, et si velit, de Sticho alia formula idem agat, quia verum est eum qui duos emerit singulos q*uoque* emisse: idque i*ta* m*axime* Labeoni visum est. sed si is qui unum emerit de duobus egerit, falsum demonstrat. idem et in aliis actionibus est, velut commodati, depositi.

§ 59. Some think that less may be properly expressed in the Demonstratio, as a man who bought both Stichus and Eros may state in his Demonstratio, 'Whereas I bought of you the slave Eros,' and sue for Stichus in another action, because the purchaser of both is the purchaser of each; and this was Labeo's opinion. But if the purchaser of one says he purchased two, the Demonstratio is false; and the same applies to actions of Loan for use and Deposit.

§ 60. Sed *nos* aput quosdam scriptum invenimus, in actione de-

§ 60. I have read in some writers that in actions of Deposit, and where-

positi et denique in ceteris omnibus quibus damnatus unusquisque ignominia notatur, eum qui plus quam oporteret demonstraverit litem perdere. velut si quis una re deposita duas res deposuisse demonstraverit, aut si is cui pugno mala percussa est in actione iniuriarum esse aliam partem corporis percussam sibi demonstraverit. quod an debeamus credere verius esse, diligentius requiremus. certe cum duae sint depositi formulae, alia in ius concepta, alia in factum, sicut supra quoque notavimus, et in ea quidem formula quae in ius concepta est, initio res de qua agitur demonstretur, tum designetur, deinde inferatur iuris contentio his verbis: QUIDQUID OB EAM REM ILLUM MIHI DARE FACERE OPORTET; in ea vero quae in factum concepta est statim initio intentionis loco res de qua agitur designetur his verbis: SI PARET ILLUM APUT ILLUM REM ILLAM DEPOSUISSE: dubitare non debemus, quin si quis in formula quae in factum composita est plures res designaverit quam deposuerit, litem perdat, quia in intentione plus po . . . [*desunt* 48 *lin.*]

ever condemnation involves infamy, a plaintiff loses the action if his Demonstratio exceeds the truth (or names one thing for another), for instance, if he deposited one thing and says he deposited two, or if he was struck in the face and his Demonstratio in an action of assault mentions another part of the body. Let us examine this question. There are two formulas of the action of Deposit, one of law, the other of fact, as we said before. The formula of law begins by defining the ground of action in the Demonstratio, and then appeals to the law in these terms: 'Whatever the defendant ought therefore to convey or perform.' The formula of fact commences with an Intentio defining the ground of action, thus: 'If it be proved that such a plaintiff deposited such a thing with such a defendant.' Certainly in the latter case, that is, in a formula of fact, if the plaintiff asserts that he deposited more than he really deposited, he loses his cause, because the excess is in the Intentio.

§ 53. When a creditor wished to be paid at one place what was due in another, he might avoid pluris petitio by employing a formula arbitraria, which noticed the difference of Place, and impowered the arbiter to make allowance for it, Dig. 13, 4.

§ 54. The penalty of pluris petitio in respect of time was reduced by Zeno, who merely doubled the term that was still to run before payment, and required the creditor to pay the costs of the former action before he brought a second, Codex, 3, 10. The effect of this was to change the meaning of the term 'dilatoria,' which, as applied to an exceptio and opposed to peremptoria, denoted an exceptio alleging pluris petitio in Time.

When Gaius wrote, such an exception, if successfully alleged, was just as fatal to the creditor as an exceptio peremptoria. It is temporary, not in respect of its effects, but of the limited period

during which it is at the command of the debtor. But after Zeno such an exceptio was temporary in its effects, and did not prevent a renewal of the action after a certain lapse of time, that is, after the expiration of the term originally fixed for the payment, and an additional term measuring the temporal excess of the plaintiff's claim. Justinian retained Zeno's law in respect of Time, and disarmed the other modes of pluris petitio of their terrors, by merely making the creditor liable to three times the amount of the loss that his exorbitant claim had caused to the debtor, particularly in respect of the fees (sportulae) of the executive officers (executores), Codex, 3, 10, 2.

§ 55. A plaintiff who had made a mistake in the subject of his claim was allowed by Justinian to amend his claim without instituting a new action.

§ 56. A plaintiff whose intentio claimed less than he was entitled to was allowed by Zeno to obtain the full amount without instituting a new action, Inst. 4, 6, 34.

§ 60. It appears that some jurist had regarded the first clause of an actio in factum, si paret . . . fecisse, as a demonstratio. Gaius himself, in speaking of this clause used ambiguous terms, nominato eo quod factum est, § 46. But it is clear from § 60 that he holds it to be no Demonstratio, but an Intentio.

The plaintiff who lost an actio in factum did not by the civil law lose his right to bring another action, for novatio or transformation of his original right into a right to have judgment, was only operated by the commencement of a personal action in jus. But this made no practical difference, for though he might bring his action, he would always be barred by the exceptio rei judicatae.

COMPENSATIO ET DEDUCTIO.

§ 61. *In bonae fidei iudiciis libera potestas permitti videtur iudici ex bono et aequo aestimandi quantum actori restitui debeat. In quo et illud* contin*etur*, *ut habita ratione eius* quod *invicem actorem ex* eadem causa *praestare* oporteret, *in reliquum* eum cum quo actum est condemnare *debeat*.

§ 61. In equitable actions the judex has full power to assess on good and equal grounds the amount due to the plaintiff, and can take into account the cross demand in the same transaction of the defendant, and condemn the defendant in the remainder.

§ 62. Sunt autem bonae fidei iudicia haec: ex empto vendito,

§ 62. Equitable actions are those of Purchase and Sale, Letting and

locato conducto, negotiorum gestorum, mandati, depositi, fiduciae, pro socio, tutelae, *commo*dati.

Hiring, Voluntary work, Agency, Deposit, Trust, Partnership, Guardianship, Loan of use, Mortgage, Partition of inheritance, Dissolution of joint ownership, Nameless contract.

§ 63. Tam*en* iudici . . . *compen*sationis r*ati*onem habere *non ipsius* formulae ve*r*bis praecipitur; sed quia id bonae fidei iudicio conveniens videtur, id*eo* officio eius contineri creditur.

§ 63. The judex is not expressly instructed by the terms of the formula to make compensation, but as it seems fit and proper in an equitable action, the power is assumed to be contained in his commission.

§ 64. Alia causa est illius actionis qua argentarius experitur: nam is cogitur cum co*m*pensatione agere, *id est ut* co*m*pensatio *v*erbis formulae compr*eh*endatur. *itaque* argen*tarius* ab initio co*m*pensatione facta minus intendit sibi dare oportere. ecce enim si *sestertium* X milia debeat Titio, atque *ei* XX debea*t Titius*, *ita int*endit: si paret Titium sibi X milia dare oportere amplius quam *ipse Titio* debet.

§ 64. It is otherwise in the action instituted by a banker, for the banker is compelled to make express recognition of compensation in his formula, and accordingly admits of any set-off from the first, and in his Intentio only claims the balance. If he owes ten thousand sesterces to Titius and Titius owes him twenty thousand, his Intentio runs as follows: 'If it be proved that Titius owes him ten thousand sesterces more than he owes Titius.'

§ 65. Item . . . bonorum emptor cum deductione agere *debet*, id *est ut* in hoc solum adversarius *con*demnetur quod superest, deducto eo quod invicem *s*ibi defraudatoris nomin*e* debet*ur*.

§ 65. Likewise the purchaser of a bankrupt's estate must notice any cross demand in his formula, and in the Condemnatio only require the defendant to pay what he owes after deduction of what was due to him from the insolvent.

§ 66. Inter conpensationem autem quae argentario interponitur, et deductionem quae obicitur *bonorum emptor*i, illa d*if*ferentia est, quod in co*m*pensationem hoc solum vocatur quod eiusdem generis et naturae est. veluti pecunia cum pecunia co*m*pens*a*tur, triticum cum tritico, vinum cum vino: adeo ut quibusdam plac*ea*t non omni modo vinum cum vino, aut triticum cum tritico co*m*pensandum, sed ita si eiusdem naturae qualitatisque sit. in deductionem autem vocatur et quod non est eiusdem generis. itaque si *a Titio* pecuniam petat bonorum emptor, et invicem frumentum aut vi-

§ 66. Between the compensation which is made against the claim of the banker and the deduction from the claim of the execution purchaser there is this difference, that compensation is confined to claims of the same genus and nature; money, for instance, is set off against money, wheat against wheat, or wine against wine; and some even hold that not every kind of wine or every kind of wheat may be set off against wine and wheat, but only wine and wheat of the same nature and quality. Deduction, on the contrary, is made of a debt of a different genus. Thus, if Titius owed money to the insol-

num *Titio* debeat, deducto quanti id erit, in reliquum *ex*peritur.

vent, and is owed corn or wine, the value of the corn or wine is deducted, and he is only sued by the execution purchaser for the residue.

§ 67. Item vocatur in deductionem et id quod in diem debetur; *com*pensatur autem hoc solum quod praesenti die debetur.

§ 67. Again, deduction is made of debts not yet due, compensation only of debts already due.

§ 68. Praeterea *com*pensationis quidem ratio in intentione ponitur: quo fit, ut si facta *com*pensatione plus nummo uno intendat argentarius, causa cadat et ob id rem perdat. deductio vero ad condemnationem ponitur, quo loco plus petenti periculum non intervenit; utique bonorum *emptore* agen*te*, qui licet de certa pecunia agat, incerti tamen condemnationem concipit.

§ 68. Again, compensation is inserted in the Intentio, and if the Intentio of the banker is one penny more than the balance, he loses his cause and his claim; whereas the deduction is introduced in the Condemnatio, where an excessive claim is not hazardous; especially as the execution purchaser, though the debt he claims is certain, sues for an uncertain sum in the Condemnatio.

§ 61. The Emperor Marcus Aurelius introduced the principle of Compensation into actions stricti juris by granting to the defendant the exceptio doli mali. Sed et in strictis judiciis ex rescripto divi Marci, opposita doli mali exceptione, compensatio inducebatur, Inst. 4, 6, 30. This exception was of the form: Si in ea re nihil dolo malo Auli Agerii factum sit neque fiat, 4 § 119. It empowered the judex, not to make compensation, but to give judgment against the plaintiff on the ground of pluris petitio. Ortolan explains that this was not as iniquitous as at first sight it may appear, for the loss of the action would only be a penalty to the plaintiff for refusing to employ a formula containing a compensatio or deductio, or a formula ex fide bona instead of a formula of jus strictum. As Gaius flourished under Marcus Aurelius, and makes no mention of his rescript, we must infer that it either was issued after the publication of these Institutions, or was mentioned in the preceding paragraphs where the manuscript is now defective.

§ 66. The balance for which the banker sued was not the balance of a Personal account, but the balance of one of the Real accounts for corn, wine, oil, &c., into which the debtor's total personal account was subdivided. The law courts, that is, took notice of the customary practice of the book-keepers, and a question naturally arose as to the extent to which a personal account could be subdivided.

In bona fide actions the Compensatio might be of an object of different nature (in dispari specie), but must arise out of the same transaction (ex eadem causa). In the action of the banker the debt might arise in a different transaction (ex dispari causa), but must be of the same nature (in pari specie). In the exceptio doli mali the transaction might be different, but probably the nature of the debt was required to be similar. In the deductio of the execution purchaser both the transaction and the nature of the debt might be different. Justinian empowered the judex to make compensatio in all actions alike, without regard to the nature or origin of the set-off. Compensationes ex omnibus actionibus ipso jure fieri sancimus, nulla differentia in rem vel personalibus actionibus inter se observanda. Ita tamen compensationes obici jubemus si causa ex qua compensatur liquida sit et non multis ambagibus innodata sed possit judici facilem exitum sui praestare, Codex, 4, 31, 14. 'Compensation shall be made as a matter of course in all actions real and personal. Provided always that the set-off alleged shall admit of summary proof and easy decision.'

A defendant was allowed to deduct his cross demand or reciprocal debt from the demand of the plaintiff by the English courts of Equity, but not by the courts of Common law, until the Statutes 2 Geo. II, c. 22; 8 Geo. II, c. 24, introduced the plea of set-off into the courts of Common law.

DE ACTIONIBUS EX CONTRACTU FILIORUM ET SERVORUM.

§ 69. Quia tamen superius mentionem habuimus de actione qua in peculium filiorumfamilias servorumque agatur, opus est, ut de *hac* actione et de ceteris quae eorumdem nomine in parentes dominosve dari solent diligentius admoneamus.

§ 69. As we have mentioned the action in respect of Peculium, we must explain this action and the others by which fathers and masters are sued for the debts of their sons or slaves.

§ 70. Inprimis itaque si iussu patris dominive negotium gestum erit, in solidum Praetor actionem in patrem dominumve conparavit: et recte, quia qui ita negotium gerit magis patris dominive quam filii servive fidem sequitur.

§ 70. Firstly, if it was at the bidding of the father or master that the plaintiff contracted with the son or slave, the father or master may be sued for the whole amount, for then the contract was made in reliance on the credit of the father or master rather than of the son or slave.

§ 71. Eadem ratione comparavit duas alias actiones, exercitoriam *et* institoriam. tunc autem exercitoria locum habet, cum pater dominusve filium servumve magistrum navis praeposuerit, et quod cum eo eius rei gratia cui praepositus fuit negotium gestum erit. cum enim ea quoque res ex voluntate patris dominive contrahi videatur, aequissimum *Praetori* visum est in solidum actionem dari. quin etiam, licet extraneum quis que*mcumque magistrum navi* praeposuerit, sive servum sive liberum, tamen ea Praetoria actio in eum redditur. ideo autem exercitoria actio appellatur, quia exercitor vocatur is ad quem cottidianus navis quaestus pervenit. Institoria *vero* formula tum locum habet, cum quis tabernae aut cuilibet negotiationi filium servumve *aut etiam* quemlibet extraneum, sive servum sive liberum, praeposuerit, et quid cum eo eius rei gratia cui praepositus est contractum fuerit. ideo autem institoria *appellatur, quia qui* tabernae praeponitur institor appellatur. quae *et ipsa* formula in solidum est.

§ 71. On the same principle the praetor grants two other actions, one to recover the debt of a ship-captain, the other to recover the debt of a manager or factor. The actio exercitoria lies against a father or master who has appointed a son or slave to be captain of a ship, to recover a debt incurred by the son or slave in his character of captain. As such a contract is made with the consent of the father or master he is justly liable for the whole. So if a man appoint another person's slave or a freeman to be captain, he may be sued by the praetorian action. The action is called Exercitoria because the shipowner or charterer who appoints the captain is called Exercitor. The actio Institoria lies against a man who appoints his son or slave or another person's slave or a freeman to manage a shop or any business, to recover any debt incurred in that business. It is called Institoria because the manager of a shop is called Institor, and it is brought for the whole amount.

§ 72. Praeterea tributoria *quoque actio* in patrem dominumve *Praetoris edicto de eorum mercibus re*busve constituta est, cum filius servusve *in peculiari merce sciente patre dominove negotiatur. nam si quid cum eo eius rei causa contractum erit, ita Praetor ius dicit, ut quidquid in his mercibus erit, quodque inde receptum erit, id inter patrem dominumve, si quid ei debebitur, et ceteros creditores pro rata portione distribuatur. et quia ipsi patri dominove distributionem permittit, si quis ex creditoribus queratur, quasi minus ei tributum sit quam oportuerit, hanc ei actionem adcommodat, quae tributoria appellatur.*

§ 72. The edict provides another action, called Tributoria, in respect of the part of the Peculium which is devoted to a certain trade carried on by a son or slave with the knowledge of his father or master. If any debts are contracted in that trade the praetor orders this portion of the Peculium and its profits to be distributed between the father or master and other creditors in proportion to their claims, and charges the father or master with the distribution; and any creditor who complains that he has received less than his share can bring this action.

§ 73. *Praeterea introducta est actio de peculio deque eo quod in*

§ 73. There is also an action in respect of Peculium and of what has

rem patris dominive versum erit, ut quamvis sine voluntate patris dominive negotium gestum erit, tamen sive quid in rem eius versum fuerit, id totum praestare debeat, sive quid non sit in rem eius versum, id eatenus praestare debeat, quatenus peculium patitur. In rem autem patris dominive versum intellegitur quidquid necessario in rem eius impenderit filius servusve, veluti si mutuatus pecuniam creditoribus eius solverit, aut aedificia ruentia fulserit, aut familiae frumentum emerit, vel etiam fundum aut quamlibet aliam rem necessarium mercatus erit. itaque si ex decem ut puta sestertiis quae servus tuus a Titio mutua accepit creditori tuo quinque sestertia solverit, reliqua vero quinque quolibet modo consumpserit, pro quinque quidem in solidum damnari debes, pro ceteris vero quinque eatenus, quatenus in peculio sit: ex quo scilicet apparet, si tota decem sestertia in rem tuam versa fuerint, tota decem sestertia Titium consequi posse. licet enim una est actio qua de peculio deque eo quod in rem patris dominive versum sit agitur, tamen duas habet condemnationes. itaque iudex aput quem ea actione agitur ante dispicere solet, an in rem patris dominive versum sit, nec aliter ad peculii aestimationem transit, quam si aut nihil in rem patris dominive versum intellegatur, aut non totum. Cum autem quaeritur quantum in peculio sit, ante deducitur quod patri dominove quique *in potestate eius sit a fi*lio servove debetur, et quod superest, hoc solum peculium *esse* intellegitur. *aliquando tamen id quod ei* debet filius servusve qui in potestate patris dominive *est non* deducitur ex peculio, velut *si* is cui debet in huius ipsius peculio sit.

been converted to the uses of the father or master. When a debt is contracted without the consent of the father or master, if any portion was converted to his uses, he is liable to that amount; if no portion was converted, he is liable to the extent of the peculium. Conversion to his uses is any necessary expenditure on his account, as payment of his creditors, repair of his falling house, purchase of corn for his slaves, purchase of an estate for him, or any other necessary. If out of ten thousand sesterces which your slave borrowed of Titius he paid your creditor five thousand, and spent the remainder in some other way, you are liable for the whole of the five thousand, and for the remainder to the extent of the peculium. If the whole ten thousand was applied to your uses you are liable for the whole. It is a single action that is brought in respect of Peculium and of conversion to uses, but it has two condemnatory clauses. The judex first looks to see whether there has been an application to the uses of the father or master, and does not proceed to ascertain the amount of the peculium unless there was no such application or only a partial application. In ascertaining the amount of the peculium, deduction first is made of what is owed to the father or master or to a person in his power, and the residue only is treated as peculium. Sometimes what is owed to a person in his power is not deducted, for instance, if it is owed to a vicarius, that is, to a slave in the peculium of the slave.

§ 74. Ceterum *dubium non est, quin is quoque qui iussu patris do-*

§ 74. There is no doubt that a creditor who contracted with the

minive contraxerit, *cuique institoria vel exercitoria* formula competit, de peculio aut de in rem verso agere possit. sed nemo tam stultus erit, ut qui aliqua illarum actionum sine dubio solidum consequi possit, in difficultatem se deducat probandi *in rem patris dominive versum esse, vel habere filium servumve peculium, et tantum habere, ut solidum sibi solvi possit.* Is quoque cui tributoria actio competit, de peculio vel de in rem verso agere potest: sed huic sane plerumque expedit hac potius actione uti quam tributoria. nam in tributoria eius solius peculii ratio habetur quod in his mercibus *erit* quibus negotiatur filius servusve, *quod*que inde receptum erit, at in actione peculii, totius: et potest quisque tertia forte aut quarta vel etiam minore parte peculii negotiari, maximam vero partem *in praediis vel* in *aliis* rebus habere; l*onge* m*agis* si potest adprobari id quod *debeatur totum* in rem patris dominive versum esse, ad hanc actionem transire debet. nam, ut supra diximus, eadem formula et de peculio et de in rem verso agitur.

sanction of the father or master with a son or slave, and therefore might sue by exercitoria or institoria, may bring an action in respect of the peculium or of conversion to uses; but it would be foolish to relinquish the actions by which he can recover the whole, and undertake the trouble of proving a conversion to uses or the existence of a peculium sufficient in amount to cover the whole of the debt. A plaintiff who can sue by Tributoria may sue in respect of peculium and conversion to uses, and will generally find it expedient to do so; for Tributoria only relates to that portion of the peculium which consists of the merchandize and the proceeds of the merchandize with which the son or slave traded, but the others extend to the whole peculium; and a man may trade with only a third or fourth or less part of his peculium and have the rest invested in land or at interest. A fortiori, if the plaintiff can prove that the whole of the debt was converted to the uses of the father or master, he should use this action; for, as I said above, the same formala lies both in respect of peculium and of what has been converted to uses.

Besides the equitable actions introduced by the praetor, a paterfamilias was rendered liable by the act of his son or slave to a condictio, that is, was liable under the civil law to an action stricti juris in two cases, if the act turned to his profit (si in rem ejus versum est), and if it had received his sanction, for a contract entered into by his order was regarded as his contract. The liability of the superior follows from the statement of the gist of Condictio, page 415. Illud in summa admonendi sumus, id quod jussu patris dominive contractum fuerit, quodque in rem ejus versum erit, directo quoque posse a patre dominove condici, tanquam si principaliter cum ipso negotium gestum esset. Ei quoque qui vel exercitoria vel institoria actione tenetur directo posse condici placet, quia hujus quoque jussu contractum intelligitur, Inst. 4, 7, 8. If the paterfamilias had neither ordered the transaction nor profited by it, the creditor's only remedy against him were the actions de peculio and tributoria.

§ 71. The relation of the free captain (magister) to the shipowner (exercitor), and of the free manager, overseer, factor (institor) to his employer (dominus), was the germ or first manifestation of the general institution of Agency (mandatum), an institution that was slow in reaching its complete development in Roman jurisprudence.

The term Institor includes a banker (mensae praepositus), bailiff (agris colendis), foreman (mercaturis), bagman (sed etiam eos institores dicendos placuit, quibus vestiarii vel lintearii dant vestem circumferendam et distrahendam, quos vulgo circitores appellamus, Dig. 14, 3, 5), and any similar agent, of whatever age or sex (nam et plerique pueros puellasque tabernis praeponunt, Dig. 14, 3, 8).

§ 74. One advantage of Tributoria was, that all commercial creditors, including the master of the slave, were treated on an equal footing, whereas in de peculio the sum due to the master was deducted before the peculium was computed for any other creditor. Another advantage was, that commercial creditors, i. e. creditors in respect of the particular trade in which the son or slave was engaged, had an exclusive right to satisfaction out of the merx peculiaris, while other creditors could only have recourse to the residue of the peculium.

A disadvantage of Tributoria was, that the creditor who received his share was obliged to bind himself to refund in case any new creditors should present their claims, whereas in de peculio the law adopted the principle, melior est conditio occupantis.

One contract with a filiusfamilias, namely, the loan of money (mutui datio) without the sanction of the father, was always invalid, in pursuance of the Senatusconsultum Macedonianum passed in the reign of Claudius or Vespasian.

DE NOXALIBUS ACTIONIBUS.

§ 75. Ex maleficiis filiorum familias servorumve, veluti si furtum fecerint aut iniuriam commiserint, noxales actiones proditae sunt, uti liceret patri dominove aut litis

§ 75. For a delict, such as theft or outrage, committed by a son or slave, a noxal action lies against the father or master, who has the option of either paying the damages

aestimationem sufferre aut noxae dedere: *erat* enim iniq*u*um nequitiam eorum ultra ipsorum corpora parentibus dominisve damnosam esse.

assessed or surrendering the delinquent. For it is not just that the misdeed of a son or slave should involve the father or master in any detriment beyond the loss of his body.

§ 76. Constitutae sunt autem noxales actiones aut legibus aut edicto. legibus, velut furti lege XII tabularum, damni iniuriae [velut] lege Aquilia. edicto Praetoris, velut iniuriarum et vi bonorum raptorum.

§ 76. Noxal actions were introduced partly by law, partly by the edict of the praetor: for theft, by the law of the Twelve Tables; for injury to property, by the lex Aquilia; for outrage and rapine, by the edict.

§ 77. Omnes autem noxales actiones capita sequuntur. nam si filius tuus servusve noxam commiserit, quamdiu in tua potestate est, tecum est actio; si in alterius potestatem pervenerit, cum illo incipit actio esse; si sui iuris coeperit esse, directa actio cum ipso est, et noxae deditio extinguitur. ex diverso quoque directa actio noxalis esse incipit: nam si pater familias noxam commiserit, et hic se in adrogationem tibi dederit aut servus tuus esse coeperit, *quod* quibusdam casibus accidere primo commentario tradidimus, incipit tecum noxalis actio esse quae ante directa fuit.

§ 77. Noxal actions follow the malefactor. If your son or slave has done a wrong while he is in your power, an action lies against you; if he becomes his own master, a direct action lies against the offender himself, and the noxal action is extinguished. Conversely, a direct action may change into noxal: if a paterfamilias has done a wrong, and has become your son by adrogatio or your slave, as I showed in the first book might happen in certain circumstances, a noxal action lies against you in place of the direct action which formerly lay against the wrongdoer.

§ 78. Sed si filius patri aut servus domino noxam commiserit, nulla actio nascitur: nulla enim omnino inter me et eum qui *in* potestate mea est obligatio nascitur. ideoque et si in alienam potestatem pervenerit aut sui iuris esse coeperit, neque cum ipso, neque cum eo cuius nunc in potestate est agi potest. unde quaeritur, si alienus servus filiusve noxam commiserit mihi, et is postea in mea esse coeperit potestate, utrum intercidat actio, an quiescat. nostri praeceptores intercidere putant, quia in eum casum deducta sit in quo actio consistere non potuerit, ideoque licet exierit de mea potestate, agere me non posse. diversae scholae auc-

§ 78. But no action lies for an offence by a son or slave committed against his father or master; for between me and a person in my power there is no obligation; and, consequently, if he passes under the power of another, or becomes his own master, neither he nor his master can be sued. Hence it has been asked whether, if another man's son or slave has wronged me and passes into my power, the action is extinguished or is only in abeyance. Our school maintains that it is extinguished, because it has come into a condition in which an action cannot exist, and therefore if he pass again out of my power I have no action. The other

tores, quamdiu in mea potestate sit, quiescere actionem putant, cum ipse mecum agere non possum; cum vero exierit de mea potestate, tunc eam resuscitari.

school maintain that while he is in my power the action is only in abeyance, because I cannot bring an action against myself, and revives when he passes out of my power.

§ 79. Cum autem filius familias ex noxali causa mancipio datur, diversae scholae auctores putant ter eum mancipio dari debere, quia lege XII tabularum cautum sit, *ne aliter filius de potestate patris* exeat, quam si ter fu*e*rit mancipatus: Sabin*us* et Cassius ceterique nostrae scholae auctores sufficere unam mancipationem; crediderunt enim tres lege XII tabularum ad voluntarias mancipationes pertinere.

§ 79. When a filiusfamilias is surrendered in satisfaction of judgment in a noxal action, the other school hold that he ought to be mancipated three times, because the law of the Twelve Tables provides that a son cannot pass out of the power of the father unless he is three times mancipated. Sabinus and Cassius and the other authorities of my school hold that a single mancipation is sufficient, and suppose that the three conveyances of the Twelve Tables are only required in voluntary emancipation.

§ 80. Haec ita de his personis quae in potestate *sunt*, sive ex contractu sive ex *m*aleficio earum *controver*sia esset. quod vero ad *eas* personas quae in manu mancipiove sunt, i*ta* ius *dicitur*, ut cum *ex contractu* earum ageretur, nisi ab eo cuius iuri subiectae sin*t in solid*um defendantur, bona quae *e*arum *futura forent*, si *eius* iur*i* subiectae non essent, *v*en*e*ant. sed cum rescis*sa capitis diminutione* imperio continenti iud*icio* [*desunt* 24 *lin.*]

§ 80. So much for the contracts and delicts of persons under power. As to persons subject to manus or mancipium, when they are sued for contracts, unless they are defended against the whole damages by the superior to whom they are subject, the goods which would have belonged to them but for their subjection are ordered by the praetor to be sold. A praetorian action rescinding the charge of status . . .

§ 81. . . . . q*uamquam* diximus . . . . *permi*ssum fuisse ei mortuos homines dedere, tamen et si quis *eum* dederit qui fato suo vita excesserit, aeque libera*tur*.

§ 81. . . . . though I said that a dead man . . . . yet if he died a natural death and the body is surrendered, the judgment is satisfied.

§ 77. Gaius explained the various modes by which a man might lose his freedom, 1 § 160. A person who fraudulently allowed himself to be sold with the view of sharing the purchase money, Inst. 1, 3, 4, a freedman ungrateful to his patron, Inst. 1, 16, 1, a woman who persisted in intercourse with a slave without the permission of the master, all forfeited their freedom, the last by a Senatusconsultum Claudianum which was repealed by Justinian, Inst. 3, 12, 1. In the older law a man who failed to register himself at the census (incensus) lost his freedom; and by the Twelve Tables the fur manifestus and insolvent debtor were assigned as slaves (addicti) to the injured party.

§ 78. Justinian decides in favour of the Sabinians, Inst. 4, 8, 6, that the action for the delict of a slave is extinguished, without possibility of future revival, when the delinquent slave comes into the power of the person aggrieved.

§ 81. The death of a delinquent slave extinguished the liability of the master. Sed et mortuo servo antequam judicium accipiatur omnino hac actione non tenebitur dominus, Dig. 9, 4, 39, 4. Si quis pro servo mortuo, ignorans eum decessisse, noxale judicium acceperit, absolvi debet, quia desiit verum esse, propter eum dare oportere, Dig. 9, 4, 42 1. 'If the slave die before an action is commenced, the master is not liable; and if an action is commenced in ignorance of his death, the master must be absolved, because his liability is at an end.'

As the Romans became more civilized the noxal surrender of a son or daughter by the parent became repugnant to public feelings, and Justinian speaks of it as a thing of the past. The delinquent, however, if unable to pay the damages in which he was condemned, was still liable to the penalty of the insolvent debtor, that is, to be confined, not in a private prison, for this Zeno had declared to be nefandissimum scelus, p. 418, but in a public prison, and there to be held to hard labour for the benefit of the creditor.

Si autem damnum ei cui deditus est servus resarcierit quaesita pecunia, auxilio praetoris invito domino manumittetur, Inst. 4, 8, 3. 'If a slave surrendered for a delict is able to indemnify the injured party, he is manumitted without the consent of his master.'

This seems originally to have been restricted to the case of a freeman surrendered for delict. Per hominem liberum noxiae deditum si tantum adquisitum sit, quantum damnum dedit, manumittere cogendus est a praetore qui noxa deditum accepit, sed fiduciae judicio non tenetur, Papinian, Collatio, 2, 3. 'On indemnification by the freeman surrendered for delict, his master is compelled by the praetor to manumit him, but cannot be sued for a trust.'

Livy relates that the consul Postumius, who, to save the Roman army, made a treaty with the Samnites, and was sent under the Caudine Forks, was surrendered by the Romans, to discharge themselves of their liability, with all the formalities of a noxae deditio, A. D. 318, Livy, 9, 10. As Postumius had not committed a delict against the Samnites, but had made a contract with them, we may either suppose that the colouring of legality which the Romans attempted to give to their violation of the treaty was defective in this respect, or that under the old law the paterfamilias could really by noxae deditio discharge himself of liability for the contracts of those in his power by which he benefited, as well as for their delicts.

With the principle of noxal actions we may compare the law of Damni infecti (damage anticipated), which allowed the owner of a dilapidated house to exonerate himself from damages caused to his neighbours' property by surrendering the house; or the rule of English law, by which the responsibility of a shipowner for damage done without his fault to another ship or cargo is limited to the value of his ship and the freight she is earning at the time, 53 George III, c. 159.

Mischief (pauperies) occasioned by an animal might by a law of the Twelve Tables be atoned for by noxae deditio.

DE HIS PER QUOS AGERE POSSUMUS.

§ 82. *Nunc admonendi sumus agere posse quemlibet aut suo nomine aut alieno.* alieno, veluti cognitorio, procuratorio, tutorio, curatorio: cum olim, quo *tempore erant leg*is action*es*, in usu fuisset alter*ius* nomine agere non licere, *nisi* pro popul*o et libertat*is *causa*.

§ 82. A man may sue either for himself or for another as cognitor, procurator, guardian, curator, whereas under the actions of the law a man could only sue for another in public suits or as an assertor of freedom.

§ 83. Cognitor autem certis verb*is* in litem cora*m* adversario substituitur. nam actor *ita* cognitorem dat: QUOD EGO A TE verbi gratia FUNDUM PETO, IN EAM REM LUCIUM TITIUM *T*IBI COGNITOREM DO; ad*versarius* ita: QUANDOQUE TU A ME FUNDUM PETIS, IN EAM REM PUBLIUM MAEVIUM COGNITOREM DO. potest, ut actor ita dicat: QUOD EGO TECUM AGERE VOLO, IN EAM REM COGNITOREM DO; advers*arius* i*ta*: QUANDOQUE TU MECUM AGERE *VIS*, *IN EAM* REM COGNITOREM DO. nec interest, praesens an absens cognitor detur: sed si absens datus fu*e*rit, cognitor ita erit, si cognoverit *et suscep*erit officium cognitori*s*.

§ 83. A cognitor for a cause is appointed by a set form of words in the presence of the adversary. The plaintiff appoints a cognitor in the following form: 'Whereas I sue you for, say, an estate, in that matter I appoint Lucius Titius as my cognitor;' the defendant thus: 'Whereas you sue me for an estate, in that matter I appoint Publius Maevius as my cognitor.' Or the plaintiff may use the words: 'Whereas I intend to sue you, in that matter I appoint Lucius Titius as my cognitor;' and the defendant these: 'Whereas you intend to sue me, in that matter I appoint Publius Maevius as my cognitor.' It is immaterial whether the person named as cognitor is present or absent; but if an absent person is named, he is only cognitor if he consents and undertakes the office.

§ 84. Procurator vero *n*ullis certis verbis in litem *substituitur*; sed ex solo mandato, et absente et ignorante adversario, constituitur. quinetiam sunt qui putant *vel eum* procuratorem videri cui non sit mandatum, si modo bona fide accedat *ad* negotium et caveat ratam rem dominum habiturum. igitur et *si non* edat mandatum pro*curator*, *experiri potest*, quia saepe mandatum initio litis in obscuro est et postea aput iudicem ostenditur.

§ 84. A procurator is appointed in any words that amount to instructions, even in the absence and without the knowledge of the adversary. According to some, instructions are not requisite if a person undertakes the office in good faith and engages that the principal will ratify his proceeding. A procurator may commence an action without producing his instructions, and in fact the instructions are often not produced until the action is before the judex.

§ 85. Tutores autem et curatores quemadmodum constituantur, primo commentario rettulimus.

§ 85. How guardians and curators are appointed has been explained in the first book.

§ 86. Qui autem alieno nomine agit, intentionem quidem ex persona domini sumit, condemnationem autem in suam personam convertit. n*am* si verbi gratia Lucius Titius *pro* Publio Maevio agat, ita formula concipitur: SI PARET NUMERIUM NEGIDIUM PUBLIO MAEVIO SESTERTIUM X MILIA DARE OPORTERE, IUDEX NUMERIUM NEGIDIUM LUCIO TITIO SESTERTIUM X MILIA CONDEMNA. SI NON PARET, ABSOLVE. in rem quoque si agat, intendit Publii *Maevii* rem esse ex iure Quiritium, et condemnationem in suam personam convertit.

§ 86. He who sues for another names the principal in the intentio and himself in the condemnatio. If, for example, Lucius Titius sues for Publius Maevius, the formula runs thus: 'If it be proved that Numerius Negidius ought to pay to Publius Maevius ten thousand sesterces, do thou, judex, condemn Numerius Negidius to pay to Lucius Titius ten thousand sesterces; if it be not proved, absolve him.' In a real action the thing is affirmed in the intentio to be the property of Publius Maevius by the law of the Quirites, and the representative is named in the condemnatio.

§ 87. Ab adversarii quoque parte si interveniat aliquis, cum quo actio constituitur, intenditur dominum dare oportere: condemnatio autem in eius personam convertitur qui iudicium accepit. sed cum in rem agitur, nihil *in* intentione facit eius persona cum quo agitur, sive suo nomine sive alieno aliquis iudicio interveniat: tantum enim intenditur rem actoris esse.

§ 87. If the defendant is represented by a cognitor or procurator, the principal is named in a personal intentio, and his representative in the condemnatio. In a real action neither the principal defendant nor his representative is named in the intentio, which only affirms the proprietorship of the plaintiff.

§ 82. If there is a genuine antithesis between suo nomine and alieno nomine, the procuratorium, tutorium, &c., nomen, which is the alienum nomen with which the procurator or guardian sues, must mean the name, not of the procurator or guardian, but of the principal or ward. When a man sues suo nomine he uses his own name in the intentio, therefore when a man sues procuratorio nomine he uses the procuratorium nomen in the intentio. But the name inserted in the intentio by a procurator is not the name of the procurator, but that of the principal.

§ 82. Eam popularem actionem dicimus quae suum jus populo tuetur, Dig. 47, 23, 1. 'A public action is one which defends the interest of the people.' A popularis actio was one brought by a common informer to recover a penalty. The informer enforced, not a private but a public right, that is, sued as the procurator of the people; and therefore an infamis, as he was disabled from being procurator, was incompetent to prosecute in such an action. To public actions and actions by an assertor libertatis Justinian adds, as maintainable by a representative under the old jurisprudence, actions in behalf of a ward. We have already mentioned, page 97, that until the ward attained the age of seven the guardian acted in the name of the ward; after the age of seven the ward acted with the authority of the guardian.

§ 84. A person who without instructions (mandatum) officiously interposed and undertook the defence of an absent neighbour was called negotiorum gestor, or defensor, or procurator voluntarius. The employment of a cognitor, from the necessity of appointing him in the presence of the adversary and by a certain formula, was discontinued as inconvenient, and Justinian only speaks of the procurator.

DE SATISDATIONIBUS.

§ 88. Videamus nunc quibus ex causis is cum quo agitur vel hic qui *agit cogatur* satisdare.

§ 89. Igitur si verbi gratia in rem tecum *agam*, satis mihi dar*e* debes. aequu*m* enim visum est *te* ideo quod interea tibi rem, quae an *ad* te pertineat dubium *est*, possidere conceditur, cum satisdatione mihi

§ 88. We next inquire under what circumstances the plaintiff or defendant is required to give security.

§ 89. If I sue you in a real action you must give me security. As you are permitted during the suit to retain possession of a thing to which your title is doubtful, it is fair that you should give me security with

cavere, ut si victus sis, nec rem ipsam restituas nec litis aestimationem sufferas, sit mihi potestas aut tecum agendi aut cum sponsoribus tuis.

§ 90. Multoque magis debes satisdare mihi, si alieno nomine iudicium accipias.

§ 91. Ceterum cum in rem actio duplex *sit* (aut enim per formulam petitoriam agitur aut per sponsionem): si quidem per formulam petitoriam agitur, illa stipulatio locum habet quae appellatur iudicatum solvi: si vero per sponsionem, illa quae appellatur pro praede litis et vindiciarum.

§ 92. Petitoria autem formula haec est qua actor intendit rem suam esse.

§ 93. Per sponsionem vero hoc modo agimus. provocamus adversarium tali sponsione: SI HOMO QUO DE AGITUR EX IURE QUIRITIUM MEUS EST, SESTERTIOS XXV NUMMOS DARE SPONDES? deinde formulam edimus qua intendimus sponsionis summam nobis dare oportere. qua formula ita demum vincimus, si probaverimus rem nostram esse.

§ 94. Non tamen haec summa sponsionis exigitur: nec enim poenali*s* est, sed praeiudicia*l*is, et propter hoc solum fit, ut per eam de re iudicetur. unde etiam is cum q*uo agitur non restipulatur: i*deo autem appellata est PRO PRAEDE LITIS VINDICIARUM stipulatio, *qu*ia in locum praedium successit; qui*a* olim, cum lege agebatur, pro lite et v*in*diciis, id est pro re et fructibus, a possesso*re* petitori dabantur praedes.

§ 95. Ceterum si aput centumviros agitur, summam sponsionis

sureties, so that if judgment goes against you and you refuse to restore the thing or to pay its value I may have the power of proceeding against you or your sponsors.

§ 90. And there is all the more reason that you should give security if you are only the representative of another.

§ 91. A Real action is either commenced by a real formula or by sponsio: if by real formula, the stipulation is called security for satisfaction of judgment; if by sponsio, security in lieu of warranty for property and interim possession.

§ 92. The Intentio of a real formula asserts the proprietorship of the plaintiff.

§ 93. In a sponsio we challenge the defendant to a wager as follows: 'If the slave in question belongs to me by the law of the Quirites, do you promise to pay me twenty-five sesterces?' and we then deliver a formula in which we sue for the sum named in the wager, and obtain judgment if we prove our proprietorship.

§ 94. But the sum named in the wager is not exacted, for it is not penal, but prejudicial, and the wager is merely a device for instituting a trial of ownership. Accordingly, the defendant does not exact a counter promise from the plaintiff. The name of security in lieu of warranty for property and interim possession is derived from the warrantors which it superseded; for anciently in the actions of the law restitution of the thing in dispute and the mesne profits was secured to the plaintiff by the engagement of the defendant's warrantors.

§ 95. In the centumviral court the sum of the wager is not sued for

non per formulam petimus, sed per legis actionem: sacramento enim re*um* provocamus; eaque sponsio sestertiorum CXXV nummorum fit, *scilicet* propter legem . . . .

§ 96. Ipse autem qui in rem agit, si suo nomine agit, satis non dat.

§ 97. Ac nec si per cognitorem quidem aga*tur*, ulla satisdatio vel ab ipso vel a domino desideratur. cum enim certis et quasi sollemnibus verbis in locum domini substituatur cognitor, merito domini loco habetur.

§ 98. Procurator vero si agat, satisdare iubetur ratam rem dominum habiturum: periculum *enim est*, ne iterum domin*us* de eadem re experiatur. quod periculum *non* intervenit, si per cognitorem actum fuit; quia de *q*ua re quisque per cognitorem egerit, de ea non magis amplius actionem habet quam si ipse egerit.

§ 99. Tutores et curatores eo modo quo et procur*atores* satisdare debere verba edicti faciunt. sed aliquando illis satisdatio remittitur.

§ 100. Haec ita si in rem agatur: si vero in personam, ab actoris quidem parte quando satisdari debeat quaerentes, eadem repetemus quae diximus in actione qua in rem agitur.

§ 101. Ab eius vero parte cum quo agitur, si quidem alieno nomi*ne* aliquis interveniat, omnimodo satisdar*i* debet, quia nemo alienae rei sine satisdatione defensor idoneus intellegitur. sed si quidem cum *cognit*ore agatur, dominus satisdare iubetur; si vero cum procuratore, ipse procurator. idem et de tutore et de curatore iuris est.

§ 102. Quod si proprio nomine aliquis iudicium *accipiat* in personam, certis ex causis satisdari

by formula, but by action of the law. We challenge the defendant to deposit a stake of a hundred and twenty-five sesterces, the amount fixed by the lex . . . .

§ 96. In a real action a plaintiff who sues in his own name gives no security.

§ 97. And if a cognitor sues, no security is required either from him or from his principal, for the cognitor, being appointed by certain sacramental terms, is identified with the principal.

§ 98. But if a procurator sues, he is required to give security for the ratification of his proceedings by his principal, as otherwise the principal might sue again on the same claim, which he cannot do after suing by a cognitor.

§ 99. Guardians and curators are required by the edict to give the same security as procurators, but are sometimes excused.

§ 100. So much for real actions. In personal actions the plaintiff is governed by the same rules as in real actions.

§ 101. If the defendant is represented by another person, security must always be given, for no one is allowed to defend another without security: but in a suit against a cognitor it is the principal who gives security; in a suit against a procurator the procurator gives security; and the same applies to guardians and curators.

§ 102. If the defendant is sued in his own name, in a personal action, he only gives security in certain

solet, quas ipse Praetor significat. quarum satisdationum duplex causa est. nam aut propter genus actionis satisdatur, aut pro*pter* persona*m*, quia suspecta sit. propter genus actionis, velut iudicati depensive, aut cum de moribus mulieris agetur: propter personam, velut si cum eo agitur qui decoxerit, cuiusve bona *a* creditoribus possessa proscriptave sunt, sive cum eo herede agatur quem Praetor suspectum aestimaverit.

cases named in the edict. These cases are of two kinds, depending either on the nature of the action or on the character of the defendant. The nature of the action is the reason in a suit against a judgment debtor, or a principal indebted to his surety, or a husband who retains a portion of the dower of his divorced wife on the plea of immorality. The character of the defendant is the reason if he has been insolvent, or if his goods have been possessed or proscribed for sale by his creditors, of if he is a successor whom the praetor pronounces to be open to suspicion.

§ 88. In a real action the defendant was required to give security; in a personal, with a few exceptions, if he appeared in his own cause, he was not required. Justinian relieved him of the necessity in real actions.

In the time of Gaius if the defendant in a real action refused to give security, judicatum solvi, the possession was transferred from him to the plaintiff by the interdict Quem fundum, Quam hereditatem, or Quem usumfructum, as the case might be, and he was reduced to the position of plaintiff. Sunt etiam interdicta duplicia tam adipiscendae quam recuperandae possessionis; qualia sunt interdicta QUEM FUNDUM et QUAM HEREDITATEM. Nam si fundum vel hereditatem ab aliquo petam, nec lis defendatur, cogitur ad me transferre possessionem, sive nunquam possedi, sive antea possedi deinde amisi possessionem, Fragment of Ulpian's Institutions of Civil Law. 'Some interdicts may either initiate or restore possession, as the interdicts Quem fundum and Quam hereditatem. For if I sue a person for land or an heritage, and he refuses to give security, he is compelled to transfer the possession to me whether I never before had possession, or once had and afterwards lost possession.' Sicut corpora vindicanti, ita et jus, satisdari oportet et ideo necessario exemplo interdicti; QUEM FUNDUM, proponi etiam interdictum, QUEM USUMFRUCTUM vindicare velit, de restituendo usufructu, Ulpian, Fragmenta Vaticana, 92. 'The plaintiff has a right to security in a real action for a servitude as well as for a corporal thing, and therefore, analogous to the interdict, Quem fundum, there is an interdict, Quem usumfructum, for the transfer of a usufruct.' Quoties hereditas petitur, satisdatio jure desideratur; et si satisdatio non detur, in petitorem hereditas transfertur. Si petitor satisdare noluerit, penes possessorem possessio remanet; in pari enim causa potior est possessor, Paulus, Receptae Sententiae, 1, 11, 1. 'In a demand of a heritage, security must be given, or else possession is transferred to the demandant. If the demandant refuse to give security, possession remains with the tenant, for in equal circumstances law favours the possessor.'

§ 91. In the Sacramentum and Sponsio two different stipulations must be distinguished. In the Sacramentum there was (A) the praedes sacramenti, and (B) the praedes litis et vindiciarum; in the Sponsio there was (A) the sponsio praejudicialis, and (B) the satisdatio pro praede litis et vindiciarum. In the formula petitoria there was only one stipulation, (B) the satisdatio judicatum solvi, corresponding to the second stipulation in the Sacramentum and Sponsio. The sum staked in the praedes sacramenti, which Gaius had told us, § 14, was a thousand or five hundred asses, he now, § 95, defines as one hundred and twenty-five sesterces.

The explanation of this is as follows: Originally the sestertius, as the name implies, was two asses and a half, and the denarius ten asses. Both the sestertius and the denarius were silver coins. In the second Punic War, about B.C. 217, in consequence of the insolvency of the State, the denarius was made equal to sixteen asses and the sestertius remained, as before, one fourth of the denarius, that is, became equal to four asses. One hundred and twenty-five sesterces, therefore, were equal to five hundred asses.

The Sponsio praejudicialis, though a personal action in form, might be in effect a real action. It resembled the Feigned Issue or issue in a fictitious action on a wager, whereby the Court of Chancery, before it had the power of summoning a jury might refer an issue of fact to trial by jury, or the parties in a court of law by consent or by direction of some act of parliament might determine some disputed right without the formality of a regular action, thereby saving much time and expense, Stephen's Commentaries, 5, 14. In the Sponsio poenalis there was both a sponsio and restipulatio, that is, both parties forfeited the penal sum if they lost the action, and the penal sum was serious, in an action de pecunia certa credita being one third and in an action de pecunia constituta being one half of the sum in dispute, § 171.

In a Sponsio based on the interdicts Uti possidetis and Utrubi fuit, both parties being both plaintiff and defendant, there were (A) two sponsiones and two restipulationes for a penal sum, and there was (B) a fructuaria stipulatio for the restitution of twice the value of the mesne profits, corresponding to the security pro praede vindiciarum, § 166. Whether it also corresponded to the security pro praede litis, or whether there was no stipulation for the restitution of possession (mere possession, not property, being the subject of dispute), from the defective state of the Gaian MS. does not appear, but the negative is more probable. If the possessor lost the action and refused to surrender possession he was liable to the judicium Cascellianum, § 166, which seems to have merely enforced an obligation ex delicto. In Cicero's time it appears that an inheritance could not be sued for by a formula petitoria. Si quis testamento se heredem esse arbitraretur quod tum non extaret; lege ageret in hereditatem; aut pro praede litis vindiciarum quum satis accepisset, sponsionem faceret, ita de hereditate certaret, Verres, 2, 1, 45. 'A plaintiff who claimed to be successor by a will that had disappeared, would either sue by sacramentum or would receive security in lieu of warranty for the thing and mesne profits and then by sponsio sue for the succession.' This shows that (B) the security for delivery of the thing in dispute preceded in point of time (A) the wager or sponsio praejudicialis.

Belonging, apparently, to the formalities of Sponsio was a proceeding which has caused commentators on Roman law no little embarrassment—Deductio quae moribus fit. It is mentioned by Cicero, Pro Caecina and Pro Tullio, but not by Gaius. It has been supposed to have been connected with procedure by Sacramentum, by Interdict Unde vi, by Vindicatio; but such connection is very dubious. It probably pertained to none of these, but to litigation respecting land by the form of Sponsio. As the securities in Sponsio (satisdatio pro praede litis et vindiciarum) were modelled on the securities in Sacramentum (praedes litis et vindiciarum) so, apparently, Deductio was a fictitious ejectment preliminary to procedure by Sponsio, just as Manuum consertio was a symbolic battle introductory to suit by Sacramentum. What was the object of the ceremony is perhaps now inaccessible to conjecture. Possibly it was merely an identification of the subject of dispute.

§ 98. We have an allusion to the security of a procurator plaintiff in the Brutus, where the negotiorum gestor is called voluntarius procurator. Mihi quoque, inquit Brutus, expectanda sunt ea quae Attico polliceris, etsi fortasse ego a te hujus voluntarius procurator petam quod ipse cui debes se incommodo exacturum negat. At vero, inquam, tibi ego, Brute, non solvam nisi prius a te cavero amplius eo nomine neminem cujus petitio sit petiturum, Brutus, 4. 'I too, said Brutus, must wait for what Atticus is promised, but perhaps I shall sue as volunteer procurator for the payment, which the principal says he will leave to your convenience. Then I shall not pay you, Brutus, said I, unless you first give me security that no one entitled to sue shall sue me on that account a second time.'

§ 102. The husband sued for the dower of his divorced wife might retain a portion on various grounds, of which Immorality was one. Retentiones ex dote fiunt aut propter liberos, aut propter mores, aut propter impensas, aut propter res donatas, aut propter res amotas. Propter liberos retentio fit, si culpa mulieris aut patris in cujus potestate est divortium factum sit: tunc enim singulorum liberorum nomine sextae retinentur ex dote; non plures tamen quam tres .... Morum nomine graviorum quidem sexta retinetur; leviorum autem octava. Graviores mores sunt adulteria tantum; leviores omnes reliqui, Ulpian, Liber Regularum, 6, 9. 'Retentions in the restitution of dower are on account of children, immorality, expenditure, donation, articles purloined by the wife. On account of children, if the fault of the wife, or the father in whose power she is, occasioned the divorce. Then a sixth is retained on account of each child, but not more than three sixths altogether. For gross immorality a sixth is retained, for slight immorality an eighth. Only adultery is gross immorality.'

The circumstances under which security judicatum solvi was required of a defendant are illustrated in Cicero's oration for Quintius. Naevius had a demand against Quintius, and alleged that Quintius had committed an act of bankruptcy by breaking an engagement to appear before the praetor (vadimonium judicio sisti), and on this ground obtained from the praetor a missio in possessionem in pursuance of the edict. Praetor ait: In bona ejus qui judicio sistendi causa fidejussorem dedit, si neque potestatem sui faciat neque defendetur, iri jubebo, Dig. 42, 4, 2. 'If a defendant give security to appear and neither appears nor is defended, I will put the plaintiff in possession of his goods.' Accordingly, when Quintius was afterwards willing to defend an action, Naevius required that he should give security judicatum solvi, § 103. Defendere debitorem sicut ante quam bona ejus possiderentur licet, ita post bonorum quoque possessionem ejus, sive ipse sui sive alius defensionem ejus suscipiat, debet satisdare, ut satisdatione interposita judicium accipiatur et a possessione discedatur, Dig. 42, 5, 33, 1. 'Missio in possessionem is prevented by the appearance of a defensor, and after bonorum possessio the debtor or a defensor may, on giving security judicatum solvi, defend the action, and put an end to the possessio.' Quintius refused to give this security on the ground that he had broken no vadimonium, and committed no act of bankruptcy, and that his goods had consequently not been legally possessed. The praetor directed a sponsio praejudicialis to try this preliminary question: Jubet P. Quintium sponsionem cum Sex. Naevio facere: Si bona sua ex edicto P. Burrieni praetoris dies triginta possessa non essent: and against the ordinary rule that a man should not be required to prove a negative, made Quintius the plaintiff in the sponsio. In the absence of Quintius, a friend had appeared (voluntarius procurator), who volunteered to undertake his defence, and thus prevent the missio in possessionem; but he was not allowed by the praetor, because he declined to enter into the security judicatum solvi, Cicero, Pro Quintio.

Besides the forfeiture of a vadimonium, fraudulent absconding to avoid the summons to appear was an act of bankruptcy, or motive for missio in possessionem. Praetor ait: Qui fraudationis causa latitabit, si boni viri arbitratu non defendetur, ejus bona possideri vendique jubebo, Dig. 42, 4, 7, 1. 'If a debtor fraudulently abscond, and no sufficient representative defends him, I will order his goods to be possessed and sold.'

A heres might, on cause shown to the praetor, immediately after his entry on the succession, be required by the creditors to give security for the payment of their claims, with the alternative of seizure and sale, on the mere ground of poverty, § 102. But after a lapse of time it was necessary to prove not only poverty, but fraudulent behaviour on the part of the heres, Dig. 42, 5, 31.

The stipulation judicatum solvi contained three clauses: Judicatum solvi stipulatio tres clausulas in unum collatas habet: de re judicata, de re defendenda, de dolo malo, Dig. 46, 7, 6. 'The stipulation judicatum solvi is composed of three clauses, for satisfaction of the judgment, for defending the action, and against malicious deterioration in case of restitution.' The action must be defended 'to the satisfaction of a reasonable man,' which was interpreted to mean that, if a defensor appeared before the judex, the second clause was not satisfied unless the defensor was prepared to give further security judicatum solvi. Si vero extrinsecus persona defensoris interveniat, aeque stipulatio non committetur, si modo ille paratus sit rem boni viri arbitratu defendere, hoc est satisdare, Dig. 46, 7, 5. 'A defensor may prevent a forfeiture of the stipulation if he defends "to the satisfaction of an arbitrator," that is, with adequate security.'

Justinian relieved the defendant in any action who appeared in his own person from the first and third clauses of the security judicatum solvi, but not from the second. The vadimonium or cautio judicio sistendi, which originally, it seems, only referred to adjourned appearances in jure, was at this period extended to the judicia, and bound the defendant to appear before the judex and remain to the end of the trial. If, then, in consequence of an adjournment in jure, there had been a vadimonium between the parties, no further stipulation would be necessary; otherwise the defendant would have had to enter into the undertaking that formed the second clause of the stipulation judicatum solvi. Sed haec hodie aliter observantur. Sive enim quis in rem actione convenitur sive in personam suo nomine, nullam satisdationem pro litis aestimatione dare compellitur, sed pro sua tantum persona quod in judicio permaneat usque ad terminum litis, Inst. 4, 11, 2. 'This is not the present rule. The defendant now is not required either in a real or personal action, if he appear in person, to give security for satisfaction of the judgment, but only for his own personal presence and continuance in court to the end of the trial.'

The procurator of the plaintiff appointed before the judex or in the record office of the magistrate by memorandum (insinuatio) in the register of his public proceedings (apud acta) was assimilated to the cognitor whom he superseded, and was not required to give security; otherwise he had to give security ratam rem dominum habiturum.

The procurator of the defendant gave no security; but his principal, as fidejussor of his procurator, gave security for the procurator judicatum solvi, including a mortgage (hypotheca) of all his property. A defensor (unauthorized representative) of the defendant gave security judicatum solvi.

DE IUDICIIS LEGITIMIS ET QUAE IMPERIO CONTINENTUR.

§ 103. Omnia autem iudicia aut legitimo iure consistunt aut imperio continentur.

§ 104. Legitima sunt iudicia quae in urbe Roma vel intra primum urbis Romae miliarium inter omnes cives Romanos sub uno iudice accipiuntur: eaque *e* lege Iulia iudici*aria*, nisi in anno et sex mensibus iudicata fuerint, expirant. et hoc est quod vulgo dicitur, e lege Iulia litem anno et sex mensibus mori.

§ 105. Imperio vero continentur recuperatoria et quae sub uno iudice accipiuntur interveniente peregrini persona iudicis aut litigatoris. in ea*dem* causa sunt quaecumque extra primum urbis Romae miliarium tam inter cives Roman*os* quam inter peregrinos accipiuntur. ideo autem imperio contineri iudicia dicuntur, quia tamdiu valent, quamdiu is qui ea praecepit imperium habebit.

§ 106. Et siquidem imperio continenti iudicio actum fuerit, sive in rem sive in personam, sive ea formula q*uae* in factum concepta est sive ea quae in ius habet intentionem, postea nihilominus ipso iure de eadem re agi potest. et ideo necessaria est exceptio rei iudicatae vel in iudicium deductae.

§ 107. At vero *si* legitimo iudicio in personam actum sit ea formula quae iuris civilis habet intentionem, postea ipso iure de eadem re agi non potest, et ob id exceptio supervacua est. si vero vel in rem vel in factum actum fuerit, ipso iure nihilominus postea agi potest, et

§ 103. Actions are either statutable or dependent on magisterial power.

§ 104. Statutable actions are those that are instituted at Rome, or within the first milestone, between Roman citizens, before a single judex; and these by the lex Julia judiciaria expire in a year and six months from their commencement, unless previously decided; which is the meaning of the saying that by the lex Julia an action dies in eighteen months.

§ 105. Actions dependent on magisterial power are those instituted before recuperators, or before a single judex, if the judex or a party is an alien, or beyond the first milestone, whether the parties are citizens or aliens. They depend on magisterial power because they can only be prosecuted as long as the praetor who delivered the formula continues in office.

§ 106. After the institution of an action dependent on magisterial power, whether it was real or personal, and whether it had a formula of fact or an allegation of law, there is no bar in the civil law to the institution of a subsequent action on the same question, and the defendant must meet it by an equitable plea alleging the previous decision or litigation.

§ 107. After the institution of a statutable personal action with an Intentio of civil law, the civil law bars a subsequent action on the same question, and an equitable plea is not required. After the institution of a statutable real action or a statutable personal action with

ob id exceptio necessaria est rei iudicatae vel in iudicium deductae.

a formula of fact, the civil law does not bar a subsequent action on the same question, and the plea of previous decision or litigation is necessary.

§ 108. Alia causa fuit olim legis actionum. nam qua de re actum semel erat, de ea postea ipso iure agi non poterat: nec omnino ita, ut nunc, usus erat illis temporibus exceptionum.

§ 108. It was otherwise anciently with the actions of the law, when a subsequent action on the same question was always barred by the civil law, and there never was occasion for an equitable plea.

§ 109. Ceterum potest ex lege quidem esse iudicium, sed legitimum non esse; et contra ex lege non esse, sed legitimum esse. *nam si* verbi gratia ex lege Aquilia vel Ouinia vel Furia in prouinciis agatur, imperio continebitur iudicium: idemque iuris est et si Romae aput recuperatores agamus, vel aput unum iudicem interveniente peregrini persona. et ex diverso si ex ea causa, ex qua nobis edicto Praetoris datur actio, Romae sub uno iudice inter omnes cives Roman*os* accipiatur iudicium, legitimum est.

§ 109. An action may be founded on statute and yet not be statutable, or statutable and yet not founded on statute. For instance, an action founded on the lex Aquilia, or Ovinia, or Furia, if instituted in the provinces, determines with the praetorship, and so it does if instituted at Rome before recuperators, or though instituted before a single judex, if the judex or a party is an alien; and, on the contrary, an action founded on the edict, if instituted at Rome, before a single judex, between Roman citizens, is statutable.

Imperium and Jurisdictio were the two component parts of Officium jus dicentis, i.e. the power of the magistrate (consul, praetor, curule edile) charged with the administration of civil justice.

Of these two elements, Jurisdictio denoted the power (perhaps originally vested in the Pontifex) of administering the civil law in the ordinary course of procedure. It consisted chiefly in presiding over the preliminary stages of litigation, and in the period of legis actiones was summed up in the utterance of the solemn words, Do, Dico, Addico; but in the formulary period it was performed, not by oral utterances, but by the delivery of written documents (verbis conceptis). In genuine litigation it was called jurisdictio contentiosa; in fictitious litigation, e.g. manumission by vindicta, alienation by in jure cessio, it was called jurisdictio voluntaria. Jurisdictio is sometimes used in a wider sense, as equivalent to officium jus dicentis.

Imperium as coupled with the administration of civil justice (imperium quod jurisdictioni cohaeret, Dig. 1, 21, 1), or as including it (cui etiam jurisdictio inest, Dig. 2, 1, 3), was called imperium mixtum, as opposed to imperium merum, or gladii potestas, the administration of criminal justice. Imperium mixtum may be divided into two functions, (1) cognitio extraordinaria and (2) actiones honorariae.

(1) Magistrates invested with imperium had the power of issuing commands (jus decernendi) to which they enforced obedience by fine (mulcta), distress (pignus), and imprisonment, and, as a preliminary to issuing a command (decretum), of summoning parties before them (vocatio) by means of a lictor, and conducting in person an investigation of facts (causae cognitio). To these functions of the praetor must be referred Restitutio in integrum, Missio in possessionem, and other proceedings which the praetor decided in person without reference to a judex, a form of procedure which finally superseded the ordo judiciorum or formulary system.

(2) But even of suits belonging to the ordo judiciorum, which conformed, that is, to the principle of appointing a judex, a portion must be referred to the praetor's imperium. All the new actions, unknown to the civil law, which the praetor invented in virtue of the powers conferred by the law of uncertain date that introduced the formulary system, the lex Aebutia; all fictitious actions and actions in factum; in a word, all actiones honorariae, were regarded, as we see by their name (judicia imperio continentia), as emanations rather of the praetorian imperium than of his jurisdictio.

Statutable actions were those which were assimilated to the actions of the law. The reason why some actions were assimilated in one of their incidents, that is, in duration, but not in another, that is, the power of extinguishing the right of action, was probably, as Heffter has suggested, as follows: Under the legis actiones, § 108, the same question could not be the subject of a second trial. The lex Aebutia, which abolished the two legis actiones, denominated condictio and judicis postulatio, and established in their stead the judicia and arbitria of the formulary system, probably enacted that these should have the same power of novation, 3 § 180, as the actions which they superseded, provided they were instituted between Roman citizens before a single judex, and within the first milestone. Proceedings, therefore, thus defined, when once instituted, extinguished the plaintiff's right of action. The provision of the lex Aebutia, however, was not interpreted as applicable to actions in factum; for actions in factum were used precisely in those cases where no right was recognized by the civil law, that is, where no right was enforceable by the legis actiones. Nor was it applied to Real actions, for these were left by the lex Aebutia to be decided by the sacramentum, and though they were finally absorbed by the formulary system, no law, apparently, ever enacted that in these cases the formulary procedure should have the same effect as the legis actio, and extinguish ipso jure the plaintiff's right of action. In Real actions and actions in factum, therefore, even though in other respects they were legitima, that is, fell under the definition of the lex Aebutia, the defendant required the protection of the exceptio rei judicatae. The lex Julia judiciaria, on the contrary, extended to all actions that satisfy the terms of the lex Aebutia.

§ 109. The nature of the lex Ovinia is not known. There were several leges Furiae: the lex Furia Caninia, 1 § 42, limiting testamentary manumission, the lex Furia testamentaria, 2 § 225, limiting donations in contemplation of death, and the lex Furia de sponsu, 3 § 121, limiting the responsibility of sponsors and fidepromissors.

The same imperium mixtum whence emanated new actions in favour of the plaintiff also issued exceptions in favour of the defendant, and in particular the exceptio rei judicatae, which supplemented the novation or consumption of a right of action recognized by the civil law (ipso jure, § 106). The aim of the legislator in barring once-used rights of action by consumption (novatio) or exceptio rei judicatae, was to protect a defendant from being harassed by successive suits, and to guard against the public evil which would arise in the shape of a general unsettlement and uncertainty of rights if judicial decisions were not conclusive. Singulis controversiis singulas actiones unumque judicati finem sufficere probabili ratione placuit, ne aliter modus litium multiplicatus summam atque inexplicabilem faciat difficultatem, maxime si diversae pronuncientur, Dig. 44, 2, 6. 'That one right of action should only be tried once is a reasonable rule to prevent interminable litigation and the embarrassment of contrary decisions.' Accordingly, it was adopted as a maxim that (in the absence of appeal or after appeal) judicial decisions should be assumed to be true. Res judicata pro veritate accipitur, Dig. 1, 5, 25. The principle may be stated more at length as follows: A judgment shall not be contradicted by a judgment in a subsequent trial between the same parties where the same right is in question (except, of course, by the judgment of a court of appeal). Exceptio rei judicatae obstat quotiens inter easdem personas eadem quaestio revocatur vel alio genere judicii, Dig. 44, 2, 7, 4. 'The plea of previous judgment is a bar whenever the same question of right is renewed between the same parties by whatever form of action.' Let us consider more minutely the import of this rule.

The parties must be the same. Res inter alios judicatae nullum aliis praejudicium faciunt, Dig. 44, 2, 1. 'A judgment between certain parties does not determine the rights of other parties.' The form of action is immaterial provided that the same right is contested. Thus a depositor, lender, pledgor, may recover damages for injury to the thing deposited, lent, or pledged, either by action on his contract or under the lex Aquilia, but if cast in one, he cannot bring the other. It is otherwise if the right contested is really different; if in one action a plaintiff claims a jus in rem, in the other a jus in personam. Paulus respondit, ei qui in rem egisset nec tenuisset, postea condicenti non obstare exceptionem rei judicatae, Dig. 44, 3, 31. 'If a plaintiff after losing a real action brings a personal action, he is not barred by the plea of previous judgment.'

The term 'the same right' must be taken to include a right and its correlative obligation; in other words, it is immaterial that the position of plaintiff and defendant is inverted. Si quis rem a non domino emerit, mox petente domino absolutus sit, deinde possessionem amiserit, et a domino petierit, adversus exceptionem: Si non ejus sit res, replicatione hac adjuvabitur: At si res judicata non sit, Dig. 44, 2, 24. 'A purchaser of a thing from a non-proprietor, sued for it by the true proprietor and acquitted, afterwards losing possession thereof, and seeking (by actio Publiciana, 2 § 43) to recover it from the former proprietor, may meet the exception by which he pleads true dominion by the replication of previous judgment.' This example further shows that the plea, though invented chiefly to protect defendants, is sometimes available for plaintiffs.

When the same right is in question it is immaterial that the subject or secondary object (2 § 1, commentary) of the right is different. Thus, a plaintiff claiming to be heir, who fails when he brings hereditatis petitio for Blackacre, cannot afterwards bring hereditatis petitio for Whiteacre as a part of the same inheritance.

Perhaps the same right may be in question even when the primary object, the benefit which the right immediately contemplates, is different. Thus, a plaintiff who fails in a condictio furtiva brought to recover stolen property, cannot afterwards maintain an actio furti to recover a penalty for theft. We might say that the plaintiff has a single compound right, to recover his property and to recover a penalty, but perhaps it is more accurate to say that he has two separate rights which, however, stand or fall together by necessary implication, and to bring this case under the following head.

It is immaterial, namely, whether a proposition was decided as the final question, or as an essential element and immediate ground of the final decision. Every judgment is a decision not only on the ultimate issue, but by implication on all the antecedent pleas, not only the exception, replication, duplication (for these are exclusively propositions valid in equity but invalid at civil law), but also on all facts, e.g. solutio, acceptilatio, novatio, which would be put in issue in English pleading, as necessary to legitimate the final decision, even if, as forming answers valid at civil law, they would not be expressed in a Roman formula. Thus, a plaintiff who fails when he sues by real action for a particular thing, or by a personal action for a debt, basing his claim on the presupposition of his succession to a person deceased, cannot afterwards claim the whole succession by hereditatis petitio. Hence we often meet with praescriptio praejudicialis, e.g. Ea res agatur si in ea re praejudicium hereditati non fiat, § 133, or exceptio praejudicialis, e.g. extra quam si in reum capitis praejudicium fiat, Cic. de Inventione, 2, 20; i.e. dilatory pleas whereby a party seeks to postpone a less important issue (causa minor) until a more important issue (causa major) with which it is indissolubly connected, shall have been decided.

Observe that the rule is, a judgment shall not be contradicted by a judgment in another action when the same right is in question, not, when the same title is in question. The latter expression would be sufficient to meet the case of personal actions. Here every different obligation is ground to support a different action, and every different title engenders a different obligation. But the rule so stated would not adequately meet the case of real actions. Here it is immaterial that the plaintiff alleges a different title. There can be many obligations between the same parties in respect of the same subject; but the same subject only admits of one true dominion, and consequently of only one true title to dominion. Hence the plaintiff in a real action was required to adduce all his fancied titles on pain of being barred by the exception of res judicata, and if, for instance, he claims ownership on the ground of tradition he cannot afterwards claim by another title, e.g. usucapion; or if he fails in a claim as testamentary heir, he cannot afterwards claim as heir by descent, Dig. 44, 2, 11, 5, and 44, 2, 14, 2. The rule, of course, does not apply to a title not in existence at the time of the former action (causa superveniens), and it is defeated if the plaintiff takes the precaution expressly to limit the former action (probably by means of a praescriptio) to the investigation of a specific title, a limitation called causae adjectio. If he was allowed by the praetor to do this and failed in his suit, he could afterwards claim dominion by a different title. Si quis petat fundum suum esse, eo quod Titius eum sibi tradiderit; si postea eum alia ex causa petat, causa adjecta, non debet summoveri exceptione, Dig. 44, 2, 11, 2. 'A plaintiff who loses an action in which he claimed property in land on the ground of delivery of possession, is not barred by exception from bringing another real action, if he expressly limited the former to a specific title.'

The exceptio rei in judicium deductae was available if proceedings had formerly reached the stage of litis contestatio. This was a powerful spur to make the plaintiff accelerate his proceedings, as if he had not obtained judgment at the end of a year or eighteen months, his action expired and, his right of action being consumed, could not be renewed.

DE PERPETUIS ET TEMPORALIBUS ACTIONIBUS ET QUAE AD HEREDES VEL IN HEREDES TRANSEUNT.

§ 110. Quo loco admonendi *sumus*, eas quidem actiones quae ex lege senatusve consultis proficiscuntur, perpetuo solere Praetorem accommodare: eas vero quae ex propria ipsius iurisdictione pendent, plerumque intra annum dare.

§ 110. Actions founded on a law or senatusconsultum are perpetual; those founded on the edict are usually annual.

§ 111. Aliquando tamen *ipse quoque Praetor in actionibus* imitatur ius legitimum: quales sunt eae quas *Praetor bonorum possess*oribus ceterisque *qui* heredis loco sunt *accommodat*. *fur*ti quoque manifesti

§ 111. But some of them are perpetual; for instance, those which are granted to the praetorian successor and to a person treated as successor. So for theft detected in the commission, the action, though

actio, quamvis ex ipsius Praetoris iurisdictione *pro*ficiscatur, perpetuo datur; et merito, cum pro capitali poena pecuniaria constituta sit.

praetorian, is perpetual; and properly so, the pecuniary penalty being a mitigation of capital punishment.

§ 112. Non omnes actiones quae in ali*quem aut ipso iure com*petunt aut a Praetore dantur, etiam in heredem *aeque competunt aut da*ri solent. est enim certissima iuris regula, ex maleficii*s* poenales actiones in heredem nec co*m*petere *nec Praetorem dare*, velut furti, vi bonorum raptorum, iniuriarum, damni iniuriae: *sed heredibus* actoris huiusmodi actiones comp*etunt* nec denegantur, excepta iniuriarum actione, et si qua alia similis *in*veniatur actio.

§ 112. The actions, whether civil or praetorian, that lie against a man do not always lie against his successor, the rule being absolute that for delict, for instance, theft, rapine, outrage, injury to property, no penal action, civil or praetorian, lies against the successor of the delinquent; but the successor of the plaintiff may bring these actions except in outrage and a few similar cases.

§ 113. Aliquando tamen *etiam* ex contractu actio neque heredi neque in heredem co*m*petit. nam adstipulatoris heres non habet actionem, *et* sponsoris *et* fidepromissoris heres non tenetur.

§ 113. An action upon contract cannot always be brought by the successor of the plaintiff, nor against the successor of the defendant; for the successor of the adstipulator has no action, nor does any lie against the successor of the sponsor or fidepromissor.

SI REUS ANTE REM IUDICATAM SATISFACIAT ACTORI.

§ 114. Superest ut d*i*spiciamus, si ante rem iudicatam is cum quo agitur post acceptum iudicium satisfaciat actori, quid officio iudicis conveniat: utrum absolvere, an ideo potius damnare, quia iudicii accipiendi tempore in ea causa fuit, ut damnari debeat. nostri praeceptores absolvere eum debere existimant: nec interesse cuius generis f*ue*rit iudicium. et hoc est quod volgo dicitur Sabino et Cassio placere omnia iudicia esse absolutoria. *De bonae fidei* iudi*ciis autem* idem sentiunt *diversae scholae auctores*, q*uod* in *his quidem* iudiciis liberum est officium iudicis. tantumdem *etiam de in* rem actionibus putant . . . . . . [*desunt 17 lin.*]

§ 114. We next inquire whether, if the defendant before judgment is pronounced, but after the formula is delivered, satisfies the plaintiff, the judex has power to absolve him, or must condemn him, because he was liable to condemnation when the formula was delivered. The authorities of my school hold that he should be absolved in every kind of action; and hence the saying that Sabinus and Cassius consider all actions to involve the power of absolution. The other school agree in respect of bona fide actions, where the judex has more discretion, and of real actions . . .

§ 110. Having considered what time may elapse between the commencement of an action (litis contestatio) and its termination (sententia lata), Gaius proceeds to inquire what time may elapse between the nativity of an action or the event which gives the right of action (actio nata) and the commencement of the action or joinder in issue.

The duration of the actions which Gaius calls perpetual was subsequently limited to thirty years, and in a few exceptional cases to forty years, though the actions were still called Perpetual. See the constitution of Theodosius, A.D. 424, Codex, 7, 39, 3.

§ 111. Those praetorian actions which simply claimed restoration or compensation were perpetual. In honorariis actionibus sic esse definiendum, Cassius ait, ut quae rei persecutionem habeant, hae etiam post annum darentur, ceterae intra annum, Dig. 44, 7, 35. 'Praetorian actions, according to Cassius, are perpetual when brought for restitution, annual when penal.' Those praetorian actions which were perpetual also lay against the successors of the defendant. Condictio rei furtivae, quia rei habet persecutionem heredem quoque furis obligat, Dig. 13, 1, 7. 'A personal action at civil law to recover stolen property, being purely remedial, lies against the successor of the thief.' The penal actions, however, lay against the successor of the defendant, with a taxation, that is, so far as he was enriched by the wrong of the original defendant. Honorariae autem, quae post annum non dantur, nec in heredem dandae sunt, ut tamen lucrum ei extorqueatur, Dig. 44, 7, 35. 'Those Praetorian actions which are annual do not lie against the successor of the defendant except so far as the successor has benefited by the wrong.' Once brought, however, they pass to the successor of the plaintiff, and against the successor of the defendant. Poenales autem actiones, si ab ipsis principalibus personis fuerint contestatae, et heredibus dantur et contra heredes transeunt, Inst. 4, 12, 1. 'Penal actions instituted between the principals pass to their successors.'

The principle may be thus stated: actions where, if judgment passes for the plaintiff, there is a gain for the plaintiff and loss for the defendant (poenales) are annual: actions where there is neither gain for the plaintiff nor loss for the defendant (persecutoriae) are perpetual: intermediate actions, i. e. where there is no gain to the plaintiff but possibly a loss to the defendant, (indemnificatory) if contrary to civil law, are annual. Thus the actio doli mali, though only for indemnification, was annual; but if the damages were limited to the amount gained by the defendant, in which case the action was persecutoria, it was perpetual, Dig. 4, 3, 28.

When a right of action was limited to a year, this was an annus utilis, that is, a year of dies utiles, of days open to jurisdiction, and on which the plaintiff was not hindered by any insurmountable obstacle, such as absence of plaintiff or defendant, illness of plaintiff and inability to appoint a procurator, Dig. 44, 3, 1. An annus utilis, though nominally a year, might really be a much longer period. Where a right of action lasted beyond a year, every day was counted (tempus continuum), 2 § 173.

The English law is more favourable to the party injured in actions ex delicto.

The executors of a testator and administrators of an intestate have the same remedy for injury to the personal property of the deceased as he would have had in his lifetime.

For an injury committed against his real property within six months of his death, they may bring an action within one year after his death. And for an injury to either real or personal property committed within six months before the death of the wrong-doer, an action may be brought against his executors or administrators within six months after they have taken on themselves administration.

Vindictive actions, that is, civil suits founded on the violation of primordial rights, and brought rather for satisfaction to the feelings than for indemnification to the property of the plaintiff, for example, actions for slander, in English as in Roman law are extinguished by the death of either party. See §§ 6–9.

§ 114. Respecting the power of absolution, Justinian confirmed the opinion of the Sabinians, Inst. 4, 12, 2.

DE EXCEPTIONIBUS.

§ 115. Sequitur ut de exceptionibus dispiciamus.

§ 116. Comparatae sunt autem exceptiones defendendorum eorum gratia cum quibus agitur: saepe enim accidit, ut quis iure civili teneatur, sed iniquum sit eum iudicio condemnari. velut *si* stipulatus sim a te pecuniam tamquam credendi causa numeraturus, nec

§ 115. We have next to examine the nature of Exceptions.

§ 116. Exceptions are intended for the protection of the defendant when, as often happens, he is under a liability by the civil law, and yet it would be contrary to equity if he were condemned. If, for instance, I have made you solemnly promise to pay me a sum of money, as a

numeraverim. nam eam pecuniam a te peti posse certum est; dare enim te oportet, cum ex stipulatu teneris: sed quia iniquum est te eo nomine condemnari, placet per exceptionem doli mali te defendi debere. item si pactus fuero tecum, ne id quod mihi debeas a te petam, nihilominus id ipsum a te petere possum DARE MIHI OPORTERE, quia obligatio pacto convento non tollitur: sed placet debere me petentem per exceptionem pacti conventi repelli.

preliminary to my advancing you the money, and then never advanced it; I can sue you for the money, for you are bound by the promise, but it would be iniquitous that you should be compelled to fulfil such a promise, and therefore you are permitted to impeach my claim by the exception of Fraud. Or if I agreed not to demand a debt, the civil law would still permit me to demand it, because mere agreement cannot extinguish civil obligations, but my demand would be avoided by an exception alleging the agreement.

§ 117. In his quoque actionibus quae *non* in personam sunt exceptiones locum habent. velut si metu me coegeris aut dolo induxeris, ut *t*ibi rem aliquam mancipio dem; na*m* si eam rem a me petas, datur mihi exceptio per quam, si metus causa te fecisse vel dolo malo arguero, repelleris. item si fundum litigiosum sciens a non possidente emeris eumque a possidente petas, opponitur tibi exceptio, per quam omnimodo summoveris.

§ 117. Real actions also admit of exceptions; for instance, if by threats of violence or by fraud you drove or seduced me to grant a thing to you by mancipation; if you sue me for it, I am allowed to plead intimidation or fraud, and if I prove it, defeat your claim; or if you knew an estate was a subject of litigation, and bought it of a person not in possession, when you claim it of a person in possession you are defeated by an exception.

§ 118. Exceptiones autem alias in edicto Praetor habet propositas, alias causa cognita accommodat. quae omnes vel ex legibus vel ex his quae legis vicem optinent substantiam capiunt, vel ex iurisdictione Praetoris proditae sunt.

§ 118. Exceptions are either provided by the edict, or, on cause shown are granted by the praetor, and are either founded on law or something equivalent to law, or on the praetor's judicature.

§ 119. Omnes autem exceptiones in contrarium concipiuntur, qu*am* adfirmat is cum quo agitur. nam si verbi gratia re*us* dolo malo aliquid actorem facere dicat, qui forte pecuniam petit quam non numeravit, sic exceptio concipitur: SI IN EA RE NIHIL DOLO MALO AULI AGERII FACTUM SIT NEQUE FIAT. item si dicatu*r* contra pactionem pecunia peti, ita concipitur exceptio: SI INTER AULUM AGERIUM ET NUMERIUM NEGIDIUM NON CONVENIT NE EA PECUNIA PETERETUR. et denique

§ 119. Exceptions take the form of a supposition opposite to the allegation of the defendant; if, for example, the defendant imputes fraud to the plaintiff in that he sues for money which he never advanced, the exception is thus expressed: 'If in that matter there was and is no fraud of Aulus Agerius.' Again, if he allege an agreement not to claim the money, the exception is thus formulated: 'If Aulus Agerius and Numerius Negidius did not agree that the money should not be

in ceteris causis similiter concipi solet. ideo scilicet, quia omnis exceptio obicitur quidem a reo, sed ita formulae inseritur, ut condicionalem faciat condemnationem, id est ne aliter iudex eum cum quo agitur condemnet, quam si nihil in ea re *qua* de agitur dolo actoris factum sit; item ne aliter iudex eum condemnet, quam si nullum pactum conventum de non petenda pecunia factum erit.

demanded;' and so in other cases. For every exception is alleged by the defendant but is inserted in the formula as a (second) condition of the condemnation, that is, the judex is instructed not to condemn the defendant unless (firstly, the intentio is proved, and secondly) the plaintiff is clear of fraud in the matter, or unless there was no agreement that the debt should not be claimed.

§ 120. Dicuntur autem exceptiones aut peremptoriae aut dilatoriae.

§ 120. Exceptions are either peremptory or dilatory.

§ 121. Peremptoriae sunt quae perpetuo valent, nec evitari possunt, velut quod metus causa, aut dolo malo, aut quod contra legem senatusve consultum factum est, aut quod res iudicata est vel in iudicium deducta est, item pacti conventi quo pactum est ne omnino pecunia peteretur.

§ 121. Peremptory exceptions are those which are of unlimited duration and insurmountable, as the plea of intimidation, fraud, contravention of law or senatusconsultum, previous decision or litigation, or agreement never to sue.

§ 122. Dilatoriae sunt exceptiones quae ad tempus nocent, veluti illius pacti conventi quod factum est verbi gratia ne intra quinquennium peteretur: finito enim eo tempore non habet locum exceptio. cui similis exceptio est litis dividuae et rei residuae. nam si quis partem rei petierit et intra eiusdem praeturam reliquam partem petat, hac exceptione summovetur, quae appellatur litis dividuae. item si is qui cum eodem plures lites habebat, de quibusdam egerit, de quibusdam distulerit, ut ad alios iudices eant, si intra eiusdem praeturam de his quae ita distulerit agat, per hanc exceptionem quae appellatur rei residuae summovetur.

§ 122. Dilatory exceptions are merely temporary obstructions, such as an agreement that a debt shall not be sued for within five years, for in five years the exception ceases to be pleadable. There are similar exceptions against division or separation of actions. After suing for part of a debt if a man sue for the remainder in the same praetorship, he is barred by the exception against division of actions. Or, when a man who has several claims against the same defendant brings some actions and postpones others in order to come before a new panel of judices, if within the same praetorship he bring any of the postponed actions, he is met by the exception against separation of actions.

§ 123. Observandum est autem ei cui dilatoria obicitur exceptio, ut differat actionem: alioquin si obiecta exceptione egerit, rem perdit. nec enim post illud tempus quo integra re evitare poterat, adhuc ei potestas agendi superest, re in iudi-

§ 123. A plaintiff liable to a dilatory exception should be careful to postpone his action, for the exception once pleaded is fatal; and although, if the matter had never been mooted, time would have removed the obstacle, yet it will not

cium deducta et per exceptionem perempta.

§ 124. Non solum autem ex tempore, sed etiam ex persona dilatoriae exceptiones intelleguntur, quales sunt cognitoriae; velut si is qui per edictum cognitorem dare non potest per cognitorem agat, vel dandi quidem cognitoris ius habeat, sed eum det cui non licet cognituram suscipere. nam si obiciatur exceptio cognitoria, si ipse talis erit, ut ei non liceat cognitorem dare, ipse agere potest: si vero cognitori non liceat cognituram suscipere, per alium cognitorem aut per semet ipsum liberam habet agendi potestatem, et *potest* tam hoc quam illo modo evitare exceptionem. quod si dissimulaverit *eam* et per cognitorem *egerit, rem perdit.*

§ 125. *Sed* peremptoria quidem exceptione cum *reus per errorem* non fuit usus, in integrum restitu*itur servan*dae exceptionis gratia: dilatoria vero si non *fuit usus*, an in integrum restitu*a*tur, quaeritur.

now, as his right has been litigated and extinguished.

§ 124. Irrespective of time, personal incapacities produce dilatory exceptions, such as those which relate to the office of cognitor, for some persons are disabled by the edict from appointing a cognitor, and others are disabled from discharging the office of cognitor. A principal disabled from appointing a cognitor can sue in his own name, and if one person is disabled from acting as cognitor, the principal can employ another, or sue in his own name, and in either way avoid the exception; but if he disregard the incapacity and sue by cognitor, he throws away his remedy.

§ 125. If a peremptory exception be inadvertently omitted, the defendant is relieved, and allowed to amend his defence: whether the same is true of a dilatory exception, is a matter of controversy.

DE REPLICATIONIBUS.

§ 126. Interdum evenit, ut exceptio quae prima facie iusta videatur, inique noceat actori. Quod cum accidat, alia adiectione opus est adiuvandi actoris gratia: quae adiectio replicatio vocatur, quia per eam replicatur atque resolvitur *vis* exceptionis. nam si verbi gratia pactus sim tecum, ne pecuniam quam mihi debes a te peterem, deinde postea in contrarium pacti sumus, id est ut petere mihi liceat, et si agam tecum, excipias tu, ut ita demum mihi condemneris, si non convenerit ne eam pecuniam peterem, nocet mihi exceptio pacti conventi; namque nihilominus hoc verum manet, etiam si postea in contrarium pacti simus. sed qu*i*a iniquum est me excludi exceptione,

§ 126. Sometimes an exception, which on the face seems just to the defendant, is unjust to the plaintiff, and then, to protect the plaintiff, the praetor adds to the instructions a clause called Replicatio, because it parries and avoids the exception. If, for instance, after we agreed that I should not sue you for a debt, we agreed that I might sue; if, when I sue, you plead the agreement that I should not sue, you bar my claim, for your allegation is true; but, as it would be unjust that I should be prevented from recovering, I am allowed to reply by pleading the subsequent agreement, thus: 'If there was no subsequent agreement that I might sue.' So if a banker sue for the price of goods sold by

replicatio mihi datur ex posteriore pacto *hoc* modo: SI NON POSTEA CONVENERIT UT EAM PECUNIAM PETERE LICERET. item si argentarius pretium rei quae in auctionem venierit persequatur, obicitur ei exceptio, ut ita demum emptor damnetur, si ei res quam emerit tradita *esset: quae est* iusta exceptio. sed si in auctione praedictum est, ne ante emptori traderetur res quam si pretium solverit, replicatione tali argentarius adiuvatur: AUT SI PRAEDICTUM EST NE ALITER EMPTORI RES TRADERETUR QUAM SI PRETIUM EMPTOR SOLVERIT.

auction, he may be met by the plea that they were never delivered, and this is a valid exception. But if it was a condition of the sale, that the goods should not be delivered to the purchaser before payment of the purchase-money, the banker is permitted to insert the Replicatio: 'or if it was a condition of the sale that the goods should not be delivered till the price was paid.'

§ 127. Interdum autem evenit, ut rursus replicatio quae prima facie iusta sit, inique reo noceat. quod cum accidat, adiectione opus est adiuvandi rei gratia, quae duplicatio vocatur.

§ 127. Sometimes a Replicatio, though just on the face, is unjust to the defendant; and then, to protect the defendant, the praetor adds a clause called Duplicatio.

§ 128. Et si rursus ea prima facie iusta videatur, sed propter aliquam causam inique actori noceat, rursus *ea* adiectione opus est qua actor adiuvetur, quae dicitur triplicatio.

§ 128. Again, if this, though just in appearance, is unjust to the plaintiff, he is protected by another clause called Triplicatio.

§ 129. Quarum omnium adiectionum usum interdum etiam ulterius quam diximus varietas negotiorum introduxit.

§ 129. And sometimes further additions are required by the multiplicity of successive transactions.

The formulary procedure contained nothing corresponding to the English system of pleading, that is, contained no method for determining the exact point in dispute between the plaintiff and defendant. For such rules we must have recourse not to the jurists but to the rhetoricians, that is, to Greek teachers whose rules contemplated originally the practice of Greek courts and were addressed to Greek orators, and betrayed their exotic origin by the vacillation in their Latin expression. Whether their doctrines are expressed in Greek or Latin, it is obvious that the ultimate source of all their rules is to be found in the Rhetoric of Aristotle. According to Aristotle the issue, *τὸ ἀμφισβητούμενον* (subsequently called *στάσις* or status) in forensic oratory is a question of fact (*γεγονέναι ἢ μὴ γεγονέναι*, status inficialis or conjecturalis), a question of law (*ποῖον*, status juridicialis), or a question of assessment (ποσόν). If the defendant simply traversed, that is, contradicted, the fact alleged in the plaintiff's declaration, or demurred to his law, no necessity was felt for distinguishing between the original and final question. In his causis eadem et prima quaestio et disceptatio est extrema, Cicero, Partitiones, 30. But the defendant might allege in his plea some new matter not mentioned in the declaration, and the plaintiff in his replication might allege some new matter not mentioned in the plea, and then it was felt desirable to distinguish the different stages of the controversy, and name the successive allegations, from the first demand of the plaintiff to the final issue. In the Partitiones, Cicero calls the first general claim of the plaintiff and general denial of the defendant prima causae conflictio; the defendant's plea in avoidance Ratio; the plaintiff's replication Firmamentum; and the final issue Disceptatio. Sed, distinguendi gratia, rationem appellamus eam quae affertur ab reo ad recusandum, depellendi criminis causa; quae nisi esset, quod defenderet non haberet: firmamentum autem quod contra ad labefactandam rationem refertur, sine quo accusatio stare non potest. Ex rationis autem et ex firmamenti conflictione et quasi concursu quaestio exoritur quaedam, quam disceptationem voco .... Nam prima adversariorum contentio diffusam habet quaestionem .... Rationum et firmamentorum contentio adducit in angustum disceptationem, Partitiones, 29, 30. 'For the sake of distinction the allegation whereby the defendant avoids the charge, and which constitutes his defence, may be called a Plea; the allegation whereby the plaintiff encounters the plea, and without which the accusation falls to the ground, may be called a Replication. The conflict of Plea and Replication produces what we may call the final issue. The opposing allegations are at first general and indeterminate, but the joinder in issue on the Plea and Replication confines the controversy to a specific question.' In the Topica he had applied the term Firmamentum to the defendant's plea, or rather, to any of the pleadings that precede the final issue. Sed quae ex statu contentio efficitur eam Graeci τὸ κρινόμενον vocant: mihi placet id, quoniam quidem ad te scribo, qua de re agitur vocari. Quibus autem hoc qua de re agitur continetur, ea continentia vocentur, quasi firmamenta defensionis quibus sublatis defensio nulla sit, Topica, 25. 'The conflict that arises from the status' (rather, the status itself) 'the Greeks call τὸ κρινόμενον; in addressing you, a special pleader, I will call it the matter in question. The grounds on which it rests, and without which no (action or) defence could be maintained, may be called continentia or firmamenta.' For a long and feeble examination of the subject, see Quintilian, 3, 6: he observes that if we define status as prima causarum conflictio we must understand prima not in a chronological sense, but as equivalent to principalis, that is, he requires us to identify status with τὸ κρινόμενον or extrema disceptatio.

The formulary system contains no method for determining the precise point in issue so as to prevent either party from being taken by surprise. The successive definition and narrowing of the question was not the work of the lawyer, accomplished before the praetor referred the action to the judex, but of the orator who advocated the cause: and the rhetoricians, whose rules were the germ of the English system of pleading, never refer to the intentio, exceptio, and replicatio of the Roman formula. When, indeed, the intentio was in factum concepta, si paret .... fecisse, it contained the final issue; but if it was in jus concepta, si paret .... oportere, there might be any number of successive pleadings, which, if they were valid by the civil law, would not be disclosed by the formula. The exceptio and replicatio consisted exclusively of equitable allegations invalid by the civil law. As the division of law into law and equity is not founded on the nature of things, and only depends on historic accidents, the English and Roman divisions do not coincide. If, indeed, it happened that what was an equitable plea at Rome was valid at common law in England, then the Intentio, Exceptio, and Replicatio of the Roman formula would correspond to the Declaration, Plea, and Replication of the English action. Again, if it happened that the same matter was a bad legal but a good equitable plea in both systems, the Roman formula and English pleading would now coincide: for by the 83rd section of the Common Law Procedure Act of 1854, the defendant in any cause in any of the superior courts, in which if judgment were obtained he would be entitled to relief on equitable grounds, may plead the facts which entitle him to such relief by way of defence; though before that Act, instead of pleading to the action he would have had to file a bill in chancery for an injunction to stay legal proceedings.

The following, however, requires to be observed. A plea is

either a traverse, that is, a contradiction of a fact alleged, or a confession and avoidance, that is, an admission of the fact alleged and an allegation of some further fact. A simple traverse would not be expressed by any adjectio, or additional clause, on the formula, and the exceptio, therefore, would only correspond to the plea in confession and avoidance. The Roman defendant, however, who pleaded an exceptio, did not by implication admit the allegation of the plaintiff. Non utique existimatur confiteri de intentione adversarius quocum agitur qui exceptione utitur, Dig. 43, 1, 9. 'The defendant who makes an exceptio does not necessarily confess the allegation of the intentio.' Nam si etiam de intentione dubitas, habita exceptionis contestatione, tunc demum quum intentionem suam secundum asseverationem suam petitor probaverit, huic esse locum monstrari (non?) convenit, Codex, 8, 36, 9. 'If you deny the truth of the intentio, although you have been allowed to make an exceptio, the intentio must be proved by the plaintiff before you are called on to prove the exceptio.' But an English defendant who pleads in confession and avoidance, as the terms imply, is precluded from disputing the truth of the plaintiff's allegation; and, originally, he could only make one plea in answer to one count of the declaration. Since, however, by the 81st section of the Common Law Procedure Act of 1852, liberty is given to each party by leave of the court to set up as many answers at every stage of the proceedings as he shall think necessary, if the defendant pleads both by traverse and in confession and avoidance he may compel the plaintiff to prove his allegation before he himself is put to the proof of the new matter by which it is avoided.

As the Exceptio merely impowered the judex to take into consideration equitable grounds of defence, no exceptio was necessary in actions ex fide bona, for here the commission of the judex expressly authorized him in the intentio of the formula to decide upon equitable grounds, § 47. Doli exceptio inest de dote actioni ut in ceteris bonae fidei judiciis, Dig. 24, 3, 21. 'The exception of fraud is implied in the action of dower as in other equitable actions.' Judicium bonae fidei continet in se doli mali exceptionem, Dig. 30, 1; 84, 5. We must except, however, the exceptio rei judicatae and others like cognitoria and litis residuae, which are founded rather on political than on equitable considerations.

§ 116. Fraud was not by civil law a cause of avoiding a stipulation, and therefore in actions stricti juris the defendant, if he meant to allege fraud, required an exceptio to be inserted in the formula. The exception of fraud, being discreditable to the plaintiff, could not be alleged against a patron, but had to be transformed into an exception of fact. Adversus parentes patronosque neque doli exceptio neque alia quidem quae patroni parentisve opinionem aut bonos mores sugillet competere potest. In factum tamen erit excipiendum, ut, si forte pecunia non numerata dicatur, objiciatur exceptio pecuniae non numeratae, Dig. 44, 4; 4, 16. 'Against parents or patrons neither fraud nor any other discreditable exception lies, but the exception must be an allegation of fact; for instance, the non-payment of money.' All exceptions in factum may be transformed into an exception of fraud. Et generaliter sciendum est, ex omnibus in factum exceptionibus doli oriri exceptionem, quia dolo facit quicunque id, quod quaqua exceptione elidi potest, petit; nam, etsi inter initia nihil dolo malo fecit, attamen nunc petendo facit dolose, nisi si talis sit ignorantia in eo ut dolo careat, Dig. 44, 4, 2, 5. 'All exceptions of fact may give rise to an exception of fraud, for it is fraudulent to claim when barred by equity: and if there was no original fraud, the present claim is fraudulent, unless made in ignorance.'

The exceptio doli was personal (in personam scripta), that is, named the author of the fraud, and herein differed from the exceptio metus, which was impersonal (in rem scripta), that is, did not name the authors of the violence, doubtless because intimidation is often the work of persons in disguise. Etenim distat aliquid metus causa exceptio a doli exceptione, quod exceptio doli personam complectitur ejus qui dolo fecit, enim vero metus causa exceptio in rem scripta est: si in ea re nihil metus causa factum est: ut non inspiciamus an is qui agit metus causa fecerit aliquid, sed an omnino metus causa factum sit in hac re a quocunque, non tantum ab eo qui agit, Dig. 44, 4; 4, 33. 'There is this difference between the exception of violence and the generic exception of fraud; the latter names the author of the fraud, the former does not name the author of the violence, but is in the terms: "If in that matter there was no intimidation," and the judge does not inquire whether the author of the violence was the plaintiff.'

The exceptio non numeratae pecuniae could originally only be alleged within the period of a year; Marcus Aurelius extended this period to five years, Justinian reduced it to two, Codex, 4, 30, 14.

There was this peculiarity about it, that while in other exceptions the burden of proof was on the defendant: Qui excipit probare debet quod excipitur, Dig. 22, 3, 9, 'The exception must be proved by the defendant;' Reus in exceptione actor est, Dig. 44, 1, 1, 'The defendant is plaintiff in respect of the exception:' in the exceptio pecuniae non numeratae the burden of proof was on the plaintiff. The effect of this was virtually to abolish Formal, i.e. Verbal (verbis) and Literal (literis) contracts in the case of loan; for the plaintiff had to prove his execution of the consideration, that is, a Formless or Real (re) contract, and was not entitled to recover on mere proof of Formal contract by stipulatio or expensilatio.

§ 117. Qui contra edictum divi Augusti rem litigiosam a non possidente comparavit, praeterquam quod emptio nullius momenti est, poenam quinquaginta sestertiorum fisco repraesentare compellitur, Fragmentum de jure fisci. 'If in contravention of the edict of Augustus a subject of litigation is purchased of a vendor not in possession, the sale is void, and the purchaser forfeits fifty sestertia to the treasury.'

Justinian enacted that a man who knowingly purchased a litigious thing should not recover the price; a man who purchased in ignorance should recover a third more than the price, Codex, 8, 38, 4. By English law Champerty avoids a contract, and constitutes a complete defence to an action. One species of champerty consists in buying or selling a pretended or doubtful title to land not in possession of the seller, but held adversely by another person. In such a sale it is immaterial whether the title of the vendor be good or bad, if the land be held adversely to him. But where the party selling land does not know that there is an adverse possession, he would not be liable to the statute penalty for selling the pretended title, even although he should know that there was an adverse claim. Again, the purchase of real estate, if made with a knowledge that it is in suit, is void for champerty, unless it be made in consummation of a previous bargain. This rule, however, does not apply to sales or assignments of personal property, whether choses in possession (movables) or choses in action (obligations). In relation to personal property the rule is, that any debt or claims may be assigned after the institution of a suit for the recovery thereof, unless the assignment savor of maintenance, i.e. be designed to stir up strife and foment litigation.

§ 118. Exceptions properly consist of equitable considerations that are not strictly speaking a portion of the law; yet we find that some laws gave rise to exceptions, that is to say, from the modesty or timidity of the legislator, or some other reason, they were merely put on the footing of jus praetorium.

Instances of this were the lex Cincia, limiting the power of donations inter vivos; the lex Julia, permitting the insolvent to avoid seizure of his person and property by cessio bonorum; the Senatusconsultum Macedonianum, prohibiting loans to a filiusfamilias without the sanction of the paterfamilias; the Sc. Velleianum, prohibiting the suretyship of women; and the Sc. Trebellianum, exempting a heres, who had been merely a trustee to convey, from the pursuit of the creditors.

§ 121. The right of action quod dolo malo factum est to recover the amount of loss incurred by fraud, being penal in respect of the defendant, only lasted for a year. After that the plaintiff had merely an action in factum for damages to the amount the defendant had gained. Sed utique in heredem perpetuo dabitur, quia non debet lucrari ex alieno damno. Cui conveniens est, ut et in ipsum qui dolo commiserit, in id quod locupletior esset, perpetuo danda sit in factum actio, Dig. 4, 3, 28. 'The successor of the person guilty of fraud may always be sued so far as he is enriched by the fraud, and to the same extent the principal may always be sued by an action in factum.'

The action quod metus causa, like that for fraud, was an actio arbitraria, § 47, and during one year was bilaterally penal and lay for fourfold damages; after that, only lay for simple damages, and was purely Conservative. Si quis non restituat in quadruplum in eum judicium pollicetur. Satis enim clementer cum reo praetor egit ut daret ei restituendi facultatem si vult poenam evitare. Post annum vero in simplum actionem pollicetur, Dig, 4, 2; 14, 1. 'Unless he makes restitution the damages are fourfold. It is sufficient clemency on the praetor's part to allow him to make restitution and avoid the penalty. After a year the damages are only simple.'

The words of the edict (Quod metus causa gestum erit ratum non habebo, Dig. 4, 2, 1; 'Duress shall be a ground for rescinding a contract or other dispositive act') are in rem scripta or impersonal; they do not specify the intimidator, but promise a remedy even against innocent persons who may have come into possession of property in consequence of an intimidation. Accordingly, the action quod metus causa, when brought for simple damages was not even unilaterally penal, but purely Restorative. Both for fraud and for violence the exception was perpetual. The reason of the difference between the action and the exception is, that the time of bringing the action depended on the party injured, the time for alleging the exception depended on the wrong-doer. Non sicut de dolo actio certo tempore finitur ita etiam exceptio eodem tempore danda est; nam haec perpetuo competit, quum actor quidem in sua potestate habeat, quando utatur suo jure, is autem cum quo agitur non habeat potestatem quando conveniatur, Dig. 44, 4, 5. 'The action of fraud does not lie after a certain time, but the exception of fraud is perpetual, because the victim of fraud can sue as soon as he likes, but cannot fix the time when he will be sued.'

§ 123. Temporary exceptions when once alleged were a perpetual bar to the plaintiff's action, until the constitution of Zeno, confirmed by Justinian, reduced the penalty of premature claim to the addition to the term fixed for payment of the amount of time by which the claim was premature.

§ 124. Soldiers and women were incapable of the office of cognitor, and infamy originally incapacitated for suing, sometimes as principal, always as cognitor. Omnes infames qui postulare prohibentur cognitores fieri non possunt etiam volentibus adversariis, Paulus, Sententiae Receptae, 1, 2, 1. 'An infamous person who cannot appear before the praetor cannot be cognitor even with the consent of the opposing party.' Justinian removed the incapacity of creating or discharging the office of procurator. Eas vero exceptiones quae olim procuratoribus propter infamiam vel dantis vel ipsius procuratoris opponebantur, cum in judiciis frequentari nullo modo perspeximus, conquiescere sancimus: ne dum de his altercatur, ipsius negotii disceptatio proteletur, Inst. 4, 13, 11. 'Exceptions alleging the infamy of the procurator or of the principal whom he represents, were formerly of rare occurrence, and are now abolished, as being merely a means of delay.'

The exceptio procuratoria was not favoured by equity. Quaedam tamen etsi sciens omittat fidejussor, caret fraude, utputa si exceptionem procuratoriam omisit, sive sciens sive ignarus; de bona fide enim agitur, cui non congruit de apicibus juris disputare, sed de hoc tantum, debitor fuerit necne, Dig. 17, 1; 29, 4. 'Some defences may be knowingly omitted by a surety without fraud; for instance, the exception against a procurator; for an equitable claim should not turn on legal subtleties, but on the merits of the case.'

§ 125. The question was decided apparently in the negative. Julian, A.D. 365, imposed a fine of a pound of gold on the advocate who should persist in arguing a dilatory exception which had not been pleaded at the commencement of the action, Cod. 8, 36, 12.

§ 126. The argentarius frequently joined the occupation of auctioneer (coactor) to that of banker. Argentarius coactor, quum paene totam fortunam in nominibus haberet, servis actoribus libertatem ita dedit, Dig. 40, 7; 40, 8. 'A banker and auctioneer, nearly all whose fortune was invested in loans, bequeathed to the slaves who conducted his auctioneering business their liberty in the following terms.' Res vendendas per argentarios dedit. Argentarii universum redactum venditionis solverunt, Dig. 47, 3, 88. 'He sold the estate by the agency of auctioneers. The auctioneers paid the whole proceeds of the sale.' The grandfather of Vespasian, after serving as centurion under Pompey at Pharsalia, coactiones argentarias factitavit, Suetonius, Vesp. 1.

DE PRAESCRIPTIONIBUS.

§ 130. Videamus etiam de praescriptionibus quae receptae sunt pro actore.

§ 131. Saepe enim ex una eademque obligatione aliquid iam praestari oportet, aliquid in futura praestatione est. velut cum in singulos annos vel menses certam pecuniam stipulati fuerimus: nam finitis quibusdam annis aut mensibus, huius quidem temporis pecuniam praestari oportet, futurorum autem annorum sane quidem obligatio contracta intellegitur, praestatio vero adhuc nulla est. si ergo velimus id quidem quod praestari oportet petere et in iudicium deducere, futuram vero obligationis praestationem in incerto relinquere, necesse est ut cum hac praescriptione agamus: EA RES AGATUR CUIUS REI DIES FUIT. alioquin si sine hac praescriptione egerimus, ea scilicet formula qua incertum petimus, *cuius intentio* his verbis concepta est: QUIDQUID PARET *NUMERIUM NEGIDIUM AULO AGERIO* DARE FACERE OPORTERE, totam obligationem, id est *etiam futuram*

§ 130. We next proceed to notice the Praescriptio, a clause designed for the protection of the plaintiff.

§ 131. One and the same obligation may entitle us to receive payment of one sum at present and another sum in future. When an annual or monthly payment of a certain sum is stipulated, on the expiration of a year or month we are entitled to present payment for the term expired, and to future payment for the future terms. If, then, we intend to claim and sue for the sum at present due, without bringing the future payments into litigation, we must employ the Praescriptio: 'Let the trial relate exclusively to the right of present payment.' Otherwise, if we sue without this Praescriptio, the indefinite Intentio, 'Whatever it be proved that Numerius Negidius ought to convey to or perform for Aulus Agerius,' brings our whole right to future as well as to present payment before the judex, and, whatever payment may be due in future,

in hoc iudicium *deducimus*, et quantumvis *in obligatione fuerit*, *tamen id* solum *consequimur*, *quod litis contestatae tempore praestari oportet*, *ideoque removemur postea agere volentes*. *item* si verbi gratia ex empto agamus, *ut* nobis fundus mancipio detur, debemus *ita praescribere*: EA RES AGATUR DE FUNDO MANCIPANDO: *ut* postea, si *velimus* vacuam possessionem nobis tradi, *de tradenda ea* vel *ex stipulatu vel ex* empto *agere possimus*. *nam si non praescribimus*, totius illius iuris obligatio ill*a* inc*e*rta actione: QUIDQUID OB EAM REM NUMERIUM NEGIDIUM AULO AGERIO DARE FACERE OPORTET, *per litis contestationem* consumit*ur*, ut postea nobis agere volen*tibus de* vacua possessione tradenda nulla supersit actio.

we only recover what is due at the commencement of the suit, and are barred from any subsequent action. So if we sue upon a purchase for the conveyance of land by mancipation, we must prefix the Praescriptio: 'Let the trial relate exclusively to the mancipation of the land,' in order that subsequently, when vacant possession is to be delivered, we may be able to sue on stipulation or purchase for delivery of possession; as, without this Praescriptio, all our right under that title is included in the uncertain Intentio, 'Whatever on that ground Numerius Negidius ought to convey to or perform for Aulus Agerius,' and is exhausted by the commencement of the first action; so that afterwards, when we want to sue for the delivery of vacant possession, we have no right of action.

§ 132. Praescr*iptiones autem* appellatas esse ab eo, *quod a*nte formulas praescrib*untur*, plus quam manifestum est.

§ 132. The Praescriptio is named from preceding the formula, as hardly needs to be stated.

§ 133. Sed *h*is quidem temporibus, sicut supra quoque *indicavimus*, omnes praescriptiones ab actore proficiscuntur. olim aut*em* quaedam et pro reo opponebantur. qualis illa erat praescriptio: EA RES AGATUR, *SI* IN *EA RE* PRAEIUDICIUM HEREDITATI NON FIAT: quae nunc in speciem exceptionis deducta est, et locum habet cum petitor hereditatis alio *genere* iudicii praeiudicium *hereditati* faciat, velut cum *res singulas petat; esset* enim iniquum . . . [*desunt* 24 *lin.*]

§ 133. At present, as I observed, all Praescriptions are inserted by the plaintiff; formerly some used to be employed by the defendant, for instance, the Praescriptio: 'Let this question be tried if it does not prejudice the question of succession;' which clause is now transformed into an exceptio, and is employed when the claimant of a succession brings another action which prejudges the right of succession; as, for instance, if he sues for a part of the heritage; for it would be unjust. . . .

§ 134. . . *inten*tione formulae de*terminatur is* cui dari oportet; et sane domino dare oportet quod servus stipulatur. at in praescriptione de pacto quaeritur quod secundum naturalem significationem verum esse debet.

§ 134. And the Intentio names the person entitled to receive, that is, the master of the slave who stipulated, while the Praescriptio confines the trial to the exercise of the stipulated power by the slave according to the true meaning of the contract.

§ 135. Quae*cum*que autem dixi-

§ 135. What has been said of

mus de servis, eadem de ceteris quoque personis quae nostro iuri subiectae sunt dicta intellegemus.

§ 136. Item admonendi sumus, si cum ipso agamus qui incertum *pro*miserit, ita nobis formulam esse propositam, ut praescriptio inserta sit formula*e* loco demonstrationis, hoc modo: IUDEX ESTO. QUOD AULUS AGERIUS DE NUMERIO NEGIDIO INCERT*UM* STIPULATUS EST, MODO CUIUS REI DIES FUIT, QUIDQUID OB EAM REM NUMERIUM NEGIDIUM AULO *AGERIO* DARE FACERE OPORTET et reliqua.

§ 137. Si cum sponsore aut fideiussore agatur, praescribi solet in persona quidem sponsoris hoc modo: EA RES AG*A*TUR, QUOD AULUS AGERIUS DE LUCIO TIT*I*O INCERTUM STIPULATUS *EST*, QUO NOMINE NUMERIUS NEGIDIUS SPONSOR EST, CUIUS REI DIES FUIT; in persona vero fideiussoris: EA RES AGATUR, QUOD NUMERIUS NEGIDIUS PRO LUCIO TITIO INCERTUM FIDE SUA ESSE IUSSIT, CUIUS REI D*I*ES FUIT; deinde formula subicitur.

slaves applies to all persons subject to our power.

§ 136. We must further remark, that when the principal promisor of an uncertain sum is sued, the formula contains a Praescriptio in place of a Demonstratio, thus: 'Let C D be judex. Whereas Aulus Agerius stipulated an uncertain sum from Numerius Negidius, whatever, IN EXCLUSIVE RESPECT OF THE SUM DUE AT PRESENT, on that ground Numerius Negidius ought to convey to or perform for Aulus Agerius,' &c.

§ 137. When a sponsor or fidejussor is sued, in the case of the sponsor the Praescriptio is as follows: 'LET THE TRIAL on the Stipulation by Aulus Agerius that an uncertain sum should be paid by Lucius Titius, of which stipulation Numerius Negidius was sponsor, BE CONFINED TO THE PAYMENT DUE AT PRESENT;' in the case of a fidejussor: 'LET THE ACTION on the guaranty of Numerius Negidius that an uncertain sum should be paid by Lucius Titius, BE CONFINED TO THE PAYMENT DUE AT PRESENT;' and then follows the rest of the formula.

§ 131. As an instance of the gross ignorance often displayed by the advocates, Cicero puts the following story into the mouth of Crassus, which shows that the praescriptio was sometimes called exceptio: Quid? his paucis diebus nonne, nobis in tribunali Q. Pompeii praetoris urbani familiaris nostri sedentibus, homo ex numero disertorum postulabat ut illi unde peteretur vetus atque usitata exceptio daretur, CUJUS PECUNIAE DIES FUISSET? quod petitoris causa comparatum esse non intelligebat: ut [ne?] si ille infitiator probasset judici ante petitam esse pecuniam quam esset coepta deberi, petitor rursus quum peteret exceptione excluderetur, QUOD EA RES IN JUDICIUM ANTEA VENISSET, De Oratore, 1, 37. 'A few days ago when I was present at the tribunal of the praetor urbanus, the defendant's advocate demanded the old and common exception: IN EXCLUSIVE RE-

SPECT OF THE PAYMENT ALREADY DUE, not knowing that it only protected the plaintiff, saving him, if his demand was proved to be premature, from being barred in a subsequent action by the exception of PREVIOUS LITIGATION.'

It seems to have been a caprice of the tribunals to decide that the words quicquid dare oportet include future as well as present payments, for in stipulations the same terms excluded future payments. Cum stipulamur, quidquid te dare facere oportet, id duntaxat quod praesenti die debetur in stipulationem deducitur, non, ut in judiciis, etiam futurum; et ideo in stipulatione adicitur verbum oportebit, vel ita, praesens in diemve, Dig. 45, 1, 75. 'In a stipulation, the words quidquid oportet only refer to present payments, though in the formula they include future payments. To include future payments in a stipulation we must add oportebitve, or, praesens in diemve.'

The mancipation of movables was incomplete without delivery, but in the mancipation of land, property might pass without possession. Res mobiles non nisi praesentes mancipari possunt... immobiles autem plures simul et quae diversis locis sunt mancipari possunt, Fragments of Ulpian, 19, 6. 'Movbales cannot be mancipated without delivery, but immovables may be mancipated without personal presence.'

One of the praescriptions of the defendant was called longi temporis praescriptio. In Italy quiritarian property was acquired by possession of a movable for one year, of an immovable for two years. In the provinces, where the absolute property of the land was in the State, qualified property was acquired in ten years if the parties were domiciled in the same province, in twenty if in different provinces; and such property could be vindicated by a praetorian action, or defended by a praescriptio, the exact form of which we do not know, but which was of the following effect: Ea res agatur si non fuit longi temporis possessio. From expressing the defendant's title (exceptio) in respect of provincial land, praescriptio came to express indifferently the title either of the defendant or of the plaintiff, so that, when the distinction between Provincial and Italic soil was abolished, praescriptio = usucapio.

The leaf containing from intentione formulae, § 134, to aut pro possessore, § 144, was separated from the rest of the Veronese codex, and seen by Scipio Maffei in 1732. It was afterwards published by Haubold in 1816, the very year in which Niebuhr discovered the rest of the codex.

DE INTERDICTIS.

§ 138. Superest ut de interdictis dispiciamus.

§ 138. The last subject to be examined are interdicts.

§ 139. Certis igitur ex causis Praetor aut Proconsul principaliter auctoritatem suam finiendis controversiis *inter*ponit. quod tum maxime facit, cum de possessione aut quasi possessione inter aliquos contenditur. et in summa aut iubet aliquid fieri, aut fieri prohibet. formulae autem verborum et conceptiones quibus in ea re utitur interdicta dec*retave* vocantur.

§ 139. Under certain circumstances, chiefly when possession or quasi-possession (possession of a servitude) is in dispute, the first step in legal proceedings is the interposition of the praetor or proconsul, who commands some performance or forbearance; which commands, formulated in solemn terms, are called interdicts or decrees.

§ 140. *Vocantur* autem decreta cum fieri ali*qu*id iubet, velut cum praecipit, ut aliquid exhibeatur aut restituatur: interdicta vero cum prohibet fieri, velut cum praecipit: ne sine vitio possidenti vis fiat, neve in loco sacro aliquid fiat. unde omnia interdicta aut restitutoria aut exhibitoria aut prohibitoria vocantur.

§ 140. Decrees, when he commands that something be performed; for instance, when he orders that something be produced, or something be restored: interdicts, when he prohibits some act; as when he forbids the violent disturbance of an unimpeachable possession, or the desecration of consecrated ground. Interdicts, then, are orders either of restitution, or of production, or of abstention.

§ 141. Nec tamen cum quid iusserit fieri aut fieri prohibuerit, statim peractum est negotium, sed ad iudicem recuperatoresve it*ur*, et ibi editis formulis quaeritur, an aliquid adversus Praetoris edictum factum sit, vel an factum non sit quod is fieri iusserit. et modo cum poena agitur, modo sine poena: cum poena, velut cum per sponsionem agetur; sine poena, velut cu*m* arbiter petitur. et quidem ex prohibitoriis interdictis semper per sponsionem agi solet, ex restitutoriis vero vel exhibitoriis modo per sponsionem, modo per formulam agitur quae arbitraria vocatur.

§ 141. The order of performance or forbearance does not end the proceedings, but a formula is delivered instructing a judex or recuperators to inquire whether anything has been committed contrary to the praetor's prohibition or omitted contrary to his injunction. Their judgment sometimes is penal, sometimes not penal; penal when the procedure is by sponsio, not penal when by demand of arbitration. Prohibitory interdicts are always preliminary to sponsio; orders of restitution or production sometimes to sponsio, sometimes to arbitration.

§ 142. Principalis igitur divisio in eo est, quod aut prohibitoria sunt interdicta, aut restitutoria, aut exhibitoria.

§ 142. The first division, then, of interdicts is into orders of abstention, of restitution, of production.

§ 143. Sequens in eo est divisio, quod vel adipiscendae possessionis

§ 143. The next is into interdicts for obtaining possession, for retain-

causa comparata sunt, vel retinendae, vel reciperandae.

ing possession, for recovering possession.

§ 144. Adipiscendae possessionis causa interdictum accommodatur bonorum possessori, cuius principium est QUORUM BONORUM: eiusque vis et potestas haec est, ut quod quisque ex his bonis quorum possessio alicui data est pro herede aut pro possessore possideret, id ei cui bonorum possessio data est restituatur. pro herede autem possidere videtur tam is qui heres est, quam is qui putat se heredem esse: pro possessore is possidet qui sine causa aliquam rem hereditariam vel etiam totam hereditatem, sciens ad se non pertinere, possidet. ideo autem adipiscendae possessionis vocatur, quia ei tantum utile est qui nunc primum conatur adipisci rei possessionem: itaque si quis adeptus possessionem amiserit, desinit ei id interdictum utile esse.

§ 144. An interdict for obtaining possession is granted to the equitable successor, beginning: 'Whatever portion of the goods;' and injoining, that whatever portion of the goods, possession of which has been granted to the equitable successor, is in the hands of the legal successor or a mere possessor, shall be delivered to the equitable successor. The legal successor includes the true legal successor and any person who thinks himself legal successor; a mere possessor is he who without any title detains a portion or the whole of the inheritance, knowing that he is not entitled. It is called an interdict for obtaining possession because it is only available for initiating possession, and is not granted to a person who has already had and lost possession.

§ 145. Bonorum quoque emptori similiter proponitur interdictum, quod quidam possessorium vocant.

§ 145. The execution purchaser in insolvency also has an interdict, which some call possessory.

§ 146. Item ei qui publica bona emerit, eiusdem condicionis interdictum proponitur, quod appellatur sectorium, quod sectores vocantur qui publice bona mercantur.

§ 146. The purchaser of the confiscated goods of a criminal has a similar interdict, which is called sectorium, because the purchasers of public property are called sectores.

§ 147. Interdictum quoque quod appellatur Salvianum apiscendae possessionis comparatum est, eoque utitur dominus fundi de rebus coloni quas is pro mercedibus fundi pignori futuras pepigisset.

§ 147. The interdict called Salvianum is an interdict for obtaining possession, and is available to the landlord against the detainers of the tenant's property hypothecated as a security for rent.

§ 148. Retinendae possessionis causa solet interdictum reddi, cum ab utraque parte de proprietate alicuius rei controversia est, et ante quaeritur, uter ex litigatoribus possidere et uter petere debeat, cuius rei gratia comparata sunt UTI POSSIDETIS et UTRUBI.

§ 148. Interdicts for retaining possession are granted when two parties claim proprietorship, in order to determine which shall be plaintiff and which defendant, and are called the interdicts: 'Whichever party has possession,' and, 'Whichever party had possession.'

§ 149. Et quidem UTI POSSIDETIS

§ 149. The former refers to land

interdictum de fundi vel aedium possession*e* redditur, UTRUBI vero de rerum mobilium possessione.

and houses, the latter to movables.

§ 150. Et si quidem de fundo vel aedibus interdicitur, eum potiorem esse Praetor iubet qui eo tempore quo interdictum redditur nec vi nec clam nec precario ab adversario possideat; si vero de re mobili, *tunc* eum potiorem esse iubet qui maiore parte eius anni nec vi nec clam nec precario ab adversario possidet: idque satis ipsis verbis interdictorum significatur.

§ 150. When the interdict relates to land or houses, the praetor prefers the party who at the issuing of the interdict has possession unimpeachable in respect of the adversary for violence, clandestinity, or permission. When the interdict relates to a movable, he prefers the party who in respect of the adversary has possessed without violence, clandestinity, or permission, during the greater part of the year. The terms of the interdicts sufficiently show this distinction.

§ 151. *At* in UTRUBI interdicto non sol*um sua cui*que possessio prodest, sed etiam alteri*us* quam iustum est ei acc*e*dere, velut eius cui heres extiterit, eiusque a quo emerit vel ex donatione aut do*tis d*atione acceperit. itaque si nostrae pos*s*essioni iuncta alterius iusta possessio exsuperat adversarii possessionem, nos eo interdicto vincimus. nullam autem propriam possessionem habenti accessio temporis nec datur nec dari potest; nam ei quod nullum est nihil accedere potest. se*d et* si vitiosam habeat possessionem, id est aut vi aut clam aut precario ab adversario adquisitam, *non* d*atur*; *nam ei possessio* sua nihil prodest.

§ 151. In the interdict, 'Whichever party possessed,' possession includes, besides the possession of the litigant, any possession of another person which may justly form an accession, such as that of a person deceased to whom he succeeds, that of a vendor, of a donor, of a settlor of dower; and if my possession added to the just possession of another person exceeds that of the adversary, my claim is preferred; but he who has no possession of his own neither receives nor can receive any accession of another's possession; for what is non-existent is incapable of receiving accession. So a possession impeachable for violence, clandestinity, or permission, cannot receive an accession, and is of no avail.

§ 152. Annus autem retrorsus numeratur. itaque si tu verbi gratia anni mensibus possederis prioribus V, et ego VII posterioribus, ego potior ero qu*antitat*e mensium possessionis; *nec* tibi in hoc interdicto *prodest*, quod *prior tua eius* ann*i* *possessio est*.

§ 152. The year computed is the year immediately preceding; so that, if you possessed during the first five months, and I during the seven following months, I am preferred, and it avails you nothing that you were the prior possessor.

§ 153. Possidere autem videmur non so*lum si ip*si possideamus, sed etiam si nostro nomine aliquis in possessionem sit, licet i*s* nostro iur*i*

§ 153. My possession includes, besides my personal possession, the possession of any one who holds in my name, though not subject to my

subiectus non sit, qualis est colonus et inquilinus. per eos quoque aput quos deposuerimus, aut quibus commodaverimus, aut quibus *gratuitam* habitationem *constituerimus*, ipsi possidere videmur. et hoc est quod volgo dicitur, retineri possessionem posse per quemlibet qui nostro nomine sit in possessione. quinetiam plerique put*ant* animo *quoque retineri* possessionem, quod nostrorum *praeceptorum sententia est. Diversae autem scholae auctoribus contrarium placet, ut* animo solo, qu*amvis* vol*uerimus ad rem reverti, tamen* retinere *possessionem non* videamu*r*. apisci *vero possessionem per* quos pos*simus*, secundo commentario rettulimus; nec ulla dubitatio est, quin animo *possessionem apisci non* pos*simus*.

power; for instance, the possession of my tenant or lodger. So also a depositary, borrower for use, usufructuary, or grantee of use or habitation, may be the instrument of my possession, as is expressed by the saying that we retain possession by those who hold in our name. It is generally allowed that intention suffices for the retention of possession, as my school maintains, when a man leaves a thing, for instance, with the intention of returning. The instruments of obtaining possession were mentioned in the second book, and it is agreed on all hands, that for obtaining possession intention does not suffice.

§ 154. Recuperandae possessionis causa solet interdictum dari, si quis vi deiectus sit. nam ei proponitur interdictum cuius principium *est:* UNDE TU ILLUM VI DEIECISTI. per quod is qui deieci*t* cogitur ei restituere rei possessionem, si modo is qui deiectus est nec vi nec *clam* nec precario *possidet ab adversario:* quod si aut vi aut clam aut precario possederit, *impune* de*icitur*.

§ 154. An interdict for recovering possession is granted to a person dispossessed of an immovable by violence, beginning: 'In the place whence thou hast violently ousted,' which compels the invader to restore possession, if the person ousted possessed without violence, clandestinity, or permission, in respect of the invader. Whereas, if his own possession was violent, clandestine, or permissive, a person may be ousted with impunity.

§ 155. Interdum tamen *etiam* ei *quem vi* de*iecerim*, quamvis *a* me *aut* vi aut clam aut precario possideret, cog*ar rei* restituere possessionem, velut si armis eum vi deiecerim: nam Praetor [*desunt* 4 *lin.*]

§ 155. Sometimes, however, the person violently ousted, though his own possession was violent, clandestine, or permissive, in respect of the adversary, must be reinstated, that is, if he was ousted by force of arms.

§ 156. Tertia divisio interdictorum in hoc *est, quod aut* simplic*ia* sunt aut duplicia.

§ 156. A third division of interdicts is into Simple and Double.

§ 157. Simplicia velut in quibus alter actor, alter reus est: qualia sunt omnia restitutoria *aut* exhibitoria. nam actor est qui desiderat aut exhiberi aut restitui, reus is est a quo desideratur ut exhibeat aut restituat.

§ 157. Those are simple wherein one party is plaintiff and the other defendant, as always is the case in orders of restitution or production; for he who demands restitution or production is plaintiff, and he from whom it is demanded is defendant.

§ 158. Prohibitoriorum autem interdictorum alia duplicia, alia simplicia sunt.

§ 159. Simplicia sunt *veluti* quibus prohibet Praetor in loco sacro aut in flumine publico ripave eius aliquid facere *reum*: nam actor *est* qui desiderat ne quid fiat, reus is qui aliquid facere conatur.

§ 160. Duplicia sunt, velut UTI POSSIDETIS interdictum et UTRUBI. ideo autem duplicia vocantur, quia par utriusque litigatoris in his condicio est, nec quisquam praecipue reus vel actor intellegitur, sed unusquisque tam rei quam actoris partes sustinet: quippe Praetor pari sermone cum utroque loquitur. nam summa conceptio eorum interdictorum haec est: UTI *NUNC* POSSIDETIS, QUOMINUS ITA POSSIDEATIS VI*M* FIERI VETO. item alterius: UTRUBI HIC HOMO DE QUO AGITUR, APUD QUEM MAIORE PARTE HUIUS ANNI FUIT, QUOMINUS IS EUM DUCAT VI*M* FIERI VETO.

§ 161. Expositis generibus interdictorum sequitur ut de ordine et de exitu eorum dispiciamus; et incipiamus a si*m*plicibus.

§ 162. *Si* igitur restitutorium vel exhibitorium interdictum redditur, velut ut restituatur ei possessio qui vi deiectus est, aut exhibeatur libertus cui patronus operas indicere vellet, modo sine periculo res ad exitum perducitur, modo cum periculo.

§ 163. Namque si arbitrum postulaverit is cum quo agitur, accipit formulam quae appellatur ar*bitra*ria. nam iud*icis* arbitrio si quid restitui vel exh*i*beri deb*eat*, *id* sine *poena* exhibet *vel* restituit, et ita absolvitur: quod si nec restituat neque exhibeat, q*uan*ti ea res est

§ 158. Of prohibitory interdicts, some are simple, others double.

§ 159. The simple are exemplified by those wherein the praetor commands the defendant to abstain from desecrating consecrated ground, or from obstructing a public river or its banks; for he who demands the forbearance is plaintiff, he who attempts the performance is defendant.

§ 160. Of double interdicts we have examples in: 'Whichever party possesses,' and 'Whichever party possessed.' They are denominated double because the footing of both parties is equal, neither being exclusively plaintiff or defendant, but both playing both parts, and both being addressed by the praetor in identical terms. For by the effect of these interdicts whichever party now possesses the land, the other is forbidden to disturb his possession; and whichever party has possessed a slave during the greater part of the year, the other is forbidden to prevent him from taking the slave away.

§ 161. After classifying interdicts we have next to explain their process and result; and we begin with the simple.

§ 162. When an order of restitution or production is issued, for instance, of restitution of seisin to a disseisee, or of production of a freedman whose services are required by his patron, the proceedings are sometimes penal, sometimes not penal.

§ 163. When arbitration is demanded by the defendant, a formula arbitraria is delivered, and if the judex directs him to restore or produce anything, he either restores or produces it without further penalty, or he does not restore or produce it, and then he is condemned in its

condemnatur. *sed* actor *quoque* sine poena experitur cum eo qu*em* neque exhibere neque restituere quicquam *oportet, ni*si calumniae *i*udicium ei oppositum fu*e*rit. *diversae quidem scholae auctoribus placet prohibendum* calumniae iudicio *eum qui arbitrum postulaverit,* quasi hoc ipso confessus videat*ur, restituere se* vel exhibere debere. sed alio iure utimur, et recte: *namque sine ullo timore ne superetur,* arbitrum quisque *postulare potest.*

simple value. Neither does the plaintiff incur any penalty for suing a defendant who is not obliged to produce or restore, unless he is sued in return for vexatious litigation. For though some have held that the demand of arbitration precludes the defendant from suing for vexatious litigation, as an admission of the plaintiff's right, the contrary view has justly prevailed; for a defendant may prefer arbitration without mistrusting the justice of his cause.

§ 164. *Ceterum* observare debet is qui *volet arbitrum* pet*ere*, ut *stat*im petat, antequam ex i*ure* ex*e*at, id *est* an*tequam a* Pr*aetore* di*s*cedat: sero *e*nim petentibus non indulge*bi*t*ur.*

§ 164. The defendant must be careful, if he wishes to demand an arbiter, to make the demand at once before he leaves the court or tribunal of the praetor; for a subsequent demand will not be granted.

§ 165. *Itaque* si *arbi*tr*um* non *pet*ie*r*it, sed *taci*tus de iure exi*erit,* cum periculo res ad exitum perducitur. nam actor provocat adversarium sponsione: *Ni* contra *edic*t*u*m Praetoris non *exh*ibu*e*rit aut non res*titu*e*rit*: ille autem adversus sponsionem adversarii restipulatur. deinde actor quidem sponsionis *formulam* ed*it* adversario; i*lle h*uic invicem restipulationis. sed actor sponsioni*s formulae subicit* et aliu*d* iudicium de re restituenda vel exhibenda, ut si sponsione *vicerit,* nisi ei res exhibeatur aut restituatur ... [*desunt* 48 *lineae*].

§ 165. If he leaves the court without requesting an arbiter, the proceeding becomes penal: the plaintiff challenges the defendant to wager a sum to be forfeited by the defendant if he has contravened the edict of the praetor by failing to produce or restore; and the defendant challenges the plaintiff to a counter wager of a similar sum to be forfeited by the plaintiff upon the opposite condition. The plaintiff then delivers the formula of the wager, and the defendant delivers the formula of the counter wager. The plaintiff, in addition to the formula of the sponsio, delivers another formula for the production or restoration of the thing in dispute, upon which, if he obtains judgment in the sponsio and the thing is not restored or produced, the defendant will be condemned in damages to the amount of its value.

§ 166. *Postquam igitur Praetor interdictum reddidit, fit fructus licitatio; et uter eorum vicerit* fructus licitando, is tantisper in possessione constituitur si modo adversario suo fructuaria stipul*atione cave*rit, cuius vis et potestas haec *est, ut* si contra

§ 166. When a double interdict, Uti possidetis, for instance, has been issued, the interim possession or mesne profits are sold by auction, and the higher bidder of the litigants is placed in possession pending the controversy, provided that

eum *de possessione* pronun*tiatum f*ueri*t*, *e*am summam adversario solvat. *nam* inter adversarios qui *Praetore auctore certant*, *dum* contentio fructus licitationis *est*, scil*icet* qu*ia possessorem interim* esse *interest*, *rei possessionem ei Praetor* vendit, *qui plus licetur*. postea alter alterum sponsione provocat: NISI ADVERSUS EDICTUM PRAETORIS POSSIDENTIBUS NOBIS VIS FACTA ESSET. invicem ambo resti*pulan*tur adversus sponsionem vel [4 *lineae*] . . . iudex aput quem de ea *re agitur* illud scilicet requirit *quod* Praetor interdicto co*m*plexus est, id est uter eorum eum fundum easve aedes per id tempus quo interdict*um* redditur nec vi nec clam nec precario possideret. cum iudex id exploraverit, et forte secundum me iudicat*um* sit, adversarium *quidem* et sponsionis et restipulationis summas quas cum eo feci condemnat, et convenienter me sponsioni*s* et restipulationis quae mecum factae sunt absolvit. et hoc amplius si aput adversarium meum *possessio est*, qui*a* is fructus licitatione vic*it*, nisi restituat mihi possessionem, Cascelliano sive secutorio iudicio condemnatur.

he gives his opponent security by the fructuary stipulation, which is conditioned for forfeiting, in the event of losing the cause, the value of the interim profits as fixed by the auction. Then each party challenges the opponent to wager a sum to be forfeited by the promisor if he has contravened the interdict by violently disturbing the possession of the promisee, and each party, after binding himself as promisor in a sponsio, becomes the promisee in a similar restipulatio; whereas in the simple interdicts, as we have seen, there is only one sponsio and one restipulatio. The judex who tries the sponsio determines the question raised in the interdict, namely, which party was in possession of the house or land in question, without violence, clandestinity, or permission, in respect of the other. If the judex determines this in my favour, he condemns my adversary in the penal sums of the sponsio and restipulatio in which I was promisee, and absolves me in the actions upon the sponsio and restipulatio in which I was promisor; and, if my opponent is in possession as higher bidder in the auction, unless he restores possession, he is condemned in an action called Cascellianum or Secutorium.

§ 167. Ergo is qui fructus licitatione vicit, si non probat ad se pertinere possessionem, sponsionis et restipu*la*tionis et fructus licitationis summam poenae nomine solvere *et* praeterea possessionem restituere iubetur: et hoc amplius fructus quos i*nter*ea percepit reddi*t*. summa enim fructus licitationis non pretium est fructuum, sed poenae nomine solvitur, quod quis aliena*m* possessionem per hoc tempus retinere et facultatem fruendi na*n*cisci conatus est.

§ 167. So that if the higher bidder in the auction fails to prove that he had possession, he is ordered to pay the sum of the sponsio, the sum of the restipulatio, and the price he offered for the mesne profits at the sale by auction, by way of penalty; and further, to restore possession of the thing in question, and restore any profits of which he has had perception; for the price fixed by the auction is not paid in purchase of the profits, but as a penalty for detaining another man's possession and means of enjoyment.

§ 168. Ille autem qui fructus licitatione victus est, si non probarit ad se pertinere possessionem, tantum sponsionis et restipulationis summam poenae nomine debet.

§ 168. If the lower bidder in the auction fails to prove that he had possession, he is only condemned to pay the sum of the sponsio and restipulatio by way of penalty.

§ 169. Admonendi tamen sumus liberum esse ei qui fructus licitatione victus erit, omissa fructuaria stipulatione, sicut Cascelliano sive secutorio iudicio de *possessione reciperanda experitur*, ita *separatim* et de fructus licitatione *agere*: *in* quam *rem* proprium iudicium *comparatum* est, quod appellatur fructuarium, quo nomine actor *iudicatum solvi* satis *accipiet*. dicitur autem et hoc iudicium secutorium, quod sequitur sponsionis victoriam; sed non aeque Cascellianum vocatur.

§ 169. It is open to the lower bidder, if he succeeds in the sponsio, instead of proceeding on the fructuary stipulation, just as he brings the Cascellianum or Secutorium action for recovering possession, to bring an action upon the sale by auction which is called fructuarium, in which he is entitled to security with sureties for satisfaction of judgment; which action, like the action for recovering possession, as following the result of the sponsio is called Secutorium; but is not, like the action for recovering possession, also called Cascellianum.

§ 170. Sed quia nonnulli interdicto reddito cetera ex interdicto facere nolebant, atque ob id non poterat res expediri, Praetor . . . comparavit interdicta [*desunt* 47 *lineae*].

§ 170. As sometimes, after the issue of an interdict, one of the parties declined to take one of the subsequent steps, and the proceedings came to a stand, a praetor . . .

Interdicts relate to sacred places or public places or possession.

§ 140. Restituere is an ambiguous term, and comprehends several acts which have little in common but the name. Sometimes it means the demolition of an unlawful structure: e.g. Quod in flumine publico ripave ejus fiat, sive quid in id flumen ripamve ejus immissum habeas, quo statio iterve navigio deterior sit, fiat, restituas, Dig. 43, 12, 1, 19. 'What you have built in a public river or on its bank, or what you have discharged into the river or on to its bank, interfering with the anchorage or passage of vessels, I command you to demolish and remove.' Sometimes it means the restoration of possession, as in the interdict Unde vi, § 154; sometimes the delivery of possession, where no possession has preceded, as in the interdict Quorum bonorum, § 144.

Exhibere is the production of a thing or person, and was usually the preliminary of a vindication. Quem liberum hominem dolo malo retines exhibeas, Dig. 43, 29, 1. 'The freeman whom you unlawfully detain I command you to produce.' Qui quaeve in potestate Lucii Titii est, si is eave apud te est, dolove malo factum est quominus apud te esset, ita eum eamve exhibeas, Dig. 43, 30, 1. 'The son or daughter of Lucius Titius, who is subject to his power, and whom you detain or have fraudulently ceased to detain, I command you to produce.'

§ 141. The formula arbitraria was, as we have said before, § 47, one which contained the clause, NISI RESTITUAT, or NISI EXHIBEAT. The formula arbitraria might be either a real or a personal action (Sed arbitrariae actiones tam in rem quam in personam inveniuntur, Inst. 4, 6, 31), restituere denoting, according to circumstances, transfer of property, of possession, or of mere detention. It might throw light on the Roman conception of Possession if we knew whether the formula arbitraria of interdict procedure was a formula of real or of personal action. As a Real action, § 91, was either by sponsio praejudicialis or by formula petitoria, and interdict procedure either by sponsio poenalis or formula arbitraria, we might be tempted by the parallelism to identify the formula petitoria and the formula arbitraria. Just as the formula petitoria recovers property or proprietary possession, so the formula arbitraria recovers me repossession; and we might suppose that the latter as well as the former initiated a species of real action. Other considerations, however, make it probable that the formula arbitraria was a formula not of real but of personal action, and was not the pursuit of a right analogous to dominion, but the enforcement of an obligation created by trespass. As it is necessary to have clear views on this subject in order to comprehend the doctrine of possession, we will examine the question in greater detail.

A jus in rem is a right to certain forbearances availing against all the world; a jus in personam is a right to certain performances availing against a determinate person. The question we have now to determine is, of what nature is the right of the mere possessor as possessor? After disseisin or dispossession he has a right to recover seisin or possession. But this is a secondary or sanctioning right, based on the violation of a previous right, just as the right of the proprietor or contractor to recover possession or damages implies the violation of an antecedent primary right to enjoy his property or to receive performance of the service for which he contracted. Of what nature, antecedently to the wrongful dispossession, was the original right of the mere possessor? the right to which he was entitled by mere possession?

Before we answer this, we must distinguish mere possession,

which we may call interdict possession (possessio), from possession combined with certain other elements, such as title and bona fides, which we will call usucaption-possession (possessio civilis). Usucaption-possession is incipient property, and is recoverable by actio in rem Publiciana, 2 § 41, that is, is treated in respect of its remedy as if it were perfect property. Usucaption-possession, then, in the eye of the praetor, is a jus in rem.

Was interdict-possession also, as some have supposed, a jus in rem, or a title to a jus in rem, that is, to a right availing against all the world (except the true proprietor) to continue in possession? If it was, the possessor could have recovered possession by a vindicatio, and the formula arbitraria would have been a formula petitoria. But Savigny has argued with much force that no such right was contemplated by the Roman legislator. The primary right of the possessor was, indeed, a right to certain forbearances available against all the world, that is, was a jus in rem, but it was not a right to continue in possession, but merely a right to immunity from violation of the body. Possession, according to Savigny, is not in itself a substantive right, nor a substantive title to a right, but merely a fact or incident modifying the redress to which a man is entitled for the violation of his body. The jus in rem of bodily inviolability is not sufficiently vindicated and protected unless redress for its violation, when accompanied by disseisin, includes a reinstatement in possession. Though not directly in itself a substantive title to continuance in possession, possession is an accidental element in the title to redress for violation of the body, and makes that redress incomplete unless accompanied by restitution. Possessory interdicts, then, as a portion of substantive law and not merely of the law of procedure, belong, not to the law of real rights, but to the law of personal rights or obligations.

The obligation on which they are founded is an obligation ex delicto, created, that is, by the violation of a real right, the real right which is violated being one of the class which we have called primordial, namely, a right to immunity from bodily molestation.

An unsatisfactory feature of this doctrine is, that it gives to so important a subject as Possession an extremely subordinate and incidental footing in the corpus juris, making it merely an appendage and concomitant of the law of bodily violence and outrage. Accordingly, we might be inclined with Puchta to make right of possession a substantive real right, co-ordinate with the other

Primordial real rights (life, limb, liberty, reputation), and we might still admit that the possessory interdicts are rather actions ex delicto than real actions, for the other primordial rights are grounds not of real actions but either of civil actions ex delicto or of criminal prosecution.

As, however, unless we exclude from the definition of primordial rights all relation to any portion of the external universe, it would be difficult to distinguish them from other real rights, and as possessory interdicts resemble real actions in being the means of recovering specific restitution, an Englishman, remembering the old division in English law of real actions into possessory and droitural, may perhaps be inclined to co-ordinate possession and possessory interdicts rather with Dominion and real actions than with Primordial rights and actions ex delicto. It then will become necessary to invent some term (such as Tenure) including Possession and Dominion, and, as relating to a certain portion of the external material world, contradistinguishing these rights from Primordial rights, which have no such relation. Accordingly, we have co-ordinated Possession rather with Dominion than with Primordial rights in the table, page 134.

If possessory interdicts were in fact regarded by the Roman jurists rather as actions ex delicto than as real actions, this may be paralleled with the fact that the actions of Trover and Detinue, though brought for the recovery of movable property, and consequently, in the eye of a Roman jurist, real actions, are nevertheless in English law (perhaps because damages or compensation for detention, and not restitution, are the only things that can certainly be recovered) two forms of action on trespass, that is to say, not of real action but of action ex delicto. And even Ejectment, practically the sole real action for the recovery of land, is theoretically a species of Trespass. The ground of the possibility of these anomalies is, that every action whatever is founded on Delict, in a large acceptation of the word (see note on 3 § 182), and hence, with the help of a little distortion and violence, any action may be pushed out of its proper place, and made to appear as an action ex delicto in the narrower acceptation.

Finally, we may observe that even if we possessed the exact terms of the formula arbitraria and of the judicium Cascellianum, which was clearly of the same nature, we might still be embarrassed to determine the question we have been examining, i. e.

whether the formula arbitraria and judicium Cascellianum were actions in rem or in personam. As praetorian actions, they were probably actions in factum; and though actions with an intentio in factum are generally classed under the head of personal actions, it is pretty certain that real actions were capable of being thus formulated. On the whole, however, it is probable that the arbitraria formula and judicium Cascellianum were not real actions (either of the form, Si paret possessionem Auli Agerii esse, or with an intention of Fact), but personal actions based on obligations ex delicto; although the arbitrium, or clause NI RESTITUAT, gave them as much power of recovering specific restitution as if they had been real actions. See page 398.

The criterion which shows conclusively that the possessory interdicts—Uti possidetis, Utrubi, and Unde vi—were classed by Roman jurists with actions ex delicto, is the fact that they were only maintainable against the wrong-doer within a year from their nativity, Dig. 43, 17, 1, pr.; Dig. 43, 16, 1, pr.; and were only maintainable against the heir of the wrong-doer so far as he was enriched by the wrong of his predecessor (quatenus ad eum pervenit .... ut tamen lucrum ei extorqueatur, Dig. 44, 7, 35, pr.). These features the interdicts have in common with other unilaterally penal actions, § 112.

§ 144. The interdict Quorum bonorum was the remedy whereby the praetorian successor, whether contra tabulas or secundum tabulas or ab intestato, having already, in response to his demand (agnitio) of the succession, obtained from the praetor the formal grant (datio) of bonorum possessio, maintained his title thereto before the tribunals if he met with opposition; just as hereditatis petitio was the remedy whereby the heres or heir at civil law would have maintained a corresponding claim to the hereditas.

The terms of the interdict ran as follows: Quorum bonorum ex edicto meo illi possessio data est, quod de his bonis pro herede aut pro possessore possides, possideresve si nihil usucaptum esset, quodque dolo malo fecisti ut desineres possidere, id illi restituas, Dig. 43, 2, 1. 'Whatever portion of the goods, granted in pursuance of my edict to be possessed by such and such a one, thou possessest as legal successor or as unentitled possessor, or wouldest so possess but for usucapion, or hast fraudulently ceased to possess, such portion do thou deliver up to such a one.'

Quorum bonorum was the proper remedy against two classes of

adversary: (1) any one who claimed as successor, either under the praetorian edict or at civil law (pro herede); and (2) praedo, or any one who seized and held without title, or merely by title of occupancy (pro possessore), in virtue of the anomalous law which permitted strangers to seize vacant hereditaments, and convert possession into ownership by a short period of usucapion, 2 § 52. If the adversary claimed on any other title, e. g. pro empto or pro donato, the proper remedy of bonorum possessor or heres was not by Quorum bonorum nor by Hereditatis petitio, but by an ordinary Real action (Rei vindicatio). The words 'possideresve si nihil usucaptum foret,' are a trace of the Sc. Juventianum, which relieved the bonorum possessor against usucapion, i. e. which rescinded the usucapion, and allowed Quorum bonorum to be brought even after usucapion had been completed and the unentitled occupant no longer possessed pro possessore, but pro suo, 2 § 57. (According to Puchta, usucapion was always unavailing against Quorum bonorum, and the effect of Sc. Juventianum was only to assist the heir at civil law, by inserting in the formula of Hereditatis petitio a clause that had always as a matter of course been inserted in the interdict Quorum bonorum.)

§ 146. The sector purchased sub hasta, and therefore acquired quiritarian property, although he was protected by a possessory interdict. He purchased the universitas juris, and proposed to make a profit by selling in smaller lots, whence probably his name.

§ 147. Instead of the interdict, a landlord might recover the goods of his tenant by bringing the Real action, called Serviana, Inst. 4, 6, 7. So the execution purchaser might proceed either by interdict or by fictitious action, § 35.

§ 148. The possessory interdicts were often used to determine which party should be defendant in a vindicatio. Commodum autem possidendi in eo est quod etiamsi ejus res non sit qui possidet, si modo actor non potuerit suam esse probare, remanet suo loco possessio; propter quam causam, cum obscura sint utriusque jura, contra petitorem judicari solet, Inst. 4, 15, 4. 'The advantage of possession lies in this, that, though the property is not in the possessor, yet if the plaintiff cannot prove his proprietorship, the possession is undisturbed, because in case of doubt judgment goes against the plaintiff.' Of the disadvantage of the onus of proof we have a typical instance in the laws of Wager of battle on a writ of right, where the tenant prevailed if his champion could maintain himself till the stars appeared in the evening; for it was sufficient to maintain his ground, and make it a drawn battle, he being already in possession, Blackstone, 3, 22. So also in Wager of battle upon an appeal of murder, if the appellee killed the appellant, or could maintain the fight from sun rising till the stars appeared in the evening, he was acquitted (Blackstone).

§ 149. The interdict Uti possidetis was of the following form: Uti eas aedes, quibus de agitur, nec vi nec clam nec precario alter ab altero possidetis, quominus ita possideatis, vim fieri veto. De cloacis hoc interdictum non dabo: neque pluris quam quanti res erit, intra annum quo primum experiundi potestas fuerit, agere permittam, Dig. 4, 3, 17, 1. 'Whichever party has possession of the house in question, without violence, clandestinity, or permission in respect of the adversary, the violent disturbance of his possession I prohibit. Sewers are not included in this interdict. The value of the thing in dispute and no more may be recovered within a year from the time at which proceedings may be commenced.' A form nearly identical is preserved in Festus: Uti nunc possidetis eum fundum quo de agitur, quod nec vi nec clam nec precario alter ab altero possidetis, quominus ita possideatis vim fieri veto. The right of the possessor was not affected if his possession was commenced by violence, clandestinity, or permission in respect of any other person than the defendant. Nam uti possidetis interdicto is vincebat qui interdicti tempore possidebat, si modo nec vi nec clam nec precario nactus fuerat ab adversario possessionem, etiamsi alium vi expulerat, aut clam abripuerat alienam possessionem, aut precario rogaverat aliquem ut sibi possidere liceret, Inst. 4, 15, 4.

The interdict Utrubi was of the following form: Utrubi hic homo quo de agitur majore parte hujusce anni fuit, quominus is eum ducat, vim fieri veto, Dig. 43, 31. 'Whichever party had possession of the slave in question during the greater part of the preceding year, the violent hindrance of his prehension and abduction of the slave I prohibit.' The same exceptions of violence, clandestinity, and permission, as in the interdict Uti possidetis, were either expressed or understood. Before Justinian's time Utrubi had been assimilated to Uti possidetis, that is, had ceased to be a means of recovering as well as retaining possession. Hodie tamen aliter observatur: nam utriusque interdicti potestas, quantum ad possessionem pertinet, exaequata est, ut ille vincat et in re soli et in re mobili qui possessionem nec vi nec clam nec precario ab adversario litis contestationis tempore detinet, Inst. 4, 15. 4. 'The modern rule is different; both interdicts, so far as possession is a title to redress, are assimilated; and in respect both of movables and of immovables judgment goes for him who proves unimpeachable possession at the moment of commencing the action.' What method of recovering possession of movables was substituted, will presently appear.

§ 153. It is necessary to distinguish between Detention (custodia, possessio naturalis, in possessione esse) and Possession (possessio), and this may best be done by an examination of particular instances.

The slave and filiusfamilias had no possession. Quod ex justa causa corporaliter a servo tenetur id in peculio servi est, et peculium quod servus civiliter quidem possidere non potest sed naturaliter tenet, dominus creditur possidere, Dig. 41, 2, 24. 'When a slave has detention on just grounds, the thing is in his peculium, and his master has possession.' Qui in aliena potestate sunt, rem peculiarem tenere possunt, habere et possidere non possunt, quia possessio non tantum corporis sed et juris est, Dig. 41, 2; 49, 1. 'A person under power has detention of a peculium but not possession, for possession is not purely physical, but partly a legal fact.' We must except the peculium castrense and quasi-castrense. Filiusfamilias in castris adquisitum usucapiet, Dig. 41, 3, 4, 1. 'What a filiusfamilias acquires in the field is converted by possession into property.'

A manager or agent (procurator) has detention, not possession. Nec idem est possidere et alieno nomine possidere, nam is possidet cujus nomine possidetur. Procurator alienae possessioni praestat ministerium, Dig. 41, 2, 18. 'Possession differs from detention in the name of another, for he has possession of a thing in whose name it is held. An agent is the instrument of another person's possession.' Generaliter quisquis omnino nostro nomine sit in possessione, veluti procurator, hospes, amicus, nos possidere videmur, Dig. 41, 2, 9. 'The occupation of a procurator, guest, or friend in our name is our possession.'

A borrower has only detention, the lender retains possession. Rei commodatae et possessionem et proprietatem retinemus, Dig. 13, 6, 8.

A lessee (conductor) has detention, the lessor (locator) possession.

Et fructuarius, et colonus, et inquilinus sunt in praedio et tamen non possident, Dig. 43, 26, 6, 2. 'The usufructuary, tenant, and lodger have occupation, but not possession.' Per colonos et inquilinos aut servos nostros possidemus, Dig. 41, 2, 25, 1. 'Our farmers, lodgers, and slaves are instruments of our possession.'

A ward may possess without his guardian's authority if he has sufficient intelligence, but not otherwise. Ofilius quidem et Nerva filius etiam sine tutoris auctoritate possidere incipere posse pupillum aiunt: eam enim rem facti non juris esse: quae sententia recipi potest si ejus aetatis sint ut intellectum capiant, Dig. 41, 2, 3. 'The guardian's authority is not requisite for a commencement of possession by the ward, for possession is rather a physical than a legal relation, but the ward must be old enough to understand the relation.'

The owner of a servitude (jus in re) has no possession. Usufructuarius usucapere servum non potest quia non possidet, Dig. 41, 1, 10, 5. 'The usufructuary has no usucaption, for he has no possession.' Naturaliter videtur possidere is qui usumfructum habet, Dig. 41, 2, 12. 'The usufructuary has mere detention.'

[It would be a fallacy to argue that occupation is possession because it is naturalis possessio, just as it would be to argue that nine is ten because it is ten minus one, for an epithet sometimes detracts from, instead of adding to, the connotation of a word.]

As the usufructuary has no possession, it follows a fortiori that the usuary has no possession. [Although the jus in re called usus must be distinguished from possession, the words usucapio, usurpatio show that in the older language usus = possessio.]

The Emphyteuta had possession as well as detention. Emphyteusis was originally regarded as a species of locatio or venditio, but Zeno decided that it was a contract sui generis, and governed by its own rules, Inst. 3, 24, 3. The relation of emphyteuta to dominus was the same as in feudal times the relation of the freeholder or copyholder to the lord. The emphyteuta was grantee of land in perpetuity, subject to payment of a rent. The property remained in the grantor, but the emphyteuta had a jus in rem nearly amounting to property, for he could alienate the land and recover it by vindication from any possessor and, as long as he paid his rent, from the grantor, Dig. 6, 3.

The mortgagor had by a legal fiction usucaption-possession, the mortgagee had interdict-possession. Qui pignori dedit ad usucapionem tantum possidet; quod ad reliquas omnes causas pertinet, qui accepit possidet, Dig. 41, 3, 16. The mortgagee could recover the pledge by actio in rem quasi Serviana, Inst. 4, 6, 7. Here, then, interdict-possession appears to be a jus in rem, for it is recoverable by vindicatio. But instead of identifying the mortgagee's jus in rem and his interdict-possession, it is more correct to regard his jus in rem and his interdict-possession as distinct though concurrent. In a hypotheca, that is, an agreement without delivery, the mortgagee acquired no possession.

The depositary has mere detention, the depositor has possession. The depositary only acquires possession in one case, that is, when he is made a stake-holder for this very purpose. Rei depositae proprietas apud deponentem manet sed et possessio, nisi apud sequestrem deposita est; nam tum demum sequester possidet: id enim agitur ea depositione ut neutrius possessioni id tempus procedat, Dig. 16, 3, 17. 'The property and possession of the thing deposited remain with the depositor, except when possession as well as detention is expressly delivered to a stake-holder: for this is the only sequestration where possession passes, the object being to interrupt the usucaption of both litigants.'

With Permissive occupation (precarium) possession passes, unless it is expressly agreed that only detention shall pass. Meminisse autem nos oportet, eum qui precario habet, etiam possidere, Dig. 43, 26, 4, 1. 'The occupant by permission has possession.' Is qui rogavit ut precario in fundo moretur, non possidet, sed possessio apud eum qui concessit remanet, Dig. 43, 26, 6, 2. 'The grantee of permissive detention does not possess, but possession remains with the grantor.'

The defendant in a vindicatio has detention but not necessarily possession. Officium autem judicis in hac actione hoc erit, ut judex inspiciat an reus possideat. . . . Quidam tamen, ut Pegasus, eam solam possessionem putaverunt hanc actionem complecti quae locum habet in interdicto Uti possidetis vel Utrubi. Denique ait, ab eo apud quem deposita sit vel commodata vel qui conduxerit . . . quia hi omnes non possident, vindicari non posse. Puto autem ab omnibus, qui tenent et habent restituendi facultatem, peti posse, Dig. 6, 1, 9. 'Although it is not expressed in his commission, the judex must see whether the defendant is in possession. Some think the same possession is required as for the interdicts; and that, accordingly, the depositary, borrower, hirer, not having such possession, cannot be defendants in a vindication. But, in truth, whoever has detention and the means of restitution, may be made defendant in a vindication.' In Personal actions the defendant is not called possessor.

Servitudes, though not the subject of possession, were the subject of quasi-possession, § 139, which was called juris possessio in contradiction to true possession or corporis possessio; though if juris possessio was the proper name for possession of a fraction of property, possession that bore the same relation to the totality of property should have been called, not corporis possessio, but dominii possessio; e.g. Fundi possessionem vel usufructus quasi possessionem, Dig. 4, 6, 23, 2. Si quis longa quasi possessione jus aquae ducendae nactus sit, Dig. 8, 5, 10. Possessionem vel corporis vel juris, Dig. 43, 26, 2, 3.

The quasi-possession of servitudes, like the possession of corporeal things, was protected by interdicts. The possession of rural servitudes, such as iter, actus, via, jus aquae ducendae, &c., was protected by special interdicts: e. g. Quo itinere actuque privato, quo de agitur, vel via hoc anno nec vi nec clam nec precario ab illo usus es, quo minus ita utaris, vim fieri veto, Dig. 43, 19. 'The foot-way, horse-way, carriage-way in question, which thou hast used within a year without violence, clandestinity, or permission in respect of the adversary, the violent hindrance of thy continuing to use I prohibit.'

Urbane servitudes, whether positive, as jus tigni immittendi, or negative, as jus altius non tollendi, being closely connected with right to an immovable, were always protected by Uti possidetis. Personal servitudes, e. g. usufructus, usus, fructus, were protected, according to circumstances, by Uti possidetis, Utrubi, or Unde vi.

Four of the cases we have mentioned, the possession of the emphyteuta, the mortgagee, the sequestrator, and the permissive holder, are anomalous; for possession is composed of two elements, physical detention and the purpose of exercising rights of ownership (animus domini), and none of these four possessors can be said to have the animus domini. In these four cases, and these alone, it is necessary to assume that the law recognized a derivative or transferred possession, in which one of the elements of original possession, the animus domini, is absent, and replaced by what may be called the animus possidendi.

As possession consists of two elements, one corporeal and one mental, it is evident that it cannot be acquired by a purely mental act. Adipiscimur possessionem corpore et animo, neque per se animo aut per se corpore, Dig. 41, 2, 3, 1. 'We acquire possession by the conjunction of a corporeal and a mental act, and not by either separately.' Neratius et Proculus solo animo non posse nos adquirere possessionem aiunt, si non antecedat naturalis possessio, Ibid. 3. 'Intention alone does not suffice for acquiring possession unless preceded by detention.' Detention necessarily implies not corporeal contact, but corporeal presence [except when a movable is by my order placed in my house during my absence], and is the physical power of dealing immediately with a subject and excluding any foreign agency. The acquisition of detention is Prehension, which is never fictitious or symbolical, but a real physical change of relation. The continuance of possession requires a continuance of both the elements which are essential to its acquisition, that is, both physical control and the intention of enjoying as proprietor. Fere quibuscunque modis obligamur iisdem in contrarium actis liberamur, quum quibus modis acquirimus, iisdem in contrarium actis amittimus. Ut igitur nulla possessio acquiri nisi animo et corpore potest, ita nulla amittitur nisi in qua utrumque (utrumque =alterutrum, or read utcunque or utrumcunque) in contrarium actum est, Dig. 50, 17, 153. 'As obligation is dissolved by a reversal of the conditions under which it is created, so possession is lost by a reversal of the conditions under which it is acquired. As its acquisition demands the concurrence of a corporeal and a mental condition, so its termination requires the reversal of one or the other.' Ejus quidem quod corpore nostro teneremus [dicam] possessionem amitti vel animo vel etiam corpore, Dig. 41, 2, 44. 'When we detain in person, possession may be terminated by either a mental or a physical change.'

The physical condition, however, is not to be interpreted so strictly in the continuance of possession as in its commencement; for continued possession permits a temporary suspension of physical control, and only requires the power of reproducing this relation at will: for instance, it is not lost if we have left a thing unintentionally in a forest, but remember the exact spot; or have stowed a thing in a place of security, but forget for the moment where we put it; or abandon an Alpine pasture in winter, with the intention of revisiting it on the return of summer. Nerva filius res mobiles, excepto homine, quatenus sub custodia nostra sint, hactenus possideri, id est, quatenus, si velimus, naturalem possessionem nancisci possimus, Dig. 41, 2, 3, 13. 'The possession of movables, excepting slaves, is terminated by loss of custody, or the power of reproducing at will natural detention.' There was an exception in the case of slaves, for a fugitive slave was regarded as still in his master's possession, and in the case of land, for a man did not lose possession of his land which had been invaded in his absence until he had notice of the invasion; that is to say, he retained possession in the interim solely by his mental disposition. Nam saltus hibernos et aestivos, quorum possessio retinetur animo, licet neque servum neque colonum ibi habeamus, quamvis saltus proposito possidendi fuerit alius ingressus, tamdiu priorem possidere dictum est, quamdiu possessionem ab alio occupatam ignoraret, Dig. 41, 2, 44. 'When a winter or summer pasture, retained in possession without the instrumentality of slaves or tenants, solely by the mental relation, is invaded by a stranger, the prior possessor is not regarded as ousted from possession until he has notice of the invasion.' It is by reference to this laxer interpretation and to these exceptions that we can understand the statement of Gaius, § 153, that possession may be retained without a continuance of corporeal detention.

§ 154. Although Uti possidetis and Utrubi are called interdicts Retinendae possessionis, they were also in effect interdicts Recuperandae possessionis. This is manifest on the face of Utrubi, and it also follows from the vitia possessionis named in Uti possidetis: if the possession of the actual possessor was tainted with one of three vices, if it was not adverse (open and unauthorized) and commenced without violence (vi, clam, aut precario), then his adversary recovered possession. What, then, it may be asked, was the use of a distinct interdict Recuperandae possessionis, the interdict Unde vi, which, like the Uti possidetis, was only available for a year? The answer is, that Uti possidetis only restored possession when the dispossessor was in present possession; it gave no redress when a third party was the present possessor: in such cases the party dispossessed required a different remedy, and this was given him in the interdict Unde vi. Further, by Uti possidetis the intermediate profits (fructus) were only recoverable from the commencement of the suit, by Unde vi from the time of the ejectment; and the remedy of the disseisee by Uti possidetis was barred by the vices of his own possession, not so his remedy by Unde vi.

The interdict Unde vi (or De vi) had two forms, one of which is called by Cicero interdictum quotidianum, and redressed cases of ordinary violence (vis quotidiana), while the other was invoked in cases of armed violence (vis armata). The former has been thus restored by Keller from indications in Cicero, Pro Caecina and Pro Tullio: Unde tu Numeri Negidi aut familia aut procurator tuus Aulum Agerium aut familiam aut procuratorem illius in hoc anno vi dejecisti, qua de re agitur, cum ille possideret, quod nec vi nec clam nec precario a te possideret, eo restituas. 'In the place whence thou, Numerius Negidius, thy slaves or procurator, hast this year violently ousted Aulus Agerius, his slaves or procurator, as he alleges, which he possessed without violence, clandestinity, or permission in respect of thee, in that place do thou reinstate him.' The interdict De vi armata may be restored as follows: Unde tu Numeri Negidi aut familia aut procurator tuus Aulum Agerium aut familiam aut procuratorem illius vi hominibus coactis armatisve dejecisti, qua de re agitur, eo restituas. 'In the place whence thou, Numerius Negidius, thy slaves or procurator, hast violently ousted Aulus Agerius, his slaves or procurator, by men assembled or armed, in that place do thou reinstate him.' This differed from the ordinary interdict by the omission of the exceptions, and the omission of limitation to a year. The interdict Unde vi only applied to immovables. Illud utique in dubium non venit, interdictum hoc ad res mobiles non pertinere, Dig. 43, 16, 6. 'It is certain that this interdict is not available for disseisin of movables.' Movables could originally be recovered by the interdict Utrubi, which probably did not change its character until a new means of recovering movables had been given by a constitution of Valentinian, A. D. 389, which, in effect, was an extension of Unde vi to movables. Si quis in tantam furoris pervenerit audaciam, ut possessionem rerum apud fiscum vel apud homines quoslibet constitutarum ante adventum judicialis arbitrii violenter invaserit, dominus quidem constitutus possessionem quam abstulit restituat possessori, et dominium ejusdem rei amittat. Si vero alienarum rerum possessionem invasit, non solum eam possidentibus reddat, verum etiam aestimationem earum rerum restituere compellatur, Codex, 8, 4, 7. 'Whoever dares to seize by violence things in the possession of the treasury or of private persons without waiting for a judicial order, shall restore possession, and, if he is proprietor, shall forfeit his property, if he is not proprietor, shall forfeit the value.' This was declared to apply both to movables and immovables, Inst. 4, 2, 1. In accordance with the spirit of this constitution, the dispossessor was no longer allowed to plead the exceptions in the old form of the interdict, and they are omitted in the new form which we find in the Digest: Unde tu illum vi dejecisti aut familia tua dejecit, de eo quaeque ille tunc ibi habuit tantummodo intra annum, post annum de eo quod ad eum qui vi dejecit pervenerit, judicium dabo, Dig. 43, 16, 1. 'The land (or, house) whence thou or thy slaves hast violently ousted such a one, and the movables which he had therein, shall be recoverable by action within a year; after the expiration of a year he shall only recover what came into the hands of the dispossessor.' That is to say, the distinction between vis armata and vis quotidiana was no longer recognized.

Although the recovery of possession by violence was prohibited, it was allowable to repel violence by violence in the defence of possession. Eum igitur qui cum armis venit possumus armis repellere, sed hoc confestim, non ex intervallo, dummodo sciamus non solum resistere permissum ne dejiciatur, sed et si dejectus quis fuerit, eundem dejicere non ex intervallo sed ex continenti posse, Dig. 43, 16, 3, 9. 'An armed aggressor may be lawfully repelled by arms, but this must be immediately, and we may not only resist disseisin, but eject the disseisor, provided that no interval has elapsed.' Qui possessionem vi ereptam vi in ipso congressu recuperat, in pristinam causam reverti potius quam vi possidere intelligendus est. Ideoque si te vi dejecero, illico tu me, deinde ego te, unde vi interdictum tibi utile erit, Ibid. 17. 'A possessor who is violently disseised and recovers seisin by immediate violence, rather restores his former position than possesses by violence. Therefore, if I oust you by violence, and am immediately ousted by you, and then oust you again, you may have the interdict Unde vi.'

As violent dispossession was remedied by the interdict Unde vi, so other interdicts remedied dispossession whose inception was clandestine or permissive. An interdict De clandestina possessione is mentioned, Dig. 10, 3, 7, 5. It would scarcely be required in the case of immovables, for as a possessor was not disseised until he had notice of the invasion, he could immediately by attempting an entry convert the clandestine into a violent dispossession. It would not be required for movables as long as the old form of Utrubi was in force, for clandestine dispossession of a movable might be redressed by Utrubi combined, perhaps, with an exhibitory interdict or order of production. But when Utrubi ceased to apply to past possession, clandestine dispossession of a movable would require a special redress. The form of this interdict is not extant.

The interdict De precario was in these terms: Quod precario ab illo habes, aut dolo malo fecisti ut desineres habere, qua de re agitur, id illi restituas, Dig. 43, 26, 2. 'The possession of the thing in question which thou holdest by the permission of such a one, or hast fraudulently ceased to hold, do thou restore to him.'

The division of interdicts into those for obtaining, retaining, and recovering possession is mentioned by Ausonius in his poem on the marvellous properties of the number Three:

> 'Interdictorum trinum genus, Unde repulsus
> Vi fuero, aut Utrobi fuerit, Quorumque bonorum.'
> Ausonius, Griphus de numero ternario, 63.

The interdicts for obtaining possession have little affinity to those for retaining and recovering possession. In the latter, possession is itself a title to possession, but not in the former. Accordingly, these interdicts belong to widely different branches of substantive law. Uti possidetis, Utrubi, and Unde vi, belong to the law of obligations founded on delict; while Quorum bonorum belongs to the law of testamentary and intestate succession, that is, to the law of property.

§ 156. Paulus mentioned a fourth class of interdicts, namely, those for either acquiring or recovering possession. Sunt etiam interdicta duplicia tam recuperandae quam adipiscendae possessionis, Dig. 43, 1, 2, 3. These are the restitutory interdicts, Quem fundum, Quam hereditatem, Quem usumfructum, which have been already quoted, § 89, whereby, if the defendant in a real action refused to give security judicatum solvi, possession was transferred to the plaintiff, who in some cases would acquire, in others recover possession.

The interdicts which Gaius calls double are called by Ulpian mixed. Mixtae sunt actiones, in quibus uterque actor est, utputa finium regundorum, familiae erciscundae, communi dividundo, interdictum Uti possidetis, Utrubi, Dig. 44, 7, 37, 1. 'Mixed actions are those wherein each party is both plaintiff and defendant, as the action for tracing boundaries, for partition of an inheritance, for dissolution of joint ownership, and the interdicts Uti possidetis and

Utrubi.' The effect of this duplicity or mixture of characters was that the plaintiff as well as the defendant was liable to condemnation and absolution. According to Justinian, the three personal actions just named are called Mixed because they involve questions both of property and obligation, Mixtam causam obtinere videntur, tam in rem quam in personam, Inst. 4, 6, 20. Another effect of the duplicity of the interdicts was, as we shall presently see, to increase the number of stipulations in the proceeding by Sponsio.

§ 162. When a slave was manumitted, his master might bind him by oath or stipulation to the performance of certain services, menial or domestic, which might be enforced by action. The requirements of the master were often exorbitant, and were repressed by praetorian legislation. Hoc edictum praetor proponit coarctandae persecutionis libertatis causa impositorum. Animadvertit enim libertatis causa impositorum praestationem ultra modum excrevisse, ut premeret atque oneraret libertinas personas. Initio igitur praetor pollicetur se judicium operarum daturum in libertos et libertas, Dig. 38, 1. 'This part of the edict moderates the recovery of services imposed on manumission. These exactions had become immoderate and oppressive to the freedmen. The praetor begins by providing an action for the recovery of services.'

§ 163. The action of calumny was one of the means of repressing vexatious litigation, which Gaius presently explains. A plaintiff proved to have sued in bad faith forfeited, if he had sued by action, one tenth, if he sued by interdict, one fourth, of the value of the subject of controversy.

§ 165. There is some doubt whether in referring to the condition of a sponsio we should use the word Ni or Si. In the sponsio praejudicialis, § 93, Gaius uses Si. We have Si in Cicero's letters: Quum ei dicerem tibi videri sponsionem illam nos sine periculo facere posse, Si [this is the reading of the MSS. but was altered by Manutius into Ni] bonorum Turpiliae possessionem praetor ex edicto suo mihi dederit, negare aiebat Servium tabulas testamenti esse eas quos instituisset is qui factionem testamenti non habuerit, Ad Diversos, 7, 21. 'When I told him your opinion that he might safely wager, That the inheritance of Turpilia belonged to him by the praetor's edict, he said that Servius Sulpicius held the will to be void because the testator was incapacitated.' In other places we have Ni. At vero hoc quidem jam vetus est et majorum exemplo multis in rebus usitatum, quum ad vim faciendam veniretur, si quos armatos quamvis procul conspexissent; ut statim testificati discederent, optime sponsionem facere possent Ni adversus edictum praetoris vis facta esset, Pro Caecina, 16. 'It is an old rule that if the plaintiff attempting an entry sees armed men at a distance, he may have the fact attested and retire, and then safely wager in the terms: Unless he was violently ousted in contravention of the edict.' Sponsio est, Ni te Apronius socium in decumis esse dicat, In Verrem, 2, 3, 59. 'He challenged Apronius to a sponsio, of which the condition was, that Apronius asserted that the praetor was his partner in the tithes.' Cogere eum coepit, quum ageret nemo, nemo postularet, sponsionem duo millium nummum facere cum lictore suo Ni furtis quaestum faceret, In Verrem, 2, 5, 54. 'The praetor compelled him, though there was no accusation, to make a sponsio with his lictor for two thousand sesterces, whether he was a thief.' It seems that Si is the proper word in the sponsio and Ni in the restipulatio, though in referring to a sponsio poenalis, the term of the restipulatio, Ni, might be employed. Apparently, then, in the passage before us, § 165, and in § 166, we ought to read Si instead of Ni. If, however, the last cited case was a sponsio praejudicialis, we must suppose with Keller that in an indirect reference to a sponsio (oratio obliqua) the term used was Ni, even when in the direct sponsio the term was Si.

We may observe that a sponsio was a stipulatio, that is, a unilateral contract; and therefore, to bind both parties and constitute a bet or wager in the modern sense of the term, it was necessary to have two contracts, that is, a sponsio and a restipulatio.

§ 166. From the two sponsiones and two restipulationes which are mentioned, it appears that Gaius is now speaking of double interdicts, and from the words eum fundum easve aedes it appears that he is speaking not of Utrubi but of Uti possidetis.

The Cascellian action was a personal action for enforcing an obligation founded on delict, that is, on personal violence; and as it was not founded on stipulation, so neither, apparently, was it accompanied with security judicatum solvi. For, firstly, it was a personal action, and it is not mentioned among the exceptional cases, § 102, where such security was required; secondly, it corresponded exactly to the formula arbitraria, § 163, and the aliud judicium de re restituenda vel exhibenda, § 165, of the simple interdicts, and in connection with these there is no mention of judicatum solvi. In the Fructuarium judicium Satisdatio was requisite to protect the plaintiff against the defendant's insolvency; but in the Cascellianum judicium, as specific restitution was recovered, the defendant's insolvency was immaterial.

Interdicts have been compared to the Mandamus and Injunction of English law: let us consider what is the amount of the resemblance. A writ of Mandamus is a command issuing in the queen's name from the court of Queen's Bench, directed to any person, corporation, or inferior court, requiring them to do some particular thing therein specified which appertains to their office and duty. The party injured first obtains by motion a rule (order) of the court directing the party complained of to show cause why a writ of mandamus should not issue. The rule is obtained upon affidavit (written statement upon oath) and cause is shown upon affidavit: and as it usually appears that the case involves questions of fact which cannot satisfactorily be disposed of upon affidavit, or questions of law which ought to be put upon the record so as to be subject to revision in a court of error, an Alternative mandamus issues in order that such questions may be determined upon the return, that is, a mandamus commanding the party to whom it is addressed either to do the act demanded or to show cause why he does not, to which a return or answer must be made on a certain day. The defendant in his answer may object to the law of the prosecutor, or traverse some fact alleged, or plead some new matter. So the prosecutor may demur, traverse, or plead to the return. If the prosecutor obtain judgment, he has a Peremptory writ of mandamus to which no return is permitted but a certificate of obedience.

The issue of the Alternative mandamus may be compared to the issue of the interdict, the point of resemblance being that the judicial authority issues its mandate before it is in complete possession of the case (principaliter auctoritatem suam interponit praetor, § 139), the merits of the case being determined by a subsequent proceeding in the nature of an action. The Peremptory mandamus corresponds to the judgment in the Cascellian action. We have hitherto spoken of the Prerogative writ of mandamus. In the action of mandamus created by the Common Law Procedure Act, 1854, the resemblance between the mandamus and interdict ceases, for here the mandamus does not issue until the case has been investigated, and the writ of mandamus is in the form of an ordinary writ of execution. Moreover, the mandamus only enforces public or official duties, whereas interdicts protect private rights of possession.

There is a greater resemblance between Interdicts and writs of Injunction. The writ of Injunction is a command of the court of Chancery requiring a defendant to abstain from some course of action, and, like an interdict or alternative mandamus, an interlocutory injunction is issued before the Court has investigated the merits of the case. In respect also of their purposes, Injunctions and Interdicts coincide: for instance, injunctions for the restraint of a nuisance, such as obstructing a highway or public river, or diverting a watercourse so as to interrupt the right of another person that it should flow undisturbed to his meadow or mill, obstructing ancient windows so that the owner cannot enjoy the light so freely as before, resemble the corresponding interdicts for preventing similar wrongs. But injunctions are not, like interdicts, used for the protection of Possession as distinct from Property, and extend to many purposes for which interdicts were not employed.

In respect of the order of the proceedings (principaliter auctoritatem interponit praetor) the interdict resembled the ex parte injunction which is obtained immediately on a bill being filed, or on motion and affidavit, and even, in particular emergencies, without notice to the defendant, when the giving of notice might only accelerate the mischief. The interdict seems sometimes to have been employed as a Summary procedure, as appears from the reference to recuperatores instead of a judex, and from an expression in the Theodosian Code: In interdicto Quorum bonorum cessat licentia provocandi, ne quod beneficio celeritatis inventum est subdatur injuriis tarditatis, Cod. Theod. 11, 36, 22. 'In the interdict Quorum bonorum there is no appeal, lest a process introduced for the sake of celerity should be injuriously protracted.' But in most cases the process must have been the reverse of summary. De loco, si possessio petenti firma est, etiam interdicere licet, dum cetera ex interdicto diligenter peragantur; magna enim alea est ad interdictum deducere, cujus est executio perplexissima, Frontinus, lib. 2, p. 44. 'The land, if your possession is clear, may be retained by interdict, but you must be careful to perform all the formalities; for it is very dangerous to have recourse to the interdict, as the process is intricate in the extreme.'

Considering the interdict merely as a conventional mode of commencing proceedings, which, but for custom, might have just as well been commenced in any other way, perhaps we may find its closest parallel not in Mandamus or Injunction, but in another institute of English law, the Original Writ. This (which is now abolished except in Real actions) was a mandatory letter from the king directed to the sheriff of the county wherein the injury is committed, requiring him to command the wrong-doer either to do the thing required by the complainant, or else to appear in court and show the reason wherefore he has not done it. Although the interdict was in form peremptory, yet in effect it permitted either obedience or disobedience with a justification. His rebus ita gestis P. Dolabella praetor interdixit, ut est consuetudo, de vi hominibus armatis, sine ulla exceptione, tantum ut unde dejecisset restitueret. Restituisse se dixit. Sponsio facta est. Hac de sponsione vobis judicandum est, Pro Caecina, 8. 'The praetor issued an interdict, as is usual in armed violence, without an exception, ordering the defendant to reinstate the plaintiff in the place whence he had been ousted. The defendant returned that he had reinstated him. The parties thereupon entered into a sponsio which you are to determine.' Here, although the return of the defendant was in form that he had reinstated the plaintiff, in fact he refused to transfer the seisin, denying the plaintiff's title. If the interdict had been alternative in form as well as in effect it would have exactly corresponded to the Original Writ.

As being initiated by an interposition of the judicial authority, the Libellary procedure which existed in the time of Justinian, having superseded the Formulary procedure, rather resembled Interdict procedure than Formulary procedure. The latter commenced with the summons before the praetor (in jus vocatio) and notice of the action which the plaintiff meant to bring (editio actionis). The stages of the Libellary procedure corresponding to these were libellus conventionis and commonitio. The libellus conventionis was a writing addressed to the court, signed by the plaintiff, stating his cause of action and binding himself to prosecute the suit to judgment: it was a form of suing out a writ or summons. Thereupon followed an interlocutio of the court, that is, a commonitio addressed to the defendant and served upon him, not by the plaintiff but by an officer of the court (executor), along with the libellus. The defendant then either gave cautio judicio sisti, security for his appearance in jure for the definitive appointment of the trial (judicio ordinando), or was liable to incarceration.

Here, then, as in Interdict process, the first proceeding of the plaintiff was addressed to the court, not, as in the Formulary system, to the defendant.

DE POENA TEMERE LITIGANTIUM.

§ 171. *Sed adversus reos quidem infitiantes ex quibusdam causis* dupli *actio constituitur*, velut si iudicati aut depensi *aut* damni *iniuriae* aut *legatorum* per *damnationem relictorum nomine* agitur: ex quibusdam causis sponsionem facere permittitur, velut de pecunia certa credita et pecunia constituta: sed certae quidem creditae pecuniae tertiae partis, constitutae vero pecuniae partis dimidiae.

§ 171. The defendant's denial of his obligation is sometimes punished by the duplication of the damages to be recovered. This occurs in an action on a judgment debt, or for money paid by a sponsor, or for injurious damage, or for legacies left in the form of judgment debt. It is sometimes punished by a wager of a penal sum, as in an action of loan, or on a promise to pay a pre-existing debt, in the former case of one third of the sum in dispute, in the latter of one half.

§ 172. Quodsi *neque sponsionis*, *neque* dupli *actionis* periculum *ei* cum quo agitur *iniungatur*, *aut* ne statim *qui*dem ab initio pluris quam simpli sit actio, permittit Praetor iusiurandum exigere non calumniae causa in*fitias* ire: unde qu*ia* heredes vel qui heredum loco *ha*bentur, nu*m*quam po*enis* obligati sunt, item feminis pupillisque *remitti sole*t po*ena* sponsionis, i*ube*t modo eos i*urare*.

§ 172. In the absence of a penal wager, and of duplication of damages on denial, and of absolute multiplication of damages, the plaintiff with the praetor's leave may exact an oath from the defendant that his denial is conscientious. Accordingly, successors and quasi-successors, who are always exempt from penalty, and women and wards, who are excused the compulsory wager, are required to take the oath of bona fides.

§ 173. Statim aut*em* ab initio pluris quam simpli actio est, velut furti manifesti quadrupli, nec manifesti dupli, concepti et oblati tripli: nam ex his causis et aliis quibusdam, sive quis neget sive fateatur, pluris quam simpli est actio.

§ 173. There is an absolute multiplication of damages in various actions: in an action of manifest theft a quadruplication, for theft not manifest a duplication, for possession or obtrusion of stolen goods a triplication: for in these and some other actions the damages are a multiple of the plaintiff's loss, whether the defendant denies or confesses the claim.

§ 174. Actoris quoque calumnia coercetur modo calumniae iudicio, modo contrario, modo iureiurando, modo restipulatione.

§ 174. On the part of the plaintiff reckless litigation is checked by the action of dishonest litigation, by the Contrary action, by oath, and by restipulation.

§ 175. Et quidem calumniae iudicium adversus omnes actiones locum habet. et est decimae partis *causae*; adversus interdicta autem quartae partis *causae*.

§ 175. The action of dishonest litigation lies against the plaintiff for the tenth part of the value he has claimed by action, and for the fourth part of the value he has claimed by interdict.

§ 176. Liberum est *illi* cum quo agitur aut calumniae iudicium opponere, aut *iusiurandum* exigere non calumniae causa agere.

§ 176. It is optional to the defendant whether he brings an action of dishonest litigation or exacts an oath of bona fides.

§ 177. Contrarium autem iudicium ex certis causis constitui*tur*: velut si iniuriarum agatur, et si cum muliere eo nomine agatur, quod dicetur ventris nomine in possessionem missa dolo malo ad alium possessionem transtulisse; et si quis eo nomine agat, quod dicat se a Praetore in possessionem missum ab alio quo admissum non esse. sed adversus iniuriarum quidem action*em* decimae partis datur; adversus vero duas istas quintae.

§ 177. The Contrary action only lies in certain cases, for instance, against the plaintiff in an action of outrage, in an action against a widow put into possession in the name of her unborn child for fraudulent transfer of possession, or an action for non-admission of a person sent into possession by the praetor. In the action of outrage it lies for the tenth of the damages, in the two latter actions for the fifth.

§ 178. Severior autem coercitio est per contrarium iudicium: n*am* calumniae iudicio x. partis nemo damn*a*tur, nisi qui intellegit non recte se agere, sed vexandi adversarii gratia actionem instituit, potiusque ex iudicis errore vel iniquitate victoriam sperat quam ex causa veritatis; calumnia enim in adfectu est, sicut *f*urti crimen. contrario vero iudicio omni modo damnatur actor, si causam non tenuerit, licet ali*qua* opinione inductus crediderit se recte agere.

§ 178. Of these repressive measures the Contrary action is the more severe. A plaintiff sued for dishonest litigation, to forfeit the tenth of the value, must have known he had no right, and have sued to harass his adversary, in reliance on the error or iniquity of the judex, rather than on the justice of his cause; for dishonest litigation, like the crime of theft, implies intention. In the Contrary action he is condemned if he merely loses the previous action, even though he had grounds for believing in the goodness of his cause.

§ 179. Utique autem ex quibus causis contrario iudicio agere potest, etiam calumniae iudicium locum habet: sed alterutro *tantum* iudicio agere permittitur. qua ratione si iusiurandum de calumnia exactum fuerit, quemadmodum calumniae iudicium non datur, ita et contrarium non dari debet.

§ 179. Wherever the Contrary action lies, the action for dishonest litigation also lies, but they are not concurrent; and an oath of bona fides excludes both the action of dishonest litigation and the Contrary action.

§ 180. Restipulationis quoque poena ex certis causis fieri solet:

§ 180. The restipulatio also is confined to certain cases, and the

et quemadmodum contrario iudicio omnimodo condemnatur actor, si causam non tenuerit, nec requiritur an scierit non recte se agere, ita etiam restipulationis poena omnimodo damnatur actor.

plaintiff who loses his cause, as he is condemned in the Contrary action, so he forfeits the penalty of the restipulatio, even though he sued with bona fides.

§ 181. *Sane* si ab *actore ea restipulationis* poena petatur, ei neque calumniae iudicium opponitur, neque iurisiurandi religio *iniungitur*: nam contrarium iudicium *in* his causis locum non habere palam est.

§ 181. The restipulatio precludes a party from suing for dishonest litigation, from exacting the oath of bona fides, and from instituting the Contrary action.

§ 182. Quibusdam iudiciis damnati ignominiosi fiunt, velut furti, vi bonorum raptorum, iniuriarum; item *pro socio, fiduciae, tutelae, man*dati, depositi. sed furti aut vi bonorum *raptorum aut iniuriarum non solum* damnati notantur ignominia, sed et*iam pacti*: *idque ita in edicto Praetoris* scriptum est. et recte: plurimum *enim interest utrum ex delicto* aliquis, an ex contractu debitor *sit*. [4⅛ *lin.*]

§ 182. In some actions condemnation carries infamy, as in the actions of theft, rapine, outrage, partnership, trust, guardianship, agency, deposit. In prosecutions for theft it is not only infamous to be condemned, but also to compromise, as the edict justly ordains; for obligation based on delict differs widely from an obligation based on contract. Condemnation in these actions, however, is only infamous to the principal, not to the person condemned as surety or procurator.

§ 183. In summa sciendum est eum qui al*iquem in ius vocare vult et cum eo* agere, et eum qui vocatus est [*desunt* 2⅛ *lin.*] patrono et liber*to* [⅛ *lin.*] et in *eum* qui adversus *ea* egeri*t*, *poena* con*stituta* est.

§ 183. Finally, a child may not summon his parent, and a freedman may not summon his patron, to make appearance as defendant in an action without the permission of the praetor, under a penalty of fifty solidi.

§ 184. Qu*ando* autem in ius vocatus fuerit adversarius, ni eo die fini*tum f*uerit negotium, vadimonium ei faciendum est, id est ut promittat se certo die sisti.

§ 184. Upon an appearance in court, if the proceedings are not terminated on the same day, the defendant must give security for an adjourned appearance on a future day.

§ 185. Fiunt aut*em* vadimonia quibusdam ex causis pura, id est sine satisdatione, quibusdam cum satisdatione, quibusdam iureiurando, quibusdam recuperatoribus suppositis, id *est ut* qui non *steterit*, is protinus a recuperatoribus in summa*m* vadimonii condemnetur: eaque singula diligenter Praetoris edicto significantur.

§ 185. The security is sometimes with sureties, sometimes without sureties, sometimes on oath, sometimes contains a reference to recuperators, so that on default of appearance the defendant may be immediately condemned by the recuperators in the penal sum of the security; all which is expressed at length in the edict.

§ 186. Et si quidem iudicati

§ 186. In an action on a judgment

depensive agetur, tanti fiet vadimonium, quanti ea res erit; si vero ex ceteris causis, quanti actor iuraverit non calumniae causa postulare sibi vadimonium promitti, nec tamen *pluris quam partis dimidiae, nec* pluribus quam sestertium C milibus fit vadimonium. itaque si centum milium res erit, nec iudicati depensive agetur, non plus quam sestertium quinquaginta milium fit vadimonium.

debt, or for money paid by a sponsor, the sum of the security is equal to the sum in dispute. In other cases it is the amount which the plaintiff swears that he honestly believes to be necessary to his security, provided that it is not more than half the sum in dispute, nor exceeds a hundred thousand sesterces. If, for instance, the sum in dispute is a hundred thousand sesterces, and the action is not brought to recover a judgment debt or money paid by a sponsor, the penal sum of the security conditioned for reappearance may not exceed fifty thousand sesterces.

§ 187. Quas autem personas sine permissu Praetoris impune in ius vocare non possumus, easdem nec vadimonio invitas obligare nobis possumus, praeterquam si Praetor aditus permittit.

§ 187. Those persons who cannot be summoned to appear without leave of the court cannot be compelled to give security for the adjourned appearance without similar permission.

§ 171. From the duplication of damages against a defendant who denied his delinquency under the lex Aquilia, 3 § 216, and against a heres charged with a legacy in the form of condemnation, 4 § 9; and from the terms, dare damnas esto = dare judicatus esto, employed both in the lex Aquilia, p. 384, and in bequest by the form of condemnation, 2 § 201, it may be inferred with much probability that both the author of unlawful damage and the heir charged with a legacy by words of condemnation were subject, in the older period of the law, to the same proceedings as the judgment debtor (judicatus); that is, in early times were suable by Manus injectio, 4 § 25, and in later times were bound to give satisdatio judicatum solvi, 4 § 102.

The condictio, or action to recover a liquidated debt, was created subsequently to the Twelve Tables by the lex Silia, § 19, and it was doubtless this law which fixed the amount of the concomitant sponsio at one third of the claim. Cicero calls the penal sum of the sponsio legitima pars, and tertia pars, and enumerates the cases in which the action lay. Pecunia tibi debebatur certa, quae nunc petitur per judicem, in qua legitimae partis sponsio facta est, Pro Q. Roscio, 4. Pecunia petita est certa; cum tertia parte sponsio facta est. Haec pecunia necesse est aut data, aut expensa lata, aut stipulata sit, Ibid. 5. 'You claimed a liquidated debt, which you now sue for in a civil action, and a wager has been made with a third, the amount prescribed by law, as the penal sum. Your claim must be founded on the real contract of mutui datio, the literal contract of expensilatio, or the verbal contract of stipulatio.' We may observe three stages in the law of procedure to enforce a strict civil obligation. The third stage, the condictio of the formulary system, was doubtless a modification of the second stage, the condictio of the legis actiones, and this again was a modification of the first stage, the sacramentum, originally the sole and universal form of action. This is called sponsio by Gaius, § 95: it differed from the sponsio of the condictio in that the penal sum was forfeited not to the party but to the State.

Constitutum was a pact (not a stipulation) promising to pay a pre-existing debt on a certain day. If the pre-existing obligation was a natural obligation of the promisor, the constitutum converted a natural into a civil obligation; if it was the obligation of another person, it operated as a guaranty.

As an extremely easy means of transforming naturalis obligatio into civilis obligatio, that is, of arming a creditor with the sharp remedies of the civil law, the invention of the Consensual contract of Constitutum sufficiently explains, as already suggested, the desuetude of the Literal contract of Expensilatio, a process which the ancient Romans employed for the same purpose.

§ 175. A charge of calumny implies guilty knowledge or unlawful intention (dolus), the Contrary action implies unlawful ignorance, that is, recklessness or want of consideration (culpa, temeritas).

§ 176. In three personal actions each party was considered as both plaintiff and defendant and had to take both the oath of the plaintiff and the oath of the defendant. Qui familiae erciscundae et communi dividundo et finium regundorum agunt, et actores sunt et rei, et ideo jurare debent non calumniae causa litem intendere, et non calumniae causa infitias ire, Dig. 10, 2; 44, 4. 'In partition of inheritance, dissolution of joint ownership, and tracing of boundaries, both parties are equally plaintiff and defendant, and therefore must swear to the good faith of both the suit and the defence.'

In the time of Justinian the action of calumny, the Contrary action, sponsio and restipulation had become obsolete, and in their place the losing party was condemned in costs, and the oath received development, being always administered to both parties and their advocates. Sed pro his introductum est et praefatum jusjurandum et ut improbus litigator etiam damnum et impensas litis inferre adversario suo cogatur, Inst. 4, 16, 10. 'Instead of the old checks the oath of the parties and their counsel has been introduced, and the condemnation of the unsuccessful litigant in the costs of his adversary.' Patroni autem causarum, qui utrique parti suum praestantes auxilium ingrediuntur, quum lis fuerit contestata, post narrationem propositam et contradictionem objectam . . . sacrosanctis evangeliis tactis juramentum praestent, quod omni quidem virtute sua omnique ope, quod verum et justum existimaverint, clientibus suis inferre procurabunt, nihil studii relinquentes quod sibi possibile est; non autem, credita sibi causa cognita quod improba sit vel penitus desperata et ex mendacibus allegationibus composita, ipsi scientes prudentesque mala conscientia liti patrocinabuntur; sed et si certamine procedente aliquid tale sibi cognitum fuerit, a causa recedent, ab hujusmodi communione sese penitus separantes, Codex, 3, 1, 14. 'The counsel at the commencement of the hearing, after the exposition of the bill and answer, shall touch the holy Gospels and swear to do their utmost for their clients so far as they believe their cause to be just, but not knowingly to support the wrong, and if in the course of the proceedings they should change their opinion, to retire from the cause.'

§ 184. Vadimonium, cautio judicio sisti, must be distinguished from the security judicatum solvi. It only referred to appearances in jure, and was required whenever there was an adjournment, whereas security judicatum solvi was only required from the defendant in real actions and in certain exceptional personal actions, § 102.

The sketch of judicial procedure which Gaius gives in this last book of his Institutions is not complete without some account of Cognitio extraordinaria.

Under the system of procedure which may be called the Formulary system, which continued in force from its institution by the lex Aebutia, about B.C. 170, until its abolition by a constitution of Diocletian, A.D. 294, legal procedure was divided into two branches, procedure before a judex and procedure before a praetor.

Ordinaria judicia were tried before a judex who received from the praetor, the fountain of Roman justice, a written commission called a formula, or instructions to hear and determine a certain issue according to the rules of equity or of civil law.

The personal interposition of the praetor in judicial proceedings may be divided into jurisdictio and cognitio extra ordinem.

Jurisdictio was either jurisdictio Voluntaria, proceedings based upon fictitious actions, such as adoption, emancipation, surrender in court; or jurisdictio contentiosa, connected with genuine litigation. This included proceedings preparatory or supplementary to trial before a judex, such as judicii ordinatio (delivery of the formula), judicis datio, execution by pignoris captio, the preliminary seizure (missio in possessionem) or final transfer (addictio) of a bankrupt's estate, personal execution by manus injectio.

In cognitio extraordinaria the magistrate superseded the regular course of proceeding before a judex (ordo judiciorum, juris ordinarii executio) and administered extraordinary relief to suitors, under special circumstances, by a decree (decretum) after an investigation (causae cognitio) which he himself conducted. The special circumstances under which the extraordinary procedure was adopted were certain claims contrary to the general spirit of the law, such as complaints of slaves against their masters, freedmen against their patrons, children against their parents, wards against their guardians, and vice versa; claims of honorarium by professors of the liberal professions, claims relating to trusts (fideicommissa) for the hearing of which a special praetor fideicommissarius was appointed, and, lastly, cases where the law itself was the instrument of wrong, petitions, that is, for relief by rescission and cancellation of legal acts and contracts (integri restitutio, in integrum restitutio) wherein equity and law were eminently in collision. There were five recognized justae causae of this extraordinary relief, minority, absence, duress, fraud, mistake. Sometimes the decretum of the praetor after cognitio gave sufficient and final relief, for instance, when he permitted a party to amend an error committed in the course of legal proceedings: sometimes the restitutio only extended as far as the ordinatio judicii, that is, judicii rescissorii: i.e. the praetor rescinded some legal act or fact (alienatio, usucapio, contractus, &c.) and the party obtained relief by trial before a judex in the ordinary course (e.g. Publiciana rescissoria, 4 § 36, commentary).

In procedure by cognitio extraordinaria, the in jus vocatio, summons of the defendant by the plaintiff, was superseded by the evocatio, summons of the defendant by the magistrate through his lictor. Obedience to this summons was compelled by a fine of which we have the formula in Gellius: M. Terentius quando citatus neque respondit neque excusatus est, ego ei unum ovem multam dico, 11, 1. 'As M. Terentius on citation has neither answered nor been excused, I fine him in a single sheep.' If the defendant continued contumacious he was summoned to appear by three proclamations (edicta) at intervals of ten days, and finally an edictum peremptorium was issued in which the magistrate threatened to hear and decide the case in his absence, in default of his appearance, which was done, if he continued disobedient, Dig. 5, 1, 68.

Procedure before a judex was properly called actio, before the praetor, persecutio. Persecutionis verbo extraordinarias persecutiones puto contineri, utputa fideicommissorum, et si quae aliae sunt quae non habent juris ordinarii executionem, Dig. 50, 16, 178, 2. 'Persecutio is the proper name for proceedings before the praetor, as in trusts and other claims which are not triable by an ordinary judex.'

ADDENDA.

In proof of the assertion (p. 79) that materfamilias properly denoted a woman sui juris, whether married or unmarried, as opposed to a filiafamilias or woman alieni juris, should have been quoted: Sui juris sunt familiarum suarum principes, id est paterfamilias itemque materfamilias, Ulpian, 4, 1.

2 § 151 has been thus restored by Krueger, who has had access to the facsimile edition (apograph) of Gaius shortly to be published by Studemund, as the fruits of a new examination of the Veronese manuscript:

Potest ut iure facta testamenta contraria voluntate infirmentur. Apparet *autem* non posse ex eo solo infirmari testamentum, quod postea testator id noluerit valere, usque adeo ut si linum eius inciderit, nihilo minus iure civili valeat. Quinetiam si deleverit quoque aut obleverit tabulas testamenti, nihilo minus *non* desinent valere quae fuerant scripta, licet eorum probatio difficilis sit. Quid ergo est? si quis ab intestato bonorum possessionem petierit et is, qui ex eo testamento heres est, petat hereditatem suam esse, vincat quidem necesse est in hereditatis petitione; sed fiscus ei quasi indigno auferet hereditatem, ne ullo modo ad eum, quem testator heredem habere noluit, perveniat hereditas; et hoc ita rescripto imperatoris Antonini significatur. *Kritische Versuche.*

A validly executed will may be invalidated by revocation: but a will is not invalidated by the mere intention of revocation. And consequently, in spite of the testator's cutting the strings by which it is tied, it nevertheless, at civil law, continues valid: and his erasure or obliteration of the dispositions does not render them invalid, though it makes them difficult of proof. What then is the result? If a claimant demand bonorum possessio by intestacy, and a devisee demand the civil inheritance under the will, the devisee must prevail in his suit, but the treasury treats him as unworthy and deprives him of the succession, in order to carry the testator's intention of excluding him into effect: and this was enacted by a rescript of Marcus Aurelius Antoninus.

Gaius, then, mentioned in this paragraph that not only the grant of bonorum possessio, but also the recovery of the civil inheritance by hereditatis petitio, might in consequence of confiscation (ereption for indignity) be rendered ineffective (sine re).

On the principle: nihil tam naturale est quam eo genere quidque dissolvere quo colligatum est (see p. 364), the only formal revocation of a will would be the execution of a subsequent will, and mere cancellation or obliteration was an informal revocation, leaving the will valid at civil law; but the devisee would not be allowed to take the inheritance against the intention of the testator. What then became of the succession? According to Gaius and Papinian, Dig. 34, 9, 12, it went to the Fiscus; according to Ulpian, Dig. 38, 6, 1, 8, and Paulus, Dig. 28, 4, 4, it went to the persons entitled by intestacy; so that either the respective claims of the Fiscus and the heirs by descent were defined in some manner not specified, or they varied at different eras.

The rescript of Marcus Aurelius is preserved in the Digest, 28, 4, 3. The institution of Ereption for indignity survived in the legislation of Justinian; see the title: de his quae ut indignis auferuntur, Dig. 34, 9, and Cod. 6, 35. Ereption for indignity had various causes, and by Sc. Silanianum passed under Augustus or Tiberius, was the penalty inflicted on the heir of a murdered person for making aditio of the inheritance, or obtaining bonorum possessio, before the slaves of the deceased had been tortured, Paulus, 3, 5.

Mortgage by Mancipatio and Fiducia (see 2 § 60 and p. 301) are illustrated by an inscription on a brazen tablet, recently discovered near the mouth of the Guadalquivir, of which Krueger gives the text and explanation in his Kritische Versuche.

The perforated margins of the tablet still contain the bronze nails by which it was attached to a wall. It is supposed to have belonged at latest to the second century after the Christian era, and to have been suspended in the chamber of a banker (argentarius, p. 446). The inscription is supposed not to have been an actual mortgage but the common form of a mortgage, indicating the terms on which the banker was willing to accommodate his customers. It runs as follows:

Dama L. Titi servus fundum Baianum, qui est in agro qui Veneriensis vocatur, pago Olbensi, uti optumus maxumusque esset, sestertio nummo uno, et hominem Midam sestertio nummo uno, fidei fiduciae causa mancipio accepit ab L. Baianio, libripende, antestato. adfines fundo dixit L. Baianius L. Titium et C. Seium et populum et si quos dicere oportet. Pactum conventum factum est inter Damam L. Titi servum et L. Baianium: quam pecuniam L. Baiano dedit dederit credidit crediderit expensumve tulit tulerit sive quid pro eo promisit promiserit spopondit spoponderit fideve quid sua esse jussit jusserit, usque eo is fundus eaque mancipia fiducia essent, donec ea omnis pecunia fidesve persoluta L. Titi soluta liberataque esset. si pecunia sua quaque die L. Titio heredive eius data soluta non esset, tum uti eum fundum eaque mancipia sive quae mancipia ex iis vellet L. Titius heresve eius vellet, ubi et quo die vellet, pecunia praesenti venderet; mancipio pluris sestertio nummo uno invitus ne daret, neve satis secundum mancipium daret, neve [ut] in ea verba, quae in verba satis secundum mancipium dari solet, repromitteret neve simplam neve (duplam).

'To Dama, slave of Lucius Titius (banker and mortgagee), the Baian estate in the municipal territory of Veneria (near the Guadalquivir?) in the village of Olba, free from praedial servitudes (Dig. 21, 2, 75: or, with all its stock, Paulus 3, 6, 45), in consideration of a single sesterce: likewise the slave Midas in consideration of a single sesterce: to assure the repayment of certain moneys, were conveyed by mancipation by Lucius Baianius (mortgagor) in the presence of A. B. as balance-holder and C. D. as antestatus (p. 91). As abutting on the estate the mortgagor named L. Titius, Caius Seius, the public highway, and—whoever else were proper to be named. The following convention (fiducia) was concluded between Dama, slave of the mortgagee, and the mortgagor. For the money which the mortgagee has advanced or shall advance, has lent or shall lend, has debited or shall debit to the mortgagor, or for which he has become or shall become fidepromissor, sponsor, or fidejussor for the mortgagor, the above mentioned land and the above mentioned slaves shall be a security, until all such moneys due to the mortgagee as lender or paid by the mortgagee as surety shall have been paid or reimbursed by the mortgagor. [Degenkolb conjectures: donec ea omnis pecunia persoluta fidesve L. Titi soluta liberataque esset: 'until all such moneys shall have been repaid to the mortgagee as lender or the mortgagee as surety shall have been reimbursed or discharged.'] If the moneys on each day that they fall due are not paid to the mortgagee or his heir, then the above named land and slaves, or such of the said slaves as the mortgagee or his heir shall elect, at the place where and at the time when he pleases, may be sold by the mortgagee or his heir for ready money (i.e. for a less price than might be obtained by a sale on credit); and the mortgagee or his heir shall not be compelled to mancipate them for more than a single sesterce (i. e. if, as mancipable things, he aliene them by mancipation, it shall be merely a formal mancipation, not one that would subject him to auctoritas, i.e. liability in case of eviction as warrantor of the title (p. 340) to the vendee); and shall not in pursuance of the mancipation give to the vendee assurance with sureties for the title; nor without sureties (p. 326) covenant with the vendee for single or double compensation (p. 340) in the event of eviction in the terms in which a mancipator gives assurance with sureties (i.e. the mortgagee shall not be bound to make himself liable as warrantor of the title (auctor) to the vendee, either by implication of law or by express covenant, and that either with or without sureties).'

We may assume that further articles bound the mortgagee, on satisfaction of the mortgage debts, to reconvey the land and slaves to the mortgagor.

4 § 170 is thus restored by Krueger:

Sed quia nonnulli interdicto reddito cetera ex interdicto facere nolebant atque ob id non poterat res expediri, praetor in eam rem prospexit et comparavit interdicta, quae secundaria appellamus, quod secundo loco redduntur: quorum *vis et potestas haec est, ut qui* cetera ex interdicto non faciat, velut qui vim non faciat, aut fructus non liceatur, aut qui fructus licitationis satis non det, aut si sponsiones non faciat, sponsionumve judicia non accipiat, sive possideat, restituat adversario possessionem, *sive non possideat vim* illi possidenti ne faciat.

As sometimes, after the issue of an interdict, one of the parties declined to take some of the subsequent steps, and the proceedings came to a stand-still, the praetor has provided for this contingency, and invented the so-called secondary interdicts, which in such a case are issued: whose effect is, that if a party decline to take any necessary step in the interdict procedure, such as the violent disseisin, or the auction of the mesne profits, or finding bail for the penal sum fixed by the auction, or the wager, or the trial on the wager, if in possession he shall be ousted, if out of possession he shall be barred from hereafter seeking to recover possession.

From this it appears that as in Real actions the defendant who declined to give satisdatio judicatum solvi, and thus impeded the unwinding of the process of vindicatio, was deprived of possession by the interdicts QUEM FUNDUM, QUAM HEREDITATEM, QUEM USUMFRUCTUM, p. 461, so a party whose contumacious refusal to play his part prevented the interdict procedure from accomplishing its course was deprived of possession, or his right of recovering possession, by interdicta SECUNDARIA. From the mention of VIS we gather that, subsequent to the issue of the Interdict and antecedent to further proceedings, one act of the drama was a conventional ejectment (vis ex conventu) corresponding to the Manuum consertio in Sacramentum, and to the Deductio quae moribus fit in Sponsio, p. 463.

APPENDIX.

The following list of passages shows the extent to which I have deviated from the text of Gaius as published by Gneist.

1 § 123. 'Si tamen quaerat ali*quis*, quare a coemptio*ne differat mancipatio*,' is the reading of Rossbach for 'Si tamen quaerat ali*quis*, quare citra coemptio*nem feminae etiam mancipentur*.'

1 § 134. 'aut *non* remancipatur patri *sed ei qui adoptat in jure ceditur ab eo apud quem in tertia* mancipatione est,' is substantially the conjecture of Scheurl for 'aut jure mancipatur patri *adoptivo vindicanti filium ab eo apud quem is tertia* mancipatione est,' and later in the same paragraph 'aut *non* remancipantur' is for 'aut jure mancipantur.'

1 § 136. '*Eae vero mulieres quae in manum conveniunt per coemptionem*,' is the reading of Huschke for '*Sed mulieres quae coemptionem fecerunt per mancipationem*.'

2 § 155. 'Velut si *ex eo quod* Latinus adquisierit, locupletior factus sit,' is the conjecture of Savigny for 'Velut si Latinus adquisierit, locupletior factus sit.'

2 § 235. 'sed et [*si quis*] si heres verbi gratia intra biennium monumentum sibi non fecerit, x Titio dari jusserit, poenae nomine legatum est,' is the conjecture of Goeschen for 'sed et si heres,' &c.

3 § 79. 'si vero mortui *per* dies xv. postea jubet convenire creditores,' is the reading of Huschke for 'si vero mortui, post dies xv postea jubet convenire creditores.' And later in the same paragraph 'itaque si vivi bona veneant, in diebus *x legem bonorum vendendorum fieri* jubet, si mortui, in *diebus v. a quibus tandem* vivi bona *die* xx, mortui vero *die* x emptori addici jubet,' is the reading of Huschke for 'itaque si vivi bona veneant in diebus *pluribus veniri* jubet, si mortui, in *diebus paucioribus; nam* vivi bona xxx, mortui vero xx emptori addici jubet.'

4 § 48. '[*sed*],' which several critics propose to insert before 'aestimata,' is omitted by Gneist.

4 § 166. '*et uter eorum vicerit* fructus licitando, is tantisper in possessione constituitur, si modo adversario suo fructuaria stipu*latione caver*it, cuius vis et potestas haec est, ut si contra eum *de possessione* pronun*tiatum* fuerit, eam summam adversario solvat' is the restoration of Krueger. Gneist reads: '*Postquam igitur Praetor interdictum reddidit, primum litigatorum alterutrius* res ab eo fructum licitando *rei* tanti*sper in possessione constituitur, si modo* adversario suo fructuaria stipu*latione satisdet cuius* potestas haec *est, ut si contra ipsum esset postea* pronun*tiatum, fructus duplam praestet.*'

The remarks on Fructuaria stipulatio, p. 463, were based on the reading of Gneist. From Krueger's reading it appears that Fructuaria stipulatio was purely for a penal sum, and was not analogous to the security pro praede vindiciarum. If a plaintiff waived the Fructuaria stipulatio and proceeded by Secutorium with satisdatio judicatum solvi, § 169, he was assured of the penal sum in case of the defendant's insolvency; but, probably, when he afterwards brought Cascellianum, only recovered possession without the interim profits: otherwise it does not appear how it could ever have been advantageous to sue on the Fructuaria stipulatio.

CORRIGENDA.

The contract of Constitutum (guaranty) is described, page 292, as operating a Novation. This is inaccurate; for it is expressly declared that Constitutum adds a second, possibly a stronger, obligation, without extinguishing the original obligation, i.e. without operating a Novation, Dig. 13, 5, 28.

The words quia tenetur ad id ipsum ut praestet actiones, Dig. 46, 1, 36, which are quoted page 324, probably mean that the creditor is compellable to cede to the surety the creditor's right of action—not against the co-sureties, but—against the principal debtor.

Compellability to cede a right of action (superseded in later times by a fiction of cession, or perhaps of succession, page 314, embodied in an actio utilis) was an incident of Correality. Correality or Solidarity, the multiplication of the creditors (duo rei credendi) or debtors (duo rei debendi) in an obligation without a corresponding division of the Object of the right or obligation, was an institution of Roman law in favour of creditors, whereby, exceptionally and usually in virtue of a special agreement, each creditor was severally entitled to recover the whole object of the obligation (solidum) from a common debtor, or each debtor was severally liable to pay the whole object of the obligation to a common creditor, subject to a right of Regress, i.e. to a right of the co-creditors to recover their proportional shares from the creditor who has received the whole from the common debtor, or the right of the debtor who has paid the whole to the common creditor to recover proportional shares from his co-debtors. The ordinary rule, to which Correality forms an exception, is, that when there are several creditors or several debtors in an obligation, the object of the obligation is divided, so that each creditor is only entitled to recover a proportional part of the advantage, and each debtor is only bound to bear a proportional part of the burden. There was a Correality between each surety and the principal debtor; but there was no Correality and no right of Regress between co-sureties (Cod. 8, 41, 11), who were protected, at least in later times, by another institution, the Beneficium divisionis, p. 328. After the institution of Beneficium divisionis, we may suppose that the right of emptio nominis against the co-sureties (which was equivalent in effect to a compellability of the creditor to cede his right of action against the co-sureties) was abrogated, and that the law, Dig. 46, 1, 17, which we have quoted, p. 324, was only inserted by inadvertence in the Justinian legislation. Savigny, Obligationenrecht, § 25.

In the commentary on 3 § 80 it is suggested that Bonorum cessio probably passed Quiritary dominion: this is a mistake, for the contrary is expressly declared in a constitution of Diocletian, Cod. 7, 71, 4.

INDEX.

M.

N.

O.

P.

August, 1871.

BOOKS

PRINTED AT

THE CLARENDON PRESS, OXFORD,

And Published for the University

BY MACMILLAN AND CO.,

16, BEDFORD STREET, COVENT GARDEN, LONDON.

LEXICONS, GRAMMARS, &c.

A Greek-English Lexicon, by Henry George Liddell, D.D., and Robert Scott, D.D. *Sixth Edition, Revised and Augmented.* 1870. 4to. *cloth,* 1*l.* 16*s.*

A Greek-English Lexicon, abridged from the above, chiefly for the use of Schools. *Thirteenth Edition.* 1869. square 12mo. *cloth,* 7*s.* 6*d.*

A copious Greek-English Vocabulary, compiled from the best authorities. 1850. 24mo. *bound,* 3*s.*

Graecae Grammaticae Rudimenta in usum Scholarum. Auctore Carolo Wordsworth, D.C.L. *Seventeenth Edition.* 1870. 12mo. *bound,* 4*s.*

A Practical Introduction to Greek Accentuation, by H. W. Chandler, M.A. 1862. 8vo. *cloth,* 10*s.* 6*d.*

Scheller's Lexicon of the Latin Tongue, with the German explanations translated into English by J. E. Riddle, M.A. 1835. fol. *cloth,* 1*l.* 1*s.*

A Practical Grammar of the Sanskrit Language, arranged with reference to the Classical Languages of Europe, for the use of English Students, by Monier Williams, M.A. *Third Edition.* 1864. 8vo. *cloth,* 15*s.*

An Icelandic-English Dictionary. By the late R. Cleasby. Enlarged and completed by G. Vigfússon. Part I. 1869. 4to. 21*s.*

GREEK AND LATIN CLASSICS.

Aeschylus: Tragoediae et Fragmenta, ex recensione Guil. Dindorfii. *Second Edition.* 1851. 8vo. *cloth,* 5*s.* 6*d.*

Sophocles: Tragoediae et Fragmenta, ex recensione et cum commentariis Guil. Dindorfii. *Third Edition.* 2 vols. 1860. fcap. 8vo. *cloth,* 1*l.* 1*s.*

Each Play separately, *limp,* 2*s.* 6*d.*

The Text alone, square 16mo. *cloth,* 3*s.* 6*d.*

Each Play separately, *limp,* 6*d.*

Sophocles: Tragoediae et Fragmenta, ex recensione Guil. Dindorfii. *Second Edition.* 1849. 8vo. *cloth,* 5*s.* 6*d.*

Euripides: Tragoediae et Fragmenta, ex recensione Guil. Dindorfii. Tomi II. 1834. 8vo. *cloth,* 10*s.*

Aristophanes: Comoediae et Fragmenta, ex recensione Guil. Dindorfii. Tomi II. 1835. 8vo. *cloth*, 11*s*.

Aristoteles: ex recensione Immanuelis Bekkeri. Accedunt Indices Sylburgiani. Tomi XI. 1837. 8vo. *cloth*, 2*l*. 10*s*.

Each volume separately, 5*s*. 6*d*.

Catulli Veronensis Liber: recognovit, apparatum criticum prolegomena appendices addidit, Robinson Ellis, A.M. 1867. 8vo. *cloth*, 16*s*.

Demosthenes: ex recensione Guil. Dindorfii. Tomi IV. 1846. 8vo. *cloth*. *Price reduced from* 2*l*. 2*s*. to 1*l*. 1*s*.

Homerus: Ilias, ex rec. Guil. Dindorfii. 1856. 8vo. *cloth*, 5*s*. 6*d*.

Homerus: Odyssea, ex rec. Guil. Dindorfii. 1855. 8vo. *cloth*, 5*s*. 6*d*.

Plato: The Apology, with a revised Text and English Notes, and a Digest of Platonic Idioms, by James Riddell, M.A. 1867. 8vo. *cloth*, 8*s*. 6*d*.

Plato: Philebus, with a revised Text and English Notes, by Edward Poste, M.A. 1860. 8vo. *cloth*, 7*s*. 6*d*.

Plato: Sophistes and Politicus, with a revised Text and English Notes, by L. Campbell, M.A. 1866. 8vo. *cloth*, 18*s*.

Plato: Theaetetus, with a revised Text and English Notes, by L. Campbell, M.A. 1861. 8vo. *cloth*, 9*s*.

Plato: The Dialogues, translated into English, with Analyses and Introductions, by B. Jowett, M.A., Master of Balliol College, and Regius Professor of Greek. 4 vols. 1871. 8vo. *cloth*, 3*l*. 6*s*.

Xenophon: Historia Graeca, ex recensione et cum annotationibus L. Dindorfii. *Second Edition*. 1852. 8vo. *cloth*, 10*s*. 6*d*.

Xenophon: Expeditio Cyri, ex rec. et cum annotatt. L. Dindorfii. *Second Edition*. 1855. 8vo. *cloth*, 10*s*. 6*d*.

Xenophon: Institutio Cyri, ex rec. et cum annotatt. L. Dindorfii. 1857. 8vo. *cloth*, 10*s*. 6*d*.

Xenophon: Memorabilia Socratis, ex rec. et cum annotatt. L. Dindorfii. 1862. 8vo. *cloth*, 7*s*. 6*d*.

Xenophon: Opuscula Politica Equestria et Venatica cum Arriani Libello de Venatione, ex rec. et cum annotatt. L. Dindorfii. 1866. 8vo. *cloth*, 10*s*. 6*d*.

THE HOLY SCRIPTURES, &c.

The Holy Bible in the earliest English Versions, made from the Latin Vulgate by John Wycliffe and his followers: edited by the Rev. J. Forshall and Sir F. Madden. 4 vols. 1850. royal 4to. *cloth*. *Price reduced from* 5*l*. 15*s*. 6*d*. *to* 3*l*. 3*s*.

The Holy Bible: an exact reprint, page for page, of the Authorized Version published in the year 1611. Demy 4to. *half bound*, 1*l*. 1*s*.

Vetus Testamentum Graece secundum exemplar Vaticanum Romae editum. Accedit potior varietas Codicis Alexandrini. Tomi III. 1848. 12mo. *cloth*, 14*s*.

Novum Testamentum Graece. Accedunt parallela S. Scripturae loca, necnon vetus capitulorum notatio et canones Eusebii. Edidit Carolus Lloyd, S.T.P.R., necnon Episcopus Oxoniensis. 1869. 18mo. *cloth*, 3*s*.

The same on writing paper, with large margin, small 4to. *cloth*, 10*s*. 6*d*.

Novum Testamentum Graece juxta exemplar Millianum. 1868. 12mo. *cloth*, 2s. 6d.

The same on writing paper, with large margin, small 4to. *cloth*, 6s. 6d.

Evangelia Sacra Graece. 1870. fcap. 8vo. *limp*, 1s. 6d.

The New Testament in Greek and English, on opposite pages, arranged and edited by E. Cardwell, D.D. 2 vols. 1837. crown 8vo. *cloth*, 6s.

Horae Hebraicae et Talmudicae, a J. Lightfoot. *A new Edition*, by R. Gandell, M.A. 4 vols. 1859. 8vo. *cloth. Price reduced from* 2l. 2s. *to* 1l. 1s.

ECCLESIASTICAL HISTORY, &c.

Baedae Historia Ecclesiastica. Edited, with English Notes, by G. H. Moberly, M.A., Fellow of C.C.C., Oxford. 1869. crown 8vo. *cloth*, 10s. 6d.

Bingham's Antiquities of the Christian Church, and other Works. 10 vols. 1855. 8vo. *cloth. Price reduced from* 5l. 5s. *to* 3l. 3s.

Burnet's History of the Reformation of the Church of England. *A new Edition.* Carefully revised, and the Records collated with the originals, by N. Pocock, M.A. With a Preface by the Editor. 7 vols. 1865. 8vo. *cloth*, 4l. 4s.

Records of the Reformation. The Divorce, 1527–1533. Mostly now for the first time printed from MSS. in the British Museum, and other Libraries. Collected and arranged by N. Pocock, M.A. 2 vols. 8vo. *cloth*, 1l. 16s.

Councils and Ecclesiastical Documents relating to Great Britain and Ireland. Edited, after Spelman and Wilkins, by A. W. Haddan, B.D., and William Stubbs, M.A., Regius Professor of Modern History, Oxford. Vol. I. 1869. medium 8vo. *cloth*, 1l. 1s. Vols. II. and III. *in the Press.*

Eusebii Pamphili Historia Ecclesiastica. Edidit E. Burton, S.T.P.R. 1856. 8vo. *cloth*, 8s. 6d.

Patrum Apostolicorum, S. Clementis Romani, S. Ignatii, S. Polycarpi, quae supersunt. Edidit Guil. Jacobson, S.T.P.R. Tomi II. *Fourth Edition.* 1863. 8vo. *cloth*, 1l. 1s.

Reliquiae Sacrae secundi tertiique saeculi. Recensuit M. J. Routh, S.T.P. Tomi V. *Second Edition.* 1846–1848. 8vo. *cloth. Price reduced from* 2l. 11s. *to* 1l. 5s.

Scriptorum Ecclesiasticorum Opuscula. Recensuit M. J. Routh, S.T.P. Tomi II. *Third Edition.* 1858. 8vo. *cloth. Price reduced from* 1l. *to* 10s.

Shirley's (W. W.) Some Account of the Church in the Apostolic Age. 1867. fcap. 8vo. *cloth*, 3s. 6d.

ENGLISH THEOLOGY.

Butler's Works, with an Index to the Analogy. 2 vols. 1849. 8vo. *cloth*, 11s.

Greswell's Harmonia Evangelica. *Fifth Edition.* 1856. 8vo. *cloth*, 9s. 6d.

Homilies appointed to be read in Churches. Edited by J. Griffiths, M.A. 1859. 8vo. *cloth. Price reduced from* 10s. 6d. *to* 7s. 6d.

Hooker's Works, with his Life by Walton, arranged by John Keble, M.A. *Fifth Edition.* 1865. 3 vols. 8vo. *cloth*, 1l. 11s. 6d.

Hooker's Works; the text as arranged by John Keble, M.A. 2 vols. 1865. 8vo. *cloth*, 11s.

Pearson's Exposition of the Creed. Revised and corrected by E. Burton, D.D. *Fifth Edition.* 1864. 8vo. *cloth,* 10*s.* 6*d.*

Waterland's Review of the Doctrine of the Eucharist, with a Preface by the present Bishop of London. 1868. crown 8vo. *cloth,* 6*s.* 6*d.*

ENGLISH HISTORY.

Clarendon's (Edw. Earl of) History of the Rebellion and Civil Wars in England. To which are subjoined the Notes of Bishop Warburton. 7 vols. 1849. medium 8vo. *cloth,* 2*l.* 10*s.*

Clarendon's (Edw. Earl of) History of the Rebellion and Civil Wars in England. 7 vols. 1839. 18mo. *cloth,* 1*l.* 1*s.*

Freeman's (E. A.) History of the Norman Conquest of England: its Causes and Results. Vols. I. and II. *A new Edition,* with Index. 8vo. *cloth,* 1*l.* 16*s.*

Vol. III. The Reign of Harold and the Interregnum. 1869. 8vo. *cloth,* 1*l.* 1*s.*

Rogers's History of Agriculture and Prices in England, A.D. 1259–1400. 2 vols. 1866. 8vo. *cloth,* 2*l.* 2*s.*

PHILOSOPHICAL WORKS, AND GENERAL LITERATURE.

A Course of Lectures on Art, delivered before the University of Oxford in Hilary Term, 1870. By John Ruskin, M.A., Slade Professor of Fine Art. Demy 8vo. *cloth,* 6*s.*

A Critical Account of the Drawings by Michel Angelo and Raffaello in the University Galleries, Oxford. By J. C. Robinson, F.S.A. Crown 8vo. *cloth,* 4*s.*

Bacon's Novum Organum, edited, with English notes, by G.W. Kitchin, M.A. 1855. 8vo. *cloth,* 9*s.* 6*d.*

Bacon's Novum Organum, translated by G. W. Kitchin, M.A. 1855. 8vo. *cloth,* 9*s.* 6*d.*

The Works of George Berkeley, D.D., formerly Bishop of Cloyne; including many of his writings hitherto unpublished. With Prefaces, Annotations, and an Account of his Life and Philosophy, by Alexander Campbell Fraser, M.A., Professor of Logic and Metaphysics in the University of Edinburgh. 4 vols. 1871. 8vo. *cloth,* 2*l.* 18*s.*

Also separately.

The Works. 3 vols. *cloth,* 2*l.* 2*s.*
The Life and Letters, &c. 1 vol. *cloth,* 16*s.*

Smith's Wealth of Nations. *A new Edition,* with Notes, by J. E. Thorold Rogers, M.A. 2 vols. 8vo. *cloth,* 1*l.* 1*s.*

MATHEMATICS, PHYSICAL SCIENCE, &c.

Treatise on Infinitesimal Calculus. By Bartholomew Price, M.A., F.R.S., Professor of Natural Philosophy, Oxford.

Vol. I. Differential Calculus. *Second Edition.* 1858. 8vo. *cloth,* 14*s.* 6*d.*

Vol. II. Integral Calculus, Calculus of Variations, and Differential Equations. *Second Edition.* 1865. 8vo. *cloth,* 18*s.*

Vol. III. Statics, including Attractions; Dynamics of a Material Particle. *Second Edition.* 1868. 8vo. *cloth,* 16*s.*

Vol. IV. Dynamics of Material Systems; together with a Chapter on Theoretical Dynamics, by W. F. Donkin, M.A., F.R.S. 1862. 8vo. *cloth,* 16*s.*

Vesuvius. By John Phillips, M.A., F.R.S., Professor of Geology, Oxford. 1869. crown 8vo. *cloth,* 10*s.* 6*d.*

Clarendon Press Series.

The Delegates of the Clarendon Press having undertaken the publication of a series of works, chiefly educational, and entitled the **Clarendon Press Series**, have published, or have in preparation, the following.

Those to which prices are attached are already published; the others are in preparation.

I. GREEK AND LATIN CLASSICS, &c.

A Greek Primer in English, for the use of beginners. By the Right Rev. Charles Wordsworth, D.C.L., Bishop of St. Andrews. Extra fcap. 8vo. *cloth*, 1*s*. 6*d*.

Greek Verbs, Irregular and Defective; their forms, meaning, and quantity; embracing all the Tenses used by Greek writers, with reference to the passages in which they are found. By W. Veitch. *New and revised Edition.* Ext. fcap. 8vo. *cloth*, 8*s*. 6*d*.

The Elements of Greek Accentuation (for Schools): abridged from his larger work by H. W. Chandler, M.A., Waynflete Professor of Moral and Metaphysical Philosophy, Oxford. Ext. fcap. 8vo. *cloth*, 2*s*. 6*d*.

Aeschines in Ctesiphontem and **Demosthenes de Corona.** With Introduction and Notes. By G. A. Simcox, M.A., and W. H. Simcox, M.A., Fellows of Queen's College, Oxford. *In the Press.*

Aristotle's Politics. By W. L. Newman, M.A., Fellow and Lecturer of Balliol College, and Reader in Ancient History, Oxford.

The Golden Treasury of Ancient Greek Poetry; being a Collection of the finest passages in the Greek Classic Poets, with Introductory Notices and Notes. By R. S. Wright, M.A., Fellow of Oriel College, Oxford. Ext. fcap. 8vo. *cloth*, 8*s*. 6*d*.

A Golden Treasury of Greek Prose, being a Collection of the finest passages in the principal Greek Prose Writers, with Introductory Notices and Notes. By R. S. Wright, M.A., Fellow of Oriel College, Oxford; and J. E. L. Shadwell, M.A., Senior Student of Christ Church. Extra fcap. 8vo. *cloth*, 4*s*. 6*d*.

Homer. Iliad. By D. B. Monro, M.A., Fellow and Tutor of Oriel College, Oxford.

Homer. Odyssey, Books I–XII (for Schools). By W. W. Merry, M.A., Fellow and Lecturer of Lincoln College, Oxford. Extra fcap. 8vo. *cloth*, 4*s*. 6*d*.

Homer. Odyssey, Books I–XII. By W. W. Merry, M.A., Fellow and Lecturer of Lincoln College, Oxford; and the late James Riddell, M.A., Fellow of Balliol College, Oxford.

Homer. Odyssey, Books XIII–XXIV. By Robinson Ellis, M.A., Fellow of Trinity College, Oxford.

Plato. Selections (for Schools). With Notes, by B. Jowett, M.A., Regius Professor of Greek; and J. Purves, M.A., Fellow and Lecturer of Balliol College, Oxford.

Sophocles. Oedipus Rex: Dindorf's Text, with Notes by the Ven. Archdeacon Basil Jones, M.A., formerly Fellow of University College, Oxford. *Second Edition.* Ext. fcap. 8vo. *limp cloth,* 1*s.* 6*d.*

Sophocles. By Lewis Campbell, M.A., Professor of Greek, St. Andrews, formerly Fellow of Queen's College, Oxford. *In the Press.*

Theocritus (for Schools). With Notes, by H. Snow, M.A., Assistant Master at Eton College, formerly Fellow of St. John's College, Cambridge. Extra fcap. 8vo. *cloth,* 4*s.* 6*d.*

Xenophon. Selections (for Schools). With Notes and Maps, by J. S. Phillpotts, B.C.L., Assistant Master in Rugby School, formerly Fellow of New College, Oxford. Extra fcap. 8vo. *cloth,* 3*s.* 6*d.*

Caesar. The Commentaries (for Schools). Part I. The Gallic War, with Notes and Maps, by Charles E. Moberly, M.A., Assistant Master in Rugby School; formerly Scholar of Balliol College, Oxford. Extra fcap. 8vo. *cloth,* 4*s.* 6*d.*

Also, to follow: Part II. The Civil War: by the same Editor.

Cicero's Philippic Orations. With Notes, by J. R. King, M.A., formerly Fellow and Tutor of Merton College, Oxford. Demy 8vo. *cloth,* 10*s.* 6*d.*

Cicero pro Cluentio. With Introduction and Notes. By W. Ramsay, M.A. Edited by G. G. Ramsay, M.A., Professor of Humanity, Glasgow. Extra fcap. 8vo. *cloth,* 3*s.* 6*d.*

Cicero. Selection of interesting and descriptive passages. With Notes. By Henry Walford, M.A., Wadham College, Oxford, Assistant Master at Haileybury College. In three Parts. Extra fcap. 8vo. *cloth,* 4*s.* 6*d.*

Each Part separately, *limp,* 1*s.* 6*d.*

Part I. Anecdotes from Grecian and Roman History.
Part II. Omens and Dreams: Beauties of Nature.
Part III. Rome's Rule of her Provinces.

Cicero. Select Letters. With English Introductions, Notes, and Appendices. By Albert Watson, M.A., Fellow and Tutor of Brasenose College, Oxford. 8vo. *cloth,* 18*s.*

Cicero de Oratore. With Introduction and Notes. By A. S. Wilkins, M.A., Professor of Latin, Owens College, Manchester.

Cornelius Nepos. With Notes, by Oscar Browning, M.A., Fellow of King's College, Cambridge, and Assistant Master at Eton College. Extra fcap. 8vo. *cloth,* 2*s.* 6*d.*

Cicero and Pliny. Select Epistles (for Schools). With Notes by E. R. Bernard, M.A., Fellow of Magdalen College, Oxford; and the late C. E. Prichard, M.A., formerly Fellow of Balliol College, Oxford. *In the Press.*

Horace. With Introduction and Notes. By Edward C. Wickham, M.A., Fellow and Tutor of New College, Oxford.

Also a small edition for Schools.

Livy, Books I–X. By J. R. Seeley, M.A., Fellow of Christ's College, and Regius Professor of Modern History, Cambridge. *In the Press.*

Also a small edition for Schools.

Ovid. Selections for the use of Schools. With Introductions and Notes, and an Appendix on the Roman Calendar. By W. Ramsay, M.A. Edited by G. G. Ramsay, M.A., Professor of Humanity, Glasgow. Ext. fcap. 8vo. *cloth*, 5*s*. 6*d*.

Fragments and Specimens of Early Latin. With Introduction, Notes, and Illustrations. By John Wordsworth, M.A., Fellow of Brasenose College, Oxford.

Selections from the less known Latin Poets. By North Pinder, M.A., formerly Fellow of Trinity College, Oxford. Demy 8vo. *cloth*, 15*s*.

Passages for Translation into Latin. For the use of Passmen and others. Selected by J. Y. Sargent, M.A., Tutor, formerly Fellow, of Magdalen College, Oxford. *Second Edition.* Ext. fcap. 8vo. *cloth*, 2*s*. 6*d*.

II. MENTAL AND MORAL PHILOSOPHY.

The Elements of Deductive Logic, designed mainly for the use of Junior Students in the Universities. By T. Fowler, M.A., Fellow and Tutor of Lincoln College, Oxford. *Third Edition*, with a Collection of Examples. Extra fcap. 8vo. *cloth*, 3*s*. 6*d*.

The Elements of Inductive Logic, designed mainly for the use of Students in the Universities. By the same Author. Extra fcap. 8vo. *cloth*, 6*s*.

A Manual of Political Economy, for the use of Schools. By J. E. Thorold Rogers, M.A., formerly Professor of Political Economy, Oxford. *Second Edition.* Extra fcap. 8vo. *cloth*, 4*s*. 6*d*.

III. MATHEMATICS, &c.

Acoustics. By W. F. Donkin, M.A., F.R.S., Savilian Professor of Astronomy, Oxford. Crown 8vo. *cloth*, 7*s*. 6*d*.

An Elementary Treatise on Quaternions. By P. G. Tait, M.A., Professor of Natural Philosophy in the University of Edinburgh; formerly Fellow of St. Peter's College, Cambridge. Demy 8vo. *cloth*, 12*s*. 6*d*.

Book-keeping. By R. G. C. Hamilton, Accountant to the Board of Trade, and John Ball (of the Firm of Messrs. Quilter, Ball, and Co.), Examiners in Book-keeping for the Society of Arts' Examination. *Third Edition.* Extra fcap. 8vo. *limp cloth*, 1*s*. 6*d*.

A Course of Lectures on Pure Geometry. By Henry J. Stephen Smith, M.A., F.R.S., Fellow of Balliol College, and Savilian Professor of Geometry in the University of Oxford.

A Treatise on Electricity and Magnetism. By J. Clerk Maxwell, M.A., F.R.S., formerly Professor of Natural Philosophy, King's College, London. *In the Press.*

A Series of Elementary Works is being arranged, and will shortly be announced.

IV. HISTORY.

A Manual of Ancient History. By George Rawlinson, M.A., Camden Professor of Ancient History, formerly Fellow of Exeter College, Oxford. Demy 8vo. *cloth*, 14*s*.

Select Charters and other Illustrations of English Constitutional History; from the Earliest Times to the Reign of Edward I. Arranged and edited by W. Stubbs, M.A., Regius Professor of Modern History in the University of Oxford. Crown 8vo. *cloth*, 8*s*. 6*d*.

A Constitutional History of England. By the same Author.

A History of Germany and of the Empire, down to the close of the Middle Ages. By J. Bryce, B.C.L., Fellow of Oriel College, Oxford.

A History of Germany, from the Reformation. By Adolphus W. Ward, M.A., Fellow of St. Peter's College, Cambridge, Professor of History, Owens College, Manchester.

A History of British India. By S. J. Owen, M.A., Lee's Reader in Law and History, Christ Church, and Teacher of Indian Law and History in the University of Oxford.

A History of Greece. By E. A. Freeman, M.A., formerly Fellow of Trinity College, Oxford.

A History of France. By G. W. Kitchin, M.A., formerly Censor of Christ Church.

V. LAW.

Commentaries on Roman Law; from the original and the best modern sources. By H. J. Roby, M.A., formerly Fellow of St. John's College, Cambridge; Professor of Law at University College, London. 2 vols. demy 8vo.

VI. PHYSICAL SCIENCE.

Natural Philosophy. In four Volumes. By Sir W. Thomson, LL.D., D.C.L., F.R.S., Professor of Natural Philosophy, Glasgow; and P. G. Tait, M.A., Professor of Natural Philosophy, Edinburgh; formerly Fellows of St. Peter's College, Cambridge. Vol. I. 8vo. *cloth*, 1*l*. 5*s*.

By the same Authors, a smaller Work on the same subject, forming a complete Introduction to it, so far as it can be carried out with Elementary Geometry and Algebra. *In the Press.*

Descriptive Astronomy. A Handbook for the General Reader, and also for Practical Observatory work. With 224 illustrations and numerous tables. By G. F. Chambers, F.R.A.S., Barrister-at-Law. Demy 8vo. 856 pp., *cloth*, 1*l*. 1*s*.

Chemistry for Students. By A. W. Williamson, Phil. Doc., F.R.S., Professor of Chemistry, University College, London. *A new Edition, with Solutions.* Extra fcap. 8vo. *cloth*, 8*s*. 6*d*.

A Treatise on Heat, with numerous Woodcuts and Diagrams. By Balfour Stewart, LL.D., F.R.S., Director of the Observatory at Kew. Extra fcap. 8vo. *cloth*, 7*s*. 6*d*.

Forms of Animal Life. By G. Rolleston, M.D., F.R.S., Linacre Professor of Physiology, Oxford. Illustrated by Descriptions and Drawings of Dissections. Demy 8vo. *cloth*, 16*s*.

Exercises in Practical Chemistry. By A. G. Vernon Harcourt, M.A., F.R.S., Senior Student of Christ Church, and Lee's Reader in Chemistry; and H. G. Madan, M.A., Fellow of Queen's College, Oxford.

Series I. Qualitative Exercises. Crown 8vo. *cloth*, 7*s*. 6*d*.

Series II. Quantitative Exercises.

The Valley of the Thames; its Physical Geography and Geology. By John Phillips, M.A., F.R.S., Professor of Geology, Oxford. *In the Press.*

Geology. By J. Phillips, M.A., F.R.S., Professor of Geology, Oxford.

Mechanics. By Bartholomew Price, M.A., F.R.S., Sedleian Professor of Natural Philosophy, Oxford.

Optics. By R. B. Clifton, M.A., F.R.S., Professor of Experimental Philosophy, Oxford; formerly Fellow of St. John's College, Cambridge.

Electricity. By W. Esson, M.A., F.R.S., Fellow and Mathematical Lecturer of Merton College, Oxford.

Crystallography. By M. H. N. Story-Maskelyne, M.A., Professor of Mineralogy, Oxford; and Deputy Keeper in the Department of Minerals, British Museum.

Mineralogy. By the same Author.

Physiological Physics. By G. Griffith, M.A., Jesus College, Oxford, Assistant Secretary to the British Association, and Natural Science Master at Harrow School.

Magnetism.

VII. ENGLISH LANGUAGE AND LITERATURE.

A First Reading Book. By Marie Eichens of Berlin; and edited by Anne J. Clough. Extra fcap. 8vo. *stiff covers*, 4*d*.

Oxford Reading Book, Part I. For Little Children. Extra fcap. 8vo. *stiff covers*, 6*d*.

Oxford Reading Book, Part II. For Junior Classes. Extra fcap. 8vo. *stiff covers*, 6*d*.

On the Principles of Grammar. By E. Thring, M.A., Head Master of Uppingham School. Extra fcap. 8vo. *cloth*, 4*s*. 6*d*.

Grammatical Analysis, designed to serve as an Exercise and Composition Book in the English Language. By E. Thring, M.A., Head Master of Uppingham School. Extra fcap. 8vo. *cloth*, 3*s*. 6*d*.

Specimens of Early English; being a Series of Extracts from the most important English Authors, Chronologically arranged, illustrative of the progress of the English Language and its Dialectic varieties, from A.D. 1250 to A.D. 1400. With Grammatical Introduction, Notes, and Glossary. By R. Morris, Editor of 'The Story of Genesis and Exodus,' &c. Extra fcap. 8vo. *cloth*, 7*s*. 6*d*.

Specimens of English from A.D. 1394 to A.D. 1579 (from the Crede to Spenser): selected by W. W. Skeat, M.A., formerly Fellow of Christ's College, Cambridge. *Nearly ready.*

The Vision of William concerning Piers the Plowman, by William Langland. Edited, with Notes, by W. W. Skeat, M.A., formerly Fellow of Christ's College, Cambridge. Extra fcap. 8vo. *cloth*, 4*s*. 6*d*.

The Philology of the English Tongue. By J. Earle, M.A., formerly Fellow of Oriel College, and Professor of Anglo-Saxon, Oxford. *Just ready.*

Typical Selections from the best English Authors from the Sixteenth to the Nineteenth Century, (to serve as a higher Reading Book,) with Introductory Notices and Notes, being a contribution towards a History of English Literature. Extra fcap. 8vo. *cloth*, 4*s*. 6*d*.

Specimens of the Scottish Language; being a Series of Annotated Extracts illustrative of the Literature and Philology of the Lowland Tongue from the Fourteenth to the Nineteenth Century. With Introduction and Glossary. By A. H. Burgess, M.A.

See also XII. below for other English Classics.

VIII. FRENCH LANGUAGE AND LITERATURE.

An Etymological Dictionary of the French Language, with a Preface on the Principles of French Etymology. By A. Brachet. Translated by G. W. Kitchin, M.A., formerly Censor of Christ Church. *In the Press.*

Brachet's Historical Grammar of the French Language. Translated into English by G. W. Kitchin, M.A., formerly Censor of Christ Church. Extra fcap. 8vo. *cloth*, 3*s*. 6*d*.

Corneille's Cinna, and **Molière's** Les Femmes Savantes. Edited, with Introduction and Notes, by Gustave Masson. Extra fcap. 8vo. *cloth*, 2*s*. 6*d*.

Racine's Andromaque, and **Corneille's** Le Menteur. With Louis Racine's Life of his Father. By the same Editor. Extra fcap. 8vo. *cloth*, 2*s*. 6*d*.

Molière's Les Fourberies de Scapin, and **Racine's** Athalie. With Voltaire's Life of Molière. By the same Editor. Extra fcap. 8vo. *cloth*, 2*s*. 6*d*.

Selections from the Correspondence of **Madame de Sévigné** and her chief Contemporaries. Intended more especially for Girls' Schools. By the same Editor. Extra fcap. 8vo. *cloth*, 3*s*.

Voyage autour de ma Chambre, by **Xavier de Maistre**; Ourika, by **Madame de Duras**; La Dot de Suzette, by **Fievée**; Les Jumeaux de l'Hôtel Corneille, by **Edmond About**; Mésaventures d'un Écolier, by **Rodolphe Töpffer**. By the same Editor. Extra fcap. 8vo. *cloth*, 2*s*. 6*d*.

A French Grammar. A complete Theory of the French Language, with the Rules in French and English, and numerous Examples to serve as first Exercises in the Language. By Jules Bué, Honorary M.A. of Oxford; Taylorian Teacher of French, Oxford; Examiner in the Oxford Local Examinations from 1858.

A French Grammar Test. A Book of Exercises on French Grammar; each Exercise being preceded by Grammatical Questions. By the same Author.

Exercises in Translation No. 1, from French into English, with general rules on Translation; and containing Notes, Hints, and Cautions, founded on a comparison of the Grammar and Genius of the two Languages. By the same Author.

Exercises in Translation No. 2, from English into French, on the same plan as the preceding book. By the same Author.

IX. GERMAN LANGUAGE AND LITERATURE.

Goethe's Egmont. With a Life of Goethe, &c. By Dr. Buchheim, Professor of the German Language and Literature in King's College, London; and Examiner in German to the University of London. Extra fcap. 8vo. *cloth*, 3*s*.

Schiller's Wilhelm Tell. With a Life of Schiller; an historical and critical Introduction, Arguments, and a complete Commentary. By the same Editor. Extra fcap. 8vo. *cloth*, 3*s*. 6*d*.

Lessing's Minna von Barnhelm. A Comedy. With a Life of Lessing, Critical Commentary, &c. By the same Editor. *In the Press.*

X. ART, &c.

A Handbook of Pictorial Art. By R. St. J. Tyrwhitt, M.A., formerly Student and Tutor of Christ Church, Oxford With coloured Illustrations, Photographs, and a chapter on Perspective by A. Macdonald. 8vo. *half morocco*, 18*s*.

A Treatise on Harmony. By Sir F. A. Gore Ouseley, Bart., M.A., Mus. Doc., Professor of Music in the University of Oxford. 4to. *cloth*, 10*s*.

A Treatise on Counterpoint, Canon, and Fugue, based upon that of Cherubini. By the same Author. 4to. *cloth*, 16*s*.

The Cultivation of the Speaking Voice. By John Hullah. Crown 8vo. *cloth*, 3*s*. 6*d*.

XI. MISCELLANEOUS.

A System of Physical Education: Theoretical and Practical. By Archibald Maclaren, The Gymnasium, Oxford. Extra fcap. 8vo. *cloth*, 7*s*. 6*d*.

The Modern Greek Language in its relation to Ancient Greek. By E. M. Geldart, B.A., formerly Scholar of Balliol College, Oxford. Extra fcap. 8vo. *cloth*, 4*s*. 6*d*.

XII. A SERIES OF ENGLISH CLASSICS.

Designed to meet the wants of Students in English Literature: under the superintendence of the Rev. J. S. Brewer, M.A., *of Queen's College, Oxford, and Professor of English Literature at King's College, London.*

It is also especially hoped that this Series may prove useful to Ladies' Schools and Middle Class Schools; in which English Literature must always be a leading subject of instruction.

A General Introduction to the Series. By Professor Brewer, M.A.

1. **Chaucer.** The Prologue to the Canterbury Tales; The Knightes Tale; The Nonne Prestes Tale. Edited by R. Morris, Editor of Specimens of Early English,' &c., &c. *Second Edition.* Extra fcap. 8vo. *cloth*, 2*s*. 6*d*.

2. **Spenser's Faery Queene.** Books I and II. Designed chiefly for the use of Schools. With Introduction, Notes, and Glossary. By G. W. Kitchin, M.A., formerly Censor of Christ Church. Extra fcap. 8vo. *cloth*, 2*s*. 6*d*. each.

3. **Hooker.** Ecclesiastical Polity, Book I. Edited by R. W. Church, M.A., Rector of Whatley; formerly Fellow of Oriel College, Oxford. Extra fcap. 8vo. *cloth*, 2*s*.

4. **Shakespeare.** Select Plays. Edited by W. G. Clark, M.A., Fellow of Trinity College, Cambridge; and W. Aldis Wright, M.A., Trinity College, Cambridge.

   I. The Merchant of Venice. Extra fcap. 8vo. *stiff covers*, 1*s*.
   II. Richard the Second. Extra fcap. 8vo. *stiff covers*, 1*s*. 6*d*.
   III. Macbeth. Extra fcap, 8vo. *stiff covers*, 1*s*. 6*d*.

5. **Bacon.** Advancement of Learning. Edited by W. Aldis Wright, M.A. Extra fcap. 8vo. *cloth*, 4*s*. 6*d*.

6. **Milton.** Poems. Edited by R. C. Browne, M.A., and Associate of King's College, London. 2 vols. extra fcap. 8vo. *cloth*, 6*s*. 6*d*.

   Also separately, Vol. I. 4*s*., Vol. II. 3*s*.

7. **Dryden.** Stanzas on the Death of Oliver Cromwell; Astraea Redux; Annus Mirabilis; Absalom and Achitophel; Religio Laici; The Hind and the Panther. Edited by W. D. Christie, M.A., Trinity College, Cambridge. Extra fcap. 8vo. *cloth*, 3*s*. 6*d*.

8. **Bunyan.** Grace Abounding; The Pilgrim's Progress. Edited by E. Venables, M.A., Canon of Lincoln.

9. **Pope.** With Introduction and Notes. By Mark Pattison, B.D., Rector of Lincoln College, Oxford.

   I. Essay on Man. Extra fcap. 8vo. *stiff covers*, 1*s*. 6*d*
   II. Epistles and Satires. *In the Press.*

10. **Johnson.** Rasselas; Lives of Pope and Dryden. Edited by C. H. O. Daniel, M.A., Fellow and Tutor of Worcester College, Oxford.

11. **Burke.** Thoughts on the Present Discontents; the two Speeches on America; Reflections on the French Revolution. By Mark Pattison, B.D., Rector of Lincoln College, Oxford.

12. **Cowper.** The Task, and some of his minor poems. Edited by J. C. Shairp, M.A., Principal of the United College, St. Andrews.

Published for the University by

MACMILLAN AND CO., LONDON.

The DELEGATES OF THE PRESS *invite suggestions and advice from all persons interested in education; and will be thankful for hints, &c. addressed to either the* REV. G. W. KITCHIN, *St. Giles's Road East. Oxford, or the* SECRETARY TO THE DELEGATES, *Clarendon Press, Oxford.*

CPSIA information can be obtained
at www.ICGtesting.com
Printed in the USA
LVHW032010171022
730904LV00007B/229